THE MISOGYNOUS PRESIDENT

THE MISOGYNOUS PRESIDENT

★ ★ ★

Corruption, Criminality, Misogyny and Racism
Inside the United States Establishment

Kevin Morley

The Book Guild Ltd

First published in Great Britain in 2019 by
The Book Guild Ltd
9 Priory Business Park
Wistow Road, Kibworth
Leicestershire, LE8 0RX
Freephone: 0800 999 2982
www.bookguild.co.uk
Email: info@bookguild.co.uk
Twitter: @bookguild

Typeset in Adobe Garamond Pro

Printed and bound in the UK by TJ International, Padstow, Cornwall

ISBN 978 1912881 352

British Library Cataloguing in Publication Data.
A catalogue record for this book is available from the British Library.

MIX
Paper from
responsible sources
FSC
www.fsc.org   FSC® C013056

To those fighting oppression and tyrany,
economic and physical in all lands.

"The great appear great because we are on our knees – let us rise"
– Jim Larkin and James Connolly

Misogyny, according to sociologist Allan G. Johnson, is: 'A central part of sexist prejudice and ideology and, as such, is an important basis for the oppression of females in male-dominated societies. Misogyny is manifested in many ways, from jokes to pornography to violence to the self-contempt women may be taught to feel towards their own bodies.' The *Collins Paperback English Dictionary* definition is put simply and inadequately: 'Hatred of women'.

Is Allan G. Johnson's description the correct one? Or is any definition in the eye of the beholder? If misogyny is 'manifested in many different ways, from jokes to pornography', what about the increasing number of men and women who watch pornography often to spice up their relationships? Are they guilty of misogyny? Some sociologists argue misogyny is not isolated to just men being culpable, but some women are also guilty of the crime. Are women taught contempt towards their own bodies? Sociologist Michael Flood argues: 'Though most common in men, misogyny also exists in and is practiced by women against other women or even themselves.' So where do we draw the line, before society becomes so engrossed that even simple conversation between people of both genders could be deemed misogynist in nature and content?

Perhaps the following could be regarded as misogynist:

1) unwelcome touching by, primarily though not exclusively, men on women;
2) comments about the nature of a woman's or women's anatomy;
3) insulting language towards women.

While misogyny means 'hatred of women', sexism is defined as 'discrimination against members of one sex, usually women'. Sexism applies often, though not exclusively, in the workplace.

Is wolf-whistling misogynist? It may be belittling but it hardly equals 'hatred of women'. We also know that wolf-whistling is not purely confined to men. However, if it is going to cause offence in any quarter, it would be wise to refrain from doing it.

There are many instances when women, with no malice intended, have commented on a man being 'fit'. Is this sexist? There was a debate on *Sunday Morning Live*, a BBC current affairs programme about whether female students should be forced to wear trousers in school. The consensus was that trousers or skirts should be optional. That sounds perfectly sensible and reasonable. But then one could ask: should boys have the same option? Why not? It is the twenty-first century, after all. It would not be my own choice, but each to their own.

This book hopes to highlight misogyny, racism, xenophobia and homophobia for the ugly fascist concepts they are. Our fictitious character, based loosely on several real-life people, bears all these negative qualities. His name is Ronald Crump and he reaches the highest political office in the Western world, the presidency of the United States of America. While the activities of our man are based around real-life happenings, I affirm that all the content herein is an unreserved work of fiction.

Ronald Crump was born in Florida, USA on 1st April 1947 to a retired colonel of the US Army, Teddy Crump, and his wife Megan, who had held a junior position in American banking before she married Teddy. As was the common thing to do for a woman who got married in 1940s USA, they married on Teddy's return from Europe in 1946. She then stopped work to raise a family. On leaving the army on a full pension at the age of fifty-two, Teddy entered the business world specialising in the arms trade, having inherited his father's small engineering firm. Then as now, this was big business, and various organisations and terrorist groups around the world were eager to purchase weapons, legal or otherwise. The legality of such sales was again, like today, of little consequence to arms dealers, including Teddy Crump.

Teddy was already a multimillionaire when Ronald came along in 1947. Whatever else Teddy may have been – some of the workers called him a slave-driver who paid the minimum he could get away with in terms of wages and ruled the workforce with an iron fist – he was a loving father by the standards of the middle classes in the USA. Teddy refused to recognise trade unions or organisations worthy of the name, as he saw them as a hindrance to his pursuit of profits. Despite all this Teddy was a considerate father, so far as US bourgeois society would allow, and Megan a doting mother. Baby Ronald was to be the apple of the couple's eyes, and for Teddy a means of continuation in the same mould as himself. He was going to have the very best money could buy.

Unfortunately, that did not include time and attention bringing him up to respect other people and considering the position of others. What the Crumps did not realise was that a child of 1940s USA needed a father to be around the place some of the time; society had not yet developed or progressed to the age of single parenthood. Teddy loved Ronald, but in a limited manner. The only time Teddy spent with his son was when he gave him private tuition. This started when the young boy reached school age. Teddy taught him subjects he felt his son would need later in life, important matters that would not be covered by Ronald's schoolteachers.

There were no baseball games played between Ronald and his father, as were enjoyed by most American children, whether they were part of the country's middle class – Teddy's position in society – or the working class.

Teddy was too busy making money which, in his warped world, he believed was the root of his and his family's happiness. In 1949 the Crumps moved to the suburbs of New York City, purchasing a seven-bedroom mansion together with games room, study, servants' quarters and private bar along with an Olympic-size swimming pool. This was at the time of Millionaires' – soon to become Billionaires' – Row. Very few who lived in this locality were worth less than five hundred million dollars and every resident had servants and at least two luxury cars, a chauffeur and a runabout.

Ronald grew very attached to his mother, as he saw very little of his father. It was Megan who took the infant Ronald on Sunday cycle rides on the nanny's day off. However, she could not fill the void left by his absent father, who was totally engrossed in his work. In his eyes the system demanded business and profits – and this superseded all other considerations, including family life. Teddy saw this mode as the best way of securing his son's future and perhaps within the confines of capitalism he had a point.

Megan could not play baseball with her son, as Teddy should have done, and Ronald would suffer for this when he started high school. Other kids' fathers who were also in business managed to find time to spend with their children, because pastimes such as baseball are very important to American culture. At school the sport was considered a key subject and most of the children, except Ronald, enjoyed playing it. Luckily, his mother taught him to swim in the family's pool at an early age. It turned out swimming would be Ronald's sport and in this he would thrive.

This was, in brief, the background of the future president during his formative years.

The Early Years

It was September 1953 and young Ronald Crump was ready to start preparatory school. His mother, Megan, took him to the gates of the private and exclusive institution for his first day at prep school. The Korean conflict, which had dominated world events for the previous three years, was still the topic of conversation among teachers and parents alike. Megan, being the wife of a retired colonel, took a close interest in the subject. 'If those nasty commies had won, the end of civilisation would have been nigh,' was a perceived belief among the brethren. Many of the parents already knew each other as they were on the school board of governors.

All the middle-class parents present at this gathering agreed that but for the United States it would have been curtains for the rest of the world, outside the then Soviet bloc, which they didn't count. They failed to mention the role played by the United Nations in securing what could only be described as a score draw in the conflict. In the eyes of Middle America, it was imagined that the USA, and only the USA, represented the entire United Nations. As far as they were concerned, the soldiers from other countries only played a 'bit part' in the fighting. They also failed to mention the many setbacks and defeats suffered by US forces on the Korean peninsula and the fact that the Soviet-supplied MiG jet fighters gave the US Air Force a run for their money.

This was the arrogant attitude of middle-class Americans, an attitude which their children, including Ronald, would grow into. Teddy, Ronald's father, took no part in the events on the Korean peninsula. He had retired at the end of the Second World War and was too old for combat in Korea. At fifty-two years old he was twenty years his wife's senior when they married in 1946. This was not uncommon in the USA at the time. An army officer returning from the war with great prospects was just the ticket for a young American bride-to-be. With his US army pension and the great wealth he had secured through selling arms around the globe, legally or otherwise, Teddy Crump was a great catch. In a world where the dollar bill trumped all other considerations, this train of thought would come to dominate young Ronald's life.

Megan Crump, having disengaged from the conversation about Korea, kissed young Ronald on the cheek and left him in the capable hands of his new teachers. She felt a certain sadness in her heart as this would be the first time she and her son had been separated for any time since his birth.

Ronald started to cry as his mother left him, shouting, 'Mommy, Mommy!' after her.

The other kids, most of whom had brothers and sisters, began to laugh at young Ronald. 'Mommy's boy' was the taunt and 'cry-baby' was one of the milder teases his tormentors offered him. One of the teachers, Miss Clarkson, intervened on Ronald's behalf and prevented the lonely child from any more torture, for now. She inwardly sighed. Even though Miss Clarkson knew several parents were acquainted, this didn't necessarily mean their children wouldn't be rude to each other.

As the name suggested, prep school was exactly that: preparation for proper school. Ronald would spend two years here, between the ages of six and eight, before moving to the junior section of this expensive complex – in future years the age for starting prep school would be lowered to three if requested by parents. Fortunately for Ronald, he was to have Miss Clarkson as his teacher, which was a relief for the shy young boy. He felt a sense of security while she was around and became a little braver.

Suddenly Ronald felt a sharp stabbing pain in his side.

'Ouch!' he screamed, as the culprit turned away.

'What is the matter?' Miss Clarkson asked him.

When he tried to explain that the other boy had poked him in his side for no reason, he was told not to be such a baby. The boy in question denied all knowledge of the incident, so the teacher could not take any action as it was one boy's word against another's. The earlier confidence Ronald had felt ebbed, as it became clear Miss Clarkson had other children, not just him, to attend to. Ronald was frustrated, as he was accustomed to having everything his own way. Mommy gave him everything, as did Daddy when he was around, usually in the form of dollar bills. In a nutshell Ronald Crump was a spoilt little brat, as his unfortunate teachers and the rest of the class would find out in time.

The first lesson on the first day at prep involved simple questions about measuring jugs and water. The intention was to get the class of six-year-olds familiar with their new surroundings and the concept of learning. The object of this exercise was to make the youngsters aware how much capacity a vessel held and that when it was full the water would flow over. Later there would be questions, like how many (US) half-pints made a pint, and if an attempt was made to pour two pints of liquid into a one-pint jug, what would the result be?

The bullies were beginning to gather, storm clouds were visible on the horizon, and young Crump was to be their target. Miss Clarkson was aware of an atmosphere developing among some of the new pupils. However, catching the others in any act of bullying would prove difficult and Miss Clarkson decided to let things go in the hope that they would sort themselves out. The main voice in the crowd was that of James Rothschild, son of a multimillionaire family, whose parents were friends of the Crumps. In Middle America the families of big business tended to be part of the same social clique. The Crumps were in arms and engineering and Rothschilds were international financiers and bankers while Bradley Morgan worked for the diplomatic corps.

Suddenly Ronald cried out, 'Miss, Miss, look what James has done, Miss.'

The teacher turned around to see Ronald dripping wet. As Miss Clarkson took stock of the situation, James Rothschild claimed Ronald had spilt water over himself and was trying to get him into trouble. As neither Miss Clarkson nor her part-time assistant, Mrs Johnson, had witnessed the occurrence, they could take no action. It was, after all, Ronald's word against the other boy's, although she suspected Ronald's version of events was the correct one.

The following day Megan Crump took Ronald to school again and engaged in conversation with some other parents and teachers. Miss Clarkson decided not to mention the previous day's unfortunate incident, but Megan Crump did.

'Ronald came home drenched yesterday,' she offered. 'What happened?'

Miss Clarkson tried to tell her the youngster had spilt water over himself, but Ronald was having none of it.

'It was like I told you, Mommy,' he said. 'James threw water over me for nothing.'

The teacher explained she could take no action, as it was one child's word against another's. Megan was not happy.

'Are you suggesting my little angel is being dishonest?' Megan protested. 'My Ronald would not lie about anything, let alone something like this. If he said they did it then that is what happened.'

The teacher tried again to explain that her hands were tied when suddenly Mrs Rothschild interjected. 'Are you saying my James is telling stories then?' she said. 'If you are, I would be very careful what you say. My James is an honest little boy.'

The two women socialites and supposed friends were on the verge of a fight when, unexpectedly, the husbands appeared.

The two men had been at an important early-morning meeting and had just secured big contracts. Crump had successfully negotiated a multimillion-dollar arms deal, which Hugh Rothschild's bank would handle on his behalf. Both were to make a mint. When the two belligerent women heard this they quickly forgot about the silliness involving the children. This was far more important so all the adults left the stage and retired for a celebratory drink. The teachers were delighted: firstly, because this meant the school would benefit financially, and secondly, because the previous day's events would be forgotten, at least for the time being.

While the Crumps and Hugh and Mary Rothschild were enjoying a social drink to celebrate their good fortune, back at the school, more problems were brewing. The children were not yet of an age where money meant a great deal, though young Ronald, due to Teddy's monetary generosity, was beginning to grasp the concept. On that day the children were learning to draw using wax crayons. Terry Morgan, one of James Rothschild's fledgling gang of bullies, scribbled all over Ronald Crump's attempts at drawing. This time Miss Clarkson witnessed the event and was compelled to act.

She called young Morgan out to the front of the class, acutely aware that the Morgans, like the Crumps and Rothschilds, were extremely wealthy, and that was the factor which decided what, if any, action would be taken. For Miss Clarkson it would have been easier if one of the warring children came from a less well-off family; she could then punish that child irrespective of guilt or innocence. The hapless teacher, not wishing to upset either family, decided she would punish neither boy but insist on a public shaking of hands.

Terry Morgan agreed to this, but Ronald Crump folded his arms and scowled at Terry.

Miss Clarkson appeased young Crump with a bar of chocolate. This had the effect she was looking for, as Ronald was used to resolutions been solved in cash or in kind. Ultimately the situation was defused, resulting in the desired handshake.

Out on the town celebrating, the Crumps and Rothschilds were joined by Brad and Ethel Morgan, young Terry's parents.

'Hey Brad,' shouted Crump, in his usual loud-mouthed fashion, referring to Bradley Morgan, 'come over and join us, we're celebrating. Have a glass of champagne or six.'

Even though Crump regarded himself as a very popular man, he was actually despised by most of this company. All they liked about him was his wallet. The Morgans gave the impression they were pleased, but privately they were jealous as hell. They briefly discussed their offspring at school and all agreed things would be great once the kids reached the age of twelve and could be packed off to boarding school. Deep down, they hated each other's guts while at the same time they were interdependent on one another. They all thought they were giving their children the best upbringing available, which was in truth totally void of any genuine love and care. They also assumed that giving their children lots of money and presents, generally turning them into the most detestable creatures on earth, was the correct way forward. The blind assumption of these rich and wealthy was that when these children grew up they would be the next generation of America's rulers or ruling classes.

Megan Crump was beginning to feel the downside of alcohol. She had reached the stage of elation and was now entering the depressive point. She began to cry for no reason. Teddy didn't mind this; he was only concerned with the deal he had secured with a foreign government for arms and the Rothschilds were primarily concerned with their huge cut for the financial transactions they were conducting on behalf of the Crumps. The foreign government in question was a right-wing dictatorship where trade unionists and political opponents were shot or had conveniently disappeared. Ethel Morgan was scheming how to benefit from all this good fortune; she had a plan, which she would discuss with her husband when they arrived home. Having spent most of the afternoon pretending to admire and like the Crumps and Rothschilds, the Morgans' real interest in the company was to procure a cut of the money for themselves. Ethel Morgan was a devious woman who would shoot her own mother if financial reward was sufficient, so stabbing her 'friends' in the back would be small fry to her. She had determined she and Brad were not going to be empty-handed and her brain was working overtime while pretending to befriend the Crumps and Rothschilds.

Teddy Crump, despite his faults, had not become a multimillionaire by being stupid. He had Ethel and Brad's intentions firmly within his sights. He had decided that the Morgans had a value so allowed Ethel a little latitude to capitalise on the deal to a limited extent. He knew if he let the Morgans believe they had pulled a fast one over on him Crump would call in the favour and another dozen similar favours, at a future unspecified date. Something would arise out of a given situation and Crump would be owed; he would have the Morgans where he wanted them. He calculated, after a brief conversation with Hugh Rothschild, that a small sum of fifty thousand dollars should be made available to the Morgans. In return, the Morgans would introduce Crump to possible new clients of mega-wealth. Put plainly, they were playing a very expensive game of 'Mouse Trap'.

On their arrival home Ethel Morgan ordered the ever-downtrodden Brad to sit down. She told him she had masterminded a plan to secure some of the money the Crumps and Rothschilds had accumulated. Brad would introduce Crump to some wealthy clients, leading him to believe that a business deal could be secured. Of course, no arrangement would be even in the pipeline but all that mattered was that Crump believed there was a deal. So, Brad arranged a meeting between the owners of a private gun club, Matthew and Sally Seddon, and Crump. The Seddon couple were millionaires, young and ambitious, with no children. Matthew Seddon was eager to meet Teddy Crump to arrange a shipment of state-of-the-art automatic weapons for his club. Crump, aware Ethel Morgan was up to no good, agreed to the meeting, which Brad arranged. Teddy offered Brad a twenty-thousand-dollar 'sweetener' if a deal could be struck, knowing full well Ethel was after more.

The three brigands met in a motel about ten miles outside New York. Brad Morgan introduced Crump to Matthew Seddon and the pair appeared to get on straight away. At a certain point Morgan excused himself to go to the restroom and Crump immediately got to work on Seddon. Before Morgan returned they had agreed in principle a deal worth around half a million dollars. On Morgan's return Crump and Seddon dragged out the already agreed deal for Brad's benefit. Ethel had left her husband instructions to get as much money he could out of Crump.

The meeting ended and as Seddon left straight away, Crump took the opportunity to tell Morgan that he was pleased with him for arranging the meeting, which had provided him with a deal worth two hundred and twenty thousand dollars, at least this is what Morgan was led to believe. Crump said he would like to offer Bradley twenty thousand dollars for arranging the deal, which he knew would be looked down on, though not refused out of hand, by Morgan. Crump also knew twenty thousand as a figure was too low for him to claim back in tax, and that fifty thousand dollars would be more beneficial. Morgan, as expected, haggled and Crump pretended to bend, eventually agreeing to fifty thousand, eighty per cent tax refundable, though this detail he omitted to tell Morgan.

Bradley Morgan left, feeling very pleased with himself having secured, for Ethel, fifty thousand dollars. For his part Crump knew most of this would be returned to him via the taxman and in the full knowledge he had in Morgan an avenue to more lucrative contacts. He had also conned Morgan into believing the low figure for the deal so it didn't bother him at all that he was being used by Brad, so long as he, Crump, was the real puppeteer. Ethel was pleased with her lapdog husband for securing fifty thousand dollars.

On his arrival home Teddy Crump was greeted by a scene of tears from his son.

'That nasty Rothschild and his friends punched me at school,' he sobbed.

Both Megan and Teddy knew the value of the Rothschilds' friendship in monetary terms and were not going to allow a kid's childish argument to spoil things. Teddy patted his son on the head and gave him a ten-dollar bill, hush money, and promised him a new bicycle. These things had the desired calming result on the young Ronald.

These early methods dealing with young Ronald's tantrums would come back to haunt Teddy and Megan in the not-too-distant future. It never entered either parent's head to teach Ronald to fight back. Perhaps this course of action would have been too time-consuming. Both Teddy and Megan firmly believed, as did many in the USA, that the dollar bill answered all questions and dealt with every imaginable problem.

Ronald Crump had been at prep school seven months now and it was coming around to his seventh birthday. He had become more accepted by the other children at school, including the junior mafia headed by James Rothschild and Terry Morgan. Megan and Teddy were organising a party for the youngster and were planning to invite their so-called friends, the Rothschilds and Morgans, and their children. The Seddons also now qualified as friends of the Crumps. These people were not proper friends, in fact they detested one another and the jealousy among them was noticeable to anybody who gave more than a cursory glance. The Seddons had no children but as they were young and energetic it was thought they would add some life to the party, bridging the gap from children to adults.

Another advantage of inviting the younger couple was that it gave Megan an opportunity to show off Ronald and his expensive presents, a kind of subtle guidance for when they would have children as to the standards which they must maintain to remain friends with the likes of the Crumps. Such actions as those practised by the Crumps, Rothschilds and Morgans, snobbery in any other country, were common in the USA then, as now, a country which claims not to practise class politics or structures. Anybody who believes such rubbish is either blind, or just does not want to see.

1ˢᵗ April, the big day, soon came around and Teddy spent what would have been about a year's worth of an employee's salary on his son's presents. Small wonder he was becoming a spoilt little brat! Even in 1954 the USA was very advanced in the field of technology, and the arms dealer spent a fortune on small presents for his son to play with. Ronald played with these gadgets for about half an hour and then, being a model of ruination, simply threw them in the bin. Young Crump's main present was a large battery-operated mini motor car, and Ronald drove it around showing off to his friends. Some of the guests at the party were girls and Ronald made a point of driving into them. He took immense pleasure in running the girls down but did not share the same enthusiasm doing the same to the boys. Perhaps he was afraid the lads would drag him out of the mini car and kick him around. Was the isolating of the girls for treatment also a sign of things to come? Young Ronald drove his machine directly at Dianna Nixon, pinning her against a wall, laughing to himself as the terrified young girl began to cry. Much to Ronald's anger his mother, Megan, intervened and stopped his activities. Despite being told off, Ronald displayed an air of importance, as if he had just distinguished himself in some heroic way. He did not express remorse at picking on somebody weaker and causing her distress, a characteristic which would follow him through to adulthood.

It was now time for the party tea. Megan had made a variety of sandwiches, or more accurately the servants had, cutting off the crusts for the little guests. The cook had baked a variety of cakes and candy with various soft minerals also available to wash down the feast. Naturally, there had to be a bun fight. The adults were prepared for this, even joining in, as the children threw cakes at each other. Once again Ronald singled out girls as targets for his amusement, hitting young Susie Carter smack in the face. The grown-ups, Jimmy and Moira Carter included, saw this for what it was, childish fun, none noticing, however, that Ronald's attention for pranks all afternoon was aimed solely at girls.

The day passed quickly, with the guests managing to keep up their pretence at being friends and the children being relatively well behaved. As everybody prepared to leave, the Carters shook hands with their hosts after Moira Carter cleaned Susie's face of cream and candy and wished the Crumps 'all the best in business and wealth', much to the arms dealer's amusement. When everybody had departed Megan, the host, surveyed the damage, such as it was, and commented to her husband, 'Oh well, Ted, the servants will have their work cut out tomorrow.'

The Crumps had several servants, or domestics, as they termed them, all African American, who were paid a pittance in the way of wages. They also had a gardener, a retired army corporal who had served under the colonel in the liberation of France. This was a historical event at which Colonel Crump arrived very late, most of the action in France being over by the time he arrived. The same applied when Staff-Officer Crump was moved to Hamburg after Germany had surrendered. The gardener was paid reasonably well and the job supplemented his army pension. Most importantly, he enjoyed the work. He was, of course, a white American and though not regarded as an equal, he was afforded more respect than the 'coloured domestics'.

The Crumps spoke to their staff in firm but polite language and kept themselves aloof from them in all but matters pertaining to their work. The retired corporal in the garden often found a quiet five minutes with Teddy to discuss the war but that was generally the scope of their conversation. On the day of the party most of the domestic staff had been given an unpaid day off, so as not to tarnish the occasion. The exceptions were the cook who prepared the feast, and Betty, the head domestic, who surveyed what needed doing. The servants arrived at the house for work the following day. Betty and her colleagues looked over the disarray in the main room. 'Lord have mercy,' she said. 'The young master and his friends sure had a wonderful day and we'll have to clean this mess up mighty quickly or the boss man be very angry.'

These servants appeared to know their place in society and accepted it without question. It never entered their heads that when Teddy and his gardener were having friendly reminiscent chats about the Second World War, many of the soldiers involved were black or mixed race. These troops played just as heroic a part as their white colleagues in defeating Nazi Germany and Imperial Japan. These domestics just accepted that they were to be treated as second class and no question about it. Young Ronald, unlike his parents, did not even afford these people the pretence of respect, mainly because he had never been told to speak respectfully to the servants: they were, after all, only blacks! Betty and her team tore into the work as if their lives depended on it. If a black employee lost their job through perceived slacking, the likelihood of finding another source of income, small as it was, was remote.

'Come on now, ladies,' Betty urged her underlings, 'we must make this a palace for Mr and Mrs Crump and young Master Crump. We can't leave a crumb of candy or speck of dust.'

Betty was a deeply religious woman who attended chapel every Sunday without exception, as were most of the poor black population. She also thanked God every night for being allowed to work for the Crumps. All these people wanted to do was serve their 'betters', people like the Crumps, and asked little reward for doing so. To the average observer very little had changed, apart from the floggings, since the days which preceded the American Civil War. The USA of the fifties was very much apartheid-based, something which was to last for many decades to follow, and the Rosa Parks incident in Montgomery the following year did not permeate to the Crumps' domestics.

It could be reasonably argued that not until the election of Barack Obama to the office of President did black people really make a mark on society in the USA. The fact that most of the country's finest athletes were African Americans, from Jesse Owens on the track to Joe Louis and Muhammed Ali in the boxing ring, counted for little in everyday life. To people like the Crumps and their cohorts this was an irrelevance, hardly worthy of consideration. Of course, if these athletic masters had been white they would have been deemed as supermen. Today black athletes continue to put the USA on the sporting map, like the Williams sisters in tennis and many black track and field athletes.

All this was a million miles away from the world inhabited by Betty and her friends working for the Crumps. When they had finished their cleaning of the rooms that had been turned into a bomb site by young Crump and his so-called friends, the place was like a palace. Teddy Crump, in typical ignorant fashion, failed to notice the work the team had put into making his home habitable again, though Megan did pay compliments to Betty and the staff. Then Ronald entered the scene.

'I want a cup of milk,' he bombastically ordered from one of the young maids, 'and hurry up with it,' he added.

'Now, now, Ronald,' Megan interjected. 'Try to remember your manners.'

She didn't really care how her son spoke to the domestics but liked to give the impression of being civilised. Ronald, on the other hand, had no respect at all for the domestics as they were only girls – and black.

Teddy had begun giving his son basic lessons in calculating figures, a subject the young Crump would shine in, making up for his deficiencies in sporting activities. Numeracy and literacy were to be Ronald Crump's strong points in the field of education. These were, according to his father, the most important subjects in business, which was where Ronald was destined. His father went on to explain that all the other work was done by other people. Scientists and men of invention and foresight did the scientific and technological work and advancements, tradesmen mastered the construction of these advancements, and men of low mental ability carried out the labouring tasks for little pay.

'In fact, the lower down the social order we go,' Crump Senior pointed out, 'the harder the work is and the less we pay in wages.' As far as he was concerned, it was an accepted fact that those with super brains – like himself – did the least work but amassed huge wealth. This, in the world of Teddy Crump, was the reason for numeracy and literacy, and everything else would follow from that. That day he was not only giving his son lessons in figures, he was teaching him how to manipulate figures to get the sum he wished. These were very early days of course, but Crump was determined his son would flourish in these departments. These subjects were also supported by the essential ingredient, deviousness!

At school things were picking up for Ronald. He had now been accepted into the junior mafia and the bullying had ceased. In fact, the young Crump was now one of the bullies himself, with most of his victims being girls. Once again, a certain trace of what would become known as misogyny was visible in his behaviour. This misogyny was to become apparent in the level of respect he gave his teachers. Even though Miss Clarkson had previously saved Ronald from Rothschild's mafia, she was now treated sarcastically by the son of the arms dealer.

Ronald never showed the same contempt for his English grammar teacher, Mr Tudor, for whom he had the utmost respect, almost to the point of grovelling. Mr Tudor was aware of Ronald's father's immense wealth and even fame in the arms and engineering industry. Unknown to Ronald, Teddy had a private chat with Tudor, leaving direct instructions this was a subject Crump expected his son to shine in. Tudor then gave him special attention to bring him along in this subject. Teddy had a similar talk with the math teacher, Mr

McArthur, leaving the teacher in no doubt of his expectations for the boy. 'Heads will roll if Ronald does not come top of the class in math and English.'

Mrs Stuart taught English literature, a subject considered important for Crump but not on the same level as English grammar. Mrs Stuart was already finding the boy a difficult student. Even at this early age he was showing unpleasant signs of the misogynist, racist and xenophobe he was to become.

To Mr McArthur and Mr Tudor, math and English, it was, 'Yes sir, no sir, three bags full sir', but to Miss Clarkson and Mrs Stuart the respect level was considerably and consistently lower. It was becoming increasingly apparent to Ronald that, due to his father's wealth, and outside the subjects he was expected to shine in by Teddy, he could do pretty much as he wished. He had more respect for James Rothschild and Terry Morgan than these female articles of fun masquerading as teachers. Mrs Johnson, the teaching assistant, stood no chance. *She was not even a 'proper' teacher, so fuck her*, was his train of thought. All the children at the prep school were developing a trend towards using bad language. This was not done in front of the teachers, especially the male ones, nothing so bold as that, but to each other the cursing became part and parcel of everyday discourse.

Ronald Crump, as demanded by his father, was shining in math and English grammar. He was now in his second year at prep school and an impression of the future adult was beginning to appear. In English literature he was above average, with much potential which later would develop, but could not really give a shit about writing essays or poetry or any other so-called aspects of the world of literature. What use would the works of Byron and Shakespeare be in the world of business? This attitude would change as would his grades in the subject.

The level of mathematics the children of this exclusive private institution were at ranged from average to, in Ronald's case, very high for the age group. They all knew their times tables from one to ten and basic adding and subtracting. Mr McArthur was contemplating moving young Crump on to multiplications which, for a child of seven, going on eight, was advanced. *Was it too early?* McArthur asked himself. He did not wish to overload the youngster and lose all the ground he had already made in the discipline – that would never do for Mr Crump and it could cost him his job. It must be remembered the importance of currying favour with the parents held for these teachers. The math teacher erred on the side of caution, at least for a month or two, and delayed Ronald's promotion to multiplications. The other children, including the rest of the mafia, were average in these disciplines but shone in the fields of physical education. Two exceptions to the rule were young Rothschild, who was showing great promise both at baseball as well as science and English literature; and Terry Morgan, who was shining in the field of American football and geography. All in all, the students were beginning to prioritise their subjects and Ronald Crump, with Teddy's private tuition, was heading in the right direction for a successful future in the world of business and commerce. He was, after all, to become Teddy's heir apparent to the business empire.

As the months passed by Mr McArthur decided the time was right for Ronald to move up to doing multiplication. Young Crump took to the subject like a duck to water and Mr McArthur was delighted with the young student's progress. His joy was because Mr Crump would be pleased with him, like a puppy being rewarded by its master. This achievement, pleasing the arms dealer, was akin to receiving a knighthood in the eyes of the math teacher. Ronald shone in this discipline so much so that Mr McArthur quickly moved him up another gear to long multiplication. Again, he flew through the math subdivision, partly due to Teddy's private lessons, and the same applied to divisions. These were the limits of mathematics at prep school, as fractions and percentages would come at junior and high schools, as would long divisions. Ronald Crump was also showing the same aptitude in English grammar and his understanding of the English language was far above that of his peers. On this subject, unlike math, he would be matched for a time by his peers as time progressed before really excelling, leaving most behind. That was, however, for the future. Ronald Crump then applied his mastery of English spelling and language to the literature side of the subject. He was beginning to see the importance of applying one to the other, grammar to literature. These would be important tools in Ronald's armoury when writing letters in later life.

It was now 1955 and Ronald's eighth birthday had been and gone in a similar fashion to the previous year. He was now in the last few months of prep school and young Crump, fully accomplished in the subjects of necessity, was preparing for junior school proper. Although the summer break from school commenced, Teddy Crump continued to give young Ronald private lessons in numeracy and literacy. He was careful not to overdo it, as he was aware that, like his employees, Ronald would need some leisure time to himself and would be more productive as a result.

Teddy Crump believed in the 'firm but fair' approach to handling his employees and he wanted his son to inherit a similar style of management.

Teddy didn't mean, by 'firm but fair', to be 'egalitarian'; it would be a mistake for anybody to think this to have been the case. If one member of staff was disciplined for an offence, usually something trivial, then the whole team would be punished. This would create disunity among the workforce, each blaming the culprit for their predicament. He wished to create the false impression, as do many employers, that they were all one team, an illusion of equilibrium and nothing more than an illusion. If a member of staff were to question this rubbish of all being the same, in that each was a valuable member of the team, that person usually received their cards. Crump instilled this form of control into Ronald in between basic math lessons. He even suggested to Ronald that he should try this method of control out on some of his son's school friends. Not the Rothschild boy or young Morgan though, as they had a similar education from their parents.

It was about eleven-thirty in the morning when the doorbell of the Crump's mansion rang. It was young Terry Morgan for Ronald. The gang was going off on an adventure and Ronald was welcome to join them. James Rothschild was the self-appointed leader, as was now the norm, and he along with Terry, Ronald, Peter Tillerson, Dianna Nixon and Susie Carter set off into the unknown. Ronald was not happy about the girls being on the outing, but it had been James Rothschild's decision they would come along and young Crump didn't dare argue. After all, he had only recently been accepted into the mafia himself. As far as women were concerned Rothschild was maturing quicker than the other three male junior brigands and was developing an attraction for Susie. Ronald was aware of something going on and decided it would not be a clever idea to bully Susie. Having reached this realisation, it still left Dianna Nixon to pick on. She was slightly overweight and wore glasses, a potentially perfect victim. Unfortunately for young Crump, James Rothschild had developed a protective attitude towards both the girls on *his* outing and although Susie was the target of his embryonic affections he would not see her friend, Dianna, bullied. Ronald would find this out almost to his cost. Peter Tillerson fancied his chances, in a childish way, with Dianna but his affections were rebuffed.

The Famous Six, as they called themselves after the Enid Blyton children's stories, *The Famous Five*, set off for the hills in the distance. Their parents' servants had made them a packed lunch for the adventure, so all provisions were taken care of. They approached a narrow stream that flowed with an abundance of fresh water. Ronald made his first and only mistake when he tried to drench Dianna Nixon for no reason. The girl began to cry.

'Shut up, four eyes!' Ronald shouted.

Suddenly he felt a sharp punch to his left ear.

'Ouch, that hurt,' blurted Crump.

'Leave her alone, you fucking bully!' shouted James. 'Do that again and I'll use your head as a football.'

James Rothschild was having none of this bullying of the girls on *his* expedition.

Peter Tillerson interjected, 'That's right, Crump,' he said. 'If you want a fight then I'm your man. Come on now.' He raised his fists and approached Ronald.

Young Crump backed away sheepishly. He knew Tillerson had joined a junior boxing gym and was looking for a sparring partner, but that was not going to be him.

'No Pete, sorry, it won't happen again.'

'It's not him you should be apologising to,' said James Rothschild, eager not to lose control to Tillerson. 'It's Dianna. Say sorry to her.'

Ronald dutifully obliged the unelected leader and directly apologised to Dianna Nixon. The incident was soon forgotten, and the six companions were soon on their way again. On arriving at their destination, the top of Sugar Hill, they stopped for lunch before their descent back to town. During the interlude they discussed school the following school year at the juniors, after which it was boarding school for all of them. Rothschild voiced the opinion he was going to be a famous baseball player, and Tillerson declared he would be the undisputed world boxing champion. Morgan had the view that an airline pilot sounded interesting while Ronald offered little about his own aspirations. Back in those days opportunities for girls were not as broad as today, so they kept quiet also. Rothschild looked up to the sky, giving the impression he knew what he was doing, and indicated dangerous weather might be on its way. He knew no more about meteorology than did the rest but wanted to keep control of *his* gang.

'Time to make tracks,' he ordered.

It was late afternoon by the time the six children made their way back to town, all a little tired after their collective expedition into nature.

On arriving back at the mansion Ronald was greeted by his parents, glad to witness his safe return. Megan indicated to Teddy not to give his son any more lessons that day. Cook had made the youngster a burger and fries supper which young Crump devoured. He offered nothing in the way of thanks to the cook who had, after all, stayed on beyond her normal hours with no extra pay, but his parents showed their appreciation by giving her some leftover vegetables. This was the contempt commonly shown at that time by the American ruling class towards their servants. The richer the employer the more contemptuous of their servants these people were. They had a very high opinion of themselves, which precluded being in any way decent to the so-called lower orders.

'Come along now, Ronald, it's time for bed. Daddy will read you a story if you're very good,' Megan appealed to her son, hoping this would entice him to retire for the night with the minimum of fuss.

After the usual 'Just five more minutes, Mommy' appeals from the eight-year-old, he eventually agreed to his parents' demands and off he went to bed. Teddy now had to read his son a bedtime story, otherwise his son would have a tantrum. He chose *Goldilocks and the Three Bears* to coax his son to sleep, and before long young Ronald was away with the fairies.

The following morning, after being tutored by his father, Ronald was free to do as he pleased, or so he thought. James Rothschild had summoned a council meeting in preparation for the new term at the Junior School. The young mafia, now renamed The Gang of Six (the Famous Six was too sissy), would discuss how they would handle the other kids at their new school. Even though the gang included the two girls, they weren't invited to this meeting as it was considered 'man talk'. They had to formulate a plan to rule the playground, up to and including physical fighting.

Ronald was none too keen on the last part, as fighting did not appeal to him. He was more of a devious little shit, a grovelling little creep where it would benefit him, and all in all, a coward. He did, however, wish to remain part of the gang but did not want to do his bit to defend the six. He furiously tried to think up a way to avoid at all costs having to fight in the playground at their new school. Ronald had the idea of sucking up to Peter Tillerson; he was a good fighter but a bit slow at academic studies. James Rothschild tied up their meeting by sharing that he wanted to make sure Susie was looked after, and the lads agreed that any threats to their domination of the playground would be met with force.

Ronald Crump began putting his plan at courting Peter Tillerson into action.

'Pete, would you like to come around to my house for tea?' he said after the council meeting wrapped up. 'I'll show you how to do multiplications.'

Young Tillerson was well behind at math.

'And in the exams later you can copy my answers,' Ronald added. Tillerson agreed to the coward's request, unable to see at that stage that what Crump was really after was protection.

'Yes, I'd love to come,' said Peter.

'Cool,' replied Ronald, 'I'll see Cook about making something nice.'

What Crump really meant by this was he would ask his mother to instruct the cook to make a special tea for him and his school friend.

When the big occasion came Peter was welcomed by Teddy at the door.

'Come in, young Tillerson, how's your dad?' Crump enquired, referring to Duke Tillerson, a large building contractor employing four thousand workers, tradesmen, semi-skilled journeymen and labourers. He also had an interest in textiles, owning two clothing factories, though building was his main interest for the present. Like Crump, he had a bombastic form of man-management and did not like his employees speaking to him in the street. Tillerson had a very high opinion of himself.

'Dad's great,' replied young Peter proudly. 'He's just landed a large contract to refurbish the leisure complex.' The young boy was pleased he could show off his interest in his father's business.

Megan then entered the scene.

'Come along, Peter, sit yourself down here next to Ronald,' she invited the builder's son.

Cook had made a special effort for the young school pals, the dinner consisting of home-made sausage rolls, spicy wedges and chicken wings. For dessert there was plum pudding and ice cream with wafers.

After the tea Ronald showed off his new toys to Peter and reiterated his offer of helping him with his multiplications. Peter Tillerson at last suspected Ronald was edging for a favour and had an idea what it might be. He had decided he would help Ronald out; he did after all need help with his math, otherwise he might fail the junior examination on the subject and this would cause a big argument with his father.

Peter Tillerson eventually asked: 'What can I help you with, Ronald?'

Ronald knew he had to call a spade a spade. 'Well Pete, I am really – you see, I'm not a very good fighter,' he admitted. 'Could you mind my back? I don't want to let Rothschild down, plus I would look silly if I couldn't mind his girlfriend, Susie.'

'Don't worry, Ron,' Tillerson said, now confident enough to call Crump by his abridged name, 'I'll look after you if you look after me with my math.'

The two boys agreed on this quid pro quo arrangement, which suited the pair of them.

The summer vacation passed too quickly, and the time came when the Gang of Six approached the gates of Wetherspoons Junior Private Educational Facility. James Rothschild had Susie Carter on his arm just like grown-ups do. James was determined nobody would ever harm a hair on her head, and today he was more vigilant than usual. Crump stuck close to Tillerson while Terry Morgan had befriended young Dianna Nixon, who had finally got rid of Tillerson's attentions.

The six walked up the school drive to be met by some older children. For the most part these were the sons and daughters of other very wealthy people, billionaires in some cases, the least well off to attend this institution the progeny of mere millionaires. The students they met appeared friendly enough. Perhaps the gang's fears of playground aggression were unfounded; they may have been comparing this prestigious establishment with those attended by the lower classes! This later realisation proved to be almost correct. These were, after all, the future ruling class and fighting each other was not part of their daily lives. It was taught from an early age that unless personal gain could be achieved by such infighting, it should be avoided. Should a disagreement occur it was usually sorted out by devious underhand methods and it was normally the richest who won through. Had Ronald been unnecessarily befriending Tillerson, whom he did not really like? Time would tell.

There was one boy whom Ronald felt a little uneasy around. His name was Mitch Brogan and he was an aggressive character. Ronald was on his own one day when this Mitch Brogan pushed him, saying, 'You're Crump, aren't you? I'm watching you. I hear you're a mommy's boy. Do you want to fight?' he continued.

'No,' Ronald quailed, and walked hurriedly away towards the classroom and headed straight for Peter Tillerson.

'I've just had a bit of bother,' he informed his minder.

'What's the problem?' Tillerson asked.

'Brogan is,' Ronald informed Peter.

'Leave it to me,' he was told, 'I'll deal with it later.'

After the geography lesson Peter Tillerson approached Mitch Brogan. 'What's your game?' he demanded.

'What's it to you?' Brogan replied.

'Listen to me,' Tillerson said. 'Crump is my friend and if you bother him then you and me will fall out.'

'Behind the gym,' said Brogan. 'We'll sort it out there at lunchtime.'

'Right,' said Tillerson. Lunchtime came and Tillerson met Brogan for the showdown. Tillerson told nobody in case he lost, and Brogan felt the same, so the encounter was a secret. Tillerson landed the first punch to Brogan's jaw and his opponent fought back with a thump to the young boxer's ears. The fight lasted about fifteen minutes and Tillerson emerged the winner – but only just. Later, he told Ronald what had happened and advised the young coward to 'avoid Brogan, or at least do not upset him,' as Tillerson had 'no wish for a rematch.'

'He won't bother you again,' said Tillerson, 'but do not antagonise him.'

'Thanks, Pete,' said Ronald. 'If I can do anything for you just let me know,' he said, hoping the offer would never be taken up.

It was a Wednesday afternoon and math, the first lesson on the timetable, was looked forward to with enthusiasm by Ronald. Remembering the private tuition Teddy had given him, the young Crump was determined to get perfect grades in this subject. As usual, though, he had a plan in mind if needed. If he found some questions difficult, he would manipulate Tillerson into forcing the answers out of those students who might be advancing quicker than he was. As it turned out Ronald's fears were unfounded, as he sailed through multiplication and division. Before long he was ready to advance to long multiplication and long division, which would not be taught until the second year. The teachers were reluctant to move Ronald on too quickly, as they wanted all the kids to develop evenly. Ronald objected, claiming it was not his fault the rest were thick, and he demanded to be moved up a grade to progress in the subject.

The school at first refused until Teddy had a word in the right ears, making veiled threats about funding and in the case of the headmaster, knowledge of his affair with a junior female teacher. The principal got the message and allowed Ronald to progress to the advanced stage of the subject. Even at this early stage of his life, Ronald was beginning to see the power of money coupled with a little suggested blackmail. He would remember how his father dealt with the obstructive school apparatus for the rest of his life. Early impressions carve a lasting image.

English was another subject Ronald was expected to thrive in. The subject had by now been unified from literature and grammar into one discipline, and Ronald harboured the same insurance plan against failure as he had for math. He found he was struggling with the writings of Shakespeare and Charles Dickens. What concern of his was it how poor people in London were forced to live by the English equivalents of his family? However, he knew mastering the subject, whether it interested him or not, was important to his father, whose disapproval the young Crump did not wish to incur. He could not go running to Daddy later, the arms dealer would begin to consider him a wimp. Maybe Tillerson could help him out. Ronald knew there was a girl Peter was interested in, but was too shy to do anything about. Her name was Judy McClean and she was nine years old. If he could get Peter 'fixed' then Ronald could demand a favour in return from Tillerson.

Peter Tillerson's parents were associates – they would like to say friends – of the Crumps, and Teddy Crump and Duke Tillerson often shared a round of golf at their prestigious golf club. Duke Tillerson was, like Crump, a billionaire though only recently had he reached this pinnacle, crossing the thousand-million barrier only a year previously. After a fire at one of his textile factories killed twelve of his employees he made a massive insurance claim, or perhaps scam would be more appropriate, as a result of which he became one of the USA's billionaires. The workers' families who perished in the noble cause of making Tillerson this mint received their bare state entitlement, as culpability was down to their own incompetent working practices and not, as was in fact the case, Duke Tillerson's corner-cutting.

The only things Crump and Tillerson had in common was a detestation for their fellow human beings and knowing how to make money, lots of it, on the backs of the workers. Tillerson also broke the health and safety guidelines on his building sites, and despite attempts to unionise the workforce, these flagrant breaches continued. To these two it was a kind of hobby, a non-professional shared amusement, which they laughed about regularly while playing golf.

Oblivious that Ronald was thinking about approaching Peter about his proposed 'deal', Peter had shared with his father his liking for young Judy McClean but said that he did not know how to go about pursuing her. One day, when Tillerson and Crump were enjoying a drink at the golf club, Duke brought up the subject. He suggested to Crump that Ronald be used as a conduit between Peter and the object of his fascination as his son was good at talking to girls. Tillerson informed Crump that the girl's father had contacts in the Middle East, particularly the Kuwaiti government, whom he knew were looking for an arms dealer to supply their military forces.

'If Ronald could get Peter on a date with Judy then I could meet the parents at some point,' mused Duke Tillerson. 'I could then get talking to McClean about securing a contract with the Kuwaiti government.'

Teddy Crump liked this idea. Of course, Tillerson would get a cut of the profits, call it a handling fee. It would be a gift but for legal reasons could not be disclosed as that.

'Not that old tax fiddle, eh, Teddy?' Duke intimated to Crump.

'No, not at all,' said the arms dealer, 'just a genuine appreciation of my gratitude.'

The two bandits laughed together at their devious little plan involving innocent children to accumulate huge wealth.

'Just kick-starting the economy,' Crump joked.

When the laughter from this hilarious little joke subsided the two businessmen had another drink.

★ ★ ★

Ronald Crump was delighted when his dad talked to him about helping Peter win his girl. *How good is this! I can kill two birds with the one stone*, he thought. *Keep in my dad's good books and get Tillerson to sort out my English problem.*

★ ★ ★

At school the next day he talked to Peter about talking to Judy on his behalf. His friend was thrilled.

'Ah thanks, Ron, you're a pal,' Peter's face lit up.

'Not a problem. I'll get back to you as soon as I can,' said Ronald, walking away.

Unfortunately, in his enthusiasm he completely forgot his father's advice about being courteous in his approach to girls. He addressed her in his usual arrogant manner.

'You there,' he said rudely. 'My friend really likes you and you're going to go on a date with him.'

'Who do you think you're talking to?' Judy replied. 'I'm going on no date with anybody, you little creep, so piss off and go home to your mommy.'

Ronald was furious at this reply, to say nothing of the humiliation in front of Judy's friends. He had not considered this could be her response – maybe it would have been better to approach her alone. Ronald did not know what to do. After a moment's consideration, he decided to grovel in his usual fashion, do a 'damage limitation', which was something he had heard his father talk about and he thought he knew enough about for it to work for him.

'I'm sorry, Judy,' he said. 'I was trying to be a big man and what I really wanted to say is would you consider meeting my friend, Peter, as he is a little nervous and asked me to ask you. Please don't tell him I was rude will you, I didn't mean it.'

This conciliatory approach had the desired affect and Judy agreed to meet the shy Peter, agreeing not to tell the boxer of Crump's rudeness. Ronald was happy with this result and could now call on a favour from Peter. In this case he decided Tillerson would coerce the kids who were shining in the literature side of English to help him out, whether they wanted to or not. This way his approving father might buy him a new surfboard, or even give him more money.

Peter Tillerson met Judy, as Ronald had arranged, on Friday afternoon behind the gymnasium, the venue of his altercation with Mitch Brogan, and unlike his meeting with Brogan he was nervous. Judy arrived, looking pretty for a nine-year-old, and Peter became all tongue-twisted. Judy was good to her word and did not repeat the ignorance shown to her by Peter's messenger, young Crump.

'You asked to see me?' she said.

Peter blushed all over his face.

'Well, did you or didn't you?' she demanded.

'I suppose I did,' replied Peter. 'I wanted to ask if you would you like to go out with me some time?'

'I hardly know you,' the girl replied, 'and even if I did I would need time to think it over. Why don't we go for a walk together first and see how we get on?'

It should be remembered that none of the kids involved with this first meeting, Ronald, Peter or Judy, had any idea they were being used by Crump Senior and Tillerson to ultimately procure her father into arranging a meeting for Crump with the Kuwaiti government.

'All right,' said Peter now feeling a little more confident. 'Let's go to the hills after school.'

This Judy agreed to. All afternoon Peter Tillerson was like the cat that had drunk the cream, concentrating not one iota on his lessons. Ronald suspected that Peter's good humour was to do with Judy, but he decided to wait until Peter reported back to him. *Best leave well alone and let nature take its course,* Ronald reasoned. Peter had agreed to help Ronald out if things worked with Judy, so all Ronald could do at the moment was keep his fingers crossed.

Yes, this was to be the course of action. Crump knew nothing of the outcome yet, he would wait. When Peter and Judy went on their short walk, they found out that they got on very well together. Peter was delighted when Judy agreed to meet him again on a more formal basis. They arranged to meet up that Saturday, hang out and see a movie later in the early evening. On the day, Peter came well prepared. He had brought plenty of his father's money, who for some unknown reason appeared very eager to bankroll his son for the day's venture. At the movie theatre, Tillerson paid for them both, and after purchasing a big carton of popcorn, they sat down to watch *Bambi*. It was Judy's choice and Peter pretended to enjoy it. The film had some sentimental parts in it, which caused Judy to cry; Peter took the opportunity of comforting her. All in all, Peter was on cloud nine.

The pair met again on several occasions and much to Duke Tillerson's delight, one evening they pecked each other chastely on the cheek outside the front door of the Tillerson mansion. Duke seized the opportunity at that moment, opening the front door as if by accident.

'Oh, excuse me!' Duke said, pretending surprise.

Both Peter and Judy reddened in embarrassment.

Duke defused the young couple's mortification. 'Why don't you invite the lady to dinner sometime, Pete?' Tillerson suggested, pretending to treat Peter like a grown-up.

'Would you like that, Judy?' Peter asked, getting bolder by the minute. 'Maybe early next week?' 'Yes Pete, I'd like to come over.'

Duke Tillerson could barely hide his delight. This was the opportunity he'd been waiting for, as he knew either his mother or father was bound to collect her. After a brief discussion it was arranged Judy would go to Pete's for tea after school on Monday.

Monday came around and the day flew by as Peter became ever more excited. He procured, with the minimum of menace, the answers to the English questions which Ronald so desperately needed. So Ronald got his papers and was happy he could keep his ever-demanding father happy, and Tillerson was going great guns with Judy.

Like the Crumps, the Tillersons had domestic servants. They were all Hispanic, and the cook was of Italian extraction. Sheena Tillerson, Peter's mother, arranged for the cook to make a special tea for Peter and his girl.

She was also aware of the financial gains this tea could bring about and was determined things would go like clockwork. Unlike Ronald Crump, Peter Tillerson spoke to the staff at the house with a certain amount of respect, not as equals, that would never do, but at least politely. Later in life Peter would become the very antithesis of Ronald, and his behaviour would eventually lead to him opposing all forms of racism. The tea which the domestics and the cook had prepared was fit for a royal dynasty, consisting of fresh salmon, caviar followed by creamed rice tarts, all washed down with lemonade. Judy arrived dressed in a pink dress, white knee-length socks and a matching pink sun hat. She was a microcosm of a grown woman about to meet her future in-laws. The happy couple sat beside one another, secretly holding hands under the table, and politely, for their age, ate their dinner. Duke and Sheena took a very much hands-off approach. It was, after all, Judy's father, Barney, they were interested in. The evening passed off well with Mr and Mrs Tillerson occasionally making small talk.

Then it was time for Duke to ask the million-dollar question. 'Is your father collecting you, Judy?'

'Yes, Mr Tillerson,' she replied.

Duke was thrilled. It would soon be time to put the second part of this master plan into action. A car approached, a large Ford Corsair, and pulled up outside the Tillerson's home. There was a ringing of the doorbell and Duke Tillerson rose to answer the front door. A large well-built man gave Duke a broad smile and offered his hand in friendship.

'Barney McClean,' he said. 'I'm Judy's father.'

'Duke Tillerson,' Peter's father replied, with a firm handshake. 'Come in, Barney. Would you like a drink?'

'Scotch and soda,' was the diplomat's choice.

'On the rocks?'

'Why not?' replied McClean.

The businessman and diplomat retired to the games room. Tillerson invited Barney to a game of pool, which Barney accepted. After a broad conversation about world affairs the two men found out they had much in common. Both hated the Soviet Union and all it stood for but also knew if any country on earth could challenge the USA militarily it was the USSR. After the game of pool, which Tillerson let McClean win, they returned to the lounge. It was time for daughter and father to go, and as they said their goodbyes, the two men shook hands and arranged to meet again the next time Judy came over to the house.

'Come on, Judy,' Barney quietly said to his daughter, 'we must be going, school tomorrow.'

'Yes, Dad,' said the young lady, 'ready when you are.'

'Good night, Barney,' shouted Tillerson.

'Night, Duke,' came the reply, and all was set for their next encounter.

Ronald Crump was beginning to feel uncomfortable as the Gang of Six were now seven. There were three couples: James Rothschild and Susie Carter, Terry Morgan with Dianna Nixon and now Peter Tillerson had Judy McClean on his arm. Ronald was the odd one out. He could not talk to women, as many once believed he could, without being rude and ignorant. Nevertheless, he knew he had to find himself a girlfriend of his own.

They were all now in their second year at Wetherspoon Private Junior Educational Facility and each was doing well in their chosen subjects. Ronald, much to Teddy's delight, was thriving at math and English, and was well ahead of the rest of the gang at the latter subject, thanks to Tillerson procuring the necessary English papers. The other lads were excelling in geography, physical education, science and international languages. All was perfect for Ronald except the vital ingredient, a girlfriend.

* * *

Benito Lugosi was an Italian American whose father, Pedro, had arrived on the shores of the USA from Italy back in the 1930s shortly after prohibition was ended in 1933. Pedro realised that with the fallout from the Wall Street Crash the country, particularly out West, was rife for extortion and other illegal rackets with a legit front. Pedro Lugosi soon had a string of casinos and took over several former speakeasies from the days of prohibition. Lugosi also had his fingers in the murky pie of prostitution, which reaped in a huge annual profit. He had several questionable business consortiums to his name, but it was the area of gambling where he really made his mark. There were strong suspicions among the legal fraternity that Lugosi was involved in criminality of the worst kind. If it could have been proved that he was the hand behind the brothels in Los Angeles, he would have been in trouble.

Having the chief of police on your payroll was a huge advantage, and Pedro Lugosi knew full well the necessity of keeping senior policemen, judges and various mayors sweet too so that not too many questions would be asked. Lugosi, some suspected, had been involved in the murder of a local gambler who owed him a lot of money. As it stood, no body was ever found and there was no evidence Pedro Lugosi was connected with the disappearance of the man. In case his bent allies in the police and judiciary could not cover for him, which was unlikely, Lugosi had a fall guy in mind if necessity called. Another customer at Lugosi's casino who had at one time won a large amount of money was found robbed and severely beaten in an underground parking lot. Lugosi acted shocked and blamed muggers for the crime, which appeared to satisfy all concerned. Pedro Lugosi died in 1950 and his son, Benito, inherited the gangster's huge empire.

Benito Lugosi moved to the Eastern United States, having beaten a murder rap in Los Angeles. This was thanks in no small way to his corrupt lawyers and judges who had their price, as did the jurors. Lugosi junior had left a string of managers looking after the business empire out West, which included casinos, drinking dens and brothels. It was the latter which Lugosi kept a good distance from. He just collected the profits, and in the unlikely event of a police raid others would take the rap. These retainers lived in constant fear of their lives if profits dropped below a certain level. However, most of the time these capital gains were on the rise, resulting in the retainers themselves being very well paid.

Under these ruthless men were the business executors (thugs) who kept a constant vigil on the gambling and prostitution circuit. If any of the girls fell out of line these thugs would beat them and, in some cases, scar them for life so that they would never work in the sex industry again. These women's only commodities were their good looks and willingness to sell their bodies for a vague promise of riches beyond their dreams. Of course, these promises of wealth were empty, but by the time the women realised this they were usually hooked on drugs. These girls believed they would be like their counterparts in New York who worked from their own premises as escorts and, in many cases, became relatively wealthy in their own rights. Even though these escorts took risks, these chances were nothing compared to those taken by the girls working for Benito Lugosi.

The girls' wages were paid sometimes in cash, most of which was spent on heroin from Lugosi's drug barons. The lower market 'employees', the ones reaching the end of their working lives as hookers and at the higher end of addiction, received their wages directly in drugs. For these poor creatures, the end of life was not too far off and the clients they entertained were from the lower end of the pay scale.

Benito Lugosi spent most of his time at the perfectly legal casinos, or he did until he decided to move eastwards, leaving others in charge. To ensure none of his retainers had their hands in the till he had a gang of entirely loyal hard men, not dissimilar to Hitler's SS in the early days of that murderous regime, to break bones and even take life should such an occasion arise. All he had to do was pay his private army well and pocket the profits thousands of miles away in the East.

The Lugosi family consisted of Benito, his wife, Maria, and three children, Benito Junior, Pedro and Colette. In 1950 his father Pedro died. Three years later, after Benito secured his position out West, he moved to New York, into the same area as the Crumps, Rothschilds, Morgans and Tillersons. The outward impression of the newly arrived Italian American was that of a successful businessman who owned a string of respectable casinos and lavish nightclubs. But there were also many whispers and rumours insinuating that he was involved in the Mafia!

Benito bought a large mansion, equal to that of Teddy Crump, and paid hard cash for the property. The family advertised for domestic help and were overrun with applicants. Benito and Maria sieved through the written submissions shortlisting seven for the five positions of cook, gardener and cleaners. Neither Maria nor Benito wanted a nanny for their children. Benito wanted to mould the boys in his own image and Maria wanted Colette to be her reincarnation. The Lugosis finally found five appropriate candidates and life began to feel good. *Just sit back and wait for the money to roll in.* Benito decided to take up golf as a pastime and mix with the locals, with the intention of checking for any situation arising which he could exploit. He was in good company with the brigands of Billionaires' Row. Later, Crump the arms dealer and Benito the gangster would find much common ground.

Colette Lugosi was an attractive girl, well mannered and a good Catholic, unlike her two brothers who couldn't care less about religion. They were like their father, who pretended to be of the devout brethren in the presence of the priest. Colette and her brothers were enrolled in the same private educational establishment as Ronald and the gang. The school made special provision for their Catholic pupils, around fifty per cent, to receive the sacraments and other specialist religious teachings. This was so they would not lose fees from the wealthy Catholic fraternity. In saying that, when it came to money, religious denominational preference counted for little and the students were of a mixed bag.

Colette was the target of many young students' attention, but most were afraid to go any further and ask her out in case they upset her brothers. One false move and Colette's brothers, who were already known as fighters, would soon sort the problem out. This was not something Colette relished. She was sick of her brothers frightening away any boy whom they considered overstepping the line with her, and she told them so. Privately, Colette Lugosi did not want to grow up like her parents. She had heard the rumours and knew people were terrified of her father – and now her brothers were turning out the same. Not for her, she privately confided to herself. She was about five feet in height, tall for a ten-year-old girl, with long flowing brown hair and always neatly dressed. In a nutshell, Colette Lugosi was every schoolboy's dream. Notwithstanding formidable obstacles, nothing was going to deter the increasingly bold Ronald Crump.

Ronald first saw Colette between lessons at school. She was going to geography and he was rushing to science. In his haste he knocked some papers out of her hand. As he lifted them up and handed them back to her, he was struck by her beauty and friendly demeanour.

'Don't worry,' she said, smiling. 'I wasn't really looking where I was going either.'

'Ah thanks,' he said, reddening. 'See you around.' He was captivated as he watched her walking away.

Ronald purposely ran late for school a couple of days later. He had missed meeting the rest of the gang deliberately in the hope he would meet Colette who was making her way to school. He set off for school alone; suddenly, to his delight, an opportunity presented itself. Colette was walking to school by the same road and she too was alone.

'Hi Colette, can I walk with you?' said Ronald.

'Yes, course you can,' replied the young beauty queen, and the two ten-year-olds walked along together, engaging each other in compatible conversation.

Ronald was delighted she had not told him to leave her alone, as he had expected, and found she appeared to like him. By the time they reached the school gates they were conversing like old acquaintances.

'How are you doing in math?' Ronald enquired.

'Not very well,' Colette answered. 'I keep getting stuck with long multiplications. I wish somebody would help me,' she mused. Then she stopped, looking at him with her soft brown eyes. 'You're very good at them, aren't you, Ron? You don't mind me calling you Ron, do you?'

'Not at all, and I'd be delighted to help you,' said Ronald honestly.

Ronald Crump's head was in the clouds all that morning. He told himself he must not be rude or ignorant with her. He held the ace card as he saw it, in his ability to help her with math.

Ronald suggested he and Colette should meet one night after school and he would give her advice in the branches of math she was struggling with. Ronald himself was advanced enough to complete the long division exam, but this was not due on the curriculum until the following year. For the time being, and so as not to confuse Colette, they would stick to long multiplication and single division. He was already showing some of the devious traits of his father in his forward planning, covering all possible eventualities, as with his plan to delay long division tutoring for a further number of months, thus creating opportunities for future dates with the young girl. His advantage in the subject meant she would be unlikely to seek the attention of other lads and he would not have to fight for her.

Unknown to young Crump, Colette was not interested in boys fighting over her, so he had no need to worry. She had already seen enough violence and certainly did not want to be the cause of any more. If Ronald could have read the girl's mind he would have found out she was seeing him because, firstly she liked him, not having witnessed his previous arrogance, and, secondly, he was good at math, which she was not. How Colette would have viewed Ronald before his attack of sudden maturity we can only guess at! All things being equal, Ronald had promised himself he would never be rude to, or in front of, Colette at any time. The question was, could he keep it up? The two of them arranged to meet the following evening, Tuesday, at the statue of George Washington in the main square. From there they would go together to Colette's house where Ronald would be introduced to her family, which included the much-feared brothers. As it was, the Lugosi household was just around the corner from the Crumps, but the statue was kept as the place of rendezvous. Colette suspected, correctly, that Ronald would be nervous going to her house alone. It was true he was anxious about going to the home of a suspected Mafia boss, but it would never do to let Colette know in case she would be offended.

'For Christ's sake,' he told himself, 'grow some balls.'

He had learned that term from his father when he overheard Crump Senior securing a dodgy deal. In relation to Colette, he kept reminding himself that his future happiness, as he saw it, might depend on this meeting. He didn't dare fall at the first hurdle.

On arriving home from school Ronald sought his parents' permission for his visit to Colette's house the following evening. He secretly planned to go anyway if they showed any hostility to the arrangement, but he preferred their blessing. When the youngster told them both, Teddy gave a long sigh and gave it serious thought. He was not thinking about the suitability of the fledgling relationship – they were after all very young and nothing long-term would come of it – he was considering business possibilities. He was also aware that upsetting Benito Lugosi had far-reaching and dangerous implications.

'Yes, that's fine, son,' Crump informed the youngster. 'Just be careful. Remember, the girl's brothers are older and very protective of their sister.'

'Don't worry, Dad, I know how to behave,' Ronald said.

Megan Crump was a little more concerned. *Were the rumours true?* she worried. *Was this man really a Mafia boss? On the other hand, it might just be idle gossip. After all, he was not in prison or wanted by the police*, she reassured herself.

'I won't let you down,' Ronald told his parents.

Teddy then hit on the idea that he would collect his son from the Lugosi household. This would give him a perfect and legitimate opportunity to meet Benito. Even though the house was only yards away from their own home, his son was only ten years old (going on eleven), after all.

Teddy suggested 9pm, but Ronald thought this a little early, as he and Colette had a lot of work to get through. Eventually they agreed to nine thirty and, like the grown-up Ronald thought he was, they shook hands on it. Teddy Crump was already working on a business deal he could put to Benito. A casino boss would surely need some kind of protection against burglars, not to mention rival gangsters! Crump could supply the latest in weapons, small arms, and a comprehensive burglar alarm system… yes, there were possibilities here all right, he thought.

On the following morning, Tuesday, Ronald purposely left it late setting off for school. He deliberately missed the gang again and set off alone hoping to meet Colette on the way. His luck was in and together the young couple made their way to the school gates, finalising plans for the coming evening. The day seemed to pass very quickly and, after school, Ronald waited for Colette at the school gates. His meetings with the girl were not going unnoticed by the other pupils, especially the lads. Colette arrived at the school gates and they walked together the same way they had come earlier in the day. Suddenly and without warning she linked arms with Ronald. He felt ten feet tall, and this gesture certainly brought about jealous looks from the other boys, all of whom fancied Colette.

'Don't worry, Ron', she said, 'I can't stand any of them, they are all mouth.'

Ronald wondered what she would have made of him if she had heard how he initially spoke to Judy McClean on Tillerson's behalf. Fortunately, that was some time ago and she would never find out, he reassured himself.

Benito Lugosi Junior was aged fifteen and Pedro was in his thirteenth year. Just as their father had inherited the business from old Pedro they too would come to take on the family empire when the time came. Benito Junior had already attended a couple of meetings, called councils, with his father and was under instructions to gradually introduce young Pedro into the way of life. Young Benito was already versed in his father's justice system (torture) and had experienced some of the milder 'inquiries' into so-called wrongdoings by individuals. The normal business rules of so-called free competition, geared to amassing profits under the veil of decency, did not apply to Lugosi's business style. The word 'negotiations' also did not enter his vocabulary and trade unions of any description were not even mentioned, let alone tolerated, in the gangster's empire.

The downmarket side of things involved inferior drinking dens and the prostitution that Benito Lugosi was never seen to have anything to do with. These were managed by subordinates and Lugosi wanted to know nothing of the managerial style of his 'retainers'. Any trouble, legal or otherwise, these people were to sort it out. In the area the family had moved to, they were accepted as equals. They could certainly match the financial clout of any of their neighbours.

Even though several of the wealthy neighbours had reservations about Lugosi and his sons, none had the courage to voice their opinions. This was a commodity these exploiters of labour lacked. The Lugosi family always fought their enemies as one, because in the Italian–American tradition, family was family and nobody spoke badly of the family. At that moment in time, Colette was only slightly aware of the rumours surrounding her father. Nevertheless, no outsiders dared say anything which might upset the young beauty in case she told her brothers, who were a force to be reckoned with.

Ronald was the girl's proper boyfriend, and the Lugosi family were determined to make the lad welcome. Amongst themselves they were cautious about him, as would have been the case with any boy Colette brought home, and they would be careful of what they said in his presence. They were also aware of the political clout Teddy Crump held and were respectful of it. Ronald was the first to get past the brothers' vetting system which, unbeknown to Colette, applied to every possible suitor. Maria had the domestics make a special dinner for Collete's guest. Pasta Bolognese with crusty bread was the main course, followed by Italian ice cream.

Ronald and Colette met at the statue of Washington and she gave him a peck on the cheek. 'Are you nervous, Ron?' she enquired.

'A little,' the arms dealer's son replied.

'Don't worry, they won't bite,' she joked.

They arrived at the door of the huge imposing mansion and Benito Senior welcomed Ronald in a traditional Italian fashion.

'Hey, Ronnie,' the gangster enthused, 'how are you?'

'I'm fine, sir,' he nervously replied.

'Hey, cut the "sir" nonsense, call me Benito,' Lugosi said. 'Come in and I'll introduce you to the family.'

Maria, Benito Junior and young Pedro were lined up, as per tradition, in the living quarters of the huge house ready to greet their daughter's guest. Ronald shook hands with each of them in turn and Maria gave him a little kiss on the cheek.

'Sit down, Ron,' Colette invited him. 'Dinner should be ready shortly.'

Young Crump was anxious and it showed, which secretly pleased the Lugosi brothers. Even though Colette's mother had reminded her sons of certain consequences if they ruined their sister's big night, Colette too was a little uneasy.

Eventually dinner was served, and Ronald Crump began to settle down. He thoroughly enjoyed the Italian food and Colette thanked the domestics for all they had done for her.

'Do you have domestics, Ron?' she asked.

'Yes we do,' replied Ronald.

'I hope you treat them well,' Colette continued. 'Without these people, none of this would have been possible.'

This was a sentiment echoed by her mother, Maria.

'Oh yes, I couldn't agree more,' young Crump replied.

He knew full well if he spoke to their domestics with such politeness they would think he'd lost control of his faculties. Then and there, Ronald decided to take a leaf out of Colette's book and try to treat his own domestic helps better. How long this sentiment would last remained to be seen. After they finished eating they retired to the study and Ronald began giving Colette instruction in long multiplications, as had been the arrangement. After about an hour, they sat back. That was enough math for one night.

'Do the sums make a bit more sense now?' Ronald enquired.

'Yes, Ron, thanks so much. You have a really good way of explaining things. I don't hate math so much any more!' she exclaimed, giving him a warm smile.

'Would you like to come over to my house for dinner sometime, Colette?' Ronald ventured.

'Yes, I'd love to,' she replied.

She moved forward and gave him a whisper of a kiss on his cheek. Caught up in sudden emotion, Ronald returned an awkward peck on her cheek. Both smiling shyly, they then leaned together for their first kiss on the lips.

Suddenly there was a ring of the doorbell. It was Teddy for his son. Ronald pulled back regretfully from Colette. 'Damn! Got to go, I'm afraid,' he said, standing up.

'It's OK,' Colette said, 'I'll see you soon.'

As Ronald cleared away his books and put them in his satchel, Benito answered the door. 'You must be Ronny's papa,' the Italian said.

'Yes, Teddy Crump,' said the arms dealer.

'Come in, Ted,' said Lugosi.

The first thing that greeted Teddy was a huge picture on the wall of Benito meeting Pope Pius XII back in 1954 on his visit to the Vatican. Crump was impressed, not with the religious connotations, but that Lugosi obviously had good contacts. Money may be made here, Teddy contemplated, but not in his usual backstabbing style of doing business. No, not in this case, as there would be consequences even for him. *This would require a different, more subtle approach – even a little grovelling – but the rewards would be worth it,* Crump reasoned to himself.

Benito Lugosi shook hands with Teddy Crump as Ronald appeared with Colette. The two tycoons bade each other goodnight, but not before Crump had invited the casino king to a round of golf at his exclusive club the following Saturday. This would be followed by drinks in the upmarket bar. Lugosi, eager to improve his image in the area, agreed to the offer. *This may be a golden opportunity,* Crump thought. He had a new range of state-of-the-art infrared-operated burglar warning and prevention systems which Lugosi might be interested in.

Taking the short walk home Crump and his son, who was strutting along like a young man who had distinguished himself in some superhuman heroic way, discussed the events of the evening.

'How did it go, son?' Teddy enquired.

'Great, Dad,' his offspring replied. 'Can Colette come over to us some evening?' 'Yes, of course she can, son, what day did you have in mind?'

'Would Friday be OK?' Ronald asked.

'I don't see why not, I'll cancel the cook's day off to accommodate you,' Teddy assured his son.

Ronald grinned to himself at his father treating the domestics like they were expendable items rather than human beings. Then it suddenly dawned on him that he would have to speak to the domestics politely in front of Colette. He knew he could not bring himself to be as nice as she was to their domestic helps, but nevertheless he would have to improve on his normal mode of communication. He discussed this with his father, who had never corrected his son for speaking to the domestics as one may communicate with a scolded dog.

'Try to be a little more diplomatic,' he advised Ronald. 'You don't have to mean it, and after all they are never going to speak to Colette independently of you, are they!'

The following morning, Wednesday, Ronald walked to school with the gang. He wanted to talk with James Rothschild about being allowed to introduce Colette to the group. In his usual begging way, Crump spoke to Rothschild: 'Would it be all right with you, James, if I bring my girlfriend into our gang?'

'Talk to me a little later when I've discussed it with the others,' Rothschild instructed his subordinate.

Ronald had to be satisfied with this short audience with Rothschild and was thankful he was not refused outright.

Later in the day James summoned Ronald to his presence to inform him of the gang's decision. 'We held a meeting to discuss your earlier request about bringing your girlfriend into our gang, Ronald,' the leader said. 'We decided it will be all right providing she obeys the rules,' he continued, obviously not understanding who the girl was and, more importantly, that her brothers could take on the entire gang should the occasion demand it.

'Thanks, James,' said Ronald.

If Ronald had any backbone he wouldn't have bothered asking Rothschild; he would have just taken Colette along whether they liked it or not. Unfortunately, Ronald lacked the courage to do this. He was also worried that if Colette knew he had to ask permission for her to join the gang he would be yesterday's news. Ronald therefore determined his conversation with Rothschild should never reach her ears.

Like most people who get rich on the backs of others, this kind of gutlessness would follow Crump all through his life. Benito Lugosi might be a gangster, even a murderer, but he had been brought up the hard way on Chicago's East Side. Not so for Teddy Crump and certainly not for his son, Ronald. Both had been born with silver spoons in their mouths and their only fighting ability was being sly, devious and backstabbing. Even Teddy's army service was questionable. The Rothschilds, Morgans, Tillersons and, to a lesser extent, the Seddons and the circles they mixed in were all the same. They had no genuine friends to call their own. Neither had Lugosi, whose friends were there through fear and fear only, and in the case of Crump all his pretend friends were bought. This flaw would become apparent with time, and as Ronald matured into adulthood the same pretentious environment would be ever-present.

Legalised robber barons such as the Crumps detest each other. They fall prey to twisted jealousies and carry a cold hatred of those who oppose them in any way. Between the monied and propertied classes, capitalists both legal and illegal make the world a living hell for everybody else. It is their sick system which eventually leads to wars resulting in the deaths of millions in the name of profit and wealth, usually in the guise of natural resources like oil. The likes of Teddy Crump are the guiltiest of the guilty: they sell weapons of mass destruction to anybody who has the money to pay for them.

At school, the bell sounded, signalling the end of science, the first lesson. Ronald gathered his books and began heading for the next class, geography. On his way Ronald spied Colette on her way to cookery class.

'Colette!' he shouted. 'Hang on a minute, I've something to ask you.'

'Hurry up, Ron, I'm late for my next class,' she said.

Ronald cleared his throat. 'Would you like to come over to my place this Friday?'

'Great, Ron, I'd love to,' the girl replied, much to Ronald's delight.

'I'll wait for you at the gates,' he said.

'Lovely, see you there,' said Colette.

That day Ronald found his geography lesson more boring than usual. It seemed to take forever to end. Finally, the bell sounded and Ronald headed for the school gates for his arranged meeting with Colette. She came running up and gave him what was now becoming habitual, a kiss on the cheek, making Ronald feel like he was walking on air.

'Come on, let's catch up with the rest of my friends,' he said. It was time to introduce her to his so-called pals.

Ronald hoped the introduction would go well. Because of his upbringing he was already aware that if the children remained friends, that made life, and therefore business dealings, easier for their parents. But if the children fell out for whatever reason, it could have rippling consequences higher up the chain. Furthermore, if there were any antagonisms from the gang towards Colette, he would have to make a choice between Colette and his gang. He had weighed up all the pluses and minuses concluding that, given the financial cost to Teddy, the gang would take priority. Ronald had worked it out that all Teddy's wealth would one day be his and given the fact he was a genius at math he was already thinking in terms of dollar bills, and the fact that he was afraid of his pretend friends.

Fortunately for Ronald the anticipated ultimatum never transpired as the gang made Colette welcome. This was fortunate for young Crump. He wasn't yet fully aware that Colette's family placed a greater emphasis on loyalty than did the Crumps, and if he had dumped her in favour of the gang it would have been taken as an insult.

Colette was accepted into the brethren especially by the girls, Susie Carter, Dianna Nixon and Judy McClean. These were the first friends she had made since moving into the area and she enjoyed the female company. Up to now she had only had her ever-protective brothers for company and frankly she was sick of their domineering attitudes, well meant as they undoubtedly were.

Friday came around quickly. It was January 30th 1958 and shortly Ronald would reach the grand old age of eleven. He and his parents were preparing for the party and Ronald saw Colette coming for her tea as a kind of rehearsal for the big day. The young couple arranged to meet at the statue of Washington again and Ronald was there a few minutes before Colette, who arrived dead on time, six o'clock. Megan Crump had instructed Cook to do a special tea for their 'distinguished guest' and much effort had gone into the preparations. Around six thirty Ronald and Colette arrived. He knew he would have to afford the domestics a little more respect than normal without going overboard. They should, after all, remember who the superior species were.

Megan made a big fuss of the girl, thinking prematurely she might have found a daughter-in-law, while Teddy saw the relationship purely through financial eyes.

'Sit down, dear, and give me your coat,' Ronald's mother said. 'Ronald tells me he was helping you with math, that's how you both became friends?'

'That's right, Mrs Crump,' the polite young girl replied. 'Ron is very good at math, he's helped me a lot.'

For a few moments they all sat chatting in the expansive living area and then they made their way to the dining room where the domestics arrived with the food. Home-made shrimp pasties with American fries was the main course followed by fresh cream cakes and lemonade, a filling meal which was enjoyed by one and all. When the staff came to clear the plates and dishes away Ronald offered his thanks, surprising the staff to such an extent it caused much gossip in the kitchen.

The talk in the dining room shifted towards Ronald's birthday party the coming April.

'Colette will be the guest of honour,' remarked Megan, and Teddy gave a ghastly grin of what passed for approval.

Colette blushed prettily.

Further discussion about the party ensued, eventually diverging to innocuous conversations about each other's families, friends and interests. All too soon the clock struck nine and the doorbell rang. The senior domestic answered the door and came face to face with Benito Lugosi. He was accompanied by his two sons and heirs apparent and introduced himself to the household helper. Teddy Crump heard his golfing partner's voice and went to relieve the situation. He didn't want the domestic saying anything untoward; better to deal with the introduction himself.

'Benito, my friend,' Crump said, 'come in and take a seat.'

'Teddy, *Signore* Crump,' he said in a phoney Italian accent. 'Good to see you again.'

Benito took his seat while the two heirs apparent took up their positions at the door, resembling the stance of prison guards during a prisoner's family visit. In years to come the two boys would become more accustomed to guarding doors during a rival's interrogation. The grown-ups soon engaged in adult talk while Ronald and Colette whispered sweet nothings in each other's ears over in a quiet corner. Teddy eventually got around to talking about Ronald's birthday party. As all the other kids' parents were attending, Crump thought it only prudent to invite Benito and Maria Lugosi.

Lugosi replied, 'Apologies, I'll be unable to attend due to commitments. But Maria will be able to come,' he said, speaking for his wife in her absence.

'Perfect, that will be wonderful,' Crump said. Megan was happy too, as she was looking forward to meeting the businessman's wife.

'Well, Colette, it's time we were making tracks,' Benito informed his daughter. 'School tomorrow.'

'Coming, Papa,' Colette said, standing up. Lugosi then clicked his fingers, calling off the guard at the door.

The Crumps were pleased the evening had gone well. Teddy had arranged another round of golf with Benito and had offered to nominate Lugosi for membership. This was accepted with thanks and appreciation by the gangster.

The days at school were becoming a little fractious as the pupils in Ronald's class were entering that transformative stage of puberty. All the gang would reach eleven years of age this year, including Colette. The gang were going to go on a hike one Sunday and Ronald invited Colette. Unfortunately, she had to disappoint him, as she always attended ten o'clock Mass followed by Holy Communion on Sundays with her mother. Ronald was not happy with this and almost showed his true spoilt self.

'Don't bother about Mass, it is all rubbish anyway,' he said.

The young lady rounded on Ronald. 'Don't you ever say that again, you philistine,' she said indignantly.

This was where Ronald's lack of understanding of both Colette and the English language came to light. He had underestimated Colette's strong faith, and had no idea what a philistine was.

Too late, Ronald realised his mistake. 'Colette I'm so sorry, I didn't mean to offend,' Crump grovelled. 'Please forgive me. I'll never say such things again and of course you must go to Mass if that's what you and your mother do on Sundays.'

The young couple kissed each other and made up. Because she couldn't go hiking with the gang they arranged to have a day together on the Saturday. Ronald arranged to meet Colette at noon, after his private lessons from Teddy. Extra lessons in ordinary math were becoming a waste of time as Ronald was so far ahead, but Teddy used the time for the more important and devious side of the subject, showing Ronald how to fiddle books and accounts.

Saturday came and they took a trip into town, just like the grown-ups. They bought ice creams and wandered around, holding hands as they browsed the different stores and landmarks. At one stage Ronald pretended to be checking out rings in the jeweller's shop window, hoping to impress the casino king's daughter. All in all, they had a relaxing and sweet time in each other's company.

The gang met at eleven on Sunday morning to set off on their hike up Sugar Hill and mess around in the stream. James Rothschild had been waiting to question Crump about his relationship with Colette Lugosi. Did Ronald know who her father was? What if he did and was well in with the suspected gangster family? Such a scenario could possibly threaten his role as gang leader, so how would he deal with the situation if this was the case? He knew that in a fight Ronald Crump would stand no chance against him, but with Colette's brothers backing him he could take over easily. Rothschild needed to secure his position, but could not let Crump see he was worried. By the same token he was in no position to threaten the arms dealer's son.

When they all met there were three couples and Ronald, alone with nobody on his arm.

'Where's Colette, Ronald?' James enquired.

'She's at Mass today with her mother,' young Crump replied.

Terry Morgan gave a shriek of laughter, only to be kicked in the shin by his far more mature girlfriend, Dianna Nixon.

'What are you sniggering at, Morgan?' Ronald bravely asked.

'Not a lot – ouch!' said Morgan, as he received a sharp blow to his ankle from his girlfriend.

The gang set off on their way. Rothschild was waiting for an opportunity to investigate Ronald's relationship with the Lugosi family, something which Ronald had actually been expecting for a while. He wouldn't exaggerate too much, just letting Rothschild, and indeed the rest of them, know he was on first-name terms with the father, Benito, and mates, which wasn't true, with the brothers. He wasn't lying in the first instance; Lugosi had invited Ronald to call him 'Benito' so this was the line he would take.

As they were walking up the incline, Rothschild broached the subject. 'Does Colette go to Mass every Sunday, Ronnie?'

'Yes, as far as I know,' replied Ronald, who then hit on the idea of pretending he might convert to the Church of Rome so as he could go with her. 'I'm thinking of becoming a Catholic,' he added. 'I'll then go with her and Marie on Sundays.'

Fuck, thought Rothschild, *he's on first-name terms with the mother.*

Ronald continued, 'Of course Benito and the lads don't bother a great deal, unless it's a friend's child's Communion, Confirmation or some other important event.'

This fuelled the speculation that Ronald was well in with Colette's family and gave credence to Ronald's lies about converting.

'Would you really convert, Ronald?' asked Rothschild. 'What would your parents say to that?'

This caught Ronald off guard. He knew if this went too far Rothschild would go and ask his father about it who would possibly in turn ask Teddy for corroboration – and then the lie would be exposed.

'Possibly, when I'm a little older,' replied Ronald.

James Rothschild, eager to secure his position as gang leader, then went into overdrive. 'Do the Lugosis treat you well?' he enquired.

'Yes of course, James, I'm like one of the family,' said Ronald, which was not a total lie; they did accept him, but 'one of the family' might be stretching it. Ronald knew that there was no way Rothschild would ask Colette any of these questions, he wouldn't have the courage. The truth was that Colette's brothers would in no way even contemplate hanging around with James Rothschild and his gang of fairies, as they saw them. They had to accept Ronald Crump as he was their sister's choice, but the rest of the middle-class dudes? No fucking way. Ronald was also eager not to alienate himself too far from the gang; after all, Colette had just voiced her anger at him but had forgiven him. He needed to stay well in with the gang while at the same time guarding his flank from possible aggression.

When the gang reached home, Terry Morgan kissed Dianna goodbye and now, away from her calming influence, he decided to try again on Ronald.

'What's this fucking Mass your girl goes to?' he ignorantly demanded. 'Tell her not to go, she's only a fucking Eyetie.'

Ronald saw red for the first time, and for once with justification. This was Colette this creep was insulting. He pivoted round on the ball of his foot, catching Morgan right in the jaw with his fist. Terry Morgan flew backwards, and Ronald took full advantage, leaping on his foe and punching him. Morgan began fighting back with a vengeance, catching Crump on the side of the cheek. The pair rolled around on the floor fiercely thumping each other. James Rothschild and Peter Tillerson reached in and after a couple of failed attempts, managed to grab each of them by the scruff of the neck. They both had black eyes and cuts and grazes on their faces and knuckles.

'Cut it out, the two of you,' Peter Tillerson demanded, a sentiment echoed by Rothschild.

'You were out of order, Terry,' Tillerson berated Morgan.

'Fucking right you were,' echoed Rothschild, eager to reassert himself as the main man.

'Both of you pack it in. Remember our motto, "All for one and one for all", like the Three Musketeers.'

The warring youngsters eventually shook hands and made up. Ronald had surprised himself as well as the rest of the gang with his defence of Colette's name. He was proud of himself. This was one of the rare occasions when Ronald did something approaching heroic, but the reader should not immediately be led into believing he had developed a spine because of it.

The following morning, Monday, Ronald called for Colette to walk to school, a habit he had recently acquired Colette enquired about her boyfriend's black eyes and cuts.

'How did you get them, Ron? The truth,' the girl demanded.

'I had a bit of trouble,' he confided. 'Somebody said something I just couldn't let them away with.'

'It was over me, wasn't it?' she said solemnly.

'Yes, it was,' he said. 'I wasn't having any of it.'

Colette Lugosi had been brought up not to ask too many questions about such incidents and she followed her family code to the letter. If her boyfriend had defended her honour that would be good enough for her and, more importantly, her brothers, who would now be more open to accept and help Ronald, if need be. This situation and perception of Ronald by the Lugosi family would change! But for the time being, Ronald was in favour.

2

The Eleventh Birthday Party

On the first of April Ronald Crump would be eleven years of age and by this time he was beginning to experience things in his body which he did not understand. A very noticeable change happening to the young man was that his penis, under certain conditions, would become very stiff. This phenomenon, he found, happened when he looked at scantily clad women or girls often found in certain newspapers. Along with this sensation he also experienced a weird feeling, not unpleasant by any stretch of the imagination, but nevertheless different to anything hitherto felt. He was beginning to have these feelings and urges when he was with Colette. There was, of course, nothing unnatural about these changes. However, Ronald found all this most strange to begin with and didn't know whom to talk with about it. He didn't feel confident talking to his parents; they had always sheltered him from the subject of sex, and he had no brothers or sisters who could have been of some help. He decided he would just let things be and see what happened.

Unbeknown to Ronald the other lads were experiencing similar changes. They were all about the same age but had not yet mastered the art of discussing with each other what was happening. Again, this would come in time, as would maturity. They were all now in their third year of junior education, after which they would have one more year to go before leaving for senior schooling and boarding school.

Colette Lugosi, like all young women of her age, was going through her own bodily turmoil. Luckily, Colette had always been close to her mother, who was more open-minded than most women of that time. Some months before her periods started, Maria explained to her daughter the biological changes and the monthly cycle that would shortly happen to her. She also talked to Colette about pregnancy and the options she would have available in the coming years. She told her about contraception, despite the Church opposing such methods at the time, and the necessity to ensure the male used a sheath. Maria even went so far as to discuss the contraception pill, which was very progressive for the late 1950s. She thought it better Colette knew all these facts now rather than later. Maria did not, however, discuss abortion in any way, shape or form or its availability in certain countries. As a devout Catholic, Maria was pleased such terminations in the USA were not generally available, though certain states differed under US state-by-state contingencies. In 1973 along came the Roe vs Wade case, when legislation allowing terminations was passed.

Maria explained to Colette these changes were perfectly normal and reassured her that she was always there for her to talk to. The other girls in the gang were not as fortunate as Colette in having mothers whom they could talk to about personal matters, especially about the sensitive subject of biological changes in boys and girls. Colette decided if any of her friends asked about it, she would give them the benefit of Maria's advice. If, on the other hand, they said nothing, she would not volunteer information.

As January surrendered to February, Ronald and Colette were becoming more intimate in their relationship as they moved towards adolescence. Colette was furnished with the relevant information, but Ronald was not which, given his domineering nature hitherto kept hidden, could possibly lead to problems, Colette knowing more than him on the subject. Maria, despite being broad-minded and equipping her daughter with the vital facts she needed, had also been very firm on the Catholic Church's views on sex before marriage.

Colette may have been a couple of months older than her boyfriend, but Maria felt she had to remind her daughter that she was first and foremost a Catholic girl. She had stopped well short of insisting her boyfriends must be of the Catholic faith. She and Benito had discussed this and decided even at an early age their daughter must be allowed to make her own mind up regarding choices of boyfriends but did hope Colette would keep the faith on no sex before marriage. Colette listened intently to her mother and did her best to heed her advice. Maria also informed Colette of the bodily changes that would happen to growing boys. She told her daughter that Ronald might try to touch her in inappropriate places and if this happened Colette should tell him not to. Colette agreed with her mother and promised, with private reservations, to be a good Catholic girl. She did not wish to alienate her mother as she was a good friend as well as parent. Maria Lugosi considered she had done her duty as a mother and as a good Catholic, which by the standards of the day, she certainly had.

It was one week on from Colette's debut at the Crump household, Friday 7th February 1958, and much of the international news was about an aircraft which had tragically crashed the previous day in Munich, Germany. On board was one of Europe's finest football teams, Manchester United, and although Association Football at the time was not very big in the USA, everybody had heard of United. This was the second air disaster involving a football team from Europe in nine years. Back in May 1949 the entire Torino team were wiped out when their aircraft crashed into a mountain just outside Turin, Italy.

Football in Europe was becoming big business, with a European competition being introduced in 1955–56. This made the disaster at Munich more significant, though no less tragic, than the event outside Turin, which the Lugosis remembered with sadness. Although the game was not very popular in the United States, aircraft manufacture was, and businesses wanted to know what had caused the accident. In the fifties, civilian air travel was a new concept and the manufacturers, such as Boeing, were concerned at the number of high-profile accidents. The engineering wing of Crumps was working on a design to minimise these accidents, so Teddy paid special attention to the news bulletins. If his company's new designs came to fruition there was a fortune to be made. Only a bandit like Teddy Crump could think how to make money out of such tragedies, a trend in business which in future decades would become the normal way of thinking. As was the case with the 1949 disaster, the US government of 1958 conveyed their condolences via the appropriate embassy.

Ronald spent less time with the gang and more with his girlfriend. Was this a sign of maturity? Time would tell. Coincidentally, the rest of the gang, James Rothschild, Terry Morgan and Peter Tillerson, were also spending less time with each other and more with their respective girlfriends.

One afternoon young Crump and Colette went for a walk in the park and he suggested they sit for a while on the bench. They began kissing, and after a few minutes suddenly Ronald felt a strange feeling, like an urge to go much further. He also had that sensation in his pants again, like a rod of iron had appeared there. He started touching Colette on the legs and began moving his hand in an upwards direction. When he got to her knee the girl stopped him. This was what Maria had meant, she thought. The young man was having none of this and made a second attempt, this time with a hint of aggression. This time Colette slapped his face.

'Why did you do that?' he said.

'I don't want you to do that, Ron. I tried to stop you nicely, but you persisted. I'm not a plaything, you know.'

'I'm sorry,' he said, feeling sheepish. 'I just get these funny feelings and urges,' he confessed. 'I… I didn't mean any harm. Please don't be angry.'

'Don't worry, Ron, I get strange feelings myself, and have felt new changes inside me. But I'm OK with them, because I know they're just about me growing up and becoming a woman. I was talking to my mama and she explained everything to me about the facts of life.' Colette told Ronald not to worry, that they'd face the problem together. But she was insistent that he should respect her, and that she would only let things go further when she felt the time was right.

Ronald felt a little more at ease after their little chat and his embarrassment began to subside. Colette touched his hand. 'Don't go all shy on me, Ron. Come on, let's walk home.'

Young Ronald Crump, if he only knew it, had an angel on his arm. As they were walking in the direction of the Lugosi house, she pointed out to him that 'Two are stronger than one,' and that they had each other. Ronald's actions towards Colette were understandable if not condonable; and if the boy had got the message, then no harm was done. Eventually Colette would find out what a little brat he really was.

As they approached her house, Ronald noticed an extensive line of large black limousines and Ford Zodiacs parked in front of the residence.

'Who owns all the limos, Colette?' he asked.

'Just some of Papa's business friends,' said Colette who, quick as a flash, had put her family head on. She knew what was happening. This was a Council of War. She guided Ronald away, explaining that her dad was involved in a big business meeting and they should not go in just yet. She didn't want to let Ronald know what she knew. Secrecy was very important when it came to family, especially her family. Inside the house all the big names from out West would be present, and most of Chicago's crime bosses would be sitting at the table with her father, the biggest crime boss of them all.

Even if Ronald had known the truth, he wouldn't have been able to criticise Colette's father as his own father and his gang of brigands were no better. Benito Lugosi may well have made his billions on terror and fear of the gun or torture for anybody who crossed him, but Teddy Crump, Duke Tillerson and the rest of his class also made their own billions on fear. In their case it was the fear of unemployment leading to poverty and, in some cases, starvation, marital breakdown and in the worst-case scenarios, suicide. If a person crossed Lugosi they could well finish up propping up a flyover or as part of the foundations holding up a skyscraper, and if someone fell out with the likes of Crump, unemployment and destitution beckoned. The difference between the 'Black Market' and the so-called 'free and open transactional market' was merely a word: legal!

Colette linked arms with Ronald and eased him in the direction of the shopping mall away from her house.

'Let's go to the mall,' she said. 'We can't go to my house while they are having a business meeting. I'm sure your papa is the same with his board meetings.'

Ronald agreed with Colette, though he could never remember his father having a board meeting at their house. All the same, they went to the mall and gave the matter no further consideration. They spent about two hours at the stores, Colette insisting they go for a milkshake, thus buying time and breaking up the afternoon. She calculated the Council of War would perhaps take around the same length of time, plus allowing for the time it would take to walk back. Colette also knew her older brother was now sitting in on his father's less important meetings, and the fact she had seen him in the garden suggested to her the meeting was of high priority. On their way back, and much to Colette's relief, a convoy of large black motor cars passed them by.

'They're the ones that were at your place, aren't they?' he asked.

'I think you're right,' she said. 'That's great. That means I can go back into the house now.'

Colette was determined not to turn out like her father or, regrettably, her brothers, but for the time being family loyalty and unity must be maintained. Colette knew her duty and carried it out to the letter of expectations; she had told no lies, it was a business meeting just not an orthodox kind and the less Ronald knew, for his own good, the better.

Due to her upbringing and her family's activities, particularly those of Benito, her father, Colette Lugosi had to learn fast. She had to become streetwise at an early age, despite living in a big house and having a wealthy family. She had no intention, unlike her brothers, of ever being part of Benito's vast empire, but she had learned how to maintain family loyalty, which despite everything was important to her. Also important was her Catholic faith – a devotion which would ebb in her mid-teens – and being faithful to her boyfriend. She was maturing physically and mentally and was already, at the age of eleven and a half, looking quite the young woman. As Colette grew into her teens she would develop a social conscience and become steeped in socialist politics, something foreign to her father as it was to Crump and his cohorts. Given Colette's strength of character, a long-term relationship with Crump could only end in tragedy for one of them, probably not her. She could more than handle Ronald in an argument, including a physical one, if need be. Her brothers had taught her to fight and, as much as she hated violence, she was well able to stand up for herself, as Ronald would eventually find out!

March arrived, and the days passed with increasing rapidity as Ronald Crump's eleventh birthday approached. The first of April couldn't come quickly enough for the spoilt offspring of the arms dealer, with the invitations for the occasion all sent out weeks in advance. The big day finally arrived, and Maria Lugosi arrived at the Crumps' with Colette. The young girl had her hair in ponytails and wore a pale yellow knee-length dress and smart shoes. Maria Lugosi was a very attractive woman and began to feel a little uneasy at the way some of the other fathers were looking at her.

Hugh Rothschild, when his wife was not in earshot, said to Teddy Crump, 'Who is the broad, Ted?'

'Forget it, Hugh, she's forbidden fruit,' Crump advised his associate.

'Ah come on, Teddy boy, you're keeping her all to yourself, aren't you? I know you, randy old fucker. Tell me, who is she?'

'Hugh, I cannot emphasise enough, she is definitely not on offer, and if I say that then take it as read.'

Crump told him whose wife she was and went on to say that if even a quarter of the rumours about Lugosi were true, then Maria was certainly a no-go area. To hear these two sophisticated members of the US ruling elite conversing, anybody taking a cursory interest could be forgiven for believing either these men were super studs or, perhaps more accurately, their mental faculties had been obliterated in some freak accident. Jimmy and Moira Carter were present with Susie who, as always, was welded to James Rothschild's arm. The Carters were leaving shortly and would return to collect Susie later in the day. Peter Tillerson and Judy McClean were there playing the happy young couple and Peter's parents, Duke and Sheena, were talking to Barney McClean and his wife, Veronica.

The party was beginning to get started. Terry Morgan arrived with Dianna Nixon linked to his arm. They had smuggled vodka in, as soon as they found out their parents were not coming. Their intention was to keep it for later when the grown-ups retired to the lounge for drinks.

The party was flowing, and soon it was time for the star, Ronald, to open his presents. Teddy had spent the usual fortune on his son. The boy's main prize was a replica AK-47 assault rifle. This was complemented by many smaller presents which Ronald characteristically tossed to one side after viewing them. He lifted up the rifle again, and played the big man, aiming the weapon at people in a menacing manner. By this stage in her life Colette had seen the real thing, so this did not please or impress her in the slightest. All the same it was his birthday, so she put up with his infantile behaviour for now. Colette had brought a friend with her, whose name was Lucy Livingwell. Lucy's father, Bertie, was in the catering and supermarket trade and was also a billionaire. He was a man who kept himself to himself. Lucy's mother had died some years earlier and her father had become somewhat of a recluse.

It was now time for the much-anticipated food and all the young guests got stuck into the feast provided by the ever-loyal domestic helps. Ronald acknowledged the maids more for Colette's benefit than anything else. The staff at the Crumps' did not expect to be spoken to as human beings, in fact even the crudest acknowledgement was regarded by them as an honour. As expected, after the food the adults retired to the expansive lounge bar at Crumps for drinks and what passed for grown-up conversation. If a passer-by could have heard these specimens of US adulthood they could be forgiven if they got the impression they were passing the local lunatic asylum, such were the levels of their boastful self-aggrandisement in all matters. Maria felt a little uneasy being on her own; all the same, she was glad Benito was not with her. Heaven only knew what he would have made of these circus clowns. She managed to strike up a conversation with Moira Carter, and then spent the next hour or so getting bored to tears listening to her.

Back in the other room, away from the parents, Terry Morgan produced his bottle of vodka. He took a slurp and handed it to Dianna who, having had a drink earlier on their way to the party, was already feeling a little worse for wear. None of the grown-ups had noticed as they were too busy trying to impress one another. Terry passed the contraband around which Susie Carter and James Rothschild refused, as did Colette. Ronald took a long pull on the drink, acting as if it was a regular occurrence for him. Once again, the young host started showing off the replica rifle and Colette couldn't help thinking, with a shiver, what would he be like with the real thing?

'Give me another slurp of the vodka, Tez,' he insisted, indicating to Terry Morgan. 'I'm gonna get pissed.'

While Colette was chatting to Susie, Ronald spotted Lucy leaving the room. He followed her, staggering a little, and found her in a room off the main corridor. Young Crump entered the room and made a lunge at the young girl.

'Give me a feel, you little tart,' he said, grabbing at her top.

'Get off! Leave me alone,' Lucy cried, trying to push him away.

'You know you want to, don't you? Come on, I bet you're feeling horny.' Crump had upgraded his vocabulary to fit what he saw as his status and hoping it would impress the girl.

'You're crazy. Let me go!' the young girl yelled, struggling to break free. Tears of fear spilled down her cheeks as Ronald pawed crudely at her.

'Help, help!' she screamed.

'I've got you, Lucy,' came a shout from the door. Colette ran into the room and stopped for a moment in disbelief as she took in the scene before her. Then she walked over and punched Ronald in the face, causing his nose to bleed.

'What do you think you're doing? You're nothing but a pervert. You just couldn't wait, could you?' the gangster's daughter continued. 'I told you we would get over all our problems together and this is how you thank me. You bastard!'

Colette then kicked Crump on the shin for good measure.

She put her arm around Lucy's shoulders. 'Come on Lucy, we're going. Let's get away from this creep and his loony family.'

'I was just looking for a restroom, and then he jumped on me...' the distressed girl sobbed, as they both left the room.

She went to the bar where the adults were socialising and went over to her mother, who was still enduring a strained conversation with Moira Carter. Colette whispered to Maria that she and Lucy wanted to leave. Maria was only too relieved to say said her goodbyes. As they departed, Colette couldn't help noticing several of the men giving her mother lingering glances. She was so proud of her mother, who ignored them all and walked away, gracefully and elegantly.

When Maria, Colette and a very upset Lucy arrived back at the Lugosi home, Maria suspected all was not well.

'All right, young lady, tell me what's been going on,' she said to her daughter.

Colette, still comforting her friend, told her mother everything she had witnessed. Maria acted shocked but in reality was not altogether surprised. She had seen these middle-class parties before, with spoilt little rich kids getting out of hand and little parental control or dialogue. It must be remembered the Lugosi family were also very rich, equal to any of those at the 'bash', but came from a different culture.

Lucy Livingwell said she might go to the police, but Colette talked her out of this course of action. It would be her word against his and, as wealthy as her father was, he did not have the political clout that Teddy Crump had.

'Ronald will be punished enough when I finish with him,' Colette told her.

This appeared to pacify Lucy. Colette was also anxious the events of that afternoon did not reach the ears of Pedro Lugosi, her younger brother. Pedro fancied Lucy and would no doubt kick Crump senseless if he found out that he'd tried it on with the object of his affections. She did not want her brother getting into trouble with the police, especially as she suspected something very big might be going down with Papa and his friends. The family did not need the police spotlight on them. Colette knew that even though Pedro fancied Lucy, the feeling was not mutual. So, when Lucy said she was thinking of telling Pedro what happened to her, Lucy advised her not to.

'If Pedro kicked the shit out of Crump, which he is more than able to do, then would you be prepared to go to the movies with him?'

'Well, not really,' said Lucy.

'Then I would urge you not to tell him. It would be different if you were with each other or you wanted to go on a date with him.'

This line of argument had the desired affect and Lucy agreed not to divulge the information to Pedro.

Back at the Crumps' household Ronald joined Teddy and Megan in their study as his parents discussed the afternoon's events. What had exactly happened? And who brought the vodka? Whoever it was, in Megan's eyes it was they and not little Ronald who were responsible for what had occurred. Her 'little soldier' was a victim of circumstances. Teddy took more of a business approach to the subject. He told his wife not to attribute blame on others so easily. It was, after all, her son who had tried it on with the young friend of his girlfriend, and although whoever brought the alcohol had a part to play, it was ultimately Ronald's fault.

'Ronald must be responsible for his own actions,' he said.

Megan did not agree. 'If the drink had not been available then the whole sorry incident would not have occurred, would it?'

Ronald quickly saw in Megan his chief way out of this mess he had created.

'Mom, it was that Terry Morgan who brought the drink and forced me to drink it. I didn't really want to, it was all Morgan's fault and that girlfriend of his, Dianna Nixon.'

Teddy did not agree. He was looking at the situation through purely financial eyes. Bradley Morgan had some great contacts, wealthy men in the southern states who owned several chains of gun clubs and although Crump did not agree with their policies, wage slavery was far more productive than was chattel slavery, which many in the southern states still believed in. Morgan could be worth a few million and Teddy was not going to allow a little eating of humble pie to get in the way. The small deal he had made with Seddon was only a taster, and as he knew Morgan could be bought at a reasonable price, it would not do to be aiming accusations at his son. Teddy aimed at doing damage limitation.

'Leave it with me, Megan, I'll have a word with Brad and see if we can sort this out in an adult fashion.'

He knew that Bradley and Ethel Morgan spoke the same language – money – as himself and he also knew Ethel would not want to lose the sweeteners Crump put their way.

'Very well, but don't you go blaming our Ronald,' Megan went on. 'It wasn't his fault, and as for that little strumpet of a girl, what's her name?' Megan pretended to forget Colette's name. 'He's better off without her and that family of hers.'

In her eyes, Ronald had done no wrong. She could not see the abomination he was growing into and how he could become a despicable person if he remained unchecked. Teddy, on the other hand, did not want any trouble with the Lugosi family. He had the resources through his corrupt connections to deal with problems, but at what price? A bullet in the head? No, best cut their losses on this one. Benito may have had some potential for Crump to capitalise on but again, at what price? He diverted Megan away from heaping unwarranted blame on the Lugosi girl, and concentrated her efforts on comforting 'her little soldier', as she saw their son.

The following day Crump had occasion to meet Morgan on the golf course.

'What happened at your lad's party yesterday, Ted?' Morgan enquired.

'Oh, some kid smuggled vodka in and Ronald, the greedy little sod, drank too much of it.'

The question of rights and wrongs of an eleven-year-old drinking vodka never entered the conversation.

'Well, Ted, I'll tell you who brought the stuff. It was our Terry. Ethel and myself gave him a damn good telling off, and Dianna's parents have grounded her for a week.'

Crump was delighted that Morgan was attributing much of the blame on his own son. This would save him face and he could tell Megan, for once with a certain amount of honesty, that he and Brad had sorted it all out amicably.

'Don't worry about it, Brad, lads will be lads after all, and our Ronald was not wholly innocent,' he conceded.

Noticeable to see in this highly charged self-analysis by these two pillars of US society that not one word of concern was voiced for the victim of this assault, young Lucy. It would appear to these two men of superior intelligence that she was a mere incidental, and neither Ronald nor Terry could be blamed for her ordeal.

In their conversation Bradley Morgan did mention Lucy Livingwell once. 'That girl,' he said. 'She's the "food man's" daughter, you know the guy who never mixes or comes to our social gatherings. She was probably making it up, that your Ronald assaulted her. You should consider suing for defamation of character,' he added.

Crump knew it would be most unwise to go down this avenue. There would be a counterclaim backed by witnesses and his son would be exposed for the person he really was.

'No, no need for that, Brad,' said Crump. 'Best let sleeping dogs lie.' He winked at his fellow conspirator. 'Anyway, Brad, what I wanted to speak with you about is the contract for supplying the Texan National Guard with new equipment and night vision sights. You were saying some time ago something may be in the offing?'

'Don't worry, Ted, I have my ear to the ground. You know how this red tape works, government contracts and all that crap. I'll give you the nod as soon as there is any mention of tendering for the arms contract. You'll have a flying start, by some distance, on any of your rivals. It will be in the bag for you, that you can rest assured on.'

Crump thanked Morgan for his manipulation in his favour. This was the main reason he wanted no bother over Ronald's drinking and sexual assault. If it was a choice between his son going to a correction centre for six months or Teddy getting the contract, then Ronald would be going for a six-month break! Fortunately, this situation would not now arise.

On arriving home, Teddy Crump was met by his anxious wife.

'Did you see Bradley Morgan and put him straight, Teddy?'

'Yes, I did, and everything is sorted out. We both agreed Ronald was not to blame. It was down to Terry and the girl, Lucy. She was the real guilty party who caused all the trouble.'

This version of events appeared to satisfy Megan, who had toyed with a similar idea to that suggested by Morgan, of suing the girl for slander.

'What about it, Teddy, could we take that little strumpet to court for falsely accusing our boy?'

'Best not, dear,' replied Crump. 'Let's just leave it now, OK?'

'Oh, very well,' his wife finally conceded, 'at least for now.'

Monday morning came around quickly, and Ronald pondered whether he should grovel to Colette, or let her come apologising to him. He decided on the latter course of action. She was bound to come to him full of sweet nothings at the end of class. Young Crump walked to school with the gang, though only Terry Morgan was speaking to him. James Rothschild and Susie, along with Peter Tillerson and Judy, blanked the arms dealer's son totally. The first lesson was science, which passed quickly and when the bell sounded Ronald gathered his equipment and set off in search of Colette. He sighted her and decided to make himself visible in order that she could deliver her apology. He was in for a shock.

Colette sighted Crump and made a beeline for him.

'You pervert, you spoilt little sod! Did your mommy tell you not to worry? That you had nothing to worry yourself about? My friend was in bits because of you, and if you ever come near me again I'll break your fucking neck!'

This was not the apology Ronald was expecting, and she had said all these things in the middle of a laughing crowd.

'Colette, don't be like that,' he said. 'I won't do it again, I promise. Please come back. I love you.'

'Love, you wouldn't know the meaning of the word. The only two people you love are yourself and that blind barmy mother of yours. Now get lost, you creep.'

Ronald was devastated but knew he couldn't show it; there were too many people present. He sloped off to the next class almost in tears and hoped he could hold off from crying till he got home to his mother.

Colette Lugosi never usually slated or even passed opinions about other kids' parents and what she said about Megan Crump was out of character.

However, these were exceptional circumstances and in Colette's eyes they warranted those derogatory comments. All the same she did feel a little remorse because Megan had always been kind to her. When she described Megan as 'blind and barmy' she had lost her formidable temper, something which was a rarity for the gangster's daughter. On the other hand, she did not regret describing Crump as a creep and a pervert. Colette Lugosi possessed many admirable characteristics and principles which would, in years to come, cause her to be a thorn in the establishment's side.

Ronald Crump arrived home and burst into tears as he blurted out that Colette had broken up with him. He cried himself to sleep that night over losing Colette.

He rose the following morning and burst into tears again, partly genuine and partly to attract sympathy from his mother.

'Oh my little soldier, don't cry,' Megan said.

'Plenty more fish in the sea, son. I lost many girlfriends for worse than what you did,' declared Teddy.

'What do you mean, Ted, he didn't do anything!' argued his wife. 'My little boy wouldn't do anything wrong,' she went on.

Teddy was in a hurry for a meeting, so grabbing his briefcase, he headed off. Perhaps Megan should have been concerned by what her husband had just said in a throwaway phrase: that he had sexually assaulted girls in his youth. Instead of claiming her boy did nothing wrong, Megan should have shown disgust and more sympathy with the victim, Lucy Livingwell.

'Leave him alone! If you can't be supportive don't say anything,' she berated Crump as he disappeared through the front door. Megan was in denial. 'That bloody girl, making things up about you,' she said to Ronald.

Megan decided to keep her son away from school for a couple of days. 'You can stay away from lessons today and tomorrow and we'll see on Thursday how you are feeling,' she told the youngster.

This was music to Ronald's ears. The longer he was off the better.

Teddy Crump arrived back home at three thirty in the afternoon, having had a short meeting and then two rounds of golf. He was exhausted. Megan fixed them both some drinks, and when he was more relaxed she informed him she was keeping their son away from school for a couple of days.

'If he is no better by Thursday I'll take him to our GP,' she said.

'Are you mad, woman?' said Teddy. 'What are you going to tell the doctor? That our son got pissed and then started groping a girl at his birthday party?

And he is sick now because his girlfriend dumped him as a result? He'll laugh you out of the surgery. Stop deluding yourself.'

At last Megan began to listen, and for a few moments she entertained the idea that her son might be guilty.

'I see what you mean, Teddy,' she said. 'I'll forget the doctor and keep him at home until Thursday and take it from there.'

Teddy agreed with his wife, if only for a quiet life. Thursday arrived and Ronald reluctantly came down for his breakfast. When his mother sought out how he felt, he lied.

'Not well, Mom, I have a sore throat.'

'Must be down to stress,' Megan told him. 'We'd better keep you at home until next week.' She conveyed her decision to Teddy on his arrival home.

'He'll have to return at some point,' Crump Senior said, concerned about him missing math and other lessons of benefit for the future.

'Very well, he can return on Monday,' Megan conceded.

So eventually Ronald Crump bowed to the inevitable and returned to the fold on the designated Monday morning. He had spent the weekend skulking around on his own, apart from a couple of hours on Saturday afternoon when Terry Morgan, his co-drunk, called round. He was not looking forward to school as not only did he no longer have Colette, but the gang, Terry and Dianna exempted, were not speaking to him either. Ronald was, at least for the time being, on his own. James Rothschild had instructed the rest of the gang to have nothing to do with Crump as he had disgraced their honour with his behaviour. And only Terry spoke up a little for Ronald.

Ronald painted a lonely figure as he set off by himself for school on that dreaded Monday morning. He half hoped that Colette would meet him, having rethought her decision to dump him. This was a forlorn hope; in fact there was more chance of a rocking horse winning the Kentucky Derby than Ronald getting back with Colette. He could see no sign of her anywhere. Perhaps this was a stroke of luck for Ronald because her mood towards him had not changed. Ronald's first priority, though, was to grovel his way into Rothschild's good books no matter what it took.

He had an idea, a moment's inspiration. If he could persuade Terry to speak to James it might help to get reinstated into their company. Terry Morgan agreed to try on Ronald's behalf. With luck, Ronald reasoned, he would be back in James's good books, and therefore back in the gang, by the weekend at the latest.

Dianna Nixon, Terry's girlfriend, had become more outgoing and assertive since the days when she broke down in tears at the thought of being picked on. She was the daughter of a multimillionaire, and since Terry introduced her to alcohol she had taken a very unhealthy liking to the drink. Since the birthday party both Terry and Dianna were picking up reputations as drunks. However, Dianna couldn't care less what the others thought and cared even less whether or not Crump was allowed back into the gang. She didn't know why Terry was so bothered about Crump. *Fucking creep*, she thought. As Terry and James discussed Ronald, she lost interest and said she would meet up with Terry later.

Having listened intently to Terry's request on behalf of Ronald, James said he would give it a high priority of consideration. James Rothschild had a very high opinion of himself and, as gang leader, a lot of self-ordained responsibility. His position was very similar to a senior army officer, deciding what was best for his troops. James deliberated all the way home what Ronald's fate would be, but the decision would actually be taken out of his hands.

James arrived home to find his father in deep conversation on the telephone. He gave this little thought until he overheard his father say, 'Yes Ted, I understand. Leave things to me, good as done.'

Teddy Crump's company did a lot of business with Rothschild's bank which had a multimillion-dollar annual turnover. Megan Crump had pestered her husband to pressurise Hugh Rothschild into getting her son back into the gang. Eventually, again more for a quiet life, he succumbed to her requests and phoned Rothschild, implying his company's business may be diverted elsewhere if his son didn't comply with Teddy's request. As we know in the world of these people the dollar bill trumped all other considerations and this was to be no exception.

'James, come here,' ordered Hugh Rothschild of his son. 'That was Teddy Crump very irate at you. You will have Ronald back in your gang pronto,' the financier ordered.

'But Pa!'

'But Pa nothing,' Hugh said. 'He is from now back in favour. Do I make myself clear?'

'Yes, Pa,' said James.

'How you word his reinstatement is up to you,' said his father. 'Just do it.'

Ronald was allowed back into the gang forthwith. 'Thanks, James, I appreciate it,' said Ronald in his grovelling way.

'You have Terry to thank, he talked me round,' lied the gang leader.

Terry and Dianna walked away, with young Morgan feeling very important in front of his girlfriend. 'Can we get some vodka?' asked Dianna.

'No we can't, I can't just walk into a shop and buy it, you know, love,' Terry reminded her.

Ronald Crump was now back with the gang thanks, he thought, to Terry Morgan. He strutted around like a returning soldier from a battle who had recently distinguished himself in conflict rather than someone who had disgraced himself in public. Colette had not been seen for over a week and Ronald kept deluding himself that she still regretted dumping him. He had convinced himself she was working out a way of apologising to him for her outrageous behaviour and was conniving a way of getting back into his good books. In fact the girl's absence was totally unrelated to Crump or the incident which had disgraced him.

Colette's absence from school was due to the fact her family were moving back west to Chicago where her father was to take a more hands-on approach to the management of his casinos. A rival gang had been trying to muscle in on Lugosi's turf, a foolish thing to do unless they could match his organisation gun for gun, so Benito was going back to lead the defence. This had been the reason for the Council of War which Ronald had unknowingly witnessed the day he was out with Colette; happier times! Lugosi had put the house on the market priced at $220,000, a fair price for the 1950s, and several potential buyers had already shown interest in the property.

One day after morning break Terry told Ronald he had seen Colette and her mother entering the principal's office. Ronald immediately headed off down the corridor so he could wait for Colette outside the office.

In the principal's office, Maria was explaining that the family was moving, and as a result Colette would no longer be attending the educational institution. Maria thanked the principal and informed him that her daughter would be away at the end of the week.

On their way out of the principal's office Maria and Colette perceived the figure of Ronald, who had positioned himself so he would be seen.

'Colette,' he called.

'Oh no,' the girl said to her mother, 'what does he want?'

'Do you want me to deal with it?' Maria offered.

'No, Mama, it's down to me. I can handle him,' she said, as she made her way over to him.

'What do you want, Ron?' she asked.

'I've been looking all over for you,' he said, with an air of superiority about him. 'I thought you might wish to apologise for your behaviour. I'm prepared to give you a second chance and forget all about it. We can start over. We all make mistakes,' he concluded with an air of paternalism.

'Start again, with you, a fucking creep like you?' Colette seethed. 'I don't see what I saw in you in the first place, apart from the fact you were good at math. That's about all you were good at! I wouldn't go back with you if there were no boys left on this planet. 'Now go away before I do something I may live to regret,' she threatened. 'Just get out of my sight.'

'That's my girl,' Maria murmured to herself. 'She's my daughter all right, that's for certain.'

Ronald Crump reeled away. This wasn't supposed to happen. It never happened to his father so why him? This was the last time for many years Crump would encounter Colette Lugosi; the end of a childhood romance which promised so much but, thanks to Ronald's spoilt and dysfunctional upbringing, ended in abject failure.

The coming September signalled the beginning of the final year for the gang at Wetherspoons. All the thoughts of the parents were on which elite expensive private educational establishment they could get their children into for the academic year beginning in September 1959. The Rothschilds and Carters had decided they did not wish James and Susie to be separated, much to the youngsters' delight. They had a relationship which would genuinely blossom, even though their parents' only considerations were financial. Their parents were already pencilling in wedding plans and, more importantly, a financial marriage which could treble the wealth of both families. The Rothschilds had applied, and James had successfully interviewed for, the Benjamin Franklin Private Higher Tutorial Institute out in Philadelphia. The Carters had also been successful in their application to get Susie into William Penn School for Young Ladies less than a mile away from where James would be boarding. They had no worries about their education being adversely affected, as they had been together for most of their time at the junior school and were well past the moony-eyed stage of their romance. The annual fees at both boarding institutions were $10,000, which was expensive even for the fifties.

'One gets what one pays for,' said Hugh Rothschild, as if everybody could afford these outlandish fees, more than most workers would earn in five years.

Teddy wanted Ronald as far away as possible, and after the parents applied to a few elite schools, eventually good news came. Ronald had been accepted into a prestigious school, Bishops Court Rise, in California. The annual fee would be $12,000. The institution catered for boys age twelve to seventeen with an optional year if a certain standard had been met. About half a mile away was a school for girls of the same age range. Occasionally the lessons were gender-mixed, from the third year upwards, in subjects such as science, cookery (optional for boys), geography and religious studies.

Now that Ronald's place had been secured, the family could head off for the summer vacation to Florida for a month, the rump of the school break.

'Four weeks of doing nothing,' Megan commented with pleasure. This statement should not mislead the reader into believing that for the rest of the year Megan Crump led a productive life full of activity. Her announcement should have been rephrased as 'doing nothing in a different place'.

The Carters and Rothschilds took a vacation together for most of the school break in Philadelphia. This was so Susie and James could get acclimatised with their new schools later in the following year.

The Nixons and the McCleans wanted their daughters, Dianna and Judy, to be accommodated at the same school. They had been friends for several years, in fact since Dianna's original friend, Susie, started dating James Rothschild. They also decided that this would be better in the advancement of their education, and Fred Nixon wanted his daughter away from Terry Morgan. Bradley and Ethel Morgan, similarly, were sending Terry as far away from Dianna Nixon as possible. They blamed her, wrongly, for introducing their son to alcohol when it was, in fact, the other way around. They were delighted to receive their letter confirming acceptance at the prestigious William Bradford Higher Educational Institute, an exclusive establishment with annual fees of $12,500.

The McCleans had nothing against their daughter's relationship with Peter Tillerson, except they could see no future or profit in it, so they decided to get Judy into the same establishment as Dianna. Freddie, Audrey, Barney and Veronica ('Ronni') were delighted when they received confirmation that both girls had been accepted at the Cranberry Boarding School for Girls situated in Michigan, with annual fees amounting to $13,000.

Duke and Sheena Tillerson were sending Peter to the exclusive George Washington High, a boarding school well away from Ronald Crump. Again, both the Tillersons and the Crumps agreed it was a good idea to separate the two boys who, they considered, hampered each other's education.

Even though all this upheaval was for the following year, the arduous work of obtaining the right schools for their children had been crucially important, and thankfully now was done. All the parents were happy with their results and congratulated each other, amid ghastly laughter on their collective good fortunes. Their offspring's final year at Wetherspoons would of course include exams, but pass or fail, the futures for these children of the US financial elite at the private educational facilities of their parents' choices were secure. All the brigands were confident their children would thrive in the disciplines their parents pushed them towards. After all, these were the heirs apparent of business empires secured through theft, bribery and exploitation of labour.

3

The Grown-Ups

Teddy Crump's claim to have taken part in the fabled Normandy landings in 1944 were questionable, to say the least. The landings themselves were largely made possible by the victories accomplished by the Soviet Union at Stalingrad and Kursk as the Red Army pushed westward. The colonel had acquired several medals for bravery – though these again were questionable as Crump had in fact been a staff officer around that time, behind the lines and away from the action. He was later despatched to Hamburg where he met his future partner in crime, Bob Tomkinson. Colonel Crump claimed he had also fought on the Eastern front against the Empire of Japan and was involved in the taking of many small Japanese islands.

Teddy often looked back on the former enemy of Nazi Germany and wondered if some of the Third Reich's political ideologies, such as banning trade unions and any other form of civil protest which the Nazis considered dangerous, were actually good for business. Put simply, if Crump could have, he would have cherry-picked the aspects of the German dictatorship which would have benefitted him, and used them. This attitude perhaps is not far away from the minds of many leading capitalists around the globe today. In fact, many governments in the so-called liberal democracies do enact certain fascist policies, without ever mentioning that this is what they are. They tend to dress them up as 'maintaining law and order' and 'suppressing threats to national security'. This way the people will never see them for what they really are, draconian 'para-fascist' laws. Whatever they call them, they are enacted to defend capitalism, which the electorate is constantly told is 'freedom'!

Teddy Crump had been very successful in the arms-dealing industry, having learned in the army how best to deceive people, a very important skill in business. As he developed his enterprise, he branched out into other forms of engineering. The administration complex of his business was called Crump Mansions and consisted of two five-storey office blocks, one of them dedicated purely to the arms-producing side of the industry. The other block opposite the arms-dealing centre was the administration section of the engineering part of the empire. Surrounding these two monuments to death, several office units sprawled across the site. These were the personnel offices of Crump Armaments and Engineering. Here office staff, usually young females, worked tirelessly in pursuit of the compelling cause of making money for Mr Crump. One wing of the complex was dedicated to science and inventing, thus keeping Crump rated as one of the most advanced arms and engineering producers on the planet. If one could have viewed Crump Mansions from an aerial camera it would be seen that the complex replicated a large prison unit with two watchtowers at the entrance. About two miles to the west of this complex were Crump's huge factories, which worked night and day.

During the 1950s and '60s the production line never ceased working. When Ronald eventually took over it was the era of modern technology and innovation, which young Crump would streamline, but in Teddy's day the conveyor system ruled supreme. Crump employed around three thousand workers at their New York factories and Crump Mansions, with a further two thousand employees six hundred miles away in Detroit. The scientists employed at Crump Mansions by virtue of their specialist skills were members of a trade association, not affiliated to any of the trade unions. Crump did not like this but could do little about it; these people were irreplaceable and, after all, this association was bound by a no-strike deal with the company. This was perhaps why he wanted some of the laws enacted in the Third Reich available to him! The engineers at his factories were also organised in trade associations – but Crump drew the line at the vast army of semi-skilled workers, unskilled employees and women workers being allowed to join such organisations, moderate and tame as they were. Crump pretended to befriend the specialist and craft association representatives, supplementing them with the firm's own staff representatives, whom Crump himself selected. He even put them, when it suited him, on a perceived equal footing as some of his junior directors. Teddy Crump realised at an early stage the importance of keeping these specialists on his side if he was to remain ahead of his competitors.

He had also studied the Japanese style of working which, during the fifties, would not have been applicable to his own industries. However, he was more concerned with their style of management regarding the unions and staff representation. In Japan's factories, certainly after the last big strike at Nissan in 1953, the union representative was regarded as a kind of manager with his own office. That representative's main task was to, under any circumstances, stave off trouble from the workers for the company. This arrangement appeared to work very well, and Crump tried to adopt a similar approach to the skilled and specialist employees at his plants. He discouraged skilled workers from fraternising with their unskilled colleagues, something which was not difficult to do due to the inverted snobbery held by the skilled workers towards the unskilled. They would not have had these people in their associations if their lives depended on it. This attitude was, of course, music to Crump's ears. Basically, Crump had those staff representatives, if that is what they were, in his pocket.

In the office complex where Crump could be found on the odd occasion he visited the place, usually for board meetings or to take liberties with a young secretary, a reign of terror existed. Word would get around that 'the big man' was on site and absolute petrification would descend like wildfire. Teddy Crump's office was a large room with a bar situated in one corner, and a huge picture of George Washington titled 'Father of Freedom', somewhat ambiguously, considering it adorned the office of a man who tyrannised his workers to ever-greater production and profits. The women employees were not allowed to be members of even these tame staff organisations. Along one wall of this office was a large aquarium containing rare tropical fish. Along the other wall was a huge sofa about twelve feet in length and covered in luxury velvet. This, Crump mockingly called his 'passion bench'. The carpeting was best thick Axminster costing a small fortune per yard. Crump had three secretaries and a personal assistant whom he took on weekend 'business trips' with him. She was married, but this did not bother Crump as marriage vows were for others to abide by, not him or his secretaries, and certainly not his PA.

One day he was in the office, killing time before his round of golf. He called Julie, his PA, in for some dictation, or so she thought. After about five minutes he told her to lock the door.

'Why?' she asked.

'Just lock the door, Julie,' he said. The woman dutifully obliged, albeit with trepidation. The tyrant then told his PA what she was going to do.

'I'm a married woman,' she demurred. 'I won't do what you ask.'

Crump then reminded her that she was his PA, his senior secretary, and she would do precisely as she was told, married or not, if she wished to keep her well-paid job with him.

The terrified woman and her husband, who also worked for Crump, had a huge mortgage and debts after purchasing goods under the hire purchase scheme. If she lost her job, she thought, then Crump would be bastard enough to fire her husband, a semi-skilled forklift-truck operator, and that would leave them homeless. Under much duress and pressure, she dutifully undressed, complaining she would not do this every day, which Crump just ignored.

This was a regular occurrence for Crump, usually with one of his unmarried secretaries, but this was the first time he tried it with a married female member of staff. Crump promised he would not tell Julie's husband what she had done behind his back, provided she was available as and when required. After the event, the young woman left the room saying nothing and feeling very low. It was these impossible conditions and abuse which eventually forced Julie to leave the employ of Crump. Her decision would at least save her marriage and husband's job.

Teddy Crump was a man full of self-importance, a man who was, or so he thought, the life and soul of any party. The truth was that people hated inviting him and his subordinate wife to any of their social gatherings, but his extreme wealth ensured he was always included. They all pretended to like 'Teddy boy' and many of the women felt sorry for long-suffering Megan.

Any sensible person, admittedly a rare species in such circles, viewed Crump for what he was, a foul-mouthed, racist, misogynous and xenophobic pig. None of his aquaintances dared say this to him and, to be brutally honest, they had no right to, as their mannerisms were identical. The irony was, these people considered themselves both academically and physically superior to other human beings. This is what happens when a person's decency, credibility and success is dictated by the amount of money they have amassed.

Put in biblical terms, standing in a room full of these people could be akin to that of being in the company of many Judas Iscariots. For any genuine person unfortunate to be in the company of Crump and his compatriots it would be very unwise to turn their back on the gathering.

Crump Armaments and Engineering supplied weaponry to the armed forces of various governments around the globe. Some of these governments, such as that of Juan Peron in Argentina, were less than savoury and openly fascist. This did not bother Crump, because he was extremely right-wing himself. He portrayed himself as an 'old fashioned conservative'. The firm also sold arms to right-wing terrorist groups around the world and, if they could afford it, left-wing would-be freedom fighters. In a nutshell Crump Armaments would sell to anybody who had cash on the hip, so to speak, and that meant anyone, legal or otherwise. The diversity of Crump Armaments during the Cold War, which followed the end of the Second World War and thereafter until the nineties, was epitomised by the countries he did business with. His company sold to both NATO and to their Cold War enemies, the Soviet-led Warsaw Pact members.

As far as Crump was concerned, patriotism was for the lower orders, an attitude unofficially endorsed by various US governments and all big business. During the Suez Crisis in 1956, his firm was selling fighter aircraft parts to the Egyptians, assault rifles to the Israelis and tank tracks and shells to the British. The US government did not pay much heed to this duplicity due to the fact the British and Israelis had hatched a plan to oust Colonel Nasser from political office, following his nationalisation of the Suez Canal, without informing US President Eisenhower. The USA took a very poor view of this 'treachery', particularly by Britain, which they considered their immediate subordinate, and would eventually make them pay. Crump made a fortune out of the Suez Crisis as did many other smaller US firms who did business with Crump.

Teddy Crump's wife, Megan, suspected her husband's infidelity and, unknown to him, occasionally got her own back. One such occasion was encountering one of her old bosses from her days working in banking. She was out socialising with Sheena Tillerson and when they went their separate ways she met, totally by chance, her former manager, Derek.

'How are you, Megan?' the bank manager said, clearly pleased to see her. 'It's been a long time.'

'I'm good,' replied Megan. 'I have a little boy now, and he's at prep school. How are you?'

The distant acquaintances from bygone days made small talk. When Derek suggested they go for a drink, Megan agreed.

'I know a nice little bar,' Derek said. 'We could go there and catch up.'

'Yes, I'd like that,' said Megan, with a feeling of anticipation.

Derek was a senior director now, rich in his own right, but had no hope of matching Crump's financial muscle.

'What are you having, Megan?' he asked, when they sat down at the bar.

'I'll have a screwdriver,' she replied.

'Two screwdrivers, bartender,' he ordered.

They remained chatting for an hour and had several drinks before they got up to leave. Megan was feeling a little tipsy, which had been her former boss's intention, and they walked for a while along the precinct.

'Imagine meeting after all these years,' Derek said for the umpteenth time.

'Yes, indeed,' said Megan, wishing he'd come to the point.

'Listen,' he said, 'why not go back to my place for a couple of hours, kill time and we can catch up further. The wife is away for a couple of days.'

This sounded like what Megan wanted to hear. If Teddy could screw anyone in a skirt at work, then she could do the same to those in trousers. She'd had a brief fling with Derek some years earlier so this would be nothing new.

They arrived at his apartment. 'Would you like a drink?' he asked.

'Sure, a vodka and orange,' replied the about-to-be-unfaithful wife.

'I'll have the same,' said the banker.

They started talking about old times at the office, before they were both married, and the conversation got around to one particular day when they were both alone in the office.

'Can you remember?' asked Derek.

'Vividly,' she murmured.

After several drinks he edged nearer and placed his hand on her knee. There was no resistance. The pair then made their way to the bedroom for a couple of hours where long-forgotten passions were remembered and reignited.

It was nearly three thirty when Megan left her former boss's apartment, almost time to collect Ronald from prep school. She reapplied her lipstick, tidied her hair and drove off. Megan had made no concrete arrangements to see Derek again, but he had given her his telephone number, so she could call him if at a 'loose end' any day. She arrived at the school playing the dutiful wife and mother, with no one the wiser about her secret rendezvous.

★ ★ ★

Whatever kind of misogynous, racist, arrogant, self-indulgent egotistic pig Teddy Crump may have been, his son Ronald would develop into a lot more than a chip off the old block. Teddy was a microcosm of what Ronald would become, due, in no small part, to the upbringing he received.

★ ★ ★

Megan Crump, née Simpson, whose parents were Quakers, had been a quiet teenage girl, brought up in a lower-middle-class environment. She was an only child who left high school and went to work in a city bank as a teller. Here she stayed, hoping to make a career in banking, and by her mid-twenties had been through a brief affair with her married manager, Derek.

One day at the bank, a late-middle-aged businessman entered the bank to discuss a transaction with the manager. Derek, the manager, had requested Megan to sit in on the meeting as part of her in-house training, and the young woman was immediately struck by the dashing mature retired colonel. When the business was concluded the colonel was escorted to the door by the young bank teller. It was at this point Teddy Crump invited the girl out on a date. The bank discouraged flirtations between staff and clients, but Megan was awestruck by the invitation and accepted.

Teddy took Megan on several dates and there was chemistry between them. To her, the couple felt compatible, and Megan liked him, despite his arrogant manner. After all, men were generally like this, weren't they? Megan consoled herself about any reservations about Crump with this calculation and ignored any tiny doubts. She was quite taken with him, or perhaps more accurately his image of a decorated and retired colonel, as well as a very successful businessman with huge wealth.

On their fifth or sixth date she decided it was time for Teddy to meet her parents. Despite early reservations, they took to Crump, recognising him as a wealthy and powerful man who could take their daughter off their hands. Despite being a self-important racist who had misogyny running through his veins, they reasoned he would make their daughter a perfect husband. The fact their future son-in-law referred to his fellow human beings as broads, tarts, niggers, monkeys and dagos appeared not to matter to these 'good Christian folk'. All that counted was his wealth and that he would, no doubt, become even wealthier. Teddy Crump considered himself a good Christian who could occasionally be found Sunday mornings at the local Methodist chapel giving thanks to God – provided a round of golf or some other pleasurable activity was not already in the offing. As we know, Crump and Megan were eventually married, both taking their sacred vows. Unfortunately, over time, they ultimately set about breaking these vows. He was first and then she followed. For Megan it was, in fairness, retaliation and revenge.

For Crump, Megan was a provider of an heir apparent. If they had a boy first, then there would be no need for any more children, he decided. She could bring the child up jointly with the domestics who would do all the dirty work, changing nappies etc., while he could screw any female he wanted at work.

It was Wednesday afternoon and an important social gathering was taking place at the New York Hilton. The guests of honour were to be Senator Wesley Vague, along with his colleague from the US Senate, Senator Douglas Dodge. Also present at this exclusive gathering as special guests of Messrs Crump, Rothschild, Morgan and Tillerson and spouses, were men from the House of Representatives: Alan Bent, Anthony Taylor and Jethro Talltail. Two of Crump's lawyers were also present, Frank Hastings and Toby Stronghold. These two gentlemen practised law and were very expensive to hire. They were top of the range and knew every loophole, as well as creating some of their own, in the legal system.

'Toby, how are you?' said Crump on spotting Stronghold. 'And you, Frank, how's the legal fraternity suiting you these days?'

'Can't complain, Ted, still paying me a fortune by the hour,' the attorney joked.

'Same with me,' interjected Toby.

'What time is the "electric current" one arriving?' said Hastings, referring to Judge Henry 'Burn 'em' Valliant. He acquired the nickname 'Burn 'em' due to the number of guilty verdicts, especially from ethnic minorities, he sent to the electric chair for murder. Many argued he would send people to their deaths, if he could, for lesser offences. This was, however, pure speculation.

'He'll be along shortly, don't panic, lads,' reassured Crump.

Megan, wearing a strapless knee-length dress, was in conversation with Mary Rothschild and Ethel Morgan, the latter being incapable of holding a conversation without shouting and uttering bitchy comments.

'That's a nice dress, Megan,' Ethel commented. 'I have to say it's very much like the one I gave away to charity the other day.'

'Oh', retorted Megan, 'you mean the one you originally purchased from the second-hand shop?'

'Now ladies, calm down,' said Mary, who was not really one for bitching; it got in the way of serious business, like making money. To the casual observer this was a gathering of lifelong friends who would lay down their lives for each other! Nothing could be further from the truth. They all hated the sight of their 'lifelong friends' and jealousy was a strand threading through the whole rotten crowd. Last to arrive were the two junior members of the robber barons, Matthew and Sally Seddon.

'Hi Matthew, how's it hanging?' shouted Bradley Morgan.

'Great, Brad,' Seddon retorted.

Sally was dressed in a flared skirt with a white short-sleeved blouse and high-heeled court shoes. Crump knew Seddon wanted to upgrade his gun clubs, which meant he could then increase membership fees. He particularly wanted the new state-of-the-art rifles which designers at Crumps had developed. Crump knew, via Morgan, just how keen and eager Seddon and his wife Sally was to secure these rifles, which would be unavailable at other gun clubs. Crump noticed his wife was fully engaged talking to the judge and his wife and saw an opportunity to follow Sally into a side room. This scene was not unlike the juvenile version at Ronald's party which finished his relationship with Colette. The difference was, at that party the subject, Lucy Livingwell, was not a willing player. Sally Seddon, for the right price, might just be.

'How are you, Sally?' Crump enquired.

'I'm good, Ted, really good,' she answered, approaching Crump softly. 'Wonderful party, isn't it? All the great and good seem to be here. I hope you don't mind me bringing up business, but you know Matthew wants to upgrade the gun club. Would you be able to give him the head start he needs for the new rifles?'

'I might be able to,' said Crump. 'What are you offering?'

Mathew Seddon knew full well his pretty young wife was going to try and seduce Crump and, given the possible lucrative reward, gave the liaison his unqualified blessing. The Seddons had discussed this before leaving for the Hilton. It was also agreed that Matthew could try his hand with Megan and, if he got a result, no hard feelings between the pair. The Seddon couple practised this form of quasi-prostitution regularly if there was a financial prize at the end.

Sally Seddon agreed to Crump's terms, without hesitation, and arranged to meet the arms dealer at a secret location the following day. Crump would be, as far as Megan was concerned, at the office when in reality he and Sally would be having an assignation outside town. Sally returned to the main room of activity looking for her husband. Matthew had disappeared and so had Megan Crump. Lucky bastard, she thought to herself, allowing herself a little giggle. Crump as per usual didn't realise his wife was missing. He was too busy being 'the life and soul of the party', or so he thought. About half an hour later Matthew returned to the room.

'Where have you been, naughty boy?' asked Sally, knowingly.

'Ask no questions get told no lies,' her husband replied with a wink.

'I shall be out tomorrow afternoon, darling,' said Sally.

'Didn't take you long, you little vixen,' said Seddon.

'Does it ever?' she quipped. 'I'll have to be careful,' she continued. 'I'll be getting a reputation as an easy ride.'

'Getting?' Seddon grinned. 'Christ Sal, your reputation went west a long time ago.'

As far as Sally and Matthew Seddon were concerned their marriage was a happy one; these were tactics purely in pursuit of money. If there had been no reward involved, the chances of Sally allowing Crump anywhere near her ranged from zero to minus ten.

Hugh Rothschild was one of the richest men in the USA. Unlike Crump, he was more laid back and quiet, though equally as ruthless when the occasion arose. Like Crump, he had no time for trade unions but in the banking sector, employing educated people, all of them proficient with figures, Rothschild adopted a friendly approach towards his staff and their representatives. He also practised what he termed 'figure manipulation', meaning the annual accounts only showed up fifty per cent of financial turnover. This way any pay increases pursued by the unions on behalf of the staff would be based only on the public figures. In case anything ever came to light, Rothschild paid off the senior personnel at the criminal fraud investigation bureau, as well as buying the senior judges. Crump also had the chief of police and all immediate subordinate ranks in his pocket.

Mary Rothschild was a smart woman in her early forties. She had put on a little weight after giving birth to James and his sister, three years younger. Mary, along with Megan, Ethel and Sheena, were all supportive of their robber baron husbands. To anybody but the blind or congenitally stupid it was plain to see all these marriage arrangements were on a purely financial footing. Marriage vows, like religion, were for the lower orders to believe in, not for the USA ruling class.

Of all the women folk under discussion perhaps Ethel Morgan had the easiest life of all. As well as the domestics she had a full-time nanny to care for Terry until he reached the age of about eight. Then, as far as she was concerned, he could fend for himself. The domestics could intervene if he needed looking after; she did not want to pay wages for a nanny when there was little or no need for one. Ethel Morgan thrived on badmouthing everyone, even those she considered friends. She could be described as a carcass of pure corruption and jealousy, tinged with outright hate. Her husband, Bradley worked for the diplomatic corps, hence all the contacts. He was a wealthy man, not in Crump or Rothschild's league, however. Tillerson, after his insurance payout for the fire, was now somewhat ahead in the financial stakes. Morgan did hold the balance of power because of his contacts. He was entirely hen-pecked and lived in constant fear of his wife. His so-called friends mocked him about his 'marriage from hell' behind his back.

Ethel Morgan could be described as a 'full woman' who was about three stone overweight. After giving birth to Terry she never regained her figure. In fairness, she never made any serious attempt to do so, and being short gave the impression of appearing more obese than she actually was. Ethel sported short curly hair tightly cropped, with a higher-than-average forehead, and wore thick-rimmed spectacles. She had a very loud voice and when in conversation it would be imagined she thought her audience to be deaf, or considered them devoid of any intelligence, unable to comprehend the simplest conversation or request. She had but one aim in life, and that was to acquire as much money as possible while exercising the least possible effort. Her self-importance dictated all those before her be considered subordinate and certainly inferior, especially her downtrodden husband. When Ethel gave the command he dutifully obeyed.

Ethel was one of these 'true Christians' in theory but certainly not in deed. By this it was meant that she preached the Bible to everybody else and practised the absolute opposite. On one occasion when she was out shopping, an elderly woman inadvertently dropped her purse. Unfortunately for the elderly woman, Ethel was behind her. Quick as a flash, and in the most unchristian fashion imaginable, Ethel snatched the purse and it was in her handbag in the blink of an eye.

The Morgans were accepted by the rest of their wealthy 'friends', who only just tolerated each other due, in no small part, to Bradley's contacts. He could point the likes of Crump in the right direction and put in a good word for the other brigands with the appropriate networking. He had put a lot of business the way of Hugh Rothschild's bank after a meeting with high-ranking Saudi Arabian officials. Morgan's work was his ace card, and he knew it, which maintained his position with the vulture squadron.

Duke Tillerson made his money in the construction industry, later branching into textiles. The big fire at one of his clothing factories, resulting in the deaths of some members of staff, had netted Tillerson a small fortune. This was the result of a successful though questionable insurance claim on top of what he already had accumulated through legalised exploitation of labour. His wife, Sheena, like the other wealthy wives, lived a life of luxury, doing little or nothing all day. She attended a club calling itself 'Help the Poor', where groups of middle-class women discussed how to relieve the lot of the unemployed and homeless. The truth was these women, well-meaning though they may have been, did not have a clue how to make a positive difference in the lives of those in dire need. The fact was that capitalism, along with these wealthy people's lifestyles, would have to go before meaningful change could take place in society. It was this system that was the cause of all the unemployment and poverty, while at the same time creating lofty positions of obscene wealth for the privileged few.

Should any form or mention of revolution ever arise the ruling elite had the National Guard at their disposal. If these proved insufficient then the regular armed forces would intervene. Even if a party were to be elected by popular vote, committed to the destruction of the capitalist system, the ruling elite would mobilise the army and all other defence mechanisms to defend their positions. The voice of the people was all well and good, providing it went the way the bourgeoisie directed it! Any revolution, in their eyes, had to be crushed at all costs. Of course, things do not always go the way the elite want them to, and in a revolutionary situation the working class might also be armed and well equipped. It could well be that the potential insurrectionists' weaponry would be purchased from Crumps; after all, he would sell to anybody who had the money.

The Crumps and their cohorts all claimed to be disciples of the be-robed son of a carpenter, Jesus Christ. This was despite practising the absolute opposite to what the Bible preached. Of the whole cabal, only Ethel and Bradley Morgan were regular churchgoers. Even so, it was sickening to watch these two 'God-fearing' hypocrites on their knees praying to something neither of them really believed in. Teddy and Megan could occasionally be seen on Sundays at their local Methodist chapel, even though she had been brought up a Quaker. Of course, they did not take their imaginary beliefs to ridiculous lengths like treating their fellow human beings as equals; nothing that drastic!

The likes of Crump, Tillerson and many thousands of other brigands would quite happily deny their workers, particularly their unskilled workers and domestic helps, the right to put food on the table for themselves and their families, if they were not profitable enough. They would preach to their workers about obligations 'before God' of abiding by their marriage vows, despite breaking their own on a near-daily basis. They hammered home at every opportunity their wholehearted belief in the Bible and how the book had assisted them in their uphill daily plight, providing work for the less educated and less well off. Of course, there was little if any mention of the inconvenient parts of the same Bible, such as 'it is easier for a camel to pass through the eye of a needle than for a rich man to enter the Kingdom of Heaven.' Should any worker ask why they did not abide by the rules themselves, they were invariably sacked.

If any employer paid their workers what they were really worth there would have been no surplus value at all, and the genuine employer who practised this would soon be out of business. The employers collectively must be blamed for this rotten system, capitalism, because it is their system, for their benefit and their enrichment. If it wasn't for capitalism there would be no capitalists, nobody to 'work with their brains', like Crump, and, therefore, no exploitation. Supporters of the system would argue that without these benevolent souls people would have no employment. This is illogical because a skilled worker would still have their skills with or without the Crumps and Tillersons of this world.

It is these people who have the power to take the workers' employment away and therefore the right to live, if profits are down. A machinist could still operate a machine with or without the brigands; in fact, without them their employment would be so much more secure. Production would be organised for the needs of all the people, not merely the greed of the few. Work would be organised differently on a not-for-profit basis. Cooperatives under workers' control would replace the capitalist sweatshops, large and small, as work would become a more harmonious pastime. Unemployment would not exist, as everybody, skilled and unskilled, specialist and general, would have something which they could do and some task to perform for the good of their fellow human beings. While the means of production, distribution and exchange belong to the likes of Crump, unemployment will always be a threat to the workers. The threat of the sack will be forever present and with it the poverty and depravation which accompanies unemployment. It is the whole rotten system which must go, not individual capitalists, bad as they are!

★ ★ ★

Irish–American James Kelly was an entrepreneur who made his millions by subcontracting his services, advertising and marketing, to the likes of Crump and Tillerson, who paid him for his considerable marketing skills. Kelly was what could be described as a middle-ranking capitalist, not in the same league as Crump, Tillerson and Rothschild – even Bradley Morgan would be well ahead in the wealth stakes. He did, however, have a lot to offer on the sidelines, which Tillerson was soon to exploit. Eventually Ronald Crump would use this same service when he took over the helm of the Crump empire, but this was in the future. Tillerson was about to use Kelly to promote both his building and textile companies. Normally Tillerson would leave such jobs to his own marketing department but on this occasion, for reasons which will become clear, he took a hands-on approach, dealing directly with James Kelly.

Kelly was in his office one morning completing some of his tax returns, or perhaps more accurately, fiddling the figures, in order to pay less income tax. The reason Crump, Tillerson, and many others used this man on occasions was that he could 'cook their books' for them. They could not do this by using their own marketing departments. It is what is often also termed 'oiling the wheels of the capitalist gravy train'.

Suddenly the telephone rang, on his private number.

'Kelly,' the man answered.

'Jim, it's Duke Tillerson,' the caller informed him. 'How's business?'

'Couldn't be better, Duke, what can I do for you?'

'What I need, Jim, is thirty thousand A5 cards; no, make them leaflets, they're cheaper, to have posted through people's letter boxes in the St George area of Staten Island. They'll be promoting my building business. Can you do that, and provide the staff for the mailing?'

The advertising agent pondered for a moment.

'Of course, Duke, thirty thousand leaflets and a team to mail them for you.'

'That's great, Jim. I also need a couple of "dudes" to parade up and down the streets wearing sandwich boards advertising my textile products.'

'Again, not a bother, Duke, I have a few mentally handicapped I can use. They'll be happy enough to wear the idiot gear for next to nothing in wages.'

Both men gave loud laughs at the thought of Kelly using mentally handicapped people as cheap labour. These people got a kick out of exploiting those unable to defend themselves through no fault of their own. To hear them talk it would be imagined they considered themselves the funniest, wisest and most popular men in town.

These particular 'mentally handicapped' individuals were at the milder end of their disability and were looked after by carers. These people were unqualified, unlike the nursing staff who took care of the more serious cases. These carers were subsequently paid much less than the nursing staff as they had no formal training at all. They were, in a word, cheap, and though considered responsible adults, they weren't overly bright and didn't grasp the level of exploitation their clients were suffering as employees of Kelly.

Kelly employed his other workers as 'casuals', meaning his workers had no contract of employment and were available as and when they were needed. They were paid a pittance, so much per thousand leaflets, and as it was cash in hand, they paid no income tax. If these casual workers were caught, they were on their own. When Tillerson paid Kelly and claimed the money on tax relief, Kelly completely covered his trail. If there were any investigations as to what Kelly had done with the money (which was highly unlikely as most tax inspectors were friends of Tillerson and his cohorts in the 'Brigands Club') Kelly was able to produce the correct forms claiming he had disclosed the money. Some of it he had, but some went on his casuals' so-called wages and the rest was untaxed profit for himself. If anybody was curious enough to dig a little deeper, they would find that all the mailing was done by Kelly himself over several weeks and months; the casuals did not exist.

'What do you want printed on the leaflets, Duke?' asked the marketing expert.

'Let me think, Jim. Let's go for: "First-class building work carried out. Conversions, extensions, renovations at reasonable prices. Painting and decorating undertaken. All work carried out by Duke Tillerson and Co., builders of distinction."'

The fact was, Duke Tillerson was neither a builder nor distinctive. He had realised at a very early age he did not have to be; all he required was enough capital to set up a business and employ tradesmen to do the work for him. He would pay them a basic wage – the least he could get away with – and call himself a builder. When he occasionally went on site he made sure a foreman accompanied him and should any of the clients ask him a technical question about construction work, the foreman was always there to give the correct answer. In return, Tillerson gave the foremen carte blanche to rule the building sites with an iron fist, bullying and threatening the workers, particularly the unskilled, for ever-greater profits. The foremen, as well as being tradesmen, were also experts in cutting corners in the name of Mr Tillerson's profits. In return they received an annual bonus called 'profit shares'. The figures and amount these lackeys received were never reflective of the actual profits made, and Tillerson warned all of them not to disclose their figures to the rest of the men.

'No problem, Duke. Is a week soon enough?' Kelly asked.

'That's fine,' replied Tillerson. 'Give me a call when the leaflets are ready.'

'Will do. Oh, nearly forgot – what do you want printed on the sandwich boards?'

'Oh yes, put on those the following: "To all retailers – Unbeatable prices from our wholesalers. Shirts, pants, denim jeans and casual jackets produced to the highest quality. Orders taken from high street shops. Tillerson textile supplies and wholesalers."

'That should do the trick. Advertising, Jim, that's the secret. Advertising,' said Tillerson after dictating the text to Kelly.

James Kelly began phoning around his casuals and the carers of his 'retarded' employees. To make up for the poor pay these carers received, they were given a fancy title, Psychiatric Caring Officers, which gave them an air of self-importance.

Kelly had a regular team leader, a married woman called Karen. Karen Cooper, née O'Rourke, was a second-generation Irishwoman who had married Tony Cooper, then a successful small-time painter and decorator. Times became hard in the trade and when Karen landed this job it was a godsend. She was in her mid-forties and had kept her looks, as Kelly constantly complemented her on. She was appreciative of Mr Kelly for giving her this work as her husband was in and out of regular employment. His small business had gone broke so he now relied on whatever work he could get. The couple's kids were grown up and had moved away some years previously.

As part of her job, Karen was instructed to treat the casuals and mentally disabled workforce as subhumans and to use whatever means she felt necessary to maximise labour. These people would be delivering Tillerson's leaflets, all thirty thousand of them, and would work twelve-hour days. Karen would drive around the area where leaflets were being distributed, making sure the job was done competently. As a reward for the slave-driving she was compelled to do, Karen was given time off to do her shopping and, if the mood took him, spend some private time in Kelly's office! She did not particularly like these 'private moments' with her boss, whom she considered a total turn-off, but knew the value of her job.

Every now and again a person possessing a modicum of intelligence would slip through the net and be taken on as a casual. It usually did not take more than a morning for such people to start causing trouble, asking for higher pay. When this happened Karen usually found an excuse to sack them without ceremony. When Kelly heard about this he rewarded her with some more private time in his office. Jim Kelly actually thought Karen enjoyed his advances when in reality she endured them as 'occupational hazards'.

Thanks to the slave-driven work of the casuals, Tillerson received several orders for building work from the well-to-do area of St George. It only took three days for the leaflets to be posted and Kelly then paid off the staff involved and grunted something roughly translated as, 'A little slow, but thanks.' He kept Karen on till the end of the week. She was on considerably more money than the rest, but she was worth it. His assault on the high street also yielded satisfactory results for Tillerson, with orders from several shops for bulk orders of denim jeans and shirts.

As we know, Teddy Crump, who considered himself some sort of philanthropist due to the fact he paid wages to his staff, practised a sort of apartheid in the workplace. At the company's social gatherings such as the Christmas party, the unskilled workers were not allowed to mingle with the skilled employees. The artisans would have it no other way, considering themselves an aristocracy of labour and that their unskilled brethren were less intelligent than chimpanzees. Then there were the scientific staff, professors and scientists, along with the white-collar workers, administration and personnel officers. This section of employment held their Christmas celebration away from both the skilled and unskilled employees, considering themselves above the shop floor altogether. Crump and senior directors would attend the office and scientific staff festive celebrations, which included a four-course meal and drinks. He would put an appearance in at the tradesmen's buffet and drinks for about an hour or so and would not bother at all with the unskilled staff.

Tillerson employed a similar system of employee control to Crump's. At the Christmas celebrations he would go out for a meal with the office staff, taking Sheena along. Regarding the clothing factory hands, he hardly acknowledged their presence. They could please themselves as they wished as, after all, they were replaceable. In his construction company he tended to associate with the foremen and occasional tradesmen. He never bothered with the unskilled labourers as they were all ten-a-penny. He adopted the same level of respect for the office staff, personnel officers and wages staff in his clothing business as he did the foremen in his construction empire. It was very important to these captains of industry to maintain this division of labour even at social functions: divide and rule was an essential system of control!

All the scenes acted out above are still performed across the USA today in what we term the 'developed world'. Similar enactments are also performed in all capitalist countries across the globe. The system and laws which belong to the employing middle class, or bourgeoisie, are made for their own benefit and enrichment. These people are forever on the lookout for new markets to exploit and new countries, conquests, to capture. Put plainly, if a visitor from another planet – something a fortune is spent annually trying to find – had the misfortune to visit Earth and witness how world affairs are organised, that visitor would in all probability leap straight back into their craft and blast back to their planet of origin!

4

Bishops Court Rise ★ Boarding School Education

On their return from Florida the Crumps resumed their normal lives of luxury, doing nothing in general apart from the usual rounds of golf for Teddy and, for Megan, socialising with her female friends, which occasionally included attending the 'Help the Poor' club. Occasionally Teddy's golf would be rudely interrupted by some pressing matter at the plant or the office which, if he couldn't offload, he would reluctantly address. Of course, these little problems were not nearly as inconvenient if one of his young secretaries were involved, and a few 'boss's privileges' were on offer. While Crump was on the golf course all day Megan began to feel like a golf widow, like so many other wives whose husbands appeared incapable of showing any attention to them. She had on several occasions considered telephoning Derek for a bit of fun, but for the time being held back the urge.

There was only one week of the long summer vacation left and Ronald, a half-stone heavier due to constantly filling his face with candy while in Florida, met with the gang for one of their final encounters before their final year at Wetherspoons. Ronald still harboured regrets about breaking up with Colette, forgetting it was her who dumped him.

All the gang were a little apprehensive about the moves to boarding school, even though there was still a year to go. Like most kids their age they had never been away from home for any length of time, so their anxiety was understandable. Perhaps the happiest of the gang were James Rothschild and Susie Carter. Fortunately for the two lovebirds this agony would not have to be overcome as they would still be close to each other. They would meet regularly at the weekends, both sets of parents having had quiet words with the principals at both schools. The headmasters were very understanding, acknowledging that even though the school did not encourage relationships among students, there were exceptions. Decoded, this roughly meant exceptions could be made if the parents were wealthy enough! The two other girls, Dianna Nixon and Judy McClean, were happy they would be boarding together, while the lads, Terry Morgan and Peter Tillerson, would be separated from both the girls and each other. Their parents thought this would be for the best. Peter was quite upset at being parted from Judy, but Duke and Sheena failed to notice their son's changed behaviour and emotions. *What would it be like next year at this time?* they all individually thought.

At the start of the new term a strange feeling of relaxation, almost complacency, befell the gang. This was their final year of relative freedom and the anxiety of the last few days appeared to have lifted.

'I feel strange,' Ronald said.

'So do I,' replied James Rothschild, 'I don't seem to feel as worried about the future as I did a couple of weeks ago.'

'Maybe it's because we're realising there's nothing we can do about it, and we may as well look forward to what's ahead,' Crump offered.

'You know what?' asked James.

'What?' said Ronald.

'Maybe you're right. Let's knuckle down and make the most of this last year,' said the financier's son.

Ronald nodded. Wise words, he thought.

The final year at Wetherspoons involved taking a final examination at the beginning of June. The time for sitting the exams came very quickly indeed and Ronald, as expected, came through math with an A+ followed by an A in English. He was especially pleased with the latter subject as he'd had quite some catching up to do on it. He also received an A in geography and a B+ in science. The other subjects were, to him, meaningless at this stage. As Ronald would find out, his cavalier attitude would have to alter once he started at Bishops Court Rise.

The other members of the gang were also happy with the results they attained in their preferred subjects. The long summer break was upon them again and it was collectively agreed that it did not feel like a year since they were all fretting about this new era in all their lives. The kids and Ronald welcomed the forthcoming break. However, Teddy had other ideas for his son; it was time for Ronald to break with the gang and he would start getting used to spending less time with them from now on. Teddy's decision on this was based on his thought that Ronald would thank him for this in years to come. There was no vacation for Ronald this year. This did not make any difference to Teddy and Megan since their lives were pretty much labour-free anyway, but Ronald could have done with some time out. So young Crump spent six weeks learning more private lessons with his father. Teddy knew his son was excellent at math and well above average in English, but he wanted to continue teaching his son the devious and conniving ways of business.

The new term beginning September 1959 came around quickly enough. It was time for Ronald Crump to leave home for the first time. It was planned that Teddy would accompany young Ronald, or Ron, as Teddy was beginning to call him, to the boarding school in California. Teddy forbade Megan from accompanying them either on the flight or even to the airport. This, Teddy reasoned, would save any maternal tears and sad farewells. From now on, from Teddy's point of view, Ron would have to grow up, and 'be a man'. Teddy Crump was not taking any account of the fact his son was still only twelve years of age; this seemed an irrelevance to him. Crump arranged a chauffeur to collect them after the five-hour flight to San Francisco International Airport, and then be ferried to the prestigious educational establishment. Teddy had also given his son ground rules in business during the break, of how to be hard-headed, devious and, if the occasion demanded, a backstabber.

'This is the only way to survive in business,' Crump had instilled into his son. Then he went on to talk about how he should use these rules to survive in his new school. He must become hardened to any previously held morals, which in Ronald's case were not many, and be prepared to tell tales to the teacher if he would benefit from doing so. He was discouraged from having any real friends (not much change there) and his studies must take preference over all other considerations.

'You are now setting out on the real journey of life,' Teddy said.

Teddy and Ronald arrived at New York International Airport – now JFK International Airport – and checked in for departure. After a light meal, they approached the gate for the specified flight to San Francisco International. Teddy had brought some in-flight reading to keep his son's mind occupied and focussed. He handed his son a book on the life of Francis Bacon, which he thought would be useful in English literature. Ronald looked at the reading material. *What a bore*, he thought, but dared not say so to his father.

Back at the Crump's family home Megan was coming to the realisation her son was entering a new stage in life. She tried to console herself that all would be well. Megan Crump, by the standards of middle-class USA, was a compassionate woman and a caring mother. She saw life a little differently than did her husband, not viewing everything through the lens of the dollar bill. Teddy told her he would be away for at least two days, as he wanted to scout for business opportunities while he was 'out West'. As she was a little bored she decided to brighten her life up a little. She would phone Derek the next day.

Teddy and Ronald arrived in the western United States and the stretch limo which Crump had ordered brought them the one hundred and twenty kilometres to the boarding school. When the pair arrived, they perceived the main building was situated in a large rural area with huge playing fields. On arrival, they encountered two large electronic gates monitored by an armed security guard. The guard appeared from his cabin and confronted the huge limo.

'Have you papers, sir?' he officiously requested.

'Yes, here they are, my name is Edward Crump, and this is my son Ronald,' Crump informed the security man.

Having checked their papers and seeing all was in order, the guard opened the gates and the car set off up the long twisting drive. They pulled up at the main entrance, a large imposing building with several arches. Parking the car, they walked into the building and down the expansive main hall towards a reception area. There they were greeted by the headmaster, who had been informed of their arrival. The principal, Mr H.A. Hardaker, then introduced Ronald to his prefect, Jefferson Jordan, who would be responsible for young Crump and his dormitory mate. Mr Hardaker shook hands with Teddy Crump and Ronald as did the prefect.

'I'll show you to your dormitory,' the principal said, 'And then Jefferson here will take over.'

'Great stuff,' said Teddy, acting the trendy father as opposed to the stuffy old traditionalist he really was.

'After that, we can go to my office and sort out the rest of the administration,' said Hardaker.

'Come on then,' said Crump, eager not to lose too much initiative to the Head, 'let's go.'

On arrival at the dormitory Mr Hardaker and Teddy Crump left Ronald in the capable hands of the prefect. They then departed to the Head's office to sort out any remaining formalities. The headmaster informed Teddy Crump that his son would be sharing for the first two years with another boy of the same age, as this would make getting used to their new surroundings a little easier.

'After the second year the boys will be "billeted" individually and encouraged to become single entities, individuals. After all,' the Head explained, 'when they leave here most of these lads will become businessmen in their own rights and companionship will become second to the competitive, often arcane, world of industry. Let's face it, Crump, he will not be distributing much of the wealth he has created, in the form of wages, to his employees, will he?'

'I would hope not,' Crump replied.

Both men exhibited ghastly grins at the thought of the workers being exploited.

'Furthermore,' Hardaker continued, 'I presume he will not be too honest and open with his competitors either.'

'I sincerely hope not, after what I've taught him about the ways of business, he will be offering nothing,' said Crump.

Mr Hardaker had a similar conversation with the other students' parents. This school would be the 'engine room' of the USA, and would produce captains of industry, without whom the entire human race would cease breathing, or so these self-appointed saviours of humanity thought.

There was a knock on the door and a middle-aged man and a boy about Ronald's age entered the room.

'Harry Johnson and Christopher, my son,' the man said, shaking the principal's hand. Johnson was an oil tycoon from Texas and would have been in the same financial league as Teddy Crump.

'Yes, we talked earlier on the phone,' Hardaker said. 'Mr Johnson, this is Teddy Crump,' he indicated.

The two men shook hands.

'Mr Crump, Christopher here will be sharing a dorm with your lad,' Hardaker said. 'And then they will go their separate ways.'

The oil baron and arms dealer viewed life through the same lens, that of the dollar bill, and had much in common. Hardaker suggested he take Christopher to the dormitory to meet Ronald while the parents could get to know each other a little better. The Headmaster introduced Christopher to Ronald and from then on Jefferson, the prefect, was to be in charge. The two students shook hands and began small talk. Jefferson laid down the ground rules which both students would find hard to adhere to due to their spoilt upbringings. Neither liked rules and would find taking instructions from someone who was only a student, like themselves, difficult at first.

'I'm from Texas,' Christopher informed Ronald.

'New York,' came the reply.

Both lads sounded each other out as to which father was the wealthiest. To be truthful there was nothing different in their positions in the wealth league; both were up there at the top and both had made their billions on the backs of others. Neither boy would admit this, or perhaps they were a little young to appreciate the full rigours of the business world at this stage. At any rate, they agreed that both their fathers were equally rich and that was all that mattered.

The two young students soon developed a rapport with one another and dialogue became much easier. They began laughing and joking with each other; they were after all only twelve years of age. Jefferson came back into the room, having gone to speak with the Head for a few minutes.

He informed his two charges, 'Lights out at nine thirty, no exceptions, and for you First Years breakfast will be at 8am.

'Yes sir, and thank you,' they both replied.

★ ★ ★

The principal returned to his office where Harry Johnson and Teddy Crump were already on first-name terms. Under Hardaker's guidance, the two men completed the appropriate forms regarding their respective sons.

'I've met with most of the new students and their parents already,' said the principal. 'A good few of the fathers and mothers are having a drink in our staff bar before I introduce some of the teachers. If you would like to join them, it is down the corridor and on your right.'

'Fancy a drink, Ted?' Johnson enquired of Crump.

'Sounds good to me,' Crump replied.

The two men retired to the well-equipped and tastefully decorated bar. Many of the parents were sizing each other up under the guise of a social gathering.

'What you having, Ted?' Johnson asked.

Whiskey, Irish, on the rocks,' replied Crump.

'Think I'll have the same,' said Johnson.

Looking round the room Teddy spotted a petite woman in her mid-thirties who was cradling a drink by herself and looking a little lost. Nearby was a group of men, one of whom was demonstrating his better golf positions to the others. Both Teddy and Harry gave each other a knowing glance which suggested they might go and relieve the woman of her boredom. Just at that moment the golf expert retired from giving his lecture and went over to the woman, putting his arm loosely around her waist. As the couple began conversing the two bandits backed away instinctively, knowing they almost made their first embarrassing spectacle.

'Oh well, Harry, plenty more where she came from, eh?'

'True enough, Ted, true enough,' the oil tycoon retorted with an air of disappointment.

A little bell tinkled and the crowd quietened. 'Listen up folks,' Hardaker announced. 'We are now going to have a brief meeting with the teachers for the coming year,' Mr Hardaker informed the congregation.

They all adjourned to a neighbouring hall where the staff were waiting.

The Head introduced the staff one by one.

'This is Mr Bob Atkinson who teaches physical education. He's a former baseball player, quite well known in his day, eh Bob?'

'Yes, I suppose I was,' Atkinson replied.

'This is Miss Madeline Copley, her speciality is French.'

'I bet it is,' Crump said, in an attempt at being humorous.

'For sure,' interjected Johnson with a smirk.

The young French teacher felt a little uneasy with these two business tycoons ogling her. She felt they were mentally undressing her; she wasn't wrong, they were.

The headmaster then introduced the next teacher.

'This is Mr Bill Wiseman, he teaches woodwork. He is also my deputy Head, and this may be of interest to you, Mr Crump, he is an ex-Marine. He was at Kasserine Pass fighting Rommel. You were in North Africa, weren't you?'

'Yes,' lied Crump a little nervously, introducing himself by his former rank.

'Good to meet you, sir,' the woodwork tutor said.

With introductions to the rest of the teachers eventually completed, that signalled the end of the social afternoon.

'See you around for some private French, eh Madeline?' Crump shouted across in less than jocular fashion to the French teacher.

The other parents pretended to laugh in an exaggerated fashion.

Crump knew the hotel he had booked into provided female company if requested, so the loss of this potential target was of no great sacrifice. Teddy Crump had a very high opinion of himself. He thought all the women, whether he was paying for their services or not, fancied him. The truth was, in most cases, they despised the man with ferocity.

It should be pointed out that all the parents of those attending Bishops Court Rise School were part of the United States 'elite golden circle', as it was termed. By this the reader should not be fooled into believing, as the assumed name would suggest, these people possessed some natural ability or preferred some physical or mental superiority over those whom they employed. To think along these lines would be a huge error of judgement and would afford these legalised gangsters a respect they did not deserve. What these people all possessed and certainly had in common was the ability to backstab, exploit, deceive, cheat and thieve off their employees and, when and if it suited, each other.

Crump, for example, never produced anything in his life. He could not even use a turning lathe or equip and arm an artillery piece. He certainly had no idea on the workings of most of the weapons his company produced, yet he called himself an arms dealer and engineer. Everything this man owned was the produce of somebody else's labour power. He knew nothing about the construction of the weapons of mass destruction he supplied to various terrorist organisations, or corrupt governments, except how many dollars they would reward him with. This was despite him formerly holding a commission in the US Army. He was devious enough to secure himself a position on the General Staff well behind the lines both in North Africa and Normandy. Dangerous life-threatening situations were for others, not him. The rifles produced by Crump's company were the work of skilled tradesmen who were rewarded with the least monetary wage Crump could get away with. Also, the machinery was maintained by skilled qualified fitters, without whom all his factories would cease producing. Crump did nothing himself yet reaped all the financial rewards.

Crump was not alone in this game of exploitation. Not one of the parents present at this dire social gathering had the right to criticise their opposite numbers. Harry Johnson's practices of extracting oil were in breach of many health and safety rules, and any employee who questioned Johnson could expect the sack. This included highly qualified engineers (experts in this dangerous field), and drillers. Johnson himself possessed none of these skills and qualities, yet he could dictate what he wanted when he wanted. If an accident occurred that was the result of a bad decision taken by Johnson, he blamed incompetent staff and somebody would be sacked or even put in prison for negligence.

Teddy Crump had his limousine waiting to drive him to his hotel, the five-star Hilton Hotel.

'Can I offer you a lift, Harry?' he enquired of Johnson.

'Not for me, Ted, I have my own transport,' the oil baron replied.

They bade each other farewell and Teddy instructed his chauffeur to bring him to the hotel. Crump checked in and retired to the bar for a nightcap. The bartender handed him a double whiskey, along with a card which read: High class services... Massage in guests' rooms, Extras available, Ask for Linda. $300 p.h. + Extras $x.

Crump fancied a 'massage', so he took the card and went to his room. From there he called the number advertised and asked for the appropriate service. This was going to be a long night!

On the following day, Crump travelled to a business meeting with a contact Morgan had put him in touch with. His name was Anthony Hogg and he was director of a consortium which owned a shooting club and deer hunting agency. Hogg boasted his agency had brought down some of the finest beasts along the Canadian border. He wanted better rifles to minimise any slight chance of escape the hunted animals might have.

★ ★ ★

Tuesday was Ronald and Christopher's first day involving lessons at Bishops Court Rise. Ronald was delighted to read the timetable, perceiving English was their first lesson, a subject in which he was now excelling. English was to be followed by art and geography, which would complete the morning's curriculum. The afternoon lessons would begin with math, again to Ronald's satisfaction, followed by the dreaded classics, Greek and Latin.

Ronald Crump's first week at boarding school passed pleasantly and quickly. He and his dormitory mate, Christopher, settled in smoothly with few if any hitches. They always had Jefferson, the prefect, to call upon should they have any difficulties. The problem with Jefferson, as Ronald in particular would find out, was that he epitomised his rearranged title, 'perfect'. He was Hardaker's eyes and ears first and foremost, and a crutch for the boys second. Ronald settled well into the lessons and more advanced teaching methods at this school, compared with the teaching techniques adopted by the teachers at Wetherspoons. He got off to a flying start in math and English, as expected, while Christopher shone in science and geography. Friday came around with the blink of an eye, or so it seemed, and the two boys struck up conversation in their dormitory.

'What did you make of the first week, Ron?' Christopher asked.

'Much easier than I anticipated, how about you?'

'Same as you, I'm pleased to say,' the oil tycoon's son said.

It was now the much-awaited weekend and the lads were deciding what to do and where to go.

'I know!' said Ronald.

'What's that?'

'Let's go and explore the town, bound to be loads to do there.'

'Yes, that's true,' said Christopher. 'I bet there will be a sports shop. I need some new shorts for games next week.'

'Let's go!' they said in harmony.

With great excitement, the two juvenile adventurers set off for the town. As they went down the front steps of the school, they were suddenly cut short by Jefferson, who seemed to appear out of nowhere.

'Where do you think you two are going?' he said. 'If you had read the timetable thoroughly you would have been aware that you're grounded for the first two weekends.'

This was unwelcome news, to say the least.

'For the first two weekends you do not leave the school compound,' Jefferson continued. 'Now get back to your dormitory. I'll not report this to Mr Hardaker this time but if I catch you again there will be trouble.'

Any ideas the pair had about Jefferson being their mate were quickly dispelled after this brief altercation. They parted company with Jefferson, frustrated and crestfallen.

Jefferson watched them leaving and suddenly felt guilty. He had, after all, not informed them about this and, perhaps more to the point, he did not want his beloved Head to think he was incompetent. He called them back.

'Look lads, I don't make the rules, but I must enforce them. It's not for long, only two weekends and it will soon pass,' he said.

Ronald immediately sensed the prefect felt a little awkward; did he pick up a hint of fear, perhaps? He remembered the tutorials given him by Teddy: if you sense fear in anybody, exploit it. Ronald was not yet ready for a confrontation with the prefect, but he would remember this occasion and would look out for any other signs of weakness.

Saturday passed quickly, considering they were grounded and Ronald decided he was going to town by himself the following weekend. The question was, should he inform Chris of his plans? Would his dormitory mate have the balls to go with him, or would he go running to the prefect to inform on him? Crump decided he could not take the chance – he didn't know Johnson very well yet, so he contrived to keep his plans to himself. He was going either through the gates or over the wall come the following weekend, and he was going alone!

The first lesson on Monday morning was French. Ronald was not a lover of languages, least of all French. Would he ever need it? Did his father understand French? No, he didn't, and he got on all right without it. That said, Ronald concluded, it was a compulsory subject and he did not wish to be seen as disruptive; his father would be less than pleased, so he would condescend to go along with the school's rules and attend the lesson. Crump genuinely believed he was doing the school a big favour by attending this class, but he was to soon come down to earth with a bang!

The French teacher was a slender young middle-class woman from Washington DC, single and aged about twenty-five years. She was the one Ronald's father had made lascivious comments about at the school initiation afternoon. She had shoulder-length wavy black hair, and she wore a pink top and a knee-length black skirt. To sum up Miss Copley's appearance in the eyes of her students, she was a sex goddess. Ronald Crump, much like his father, had only one thought on his mind when he spotted the young teacher. He also felt the sensation he had the day he was with Colette on the bench in the park, except this time he had a better idea what it was all about. Thanks in no small way to his ex-girlfriend, Colette, Ronald was advanced in knowledge of the birds and the bees.

The lesson flew by very quickly with Ronald taking little notice of what he was being taught and when the bell rang, before he got up to go to the next lesson, he had to adjust himself to hide the bulge in his pants. Then he packed his pen and pencils and left for the next class which, ironically enough, was religious education.

Religious studies were conducted on a denominational basis. There was instruction for Roman Catholics and the various Protestant groups, and a rabbi to teach a small Jewish group. There were no Muslims in those days at such prestigious schools; all the students were white Americans. Crump was a Methodist, in theory, and Johnson belonged to another Protestant sect. Neither of their families really believed a word of what the Bible said and certainly did not practise its teachings.

Father Ciaran McKeon took the Roman Catholic classes and was always available for the confessionals. A rotund gentleman and partial to a drop of

Irish whiskey, he had a Kaiser Wilhelm pre-First World War bicycle moustache which extended about three inches either side of his cheeks. He had studied theology at a major Catholic seminary and had been appointed Head of Catholic Studies at Bishops Court Rise about a decade previously.

The Protestant religious instructor was the Reverend Jethro Pilkington, a tall thin man with a bony physique whose clothes hung off him like a line of washing hanging on a clothes line. He had been an army chaplain in the Second World War. Ronald spent most of the time during this lesson, which was compulsory, thinking about Miss Copley, the French teacher. The hour soon passed – thank God, he wryly thought – and he left the class as clueless as when he had entered.

The day passed quickly and back in the dormitory that evening Ronald broached the subject of the French teacher with his friend.

'What did you think of her, Chris, did you see that body?'

Christopher had not had the benefit of having a knowledgeable girlfriend, as had Ronald, so he was a little behind Crump in this department.

'Very nice,' said a slightly embarrassed Christopher. 'Well, actually, I… I had a strange sensation when she stood near me to explain something.'

Ronald sensed he had the upper hand in the subject and began acting like someone who had a lot of experience with girls. He began to recant some of the filth he had overheard Teddy speak of to his business friends and concocted them as his own. He guessed this would give his roommate a feeling of inferiority, knowing he could tell Johnson anything and he would not be able to contradict him. How should he use this new-found advantage? How could his friend's ignorance benefit him?

'Well, Chris, in my experience,' he said with an air of somebody twice his age, 'they are just "teasers".' He was not too sure what the phrase he had just used meant, but knew Christopher would have even less of an idea if he could ride it out.

'What's a teaser, Ron?' Johnson asked.

This was the question Ronald hoped would not be asked but he could make some trash up.

'A teaser is…' he began, 'a teaser is, is – someone who, who, well, it's like this,' he bluffed not very convincingly,

'You don't know, do you?' the roommate interjected.

'Yes, I do,' protested Ronald. 'It is somebody…'

'Yes, you've said that. Get on with it,' Christopher insisted.

'Who teases,' Crump finally informed his bemused friend.

'Hmm,' muttered Johnson, still not convinced his roommate had any more idea than he did.

Ronald Crump was not accustomed to doing as he was told; he had never really had to, and he had certainly never been grounded before. His mind was made up, it was about time this school and idiot prefect discovered who was the boss! Crump had decided he would begin a crusade and become the leader, and when the rest saw how successful he had been they would fall in behind him – or so he thought. Rules or no rules, prefect or no prefect, he was going to town and that was final. Previously at prep school and later at Wetherspoons Junior School nobody, least of all the teachers, had disciplined him; they didn't dare. His father was far too powerful for the staff at either establishment to risk telling 'little Ronald' what to do. In fact, James Rothschild and Peter Tillerson had much more influence over Crump than those in so-called authority. *Why should this place be any different*, he thought?

If he had taken a moment to calculate the difference between the school he was attending now and his former establishments, the answer would have been clear. At this school his father, wealthy as he may well have been, was just another billionaire. All the kids' parents were in the same wealthy bracket, not just Teddy Crump. At the previous establishments the parents of all those in 'the Gang of Six' were wealthier than most other pupils' parents. This gave them special status, something which did not exist at this institution.

It would be fair to say that Ronald had been brought up to believe the rules of society were for the working-class and not for his sort. This was to a considerable extent correct, certainly within a capitalist world of haves and have-nots, and, as his father had drummed into him, this notion of the 'free world' was actually a lie. 'The freedom often preached by politicians when referring to this "great land of ours", is designed for most of the population to believe and for us, the ruling-class, to promote. We are not supposed to believe this nonsense ourselves, but we must maintain the illusion held by the lower orders that they are free. That way they will continue, with a few exceptional "troublemakers" who are members of trade unions, to be unquestioningly obedient. We will continue to become ever richer and they, the workers, under this misguided belief, will die poor because all their wealth created by their labour will have been given to us! Brilliant, isn't it?' said Crump to his ever-adoring son.

'When you grow up, Ron, all this will be yours but, in the meantime, it may be necessary for you to do as the school rules say. But do question if you think a point needs raising. In order to maintain the system when it becomes your turn to take up the position of leadership, this illusion among the lower classes must be maintained. Whatever you do, son, do not allow those trade unions through the door. Some of them are sponsored by Moscow and the communist regime in Russia. We must keep the workers believing that the Soviet Union is a terrible thing, despite its free health care, full employment, free education and abolition of homelessness. We must highlight the bad areas of Soviet policies,' Teddy continued.

'Such as?' interjected Ronald.

'Well,' said Teddy, 'people are not allowed to make money over there.'

'That is very bad, isn't it, Dad? What would happen to people like us, the real workers, if those policies came here?'

'Exactly, Ron, you're getting the picture.'

These lessons were given by Teddy to his son on a regular basis. This is one way the bourgeoisie maintain their rule over the numerically superior workers. The object was to get Ronald to accept school discipline for a few years, to make him a better man when the time came. Other lessons the arms dealer gave Ronald, apart from 'cooking the books', were about how to use the brilliant education he was receiving by twisting it into a corrupt metamorphosis of what he had actually been taught.

Christopher Johnson, like Ronald, did not particularly like the rules either. Unlike Crump, he had been subject to a limited form of discipline by his parents. Harry believed self-discipline was a crucial factor in business which, after all, was where his son was going. He may have had a point. Teddy Crump, in contrast, believed in teaching his son from an early age that everybody had to do as he said which, to a point, was correct certainly in the business Crump was in. Unlike Johnson, who spent time at his oil wells even though he knew little about drilling, Crump delegated responsibility to others who, if they got it wrong, were sacked. The workers on the shop floors in turn lived in fear of their immediate bosses and supervisors who themselves feared Crump. Fear was Crump's ace card in business whereas a more direct hands-on approach, more involved and a little less delegating, was the business model of Harry Johnson.

When it came to corruption and class rule, Harry Johnson could be just as corrupt as Crump. He too held periods of private schooling with Christopher, teaching him pretty much the same as Teddy taught Ronald. These private lessons went on in the homes of all the US bourgeoisie and the theme, class domination, was generally the same. In the homes of the working-class, lessons were also being taught, albeit with one major difference. Working-class kids were taught to obey their teachers always, without question, and, when they left school, to afford their employer the same unswerving obedience and loyalty.

The weekend came around again with the blink of an eye, and Jefferson reminded the lads it was another weekend on site for them.

'That's what you, think,' Crump muttered.

'What was that Ron?' said Christopher.

Oh, eh – it stinks,' said Ronald believing for a moment he had let the cat out of the bag.

No need to worry; he realised Johnson had not discovered the plan. Saturday morning came, and Ronald rose early. He did not want to waken his roommate and alert him to his plans. He gently opened the door and sneaked along the corridor to the exit. Peeping around the corner, he saw all was clear.

'I bet that creep Jefferson is still in bed,' he assured himself.

From there he ran across the fifty yards of open ground to the first fence. To his left were the huge playing fields and gymnasium, to his right the canteen and auxiliary buildings. Then from there, he climbed over the fence and headed towards the high perimeter wall. To his dismay he realised that he would never make the climb over the wall, and to make matters worse, he saw that the security guard was in his box. So Crump turned and followed the wall the other way for about half a mile, just under a kilometre, and the wall lowered in height. He would make this, he calculated. Ronald had not yet considered, assuming his plan went to script, how he was going to regain entry to the school on his return from this excursion.

Back in the dormitory Christopher had woke up. He noticed his roommate was missing but paid little attention to this until half an hour passed. Knowing they were both grounded, there was nowhere Ronald could have gone that would take half an hour. He began to feel concerned. What could have happened? Had he had an accident? Better tell Jefferson, Christopher thought. Jefferson pre-empted Christopher going in search of him and entered the room.

'Where is Ronald, Chris?' he enquired.

'I don't know, sir,' the youngster replied.

'I see,' the prefect exclaimed. 'I reckon he is trying his luck at escape.'

'I really don't know, sir,' Christopher said. 'He hasn't said anything to me.'

'I'll sort this out. Leave it to me and not a word to the Head,' Jefferson told Christopher. 'It will be harder on your friend if Hardaker finds out.'

What the prefect really meant was that it would be harder on him, Jefferson, if the headmaster were to get wind of this escape. In a flash, the prefect left the room.

In the meantime, Ronald had come to a part of the wall that tapered down to about six feet in height. He had found some debris and piled it up, thus giving himself more height. Scrambling up, he grasped the top of the wall with both hands. As he pulled himself up he suddenly felt hands around his ankles.

'Come here, you young scallywag,' said Jefferson, pulling him down. 'You're going nowhere except back to the dormitory.'

Shit, thought Crump, *how did he find out?* Jefferson pulled Ronald down from his lofty position and began marching him back to the dormitory.

'I'll have to inform the Head,' the Prefect informed Crump. 'This is a serious breach of school discipline.'

Jefferson Jordan had every intention of informing the headmaster if he caught Ronald. It was only to be kept a secret between himself and Christopher if he failed in his mission. This is how he had got to be prefect in the first palace, by being devious and a liar. He knew the principal would be pleased with him for bringing the young would-be fugitive back into captivity. Like a dog which had pleased its master, the Head would give Jefferson a favourable consideration over the other prefects. It was the equivalent of receiving a large bone.

When Jefferson had left the dormitory, Ronald and Christopher faced each other. Crump had made up his mind that Johnson had 'grassed him up'.

'You ratted me out,' Crump accused Johnson.

'No I did not!' retorted Christopher. 'I woke up and you were missing. When you didn't come back, I thought something may have happened to you. I was concerned.'

Ronald looked at Christopher, who, although a little shorter than himself, was stockier in build. A fight could result in humiliation for Ronald, and he didn't want that. Instead, he wanted an honourable way out of the predicament that he had created.

'Right, I'll let you off this time but if I find out you touted, I'll...''You'll what?' said Christopher, giving Crump notice he wasn't afraid.

'Forget it,' said Ronald before defeat became apparent.

'Right,' said Johnson. 'But don't you threaten me, or we'll fall out.'

The headmaster decided, on hearing of Ronald's exploits, to ground him for a further two weekends. He called him to his office and explained the situation Crump was in.

'We don't like using corporal punishment,' Hardaker said, 'but if we have no other choice we will. We use the strap here for the worst cases of indiscipline, but as this is your first and, I might hope, last deviation from the rules, I'm not going to use it. You will be grounded for a further two weekends.'

'But sir—'

'No buts, Crump. Be appreciative you're not receiving four lashes across each hand. Now run along and be pleased you've got off so lightly.'

Monday morning came around again, and Ronald had forgotten the weekend's event, happy not to have been flogged, as he saw it.

'Morning class,' Miss Copley said.

'Morning, Miss.'

'I'll do the register now, starting with Crump. Are you staying here for the class, or thinking of going on a walkabout, are we?' she said, half-jokingly.

'I want to talk to you today about growing up in France, and reaching adulthood, and, in your cases, becoming men. Something about which Ronald Crump still has a lot to learn,' she continued, giving him a disparaging glance.

Ronald coloured up a bright crimson at this humiliation. Jefferson must have mentioned his escape attempt to her. He would not forget this; like his father he could be a very vindictive person indeed.

Ronald Crump was experiencing acute ambivalence; his emotions were all over the place. On the one hand he was feeling extremely angry at being shamefully singled out like this, and on the other, he fancied Miss Copley. He couldn't get her out of his head. He imagined getting her in a compromising position and then, out of the goodness of his heart, letting her off. Then she would fall in love with him for being gallant. Of course, this was a mixture of Ronald's hormones and emotions playing tricks on him, perfectly natural for somebody in the initial stages of adolescence. It would be the bitter, angry Crump who would win through in years to come when he would get his revenge.

He was also angry at not getting his own way and being put down by some upstart prefect. In saying that, he knew Jefferson would make a bad enemy. He decided he would bide his time, forgetting that when he would be Jefferson's age the prefect would be long gone to some top job in one of the big cities.

On Monday afternoon the first-year students all gathered in the gymnasium. It was to be their first encounter with the games master, Mr Atkinson. Atkinson was once a household name as a professional baseball player and was also an able middle-distance runner. On retiring from the big league Atkinson did a teaching course at university, qualifying with honours. He then applied and was successful for the post of Physical Training Instructor at Bishops Court Rise. He was known as a hard man but was also professional enough to realise these were first-year students and needed the 'kid gloves' treatment – without being too soft.

'Right, you lot,' he said as an introduction, 'my name is Mr Atkinson, or God, depending on your disposition. All of you will become first-rate athletes. Nobody in my class fails, I won't allow it. Do I make myself clear?' he bellowed.

'Yes, sir,' came the reply in unison.

'Some of you look like wimps. That will change, believe me,' he continued. 'I don't stand slackers in my class. From the word go it will be arduous work, do you all understand?'

'Yes, sir,' again was the collective reply.

'Right, we are doing rope-climbing for starters, so I can judge the weaklings among you maggots.'

Atkinson had picked up this terminology during his two-year voluntary service in the National Guard.

'Right, in groups of three, one, two, three up those ropes now.'

The first three started off up the dangling ropes.

'Come on, Johnson, you little weasel, I've seen broads with bigger biceps,' he shouted.

'Right, Crump, I've heard all about you, think you're above the rules, don't you! Well let me tell you, not in my class, I don't care if your father owns half of New York, here you are a nobody.'

Ronald wondered how he had found out about his altercation with authority over his escape attempt the previous weekend. It was probably Jefferson again!

Atkinson then had them all springing over the vault, a large wooden construction resembling the saddle of a horse.

'Come on, faster,' he encouraged. He kept them all going until he could see they were tiring.

'Right, that will do for today. Well done, all of you, for a first time.'

Ronald soon found out through the school grapevine that Mr Atkinson was having an affair with Miss Copley. Crump was furious; he desired the French teacher and a strange feeling of jealousy permeated through his body. He knew he stood no chance in his imaginary dual with Atkinson, but this didn't stop him hating the man. Ronald Crump was lovesick and angry. Truth be told, just about every young man in the first form had some kind of imaginary desire on the French teacher, so Ronald Crump was not alone. Christopher had also passed comments about her, slightly milder in content than his roommate's, but nevertheless in a similar mould. At one stage Ronald was on the verge of striking Christopher in a fit of jealousy but remembered how Johnson had stood his ground earlier, and so yet again fear of defeat decided the issue for Crump.

The week flew by and the weekend was once more upon the school. Jefferson entered the dormitory on the Friday evening and informed Christopher Johnson he was free to leave the compound this weekend if he wished.

'Thank you, sir,' said Christopher.

'And me?' asked Ronald.

'Not you, Crump, you've another two weeks grounding to do thanks to your foolish antics.'

'Very good, sir,' Ronald mumbled.

'Are you going out, Chris?' asked Ronald, after Jefferson left them.

'No I don't think I'll bother, I'll wait for you. It doesn't seem fair really and I wouldn't feel right, so I'll wait,' the oil baron's son said considerately.

'Thanks, Chris,' said Ronald, knowing full well if the boot was on the other foot he would be off with or without his roommate.

It was time for the lights out and after half an hour's chatting the two lads were feeling sleepy. Christopher was out like a light, but Ronald stayed awake for a little longer. He was thinking about digging a tunnel under the dormitory, below the canteen and out to the open country. He was sure it could be done, just like the Allied prisoners of war escaping from Colditz in a film he had seen. *Should he suggest this scheme to Christopher?* he wondered. They could use the tunnel even after his grounding was over, and that meant they could go out every night after lights out!

Ronald fell asleep and dreamed he was a downed US pilot in 1943 who was captured and sent to Colditz. There he was appointed leader of the Escape Committee holding the rank of colonel, like his father, and immediately got down to liberating his comrades. They would tunnel under the castle starting right now. No sooner had the first spade gone into creating the underground subway than the door flew open. It was a German guard who looked very much like Jefferson in a German military uniform. Suddenly he woke up with a start, and looked around him. His roommate was asleep in the darkened dormitory. As he lay there mulling over the dream, he eventually dropped off.

The following morning Ronald decided against the tunnel idea so there was no need to mention it to Christopher; only two more weekends and they could both go to town, legally.

The next few weeks flew by and Ronald was well ahead in math and English. The embarrassing incident which occurred in the French lesson was all forgotten, well not quite, in Ronald's mind he was still going to have his revenge, but in the eyes of the rest, all was water under the bridge.

Thanks to Mr Atkinson's rigorous keep-fit programme, the boys were beginning to fill out. Ronald had not forgotten that the games teacher was with 'his woman', as his imagination dictated. Still, he realised he could not do anything about it, so maybe he would let it go for now… but one day?

All the young students were now looking forward to their first holiday and an opportunity to visit their families for a week. Teddy and Megan Crump had decided to let Ronald remain at school for the half-term break. This was done without even consulting the youngster. He was, after all, on the other side of the USA. To all intents and purposes young Ronald might as well have been on another planet for all these two cared. Megan had got over her initial maternal separation from her son and had now settled down to an enjoyable, if not honest, way of life. Teddy was only interested in his business, making more money, and the frequent groping of his secretary and sexual encounters with his PA. He would see his son at the end of term for a progress report and would judge for himself when he would be ready to be introduced formally into the business. It would not be for at least two years from this date anyway, but Crump wanted to ensure the skills he had taught Ronald in the murky way of the business world had not been forgotten. Megan was continuing her affair with Derek behind her husband's back and Ronald being around would be an inconvenience and certainly an unnecessary distraction. This was why she agreed wholeheartedly with her husband when he suggested leaving their son at school for the break.

Teddy Crump informed his son by letter that he would be remaining at boarding school. The letter was a brief note just outlining some reasons why his parents had not the time for him, despite not having conversed on a personal footing with him for nearly eight weeks and despite the fact Ronald had never been away from home before. The note said in brief: 'Due to business commitments it is not possible at this juncture for you to return home for the half-term break. We feel sure you will understand that business is business and your father will be away for the week.' The document did not say where his mother might be for the week's duration, which in itself spoke volumes.

Ronald had no idea about his mother's assignations with her former boss and now lover. Neither, for that matter, did Teddy, who didn't even question why his wife had remained silent when he offered an explanation for his week's activities. She thought, the least said the soonest mended. To make things worse for Ronald, his roommate was going home for the half-term break. Christopher had received a three-page letter from his parents coupled with an air ticket for Texas. He saw Ronald was a little upset and tried to console him.

'Never mind, Ron, it's only a week, hardly seems worth it. I'll no sooner disembark the airplane and it will be time to board again. I'm sure there is a logical explanation as to why your parents on this occasion are busy.'

'I'm not bothered,' lied Ronald. 'As you say it's only a week and it will soon be over. I hope you enjoy yourself.'

The truth was Ronald couldn't really give a monkey's toss whether Johnson had an enjoyable time or not, but he pretended all the same to wish him well. It wouldn't do to be seen as envious; after all, he might need Johnson at some future date so best make things look good.

With the blink of an eye, half-term was upon them. It was Saturday morning and Christopher had his bags packed.

'See you in a week, Ron!' he said with a grin, before hurrying out of the dorm.

'Yay,' Ronald mundanely replied.

Harry Johnson had hired a private chauffeur to collect his son for the airport, as was customary for the upper tiers of the US bourgeoisie, and as the car sped down the long driveway to the school gates Christopher waved at Ronald from the rear window.

'That's him out of the way,' Ronald muttered under his breath, pretending to himself he was not bothered.

A skeleton staff remained at the school to look after the students who were not going away for the break. These were mainly single teachers. A handful of prefects were also in attendance. The teaching staff who remained were Mr Atkinson, Miss Copley, Mr Simpson, who taught third-year geography, and Mr Wiseman, the deputy Head.

During the break the teachers who remained left most of the supervising to the prefects. Jefferson was one of those who stayed, hoping to promote himself into the headmaster's good books for forfeiting his vacation for the good of the school. Sunday came, and it was quite a fine day for mid-October. The sun shone and it felt like spring as opposed to autumn. As the weather was so pleasant the teachers, under the guidance of Mr Atkinson, had organised a fun baseball game that would take place in the afternoon. Jefferson knocked on Ronald's door to inform the youngster of the event.

'You can come and take part if you wish, Ronald. It's voluntary, of course, and Mr Atkinson and Miss Copley are organising it.'

Ronald was delighted to hear this, as here might be his chance to impress the French teacher who, he felt sure, would be unable to resist him and finish her silly affair with Atkinson. The game was due to start at two o'clock and Ronald made his way to the field of play at the appointed time. Atkinson captained one team and Miss Copley the other.

Ronald was on Atkinson's team, much to his disgust, but would endeavour to impress the French teacher with his batting skills – which he did not possess. When it came to his turn to take his position to bat he acted like one who was well versed with the game, pretending to judge the air currents for the best strike. The ball came towards him and he lashed out, more in hope than with any natural ability for the game, and by luck he struck the ball. High into the air it rose and began its descent into the waiting arms of the very person Ronald was hoping to impress, Miss Copley.

'Out, Ronald,' she shouted, and Crump pretended he had purposely delivered the ball in such a way as to allow her to catch him out. He gallantly marched away, magnanimous in defeat, acting like Sir Lancelot at King Arthur's round table, having just saved a fair maiden's honour.

The game finished as a respectable draw as the afternoon ended. As the onset of winter was just around the corner, the sun was going down earlier every evening now. Mr Atkinson instructed the prefects to gather the equipment together and return it all to the gymnasium. He and Miss Copley then retired to the gym instructor's office. On seeing this, Ronald felt a jealous rage permeating through his young body. This was compounded by Miss Copley not acknowledging the fact he had 'allowed her' to catch him out.

On his return to the dormitory Ronald was tired. 'It has been a very energetic Sunday,' he yawned.

Ronald was asleep for about two hours when he woke up with a start. The idea was back in his head again; it was something that was formulating in his head far in advance of his years, regarding his takeover at an as-yet-unspecified future date of the Crump empire. Although he was only twelve years of age Ronald had been acclimatised gradually to the world of business by his father for some years now. During his private lessons Teddy had not only refined his son's business skills but also advised Ronald about following innovative ideas, even if they came to nothing.

'Don't just get an idea, son, or think it too adventurous and drop it without first at least giving it some time for primary exploration,' Teddy had told him.

This was such a time for Ronald. He would, one day, expand the business into the world of scientific engineering. He had often heard Teddy talk of 'international law' and substances 'banned by treaty'. 'International law is all well and good,' his father had said. 'Depending on whose government is breaking it. Banning various substances by treaty is again a great scenario and, once more, it depends who wants to break the treaty. For example, a treaty by the US government with a country which could fight back, the USSR, should not be broken by either side unless they felt it could be got away with. On the other hand, a treaty between say, Kenya, a sub-Saharan African country and the US government, could be broken with the stroke of a pen.' Ronald's twelve-year-old mind had not yet expanded beyond the information Teddy had given him, but he determined to further inform himself.

Ronald Crump lay on his bed thinking things over. He was already miles ahead in math and English, but he would need to develop his skills in the science lab to stand any chance of developing this embryonic idea. He decided tomorrow, Monday, he would visit the extensive school library and begin to learn more about science and chemistry. For the time being that evening, he would revise his math and recap on Shakespeare for his English literature.

The following morning he ventured into the school library, which had remained open during the half-term break especially for students who had stayed on at the school. For this, Ronald was grateful as he had spare time and no other distractions. With Christopher away, he could give himself a crash course in advanced science, obviously using the information he had learned in his basic science lessons. He dug out his notes from the classroom and noted the appropriate books he would need. The reader should remember this was still his first year, so the level of reading could not as yet be too advanced. Nevertheless, he was showing great initiative. This would serve him well through his later life in business. Added to that, his innate ruthlessness and deviousness would make Ronald Crump a very rich man.

The library opened at 10am and Ronald was there when the doors opened. The fact that there was little else to do all the half-term week added extra impetus to Crump's drive to catch up on his subject of interest. He selected three books from the shelf in the library relative to the lessons he had already had in the subject and complemented his reading with notes. He wondered if he should tell Christopher of his new-found interest in the world of science and decided against it. It would never do to tell him too much and remembering his father's advice, he proceeded to immerse himself in his studies.

He had spent most of the day lying on his bed reading, and it was now early afternoon. Ronald felt he needed some air and took appropriate action, heading for the playing fields. He decided to do a short run. Atkinson had impressed on the students the importance of keeping fit and, although he hated the man for 'stealing his woman' as his adolescent mind perceived it, he decided on this occasion the gym instructor was right. He set himself a target of two laps of the fields, about a mile and a half or 2.4 kilometres, and set off accordingly. Another piece of the games teacher's advice that Ronald reluctantly adhered to was the importance of pacing oneself over a distance. While he was jogging he repeated to himself his readings from the science book, and the time and distance passed rapidly. Now tired, he retired to his dormitory, taking with him a sandwich from the school canteen shop. He hit his mattress and was soon fast asleep.

The following days were spent pretty much the same as that first lonely Monday had been occupied, reading and cross-referencing with notes. Every other day he took a run and a shower. Before he could say 'hydrogen chloride', a gas he had read about, it was the weekend and Christopher would soon be returning. Ronald was not looking forward to hearing the fanciful stories Chris might have. Saturday afternoon arrived fast enough, and Christopher's car pulled up outside the main hall, delivering the oil baron's son back to captivity.

'Hi Ron, how are you doing?' he enquired of Crump, who casually replied. 'Not bad, not bad, very busy.'

'Why, what are you up to?' Christopher asked.

'Nothing you would be interested in,' replied the superior Crump.

'My dad had just struck another deposit of oil, going to be worth billions, what about that?' Christopher boasted, feeling such earth-shattering news would be certain to arouse more than a passing interest.

'When can we expect this discovery to hit the world's press?' Crump asked.

'It's already been in most of the nationals,' Christopher told him, oblivious to Ronald's sarcasm. 'Work begins on the drilling around Easter next year.'

'Very good! I'm pleased for you and your family,' replied Crump, who could not really give a damn about Johnson's oil deposit discovery.

Christopher talked on for about an hour while Ronald intermittently went through the pretence of reading. Eventually young Crump put down the material he was perusing and engaged in conversation, feeling he had made his point about his work being more important than Johnson's oil find. The two young futuristic business tycoons chatted till late and eventually put the lights out and went to sleep.

The following day, Sunday, was very quiet. There was no entertainment this week because it was felt the half-term break was over and the school wanted the students in learning mode. Christopher continued boring Ronald about what he had done during the break and he, Ronald, in turn pretended to be interested. The day passed without incident and all awaited the arrival of Monday morning and their first lesson.

Monday morning arrived and the first point of call for our intrepid young students was French. Ronald felt certain Miss Copley would show her appreciation to him for delivering her such an easy catch in the rounders game. Alas for Crump the French mistress just continued the lesson without even mentioning the event. One thing which never entered Ronald's otherwise advanced head was the fact that Miss Copley no more fancied him than did Marilyn Monroe. Such a thought was beyond young Crump's imagination. He told himself that the reason she didn't let her true feelings towards him be known was that pest Atkinson wouldn't leave her alone.

The following lesson this Monday on the school rolling timetable was math. By 'rolling timetable' it is meant that one Monday French could be the first lesson, but it did not automatically follow every Monday this would be the case. The thinking behind this system was to get the young students in a frame of mind where the unexpected could arise. This way they would revise all subjects, not knowing with any degree of certainty on any given week what order they would be sitting. This way they would learn to be flexible. This system would be practised for the first three years and for the final two, when students had decided which disciplines they were going to study as priorities. Then, timetables would be written accordingly for each pupil, giving extra time to the priority subjects. The thinking behind this was that the students could get used to organising their future lives in the world of business.

The math teacher was Mr P. Bradley, who was known as a disciplinarian. This did not bother Ronald as he liked math and knew he would not need to be chastised. Mr Bradley – 'Brad' behind his back – let all the boys know who was in charge and said he would not hesitate to use the strap if he felt it necessary. Today long division was the subject matter, which to Crump was easy, but some of the class were struggling. Mr Bradley gave them a little more encouragement and individual attention.

Suddenly there was an interruption to the lesson. Miss Copley entered and called Mr Bradley over. 'Peter,' she said, 'I have an unruly young man who will not behave. Could you come and have a word?'

'Yes, certainly, Madeline,' Bradley replied.

'Right you lot, sit still and no messing while I'm out of the room. Crump, keep an eye on things for me.'

'Yes, sir,' Ronald replied.

When the French teacher had first entered the room, Ronald thought it had to be to tell him she was grateful for his gallant act in the baseball game. Unfortunately, once again she did not mention the game. Not to worry, Ronald thought, the fact he had been left in charge was bound to impress her. About five minutes later Bradley arrived back.

'Any problems, Crump?' he asked.

'None, sir,' Ronald said.

'Creep,' one of the boys commented, which was an opinion held by most of his classmates. However, none of the others joined in as they knew they might need Crump for help at some stage in this subject.

Very shortly the bell sounded, signalling the end of the lesson and lunchtime. Ronald was very hungry.

'Where are you going for lunch, Chris?' he asked.

'We're going to town to the café, the canteen grub is rancid.'

'I'll come to town with you, if that's all right?' Crump asked.

'Yes, of course it is,' the future oil tycoon answered.

The lads frequented a café in the town centre for lunch which did great food and at reasonable prices. Some of the fifth-form students were there but had little to do with 'the little kids' who, they felt, would cramp their style. Ronald, Christopher and a young lad called Quentin, whose father was a top-class lawyer, all sat at the lower end of the room, leaving the top part for the older boys.

One of the older lads had a reputation as a ladies' man and he was working his charm on a young waitress. The fifth-form students were in their later teens, so such chat-ups were not out of the ordinary. Ronald observed his technique, and in his fanciful imagination thought he might learn something useful about possibly chatting up Miss Copley.

'What are you doing tonight, Rosie?' the fifth-former asked the girl.

'Nothing much,' the waitress replied.

'Right, you're coming to the movies with me. Pick you up at seven,' the senior pupil said.

'You're very confident of yourself, aren't you?' the café worker said. 'What if my boyfriend objects?'

'Never mind him, just say you're going with me.'

'No, I'm sorry. We are going out tonight when he has finished work. He works down at the beach, he's a lifeguard,' she told the student.

This was sufficient to shut the fifth-former up. Lifeguards were fit and strong, and, therefore, this guy was probably more than a little competent with his fists!

'OK, another time,' the student said, hoping not to lose too much face.

A valuable lesson, Crump thought. Do not bite off more than you can chew, or your teeth might be knocked out and you will chew no more. Christopher ordered his food as did Ronald. Quentin was a little shy, so Johnson ordered for him. The lawyer's son took a lot of stick because of his name, so Christopher had taken him under his wing. Ronald thought about taking the piss out of him, but guessed this might antagonise Christopher so he quickly dropped that thought.

The afternoon flew by and at four fifteen the last bell rang out signalling the end of the academic day.

'We are all going to play baseball, Ron,' Christopher informed Crump. 'Are you coming?'

'No,' said Ronald, 'I've something in the dorm to be getting on with.'

He couldn't play baseball, as his father never taught him. Furthermore, he did not want Johnson to know what he was doing. Ronald made his way back to the dormitory and began to revise his science, which would be the first lesson the next day.

The two roommates made their way to the science laboratory on Tuesday morning where Mr Hughes, the first-year science teacher, was eagerly waiting. Ronald had been revising the properties of alcohol as a chemical and the differences between ethyl alcohol, which goes into alcoholic drinks, and the much more potent and toxic industrial alcohol. This, he felt at this early stage, could come in useful for the engineering side of his father's empire, which he knew would be eventually taken over by him.

'What would happen, sir, if industrial alcohol were to find its way into a regulated alcoholic drink, not including the unregulated moonshine?'

'Well,' the teacher said, 'the consequences could be fatal depending on how much of the industrial variant was applied to the drink. The effects could vary from acute sickness to permanent blindness and even death. It would be a very foolish thing to mix the two, even for a prank.' He continued, 'The two different forms of alcohol have alternative uses and should never be mixed, for example, in engineering, industrial solvents containing alcohol can be used very successfully as a cleaning agent, resulting in an immaculate finish for certain products. Ethyl alcohol, which goes into drinks, would not give this result. Now there have been occasions, for example, teenagers' parties, where industrial alcohol has been added to give alcoholic drinks some extra bite. On one occasion a young man temporarily lost his sight and was very lucky the situation did not become permanent. Never indulge in these foolhardy activities, boys. It could be fatal for the victim.'

'Thank you, sir, that is the conclusion I came to during my revision last evening,' Crump obsequiously replied, expecting a 'Well done, Ronald, for good revision.' Hughes just nodded and grunted.

Having failed to promote himself to Mr Hughes's good books, Ronald bombarded the scientist with more questions and probes into the subject. This way, Crump thought, Hughes would get the impression that Crump was a more interested student than the rest and would give him more time. This he could report to his father, who would be pleased. Unfortunately for Ronald, the science teacher was not one for favouritism and although highly knowledgeable in his field, he was grumpy and boring to all his students.

By the end of this lesson Ronald realised that all the grovelling in the world was not going to improve his standing in the eyes of Mr Hughes. He would just have to get a good mark on his own merit!

The bell sounded for the end of this lesson and the class made their way to their next point of call, religious studies. At this point the class split into their denominational and religious categories, Catholics, Protestants and Jews. As the reader may recall, in the 1950s and '60s, unlike more recent times, Muslims were very few in the USA and certainly would not have been given their own religious teaching slot – that was if any of the schools would have them. The same applied to black people, whether they were Christian or Jewish or neither: society made it known they were second-class citizens, if citizens at all, and would just have their own shanty schools.

Some may be familiar with the case of Rosa Parks, often today titled the mother of the civil rights movement, and the incident where she refused to give up her seat on a bus for a white passenger in 1955. These racist attitudes prevailed in the USA when Ronald and his friends were at school and were also reflected in the education system. The class Ronald was with was the Protestant congregation under the Reverend Pilkington, while the Catholics awaited the arrival of Father McKeon. He eventually arrived to take his flock to the other chapel across the yard. Ronald noticed how the well-fed priest almost filled the door, and that his huge bicycle moustache made him look like Kaiser Wilhelm. Ronald became lost in thought and imagined he was in France with General Pershing during World War One, fighting against the German kaiser and his army. Pershing had given him an order to go on a secret mission to Berlin and assassinate the German leader.

Suddenly Ronald came back to earth as the Reverend Pilkington flicked his ear.

'Stop daydreaming, boy,' he thundered.

Ronald remembered conversations he had had with his father about religion and the fact-versus-fiction aspect of the subject. Teddy had always told his son that religion was one of the best weapons in the armoury of the ruling classes in keeping order in their society. It was therefore very important that, without necessarily believing a word of it, Ronald and the rest of the brigands' children got the tale right.

'The further down the social order, or the poorer people are,' Teddy explained, 'the more important religion is. It is important to us as a means of keeping these people poor in order that we stay very rich. It is important to the poor to believe it is their place to be poor on this Earth, and work hard for us rich people, and they will secure a place in Heaven. It is important they believe it's God's will they are destitute on this mortal Earth but will be rich in the afterlife.'

'Do they believe this rubbish, Dad?' Ronald questioned his father.

'It is part of our job to make sure they continue to believe, son, because if they ever catch on that all is not quite what we and the church ministers, priests and rabbis tell them, they might get ideas above their station. Should that ever happen we should, and would, send the troops out to shoot them down, which would, of course, cost money. Of course,' he continued, 'the further up the social ladder we go the less strong this belief is so for the better paid workers we modify the story a little to make them feel a little more inclusive. That is why we must be seen at church every now and again at events like Thanksgiving, Easter and Christmas, leading these poor unfortunate souls by example, whose poverty ensures our wealth. Therefore, at school, son, it is important to listen, not because the story is true – in fact even those doing the teaching don't believe that – but so you have got the story right for later in life. Now do you understand?'

At the end of this lecture Teddy gave a ghastly grin and patted his son on the head.

In the classroom the Reverend Pilkington was giving instruction about the Sermon on the Mount and that 'all are God's creatures'. *This is the bit Dad said is just for the benefit of the lower orders,* Ronald thought, *but I must listen and get the thing right. After all, if a man is going to tell a lie he must be consistent,* which was another bit of Teddy's advice. A translation of what the Reverend was really saying was, 'All are God's creatures, but the majority, according to God, must work all their lives for the minority and be rewarded in Heaven. This is what God really meant and that is why the story is for our benefit and to the cost of those who do believe it.'

Suddenly, as if sent from the Almighty, the bell sounded, signalling the end of the lesson and lunchtime.

The two students, Christopher and Ronald, were heading into town for their lunch. The benevolence which Johnson had shown Quentin over him being bullied over his name, taking the attorney's son under his wing, did not stretch as far as black people, Hispanics or Native Americans. These were views shared by Crump, who had also been brought up in a racist environment.

'My dad,' said Christopher, 'says the worst day in US history was the 9th May 1865 when General Robert E. Lee surrendered in the American Civil War. It signified the defeat of the South and the freedom of the slaves. Dad says black people are only good for slavery.'

The Crump family shared this view to a certain extent, but their families had supported the North. This, though, did not necessarily include approving of the abolition of slavery. Their main concerns were to do with the advancements in banking brought about by the European Industrial Revolution. The old ways of the southern states were obsolete and had to change. However, they shared many of the South's views on slavery, although they recognised that wage slavery was cheaper than chattel slavery.

At that moment two black lads, minding their own business, approached in the opposite direction. They both looked younger than Ronald and Christopher.

'Look at these two black bastards coming,' Chris Johnson exclaimed.

Ronald was a little taken aback by his friend's attitude and language, but endorsed his mate's opinions all the same.

'Yes, let's give them a tough time,' suggested Ronald.

'What you looking at, n****r? Cross the road when you see us whites approaching in future,' Christopher called out.

'That's right,' said Crump, feeling confident their targets were not going to retaliate. Christopher then approached the older of the two and pushed him into the road.

'This is white man's territory and we don't want you here,' Johnson stated.

The two students felt as though they had just taken a great step for the white race. Of course, the two boys had just epitomised the backward thinking of what they liked to think was the most advanced nation on the planet. This act of blatant racism would come back to haunt them soon.

They went to the café where the fifth-form student had been rebuffed by the waitress the previous day. Crump decided he would try his luck with one of the other girls.

'What you doing later, darling?' Crump rather clumsily asked.

'Piss off, you little twerp,' the young mixed-race girl retorted.

Ronald Crump was again taken aback. How dare a half-breed, as he saw it, speak to him like that?

'What did you say, tart?' Crump enquired.

'You heard. Go away now if you don't want this tea over your head,' the young woman said.

Ronald and Christopher left the counter area, the former feeling slightly belittled. Then things suddenly got worse.

'That's them there, them two,' came a shout.

As the two boys looked over, they saw the young boys they had insulted on the road. Now they were accompanied by two big black lads, about fourteen, who looked very like them. One of the younger boys was pointing at Ronald and Christopher.

'Come here, you two,' shouted one of the older lads.

The two racists made a tactical and rapid retreat. Ronald caught a clip from the taller of the two's fist, making his ear throb.

'Run!' shouted Johnson. The white race was in an all-out retreat. It appeared their self-perceived supremacy was only applicable when their opponents were younger and weaker.

On arriving back at the school gates, they looked at each other.

'We just made it, Ron,' Johnson panted.

'Only just,' replied Crump.

'We should keep out of town for a few days, those two bucks were annoyed and up for it,' said Christopher.

'I know, I tried to smack one of them and just missed,' Crump lied.

Johnson doubted this but was in such a hurry to save his own skin he had not seen anything to disprove Ronald's claim.

'At least there will be no comeback on the school, the teachers hate the n*****s more than we do,' said Christopher.

'Yes, especially the Head,' retorted Crump.

'We're safe enough on that front,' they both agreed and complimented each other on their heroic lunch break.

Games awaited them in the afternoon. Ronald's mind soon drifted as to what he was to do about the ridiculous affair between Atkinson and his natural suitor, Miss Copley. *This cannot be allowed to continue*, he thought to himself, *the question is not if but when to put a stop to it!* Of course, this was all in Ronald's adolescent imagination; there was nothing he could have done even if he had been older. That said, if he had been older such stupidity would not have entered his head – or would it? Time would tell.

★ ★ ★

Teddy Crump had been involved in sensitive negotiations with the US Government to secure a lucrative contract. He hoped to secure for Crump Armaments and Engineering the state contract for ten new state-of-the-art Blood and Guts tanks. The tank's title came from the nickname given to Second World War General George S. Patton by his men. The tank could reach speeds of sixty km/h over land and shallow water, reaching eighty km/h if the extra road wheels were to be lowered. The caterpillar tracks and bodywork were to be constructed at Crump Engineering while the cannon and sidearms would be manufactured and sighted for accuracy at the armaments department of the company. The contract would be worth $2 million to Crump, and Teddy with his team had worked night and day as well as lobbying to see off their competitors. Of course, a few palms were crossed with silver to make sure the contract would be awarded to Crump. This is normal practice in the corrupt world of big business.

Once the contract was signed by representatives of the US government and Crump himself, Teddy and his negotiating team, along with their departmental secretaries, retired to a local hotel for a few nights' celebration. One of the secretaries, who was married, phoned her husband, explaining she would not be home for the weekend due to work commitments. Her husband was not pleased, he had an idea what these 'commitments' were but was powerless to stop his wife's extra duties.

So it was on the Thursday that Teddy Crump phoned Megan, informing her of the good news and that he and the team would be away for the weekend.

'That's great news, Teddy,' she said – *in more ways than one*, she thought!

Megan Crump was still under the impression her husband was unaware of her extramarital affair with Derek. The truth was somewhat different. Teddy had suspected for some time she was playing away but decided for tactical reasons to let it go. Crump himself had two affairs on the go, one with his leading secretary, which Megan was aware of, and one with his PA. Crump calculated that Megan might one day discover the truth and he wanted ammunition to fight back with. Should his infidelity be unearthed, he could fire back with her misadventures. Teddy Crump never did anything unless there was an ulterior motive and allowing his wife to sleep with another man, believing him to be blind to the fact, was no exception.

No sooner had her husband replaced the receiver than she was on the same telephone to Derek, her lover.

'He said he'll be back next Tuesday,' she told him. 'To be safe we can spend Friday, Saturday and Sunday together, but you must leave on Sunday evening,' she informed Derek. 'I'll give the staff the weekend plus Friday off, they'll think it's Christmas, no pay of course but all the same they'll be glad of the time off. Can you come here tomorrow?' she asked.

'You bet, honey,' was her former boss's reply. 'Wild horses wouldn't stop me.'

Everything was in place for the following morning. She called the staff together and informed them of their unexpected mini vacation.

'No need to mention this to Mr Crump,' she advised them.

'No Missy, we'll keep shtum,' Betty assured her.

'Good, enjoy your break and I'll see you all on Monday morning,' said Megan.

She had decided to entertain her lover at the mansion. That way, if her husband called she was on hand, and wouldn't suspect a thing. Derek arrived late Friday morning as arranged, and the pair headed straight to the bedroom, starting as they meant to go on! Megan took a bottle of champagne to keep them both refreshed between bouts.

It was as well Megan had arranged for Derek to depart the mansion on Sunday evening because Crump, as he had a habit of doing, returned a day early on the Monday around lunchtime. He had brought with him a case of champagne so that he and his wife could celebrate the great news about the contract. Fortunately, Megan had arranged the staff to be back early on Monday morning.

'I'm home, honey,' Teddy called out. 'I have a surprise for you.'

'Hi, darling,' Megan greeted him. 'What have you brought, anything nice?'

'A case of champers here,' he replied. 'I'll open a bottle, shall I?'

Crump settled back in at the mansion and they both enjoyed a few glasses of bubbly.

'I thought I'd invite Hugh and Mary over to celebrate, honey, what do you think?'

'Great idea,' Megan replied, and with that Crump was on the phone to the Rothschilds. Teddy wanted to discuss a way of evading some income tax on this new contract and there was no better man than Hugh Rothschild to advise on this subject. And of course, what better way to discuss the matter than over a couple of bottles of champagne?

The Rothschilds arrived and the small celebration was soon in full swing. To look at both Teddy and Megan it could be thought that they were a devoted couple and butter wouldn't melt in their mouths.

★ ★ ★

The winter months had well and truly arrived and at Bishops Court Rise the students were preparing for their pre-Christmas exams. Ronald was expecting an A in math, English and geography. He was also hoping he had made up some lost ground in science, and maybe could get a B+ or at least a B.

Crump was behind in history. He could never remember dates and didn't see the point of the subject. In his mind, because the subject did not involve exploiting people in order that huge profits could be amassed, he saw little mileage in studying the subject too earnestly. He had not grasped the concept that to understand the events of today they must be viewed through the lens of history. In many years to come his neglect of history as a subject would come back to haunt him and would contribute to his downfall.

The next milestone in the school calendar would be Christmas and the three-week vacation. This time Ronald would be going home, as would all the students. Teddy had sent him his flight tickets early, in late November, to avoid the Christmas rush, and the school was due to break up on 20th December. They would then return on 8th January. Christopher Johnson's father had sent his son the air tickets, which arrived the same time as did Ronald's. The two students were looking forward to going home to see their parents and their respective friends, or people who qualified as friends in bourgeois USA. Before any of this could happen though, the exams had to be sat. As both Ronald and Christopher had been diligent in their studies, they were confident in their expectations. The exams were to start on 20th November and would finish four days later.

Monday 20th November arrived. The school students made their way from the dormitory to the main hall, through the snow which blanketed the ground, for the geography examination. The adjudicators were in position as the students took their places.

'Take your time, and read the questions thoroughly first,' were the instructions received from the teacher who then left the room.

'You may pick up your pens now and begin,' said the adjudicator. 'You will have two hours, after which all pens must be placed on your desks and papers handed in to those collecting. Begin.'

The two hours soon passed, and the adjudicator signalled that time was up. 'Put down your pens and sit quietly,' he instructed them.

Walking out, Christopher asked Ronald, 'How did you do, Ron?'

'No problem,' said Crump. 'I think I did enough to get a decent mark.'

'Me too. I was a little stuck on the average precipitation for Rhodesia but managed in the end,' Christopher stated.

'No point worrying now, Chris,' said Ronald. 'We can't do anything now, the job is done.'

'True enough,' agreed Johnson.

The two students got back to their dormitory a little drained. In the afternoon there was an hour of games with Mr Atkinson and then, due to the exams, it was the end of the day. On examination days the school schedule was shorter, and Atkinson had given them an easier time than usual, so as not to exhaust the pupils for the following morning.

Tuesday morning offered the math exam, which both Ronald and Christopher looked forward to. They were both satisfied with the paper and gave each other a thumbs up as they left the hall. More exams followed, with the final test, English, taking place on the Thursday. It would be the new year before the results would be posted, so the students would have to wait until after the Christmas break for their results.

After the final paper was sat, the examination papers were sent to the external examiners' board where they would be marked. The teachers at Bishops Court Rise had nothing to do with the marking and were busying themselves making out the students' individual reports for the coming break. Ronald was hoping for a good report; he wanted to please his parents, his father in particular.

The exams over, Ronald lay in his bed and his thoughts, as was now common, drifted away towards the relationship Miss Copley was having with Mr Atkinson. There was nothing sordid about this affair except in the mind of Ronald Crump. Ronald was thinking to himself: how could he sort this mess out for the French teacher in the new year? Every time he thought of Miss Copley he felt a twinge in his groin. In a few months, next April, Ronald would be thirteen years old, and biological and hormonal changes were a normal part of reaching adolescence. Unfortunately for Ronald, his imagination ran riot to the point where he believed his thoughts and emotions at this moment in time to be rational and coherent which, of course they weren't. He told himself he would sort out Miss Copley's problems for her next year, and she could then show her gratitude.

20th December arrived, the day when students and staff at Bishops Court Rise vacated the school for the Christmas break. A convoy of large black cars made their way up the long school drive to collect the next generation of the ruling class. Similar cars were also going to the nearby girls' boarding school. All these vehicles had been hired by parents to ferry their offspring to the airport or if they lived locally, to their parents' mansions.

'Crump,' Jefferson called. 'Your transport is here, get a move on. Have a good Christmas and see you next term.'

Ronald shook hands with Christopher who was waiting for his transport to the airport. Crump was flying to New York and Johnson to Texas, so they were going to different terminals.

'See you next year, Chris.'

'Will do, Ron,' he said, waving as young Crump ran down the steps towards his car.

The chauffeur opened the door for Ronald, who pushed past him in an arrogant manner. The words 'thank you' never entered Crump's head.

'How was school, sir?' the chauffeur asked, but Crump just ignored him and acted as if he was alone in the car.

Ronald considered himself above conversation with such lowly people as his driver. Who did the chauffeur think he was trying to engage him in conversation? As far as Ronald was concerned the driver was getting paid for driving him to the airport, and this did not give the man any right of conversation. On their arrival at the airport the chauffeur opened the car door for Crump who, once again, ignored him. Ronald Crump broke his silence only to instruct the chauffeur to bring his luggage to the terminal where he was to check in.

* * *

Teddy and Megan, still playing cat and mouse with one another, were looking forward to having their son home for Christmas. They had spent a small fortune on Ronald's Christmas presents. For what they termed stocking fillers, they had purchased three pairs of handmade leather shoes: a pair of brogues, a pair of tasselled slip-on shoes and a pair of elastic-gusseted ankle boots. All were made of the highest quality leather with leather soles and velvet and silk lining. Another smaller present they bought him was a solid gold pendant and chain which he would show off on his return to school.

His major present was $2,500-worth of photography equipment. There were cameras of varying sizes including the tiny pocket camera as used by CIA personnel, the companion set consisting of an orthodox top-of-the-range camera and a tripod. The set also consisted of a video camera which enabled the user to produce their own home movie. Also included was the necessary equipment for the budding photographer to develop their own film. This was one time when Ronald's parents got him the perfect present. Photography would become a huge interest for him, and over the years he would further refine and improve his skills in the subject. One particular reason for this interest would become apparent as his education progressed.

Ronald Crump had also developed an interest in swimming and diving and for this reason his parents had bought him a full scuba-diving wetsuit, flippers and oxygen tank. Ronald's reason for this interest, which he never disclosed, was to escape some of Atkinson's games. The swimming classes were taken separately by a former US Olympic swimmer, Guy Spitz who was a Gold Medal winner in the 1950 Olympics. It was true young Crump did enjoy swimming but not to the extent he claimed. To hear him talk one could be forgiven for thinking he had an eye on making the US Olympic team, which he certainly did not. He just preferred this mode of keeping fit to being in the company of the aggressive and hated Mr Atkinson, who was knocking off his woman!

Ronald's plane touched down at New York Airport and waiting for him were Megan, Teddy and their chauffeur.

'Hi, Ronnie darling,' Megan shouted, 'we're over here.'

'Hey, son, have you forgotten what we look like?' Teddy shouted trying, and failing, to create amusement.

Megan gave her son a big hug, and now they were all together for the Christmas break.

5

The Christmas of '59

Teddy Crump and Megan were chauffeured back to their suburban mansion with Ronald, who sat like a lord with his parents in the rear of the stretch Limousine. They approached the huge electronic gates which the security guard opened by pressing a button – but not before he had checked it was really them. All the houses in 'Billionaires' Row' were of this nature and the land, including the large gardens, taken by four of these unnecessarily large buildings, could have accommodated an estate of one hundred average homes. The Crumps arrived home to a delicious meal Cook had made for the family. Megan thanked Cook for her extra effort, as in a roundabout way did Teddy. Ronald just exclaimed an ignorant grunt for Cook's efforts.

'I'm tired,' said Ronald, understandable after his long flight.

'Well, go to bed, darling. Daddy and I won't mind, will we, Teddy?' she expressed on behalf of them both.

'Thanks, Mom, I think I will,' said the youngster and off he went to bed. It had been a long old day.

The following morning Ronald awoke much refreshed.

'What are you doing today, son?' his father enquired.

'Not sure yet. Thought I might do some catching up. Do you know if James is back from school? If so, I'll visit him.'

'Yes, I heard from his father that James and Susie are both coming back on the same flight,' Teddy informed him. 'They might be home by now.'

'Is he still with her?' asked Ronald.

'Yes, he certainly is – and don't let him hear you referring to Susie as *her* if you have any sense,' Teddy warned his son. 'But before you go anywhere, Ronald, haven't you got something to show your mother and me?'

'What do you mean, Dad?' Ronald said.

'The school report! You know we are interested. Call your mother and we'll all sit down and go through your progress, or lack of!'

Ronald was still going through his bag when Megan came into the room.

'Here you are,' he said at last, handing the sealed envelope to his father.

Megan sat opposite her husband, who opened the envelope. The first subject was math, and the review was good: 'Ronald shows terrific interest in this subject and excels and enthuses in all branches of the subject. There is no reason why Ronald should not thrive in math and make it one of his core subjects in later years.' In the margin provided, an A+ was placed, indicating his performance level. This was not to be mistaken for the exam results. The next subject was geography. 'Ronald has a little difficulty map reading but this should become easier over time as he shows great aptitude in all other areas of geography. His knowledge of international precipitation is wide and vast and there are no reasons why he could not, with a little more concentration, develop and, if he wishes, take this as a core subject or an optional core in reserve.' In the margin was B+. The next on the list was French. 'Ronald has a tendency to allow his thoughts to wander in this discipline. He needs to concentrate a lot more and put more effort in his verbs and adverbs.' In the margin was a disappointing C–. Teddy recalled his afternoon at the school and meeting Miss Copley and could empathise with his son's mind 'wandering' in her class. The next subject listed was English. 'Ronald has a great aptitude in this subject. His essay writing has improved over the last few months from his early days. I have great hopes for Ronald taking English as a core subject.' The mark in the margin was A+. Then came the report for science: 'Ronald has come along in leaps and bounds in recent months. His revision is second to none and if this level of improvement continues at his current rate science may well be one of his core subjects.' The all-important mark was A. Religious Instruction was the next. 'Ronald tends to ask silly questions about the viability of the subject, though all in all he shows a grasp as to what he needs to concentrate on.' The margin afforded Ronald a respectable B.

The Crumps went through all the subjects and were very satisfied because their son's results were well above average. His father was not too worried about the French result, as he saw it as unnecessary and the teacher, Miss Copley, in Teddy Crump's mind, was only good for a screw. This was Crump's view of most women, though in his wife's company he kept this to himself. In years to come his son would make these opinions look moderate.

'May I leave now, Dad?' Ronald asked.

'Yes, run along, son, see you later.'

Ronald ran down the road to the home of James Rothschild. He rang the bell, which sang a verse of Beethoven's sixth symphony, and Hugh Rothschild answered the door.

'Is James back from boarding school, Mr Rothschild?' Ronald enquired.

'Yes he is, Ron. I think he's out on the veranda with Susie,' the banker informed him.

Ronald thanked Rothschild and made his way out to the veranda, which was tastefully decorated in pine and had two sets of wooden chairs and tables along the length of the house.

'Hi James, how are you? Hi, Susie,' he greeted them.

'Great, Ronald,' said James, standing up and offering his hand in friendship. The two lads shook hands and swapped a few tales about their first few months at boarding school. Susie was content to sit back and let the lads chat away.

'Are you coming into town, James?' Ronald asked.

'No, Ron, Susie and myself have plans for today, maybe we can catch up tomorrow for an hour,' James said.

'Don't forget, James, we are going to the cinema tomorrow,' Susie reminded her boyfriend.

'Oh yes, sorry Ronald, another time perhaps. Tell you what, I think Terry and Peter are back.'

'What about Dianna and Judy?' Ronald asked.

'I think Judy has something of a personal nature to tell Peter which, frankly, is none of my business. If I were you, I would give Terry a call and try to give Judy and Peter some space,' James advised.

'Yes, I'll do that,' a bemused Ronald said.

Ronald moved on to Terry Morgan's house, curious as to what the mystery was with Peter and Judy. He also got the distinct impression James did not want to be as much a part of the gang he was once upon a time – certainly not as a leader.

'How are you doing, Terry?' Ronald asked young Morgan.

'I'm good, Ronald, brilliant results in my first report. Mom and Dad are delighted.'

'Same here,' Ronald told his friend. 'I've just called on James. He doesn't seem interested in the gang any more,' Crump continued.

'I think he thinks he's in love, maybe he is – I don't know. One thing is sure: he is not the James who went away,' Terry said.

'Look,' said Ronald, 'Is there something up between Peter and Judy?'

'Leave well alone,' Terry advised. 'If it's what I think it is,' Terry said, 'he'll need our support and friendship, but he'll ask for it when he needs it.'

'Why?' Ronald persisted.

'She is going to finish with him, dump him, you watch,' Terry said.

* * *

Judy McClean rang the bell at Peter's house. It was answered by Duke, his father.

'Hi Judy, how are you?' the builder asked.

'I'm fine, Mr Tillerson,' Judy replied. 'Is Peter in?'

'Yes, come in, dear,' Peter's father invited. 'He's through there, in the games room.'

'Peter, how are you?' she said.

Peter looked up in surprise. 'Judy!' he exclaimed. As he looked at her solemn demeanour, he knew for sure something was wrong. She had not replied to the letters of love he had constantly sent her. 'What's wrong?' he asked.

'I wanted to tell you face to face,' Judy said.

'Tell me what?' Tillerson enquired.

'It's like this, Pete, I was out in the town near the school with Dianna, and we met – I mean I met this boy, Cecil…'

'Cecil,' Tillerson interjected.

'Yes,' said Judy, 'And we—'

'What kind of a name is that? Cecil!' Peter felt unaccountably angry.

'I knew you'd fly off the handle Pete, I knew it, I always felt trapped when we were together, you're too aggressive and possessive and that boxing doesn't help,' Judy explained.

'I'll give him fucking Cecil, I'm coming down there and Cecil will be lucky if he ever gets near you again!' Peter spat out.

'No, Peter, you are not going to my school or anywhere near it. I did all the running! I'm not your property, just accept it. Cecil treats me like a person, not a possession like you do.'

The truth of what she said dawned on Peter, and he became red-faced with shame.

'I'll change, Judy, you see if I don't, I promise.'

'No Peter, it's over.'

At this juncture Duke Tillerson, alarmed by the loud voices, entered the room.

'What's the problem?' he asked.

'Ask her, ask Marilyn Monroe there,' Peter said, his voice shaky with emotion.

Duke put two and two together pretty quickly. 'Peter will you calm down, son.'

'I'm afraid I'm breaking it off with Peter,' Judy said, looking at Peter with sad eyes.

'Oh,' he said, 'I see. I'm sorry to hear that, Judy. And I'm sorry, Peter. I know this must be hard for you. Judy, I think you should leave now, but thanks for having the courage to tell my son to his face,' Duke acknowledged.

Judy gave Peter one last look and left.

'Whose side are you on?' Peter asked his father, feeling hurt.

'Son, you can't hold the girl, any girl, against her will,' Duke told his son. 'Let her go.'

Duke was secretly delighted at the outcome of this affair. He had wanted them to separate for some time and would have intervened himself if nothing had happened. Judy had saved him the trouble. There was no profit in this relationship, and Duke had his own suitor for his son in mind. Duke's building friend and conspirator, Arthur Chappell, had a daughter the same age as Peter. Angela was not as attractive as Judy but when they married their children off to one another, whether they liked it or not, the merger would be worth a mint to all concerned. Duke and Arthur, with their wives, Sheena and Betty, had arranged for the children to meet the following year. The plan was to arrange a meeting and a relationship would be struck up. However, this was not for months yet, not this Christmas. If the cursory observer could draw an analogy of this scene, they might conclude it was similar to that of a stud farm involving the preparation of racehorses for mating.

Duke engaged Peter in conversation. 'She could have two-timed on you, son. She could have had you here and the other guy down there, near the school. At least she had the decency and courage to tell you to your face,' he said again.

'That's true, Dad, I'll be grateful for small mercies, and she was nice about it.'

'That's the spirit, son, plenty more fish in the sea,' Duke said.

He actually hoped not, as he didn't want his son involved with any other girls until he had 'got it on' with Angela Chappell. Duke and Arthur would ultimately be disappointed, as events conspired against their plan to mate Peter and Angela.

* * *

As the month of November drew to a close, high-level talks were taking place at a summit in which Bradley Morgan was involved at a junior level. The prospect of a US company, Megga Oil, drilling for oil in Kuwait where deposits had been found was the reason for the summit. Morgan was not involved at this level. Instead, along with a few other junior diplomats, he attended fringe talks which allowed the major players time to negotiate the bigger issues. Although the talks were on the periphery, it still gave his wife, Ethel, something to boast of to her pretend friends. To hear Ethel talk, one would think her husband was involved in a big top secret project. It suited her just fine that she couldn't divulge much information, as she didn't know very much about it anyhow.

Should the talks conclude with the US transnational company securing the drilling contract, accommodation for the workers would be required. A junior Kuwaiti minister had been given this portfolio and Morgan would be the senior person for the United States at this level. The money talked of at the higher level was in the tens of billions of dollars making the half a billion, top figure, at Bradley's level, look like loose change. Nevertheless, it would be Bradley's role to find a suitable contractor to construct the workers' accommodation, and he immediately thought of Duke Tillerson. Bradley also knew he would receive a 'sweetener' from Tillerson should he be awarded the contract. All depended on what happened in the big talks. Morgan, for the time being, kept things under wraps, not yet informing Tillerson of the possibilities which might come his way.

Duke Tillerson had handled much bigger jobs than this one which was why he had one of the biggest domestic companies in the USA. However, all his other jobs had been in the US and should this one come to pass he would be operating overseas. Morgan was banking on this factor as the main bait to tempt his friend and conspirator. News filtered through that US giants Megga Oil had secured the drilling contract from the Kuwaiti government, and drilling was to begin in three years' time. This meant the jerry-built accommodation had to begin in earnest early in the new year, 1960.

Morgan was having lunch with the junior Kuwaiti official, Mr Abdul Abdula, and the discussion drifted in the direction of the contract for accommodation. Mr Abdula had a certain budget to work to, from which he, naturally, wanted his personal share. Therefore, corners had to be cut by the successful contractor. Morgan, a veteran of such workings, understood perfectly and he also wanted his cut, which Tillerson would cross his palm with. This part he kept from Ethel; she was too greedy by far and life had taught Bradley to reveal as little as possible to the money-grabbing little gold-digger. He knew his wife was a liability and would therefore act accordingly as to how much he would tell her. Therefore, 'what she didn't know she couldn't chase', was Bradley's motto.

Mr Abdula wrote a figure down on a piece of paper as to what he wanted to pay for the job. Morgan looked at it.

'This is tight, Abdul,' he commented.

'That's the figure,' the official said.

'Any room for manoeuvre?' enquired Bradley.

'Perhaps a little, see what you can come up with,' he advised Morgan.

Bradley Morgan left the table and phoned Duke Tillerson. The two agreed to meet on Morgan's return. When they got together, Morgan showed Tillerson the figure and hoped for the best.

'You're joking, Brad, tell me you're joking,' Tillerson remarked.

'No, Duke, that's the figure he gave me.'

The builder was not impressed. 'Can you get him to go up a little? There's something in it for you, Brad, if you can.'

Morgan had been around long enough to know he could squeeze a little more profit for his fellow brigand if he tried.

'Leave it with me,' he told Tillerson.

There were to be clauses in the contract for delays or overbudgeting, but these did not worry Tillerson a great deal. He knew with some diluting of material quality and cutting corners generally as well as paying the least for labour he could get away with, he could fulfil the terms of the contract. He was aware that after three years the buildings would be in a state of disrepair, but he also knew that the oil barons were more concerned with how many billions were coming out of the ground than the quality of their workers' accommodation.

Bradley Morgan arranged to meet the Kuwaiti official again to renegotiate the figure.

'He says this figure will not cover the costs and profit, he will need some more, Abdul.'

'How much more?' asked Mr Abdula abruptly.

Morgan knew to go higher in order that he could come down. 'An extra million dollars on the overall cost,' he informed the Kuwaiti.

'Out of the question, far too high,' the official retorted as expected. 'You'll have to come down some otherwise I'll have to look elsewhere, perhaps at home in Kuwait.'

After much haggling the two conmen came to a figure which Bradley knew would be acceptable to Tillerson who was, after all, trying to get a foothold in the overseas market. He arranged to meet Duke that evening and he gave the new figure, which was for the entire building contract. It was worth $4,500,000 pre-tax which would be taxed at the lower end in Kuwait. Not exactly legal but not criminal either under the rules of capitalism.

Tillerson met Abdul Abdula and Bradley Morgan the following day to sign the contract. The work would begin in Kuwait at the end of March 1960. It was due for completion by the end of November 1962 with penalty clauses included for excessive delays. When Tillerson read the contract, he was privately pleased with the profit ratio he would make. He knew using inferior materials would be easy and salaries for his workers would be cut to the bone, and if they didn't want the job, there were plenty out there who would. The three thieves shook hands and signed the contract. This would be a very, very merry Christmas indeed.

All that remained was for Tillerson to hand Morgan a cheque for $30,000 and everybody would be happy. The $30,000 was the sweetener Tillerson paid Morgan for doing the groundwork and arranging the meeting between himself and Abdula, the Kuwaiti government representative. The money would ultimately come from the $4,500,000.

This was what Christmas was all about, the men agreed – even Abdul, who wasn't a Christian. This year he joined in the festivities in a very Christian way as he had secured $300,000 of this final figure for himself, unknown to Tillerson and, for that matter, Morgan. The real figure was $4,200,000, payable to Tillerson. All three bandits were happy.

Morgan made more money on corrupt contracts than was his actual salary. His superiors were aware of what was going on but turned a blind eye; after all, they were also milking the system. The rules were: do not get too greedy, keep the wheels of the capitalist gravy train lubricated and we can all do very well. These rules were practised just in case somebody competent and honest ever got the top job in the USA, which was unlikely as the top men in government and commerce had enough checks and balances to throw that man (women were not yet considered as candidates for this post) off the scent. It would be another fifty years before such a man entered the Oval Office.

It was Christmas morning and it was the Crumps' turn to hold the feast at their home. All the brigands and families were present: Duke and Sheena Tillerson, Bradley and Ethel Morgan, Hugh and Mary Rothschild and Matthew and Sally Seddon. It was Sally whom Teddy had the assignation with previously; such an opportunity would present itself again, Teddy hoped. Jimmy and Moira Carter were there with Susie, who would sit with James at the table, as were Fred and Audrey Nixon with Dianna, and Barney and Veronica McClean with Judy. It was the latter's presence which caused a little unease due to the situation between Peter and Judy, but both sets of parents had spoken to their children and agreed to keep them apart. They had no need to worry as Peter appeared to have got over the initial shock of being dumped and a civilised atmosphere prevailed throughout as 'glory shone around', as the Christmas carol suggests, in true Christian fashion.

Before the day really got under way, the Christians attended Christmas morning service at their relevant church. This hypocritical act was aimed at the working class, some of whom were employed by Crump and Tillerson and some by Rothschild and McClean. This hypocrisy did not present itself as a problem to the brigands because they did not believe in what the church minister was saying any more than the orator did. The latter received a salary from bourgeois society for preaching this method of control from the pulpit.

There were, however, those in the congregation who did believe every word, and the lower down the social order the more the devotion of the followers in this belief became. For this reason, in order that those who really did have a gripe with society and perhaps should take up arms in revolution to better their conditions, it was important that the likes of Crump were seen to show the same level of devotion. It would not do for the lower orders to start asking questions about the entire charade; after all, God would not like it! He had, when all was said and done, decreed these people to be poor and the likes of Crump to be wealthy. Better to keep these people in blind ignorance and, of course, subordinate. Perhaps one of the more sickening sights at this spectacle of hypocrisy was the ghastly image of Crump singing Christmas carols like a man auditioning for an operatic role.

With this obscenity out of the way, it was back to the Crumps' where the domestics and Cook had prepared a banquet for the family and guests. The staff genuinely did believe in the oration delivered by the minister, but they would have to wait until the evening service to show their appreciation to God for being allowed to work for the Crumps, and celebrate his son's birth. They were not allowed to attend the morning service, as there was too much work to be done preparing the feast for their betters.

And what a meal it was, along with the finest wines and champagne. As usual, Teddy Crump considered himself to be the life and soul of the party, but even his fellow brigands, all equally as boring and pathetic, found him nauseating. With the feast over, the gang of thieves retired to the lounge and luxury seating. The telephone rang and Sylvia, one of the junior members of staff, took the call.

'Mrs Crump, telephone call for you, madam,' she informed her mistress.

'Won't be a minute,' Megan advised her company. 'I'll take it in the study where it's quieter,' she said to Sylvia. Teddy suddenly felt he had to go to the toilet.

'Just going to adjust the pluming' he humourlessly informed the audience. 'Won't be long.'

Ronald had an idea something was a little untoward and for this reason he sneaked out after his father. His suspicions were correct. As he peered through the crack in the bedroom door he perceived his father listening in on his mother's call from one of the other telephones.

Teddy grinned to himself as he heard every word said between Megan and Derek. Teddy now had the ammunition he needed; he could play and control Megan all he liked. If she ever caught him out with any of the women at work or even with Sally Seddon, he had this in his back pocket to fight back with. He was almost turned on by the power he now had over his wife. If ever she said she was going somewhere, and he thought she was going to meet Derek, he would just make a last-minute excuse why he and Megan would have to be elsewhere! If she was to meet her lover on, say, Monday afternoon, he would wait until the very latest possible moment and drop a bombshell. This could be some important occasion that had just cropped up which they both had to attend. This was brilliant, Teddy thought. What Crump did not know was that Ronald was also aware of the conversation.

When Ronald had seen enough he sneaked back to the lounge acting as if all was well. Although did not hear what was said on the phone, he had a good idea what was going on. He would possibly use this to his advantage when the time came. Teddy Crump had not given up all hope of a few minutes alone with Sally Seddon. As the reader may recall, at an earlier social function Crump and Sally had arranged a liaison seemingly behind her husband's back. The fact was Matthew Seddon and his wife had planned the whole affair in order to gain a contract for rifles from Teddy Crump. In a nutshell, the Seddons were prostituting Sally, who did not mind, providing the action paid dividends. Crump was unaware he was a tool in the couple's little game and thought the same rules applied today, Christmas Day. He was to be disappointed. Crump made a move towards Sally.

'Enjoying yourself, Sal?' he enquired.

'Yes, very much, Ted,' the young service provider replied.

'Listen, Sally, Megan will probably fall asleep, she cannot take alcohol. We could find a quiet corner for some private time.'

Sally was aware this had not been arranged with her husband and although she felt a little tipsy, she declined the offer. Perhaps if Crump had been twenty years younger she may have risked it as she liked a little danger, but not for a boring old fart like him.

'Sorry, Ted, nothing doing, darling, what kind of girl do you think I am? I'm a happily married woman and you... well, you're a married man, sorry.'

'Come on, Sally,' Crump persisted. 'Remember the other month. It was great.'

'For you maybe, darling, for me, well, let's just say it was average and leave it at that, besides Matthew is getting suspicious.'

Crump glanced across the room and noticed Matthew was looking across. Crump offered a friendly smile which Matthew returned.

James and Susie sat on the couch together acting like the grown-up couples – well, perhaps not quite like them; they actually did love each other, albeit in a childish kind of way. They had not yet learned the ways of the brigands and how one had to act as adult members of the US bourgeoisie.

Ronald was discussing the finer arts of photography with Terry Morgan, explaining he had a full Kodak camera outfit and projector for making home movies.

'That's great, Ron. Can we make a movie before school restarts?'

'Yes, I don't see why not,' Crump obligingly informed Morgan.

'It's good to see Peter and Judy are still at least talking to each other,' Terry remarked.

'Yes, it is, I'm glad there is no bad blood,' said Ronald not really caring one way or another.

'Who is this guy she has got down near her school?' enquired Terry.

'Someone called Cecil,' Ronald told him.

Both of them then went into a fit of laughter at Judy McClean's new boyfriend's name. Judy looked sharply across at the two adolescent males laughing, and they both abruptly stopped.

The day came to an end, all the adults by now the worse for wear due to alcohol consumption. Fortunately, none of them had to drive, as they all lived in the same neighbourhood. Even if they did have to drive it would not have presented a problem because the local police were in their pockets. With Christmas Day over Teddy and Megan retired to their bedroom, as did Ronald, with the day's secret firmly on his mind. Teddy acted as though nothing was wrong, and Megan never suspected a thing.

The rest of the festive season passed without incident. Peter Tillerson appeared to have recovered from the disappointment of his break-up with Judy, spending more time down at the gymnasium preparing for his next junior boxing bout. Ronald and Terry spent much of their time in each other's company while James and Susie became increasingly inseparable. Within the time it would take to have a long yawn the holidays were over and the 8th of January, the day of return to boarding school, was upon them. Ronald was to catch a flight at 9am and Teddy had instructed the chauffeur to be at the front of the house at 6am. His luggage was loaded into the limousine for transportation, and Ronald took up his position in the rear seat. Teddy shook hands, wishing his son good luck, while Megan gave him a loving kiss on the cheek.

'Take care, darling,' she said with affection.

'Yes, good luck, son, remember to write,' his father added.

With that it was off and away to the airport. During the flight to California, Ronald reflected on his first few months at Bishops Court Rise boarding school and concluded these thoughts by determining to do better in both science and swimming.

Ronald arrived back at the school at about four o'clock in the afternoon. There had been no lessons that first day as students were returning in batches, depending on how far they had travelled. He got back to the dormitory and lay down on his bed. Suddenly the door flew open. It was Christopher back from Texas. The two lads shook hands, genuinely pleased to see each other. They briefly exchanged stories about the Christmas break, swapping experiences and trying to outdo each other as to who got the best and most expensive presents.

'I'm going to take swimming for two of the games periods with Spitz,' Ronald informed Christopher.

'I was thinking along those lines myself, still am in fact,' Christopher replied.

'Go on, Chris, it will be great, the two of us, we can encourage each other.'

'You've talked me into it, Ron,' Johnson told his roommate. 'Let's go and see Atkinson before the first games period.'

That would not be until Wednesday under the new changed timetable, and the two would-be Olympic swimmers decided they would approach Atkinson together. The impression these two were giving was that a momentous decision had been taken of such magnitude the entire future of the Olympic movement might depend on it. They would present a united front to Atkinson. The truth was, the chances of the games teacher saying no were remote, to say the least. The swimming class was crying out for young participants, so they were both certain to be accepted.

The following morning the two boys rose early and agreed something of such importance could not wait until Wednesday. They would approach Mr Atkinson that morning. They set off for the games teacher's office and knocked on the door. 'Come in,' a voice beckoned.

'Sir,' Ronald addressed the teacher, 'we would both like to take swimming as an option during games if that is OK?'

'Yes, no problem lads, I'll see Mr Spitz. Just bring your kit on Wednesday and you can go along with him.'

'Thank you, sir,' they both said, and with that headed off in the direction of the main building.

The school had three swimming pools, all Olympic-sized. The first was just a pool with a maximum depth of two metres. The second pool was the same length with a three-metre spring board and was generally for the fourth- and fifth-form students. The pool itself had a maximum depth of five metres. The third pool, again the same length, was reserved for the sixth-form students who had taken swimming as one of their three specialist subjects, and who were also doing high diving. This pool had diving platforms of five metres and ten metres with a maximum pool depth of ten metres. Ronald was already a competent swimmer as his mother had taught him back home in the family's private Olympic-sized pool located in the grounds of the house. Christopher also enjoyed similar facilities at their large mansion in Texas.

The first lesson proper for Ronald on Tuesday morning was science. Following this was ninety minutes of fantasising over Madeline Copley in French class, as he still had his crush on the teacher. With the morning over and math and English completing the day in the afternoon, it was back to the dormitory and revision.

Wednesday morning could not arrive quickly enough for the lads as it was their first day with Mr Spitz. Both were eager to impress this national icon. The former Olympian entered the pool area looking lean and fit. The class consisted of ten students. *Just enough*, Ronald thought, *to leave plenty of room in the pool for us all to swim properly.*

'Right, let's see who's who and what is what. I want you all to do five lengths of the pool, if you can. Should you get into difficulty do not hesitate to let me know. There is no shame, lads, just indicate if you're having problems.'

'He sounds great, Chris, treats us like human beings instead of monkeys as Atkinson does,' said Ronald to his friend.

Crump and Johnson completed the five lengths as did most of the class except two who were flagging after three lengths. However, even though the two boys completed the task, they were both out of breath.

'It's a long way, isn't it Ron?'

'Too right it is. Does this mean we are unfit?'

'No lads,' Spitz interjected. 'This is a long pool and I just wanted to see what you are all capable of.'

With that the ninety minutes were over and the gallant duo got dried, dressed and headed for the geography class.

The weeks flew past at Bishops Court Rise and before they knew it the spring and summer months were upon them. Ronald achieved his goal in science by bringing his marks up to A+, the same grade he received in English and math. He was pleased with himself. Both Christopher and Ronald were also excelling at swimming and Mr Spitz was happy with them both.

Most of the term was incident-free and all were looking forward to the long summer break, having got past Easter and all the religious ceremonies and symbolisms which accompanied it.

Both Ronald and Christopher's overall exam results were very good. They reflected the marks given, certainly in Ronald's case, in his school report, which Megan and Teddy were very satisfied with.

6

The Kuwaiti Desert

It was now July and summer was well and truly upon the whole country. Megan Crump was speaking on the telephone to whom she thought was her secret lover, Derek. Her adulterous affair had been known to her husband since he eavesdropped on her the previous Christmas and he was playing it to the full. Megan had no idea Teddy was in any way alerted to her little carry-on and she thought to herself that if he ever found out she would deny the affair. She would then voice her suspicions about his flirtations with young females at work, abusing his position as an industrialist and the power he had over his staff. Unbeknownst to her, Teddy was once again listening to her conversation, as he had on many occasions over the last few months. Neither of them considered for a moment that Ronald had his own suspicions that his mother was 'screwing around'. Ronald had no proof but what he witnessed that Christmas certainly aroused his curiosity.

Teddy was listening intently to every word his wife said to her lover.

'Yes, I think he'll be working late on Thursday, we could meet for coffee and then go back to your place,' Megan said.

Crump gently returned the receiver to the call position, as he did not want any suspicious clicking to give the game away. Teddy had decided that on this occasion Megan would not be making her rendezvous with Derek. In the past he had allowed two liaisons to go ahead simply because he had something planned with either his secretary or his PA. On this occasion, though, he would put a block on his wife's little game. This would prove who was really calling the shots, because that was how he liked it.

It was Wednesday morning and Crump was in his office, which was unusual for him as he played golf on this day. For a while he pretended to be engrossed in a pile of paperwork. Then he summoned his secretary, a new girl aged about twenty-three he had not tested out yet, and informed her she was needed for some shorthand and other dictation.

'How is your boyfriend, Sandra?' he asked, when she sat down opposite him. He knew full well the girl and her partner had split up. 'When are you getting married?'

'Don't talk to me about that waste of space, Mr Crump,' the secretary said. 'I couldn't care less if I never see him again.'

'Must be lonely on your own,' the arms dealer probed.

'Yes, it is a little,' she said giving Crump an encouraging grin. She was on the rebound and Crump knew it.

'Would you like a drink before we start?'

'Thank you, Mr Crump, I'll have a Tequila Sunrise.'

'Expensive tastes,' said Crump. On his way to the drinks cabinet Crump leaned over and patted his secretary's rear.

'Why don't you lock the door, dear?' he said.

'Mr Crump, what kind of girl do you think I am?' she said, getting up and putting the latch on the office door.

★ ★ ★

Crump arrived home around six thirty.

'Are you home, honey?' he called.

'Yes, in here, darling,' Megan replied.

'Darling, I need you to come to a convention with me tomorrow. I know it's short notice, but I need you there. You're not doing anything, are you?'

'No dear,' she lied, 'Nothing at all.'

Teddy knew this to be a lie but this was exactly the reaction Teddy wanted. It was true that a convention was going to take place but normally nobody of Crump's standing would be present; it was generally for the lower management.

'Do you really need me there, dear?' she asked nonchalantly.

'Oh yes. It's of the highest importance – we both need to be present.'

'Very well, then,' Megan said, gritting her teeth. 'I'll be by your side.'

Crump knew when they both arrived at the event, the lack of importance of the mini-convention would automatically tell Megan she had no need to be there at all. She would, however, not dare complain in case her secret came out. Megan then left for the bedroom, checking Teddy did not follow her, and phoned Derek.

'He wants me with him tomorrow, darling, a damn nuisance I know, but I'll have to cancel our date.'

'Don't worry, dear. We'll arrange it for another day. You do what you have to do.'

Of course, Teddy was listening in to this conversation and it was all he could do to stop himself from bursting into laughter. Here was a man who knew his wife to be having an affair and was turned on by it. In reality it was not the affair which turned Crump on, it was the knowledge that he had the power to dictate when events would or would not happen, and even for how long.

★ ★ ★

Hugh and Mary Rothschild had invited their expected future in-laws, the Carters, to a candlelight supper.

'How's Susie doing at boarding school, Moira?' Mary asked of Mrs Carter.

'She's doing fine, Mary, coming on excellently in cookery lessons, and in mathematics she has top marks.'

'Well that's great, math is the subject every businessman or woman will need. I'm sure we are all in agreement on this one. We keep emphasising to James the importance of math.'

All this was just small talk when the real subject was their children's future together and what amount of manipulation would be needed from themselves. The cook had made a lovely supper for the company beginning with mango and pear, followed by lightly poached salmon and finishing with pineapple and cream. After the meal they retired to the study for drinks.

'I think,' said Mary Rothschild, with an air of sensibility which was a novel occurrence, 'that we should not interfere too much in the personal side of their relationship. There appears to be a lot of chemistry present already and when the time comes, I imagine they will need little encouragement in the bedroom department.'

'Too right', roared Jimmy, a little worse for wear after half a bottle of the best cognac. 'Won't take much for your James to—'

'Jimmy, shut up,' Moira interjected swiftly. 'I think Mary is right. The chemistry is already there and we should let nature take its course there, unless there are any major bust-ups, which I can not envisage happening. We should concentrate on the financial aspects and, naturally, benefits to ourselves,' she concluded.

'That's right, Moira,' Hugh Rothschild agreed. 'When Jimmy merges his business with our financial empire we shall be worth collectively, on present figures and estimations, around ten billion, including all assets from your real estate empire and my bank.'

The four schemers then drank a toast to the future and even bigger profits.

Susie Carter would inherit her father's real estate business, but Jimmy wanted her married to James before such a transfer of deeds could go ahead. He did not trust a young woman to carry out the demanding tasks such a high-powered role demanded.

'She could not play golf or go shooting, could she?' Carter bullishly remarked.

'That's true enough Jimmy, we must get our priorities right,' a slightly drunk Rothschild replied.

They all agreed that 1965 would be a good year to edge the couple towards the church and wedding bells. However, despite all the chemistry and genuine love between James Rothschild and Susie Carter, the brigands would manage to besmirch this natural flow. By the time the wedding came about their relationship would have been relegated to that of a financial arrangement. If the brigands had a modicum of practical intelligence outside that of finance, Susie and James could have gone on to enjoy a normal loving marriage along with all the financial considerations and benefits. Because their own marriages were shambolic they expected those of their children to follow this abysmal road.

★ ★ ★

Duke Tillerson had placed advertisements in every newspaper, local and national, to aid his recruitment drive for tradesmen and labourers for the big Kuwaiti contract. The advertisement was attractive and aimed mainly at single men:

MEN WANTED FOR WORK OVERSEAS
TRADESMEN, LABOURERS and SEMI-SKILLED 2+1 GANGS
CARPENTERS & ELECTRICIANS, PLASTERERS
GOOD RATES OF PAY, THREE YEAR CONTRACT, 50% EXPENSES PAID
APPLICATION FORMS AVAILABLE FROM D. TILLERSON & CO.

For those not familiar with the building trade, a 2+1 gang equals two bricklayers and one bricklayer's labourer. A bricklayer's labourer was paid significantly more than a general labourer as were plasterers' labourers. Tillerson was looking for 2+1 gangs. They had to keep two bricklayers supplied all day with bricks by use of a carrying hod. A good labourer was also looked after by the bricklayers, who were often on bonus on top of the wages received from the company. Usually bricklayers and their labourers travelled in gangs from site to site; it was very much teamwork. Tillerson Construction Ltd had been flooded by applicants for this apparently lucrative employment in Kuwait. Tillerson had left the interviewing to his local managers and personnel departments while he sorted out which supervisors he would choose. He wanted slave-drivers for this job, foremen who cared nothing for health and safety and who put the company's profits over and above all other concerns.

Tillerson selected ten foremen and one general site foreman, Ben Thompson, to cover the work. He would be over in Kuwait himself, as he wanted to meet with Mr Abdula while there to examine the possibility of more contracts for his firm. Tillerson was aware of penalty clauses written into the contract and for this reason he wanted his hardest slave-drivers as foremen. No time should be lost; they were already behind schedule, but thankfully there was a little latitude on this. Tillerson did not want any of the clauses invoked and the foremen knew if this were to happen, thus costing Mr Tillerson money, it was their heads which would roll. Duke wanted as much of the four million plus which remained after tax to be solid profit. No penalties incurred was the order of the day.

It was early July and Peter would not be home from boarding school until the beginning of August for the summer break, so Duke said Sheena could come with him for a short holiday. Fortunately, she did not drink excessively as the laws on alcohol in Kuwait were very strict. Overseas workers could drink only on the compound where they resided. However, because Tillerson's men were building accommodation for workers who would be working on the rig, they themselves stayed in low-standard hotels, which Tillerson & Co had paid for. However, in these establishments alcohol was out of bounds. The company also paid for the workers' flights out to Kuwait but if they wished to return home early, they had to foot the bill themselves.

If the workers wanted to stay in one of the very few hotels where limited alcohol consumption was tolerated, they had to pay for it themselves. As these hostelries were few and far between they were also very expensive. Some had toyed with the idea of risking drinking, but having found out the penalties were severe if caught, decided against the idea. To make matters more teasing for the construction workers, they were to build a social club, complete with bar for the future inhabitants, who would be employees of Mega-Oil.

In sharp contrast to his employees, Tillerson and his wife stayed in a five-star hotel in Kuwait city, financed by the Kuwaiti government. Sheena was to stay for the first two weeks of July and then head home for Peter's return for the vacation. In this hotel limited alcohol consumption was permitted during certain hours of the day, and strictly in the hotel. As Sheena could take or leave a drink, she was little bothered by these restrictions. Duke, however, was a drinking man and a bar nearby was mandatory. The Tillerson couple arrived by chauffeur at the hotel and Duke decided he needed a drink. Unfortunately the bar was closed, as it was outside the permitted hours.

Sheena explained to her husband, 'It might be a good idea not to drink at all, darling. You know what you're like if a hair of the dog can't be found. A bear with a sore head does not come into it.' This was sound advice and Duke knew it. If he got pissed he would need a 'cure': better not to start than be unable to stop!

'Yes, you're right, dear,' the building tycoon agreed. 'Better leave well enough alone.'

The couple took their belongings up to their room and relaxed on the bed. Placing the 'Do Not Disturb' notice outside, Duke and Sheena enjoyed the afternoon immensely.

The temperatures were in the nineties and after the couple's antics they both needed a shower. Tillerson then phoned his supervising foreman and arranged a meeting at ten o'clock the following morning, before the job began. When Tillerson arrived on site, the temperature was already soaring, and he gave his site foreman explicit instructions.

'No slacking, any man not pulling his weight is on the next flight home, out of his own pocket. By the end of the day all the men should be here. There will be no fucking around. They start tomorrow seven o'clock sharp. I'll be on site myself a lot of the time to keep an eye on things, and when I'm not, you, Thompson, are my eyes and ears. Do you understand me?'

'Yes sir, perfectly, Mr Tillerson,' the subordinate replied.

The following morning the men gathered on site. Because Tillerson wanted to save on wages he had merged the separate jobs of machine workers and labourers. Thompson stood on the steps of his office issuing

Tillerson's orders. The sub-foreman had their instructions and carried them out accordingly.

'Now,' said Thompson, 'get started on the foundations. Why are those machines idle? Get them operational now!'

The machine operators/labourers started trawling the ground for the foundations of the oil workers' compound.

'How fucking deep are you going with those foundations? There's no need to go too deep, takes too much time,' Thompson bawled.

'But—'

'No buts, if you can't do the job you shouldn't have said you could. If you don't want to be on the next flight home, do as I say.'

The machine operator kept his mouth shut and followed the foreman's instructions. He knew the foundations were inadequate and would last no more than five years, but Tillerson wasn't bothered about that. Three years' life expectancy would do. After that his warranty was up and he could not be sued. Besides, the oil barons would not care a shit about their workers' living accommodation – all they were interested in was the amount of black gold in barrels per day that could be extracted.

The heat was scorching, and the men were dehydrating, so a makeshift canteen had been hurriedly constructed, providing water and sandwiches for lunch. Mr Thompson realised he would have to make small allowances for the men to take water outside their normal lunch break. This thought broke Thompson's heart; it would cost the firm time and he was on a two per cent commission if the job was completed on time. 'Let the men have a fifteen-minute break halfway through the morning. No longer, mind. We are making nothing in profit on this job, it's more of a favour for the Kuwaiti government,' he lied.

By the end of the week the foundations were dug, not as the contract had specified (that would have taken too long), but this work would be out of sight. Out of sight out of mind was Thompson's motto, and once building above ground level began, a viewer would have the optical illusion of a good job having been done. If the Kuwaiti government's site agent had taken the trouble to come on site at the start and surveyed the work, he would have seen the inadequacies and certainly would not have certified the substandard construction job. As it was, he wasn't bothered and passed the work without looking. This had cost Tillerson, via Mr Abdula, a few grand ensuring the site agent would not be over-observant, but it would be worth it

Thompson constantly complained to the sub-foremen who were well and truly sick of listening to him. They were not, after all, on a commission and had no idea how much Thompson was on. This was a closely guarded secret known only to Tillerson, Abdula and Thompson himself.

It was now the second week in July and Sheena Tillerson was preparing to leave Kuwait. Tillerson had decided to remain for the duration of the first stage of the work. He wanted to ensure the correct corners had been cut and weaker-than-specified materials were used. Where they could get away with it, watered-down concrete was used and one coat of paint applied when two were specified. He could do this in the full knowledge there would be no visit from the site agent until completion. By then all the inferior quality work would be hidden from the naked eye. With Sheena out of the way, Tillerson would be on site to bully Thompson who in turn continued to terrorise the men.

One morning Tillerson arrived on site dressed as a worker so that only Thompson and a limited number of employees knew it was him. He found a man who was taking a break from the blistering heat.

'What are you doing, idling, are you?'

'What's it to you?' the unsuspecting man asked.

Tillerson just stared at him.

'What are you fucking staring at?' the worker said.

That was his death warrant. Tillerson charged into Thompson's office.

'What are you doing with the men? Who do they think they are, cheeky bastards, lazy no-goods? I want that man off site in five minutes,' he shouted.

The foreman, quaking in his boots, went to the man and told him he was dismissed forthwith under Mr Tillerson's orders. The man knew there was no point pleading to Thompson's better nature; firstly, he did not have one, and secondly even if he had, the order came from Tillerson. The man collected his gear together and made his way back to town, and luckily, he just about had his airfare home. The rest of the men tore into their work like their lives depended on it which, in many respects, was the case. They all agreed, rather than stand together, that Thompson was quite right, that the bloke was a lazy bastard and frankly should have gone weeks before.

If the site inspector had actually turned up, Tillerson and his gang would have been sent packing on the first day of their so-called construction.

★ ★ ★

Sheena Tillerson arrived back in New York to give instructions to Mabel, the head domestic, who held the same position as Betty over at the Crumps. She told Mabel what was needed for Master Peter's room when he arrived in a week's time for his vacation.

'Now Mabel, I want you to clean all the paintwork down and wash all the bedding. I also want you to have all the windows in the house cleaned, designate as you see fit, but make sure they are done. If any member of staff voices any complaints, remind them the orders came from me and I won't stand any insubordination,' the mistress demanded.

'Very good, madam, I'll see to it. Leave everything with me and don't you worry about a thing. The young master must be well looked after and want for nothing, I'll see he doesn't, madam.'

Mabel was only short of offering her soul to the devil if the young master demanded or performing cartwheels in the garden if he wished – anything to please the Tillersons.

★ ★ ★

In the searing heat of Kuwait, Duke Tillerson took it upon himself to personally supervise on site. He wasn't used to outdoor work, or come to it, any physical work at all, but felt he could not leave this to Thompson alone. There were so many corners being cut and so much to hide from the Kuwaiti governmental authorities that he felt his presence was needed. Even though the site inspector had been paid well to keep away until the closing stages of the work, there was no law against the authorities coming for a look themselves. That was Tillerson's worst nightmare: somebody not in the script coming along and interfering.

'Thompson, come here,' he roared.

'Yes sir,' the site manager dutifully responded.

'I'm going up to the office. You take personal charge and make sure the men don't slack and also don't let them mix the concrete strongly. Water it down wherever possible. Remember, your two per cent depends on how much we can save.'

'Very good, Mr Tillerson, sir,' Thompson replied.

Tillerson climbed the steps to his makeshift office, which was as hot as an oven. The phone rang just as he sat down. It was one of his senior directors in his textile business back in the US.

'Duke, you have to get back here,' was the urgent message from George Cleveland, one of his directors. 'We have a major problem.'

'Well sort it out, man. You're management and in my absence you have, along with the other four board members, ultimate power,' was Tillerson's response. 'What is it anyway?'

'I think this is outside our remit. It will need all the board and you as leader and managing director to sort it.'

'Look, George, it's so hot here I have sweat pissing out of me and you phoning me about some problem in one of my factories,' the frustrated chief responded.

'If that were all, I wouldn't be bothering you, but the situation is that all of your factories are involved. They are all demanding trade union recognition. They say they have certain demands and will go on strike if we don't meet them. We've tried the carrot and stick approach, threatening dismissals then even offering a small pay increase, but the staff will not have it. You must come back.'

'Fuck it, if I must I must, but I'm telling you if I come back there and it is a small problem after all I shall be less than happy,' Duke growled.

Duke Tillerson summoned Ben Thompson and told him he would be away for a few days.

'Something's cropped up back home,' he told Thompson. 'You are in sole charge while I'm away. If anything, and I mean anything, goes wrong, Thompson, you will be on the next flight home. Do I make myself clear?'

'Yes sir, crystal,' replied the site manager, wiping fresh beads of sweat from his brow.

Back in New York, Tillerson's textile employees in all his factories, which were spread across several states, were demanding trade union recognition. Tillerson had dealt with a similar problem on some of his construction sites and had got over it by courting corrupt union officials and allowing tradesmen to become members, but forbidding his unskilled employees the privilege. The problem this time was that the trade union involved, the United Textile Workers Union, was militant and incorruptible. Their officials had been accused on more than one occasion of being in the 'pay of Moscow' of which there was no evidence, and not even tainted lies could be brought to bear to support these allegations. The UTWU was a large trade union which represented workers across the United States. They were aligned to the American Federation of Labour, a body similar to the Trades Union

Congress in Britain or the Irish Congress of Trade Unions in Ireland, and could call on support from other unions also affiliated to the AFL. New York was a state where the UTWU was not as strong as in other states. They were trying to change this state of affairs. A number of Tillerson's employees had approached the union with a view to joining as a body. They had not had a pay increase for a number of years and were sick of Tillerson cutting corners on health and safety, thereby putting their lives in danger. There had already been a disaster in one of Tillerson's other factories, costing some workers their lives. The workers had been blamed in a sham enquiry which resulted in a massive insurance pay-off for Tillerson. They feared such a scenario was in the waiting again and this time they were not going to carry the can; they were determined to have strong representation.

The workers had meetings at the Michigan, Kansas and the two New York factories, as well as with the dyeing and specialist plant in Nebraska. The staff had held meetings with UTWU officials and workers were queuing up to join the union. The directors had tried the carrot and stick technique to control the situation, to no avail. They had offered a three per cent pay increase and the formation of a 'works committee' consisting of management and selected workers representatives to meet quarterly. The committee would have no right to strike or order a work to rule; in fact, it was absolutely powerless, which was the object of the exercise from the management's point of view. This joke was rejected by the staff out of hand: they wanted to be represented by the UTWU and elect their own shop stewards. These were their demands and no imitation committee would suffice. In fact, they told the directors in no uncertain terms what they could do with their 'committee'.

As we know, when the news reached Tillerson in Kuwait he was not a happy man. He had never really had serious insubordination in the past; no worker or group of workers would ever dare. Tillerson then took his anger out on Thompson, which almost gave the man a heart attack. It would not have bothered Tillerson if his site manager had dropped dead on the spot. He could always find another mug! This, back home, on the other hand, was potentially serious and needed nipping in the bud. This kind of communistic disobedience would not be tolerated, and he would soon sort out these Moscow stooges.

At all costs he would keep the news of this domestic mutiny back home from his Kuwaiti paymasters. He wished he had the power the government had in this country, he could have men publicly flogged for less. Tillerson explained on the phone that this behaviour would not be tolerated and if these troublemakers valued their jobs they would stop this union silliness forthwith and he, Tillerson, would say no more about it.

'Duke, we've tried all that and more. They are adamant. It's union recognition and ten per cent or strike action and pickets will commence. The UTWU are backing the workers all the way,' said Cleveland on the other end of the phone.

'Fuck it, George, I'll be back by the end of the week. I'll sort these troublemakers out once and for all. '

George Cleveland doubted this but was not going to argue. He would await the chief's arrival with anticipation.

By Thursday, Tillerson was back in New York.

'Now, what the hell has been happening in my absence? I have arranged meetings with senior Kuwaiti officials regarding more contracts in the construction game. If these commies put me in a bad light out in Kuwait, I'll swing for them,' the besieged chief said.

'Well, Duke, the other board members said in agreement that we will probably have to recognise the union – at least that way we can try and limit the damage they can inflict on us.'

This was the board's way of solving the problem, but it was not, certainly initially, Tillerson's.

'No fucking commie is telling me what to do. I don't care if they call themselves trade unionists or not, they are all in the pay of the Kremlin.'

This of course was pure fabrication; if the union had been in the pay of Moscow they would have had much more clout than was the case. They would be taking their instructions straight from Khrushchev and the Kremlin direct.

'The staff have given us until the end of the week to respond to their demands, after that a strike will commence at all our factories and plants,' they informed their leader.

Tillerson began to see the impossibility of the situation he was in. He would have to buy time, at least a week to cobble together some con trick. That should not be difficult. They were, after all, only machinists and easily replaceable. He would arrange a meeting for the following week in New York inviting delegates from all his factories and plants to discuss their differences.

'Put a circular out, George,' he told Cleveland. The circular went to all factories and the dyeing and specialist plant informing the staff to send delegates, paid time off as a concession, to the meeting.

'Well, Duke, they will want their union representatives to do their talking. They have already signed up to the UTWU to a man,' George Cleveland informed his chief.

'What!' bawled Tillerson. 'You mean I have to talk to these communists before I've agreed to recognise them?'

'That's right, I'm afraid so,' said Cleveland.

This was not going to be the walkover Duke Tillerson had in mind. He was used to speaking to his workers as one would address a dog. This time he was dealing with his intellectual equals, in fact betters, as these union officials were well versed in their roles. Hitherto Tillerson, like Crump, had not needed to use a high level of intelligence when dealing with employees. These times were changing.

News of the problems being faced by Tillerson reached New York's other brigands, including Teddy Crump. They all demanded a meeting with Duke to discuss the situation and how it might affect themselves and business in general. They all met in the large City Hall on the Friday evening. Crump, Rothschild and Morgan were present, not as friends of Tillerson's but as concerned businessmen. As we know, these people were never proper friends in the first place and an incident like this brought to the surface the simmering detestation they all had for each other. Tony Smallman, a competitor of Tillerson's, but on a much smaller scale, having just one 'pocket' factory on New York's East Side, had already had dealings with the trade union in question. Duke Tillerson was reluctant to ask an inferior operator for advice but saw little option in this case. He would not, under any circumstances, treat Smallman as an equal, and was determined to make it appear the rival was privileged to be speaking to a man of his importance. Smallman employed around three hundred machinists and embroiderers along with finishers and dyers. Tony Smallman Quality Clothing Limited had had dealings with the UTWU and found, much to Smallman's surprise, that although the meetings were not exactly cordial, they were certainly not belligerent. The union had given him advice about his health and safety measures being inadequate, which he attended to. All in all this saved him a lot of money in fines, in case a factory inspector ever visited. Unlike Tillerson, Smallman did not have the inspectors in his pay; he was not a large enough operator for those tactics. He had reached an agreement with the union lasting for five years regarding pay and also a facility time agreement for his factory convenor to carry out his union duties properly. He also saw the benefits of dealing with one of three shop stewards on local issues which was leading to a better, more relaxed working environment. Although he initially had problems with the union, these difficulties were not as prevalent as he first thought. The union reserved the right to take strike action if management failed to live up to their commitments and, likewise, Smallman could expect productivity in return for higher pay. This system is sometimes referred to as pluralism as a mode of industrial relations, representing dual power.

At the City Hall a packed bourgeoisie and petty bourgeoisie sat to hear Duke Tillerson outline his plan for the UTWU. Before the meeting started, Tillerson summoned Smallman to a private audience.

'Tell me, Smallman, how did you deal with your bunch of troublemakers?' he asked.

'Well, I went in with a superiority complex which, I must admit, was a big mistake. These fellas are not dudes, Mr Tillerson. They are experienced negotiators, so underestimate them at your peril.'

'Are you telling me these commies have an intelligence level equal to mine?'

'That's precisely what I'm telling you.'

Tillerson pondered. 'In your case, what kind of demands did they make?'

'A decent pay rise, which I could afford, and improvements in health and safety, which saved me a fortune should the inspectors have called. Of course that won't—', at this point Smallman stopped short of accusing Tillerson of being corrupt. He was going to say 'won't affect you as they are all in your pay', but for the moment thought the better of this.

'So, if you were me, you'd listen to them as equals?'

'Yes, most definitely, Mr Tillerson,' Smallman advised.

'And I could do a deal with this union rather than have a strike?'

'Possibly, if you go in with an open attitude,' the small operator replied. 'Look, tell me to mind my own business if you wish but you asked my advice so here it is. When was the last time your staff had a pay increase? From what I've heard, some of them were burnt to death in an accident from which you escaped scot-free; in fact you received a huge insurance claim while blaming your staff.'

'How dare you speak to me like that, you little shit! That accident was all the workers' fault, as the court of enquiry found in my favour.'

'You know, and I know, Mr Tillerson, that court was a farce, a fucking joke, everybody knows it but just daren't say so. You know you paid the judges off like you pay everybody else who gets in your way.'

'Fuck you, get out of my sight,' the chief brigand told Smallman.

But Smallman stayed sitting in the chair looking at him calmly, and it was Tillerson who grumpily got up and left. He entered the hall and sat at the head of the room on the stage along with Crump, Rothschild, Morgan and several other leading New York businessmen. Tillerson told the audience that he was being bullied by the agents of the Soviet Union and would not stand for it.

'Come on, Duke, that's all well and good for the newspapers but not us. The union are no more agents of Moscow than are you,' a leading automobile dealer said from the floor. 'We want to know how you intend dealing with this threat. They are, after all, only plebs. What have they got to put up against our combined might?'

After a brief consultation with the quiet and wise Rothschild who sat next to him, Tillerson replied. 'I'm going into the meeting with an open mind, a mind willing to talk and we will see what happens.'

'Very well, but if you go under through your inability to put these dudes back in their box, you are not taking the rest of us with you, get that straight,' was the consensus from the floor.

Tillerson was acutely aware he had to keep this dispute out of the nationals. He must prevent it escalating and news reaching Kuwait where, hitherto, more construction contracts might be waiting. This must be kept out of the national news at all costs. He told Rothschild and Crump he intended to do a deal with the UTWU next week, granting recognition and a pay increase. He could not afford a long strike and pickets at his gates, or any bad publicity. Crump advised his so-called friend not to endanger the rest of the city's business establishments, or Tillerson would be in more serious trouble. Rothschild listened and said little, but later took Tillerson to one side and suggested he should ignore the 'mouth on a stick', referring to Crump, and follow common sense.

'If you need advice talk to me, but I'll tell you for nothing, if you think these union fellas are stupid I strongly recommend you think again,' he urged Tillerson.

The meeting took place as arranged the following Wednesday with Tillerson asking for union agreement not to talk to the press. This the UTWU agreed to, suspecting Tillerson had a reason for this, a weakness they might exploit. Bill Haywood, chief union negotiator, had a deep suspicion of Tillerson's attitude and his apparent willingness to meet the union at all. He would have liked to delve deeper, but time was not on his side. However, he decided to push for extra concessions on the back of the press blackout. He knew his adversary had something to lose by the media finding out what was happening. Why was a man, usually eager for any publicity, so desperate for a media blackout? All might come out through the process of the negotiating machinery, Bill thought. He had no idea of Tillerson's involvement with the Kuwaiti contract; if he had, the cards would have been stacked greatly in the union's favour.

The negotiations began on the understanding, by both parties, that a media blackout be put in place. The trade union side, with members of Tillerson's workforce in attendance, fired the first salvo: a minimum of ten per cent increase in pay. Bill Haywood and his team, in consultation with the workforce, argued that the workers had had no meaningful pay increase for more than five years. The way the company were carrying on it would be thought the year was 1929, the time of the Wall Street Crash, and not 1960. In real terms each year with no increase in pay, allowing for inflation, represented a pay cut.

The union chief continued: 'In real terms these workers have suffered pay reductions for a number of years as inflation is running at seven per cent and the company have, reluctantly, given pay awards of three and four per cent. This equals a pay reduction over a two-year period of, calculating all the figures, seven per cent.' In addition to this, the union side demanded that on top of the ten per cent they would be looking for two dollars per hour extra on the basic pay of the lower grades, thus bringing them in line with national rates.'

Duke Tillerson, George Cleveland and the company representatives glanced at each other.

'We cannot possibly contemplate anything near your claim. We were considering two per cent for the higher paid grade and one per cent for the lower graded employees. This is all the company can go to,' Tillerson apologetically claimed. He then threw another spanner in the works by insisting this be linked to productivity.

'You mean the machines that were over-producing to a dangerous extent, which was what caused the fire previously and which the workers were blamed for, for not following procedures – you want them to produce more! This was rubbish and you knew it, Mr Tillerson,' Bill Haywood stormed. 'Perhaps our friends in the press might like to hear the truth,' the union boss continued.

'We had an agreement, no talking to the media. Are the union going back on their word?' asked Tillerson.

'That was before you insulted your workers' intelligence, to say nothing of ours in the negotiating team. You also besmirch the memory of those workers who lost their lives in the fire. If you want to maintain a media blackout put something sensible on the table,' Haywood concluded.

It was agreed the negotiations would break off for lunch to give both sides time to cool down.

'No communication with the press?' said Tillerson with an element of panic in his voice.

'Not for the moment,' the union agreed.

Outside the negotiating rooms the press, local and national, had gathered, hoping for a report from both sides. This would not be forthcoming. Despite UTWU's anger with Tillerson for his measly offer they would be good to their word: no communication with the press. Duke Tillerson, seeing the press, stayed inside the building. The union team and Tillerson's workers headed for a hotel opposite the City Hall for lunch.

The meeting reconvened at 2pm and the union side expressed an off-the-cuff opinion that if they had reached no sensible agreement by the end of the working day the press might make up their own story. This possibility, which showed Tillerson's naivety at negotiating, prompted the management side to come up with a more realistic approach. They agreed to recognise the UTWU as the trade union of their employees' choice and would also recognise their elected shop stewards. Tillerson hoped this would soften up their pay demand and make them more open to a small increase. He was wrong. This union team were skilled at what they did and stuck out for the ten per cent and two dollars per hour on the lower graded workers' basic pay.

'Mr Tillerson, ten per cent for this year is not unreasonable, with a pay increase above that of inflation for the next five years. This would only put our members at your factories in line with comparable work nationally.'

Tillerson asked for a short adjournment to discuss the union's demand. The union agreed. Half an hour later the management side returned with an offer. Tillerson stood up and put the cards on the table.

'Eight per cent for this year with one dollar on the hourly rate for the lower grades. We can discuss the next five years on a yearly basis.'

This was nearer the union's demand but they wanted ten per cent; anything less would not bring the workers at Tillerson's in line with the national pay scale.

'We agree to the one, instead of two, dollars on the lower grades basic,' Haywood said, 'but we cannot budge on the ten per cent. If we can't get agreement on this the strike, which we have a mandate for, will go ahead. Pickets will be on the gates from 7am on Monday.'

Tillerson knew this would make the national press and this he could not afford. He did not want his potential paymasters in Kuwait thinking he could not handle staff relations, as they might then consider him unreliable.

'Very well, ten per cent and one dollar on the basic of the lower grades it is.'

'Plus union recognition for the UTWU,' insisted Haywood.

'That is one dollar net per hour, Mr Tillerson, not one dollar gross,' interjected Elizabeth Flynn, another of the union team. Sensing weakness, she threw in another claim on behalf of the women workers. 'Due to the biological differences between women and male employees, we want a special concession time for women of a certain age to deal with problems only they experience with no loss of pay.'

Surprisingly Duke Tillerson agreed to this on top of the initial claim.

'We will put this offer to the workers with a recommendation of acceptance. Our shop stewards will deliver the result to you on Monday, Mr Tillerson,' Haywood explained.

As promised, the union put the offer to the workers. This was the first time the newly appointed shop stewards had organised anything, and it would not be the last. They urged employees to accept, which they did. Tillerson was less than pleased but he could now give a glowing statement to the press about being a considerate employer who could handle disputes without the workers resorting to strike action. This would reach Kuwait and he would be seen as a reliable contractor whom they could depend on. The trade union side also put the deal across as 'a victory for common sense and fair play'.

Duke Tillerson arrived home with his chauffeur and kissed Sheena on the cheek.

'What a day,' he exclaimed. 'I'll be going back to Kuwait on Monday, dear. The red-hot temperature of that country will appear pretty cool after this.'

7

An Eventful Vacation

1960 was a presidential election year in the United States. Teddy Crump was a republican and, in the past, had given sizable funds to the Republican Party. He considered himself to be part of the often-termed 'religious right', self-convinced that God was on the side of the righteous and the bourgeoisie and intended the vast majority of people to be less well off than the ruling class and therefore compelled to wage-slave for them. Crump, however, had been rethinking his political position in light of the Democratic Party's new young dynamic candidate, John Fitzgerald Kennedy. Dwight D. Eisenhower, the soon to be outgoing president, had been good for the United States – meaning good for US business – but Crump liked Kennedy's position and apparent harder line with the Soviet Union.

Crump was no expert on the murky world of US politics, but he did know that like in business any candidate who wished to gravitate to the White House had to be a good and consistent liar. The same rule applied to any successful businessman. The Republican incumbent vice-president Richard Nixon appeared to Crump a little wide open when it came to telling lies. Kennedy had told the population, wrongly, that the Soviet Union had overtaken the USA in the atomic arms race, which was a blatant lie. The Republican incumbent, President Eisenhower, could have countered this lie by telling the electorate the truth that the USSR had not surpassed them and the USA was still in front. The truth was that after a certain number of atomic weapons, even back in those days, had been reached, their destructive power would have been so great that any warheads above this number were largely irrelevant. Eisenhower should have told the electorate the truth, which would have taken the wind out of Kennedy's sails. He didn't. The question was, why not? It would have been in the Republican Party's interests and those of their candidate, Nixon, for this lie to be exposed.

Perhaps the arcane reason it was not made public could well have been to do with not letting the USSR know the truth. Providing their Cold War enemy believed themselves to be ahead in the arms race, they might ease off production, believing themselves to have the superior numbers of warheads. It could give the Soviet Union a false sense of security by underplaying the size of their, the USA's, nuclear arsenal, implying they were behind the USSR. This was done by Hitler prior to the outbreak of hostilities, who actually overstated the size of Nazi Germany's arsenal, making his potential enemies reel in shock. For reasons best known to the US establishment and the security family of the CIA, NSA and FBI, this tale spun by Kennedy was told and believed. As in most liberal democracies, then as now, it is better to win an election on a pack of lies regarding foreign policy, thus diverting the electorate's attention from important domestic issues like working-class poverty, unemployment, absence of a health service and poor economic growth. Keep the population in a state of semi-terror, and for the government of that time, it served well to cite the USSR as the permanent threat and bogeyman.

Teddy and Megan Crump were waiting anxiously for their son to return home for the long summer vacation. The domestics had his room freshened up and the chauffeur was waiting at New York International Airport for his arrival. Ronald arrived, exiting the arrivals lounge with his case, which the chauffeur eagerly removed from his person to save the boy unnecessary labour. As the car sped through the city, Ronald noticed all the election posters. For a moment he thought of making conversation with his driver about the election but decided against it. He did not want the chauffeur getting the idea that he was Crump's intellectual equal, certainly not in politics. Besides, Ronald had not yet formulated an opinion on who to support, but did not want the driver to be aware of this.

At last the vehicle pulled into the driveway at the Crumps' mansion. Teddy came to the door to greet his young heir apparent.

'How are you, son?' the tycoon greeted Ronald with a solid handshake.

'I'm great, Dad,' Ronald enthusiastically replied.

Megan greeted him with a kiss on the cheek and a maternal hug accompanied by regulation tears. The domestics were lined up to pay homage to the young messiah's safe homecoming.

'Well, well, Master Ronald, how you've grown,' said Betty. 'You must have grown a full six inches, praise the Lord.'

Ronald Crump paid no attention to Betty's exaggerated deliberations and, ignoring the woman's attentions and praisings of the Lord, brushed her aside and accompanied his parents to the study. This was systematic of the way servants were treated in the United States, especially the black domestics who, five years after the Rosa Parks stance in Montgomery, were still regarded little better than a domestic pet.

Ronald rose the following morning just after eight and headed to the kitchen for breakfast. Both his mother and father were already at the breakfast table. Betty tried to serve him his cornflakes, but he pushed her away.

'Go away and annoy somebody else,' the spoilt teenager rudely told her.

'Now Ronald,' Megan said, 'where are your manners?'

Ronald paid no attention to her.

'Where are you going today, son?' Teddy enquired.

'Thought I'd go and see Terry and Peter, no point bothering with James as he's only got eyes for Susie these days,' Ronald replied.

'Well, before you go anywhere I have some lessons for you,' his father said.

'But Dad—'

Crump Senior had designed some lessons on 'figure transformation and manipulation' which, he felt, would be a compliment to his son's natural ability in mathematics.

'No buts, this is non-negotiable. One hour every morning before you go out. It's very important. You'll see why as we progress,' the tycoon told the youngster.

'All right, Dad, I suppose it's for the best.'

'That's the ticket, son, you'll thank me for this in years to come.'

Ronald and Teddy finished their breakfast and retired to the study for the hour-long lesson.

'Well it's like this,' Teddy began, 'we have two rows of figures but only one do we declare for tax. We take the lower of the columns, add them all together and go to the nearest hundred thousand. Now the trick is, son, we want the figures to be such that the nearest hundred thousand is at the lower rather than the higher end.

'For example, if we add all one lower column up and they come to $144,000 we submit $100,000 for tax, thus saving $44,000 evading tax. We then place this windfall into the other higher column which are the profits for the year. On the odd occasion we must go to the higher ten thousand, for example, the figures come to $147,000 meaning on the rare occasion this happens we submit $150,000 as that is the higher ten-thousand. Note, son, when it is to our benefit, and there is no need for you to share this information with your teachers, we go to the lower one hundred-thousand. However, when we must go higher we submit only to the nearest ten thousand. Do you see?'

'Yes, I think so, Dad. Does it mean we save $44,000 on the first set of figures but only lose $3,000 when we have to go to the nearest ten thousand?'

'Yes, I think you are getting the picture.'

'Is this what they call "cooking the books"?'

'We never use that term, son, neither do we say tax evasion. Only if any questions are asked, say it is tax avoidance. Normally nobody asks questions, providing the returns are regular and reasonably consistent, always remember that.'

'Thanks, Dad, I will, and this is between us two?'

'That's right, Ronald.'

'I won't say a word to anybody, not even Christopher.'

'Especially Christopher, he has no need to know,' Teddy told his protégé, guessing Harry would be having a similar talk with his son at some stage.

After the conversation Teddy continued teaching his son until the hour was up.

'That's all for today, then. Off you go to your friends, son.'

Ronald called Terry.

'Great to hear from you, Ron! Come on over,' Terry enthused.

Ronald's friend was also happy to be home for the summer break and was also raring to go out and have some fun. When Ronald arrived at Terry's house he suggested paying James a visit.

'What do you reckon, Terry?'

'Not much point, he's obsessed with Susie Carter, they're inseparable. He won't be back with the gang,' Terry said. 'In fact, the gang is no more as Peter, since he split up with Judy, is only interested in boxing. I reckon Judy dumping him had a much greater impact on Pete than he would ever admit to, and I for one am not going to push the issue with him.'

'See what you mean,' Ronald said. 'But a call would do no harm, just so he knows we have not forgotten him.' Such sentiments were uncharacteristic of Crump, perhaps it was a kind of insurance policy for some unspecified later date.

Terry agreed, and the pair headed off to Peter Tillerson's house. On arriving they rang the bell and Sheena, Peter's mother, answered the door,

'Peter,' she called, 'your friends are here.'

Peter greeted his friends as he ran down the stairs to the foyer. He was dressed in training gear.

Terry asked if he would like to hang out with them.

'Not really, lads, I'm going to the gym, training for a fight. It'll be on just before we go back to school. Do you want tickets?' he asked.

'Thanks, Pete,' both Terry and Ronald said, voicing their appreciation.

The three of them chatted for a few minutes about this and that, and then the gang of two headed off.

On the edge of the billionaires' paradise were the houses of the 'petit bourgeoisie', or the small business class, which although not in the same league as the Crumps, Rothschilds and Morgans of this world, were all reasonably well off. These were the shopkeepers, artisans who had small building firms, doctors and dentists. A few miles further down were the sprawling estates of the working class, the proletariat who were forced to sell their labour power to the likes of Crump for as little as he could get away with paying in wages.

Ronald and Terry never ventured that far away from their own area, where they were a little unsure of the terrain. Crump, after the self-inflicted fight with the two black lads, had shown how much mettle he had in a fight: less than impressive.

However, these two fancied some fun but not in the 'badlands' where the working-class gangs ruled supreme. Mr Boardman owned a small hardware store as well as a seasonal fruit stall which he kept stocked with apples and strawberries from his garden. This small concern supplemented his daily income, and every Saturday during the summer he erected his stall outside the store. He grew some of the finest apples in the area and Ronald decided along with Terry they were going to relieve him of a few of them. They climbed the outer wall of the garden and from the top, about five feet, they shook apples from the trees.

Suddenly there was a shout from the house.

'You there, yes you two, stop that!' Mr Boardman shouted.

'Fuck off, get back to your shop,' Terry Morgan yelled back.

Ronald stayed quiet, not daring to shout anything. He lacked any form of fibre when any risk, no matter how small, was involved.

What these two did not know was that Boardman had called the police, who were there in minutes. Ronald felt something grab his feet, similar to the day at school when Jefferson caught him trying to escape for the first weekend.

'Come on, you two rogues,' the policeman said.

Mr Boardman had come around to the front of the house and was waiting by the patrol car for the officers to apprehend the two 'thugs'.

'Rest assured, sir,' one officer told Mr Boardman, 'we'll take these two down to the station.'

'Thank you, officers,' Boardman replied.

The policemen had no intention of taking Ronald and Terry to the police station. That response was reserved for crimes committed by working-class kids, not the children of the elite. Instead, the police took the boys back to their respective homes.

'As it was a minor misdemeanour we did not really want to respond to the call but, as it was from the small business area, we thought we'd better,' the policeman said to Teddy Crump. 'There will be no charges, Mr Crump. Just make sure you tell him not to do it again.'

A similar conversation took place between the forces of law and order with Mr and Mrs Morgan. Neither Teddy Crump nor Bradley Morgan had any intentions of reprimanding their offspring. It was, after all, only stealing apples. Anyway, who did Boardman think he was, calling the police? *Damned cheek of him*, both entrepreneurs thought. Both Crump and Morgan really did believe the law was not for them and that the police were there to protect them and only them, the ruling class.

Ronald Crump had started taking an unusually strong interest, for a lad of thirteen, in politics. The reader should remember that families like the Crumps did not bring up their kids in the same way as working-class parents did. From the day Crump was born he was to be moulded to rule both politically and economically. Teddy was delighted his son was taking an interest in politics and wished he had done the same at an earlier age. Ronald listened to the debates involving the two presidential candidates, Richard Nixon and John F. Kennedy. He was interested to find out if either of them would discuss any of the things his father had taught him, especially economics. He was to be disappointed. Neither man was sufficiently knowledgeable in the subject to discuss it in a sensible way.

Whoever won would have advisers in the civil service to deal with such issues, as both had little knowledge about politics; they were, after all, only standing for president. Kennedy appeared to speak of nothing else other than what he considered a threat from the Soviet Union and communism. This was a position endorsed by Teddy Crump, whose fear of the working class was one of the few genuine aspects about the man. Teddy Crump was supporting the Democratic Party candidate, Kennedy, breaking with Crump tradition. He argued this man's hatred of communism and aggressive attitude towards the USSR was what the USA needed. The Republican Party nominee, Nixon, on the other hand, had failed to put forward any realistic economic policy, as Crump saw it. He had said nothing on increasing profits and legislating against trade unions and greedy pay increases.

Ronald asked his father to explain his anti-communist position, which Crump senior was only too happy to do.

'Communism is an evil ideology, or set of ideas,' he explained to his son. 'It advocates free health for the entire population, but never tells us who is to pay for it. Well I can tell you son, we are to pay. We are the ones who have worked hard to build up our business and benevolently provided employment for these people. We are to pay for their health if the commies ever get their way. If they think they can take money off us to pay for the health of some low-life, they can think again. The communists of the so-called USSR are hell-bent on destroying our freedoms and benefits which we, the capitalist class, have engineered for the provision of everybody. They have only one end, son, and that is to take over this great country of ours either through invasion or ideologically. We must strengthen our defences against this rising tide of communism and Mr Kennedy is about that.

'It's all very well that the communists talk about full employment and housing for all, but they never tell us it will be at our cost. They brainwash working people into believing in something which is against everything God intended. That is why we must know the story pertaining to religion so as we can encourage the poor to stay poor – that it's God's will. We must make sure they continue to believe the tale! Now do you see, son?'

'Yes, I do, Dad. If any of those communists try to take our wealth I'll fight them.'

'No need, son, we have an army to fight for us. They are our army, which is why all officers of senior level come from wealthy families. The population only think they are there, like the police, for everybody. They are not, and if any demonstrations get out of hand at home we have the National Guard to batter them to keep order.'

'It's good to know we are safe and those Soviets cannot get near us. Most of the poor people believe in us, don't they, Dad?'

'Yes, son, that's the beauty of our system. We control everything, including information.'

'That is why you want Mr Kennedy?'

'That's correct. Mr Kennedy is getting the message across both at home and in Moscow better than Mr Nixon.'

During Teddy's lecture on the merits of capitalism against the horrors of socialism and communism, young Crump was forming the misconception that when his father said 'their army' and 'their police force' he really meant 'Ronald's army' and 'Ronald's police force'. Though these erroneous thoughts would eventually give way to reality, and young Crump understood that when Teddy spoke of 'their army' he was actually speaking of the bourgeoisie or capitalist ruling class, Ronald Crump would always retain a certain arrogance on such issues. Such arrogances would, in the distant future, come back to haunt him.

As we are aware, Ronald Crump was brought up by a father who held very racist and misogynist views. These negatives of the immediate post-war years leading into the sixties gave rise to progressive movements against sexism and racism as people, particularly from within the black community, began to take action. During the sixties, the decade we are presently at the dawn of, organisations such as the Black Panthers came to the fore and individuals like Malcolm X and Dr Martin Luther King began street orations against inequality and racism. Feminism also began to take a more public and proactive stance as the actress Jane Fonda took part in many progressive movements, particularly combating the war in Vietnam.

Teddy Crump hated these organisations as his sexist, racist and xenophobic views spewed out of his mouth on a daily basis. Ronald's mother, Megan, though perhaps not sharing the extremities of her husband's views, did little to contradict them. Teddy Crump's opinions had a great effect on Ronald, as seen with the incident when he and his mate at school picked on the two younger black lads in the town.

Most of the US ruling classes held similar views to a greater or lesser extent; they were employers and it was in their interests to maintain racial segregation if for no other reason than to prevent workers' solidarity. The racist views preached by them had the desired effect on many, though not all, white working-class males. They avoided any communication, let alone solidarity, with their black counterparts. Teddy Crump was a microcosm of what his son would become!

★ ★ ★

On a beautiful day in July, Megan Crump took a cab to downtown New York, and waited in a trendy café for Derek to arrive. Megan still believed her husband knew nothing of her assignations. Her husband not only knew exactly what was going on but, due to his eavesdropping, was furnished with the knowledge that today's little encounter was going ahead and at what time. Crump was playing his wife for his own amusement and was going to gatecrash today's rendezvous when the right moment presented itself. Crump had decided his wife was leaving the café with him, and not with Derek.

Megan sat nurturing a coffee when the door opened and Derek entered. Teddy was watching proceedings from a safe distance. Megan and Derek greeted each other with a kiss and talked for a short while. They had almost finished their coffee and were about to go back to his apartment when Teddy walked in.

'Hello, darling,' said Crump, pretending to be surprised. 'What a coincidence to see you here.'

'Yes it is,' said Megan, barely hiding her shock.

Crump made some silly, barely believable excuse as to why his presence in the café came about as his wife tried to explain why she was there.

'This is Derek, we once worked together in banking,' she explained. 'Derek, this is my husband Teddy.'

'Nice to meet you, Del, you don't mind me calling you Del, do you?' said Crump.

'No, not at all, Ted. Is it all right for me to call you Ted?' Derek retorted.

Megan went on to say they had met by accident, which Crump pretended to believe.

'We were just saying goodbye before going our separate ways,' Megan said, blushing despite herself.

'No worries, I can give you a lift, Del, if you wish. I'm parked over there. It's not out of my way.'

'Uh – no, it's fine, thank you. I have to be elsewhere and only popped in for a coffee and bumped into your wife,' Derek said as he hastily stood up.

Teddy Crump offered his hand and shook hands with the banker.

After Derek left, Crump turned to his wife. 'Well, darling,' he said, 'we should be getting home if we are to beat the traffic.'

'Yes indeed, dear,' said Megan, trying to put on a fake smile.

The pair got into the car and Teddy struck up conversation. 'Seems a nice guy, honey. So, he's an old acquaintance?'

'Yes, I've known him a long while, as I explained. He was my former boss,' she said.

'I bet it was one of those boss–clerk relationships,' joked Crump nastily, almost describing his own relationships with his female members of staff.

'No, not like that, Teddy.'

'Sorry, darling, just making light conversation,' Crump said.

Teddy then suggested she invite Derek to supper some evening.

'Yes, that would be nice.' Megan was feeling increasingly uneasy with every passing moment.

The following morning Megan phoned Derek. 'We'll have to cool it, darling. Yesterday was too close for comfort.'

'That's right,' Derek agreed, 'too darned close. Are you sure he knows nothing?'

'I'm beginning to wonder,' confessed Megan.

Crump was at work, so he definitely had no knowledge of that particular conversation. However, he knew so much he could probably hazard a reasonable guess that a conversation along these lines would take place between his wife and her lover. As it was, the couple agreed to put a hold on things for a while, but in reality Megan was thinking of ending the whole affair. She did not relish forfeiting her lavish lifestyle, as Derek could never match Teddy for financial muscle and could not hope to keep her in the lifestyle she had become accustomed to. So, after considerable reflection, and in spite of reassuring Derek she would contact him when the heat was off, she decided to call it a day and break off all contact with him.

★ ★ ★

The long summer vacation was coming to an end and Ronald Crump had experienced his first brush with the law. He had also found out that laws pertaining to working-class kids did not apply to him so there was little need to pay any attention to them. It was the final week before school and as Ronald prepared for his return to Bishops Court Rise and the start of his second year, his thoughts drifted back to his French teacher. He still had feelings of lust for her and, equally, the need for revenge. This he would address in the coming years as one day an opportunity would eventually present itself. That future event would be another milestone for Ronald on his journey towards becoming a soulless, devious and despicable man.

8

The 1960s, Invasion, Crisis, Assassinations and Teenage Blackmail

It was September 1960 and Ronald Crump returned to his studies at boarding school. It was a new year, the last he would be sharing a dormitory with Christopher. His thoughts wandered again in the direction of his sexy French teacher and what he should do about her boyfriend, Mr Atkinson. The fact was, there was nothing he could do unless an unforeseen opportunity came his way. For this unlikely chance he would have to wait.

He arrived back at the school gates where the security guard gave his chauffeur-driven car the usual once over before opening the gates. He took his gear to the dormitory and lay on his bed. It had been a long journey, even though it was classified as a domestic flight. Christopher had not yet arrived back at the school but Ronald knew it would not be long before he would come rushing through the door.

As if to script, after about half an hour his roommate arrived. With boyish excitement the pair started swapping experiences about the long vacation. Ronald got in first with his brush with the law and how he had sorted two officers out with the minimum of fuss. This greatly exaggerated version of events had Crump forcing the officers to give Mr Boardman, the man whose garden he had been raiding, a good telling off for causing trouble. He then explained to a disbelieving Christopher how he warned the two police officers that if there were any repercussions of their behaviour the men would be relegated to directing traffic when he had a word with their commissioner.

For his part and not to be outdone by Ronald's fanciful tales, Christopher Johnson had his own experience to tell. Like Ronald Crump, the telling of a truthful story was beyond Johnson, and to say it was another exaggeration of the event was an understatement. According to Christopher, he and some of his friends, who were all from the same business class as Ronald, were in downtown Dallas. Suddenly a group of native Americans and some lowlifes started trouble with them. Christopher and his pals told the townspeople not to worry; they would sort this out for them. Christopher then told the tale, a very tall tale.

'They came down the main street, a big mob of them, and me and the guys were having none of it. I said to them, "Look here, you are a conquered people so start acting like it." One of them said something I took offence to, so I walked over and smacked him right in the jaw. Well, that was it, the rest of my gang were in on my command and the natives scattered.

'The townspeople were very pleased with us and one recommended me for a commendation. I explained my honour at the thought but had to turn it down.'

When Ronald had told his pack of lies Christopher had believed none of it but pretended to express an interest. Ronald Crump was now repaying the compliment to Christopher and let him rant on, pretending to be impressed. The reader will be aware of the truth surrounding Ronald's story but not so with Johnson. It was true Christopher and his friends had been downtown, but not in Dallas, nearer a small township about half a mile from the billionaires' row where he and his mates lived. A group of Hispanic lads were minding their own business with their girlfriends when they came across Christopher and his gang. With an attitude of superiority Johnson made an offensive remark about one of the girls in the Hispanic crowd. Her boyfriend took offence and gave Christopher a thick ear and a kick up the behind. Johnson and his mates ran away as fast as they could for fear they may receive a right hiding.

When he got home, Christopher was exhausted and almost dying of fright. His mother calmed him down as he told her how he'd been attacked for no reason by some Hispanic boys. As we can see, the reality of what occurred was a far cry from the versions expressed in both cases.

It may be necessary to clarify to the reader what is meant by 'Billionaires' Row'. Back in the late fifties and sixties billionaires were actually few and far between. Teddy Crump via his business enterprises was one such person as was Harry Johnson, Christopher's father, from Texas. However, it was true to say everybody living in what was termed Billionaires' Row were extremely wealthy. Some were multimillionaires and others mere millionaires, but few had reached the status of billionaire. This would change as the sixties gave way to the seventies but at the moment in time we are now at, the early 1960s, the billionaire club was still small. Hugh Rothschild had reached this status along with Crump. Duke Tillerson had been knocking on the door to get into the club when the 'unfortunate' accident occurred, killing some workers in his textile factory. The insurance payout received by Tillerson for the tragedy, plus the profits from Kuwait, secured his place in the club. Perhaps a more appropriate title for this exclusive luxury housing area would have been 'Brigands' Row', as all these people's wealth had been gained through exploitation of the labour of others.

The year moved rapidly and before an eye could be blinked it was nearly the end of the year. John Fitzgerald Kennedy, much to Teddy Crump's delight, won the presidential election, greatly though not exclusively, on lies. Nothing new or old there. Teddy sent Ronald a letter informing his son of the result and emphasising Kennedy would be the man to sort out the commies. Christopher Johnson received a message from his father expressing similar sentiments to those of Crump. Time would prove these two mega-brigands' assumptions about being hard on the USSR to be perhaps not as well founded as first proclaimed! Ronald and Christopher both believed themselves to be experts on the subject of US politics, despite having not a notion outside what their parents had told them.

As the year drew to a close, the school term was so far pretty uneventful at Bishops Court Rise. Christmas came and went in much the same fashion as previous years. It was the dawn of 1961 and concern was mounting over the tiny island of Cuba. In 1959 Fidel Castro's revolutionary forces commanded by communists such as Che Guevara had overthrown the right-wing dictator Fulgencio Batista, who had been an ally of the USA. The revolutionary government on the island of Cuba was swinging further into the communist camp with its ideology and had recently nationalised certain United States economic interests, banks, oil refineries (one of which was owned by Harry Johnson) and sugar plantations. The government of Fidel Castro had also closed child prostitution establishments, playgrounds for elements among the US wealthy, hitherto under the dictator Batista allowed to function albeit with a blind eye turned.

This 'unreasonable' behaviour by the Castro government was causing much concern within the ranks of the US bourgeoisie. A plot was hatched by the CIA to invade the island using, as combatants after training, former Cuban propertied classes. These men, who had fled after the revolution, would fight along with US military advisers and hardware. The invasion, which became known as the Bay of Pigs, took place in mid-April 1961, about two weeks after Ronald's fourteenth birthday. Teddy and an increasingly ruthless Ronald were delighted at this plan to put the communists in their place but were to be disappointed. The Cuban revolutionary forces repelled the invasion within two days to the annoyance of the United States bourgeoisie and government. Crump had hoped for a massive arms contract had the invasion been successful and was seething that this would not be. So too was young Ronald.

'Nuke the fucking place,' was Teddy's advice, forgetting that even if somebody was mad enough to carry out this loony suggestion, Cuba was a mere ninety miles off the coast of Florida.

After this failed attempted invasion, Cuba began talking directly to the Soviet Union, eventually becoming an ally of the USSR and declaring itself socialist. So much for Kennedy 'sorting out the communists'. They were now nearer the USA than ever before. Back at school, Ronald and Christopher, whose father had lost a small fortune after the nationalisation of his oil refinery, were discussing what the USA should do about Castro and, given the chance, what *they* would do! Much of these discussions were, of course, adolescent dreams rather than practical ideas but, in Ronald's case, one day these dreams would potentially become reality.

What neither father of these two apprentice brigands ever mentioned was that Fidel Castro, Che Guevara and Raul Castro to name but a few had put an end to the blatant exploitation and sexual abuse of children on the island of Cuba. Regarding the industries in Cuba that were formerly owned by the USA and from which profits were gained through exploitation, these properties now belonged to the Cuban people, where profits began to be shared ethically. Of course, it would not, then as now, be in the interests of the bourgeoisie to even contemplate this avenue of thought and the offspring of these brigands would grow up in the same mould, greedy, selfish and ruthless.

Just before the Bay of Pigs, Ronald Crump had his fourteenth birthday. His thoughts often drifted back towards Miss Copley. On the one hand he had neither forgiven nor forgotten the incident when, in his opinion, she humiliated him and he still felt that she should suffer for that crime. On the other, he fantasised over her. Many teenagers of this age fantasise over their female teachers and in most cases that is where it stops. In the case of Ronald

Crump these fantasies were becoming misogynous and would grow stronger. A potentially dangerous state of mind was beginning to formulate inside his head. Had anybody known or even suspected what he was thinking he might have been sent for psychiatric treatment. However, Ronald was a very devious and close-minded person; his father taught him well in this respect, so nobody knew. This situation would develop over the coming months and years.

On the other side of the planet Soviet leader Nikita Khrushchev was on his vacation beside the Black Sea. He told an aide, pointing with his stick in the general direction of Turkey, that the USA and NATO had nuclear missiles based there aimed at the heart of the USSR.

'This is a situation I can't allow to continue,' he said.

The aides looked at each other wondering what the Soviet leader had in mind. They would find out, as would the USA, very shortly.

The year was 1962 and back in the USA Kennedy was enjoying great support for his presidency. He was making all the right noises about catching the Soviet Union up in the space race and was in discussions regarding how to prevent any further US involvement in Vietnam. Khrushchev was planning to redress this unfair balance by placing his own nuclear missiles in Cuba. It should be remembered that all Khrushchev wanted was the US missiles out of Turkey and Italy. He had no desire to set up a Soviet base on the island of Cuba, but he knew that simply asking the USA to remove their missiles would be fruitless. A deterrent was needed, even if a dose of bluff was involved. If he could convince the USA and NATO that he intended to place nuclear missiles and troops in Cuba it would give him the leverage required to force the US to remove their missile system from Turkey and Italy. The events which were to unfold became known as the Cuban Missile Crisis.

As events slowly unfolded and it became apparent that the Soviets were up to something, Teddy Crump, with no regard for national security – his sort never do – was once again thinking about an arms contract. As history turned out, such thoughts were useless because ultimately common sense prevailed, with the USA blinking first, if this is the correct term. The Soviet reasoning for the deployment of missiles in Cuba was to restore the balance regarding deployment. The Cubans wanted the missiles in order to deter the USA from any repetition of the Bay of Pigs the previous year. The whole crisis lasted for twelve days in October 1962.

The result of the crisis was one of sound judgement. US President John F. Kennedy agreed never, without provocation, to invade Cuba. This appeased

Fidel Castro. The Soviets demanded the USA remove their missile-functioning Jupiter missile systems from Turkey and Italy, which the USA agreed to. In return the USSR agreed to remove their not-yet-functional missile system from Cuba, a victory for rational behaviour given the magnitude and potential of the crisis. The two leaders, Kennedy and Khrushchev, agreed to the setting up of a nuclear hotline between Washington and Moscow to prevent any future 'misunderstandings'.

This settlement did not satisfy the hawks within the CIA or, on the Soviet side, the KGB. Arguably the Cuban Missile Crisis cost Kennedy his life the following year. Did the hawks arrange his assassination for backing down, in their eyes, to the Soviet Union? Was the man credited with the assassination, Lee Harvey Oswald, an unsuspecting tool of the CIA? In 1964 Khrushchev was replaced by his former press secretary, Leonid Brezhnev, a hardliner, as head of the USSR. Was this the result of hardliners within the KGB who were unhappy with the settlement? Whatever the case, Khrushchev and Kennedy showed great negotiating skills and good leadership in the face of planetary destruction.

Teddy Crump was scathing over this climbdown to the communists; he had also hoped to make money out of the crisis. Ronald echoed his father's disapproval with curses of Kennedy, accusing the man of cowardice.

'So much for standing up to communism,' he told a meeting of students at Bishops Court Rise, and wrote anti-communist propaganda in the school rag.

These views were reflective of the US bourgeoisie who viewed any compromise, even one which may have saved the planet, as a climbdown by capitalism towards communism.

'Fucking Kennedy, he said he would take a hard line towards communism,' Crump Senior ranted to all who would listen. 'I voted for him on this understanding.'

Ronald repeated his father's rhetoric in the school with some extra hardline statements thrown in.

Ronald Crump was now in his fourth year at boarding school in September 1962. At the time of the Cuban Missile Crisis, he was well settled in to this year. His exam results hitherto had been exceptional in his chosen subjects of math, English, science and his geography had made up ground. The swimming with Mr Spitz was proving a success and in his spare time he built up his skills in photography, using his own extensive camera kit. It would be this hobby which would give Ronald Crump his long-awaited opportunity for revenge on Miss Copley.

One day Ronald Crump met Christopher Johnson in the school canteen. Both students had single dormitories since beginning their third year, and therefore didn't keep each other as updated as before regarding stories or useful information.

'How's it going, Chris?' enquired Ronald.

'Great, Ron,' Chris replied. 'Listen, you still barmy over that French teacher?'

'Yes, you fucking bet I am,' Ronald answered.

Christopher had some vital information for Ronald. 'You know she meets Atkinson every Wednesday afternoon at his office near the gymnasium?'

'No, I didn't know,' admitted Ronald, 'but go on, I'm interested, very interested.'

'The word is that they're both getting it on in that room,' Johnson informed his friend.

'Every Wednesday, you said?' asked Crump for clarification. 'Thanks, Chris, I owe you.' A ghoulish grin spread across Ronald's face.

Ronald Crump decided on a reconnaissance trip to ascertain the validity of his friend's claim. He decided to go to the gymnasium that coming Wednesday at 2pm to see what he could glean. He arrived in the area and waited. Sure enough, the target of his twisted attention, Miss Copley, turned up. Within a few minutes Atkinson also appeared.

Suddenly the games teacher spotted Ronald. 'What do you want, Crump? You have no lesson with me this afternoon so on your way,' he ordered.

'Sorry, sir,' said Crump meekly.

'Get out, I don't want to see you here again with no good reason,' Atkinson continued.

Ronald strongly suspected the couple were going into the gymnasium for sex. He now began formulating his plan for the following Wednesday. A week is a long time when excitement for the following week is anticipated. During the French lesson Ronald never let on what he had in mind, but he could not take his eyes off Miss Copley. Twice he nearly got caught out ogling the young woman. Over the weekend Ronald worked at his photography. He could also do his own developing, a skill he had learned in the science lessons.

Wednesday arrived and Ronald prepared to put his devious plan into action. He headed for the gymnasium around one thirty and found a safe place of concealment. He had armed himself with his state-of-the-art pocket camera, and made sure the sun shining through the window was at his back. His camera was virtually silent so the chances of him being caught taking photos of the courting couple were virtually nil. Right on time at two o'clock Miss Copley and Mr Atkinson arrived, locking the door behind them. They both got undressed and the young woman performed oral sex on the games teacher.

Ronald took his first snapshot. The slight click was unheard with all the moaning going on. This was followed by acts of sexual intercourse which Crump photographed with at least three perfect shots. The couple were at it for about half an hour and Ronald Crump had it all on film. This was going to be his long-awaited revenge for what he considered was the humiliation she had inflicted on him all those years earlier. This was the kind of twisted mind Ronald had inherited from Teddy, his father, with a lot more added on. The couple eventually left the gymnasium and Ronald stayed hidden until he felt the coast was clear. Then he made his escape. Time was no problem as he was on a free afternoon, supposedly for revision.

Ronald Crump took his camera back to his dormitory. He turned his bedroom into a darkroom and began developing the films. They came out perfectly. It was now time for the most devious form of blackmail imaginable, certainly for an adolescent of his age in those times. Ronald Crump waited a couple of days before he approached Miss Copley when she was alone in her classroom.

'Can I have a word, Miss?' he asked.

'Certainly Ronald, what can I do for you?' she replied.

'Quite a lot, Miss, I think you'll find,' said Ronald.

He then produced the compromising photos of her and Atkinson. 'Not bad, Miss. What do you think?'

'I… I… I… where did you get these? I'll tell Bob, uh, Mr Atkinson.'

'I don't think you will, Miss, because if you tell anybody these pictures go in the school magazine and copies to Mr Hardaker.'

The young woman was mortified with these revelations. As she went to grab at the photos with the intent of destroying them, Ronald informed her that he had made copies that he had stored in a safe place where she would never find them. She looked at the young man in shock, disbelief and disgust.

'Why are you doing this?' she whispered.

'You should know, Miss,' Ronald sneered. 'No need to worry, it can be our secret,' Ronald said not very reassuringly. 'All you have to do is come to my dormitory this evening and I'm sure we can come to an arrangement,' he told her.

She saw for the first time how earnest in his evil intentions this young man was. His eyes were cold, heartless. If she said no, she had no doubt that he would carry out his threat and put the photos in the school magazine. If that happened, she and Atkinson would certainly be fired. As she digested this awful information she realised there was no way out.

'Shall we say seven o'clock, Miss?' he said.

'Very well, you little bastard,' she muttered.

What Crump had in mind was nothing short of rape, rape by blackmail. No physical force as such but still no less rape. Miss Copley arrived on time at seven o'clock and Ronald told her to undress. What took place does not need describing only to say that from her point of view it was far from consensual. The young woman left Crump's dormitory in tears. She would neither forgive nor forget, as we shall eventually see.

Ronald Crump now had his long-awaited revenge for, as he saw it, the humiliation bestowed upon him during his first year at Bishops Court Rise. Any sane person of the same or similar age would have forgotten the insignificant incident soon after it occurred, but not Ronald Crump. The fact that Crump allowed a bit of fun at his cost to fester over a number of years must say something about the internal turmoil of his mind.

He decided to let the matter drop, providing she gave him no more trouble. He convinced himself she had deserved what happened. As ever, it was easy for him to conjure up an imaginary story: it was her fault, she fancied him and should never have gone to his dormitory, putting him in a compromising position. He also decided to keep the incident to himself, the others may get jealous if they discovered the young sex goddess fancied him, which she evidently did! Before the next French lesson, he decided to approach Miss Copley to reassure her he would tell nobody about what *she* had done, and that her secret was safe with him!

A pattern was beginning to appear where Ronald would commit a crime against a female and then forgive *her* for what *she* had done. This was obviously inherited from his father, Teddy, and would follow Ronald throughout his life, putting Teddy into the shadow regarding severity until his final demise. Before Ronald Crump would meet his end, many women would be abused, ethnic minorities insulted, racial remarks and actions taken against non-whites, gays and lesbians belittled; in fact, just about every person or group that Crump found fault with would be offended to a greater or lesser degree.

It would shortly be Christmas 1962 and the school would be closing as per usual until the 8th of January. Ronald Crump, now fifteen years of age, was going home for the duration. Teddy had decided it was time for his son to accompany him at minor board meetings; get to learn the ropes, so to speak. Teddy had accepted an application from Matthew and Sally Seddon to become board members and he would put their application, and investment, to the rest of the board at the next meeting. Ronald could accompany him to this decision-making gathering.

Before leaving for the break Ronald armed himself with his exam results which, despite all other distractions, were exemplary. In the subjects of math and English he was out on his own with A++ for both. In science he had an A while in geography he was catching up with a B+. Not surprisingly, French was poor with a C–. Ronald left Bishops Court Rise on 20th of December and was chauffeured to the airport for his flight to New York. During the flight Ronald took a liking to one of the air hostesses, an attractive woman in her early thirties. Fortunately for all concerned as Crump was about to begin his chat-up line – which would have been pathetic – a male colleague of the woman came along and took over.

On arriving home Megan and Teddy were waiting to greet their son with open arms.

'Tell us all about school, dear. How did you get on in your exams?' his mother asked.

'I've done very well, Mom,' Ronald informed the woman who thought butter would not melt in his mouth.

'Let's see the results, son,' Teddy asked.

'Oh Ronald, I'm so proud of you, dear,' Megan exclaimed, on viewing the results and report.

'Yes, well done, son,' Teddy interjected. Teddy then told his son about his plan to introduce him to the board at work.

'What do you think about that, Ronald?' asked the arms dealer.

'Fantastic, Dad, I can't wait,' an excited Ronald told him.

The great day finally came to pass, the last mini-board meeting before Christmas. On the short agenda was the proposal by the chief, Teddy Crump, that Matthew and Sally Seddon be elevated to the status of non-voting members of the board. The couple were prepared to invest two million dollars into the arms side of Crump's empire. According to protocol, Crump was obliged to ask the board for permission for Ronald to sit in. This was merely a formality as nobody would dare object. The agenda settled, Crump then took a vote on the Seddons' application, which was carried. The next step was to introduce the two new board members, who were waiting in the lobby.

'See how it's done, son?' Teddy spoke quietly to his protégé.

'Yes, I'll get the hang of things, Dad,' Ronald replied.

Matthew and Sally then entered the hallowed room and were informed of their acceptance.

'Take a seat,' Crump invited them. The reader may recall Sally Seddon had already prostituted herself to Teddy Crump some time ago with her husband's connivance. She had turned Teddy down at the Crumps' Christmas party, but now, with the promise of further financial gain, she allowed him to flirt with her again.

Wearing a short skirt, she placed herself at Teddy Crump's side while Matthew sat opposite. Crump placed his hand on her leg, which she politely removed.

'Naughty,' she teased him.

The meeting was over within half an hour and the offices were soon to close for Christmas. However, this was not the case for the blue collar employees who had to work up until Christmas Eve.

'Like a drink?' Teddy asked Sally and Matthew.

'Yes, why not,' they both agreed.

'This is my son, Ronald. He will eventually be taking the reins,' he informed the newcomers.

'Nice to meet you, Ronnie,' Sally coyly said.

Matthew echoed the same sentiment.

'Likewise,' replied the budding tycoon.

After drinks and sandwiches the gathering dispersed and the Crumps were driven home by their chauffeur.

'Who was the pretty woman, Dad, the one who called me "Ronnie"?' the youngster asked.

'That, son, is Sally Seddon, Matthew's wife. Why, do you like her?' he asked, sporting a ghastly grin. Teddy had no idea his son was so well versed with this subject.

'Yes, she's not bad, very smart and, well, you know,' said Ronald.

'I see, son, you'll get to know the pair of them better, but why do I get the feeling it is only Sally who is of any interest to you?' Teddy said rhetorically.

Christmas arrived, and all the brigands met at the Rothschilds' house after attending a church service. They sat down for the Christmas dinner at a huge oak table, saying grace and insincerely uttering the words, 'Lord, make us truly thankful'. After the meal was over they began cracking less-than-funny jokes about the cooking, which the cook and domestics had taken great care to prepare and serve. Ronald was allowed a couple of glasses of wine and began engaging Matthew and Sally Seddon in what passed for conversation. Ronald was trying to sneak a look up Sally's skirt, which she was aware of, and she eventually teasingly gave him a quick glimpse.

James Rothschild and his girlfriend Susie Carter were watching events unfold, including Ronald making a fool of himself with Sally Seddon. James and Susie considered themselves aloof from this kind of amateur dramatics and saw themselves more adult-like than Crump, or, indeed some of the actual grown-ups.

'I think it's disgusting. He is acting in much the same way as he did at his birthday party the other year,' exclaimed Susie, referring to Ronald's assault on Colette's friend, Lucy Livingwell. 'This time he's trying it on with a grown woman, who appears to be playing with him.'

James took a philosophical view of the situation, refusing to cast judgement but not disagreeing with his partner. In truth James was a little envious of young Crump, but could not let Susie get wind of that!

'She's old enough to be his mother,' Susie commented with an air of superiority.

'Not to worry, Susie, they'll have all gone soon,' James replied.

Peter Tillerson was present with Duke and Sheena, now in great shape due to his boxing training. He was bored with the whole cabal; in truth, he had not really recovered from splitting up with Judy. He couldn't wait to leave and made his boredom very apparent. He also knew he was to inherit Duke's building and textile empire soon, so tolerance was the order of the day. Bradley and Ethel Morgan were also present. Terry had stayed on at school at Ethel's insistence to save him getting re-involved with Dianna. Ethel was ostensibly a non-drinker but was slipping vodka into her bitter lemon drink when she thought nobody was looking.

If a description could be applied to this festive scene it would be one of semi-drunken sexual innuendos, silly, less-than-humorous jokes told by persons lacking their mental faculties. Ethel Morgan was monitoring the situation going on with Matthew, Sally and Ronald, principally to ascertain if there could be any gain for her to be achieved. After all, Ronald was only fifteen and this older woman was plainly flirting with him. She was hoping these flirtations would go up a gear and the possibility of causing unpleasantness over it was in her mind. She was, on this occasion, to be disappointed.

The Christmas and New Year period and festivities which accompanied this time of year came to an end and shortly it would be back to school and business as usual for Ronald. On 7th of January 1963 he was chauffeured from the Crump mansion to the airport and his flight westwards. His attitude towards the chauffeur was as rude and ignorant as always, despite his mother's half-hearted pleas to change. He was soon in the departure lounge, having checked in for his flight, and would shortly be on board the Boeing 737 in his first-class seat. Ronald's thoughts drifted back to Sally and he was thinking how he would love to fuck her. She was a teasing bitch, he said to himself. Had a psychiatrist assessed him, the results would show that Ronald Crump was clearly showing all the warning signs of being a danger to women. The aircraft taxied and then launched into flight. A little while later along came the air hostess with drinks and other refreshments.

'I'll have a white wine, please,' said Ronald chancing his arm.

'No, you won't, you're far too young,' the woman replied. 'Now behave yourself.'

Ronald took this as another affront to his manhood, as he had in the French lesson three years previously at school. The difference here was he was not at school but thirty thousand feet in the air. He consoled himself with thinking about Bishops Court Rise and Miss Copley. He considered having another go at her but, surely, she would not take it 'lying down' again, would she? He chuckled to himself and decided not to pursue this train of thought. He had got away with it once, even though it was all the French teacher's fault, so maybe he should just forget about it. Ronald then drifted off into a sleep and did not wake up until his arrival in California.

At the airport his chauffeur was waiting to take him back to school. On his arrival back, checking in at the gates, he collected his bag from the car boot. The first person he came across was Miss Copley, the victim of his rape by blackmail.

'Hello, Miss Copley,' he sarcastically called out.

'You little shit,' she uttered under her breath.

Whether the young rapist did or did not broadcast the incident would make no difference to the way the young teacher felt; she understandably wished he was dead.

Ronald was in his fourth year and had been advised to consider, in view of his high marks, whether he wished to stay on at the school for an additional year and take a specialist subject. There was no rush for a decision, but Ronald was toying with the idea of real estate. He had plans for his father's business, which would soon be his, and was considering expansion into the property market. He would give this serious thought over the next year and decided he would, at a future date, discuss this plan with his father.

★ ★ ★

Back at the ranch Megan Crump was still enjoying what she thought were secret assignations with her lover, Derek. As agreed with Derek, after the café incident she stopped seeing the banker until she felt the coast was clear. Time had now passed and they both took up where they left off. She still had no idea her husband was aware of what was going on. Perhaps this was a common factor in US bourgeois married life: after all, the Seddons were what today may be called swingers, and Sally had been known to prostitute herself for capital gain. So maybe Teddy's behaviour and attitude towards his wife's games was not so unusual.

As we have seen from Ronald's behaviour towards women, like his father, he was a control freak. Teddy was still having sexual relations with his secretaries and his married PA. None of these women enjoyed their pervert boss's attentions but lived in constant fear of being fired if they refused, believing there was no option but to appease the boss. Crump often made innuendos reminding staff of their positions and caused constant discord and fear among all employees, not just the more vulnerable women in his office. He made it quite clear on more than one occasion that there were certain guidelines for him and a separate set of rules for the staff.

'You lot do as you're told and never question me, and we'll all get along fine,' he often told them.

Teddy Crump was plotting a surprise for his son on his sixteenth birthday, 1st April. He arranged a meeting with Matthew and Sally Seddon with this treat in mind. He was planning to elevate their position on the board from non-voting to limited-voting status. Crump knew he had enough power on the board to outvote all other directors, he had made sure of that, so giving this couple slightly more clout than they presently enjoyed would be no great threat to himself. It must be remembered Teddy Crump had no code of ethics or morals. These words were not in his vocabulary, either at home or in the workplace.

Crump arranged to meet the Seddons, unknown to his wife who probably wouldn't have cared less anyway. Her main interest these days lay elsewhere. The meeting was to take place at the New York Hilton. The trio met at seven o'clock in the bar on the evening of 28th January 1963 to discuss Ronald's birthday treat.

Teddy Crump ordered the drinks. 'Scotch on the rocks for me, and…'

'Dry martini for me,' Sally interjected.

'I'll have a brandy,' said Matthew. With their drinks, the three retired to a plush seat.

'How would you like your positions on the board to be elevated to allowing you both limited voting rights?' Crump enquired.

'Great, Ted,' said Matthew.

'Hold on, what's the catch?' asked his wife, already suspecting something unethical.

'No real catch, just a favour,' replied the tycoon.

'What sort of "favour"?' Sally queried.

'Well, my son's birthday is coming up,' Crump advised them both. 'I have something in mind which he will never forget.'

Sally and Matthew looked at Teddy in silence as he continued. 'I understand the pair of you attend these so-called wife-swapping parties?'

'That is our business,' Matthew indignantly said.

'Not on my board,' answered Crump arrogantly, but Sally saw an opportunity here, a bargaining chip.

'What do you want?' said the young woman.

'I noted at Christmas you and my son were getting on very well,' observed Teddy.

'Yes we were, he seems a bright young man,' replied Sally.

'Where is this going?' Matthew enquired of his chief.

Sally asked the six-million-dollar question. 'In return for these limited voting rights on the board what would be required in return by you, Teddy?'

Teddy Crump then outlined his proposal to the Seddons.

'My son will be sixteen this April and I'd like you to visit him, Sally, in his dormitory at school. They are allowed visitors. All you'll need is identification for the security saying you're his aunt, which I will supply. Then I want you to make a man of him.'

'You mean you want me to sleep with your son, for him to lose his virginity with me.'

'That's about the strength of it,' replied Crump, unaware this had already been done through his son's blackmailing.

'Now hang on, Teddy,' Matthew protested.

'No, wait,' said Sally having recovered from the initial shock. She had hitherto believed it was Teddy who wanted a repeat performance with her.

'Let's talk this over, Matt.'

'Can we have five minutes alone, Ted,' said Matthew.

'By all means,' replied Crump.

The Seddons left and retired to the hotel lobby where they discussed the tycoon's proposal.

'Listen, Matt, we can gain out of this. We should agree to what he wants, perverted as it may be. But we must demand full voting, not limited, rights on the board.'

'OK,' said the ever cash-hungry Matthew.

They returned to Crump and told him their terms in order his request be granted. Crump pondered, or pretended to. He was half expecting this and had contingency plans already in his mind. He could reduce the voting weights of two junior members thus accommodating the Seddons, thereby keeping his overall control. Any opposition would be dealt with in his usual ruthless fashion.

'Very well, you have a deal, full voting rights it is,' said Crump, offering his hand to shake on it.

A little nearer the date he would inform his son to expect a visitor on the evening of his birthday. His 'Aunt Sally', he laughed to himself. The trio departed the Hilton and went their separate ways.

Teddy Crump arrived home to find Megan was not at home. He had an idea where she might be but decided not to act. He wasn't really attracted to his wife any more with all the younger women available to him and, in the future, he was in no doubt Sally would also be available for sex. Why then should he spoil his wife's little fling? She was, after all, handy for social functions: she knew how to behave, and he was at the end of the day in charge of her little arcane activities. No, he would allow his wife to continue her affair, providing it went no further. This way, if ever she found out about his numerous assignations he had ammunition to fire back with.

Back at Bishops Court Rise, Ronald was improving his swimming under the tutorship of Mr Spitz. He and Christopher had been shortlisted as possible candidates to join the team and represent the school in the California State

Swimming Championships. Mr Spitz had suggested to both students that they had a great future in the sport and might one day go on to represent the USA internationally. As much as Ronald enjoyed the sport he, like his father, only viewed life through the lens of the dollar bill, and how many of these could be accumulated. Medals were all very well and certainly prestigious but financially worthless. On these grounds, swimming was never going to be an alternative to the world of corruption passing as big business. All that considered, a long-term future in swimming was a non-starter. However, representing the school might have benefits for his remaining time there.

Back in his dormitory Ronald Crump pondered over what to do when his time at high school was over. He was in his fourth year with one more to go. Would he leave and move straight into business with his father or, providing he could maintain his high grades, stay on an extra year studying real estate and go to university? Long term this was the practical thing to do. He intended to eventually expand what would by then be his business, into the property world. He didn't have to give a decision until after September, the beginning of his fifth and final year, so there was no immediate hurry. He was leaning towards university but would hold fire on a final decision. He would discuss it with his father, explaining the pros and cons to him. He was also aware that Teddy would be well into his seventies by the time he was ready to assume control if he took the longer-term option. Yes, he would talk it over with the supremo. His grades in math and English were excellent and he knew he could maintain these. He was also continuing to improve in Geography as well as science. As for French, fuck that, he thought, then reminded himself he already had, laughing fiendishly at his rape by blackmail antics. This action would come back to haunt Ronald in later life at a time he could do without it.

It was Saturday morning in late January and Ronald was, along with Christopher and other students, heading to town. As they were walking down the main street Ronald noticed a headline on an advertising hoarding for a newspaper: 'CHICAGO GANGSTER TO FACE CHARGES'. He bought the newspaper and read the subheading. 'Infamous Chicago Mafia boss, Benito Lugosi, to face charges of blackmail, three counts of murder, extortion and living off immoral earnings.' Young Crump then made his excuses and headed back to his dormitory to read and absorb the article. He did not wish his colleagues to know of his past childhood friendship with Colette Lugosi and yet he wished to pass an opinion on what was in the paper. When he arrived back at his dormitory he read the article in depth.

'Fucking hell,' he said to himself. 'To think I was friendly with that tart of a daughter of this murderer.'

Firstly, Colette Lugosi was a decent girl, not a tart, and she was not, unlike her brothers, a chip off the old block. She was nothing like her father and bore strong similarities to her mother, Maria. Colette may not have agreed with what she suspected her father was up to but neither would she inform on her family. What Ronald Crump should have remembered was that she saved him receiving a severe hiding from her brother Pedro after his drunken sexual assault on her friend Lucy Livingwell. Of course, Ronald conveniently forgot things when it suited him; he was that kind of youth and would become the same in manhood.

Later, Christopher Johnson called on Ronald.

'Where did you get to, Ron?' he asked.

'I'd forgotten something at school and then fell asleep,' Ronald lied.

'Have you seen these headlines, Ron?' asked Christopher.

'Yes, and I'd send him and his type straight to the chair. They, that Mafia crowd and particularly the Dons, give honest hard-working businessmen like my dad and yours a bad name.'

'Well, put like that I'd do the same,' said Johnson.

To hear these two future brigands talking it would be imagined their parents were honest, fair-minded, hard-working business people. Nothing could be further from the truth. Both Teddy Crump and Harry Johnson epitomised the legalised variant of everything Benito Lugosi and the Mafia Dons stood for. They, the 'hard-working' businessmen, ruled by fear: fear of unemployment, poverty, matrimonial breakdown and in some severe cases, suicide.

Lugosi ruled through fear, the fear of the gun and torture, resulting in death or at least pain, much the same as did Crump and Johnson. It is unlikely that Lugosi would force young women into having sex like Crump did. Crump was not the only 'hard-working' businessman who ruled his employees with an iron rod; most of them did. Whether they all participated in what amounted to forced sex with their female members of staff was open to conjecture.

So, for Ronald and Christopher, wishing this man Lugosi to be sent to the chair was hypocritical at the very least. It must be remembered these were charges aimed at Benito Lugosi by an equally corrupt police force; nothing was really proven. Yet Ronald deemed it fit to pass judgement, more than likely in a vindictive way to heap revenge on Colette for something which happened when they were essentially children. Whatever the case, he knew not to go on about it too long in case Christopher became suspicious about Ronald knowing more about this Mafia family than he was letting on. Ronald then allowed Christopher to do most of the talking on the subject, but one thing was for certain: this vindictive attitude would follow Crump all through his life and would get worse.

Though only fifteen, going on sixteen, Ronald could just about pass for eighteen. He had purchased a bottle of Scotch whisky and offered his friend a glass.

'Thanks Ron, where did you get this?' Christopher enquired.

'I bought it in town but keep it to yourself as we're not supposed to have alcohol. Still, a glass will do no harm.'

The two students then proceeded to polish off most of the bottle, having a drunken conversation on how, if they were in charge, they would tackle crime, especially among the working class. Both agreed capital punishment for most crimes and all murders was the appropriate way to go. If these two teenagers were ever in charge people would be sent to the chair for such crimes as armed robbery, rape, blackmail, cattle rustling and car theft. Christopher then decided to add shoplifting to his list. Both intoxicated youths roared with laughter. If they were in charge the country would be a safer place, that was for sure. The irony was, one day Ronald Crump would be in charge and his views would not have changed a great deal from the drunken variant he was spluttering out with Christopher. He would hold very similar views with a refined vocabulary attached.

Sunday morning dawned. If lessons had been taught on this day, outside of religious studies for those who were interested, Ronald and Christopher would have had problems. Christopher had fallen into a drunken sleep in the armchair while Ronald was lying on his bed fully clothed with a pool of vomit to his left side. The two students eventually came to, but within a short time they both had to run to the lavatory to be sick. This condition was due to the amount of alcohol they had consumed the night before – they were in many respects lucky to be fit and that their bodies could handle the toxins.

The prefect, Grover, called on them as was usual on Sundays to enquire whether they wished to attend chapel.

'Fuck off,' said Christopher, echoed by Ronald.

Grover could smell alcohol and vomit. His suspicions were confirmed by the empty bottle which had once contained whisky.

'What has been going on here?' he enquired.

'We won't tell you again. Fuck off,' said Ronald. They were no longer afraid of prefects as next year they would be eligible for the post themselves if they wished.

The prefect knew better than to hang around and beat a hasty retreat, immediately heading for Mr Hardaker's office. He reported the incident to the headmaster who acknowledged the fact and told the fifth-former to depart.

'I'll deal with it,' he said.

Hardaker was furious and saddened. He was furious at the thought of two students of their ability stooping to this and breaking his rules and saddened by what it might lead to if he did not address the problem now. This he would do, having visited a similar situation in the past. Laying down the law was not the way, not at least for their first and, hopefully, last offence. Tact was the order of the day, tact and advice.

Mr Hardaker decided to wait until the early afternoon before tackling Ronald and Christopher. He calculated, correctly, that by about two o'clock the vomiting would have ceased, and they would be feeling remorseful and delicate. He arrived at Crump's dormitory and knocked on the door.

'Come in,' a timid voice meekly said.

'Now Ronald, what have you and Johnson been up to?' asked the headmaster.

'Sorry, sir, we got drunk,' said Ronald.

'Go and get your fellow drinker. I'll wait here.'

'Yes, sir, I'll be as quick as I can,' Ronald said.

The two arrived back at Ronald's dormitory.

'Sit down, the pair of you,' the Headmaster instructed them. Dutifully they obliged.

'I'm disappointed in both of you,' said Hardaker. 'Have you been drinking long?'

'No, sir,' they replied in unison.

'This was the first, and only time, sir,' said Ronald apologetically.

The headmaster then lectured them both in a calm and rational way about the dangers of alcohol abuse. Not as much was known about alcohol abuse in the early sixties as today, but enough to warrant concern. Hardaker explained, as he had done once before with success, the dangers to their livers and kidneys.

'You are both very young. Your organs are still developing and are susceptible to damage,' he explained. 'You are both intelligent and are achieving good grades. You stand to be businessmen in the future; you are the future of the United States. If you continue like this it could cost you a lot, including your capital and monetary wealth.'

He then reminded them of the school rules regarding alcohol. It was the thought of losing all that money, plus the businesses which their fathers had created, exploiting other people's labour power, only for them to throw away through drinking, which caused most concern. More importantly, it could mean they would reach rock bottom and might have to find employment, thus becoming one of the lower class of people their fathers employed and enjoyed power over.

This thought, above all others, made them both think very hard, and it had the desired effect. This mattered more than breaking silly rules which neither could care less about, and more than the possible long-term damage to their health – these were minor details compared with the possibility of losing their lives of luxury. This was what frightened them both. Mr Hardaker then informed them he would take no action on this occasion but should there be any repeat he would have no choice but to write to their parents advising of possible expulsions.

He then left the room with the parting statement, 'We'll leave it at that.'

'Thank you, sir,' they both said in a grovelling way.

February was a quiet month at Bishops Court Rise. There were no exams for Ronald so it was about improving his geography and science and bringing his grades in those subjects up to his math and English levels. He maintained his position as leader in the two pole subjects but desperately wanted the other two disciplines to reach the same heights. In the swimming both Ronald and Christopher were down to represent the school during the long summer break, if they wanted to. This would mean staying at school for two of the six weeks' break but this thought appealed to both buddies. Ronald wanted some time to discuss his future with his father, but he would not need the full six weeks to do that.

Ronald received a letter from Teddy informing him to expect a visitor on his birthday just over a month from then. Ronald answered the letter outlining his plans for the summer break and enquiring who this visitor would be. Teddy held fire on answering his son's letter; he could wait until mid-March when he would reveal all about his son's surprise. Teddy also thought Ronald's plans for the summer break to be a good idea, and that it would be good for him to represent the school at state level. February came and went and with the blink of an eye it was March.

Early in the month news was broadcast on the television and newspapers of the acquittal of Benito Lugosi. 'LUGOSI FREED', read the headlines. The paper went on to explain how insufficient evidence forced the judge to order the acquittal of suspected gangster, Benito Lugosi. Had Harry Johnson or Teddy Crump been in a similar situation it would have been highly likely the same outcome would have ensued.

On 17th March Ronald received a letter from his father in reply to the memo Ronald had sent home in February.

Dear Ronald

Firstly, I would like to fully endorse and support your decision to represent the school at state level during the summer break. Both your mother and I think it is a brave decision and wish you all the best in the swimming tournament. We are both confident you will be among the medal-winners. We can discuss your future when you land in New York for the remaining four weeks of the vacation and I must agree with your suggested preference to stay on for an extra year studying real estate with a view to studying it in university. I was hoping to step down from the company at around the age of sixty-eight or sixty-nine but can hang on another year or two if we can look forward to an even better future for the company. I think your extra studies will bring financial benefits to the company and we can discuss the details face to face. I will have an agenda for our meeting drawn up.

As I intimated in my previous correspondence you will be receiving a visitor on your birthday around seven o'clock in the evening. That visitor will be Sally Seddon, who will pose as your auntie, so make arrangements for her to see you. She and Matthew will be in the West on business, so she will deliver your present in person. That's all for now son, look forward to our meeting in the summertime.

Dad

Great, Ronald thought, not suspecting for a moment Sally's real reason for visiting him in person.

Ronald had now made up his mind about his future. He was going to study real estate for an extra year, knowing he would need at least a B+ to stand any chance of a place in university. He did not anticipate any problems achieving better grades, so the decision had been made. All he had to do was inform the headmaster, which he would do first thing the following day. Ronald was up at the crack of dawn and went for a short jog before breakfast. He then headed for Mr Hardaker's office to inform the Head of his decision. Hardaker was delighted. The drinking incident was now well and truly behind them and together they completed the forms, guaranteeing Ronald a position for a sixth-year placement studying real estate.

Ronald Crump's birthday came around quickly enough and Teddy had everything planned and ready to execute. The Seddons would travel to California, stay overnight at the Ritz, and travel back to New York the following day. He had arranged for Sally to be chauffeured from the hotel to the school and Ronald's dormitory. On entering the school surrounds, the security would ask her for ID and she would present herself as Ronald's auntie. Sally Seddon was anything but the figure represented in the old English pub game, 'Aunt Sally'. While his wife was playing the seductress, Matthew would remain at the hotel and the whole operation was expected to be played out in about two hours.

Matthew and Sally Seddon arrived at the Ritz and checked in at reception, their reservations having been made a month earlier by Teddy Crump. Then they retired to their luxury suite.

'What are you going to wear, dear?' asked Matthew.

'Nothing, darling,' was Sally's answer.

'What, nothing at all?'

'Well, only this long coat to travel in. It fastens well and will reveal nothing until I decide the time is right,' she explained.

'You mean, Sally, to be chauffeured to the school in nothing but your birthday suit, apart from your coat?'

'Exactly,' she giggled.

Matthew felt a little aroused at the thought of his wife travelling naked, underneath a coat. However, he also had an uneasy sense of apprehension.

Matthew actually had a bad feeling about this entire venture since Teddy first suggested – or more accurately ordered – it, though he said nothing as his wife appeared to be excited by the whole venture. He also was aware of the financial benefits he and Sally could accrue with full voting rights in Crump's empire, so he kept his mouth shut. He could not help thinking that this was different from when he and his wife had conspired and prostituted her to Teddy in return for a head start for her husband's gun club with new rifles leading to financial gains. It was also a departure from the wife-swapping parties they attended when consenting adults were all in the same building with different partners other than their own.

What they were undertaking here were uncharted waters, a journey into the unknown in many respects. All the same the arrangements were in place and Sally did not appear in the least bit bothered.

'Right, I'm going. Wish me luck, darling,' said Sally.

'I can't believe you're wearing nothing under that coat of yours,' exclaimed Matthew.

Sally opened her long coat, revealing her nakedness.

'Satisfied?' she said.

'Jesus, you're not kidding, are you?'

'I never joke where money is concerned. You should know that, dear,' his wife replied.

She securely buttoned up her coat and departed for her chauffeured transport to the school and Ronald's dormitory. Her prearranged chauffeur was waiting and Sally, wearing black stilettos, got into the car. She was careful not to reveal anything to the chauffeur (mustn't let him get any ideas!); his job was to drive and nothing more.

'To Bishops Court Rise school,' instructed Sally.

'Yes, madam,' he replied. On arriving at the gates, the security guard asked for ID.

'I'm Sally, Ronald Crump's auntie. Here is my identification,' she said, producing her passport.

'Very good, do you know where to go? It's Number 16 on the second floor,' the guard advised her. This was all a formality, as Ronald's aunt had been expected.

On leaving the car Sally was careful to keep herself well covered until she got to her destination. She knocked on the door and young Crump answered.

'Come in, Sally. Dad said something about you and Matthew being in the area on business, and that you would be giving me a present.'

'Well, not strictly true, Ronnie,' Sally said, slowly removing her coat to reveal her curvy body.

'Holy shit!' exclaimed Ronald, his jaw almost touching the ground.

'What are you waiting for, a written invitation, Ronnie?' Sally said seductively.

Back at the hotel Matthew sat in the bar, periodically glancing at the clock. The time seemed to be going backwards as his head filled with apprehension and worry. Perhaps he should have considered the possible consequences of these actions instead of dollar bills. He ordered another large scotch and soda to calm down.

At about nine o'clock a distraught Sally left Ronald Crump's dormitory shaking, and more than a little afraid. Ronald had gone further than she had wanted and would not stop. There had been no tenderness or foreplay that one would expect from a virgin male. Of course, this was because Ronald Crump was not a virgin: he was a cruel blackmailer and rapist. Of course, Sally and for that matter Teddy knew nothing of young Crump's previous sexual encounter, let alone the circumstances surrounding it.

Sally got in the car and, as calmly as she could, instructed the chauffeur to take her back to the Ritz. The driver noticed all was not well.

'Everything all right, madam?' he asked.

'Yes,' she snapped, wiping her eyes. 'Just drive.'

On arriving back at the hotel Sally went straight to the room and put some clothes on. She was sore all over, her arms bruised and aching where Ronald had been very rough. Her anus was also sore; that was absolutely not part of the deal. No matter what circumstances were involved in arranging this stupid stunt, when Sally said 'no' that should have been Crump's cue to stop. Not so with Ronald. He just got rougher. He had quickly worked it out that all this had been arranged by his father, so he gambled that no matter what he did to Sally, she would not dare tell Teddy. He bet correctly.

Sally, now fully clothed and still sobbing, met her husband in the bar.

'Jesus, Sally, what happened?' Matthew was shocked at her appearance.

'Don't ask, it was horrible, he was rough to the point of being sadistic. That boy is an animal and I do not mean that in a complimentary way. I tell you, he's going to be a danger to women in years to come.'

The Seddons knew they were powerless to do anything about what had happened. If they told Crump Senior he would not believe them, as his son would deny everything and they would, in all likelihood, be kicked off the board. They would just have to take it lying down. They had, after all, gone along with this foolhardy game from the off.

'I am saying to you here and now, Matthew: never, never again. I don't care if he offers us the company. I thought that demon was going to kill me!'

The Seddons had a few drinks and retired to their suite, sorry they had embarked on this stunt in the first place. Matthew consoled his wife and they agreed they would not do anything like this again. Wife-swapping was one thing, even sleeping with Teddy Crump if financial circumstances dictated, but Ronald? No, never again.

With the birthday events over and done with and another woman essentially raped by Ronald Crump, it was time for the young man to train hard for the California state swimming championship. Christopher Johnson, who shared

Crump's racist and xenophobic views, had no idea of the level of misogyny held by his friend. Neither did Mr Spitz or anybody else in the school apart from his first victim, Miss Copley, who was too terrified to speak out. Had the real Ronald surfaced, it is questionable whether he would have been allowed to be involved in the coming swimming contest. Ronald and Christopher had informed Mr Spitz of their willingness to forfeit the first two weeks of their summer vacation to take part in the contest and represent the school. Spitz was delighted because despite their faults they were good swimmers. Most training for the prestigious event was to be done after school in the evenings, three nights per week and at weekends. This way studies and revision for their final year exams would not be neglected.

Ronald Crump in his swimming trunks cut an athletic figure: dark in appearance, almost Italian in looks, about six feet three inches in height and slimly built. Christopher Johnson was almost the opposite: blond, short and very fair. The venue would be in mid-state California in an Olympic-sized pool. Tension was already riding high among the competing athletes from all schools taking part. Mr Spitz, himself used to pressure from his days as an Olympian representing the USA, was feeling a paternal pressure on behalf of his young swimmers.

The school stood down for the summer vacation in the second week of July. Most students returned home, leaving the team of young athletes representing Bishops Court Rise to put the finishing touches to their preparations. On the day they left for the venue Mr Spitz gave them all a final pep talk.

'Right boys, you have all trained very hard for this. Now go and give it your best, but above all, enjoy the tournament.'

The whole bus applauded the former champ.

The swimming contest had four events: the 50-metre one-length sprint; the 150-metre three-lengths distance swim; the 200-metre four-lengths mini-marathon; and the 400-metre eight-lengths marathon. They were all very demanding contests in their own right. Christopher thought his best shot at a medal lay in the 50-metre sprint, as he was fast over a short distance. There would be three qualifying heats before the final of each race. In the first heat the first two would qualify, and thereafter only the winners of the remaining two heats would progress.

Christopher, as expected, came first in the 50-metre first heat, thus gravitating to the second heat, while Ronald came fourth, failing to qualify.

Christopher consoled his friend. 'Never mind, Ron, you did not expect to do well in the sprint,' he said.

'That's right,' said Ronald in an uncharacteristically sportsmanlike manner. 'I'll do better in the longer races. Maybe not the 150 metres but certainly I expect to have a good chance in the 200- and 400-metre contests.'

Christopher walked the remaining two heats and ended up coming first in the final, collecting a gold medal for his efforts. It was time now for the 150-metre contest. Ronald came second in the first heat, managing a qualification place – but only just. There was an inquiry into the result as it was a close shave, with the judges awarding the qualification to Ronald. Christopher came a disappointing fourth, failing to gain qualification. It was Ronald's turn to console his friend, expressing similar sentiments as Christopher had to himself. Christopher then informed Mr Spitz he would not be competing in the longer distance races. 'I am not a distance swimmer,' he said. 'Give one of the reserves a chance, sir,' he said to Spitz who appreciated his honesty. If Christopher was honest at all, it was more about his vanity: he didn't wish to be seen coming outside the first three.

In the second heat Ronald came second again, which was insufficient for qualification. Undeterred, he was ready for the 200-metre mini-marathon. Ronald Crump won his first, second and third heats, easily qualifying for the final where he came third, securing a bronze medal. It was now onto the marathon, the 400 metres, eight lengths, and Ronald qualified for the second heat, finishing second in the first bout. He came first in the remaining two heats, gaining qualification into the final 400-metre marathon front crawl.

'Go on, Ronald, give it to them,' Christopher encouragingly said to his friend.

Tensions were high as the competitors took up their positions. The whistle went for them to dive and the race was on. It was a gruelling contest with Ronald finishing a very close second, after another inquiry. He lost to a swimmer from Saint Brendan the Navigator Catholic School. After they were awarded their medals all the winners shook hands. What a pity Ronald Crump could not conduct himself in the same civilised manner on dry land as he did at these games in the swimming pool! Bishops Court Rise came away with one gold medal, one silver and a bronze, all won by Ronald Crump and Christopher Johnson collectively. Mr Spitz was very proud of his boys and told them so.

Ronald Crump arrived back in New York after a long flight and another failed attempt at picking up an air hostess. These globetrotting women are educated as well as streetwise, a combination well outside the remit of

Ronald Crump at this stage of his development. On arrival at the airport he was met by Teddy's chauffeur and taken home to be greeted by Megan and Teddy. Ronald showed them both his silver and bronze medals from the swimming contest.

'I'm so proud of you, Ronald,' Megan said with exaggerated enthusiasm.

Teddy was a little more reserved with his congratulations. He had little time for Ronald getting second place but he did not wish to ruin his wife's party.

'Yes, well done, son,' he said.

Teddy Crump was in the process of turning his father–son talks into mini-meetings.

'I have an agenda drawn up for our meeting tomorrow, Ronald,' he informed his protégé. To an observer blessed with a knowledge of history this could be a re-enactment of Augustus Caesar speaking to Tiberius, his successor. Teddy would be represented as Caesar and Ronald young Tiberius.

'We meet tomorrow morning in the study, ten o'clock,' Teddy informed his son. There was no debate on this time and venue. When Caesar says, 'Cometh to me', then Tiberius follows.

The following morning after breakfast, Teddy and Ronald retired to the study as arranged, leaving instructions not to be disturbed. The agenda was: Ronald's future, immediate and long-term; the future of the empire; and the coming board meeting.

Ronald outlined his plans to stay on at Bishops Court Rise for an extra year, and then go onto university with the intention of graduating with an honours degree in real estate.

'I then hope to expand the business into the property market. Let me explain why and bear in mind, Dad, these are protracted plans, not immediate or even medium-term. The engineering world is changing, and our products will be obsolete in years to come. Now we can either retrain the staff, some of whom, frankly, do not have the ability to upgrade – or we can rationalise that side of the business and expand into another field. The money will be in property, that I am sure. We can eventually sack staff or, if necessary, make them redundant, paying the legal minimum; those who are older, we can retire. Of course, there will be no mention of pensions, as we don't have – and never will have – unions who insist on this happening. Therefore, the whole operation will cost us, after we claim on our tax, virtually nothing. This is all, however for the long term,' Ronald concluded.

'Yes, that sounds good. I like your plans, son, but remember these are for the long term when I have retired. For the time being I am in charge and will be for the next number of years, and you are very much the deputy. I also like your ruthless streak, particularly on how to get rid of staff, paying them next to nothing. If they want pensions we can send them in Hugh Rothschild's direction: his banks run pension schemes.'

At the thought of this underhandedness the two bandits shared knowing grins.

'I should have no need to tell you, son, we do not repeat any of this to those vegetables on the board,' Crump Senior said. 'Not a word. We won't really need their support anyway, but they do have their uses, albeit limited.'

At this point Teddy moved on to the third item of business, the up-and-coming board meeting at which Sally and Matthew Seddon would be present. Teddy was unaware of what had gone on as a result of his sick plan, and Ronald intended it to stay that way. Even if he had known he would not have cared too much; he'd had his fun and so had Ronald.

'I have arranged for Bob Tomkinson to table a motion recommending sharp staffing reductions in our offices – not secretaries, but clerks and wages staff. I'll recommend rejection of Bob's proposal and you will second me. This way the staff will see me and you as good people who look after their employees, defending them against those who wish to dismiss them. I will give an impassioned speech about not throwing people out of work when there is no need. We will carry the day and be trusted by the fools for evermore!

'The rationale behind this train of thought and strategy is this: the militant trade union, United Automation Workers, have been trying to recruit our engineering works and offices. Most of the staff are not interested, they have their own representatives, or so they think. These representatives are in my pocket, and we've managed to breathe enough common sense into most of them. However, a few are interested in having a proper trade union as opposed to the puppets presently in house. If they see, being the gullible simpletons they are, that their interests and those of senior management and owners are the same, they will send the commies packing. If I'm seen to defend their interests to the hilt they will feel a union is unnecessary. They will send the UAW away and in six months' time we will be able to do as we like with the fools! It is about creating a false confidence among the staff in the company.'

'Sounds a good strategy, Dad. Is Bob aware of your plan?'

'Yes, I've briefed him, but nobody else knows.' Both of them laughed. 'Let me tell you about industrial relations at Crumps, son. People think we have no unions, but this assumption is not strictly true. We have staff representative groups, which are not affiliated to any of the federations such as the American Federation of Labour, and I pick the representatives. They are, therefore, in my pocket and when you take over they will be your property to select or deselect. This is why we do not want proper trade unions interfering. Get the picture?'

'I sure do, Dad.'

At this point both business rogues retired. It was one o'clock and the servants had served up lunch. They left the study laughing and joking with each other.

'You two boys sound happy,' observed Megan. The family sat down for lunch, dismissing the domestics from the room so they could eat in peace.

The day of the board meeting arrived and a full attendance, including the Seddons, were present. Teddy and Ronald entered the room and Caesar took up his seat at the head of the long oak table, Tiberius sitting to his immediate right. To Teddy's left sat his newest young secretary preparing to take the minutes of the meeting while the rest of the board members sat along each side of the table. Ronald began making subtle signs in the direction of Sally Seddon, inserting his middle finger in and out of his left palm, and occasionally putting the pen in his mouth while looking at Sally. To all other board members, apart from Sally, he was just concentrating. Sally Seddon knew full well Ronald Crump was making these suggestive signs at her, reminding the woman of that night in his dormitory. Matthew had an idea but said nothing. Both of them were too afraid of incurring Teddy's wrath and possibly losing their seat and votes on the board.

Ronald Crump may have held all the cards at this juncture and would do so into the distant future, but this state of affairs would not last for ever and Sally Seddon, along with Miss Copley and other individuals and groups whom this fascist went on to offend, would ultimately exact their revenge. As if to rub salt into the wound, Ronald, as a point of observation, noted the toilet paper in the executive loos was too hard. He suggested softer paper as people may be 'sensitive' in this area and suffer mild discomfort. Everybody on the board agreed and saw nothing sinister in this suggestion – everybody, that was, apart from Sally Seddon who knew what Ronald Crump was getting at.

After the reading of the minutes Teddy Crump requested Bob Tomkinson to read his prearranged covert proposal. The rest of the board were under the belief this was all Bob's own work and suggestion: so much for honesty among thieves. The proposal was principally about staff reductions in the engineering side of the empire, primarily in the cooling shops and offices.

Tomkinson began his speech. 'We are overstaffed in the cooling shops in the engineering sector of the business. We are also overweight with personnel in our offices, particularly the wages department and human resource management area. We need to reduce levels and as a result the wages bill.'

Tomkinson then outlined the sections in the offices which could not be chopped. 'Secretarial positions and Mr Crump's PA cannot be reduced, as Mr Crump needs these staff at his disposal due to his exceptionally heavy workload. We can, however, reduce the number of wages clerks by around thirty per cent and two positions in the personnel department, one senior and one junior, can be got rid of according to my calculations.'

Bob Tomkinson then handed a copy of the figures he had drafted to each board member, including the increasingly involved Ronald. All the members looked seriously at Tomkinson's figures.

'Could we not be a little less severe?' asked Matthew Seddon. 'These seem more like butchery than rationalising.'

'No!' said Tomkinson abruptly.

'Hang on a minute,' said Teddy. 'These people are human beings, not chess pieces. Some of them have families.'

He then gave a worthy speech in defence of these jobs. 'We cannot just throw people on the scrapheap with no good reason, and I will not accept economics alone as a reason,' he lied.

'Excuse me, sir,' interjected Tomkinson, 'new technology is coming which will do away with numerous jobs. These estimates are on the low side. To be honest, we could do with reducing by even greater numbers.'

'How do we know this technology will do the jobs of the men in the cooling shops? Have they been tested?' Crump said. 'Do we know they can deliver the same level of quality as our present loyal staff? If the answer to either of these questions is no or we don't yet know, then I recommend we hold fire before throwing good workers and loyal staff onto the scrapheap.'

This speech by Crump carried the day, and it was decided to revisit this subject in two years. Of course, Teddy Crump had no intention of waiting two years. He just wanted the shop floor and office personnel to send the trade unions packing. Then it would be open season and the staff, who foolishly listened to the board and, most importantly, Teddy Crump, would be defenceless. The board voted overwhelmingly to support their chief who made sure his secretary had recorded in writing every detail.

'Did you get all that, Susie?' asked Crump.

'Yes sir, every word,' she assured him.

'Wait for me in the office, I need a word,' Crump instructed her.

'Yes, sir,' the young woman said. The board then broke up, all going their separate ways.

'I'll see you back home, Ronald,' Teddy informed his son. 'I've a bit of business to sort out. Tell your mother I'll be about an hour.'

'Sure, Dad, will do,' Ronald said.

Teddy Crump retired to his office where young Susie was waiting.

'I want you to make sure the staff hear about the part of the board meeting where I defended their jobs. There's no need for them to know any more, just that their interests are being looked after at senior level.'

'Very good, sir, I get the picture and will ensure your instructions are carried out to the letter.' Crump then suggested they both have a drink, producing a bottle of Scotch from his drawer.

'Thank you, sir,' Susie said, grateful that a man of Teddy Crump's importance deemed her fit to have a drink with. This was an honour indeed.

'Come and join me on the couch,' Crump suggested, pointing towards a luxury sofa. The secretary willingly joined him, and they sat close to each other.

As they exchanged superficial chit-chat, Teddy put his hand on his secretary's knee. Susie knew what was expected and was too afraid to question. This was going to happen anyway, as Teddy obliquely intimated when she first started that his secretaries might, from time to time, be expected to carry out extra duties. This was going to be a long and intimate meeting.

Ronald arrived home and explained to Megan his father would be a little late and to instruct the domestics accordingly.

'Very well dear, your father is a very busy man,' she pretended to acknowledge. 'He must be rushed off his feet.' She was in a good mood because just before Ronald entered the building she had been talking to Derek over the phone and had arranged to meet the following day. Teddy eventually arrived home, and he was in a very good humour himself.

The reader may question why Derek's wife had not already been mentioned. The fact was, he and his wife, Mavis, lived separate lives despite living under the same roof. They exchanged pleasantries, slept in separate beds and were civil towards each other but apart from these superficial gestures, their lives were poles apart. When Derek accidentally bumped into Megan that afternoon he thought it was a gift from heaven. He was unaware at this point and hitherto remained oblivious to the power Teddy Crump had over his wife and, indeed, most other people. For this naive reason, when the time was right, he intended to ask Megan to leave Teddy for him. He did not realise the absurdity of such a request, but soon would; should Megan ever be suicidal enough to go along with Derek's innocent but crazy plan, Teddy Crump would break the pair of them. Within weeks they would be penniless and homeless, living in the gutter. There was no way this well-meant act could ever bear fruit.

The following morning, Teddy and Ronald retired after breakfast to the study to discuss applying Ronald's advanced mathematics into accounting and cooking the books. They explained to Megan no lunch would be required.

'If Cook could do some sandwiches and bring them in about two thirty that would be fine,' Teddy instructed.

'In that case, I shall be out most of the day,' said Megan.

'Fair enough, dear, enjoy yourself.'

Megan cancelled lunch with the cook and domestics leaving instructions for the requested sandwiches. She then drove off to a telephone kiosk to ring Derek. At this stage she didn't dare risk phoning him from the house. They arranged to meet in a downtown coffee shop about ten miles from Billionaires' Row and three miles from the private road where Derek resided. Derek had informed his deputy at work he would be taking an extended lunch and not to expect him until the following morning. Derek had genuine feelings for Megan and resolved he would broach the subject, at some point, of her leaving her husband. He would argue Ronald was now at an age where he was no longer dependent on his mother, so this could be a good time to do it. He was unaware of the complications which would accompany such a bold move. He decided to broach the subject after sex as he did not wish to spoil the main event! Megan arrived, and he ordered two coffees.

'The wife's away at her sister's so we have the place to ourselves, darling,' he informed Megan. 'You can stay the night, we won't be disturbed.'

'That's not an option, Derek, I can stay the afternoon and even into the early evening – but not all night. Teddy would go berserk, he would definitely suspect something was going on. I'd love to spend the night with you,' Megan assured Derek, 'but it is just not possible.'

The couple arrived at Derek's modest-by-comparison detached house and they made for the bedroom. They took with them a bottle of wine for periodic refreshments and engaged in an afternoon of lustful activity. When they emerged from the bedroom Derek once again poured them both a drink.

'That was fantastic,' he complemented Megan.

'You weren't too bad yourself,' she replied.

'I have something to ask you. Are you happy at home with your husband?' Derek blurted out. 'Do you feel fulfilled and contented? Do you get the care and attention you deserve?'

'Well,' said Meghan, surprised at his barrage of questions, 'most of the time I feel wanted and appreciated. Teddy does not let me want for anything and we go to some great social evenings. Intimate relations are infrequent, possibly due to my husband's age.'

She did not want to face her suspicions that Teddy had a stream of younger models at his work which might, in his eyes, make her surplus to sexual requirements. What these younger women could not compete with was that she was the ideal partner at social evenings and the perfect hostess when he had business people at their place. This was Megan's domain and Teddy would not swap her for the world. All in all Megan was quite happy with her lot. She asked for and received everything she wanted from Teddy and was having great sex at least once per month with Derek. Yes, she was contented enough; she would prefer more time with Derek but would not risk losing everything else in pursuit of this.

'Have you ever thought about leaving him, darling? We could move in together as Mavis and I live completely separate lives. If I were to leave her it would make little difference.'

Megan Crump could not believe what she was hearing: leave Teddy? No, this could not happen. If Teddy had been an ordinary medium-sized businessman with no real power there would have been no problem. Unfortunately, he was not, and she knew he wielded much power and authority over others including judges, police chiefs, property developers and senior civil servants.

'I couldn't do that, Derek. It would not be worth the trouble which would certainly follow. If I were to leave my husband he would crush us both within a month, and we would be living in the gutter. That much I am certain of.'

'You are prepared to spend the rest of your life with a man who does not love you, nor you him?'

'It's not like that, darling, it is more a case of the end would not justify the means. Teddy, if pushed, could even make you disappear,' she informed him reluctantly.

'Does he really have so much power at his disposal?' asked Derek.

'Yes, he does. We are taking a huge chance meeting as we do. Can we settle for that? If Teddy was dead things would be different but he's very much alive. Can we just leave things as they are? I beg of you.'

'Very well, darling, if that is what you really want, let's leave well alone,' Derek conceded.

They both kissed passionately and arranged to meet the following morning. Teddy would be in conference with his son, so Megan would be able to get away for a couple of hours and Derek could make an excuse for being late for work. He was, after all, the senior member of staff in the branch of the bank.

★ ★ ★

In 1963 the USA had 20,000 troops active in Vietnam and opposition was beginning to mount at home. The seeds of what would become a large anti-war movement were in the early stages with people like actress Jane Fonda playing a prominent role. Both Teddy and Ronald opposed these groups with a vengeance, describing them as traitors. President Kennedy, despite the settlement which ended the Cuban Missile Crisis, was determined to stem the flow of communism in Indochina.

The Crumps believed strongly in their President's stance and only regretted he had not gone to war over Cuba a year earlier. Such movements as the anti-war campaign and campaigns against racism and racial segregation would become a prominent part of Sixties life in the USA. Many people involved with one cause would also be associated with the other.

Universities played prominent roles in the development of these campaigns. When Ronald eventually began his studies at college and became involved in his brand of politics, there would be considerable opposition from other individuals and groups there.

★ ★ ★

Megan arrived home in the early evening.

'Hello, darling, did you have a nice day?' enquired Teddy.

'Yes, fantastic, Ted,' she replied.

Teddy had a good idea where she had been but would let it go. She was only doing what he did at work regularly. Teddy was in great form because

Ronald had introduced a foolproof system saving millions if not billions in tax while still being seen to be paying their full amount. For this reason, Crump was in no mood for a fight with his wife, especially when it was not necessary.

'I have to go out again in the morning, Teddy. You and Ronald will be busy again, won't you?'

'Yes, of course we will, dear, until about three o'clock. How about if then we all go out for a meal? I'll make the booking,' Teddy suggested.

'That sounds great.' Megan breathed a sigh of relief. She could have her magical couple of hours with Derek.

The following morning Teddy and Ronald retired to the study, as was now customary after breakfast, and Megan made her escape. She met Derek for her usual assignation, which was blissful. She arrived back home around midday just as the boys were finishing up their plans for corruption, earlier than they had anticipated. Teddy Crump had reserved a table for three at the New York Hilton and instructed the chauffeur to collect them from the mansion at one thirty and to drive them to their appointed luncheon venue.

'Pick us up here at four thirty,' instructed Crump.

'Yes, sir,' replied the chauffeur.

Teddy informed the head waiter of their presence and reminded the man of their reservation. 'Certainly, Mr Crump, sir. This way, and may I say how wonderful you and your lovely wife are looking today.'

Crump just gave him a grunt and then dismissed the waiter as one would dismiss a dog which had displeased its master. Teddy Crump was used to being spoken to in a grovelling way; he even expected the lower orders to conduct themselves in such a manner.

Crump considered himself superior to all who passed him, except those fellow brigands to whom he pretended to offer some sort of equality, depending what he wanted, while in reality detesting them. Crump was not alone with these trains of thoughts and opinions of others; all the bandits across the USA thought in much the same way. None of them had a very high opinion of their fellow human beings: the lower down the social ladder, the more contempt was shown.

Halfway through their meal Teddy decided on some light entertainment for himself at his wife's unsuspecting failings.

'What was the name of that chap I saw you with some time back, dear?' he enquired. 'You know the man you once worked with, I believe. Oh, what was his name?' Teddy pretended to be puzzled and interested in remembering.

'You remember, darling, you were having coffee with him that afternoon and I coincidentally walked in. What *was* his name?'

'Derek, darling,' she said with an element of guilt about her tone.

'Derek. That's right, dear. I do hate not being able to remember, people think I'm going senile,' he said, chortling. 'Derek, that's right, works in banking at a lower level. Have you seen him since then?'

'No, no I haven't dear,' Megan lied. 'No reason to.'

'I just wondered,' Teddy said in a semi-accusing manner, holding back the urge to laugh.

'Yes, yes really,' Megan reacted, almost giving the game away.

'Are you looking forward to getting back to school, Ronald?' asked Crump, deliberately changing the subject when he thought his wife was embarrassed enough.

'Yes, Dad, I am,' Ronald replied, suspecting his father had an ulterior motive for his mother's grilling then deliberately changing the direction of conversation. This outing would be the family's last before Ronald returned to school for his final scheduled year.

It was finally the end of the long summer vacation. Even though Ronald had forfeited the first two weeks for the swimming contest it had still been a decent break. Ronald had learnt a lot. He had sat on the board which he would be doing much more of, he had reminded Sally Seddon and her dimwit husband who was in charge and had worked out an aggressive plan with his father on cooking the books. Now it was back to Bishops Court Rise for his final year before he took the sixth-year option studying real estate. His task for the fifth year was to continue elevating his grades in geography and science.

He also decided to do a series of articles for the school magazine attacking these anti-Vietnam war groups and the communists he believed, or more to the point, his father had told him, were leading them. He also determined to counter these civil rights groups promoting racial equality as being abnormal and an affront to God. Who had ever heard of the black man being on the same level as his white superiors! Christopher Johnson shared these views, coming from Texas in the south. Prejudices in that part of the USA dated back to the Civil War of 1861–65. He would make his views known and also organise a series of meetings. Perhaps Christopher would accompany him, helping to ensure Bishops Court Rise remained patriotic and behind the war as well as being white supremacists.

Apart from the obvious communist infiltration and leadership of these groups there was another denominator. A number of women were involved in the anti-war groups. They included celebrities such as actress Jane Fonda, and ordinary women who should be serving their hard-working husbands with meals and keeping house. Perhaps many of these women were lesbians who had no husbands. *Fucking dykes*, Ronald thought to himself. This was at a time in the USA and, indeed most of the world, when homosexuality and lesbian relationships were illegal. If Ronald could cast aspersions in these directions, without actually accusing anybody, then support for these groups would almost certainly shrink. What about these rich women, wealthy enough to have domestics? They should be more patriotic. Why can't they busy themselves with useful causes such as joining 'Christian Women Fighting Poverty'? That was a very worthwhile group of bourgeois women fighting a good cause, not causing trouble with impossible ungodly demands like racial equality or committing treason. Ronald approached the editor of the school magazine who greeted his ideas with open arms.

'Great, Ronald, I like the style. Just be careful of the libel laws. Do not name anybody or accuse any individual by name unless you can prove it in a court of law. Remember, some of these celebrities are wealthy themselves and can afford the best lawyers. Still, if you name nobody directly, just subtly suggest, they cannot touch you,' the young editor said.

Having received the green light, Ronald put together his first of a series of articles attacking the unpatriotic behaviour of the anti-Vietnam war groups. The first headline read: TREASONOUS VERMIN ON OUR STREETS, by Ronald Crump, Year Five. He aimed his first prong of attack at the women involved, suggesting their sexuality was questionable. His aim, though he did not print this, was to encourage a police inquiry into the groups regarding illegal 'unnatural' sexual behaviour. If he could at least cast doubts in the minds of the public, it would be a start. He would then go on the offensive against the obvious communist infiltration, perhaps citing President Kennedy's weak stance against the Soviet Union over the Cuban Missile Crisis as the touchpaper which encouraged the communists. By communist, what Ronald really meant was anybody whose views differed greatly from his own or his father's.

Ronald Crump was also going to try and bring down as many well-known people as possible who were foolishly involved with these anti-American organisations. The better known the person the more bad publicity they would get for their racial equality and anti-Vietnam movements. These organisations often interwove, for example, many people involved with one, or on the steering committee of a certain group could well be involved with the other or even numerous other like-minded groups. Ronald fully intended taking this right-wing fascist campaign with him to university. Here would be a larger audience all, he was sure, who would agree with him and his position. He would be disappointed in this hope. Universities were a different world from boarding school with an equally large, if not larger, left-wing students' union! This was, however, for the future. For the time being Ronald Crump began his political ideology based on hatred of anybody who did not fit with his ideal persona at boarding school. The first lesson for Ronald this year was science. He had to specialise in a particular field and the works and projects of one or more famous scientists. As Ronald was the heir apparent to Crump's Armouries, now renamed Crumps Arms & Engineering, he chose the works of Robert Oppenheimer and the Manhattan Project, the project responsible for developing the first atomic bomb. Ronald's long-term interest was, of course, financial and what benefits the Crumps could gain from this knowledge.

The arms race was going to gather momentum in the decades to come and Ronald was determined his company would be at the forefront of this race. In the meantime he felt positive a good project would catapult his grades through the roof. His marks were good enough now, but Ronald wanted the highest grades for the future of the company. He would keep his long-term plans secret from his father who might not agree with him and might try to stifle the progress Ronald had in mind. He would introduce his ideas when he was holding the reins and not before. To have any impact and be taken seriously he needed to know his subject, which was why this avenue was chosen. The huge school library had plenty of texts on Robert Oppenheimer and the Manhattan Project, so Ronald decided to spend a lot of his time there. When he was not engaged 'chasing Oppenheimer' he wrote his hate-filled literature for the school magazine.

On arriving back at his dormitory Ronald began working on his first article about the 'Treasonous Vermin'. Women's participation in the anti-Vietnam War movement was still in its early stages as was US involvement in the war, by comparison with things to come. Ronald questioned why these otherwise no doubt sensible women were getting involved in treachery against their country. They should be behind their men defending the US from the evils of communism, to say nothing of protecting the peoples of Indochina from these red menaces. He failed to mention, possibly through ignorance or more likely because it did not suit his purpose, that the majority of the landless peoples of Vietnam supported the communists, and they certainly needed no protection.

'Should women not be at home cooking their hard-working husbands' meals?' Ronald's article continued in a sexist vein. 'And why are single women involved? Should they not be supporting their boyfriends as they wage war against the communists?' Ronald cast certain aspersions regarding some of these women's sexuality, without mentioning anybody by name. The celebrities would know who he was aiming at. The following month he intended attacking the movements for racial equality, claiming it to be against the natural order and an affront to God, which he pretended to believe in, only for the purpose of deceiving the working classes. These articles and meetings he had planned would go down well with the right-wing readership of Bishops Court Rise. All the students at this institution were the offspring of the powerful US bourgeoisie, a ready-made audience and readership for his hate-filled works.

★ ★ ★

Back in the eastern USA, Teddy Crump had warned all his employees of the consequences they would suffer if even an utterance of support for any of these communist groups was to be expressed. Instant dismissal was what awaited anybody who considered backing these movements. So much for free speech, a concept which although written somewhere in the constitution of the USA, did not apply to US citizens working at Crumps.

Teddy wrote to his son suggesting he used Crumps Arms and Engineering as a shining example of USA patriotism. Teddy also put it to Ronald to suggest that the other students should advise their parents to take a similar line at their companies. Teddy called this class solidarity. However, if his employees had adopted a similar position in order that they improve their working conditions, each and every one would be dismissed. Class solidarity was designed for the bourgeoisie and not, irrespective of what Karl Marx had written, the proletariat! Teddy Crump informed his staff at a compulsory meeting in their lunch break that those anti-Vietnam protesters were nothing more than traitors.

'I will not have traitors or those who support such actions working at Crumps, do I make myself clear?' he stated.

All the staff nodded or muttered, 'Yes, Mr Crump' or 'Yes, sir.'

'As for these lovers of racial equality, they are an affront to the word of God, and you all know I'm a God-fearing man, a Christian and regular churchgoer. I will not have blasphemy in any establishment owned by me,' he added.

All the staff, including those on the shop floor, murmured agreement with their boss.

Each member of staff then made a promise to tell Mr Crump of anybody they heard uttering such evils as ending US involvement in Vietnam or suggesting that black people were equal to any of them.

1963 was moving apace and it was already November. Ronald Crump had embarked on his final scheduled year with enthusiasm. His studies of Robert Oppenheimer and the Manhattan Project had been accepted as his project and his right-wing hate articles and meetings were gathering momentum. One major talking point in all circles was the emergence of a brilliant young boxer, Cassius Clay, who had won a gold medal at the Rome Olympics back in 1960. This young athlete had now turned professional and had a style of fighting hitherto unseen. He was preparing for a tilt at the world heavyweight champion, Sonny Liston. Both Liston and Clay, shortly to change his name to Muhammed Ali, were black Americans and, as in most sports, represented the hopes of the USA much to the denials of the so-called white supremacists.

'This makes no difference to the black man's status in society. They may be able to knock the shit out of each other but when it comes to running business, having jobs which require a modicum of intelligence and running the country and economy, these are jobs only educated civilised white men can do,' boasted a bitter Ronald Crump. Could it be their deepest selves felt inferiority to these athletes? Of course, Crump could never confess to such an absurdity, even if deep down he felt it could well be true!

'It's only a matter of time before a good young white fighter comes along and the natural order, as God intended, will be restored,' Ronald continued. This assumption was said more in hope than expectation, but he had to sound convincing, and as any student of boxing will be aware this 'Great White Hope' is still being awaited. Ronald Crump went ballistic when he found out that Cassius Clay had become embroiled in both the civil rights movement and the anti-Vietnam war campaign. Clay – Ali – would become more involved, and his orations on both subjects, which he interlinked, would become much more radical in the years to come. These boxers had hitherto been the major talking point nationwide until on 22nd November 1963, news came through of the assassination of President Kennedy.

Teddy Crump was privately pleased at this assassination. He was careful to keep his opinions to himself until he found out the mood and opinions of his peers. He did not, after all, wish to lose contracts and profits over an opinion. Teddy pretended to be outraged at the thought of a US president being assassinated, particularly on US soil. Kennedy was killed in Dallas, Texas as he was travelling in an open-topped vehicle. Teddy tried to blame the communists, but this tended to fall on deaf ears. Nobody believed even the USSR would commit such an atrocity. Besides, for what reason? They had got the better deal, if that is the correct term, out of the Cuban Missile Crisis and a certain amount of semi-détente had evolved between Kennedy and Soviet leader Nikita Khrushchev as a result of a very dangerous situation.

Crump dropped this propaganda as even his allies thought it beyond the pale. He then came up with a suggestion which might hold water. A man called Lee Harvey Oswald had been arrested for JFK's murder. Crump reasoned this man had, either wittingly or unwittingly, been used by the intelligence services. Teddy suggested to Duke Tillerson: 'Could Kennedy have been assassinated by the hawks because they perceived a climbdown over Cuba? After all, we gave up a perfectly good state-of-the-art working missile system in Turkey and Italy and they removed a missile system not yet working from Cuba. We could have bombed the island and destroyed their missile parts. Could this Oswald fella be a pawn in the game played out by the hawks?'

'Good point, Ted, it's certainly a possibility,' Tillerson agreed.

Shortly after this conversation Oswald himself was assassinated. A man named Jack Ruby was credited with this killing, which for Crump confirmed his suspicions.

'They had to get Oswald out of the way in case he spilled the beans, Duke, what do you make of it?'

'Good point, Ted. In fact, the more I think about it I am sure you are right.'

Ironically the following year, 1964, Nikita Khrushchev was replaced as Soviet leader by the hardliners in the USSR. He was replaced by his press secretary, Leonid Brezhnev, after he went on his Black Sea vacation. The Cuban Missile Crisis had cost both leaders, both of whom had pulled the world back from the brink of destruction. Both men paid the price for this diplomacy by hawks on both sides who might have, in each case, preferred war! It cost one leader, according to Crump, his mortal life and another his political life.

Teddy Crump and Duke Tillerson, in their own eyes both educated worldly statesmen superior to all others, agreed Kennedy deserved nothing less for his betrayal. Of course, the late president had betrayed nobody. Telling lies in an election campaign is common practice around the globe, but to accuse the man of treachery was stretching it, to say the least.

'We should have bombed Cuba and the commies' weapon sites,' Teddy argued.

'I agree, Ted,' Tillerson said. What both these would-be world leaders were not taking into account was that there were Soviet nuclear submarines around the Cuban coast and they were, in all probability, armed.

Back at Bishops Court Rise Ronald Crump was delivering anti-Kennedy speeches, trying to tie them in with his right-wing ethos over civil rights and the anti-Vietnam campaigns. Ronald was careful how far he went on condemning Kennedy and his legacy, particularly over Cuba. He was aware most students at the school shared some of his views, but not all of them. He did not want to lose support for his fascist line simply because he had pushed the Kennedy incident too far.

Lyndon Baines Johnson succeeded the assassinated President Kennedy and was sworn into office the same day his predecessor was killed. Johnson signed into law a series of civil rights bills, much to the annoyance of Teddy Crump and his bigoted hate-filled son. He also banned, at least in theory, racial discrimination in public facilities, the workplace and housing. President Johnson also introduced the Voting Rights Act prohibiting certain requirements in the South designed purposely to deny African Americans the vote. The Act made these requirements themselves unlawful.

On hearing this Christopher Johnson flew into a rage, as did his father, Harry.

'This n****r-loving wanker of a president giving the n*****s the fucking vote. My dad is fuming. He's getting businessmen of repute to sign his petition against the Act.'

The reader will recall Harry Johnson was an oil tycoon from Texas, one of the Confederate States in the American Civil War. Many racist views from that period were still held in these states by the likes of Johnson and his son.

'Yes, my dad is none too pleased. I can assure you no fucking n*****s will be employed by our company either by my father or myself when I take over,' Ronald Crump assured his friend.

'My dad reckons the business class, people like your father and others who have made it big through hard work, should run the country as a business. Anybody or any country which gets in our way should just be trampled over,' said Christopher Johnson in true Hitlerite fashion, though he did not realise this.

'Couldn't agree more, Chris,' Crump said. 'My dad says something similar to yours, Chris. In the North and certainly New York there is opposition to this Act.'

It should be remembered New York was on the opposite side to Texas in the Civil War which was not, contrary to popular belief, solely about the issue of chattel slavery. There were many other factors, of which slavery was one, which sparked off the American Civil War. Many in the North shared, to a certain extent, the beliefs regarding slaves held by their southern counterparts in the South. Such shared beliefs among a minority were once again surfacing.

As '63 gave way to '64 the Christmas and New Year periods were upon the population of the USA once again. Peter Tillerson was home for the break. Duke began telling his son of his abhorrence at the new President's Act and bills on racial equality.

'The fucking n*****s will be running the place before we know it. We should take direct action now, what do you say, Pete?'

Duke was not expecting the response from his son.

'Do you really want to know what I think, Dad?' Peter Tillerson suddenly let loose with both barrels, something he had wanted to do for many years. 'I think you and your so-called friends, who are not friends at all, are the most bigoted, hate-filled shits I have ever had the misfortune to meet, let alone be the child of. You people are no better than Adolf Hitler, the guy you were fighting against from 1941, remember? I ask myself: were you and your so-called cohort Teddy Crump on the right side? It certainly raises questions for me, Dad. You all pretend to like each other when it is plain to see not one of you is genuine. There's that woman, if that is what she is, Ethel Morgan, who cannot say a nice word about anybody, and her henpecked husband Bradley whose pants are full of brown stuff every time she looks at him a little displeased.'

Tillerson Senior looked at his son in disbelief.

Peter continued. 'All you lot can do is try to keep good honest working-class people down, especially if their pigmentation is a different colour to your own. They must know their place. You all make me sick. Down at the gym I'm sparring with a great up-and-coming fighter, who will one day be a challenger for the world title and who is a perfect gentleman outside the ring as well as inside it. His name is Joe Frazier. He is one of the greatest sportsmen and people I have ever had the pleasure to meet. Then I come here and listen to this shit which you and your friends spew out.' Peter regarded his dad squarely, red-faced but resolute.

'How dare you speak to me like that, boy, who do you think you are? I do everything for you. The business and all the wealth including contracts abroad will one day be yours, and you speak to me, your father, like that.'

Peter felt no remorse at what he had said. Perhaps he could have phrased it in a more civilised manner, but civilised wasn't on the agenda when he had to finally come clean about these issues.

'Look, Dad, can't you see people are people, irrespective of skin colour, ethnic origin, sexual orientation or any other fictitious prejudice which you hold? Look at the company you keep: Teddy Crump and his spineless son and Megan who hasn't a clue what is going on behind her back. Teddy Crump's employees are so afraid of him they will do anything he demands. Young women too afraid to keep their pants on in case Crump wants them off. What kind of a man is that?'

Peter finished by saying, 'I'm grateful for the business, Dad, but if the price of inheritance is becoming like you, I'd rather not. If I take over, I will employ people on merit not skin colour and if the staff want trade union recognition I will not just dismiss the request out of hand. Look what happened to your textile business when you tried. The union almost broke you. All that had to be done was a little talking, taking into account staff grievances. I've said my piece now, Dad, as best I can. I'm off to the gym.' With that, Peter strode out of the room.

Duke sat back and pondered what Peter had said. Unlike Crump, Tillerson was, albeit reluctantly, open to change at a push. He would certainly take aspects of his son's opinions on board.

Back at school for the beginning of 1964, Ronald was again studying the Manhattan Project and something called 'nuclear fission'. If he could master the basics of this, he would be in good stead for the exams later in the year. He had also been listening to President Johnson's foreign policy and in particular Vietnam. He was pleased to hear the president intended increasing US involvement in the war. This, to a certain extent, dampened his hatred of Lyndon Johnson after his ridiculous Voting Rights Act. He would concentrate most of his speeches on promoting the war, threaded in with occasional racism and racist comments. Sometimes one would complement the other, especially if he could prove black soldiers showed more fear than their white counterparts. This he would have problems with, as it was not the case. Sometimes it was the black soldiers who showed most bravery, though their white officers would never admit to this!

President Johnson's policy on Vietnam also pleased Teddy Crump, who wrote to his son telling him so. Anti-black feeling in New York was ever-present but not as aggressive as the southern states. The president's foreign policy helped make the Voting Rights Act more palatable to the northerners. Ronald Crump had booked the main school hall with the assistance of the school magazine editor for a meeting about the Vietnam War. He began the meeting by applauding the president's stance on Vietnam and his pledge to increase US involvement against the Viet Cong and North Vietnamese Army.

'We must hold firm against this communist threat, if necessary be prepared to nuke them.'

This was met with rapturous applause from the audience.

'Even if the Soviet Union are supplying the Viet Cong and have the capability to send nuclear bombs our way, we should call their bluff. They wouldn't dare attack the USA and we could finish it in a day!'

Once again, the audience applauded with enthusiasm. There was no doubt in Ronald's mind he would one day become a great leader of his nation. He was beginning to hold romantic delusions for the future when he realised he was only halfway through his speech. 'We must give the south Vietnamese all the assistance they require to beat the communist threat. Victory to the USA and victory to south Vietnam!'

The crowd rose to their feet applauding enthusiastically and Ronald waved as if he was already the great leader he believed one day he'd become. He retired back to his dormitory, wishing Miss Copley had been present. In his deluded mind he imagined she would have wanted to witness her beloved Ronald in action. In actuality, she hated his guts and one day would take her revenge.

Ronald Crump was now preparing for his midterm exams. The science report he was working on was going to be saved for his finals, which would involve essays of four thousand words as well as a written exam. The finals would be sat in late June and the results would be available before the long summer break.

The knowledge Ronald had acquired in the discipline of science had improved greatly and he was also working to bring his geography marks into the high B or even A bracket. He had also been studying the Hispanic countries of Central and South America, all about their evolution, climate and peoples. He was also undertaking a project, again for the finals, on the Spanish conquistador Hernan Cortes. Cortes represented the first stage of the Spanish conquest of the Americas, North America exempted, and was an example of how European technology overcame superior numbers of the natives. European illness also played a major part in conquering the indigenous population. Smallpox, to which the locals had no resistance, along with the common cold, had a devastating effect. Ronald Crump would, like many historians, play this factor down as it did not swerve his racial superiority purpose. Between 1521 and 1524 Henan Cortez personally ruled what today is called Mexico. Like his science project, his geography topic would be more geared towards his finals than the midterms.

The midterm results came through and Ronald's efforts had delivered fruit. His English and math were really forgone conclusions; he knew he would receive top marks for both. It was the other two subjects he needed to improve on and improve he did. The final marks were: English A++, Science A+ (a great improvement), math A++ and geography A. Other subjects like history were also on the up and up, his history mark a B+. As expected, French was very poor but that did not bother him too much. He felt secure that enough had already been done to attain good overall marks for his finals.

Ronald Crump decided to organise another meeting in the school hall where he intended to whip up support for Lyndon Johnson's foreign policy in Vietnam. He wanted to ease off a little on his anti-civil rights campaign and embark on a path of phoney harmonisation. By this it was meant he, as the main orator, would try to convey a message appearing to be more inclusive regarding black people. Although there were no black students at Bishops Court Rise Ronald was aware his speeches reached the local media. It would also be good practice for when he eventually picked up the gauntlet at university.

The headline advertising the meeting read: 'African Americans; Your President Needs You!' It was a warm early May evening and the hall soon became full. Crump arranged for a public-address system to relay his speech to those basking in the sun outside, as the topic of the meeting had attracted interest. Ronald began.

'My fellow Americans of all colours and creeds, especially the black man,' young Crump pretentiously quoted former President Franklyn D. Roosevelt. 'President Johnson is benevolently trying to introduce his Voting Rights Act which he successfully steered through the Senate. This will prohibit any state enacting state rules which may inhibit your right to vote. You will no longer have to get through any state legislation to exercise your right once he gets it through the House. You people owe him. Now he needs you as you needed him. He needs you to volunteer for service in Vietnam where your country is at war. So, don't be found wanting, enlist and do your duty.'

This was the basis of Ronald's discourse and a practice run for university where the national media would be present for such meetings.

After the great oration Ronald retired to his dormitory for a well-deserved rest. Suddenly there was a knock on his door, it was Christopher Johnson. He was in a foul mood with all the bigotry and racism which would be expected from a son of the Confederacy.

'What the fuck do you think you're playing at, Ron? You've been inciting the n*****s to believe there is a hope of them becoming equal in status to the white man. Even your own gang in New York don't believe in this fairy tale. A civil war was fought in this country and a major reason for that conflict was the very ideas you appear to be spewing out today.'

'Calm down, Chris,' Crump replied, 'think about what I was saying. Let's get one thing straight: I do not believe in racial equality. The pecking order is the white man rules supreme. A good distance behind are the Hispanics; then native Americans, if that is what the defeated tribes are; and finally the black man to be used for the menial jobs. I said what I said to create an illusion, pretending to support the Voting Rights Act to encourage the negro into joining the white man's army for service in Vietnam. Make them believe our great and charitable president has given them or is in the process of giving them something and they, therefore, owe him and, more to the point, us. This way they, the n*****s will be lining up to become cannon fodder against the commies and we kill two birds with one stone.

'The commies will kill a number of black troops and, in the name of the USA, the blacks will kill a load of commies. There will be no need for good white stock to join up' – he was thinking primarily of himself here – 'as there will be enough black sacrificial lambs to fill the ranks. Then when the commies have been put in their place these troops will come back to nothing except the third-class citizenship they went off to defend. By such time we will have a sensible president who will reverse Lyndon Johnson's Voting Rights Act and normality will prevail. Then you, me and the rest of the level-headed, hard-working business class can get on with making money without lifting a finger. The workers, then as now, will do all the work for us. We will also have a reserve labour force in the enslaved black man, not chattel slavery as previously but nevertheless slaves!'

'Ron you're a political genius, you may be president one day!' Christopher remarked admiringly.

Ronald Crump submitted his dissertations as part of the final exams to the headmaster one week before written examinations in the first week of July. The results would be in the following week just before the long summer break. Ronald felt confident, with good reason: he had worked hard on the project, even if he had omitted some facts which did not fit his ideology. Christopher Johnson had worked hard also and was staying on for the optional extra year to study petro-chemistry. It must be remembered that Johnson, like Crump, would inherit a huge business empire so he needed to keep abreast of developments in the oil business. When the final results including the dissertations came through, Ronald was ecstatic. Both his projects were in the nineties and his written exam marks in all the subjects were As or A-pluses. All things considered, he was up and running. The next port of call was his sixth year studying real estate. He left for his summer break in great form.

It was the third week of the vacation, Ronald having spent the previous weeks in meetings with his father and attending a board meeting. Ronald was out relaxing when he met Peter Tillerson and Terry Morgan.

'How's it going, guys,' Ronald greeted them.

'Fuck off, you racist. We've heard about your articles in your school magazine and the meetings you have been holding,' remarked Peter. 'Not for me, you neo-fascist bastard,' he continued.

'Nor me,' said Terry.

It was at this point Ronald Crump came across the first real physical opposition to his racism. He was soon to find out that his views were not universally shared by the population of New York, let alone the USA.

'Don't tell me you support all this equality crap, do you? And I suppose you oppose our boys in Vietnam?'

'That's right, what of it?' Peter Tillerson asked.

'You fucking traitor, you should be tried for treason,' said Crump.

This was the last he would say on the subject, for that day at least. Adopting a boxer's stance, Peter approached Ronald and let loose with a left, knocking him to the ground. Terry entered and was about to put in the boot, but Peter prevented him.

'Leave it, Terry. The little shit isn't worth it.'

Peter Tillerson had mastered the art of boxing over the years and hated himself for using this gift in the street, but Crump had ignited the touchpaper, something he would not do to Peter again.

'To think when your pants were brown at junior school I defended you in return for some simple math questions, more fool me,' Peter said. 'I'd love to take you to the gym and let you make one of your sick speeches down there. We are a mixed bag: black, white, native American, Hispanic, and the one thing we all have in common is that we are all human beings with real camaraderie, something a person like you would never understand.'

Ronald Crump was mortified, and almost welded by fear to the ground.

'I don't want to see you, talk to you or breathe the same air as you,' said Peter.

'That goes for me too,' Terry added.

Terry Morgan was not so anti-racist as was Peter. Truth be told, he understood little about the subject, but what he did know was, if his mother, Ethel, spouted racist views it must be a nasty concept. He had latched on to Peter who had given him some literature on the subject and he was beginning to form a picture of what the likes of the Crumps, as a family, really stood for. He also knew his father, Bradley, was not one of these morons but was so afraid of Ethel he pretended to be like-minded. Terry was determined this would not apply to him.

When Ronald eventually picked himself up, making sure Tillerson and Morgan were well gone, he headed for home with a cut lip and bruises.

'Ronald, my darling little soldier, what happened?' his mother fussed.

'I fell over, or more to the point I tripped,' said Ronald, too ashamed to tell the truth.

'Is that really what happened, son?' enquired Teddy.

'Yes, Dad, that's the truth,' he lied.

'Very well, don't forget tomorrow morning, we have a meeting with a potential customer. I'd like you to sit in. Roughly translated, that means you are sitting in, no argument.'

When the domestics brought the Crumps' evening meal to the table, Betty commented sympathetically on Ronald's cut lip.

'How did it happen, sir?' she asked, genuinely concerned.

'Oh, it's nothing, just get on with what you are paid for and stop bothering about matters which do not concern you,' Ronald snapped.

Betty took no offence at his rudeness; she was used to being spoken to like a dog.

The following morning a chauffeur-driven limousine arrived on the long driveway of the Crump family home. The guest was a representative of a Palestinian group intent on the overthrow of the Israeli state. It was the policy of the United States to support Israel in any conflict with their Arab and Palestinian neighbours who received, at least, tacit support from the USSR. In a nutshell, the two superpowers, the USA and USSR, were fighting a war by proxy in the Middle East. Crumps Arms had done deals with the Israeli government on many occasions, supplying the Israeli Defence Forces (IDF) with weapons and fighter aircraft parts. It was illegal for arms dealers to supply the enemies of Israel in that region as it was tantamount to supporting the Soviet side.

Teddy Crump cared little for patriotism or the law when it came to money and neither did his son, despite his phoney speeches promoting the USA in his patriotic crusade. For them the dollar bill trumped all other considerations, and it was not unusual for Crumps Arms to supply the allies of the US's enemies. Back in 1956 he had supplied the Irish Republican Army (IRA) with weaponry to launch their 'Operation Harvest' against British rule in Northern Ireland.

'The trick here, son, is not to get caught,' Teddy explained to Ronald.

For this reason, Teddy Crump had insisted this preliminary meeting took place at his private residence and no actual deals were to be signed or handshakes exchanged. The meeting was to ascertain what the Palestinians wanted and the best avenue of transportation to get the merchandise to them. Once these details had been verbally agreed Teddy would put the representative, Achmid (a codename), in touch with his senior representative and director of Crumps Arms, Bob Tomkinson. He was the director in Teddy's pocket, his troubleshooter and, if necessary, fall guy. Should anything go wrong, Teddy would know nothing of this transaction, and neither would Ronald, who was beginning to feel very important.

The Crump family butler answered the door and allowed the visitor in, directing the man to the study where Crump and his son were waiting to greet him.

'Good to see you, Achmid my friend,' Teddy said, welcoming the guest to his home.

For the lucrative purposes of this visit, both Ronald and his father put aside their white supremacist beliefs.

'This is my son, Ronald,' said Teddy.

'Great to meet you, sir,' said Ronald by way of polite introduction.

'Now Achmid, I understand you wish to be supplied with two hundred high-powered assault rifles, do I understand correctly?' enquired Teddy.

The Palestinian looked suspiciously in Ronald's direction.

'Oh don't mind my son, he's my heir apparent,' Teddy said reassuringly.

'Yes, Mr Crump, two hundred plus night vision sights for our forces.'

'Very well, the rifles plus sights are no problem and because you have indicated future orders we can agree a price of $1,000 per rifle,' Teddy explained.

'That sounds very reasonable, Mr Crump. I think we can do business.'

'No, not today,' Crump told Achmid. 'We will make a verbal and, as gentlemen, binding agreement today and from now on you will deal with my most trusted man, Mr Tomkinson. He will sort everything out including safe passage, payment method and any liaison you may require.

The Arab nodded. 'That is suitable.'

'I'd trust Tomkinson with my life,' Teddy added, exaggerating just a little. 'May I recommend passage via Saudi Arabia?'

'Yes, if your Mr Tomkinson can guarantee to get them to our contacts in Syria,' the Palestinian cautiously said.

'Very well, I'll arrange everything with Mr Tomkinson. This is the last time you and I shall meet person to person. The less contact we have, the less chance of anything going wrong,' Crump told Achmid.

'I agree,' said Achmid.

At this point the meeting ended. Teddy informed his guest that Tomkinson would contact Achmid's Syrian office directly, and with that, they said their goodbyes.

Teddy now went to work on his son.

'You see, son, always put clear blue water between yourself and anything which may backfire. Of course, we don't want that to happen but should it, both you and I are in the clear. It is Bob Tomkinson who will take the rap. He gets paid extra for these jobs and the chances of anything going wrong are miniscule. For Bob it's money for old rope but should anything happen, I know nothing of the deal. When the rifles are passed over Tomkinson will ensure false hallmarks and numbers are etched onto them.

'Now so this is where you come in, with that mathematical brain of yours. We shall be receiving $200,000 from the Palestinians in a money transfer from a respectable account. During the transaction you will make $200,000 become half a million, get my drift? As no actual money will change hands, the final amount will finish up not in the business account but our undisclosed special reserve account we have with Hugh Rothschild. We do not put these through the books and therefore do not pay tax. To all intents and purposes the money does not exist. Should anybody get caught it will be some teller at Rothschild's bank whom he will not only dismiss but also prosecute. It's an extra insurance. Of course if nothing goes wrong the employee is safe, providing they do not ask too many questions.'

'That sounds great, Dad. I'm learning fast under you,' said Ronald.

'Sure you are son. I'm not handing all this over to an idiot,' Teddy said with a confiding grin

Bob Tomkinson was an engineer in his own right and by trade. He had been in the US Army with Teddy Crump; in fact, Colonel Crump was his commanding officer towards the end of hostilities. On leaving the army Tomkinson had ideas about setting up on his own, ideas which had come to the attention of Crump via the barracks grapevine. The Colonel decided he had to stop Bob's endeavour. It would be competition which he could do without, especially since he knew nothing about engineering himself. Crump was to inherit the family's engineering company and had plans to expand into the arms trade. He did not need a competitor who knew what he was doing. He summoned Sergeant Tomkinson to his office.

'Now Sergeant, uh Bob, let's cut the formalities. We will both be in civvy street shortly. I understand, or I've heard through the grapevine, you are intending to set up a business of your own?'

'Yes, sir,' replied the sergeant.

'Well, Bob, why not consider coming in with me instead of starting from the bottom on your own? I will have a ready-made business and you could be, if you wish, my deputy, my number two, answerable only to me. You will be a senior director, in fact *the* senior director and you will not have to invest a cent, unlike the other board members. You know the trade so nobody on the shop floor, where you will be king, will be able to pull the wool over your eyes.

'You will be on five per cent of all profits per annum along with your director's salary which will be pretty much the same as the other board members. I can't be seen as too preferential, as I am sure you will understand. And you will be my troubleshooter, Bob. We have been through the war together [not strictly true – Crump had been a staff officer for most of the conflict; only towards the end was he in France with Bob], and I need a man who is one hundred per cent trustworthy – and that man is you.'

Tomkinson was beginning to feel like a man who had shaken hands with destiny, the Almighty himself. His head was up in the clouds with this unrivalled blessing.

Crump elaborated further. 'As you know business is a little like the army: there will be times when the game gets dirty, and you will cover my back just as we cover each other's backs in the field of conflict [Crump had never actually been in the field of conflict]. Should circumstances demand, you will be my barrier man: to get to me they must get through you. For these very rare occasions, if ever, you will receive a payment of $10,000 cash tax free.

'I'd appreciate it if you would take this offer, sergeant,' Crump said, reverting back to military conversation momentarily, reminding Tomkinson of the difference in their ranks.

Tomkinson, being used to unquestioning obedience, took this request of his colonel to be more of a subtle order which he could not refuse, just as Teddy Crump was hoping. Bob Tomkinson accepted the offer without hesitation, and with this disappeared any chance or hopes he may have held about going into business himself.

'Good man, I knew I could rely on you, sergeant, sorry, Bob. I'll have a contract drawn up for this afternoon,' a delighted Crump enthused.

Bob Tomkinson saluted and left Crump's office. As he came back to earth after the initial euphoria, he felt like a man who had just sold his entire future and those of his children to the devil. It was too late now to change his mind, and the colonel would be most annoyed if he did. On the bright side, he thought, I will have a regular salary, plus my five per cent, and the occasional ten thousand dollars in my account. *Colonel Crump would never put me in any real danger, it will be easy money*, he convinced himself.

Now, twenty years after the Second World War ended, here he was, still on his miserable five per cent and the fall guy for a man who was quite obviously up to no good at times. True enough, he had become reasonably wealthy himself over the years but Crump was one of the wealthiest men in the USA. If anybody ended up in prison it would be him, Tomkinson, and certainly not Crump or his son. *There was no point crying over spilt milk*, Bob thought. Even if he wanted to set himself up in business he was now too old and even if he were twenty years younger Crump was now so powerful he would make a terrible enemy and competitor. He consoled himself by reasoning that the chances of him doing time for Crump were very low as Teddy had the commissioner of police and many senior judges in his pocket. There were enough safety nets in place to prevent Tomkinson ending up in prison, unless he did anything stupid. Teddy would not allow that to happen, would he?

It was now August and here occurred an event which caught Ronald and Teddy's attention. An incident occurred in the Gulf of Tonkin involving two Vietnamese gunboats and the US Battleship, Maddox. According to reports, the Vietnamese vessels attacked the US ship in international waters on 2nd August. The navy retaliated but another similar incident took place two days later on 4th August with a similar result. Minor damage was done to the US ship and one of their aircraft.

'Fucking commies attacking our boys in neutral waters, in clear breach of international law,' raged Teddy Crump.

Ronald agreed wholeheartedly and suggested he hold a public meeting when he returned to school.

'Good idea, son,' agreed his father. 'Lay it on thick.'

In years to come this incident was proved to be purely an invention of the White House to justify President Johnson's plans to send more US troops to Vietnam. This phoney incident had, in the short term, the desired effect as public opinion began to swing behind the president.

Ronald decided to return to Bishops Court Rise on the Sunday instead of Monday. Today being Thursday, he had only a couple more days to avoid Peter Tillerson and Terry Morgan. He wanted to go into town to buy two key text books, *Property Markets and Transactions* and *Modern Real Estate*. He left early to avoid meeting Tillerson on his way to the gym and was a nervous wreck on the bus. *What if Tillerson boarded the vehicle?* he thought. What would he do? There was nowhere to run, and he would be exposed for the non-fighter he was.

By the time the bus stopped at Ronald's destination, Ronald's nerves were almost at breaking point. Thankfully, he had arrived in town without incident, and the bookshop was only a matter of yards away. In the distance he thought he spotted Terry Morgan who, though not the menace Tillerson would be, could still knock Ronald about. Crump found some inner strength and pulled himself together. He looked again and much to his relief noted the individual in question, on closer inspection, was not Morgan. Phew, thought Ronald. He entered the bookshop and located the required literature. He took the books to the assistant, a young attractive woman in her early twenties, who noticed Ronald was shaking.

'Tire you out, did she, love, or was it your right hand?' she asked teasingly.

Of course, it was neither of these.

'Something like your first guess, darling,' he said, trying to act all manly.

'Don't lie, you've been ham shanking,' the woman from the Bronx teased, using something like English Cockney slang.

Not to worry, thought Ronald, *all I have to do now is get back home safely.* This he accomplished and never ventured out of the house unaccompanied again until he returned to school. The weekend flew by, much to Ronald's delight, and on Sunday afternoon he said his goodbyes to Teddy and Megan as he was driven to the airport. On the flight he decided against trying any fancy chat-up lines with the hostesses. It had not, after all, been a great holiday in the department of popularity, and he didn't want to make things worse. He began planning his public meeting. He thought the best time to hold it would be before the start of term if he could manage it, because even though he had promised no meetings in his sixth year, the Gulf of Tonkin incident could not be allowed to pass. Yes, he would book the hall as early as he could. One last oration then heads down to studying.

Ronald arrived back at his dormitory, the first week in September, and flaked out on his bed. After a short nap he produced one of the text books he had purchased from the shop and began to read. He took a pencil and began drafting some figures regarding property and inflation projected over a two-year period. These figures would be of no use to him in a real business deal. They were purely for practice purposes so when the course began he would have perfected a calculating formula which would be of use in exams. The student was then supposed to answer the questions by cross-referencing. Cheating would only give a false picture. Ronald was aware of this and avoided such folly.

Ronald Crump had booked the main hall for his meeting to discuss the events of the 2nd and 4th August 1964 in the Gulf of Tonkin. There was a huge attendance expected on the evening of Wednesday 10th September, the earliest he could book the room. He did not want the events under discussion to fade from memory, so it was important to have the subject talked about as soon after the incident as possible. He intended to drum up support for the war and inject as much hatred for an alternative political ideology, communism, as possible. He would also once again appeal to the black population of the USA to enrol and do their duty. Ronald also invited the local media to the meeting with a view that if his oration was good enough the national newspapers could get a copy via the locals selling to them.

The evening came to pass quickly enough and Ronald opened his address.

'My fellow Americans,' he said, 'on the second and fourth of August this year, 1964, our naval patrols were attacked with no good cause in international waters by communist terrorist gunboats. We, the USA, have been more than patient with these terrorists and can no longer stand idly by and allow these actions to continue with no retaliation. We must all support, despite a handful of mindless commie sympathisers opposition calling themselves the "anti-war movement", President Johnson's policy of increasing our military presence and activity in Vietnam.'

This was met with rapturous applause by the junior ranks of the US bourgeoisie, and the media gave the oration a glowing report. It was true that, at the time, both the anti-war movement and US military involvement were small compared with a year later. Later in the conflict when TV pictures broadcast the horrors of Vietnam, the anti-war movement would mushroom in size.

Ronald's oration of that evening for the first time made national newspapers – those which were supporters of the Democratic Party, at least. This would be Ronald's last public discourse before university where he intended carrying on with his racist views and opposition of the anti-war movement. But he would find life surprisingly different there.

The local media were delighted to act as a conduit for the nationals, thus promoting Ronald Crump as a future politician. Ronald Crump was already beginning to feel like Joseph Goebbels, Hitler's propaganda minister, despite claiming to have nothing politically in common with him. He had studied this madman and his posturing with the intention of imitating the Nazi, hoping nobody would notice any similarities. He had no need to worry on that front. His posturing was nothing like that of Goebbels or, for that matter, any other political orator.

Ronald began his studies with enthusiasm. The mock work he had prepared would serve him well in his studying of real estate proper. Ronald was applying his math skills into property valuations and these skills would give him an impressive edge over his peers. He was a quick learner, particularly if he had an ulterior motive as he had in this subject: making money. One very important issue Ronald did learn about was regarding properties to be purchased and what these properties entailed. If a potential buyer decided upon a property, that property would be bought as seen. This would include all land surrounding the property as part of the actual building until such a point as that estate stopped in law. If there were any natural resources on this land and if the seller was unaware of this fact, and if at a later date the purchaser discovered this, they were under no legal obligation to inform the former owner. If the purchaser was aware of any resources which added value to the property being present before the sale, but the seller was unaware, then the buyer was again under no legal obligation to bring this to the seller's attention. The buyer would purchase as seen and as described by the seller or that person's agent. If the seller was aware of any resources on their land for sale, they were legally entitled to add this accordingly on to the selling price. This aspect of the subject interested Ronald and already his mind was working overtime. There had to be a way, if selling, to con a potential buyer into believing that natural resources *might* be present without actually stating it as a fact. This implication could be added on to the price. No law would be broken – at least, strictly speaking.

Ronald's sixth form dormitory was larger than his previous accommodation at the school, and it was here he began his early plans for a 'Property Survey Department' for Crumps Ltd. As we know, Ronald Crump was eventually to take over the reins of his father's empire. He had already outlined his provisional plan for expanding into the realms of real estate which Teddy had agreed in principle. He knew the days of heavy engineering were numbered and planned to reduce the size of this area greatly, perhaps concentrating on micro-engineering which would require two small workshops only. The cooling shops would no longer be necessary, nor would the huge turning rooms. The blacksmiths' department could go with the loss in total of around two thousand jobs. All this was, however, for the future. United States scientists were working on many new projects which in decades to come would change the face of industry, including Crumps. Ronald was considering, again in the future, of changing the company's trading name, dropping the 'Engineering' part of the title. He would eventually name his company 'Crumps Arms Developers and Real Estate'.

Early November saw the mock exams take place. The course Ronald was sitting held their mocks in the second half of November, about five weeks before Christmas. This way the students would have an idea how they were doing and where they needed to improve before the Christmas break. The real exams were in March the following year. Ronald was disappointed in his result, just scraping a B. If this was his mark in the real exams it would be touch and go as to whether a B would be high enough to get him into university. As was his entitlement, Ronald decided to see his year tutor for an explanation.

'Well, Ronald, your plan for properties which may or may not hold natural resources, though not illegal, is very close to the line between lawful and unlawful. In property, the area between legalities and illegalities is very grey indeed, and you are certainly trawling deep waters by ignoring all ethics. Do you see why we marked you down?'

'I do and you're wrong,' an indignant Crump told his lecturer, not perhaps the best way of promoting ideas with the person who could make or break him. Ronald went on to explain. 'In the real world of the property market such ideas and moves as I suggested would be considered mild by comparison, perhaps even professional.'

'Yes, Ronald, that may or may not be the case, but you are not in the real world yet and if you really wish to get there you will dilute these ideas down. The idea of mock exams is for students to learn from their mistakes and put them right for the real thing,' said the lecturer. 'Imagine, Ronald, you are taking your driving test and you adopt the habits of experienced drivers. These habits may not be illegal, but an instructor would not expect a learner to be using them in their test. Do you get my drift? These mocks are your "mock driving test", an opportunity to put good any slapdash errors. If you have any sense, for your real exams you will stop these suggested conman tricks and stick to the straight and narrow. When, or indeed if, you enter the murky world of real estate, there will be plenty of room for this kind of trickery.'

'You're right, sir. I'll revise those ideas accordingly.'

'That's better, Ronald, I've no doubt you will pass with flying colours come March,' said the lecturer.

The sixth year at Bishops Court Rise was different from the previous five because every student was doing their access course by choice. Ronald decided to follow the advice his tutor had given him and use the text books which he had invested in, along with the school library recommended reading, as they were supposed to be used. No more ideas of pretending he was already a high-flying property speculator; plenty of time for that once he had reached the required standard to enter the field.

He also determined over the Christmas break that he would divide his time between meetings with his father and revision. If there was an overlap, then his studies would take preference and if his father did not like it then that would be unfortunate. Of course, Ronald thinking like this immediately after a meeting with his lecturer and actually conveying such feelings to his father were two entirely different things. Although Teddy was very supportive of his son's studies he would not tolerate insubordination from Ronald. Talk like 'that would be unfortunate' Teddy would not accept. Ronald would have to word it more mildly but mean the same thing. Ronald was hoping Teddy would understand, especially as these studies would benefit the company in the protracted vision, which they would. The language conveying these thoughts must be tactful though.

Ronald knew he had to get at least an A or preferably an A+ to guarantee himself a place at university. A lower mark might not be sufficient, and it meant leaving a lot to chance! It would serve him well to bury himself in his studies over Christmas, and it would also give him the perfect excuse for not leaving the house. He was still afraid of encountering Peter Tillerson and Terry Morgan, who seemed to hate him for his fascist ideas, as they saw them. However, he would have to leave the house on Christmas morning to attend church service, but he would be with his parents.

As it was, Peter was growing away from Duke and Sheena Tillerson and might not be at church. He seemed to be heading down the atheist road. On Christmas Day all the brigands' families were going to the Rothschilds' and again if Peter was there it would be with his parents. There was also a possibility Judy McClean would be present with her parents so enough alternative activity would be present to keep Peter away from Ronald, he told himself.

The Christmas and New Year period went off with no major incident; Ronald had managed to avoid his two erstwhile friends. *What had happened*, he thought, *to these two morons?* They sounded like communists. And what could he do about it if this were the case? Once again Ronald's mind began to drift into the realms of fantasy, imagining he had the power to have these two arrested and thrown in irons.

Just before Ronald returned to school President Lyndon Johnson came on the television outlining his plans for the coming year. He intended increasing US ground troop numbers in Vietnam, as requested by the generals. Hitherto, most operations carried out by the United States were done by the United States Air Force but after losing many aircraft to the Soviet MiG fighters, Johnson decided on the use of more ground troops. It had been recently revealed that the Soviet Union were backing the North Vietnamese Army and, therefore, the Viet Cong Guerrilla fighters in the south, with military hardware including aircraft. 'Boots on the ground,' was President Johnson's response.

'Now we'll see the commies get a roasting, son,' Teddy commented.

'That's right, Dad, I only wish I could be there,' said Ronald, knowing full well this would be unlikely to happen, and even if there was a draft it would only affect working-class kids, not the likes of him who were far too valuable to lose in battle. If one day the draft came into being and did reach as far up the social ladder as himself, he knew his father would pull enough strings to get him out of it! This did not stop the armchair soldier pretending to bite at the bit to get out there and sort out the communists.

Ronald arrived back at school and, as he had promised himself, got straight down to his revision. The final exam in late March had to be better than his mocks. He was confident, now he was aware of his mistakes, he would get at least an A. Despite his promise to himself about taking time out from what he considered political activity, on 7th March 1965 an incident occurred which tested his resolve to this commitment.

The incident in question lasted from 7th–25th March and made national television. A civil rights march from Selma to Montgomery, Alabama, along a fifty-four-mile-long highway in support of President Johnson's Voting Rights Act was brutally attacked by State troopers, despite being non-violent. The majority of the marchers were African American and were protesting against attempted state legislature in the racist state of Alabama and its racist governor George Wallace. Alabama had invoked sixteen state legislatures which were passed, leading to a series of discriminatory requirements which African Americans were to fulfil in order to exercise their democratic right to vote. If these legislatures went unchecked millions of African Americans would face being disenfranchised. Ronald Crump, as was his father, was fanatical in his support for the racist policies of George Wallace and in a conversation with his equally racist friend, Christopher Johnson, he voiced, 'They should have shot the lot of them, blacks and the rotten white traitors alike: gun them down like dogs.'

'Too right, Ron, my dad says, "The only good n****r is a dead one". What fucking right have they got to demand anything?'

'No right whatsoever, Chris,' Ronald agreed.

The truth was, neither Ronald or Christopher had any idea about politics in the USA. They both parrot-fashioned what their parents had told them who, in turn, merely aped their own forebears. This kind of racial prejudice in the USA, particularly in the South, had been passed down from generation to generation since the days of Robert E. Lee, Stonewall Jackson and the Civil War.

Of course, there was an ulterior motive for this racism, certainly from Teddy Crump and Harry Johnson's viewpoint, and the same would apply to Ronald and Christopher very shortly. The last thing the bourgeoisie needed was black and white workers uniting, together with native Americans and Hispanics, against the common cause which they all shared: poverty, shit working conditions and uncertainty in life, while the likes of the Crumps got richer by the minute. For this reason, these tycoons hated trade unions who bridged the artificial gap which divides workers.

In union firms, workers are certainly more united and enjoy, as a result of this solidarity, better working conditions and wages. The last thing the Crumps and Johnsons, senior and junior, wanted was workers' solidarity. Therefore, the more division they could create dividing these workers the better. What easier way than the grounds of skin colour. Tell the white workers they are superior to the blacks and encourage white workers in the name of this supremacy to have nothing to do with their 'inferior' black brethren. Even though white workers were also living on the breadline they were marginally better off than their black counterparts. These white workers would fight to the death to defend these miniscule advantages. As far as Ronald and Christopher were concerned, these traditions of racist disharmony would continue on their watch just as on their parents'.

What these people did not realise, or refused to conceive, was that industrial relations were changing in the USA as was society in general. Duke Tillerson was forced into recognising the trade unions at his textile factories, a trend which had spread to the construction side of his empire. With the trade unions came better working conditions and pay for the workers plus improvements in health and safety, which also benefitted the employer. Tillerson consequently enjoyed unprecedented industrial peace in both his avenues of commerce and, though he was loath to admit this, had no regrets generally in recognising the unions. He now dealt with a committee of shop stewards instead of the countless individual grievances. Teddy Crump and, later, his son, would not even contemplate accepting what they perceived as a climbdown.

Ronald decided against involving himself in the events unfurling in Alabama. Despite supporting Governor Wallace unreservedly, he needed to concentrate on his studies. He told his fellow racist and so-called 'patriot' Christopher Johnson, 'I have done enough to save this great nation from the n*****s and the commies. I have worked all hours in this great crusade against the Reds and, the way I look at it, the USA owes me a lot. Now somebody else can lead the way. Let them show the courage I have espoused.'

'Too right, Ron,' Johnson said sympathetically.

Teddy Crump was one of the top ten richest men in the USA. His disclosed wealth, taxable, was around nine hundred thousand million dollars plus, just short of the billion-dollar figure. However, it was his undisclosed monies which pushed him over this magical figure: the wealth he had not disclosed to the government. These were monies he had accumulated through dodgy deals, such as the small one he was conducting with the Palestinians against the allies of the USA, Israel. Most, if not all, of the top ten richest men in the US had become rich by adopting such tactics which were broadly accepted, provided tax was paid at the normal rate on the disclosed income. These were some of the underhand dealings that Teddy had taught his son. He actually had no need to worry because Ronald understood the way of the world and had already perfected some more advanced ideas of his own in this department.

In the second from last week in March, Ronald Crump sat in the great hall ready to sit his final exams on the subject of his choice, real estate. He would have his results in time for his eighteenth birthday in April. After that, there was only a four-thousand-word dissertation to submit before 30th May and that would complete his sixth year. The exam marks carried sixty per cent and the dissertation forty per cent.

In late March Ronald received his final exam results. He had reached his target with a respectable A, at eighty out of a hundred points. Providing his dissertation received more than forty-five out of a hundred, he was on his way to either Harvard or Yale. It would shortly be Ronald's birthday, which he was to spend at Bishops Court Rise with his so-called friends. When the day arrived, and as it was an optional year, Ronald and a select group took the day off studies. He was halfway through his dissertation, so time was now on his side and the gang decided town was a good idea. After a pub crawl and a great deal of alcohol consumption they finished at a small bar frequented by local people. Of course, Crump and his gang thought the rules of the shop did not apply to them so, fuelled by alcohol, Ronald decided the woman behind the bar was his for the taking.

He lunged forward making a grab for the upper regions.

'Get off me, you pig,' the barmaid shouted.

'Come on, sugar, you know who I am, and I want you for the night,' Ronald told her, much to the moronic laughter of Johnson and the rest.

At that moment a local lad, the woman's partner, was on his feet, and so were his friends.

'Keep your fucking hands to yourself or I'll break you in two,' the local said.

'You and whose army?' Crump replied.

At this point the young man, the barmaid's partner, smacked Ronald, putting him down in one. Even the alcohol could not hide the fear which

Crump was experiencing and, similar to the event with Peter Tillerson, he stayed curled up on the floor. Christopher Johnson made a half-hearted move in his friend's defence and was met with aggression from another of the man's company.

The bar manager came out.

'What is going on?' he asked.

'This guy just molested Kathy,' the young man said. 'He tried to grab her against her will.'

'Right you lot, out! You're barred,' shouted the manager to the locals and the barmaid.

'Were you encouraging these lads again?' he accusingly asked Kathy.

'No I wasn't! He tried to grab my breasts,' she protested.

The manager did not believe her or her boyfriend. After he barred the locals he apologised to the students of the bourgeoisie for any inconvenience which they may have suffered.

'They won't be served in here again, goddamn rabble,' the manager assured the students. 'Of course you lads are welcome anytime.'

'Thanks, Mr Barman, we'll think about coming to your crummy little bar again if we are desperate,' Ronald Crump insultingly told the bar manager, having recovered his composure.

'Fucking dump,' interjected Johnson and at this point they left, kicking a couple of chairs over on their way.

The publican had, by creeping to his so-called betters, just lost his regular customers, his barmaid and his dignity in one fell swoop.

Ronald Crump received his marks for the coursework he had submitted, the four-thousand-word dissertation. He was given a mark of 2–1, a high second which, coupled with his exam results, would almost certainly guarantee him a place at university. In mid-June he received a letter from Yale university in Connecticut, not too far from New York, accepting his application and securing him a place in the discipline of his choice, real estate. He would take his place in September, the start of the academic year, and would spend three years at the prestigious educational establishment.

The long summer break this year was very quiet for Ronald. He spent most of his time with his father discussing plans for the business, as there was no studying for once. He was an almost permanent fixture at his father's side and was even given a temporary office in the admin block at the arms factory. At the board meetings Ronald still had the urge to remind Sally Seddon of the ordeal he had subjected her to, despite her playing her own part in bringing the terror about. The novelty of this sick amusement was beginning to wear a little thin as important business decisions, involving Ronald, were now being taken. He felt more involved and that his opinion counted. He even considered a 'kiss and make up' meeting with Sally but decided, as the whole rotten saga was her fault and he was the injured party, he would 'let sleeping dogs lie'. After all, the last thing he needed were further distractions from her!

Ronald arrived at Yale university on his first day with all his belongings. He was to reside in the halls of residence and was heading in that general direction when he was confronted by something he was not expecting. Facing him at the end of the main lobby was a life-size portrait of Martin Luther King Jr. Dr King had given a very successful speech at Yale back in 1962 and many students had been won over to his way of thinking. This had started a leftwards tradition at the university encompassing civil rights, which prevailed on campus at the time of Ronald's arrival. To make matters worse for Crump his hero, George Wallace, the racist governor of Alabama, was forced to cancel his talk at the university. Initially, some students spoke to him, but he had to pull out due to opposition to his views from the powerful students' lobby.

Ronald was met at the halls of residence by a welcoming committee of four men and two women. 'Are you Ronald Crump?' the leading male requested.

'Yes, and you are?' was Ronald's reply.

'We are from the students' union and these two gentlemen are supporters of the Black Panther Movement. We are here to tell you that any of your racist crap will not be tolerated.'

The Black Panther Movement was a fledgling black liberation organisation.

'Now you listen to me—' Ronald began, leaning forward aggressively.

He shrank back when one of the men stepped forward confidently. 'No, you listen, Crump. We don't have people like you creating racial disharmony here, and if you make any attempt at pathetic speeches you will feel the consequences. Do you understand? This is your first and final friendly warning.'

One of the women then interjected. 'We are from the women's section supporting feminism, and any sexist, misogynist anti-women discourse will be disposed of in much the same way.'

'So you just get on with your studies and bother nobody and we'll all get on famously. Oh, if you change your views and become human you will be welcome to join us,' another man said.

Not likely, Ronald thought, but had the good sense to keep his mouth shut.

The first semester of the commencing year began well for Ronald. He had received his information package outlining each of the three courses which completed the semester and the recommended reading which he could acquire in the college library. He also had his key text books, which were always advisable to purchase, and would read and act accordingly. He decided, in view of, but not solely because of, the conversation he had with members of the students' union, not to involve himself in the political scene at Yale. The students' union was quite obviously controlled by terrorists and communists, he thought, and his brand of political theory would not be appreciated. Translated, this roughly meant the students' union representatives had frightened the brave fascist to death.

Ronald knew he had to get over forty-five per cent in his first year; this was the benchmark which decided who would progress to the second and third years and who would be sent home. He also knew, despite the low mark as the benchmark, that in the first year and because of only forty-five per cent being the pass mark, the marking would be much tighter. He settled into his dormitory in the halls of residence and unpacked. His thoughts wondered back to the ugly reception he had faced.

'These people will pay for their treachery one day,' he told himself.

For the time being Ronald's sole aim was getting through the next three years and moving on to the serious world of big business.

The students' union at Yale was large and well organised. It was not, as Ronald suggested to himself, run by communists, though there were many Marxists involved. The majority were centre-left in their outlook and for many the union was a phase of university radicalism which they were going through. The majority of student activists at Yale, as at any other university, would, on leaving higher education, drop their radical ideas and move into the world of business and commerce. Others, perhaps more dedicated to the Marxist and revolutionary cause, would possibly become trade union leaders, moderating their views a little, and would forget about overthrowing the system and would operate within it for the benefit of their members. A tiny minority would become full-time revolutionaries in such organisations as the Red Brigades, Red Army Faction and other groups, possibly purchasing illegal arms from such people as Ronald Crump! One thing all these student activists shared was a detestation for racism and the Vietnam War. For these reasons Ronald kept his counsel to himself.

★ ★ ★

Megan Crump was at home alone, as was the case most days, with only the domestics for company. Megan did not wish to be available for conversation with her staff; she preferred to keep a distance from them because she did not believe in too much familiarity. Teddy was at work, or what passed for work, so she telephoned Derek. After a period of caution regarding covering her tracks, she had become more confident again about using the phone from home. What she was unaware of was that Teddy now had their telephone rigged so he could listen in on her calls at his office. And today would be one of those days when he would do just that.

'Hello, Derek darling. What are you doing tomorrow?' the bored housewife enquired.

'Nothing, dear, I can get the morning off to meet you.'

'Wonderful! Meet in Bishops Hotel at eleven?'

'Perfect, darling, I can't wait,' her lover said. 'Till tomorrow.'

Teddy listened to this and decided his wife would not make her meeting. He was bored himself and wanted some amusement. Teddy arrived home about six o'clock.

'Hi, darling, busy day?'

'No not really,' replied his wife, 'very quiet. The dinner will be served shortly, dear, Cook has made a special effort for you to show her appreciation to you as an employer.'

'Oh, I am honoured,' Crump sarcastically said.

The following morning Teddy delayed his time for setting off for the office. 'I'll need you this morning, dear,' he informed his wife.

'What for? I… I… I'm going out.'

'Sorry, dear, duty calls,' Teddy informed her. 'Your friend will understand.'

'Friend, what friend?' said Megan with an element of panic in her voice.

'Why, Mary Rothschild. I assumed you were meeting her for coffee when you said you were going out. I'll phone her and let her know you can't make it.'

'No, no. I'll tell her, dear, no need for you to bother yourself,' Megan said.

Derek would be waiting. It was too late for him to cancel his arrangements for time away from work. What could she do? Of course, Teddy was aware this would be the case, which was why he left it until the last minute to inform his wife she was needed elsewhere. Megan was supposed to meet Derek at eleven and it was now half past.

Teddy then dropped his bombshell, again pre-planned. He told Megan he would not be needing her after all so if she wished a coffee with Mary that was, after all, possible.

'Would you like to phone her, darling? I'm going to the office now,' he said chuckling away at his mischievous actions. As soon as Teddy was out of the drive Megan phoned Bishops Hotel to ask if Derek Riley was still there.

'Hold on, madam, I'll just see for you.'

Derek came to the phone.

'I was just about to leave, Megan, where were you?'

The distraught Megan explained what had happened. 'It was almost like he was playing a game with me, like he knew what's going on!'

'Don't be silly, darling, how can he?' Derek replied with mild laughter in his voice. 'He has no idea what we're up to, don't worry.'

Megan agreed, feeling a bit better. Little did she know what other games Teddy had in mind, games which would never actually be played due to a sudden deterioration in the tycoon's health.

Ronald was preparing for his first exams at Yale University. He had revised hard but was acutely aware the marking here was on a different level to Bishops Court Rise. He had not mixed well with his fellow students as he was unsure who was who. They all seemed to be part of the union, and he had been told in no uncertain terms he was not welcome to join it with his current political views. He fancied one of the girls who was active in the union and had even tried to talk to her.

'Fuck off, I don't talk to racists,' she had told him.

'Bet you're a lesbian,' he muttered to himself.

It was a lonely life for Ronald, but it was mostly of his own making. Nobody likes a racist and misogynist and certainly not in a progressive institution like Yale. He sat his exams and presented his coursework on time. His essay marks were very good, which allowed a little room for manoeuvre in his exams. For his essay on Fluctuating Property Values he was in the 60s or 2–1 bracket, which was good; and his exam marks, despite the complexity of the questions, were better than he expected – 48, 53 and 55 respectively, a third and two 2–2 marks. There was no pressure on Ronald to achieve a first in this discipline. That would be only for self-gratification. He would not be applying for a job which demanded at least a 2–1 or even, at a push, a 2–2, as his father's company was, or soon would be, his own.

Teddy Crump was now in his mid-seventies and was beginning to lose interest, or perhaps more accurately, was beginning to show signs of being unable to hold his interest. The vultures in waiting on the board had not yet come to the realisation their chief was beginning to lose his grip. Teddy was privately aware he was not the man he had been even six months previously, but still had enough about him to hold on for the arrival, full time, of Ronald. He had pencilled in the year 1970 at the latest for his final exit from the business but privately hoped his son would be ready to take over earlier. It was now approaching 1966, only four years to go, maximum, and that was it for him. Teddy would enjoy his retirement, though what difference it would actually make to his daily life was unclear: he did little enough in the way of work as it was!

Teddy was aware Ronald would graduate in 1968 and privately hoped that within six months of this graduation his son would be ready. He could not allow the board or more importantly his employees to realise what was happening. Teddy had made a master plan to finally catch Megan and her lover out in the open with no argument. He would catch them in bed red-handed. The problem was, on the day he was to execute his devious plan he just could not be bothered. He could not find the energy. Therefore, Megan and Derek continued their assignations in blissful ignorance. Crump even reduced the amount of sexual assaults and abuse he subjected his young female employees to. This change went unnoticed as Crump seldom used the same member of staff more than once in a fortnight. Occasionally he might molest the same woman regularly for two or three days and then move on to somebody else. The same applied to him having sex with them, either in the office or at a hotel. The staff never discussed this abuse with each other. They were either too ashamed, too afraid or both and because there was no dialogue on the subject, and because of the irregularity with individuals, no attention was paid to Crump's deterioration in health.

Over the Christmas and New Year period Ronald had noticed his father had lost some of the bounce in his character. He had an idea what was happening and made it his business to keep any notions private and away from the board. During this break from university Ronald undertook a few more duties, the unseen work, from his ailing father. He would soon be in his second year at Yale and had every reason to believe he would graduate in 1968 with at least a 2–2. So long as he could sign his name 'Ronald Crump BA (Hons)', that was all which counted. He worried less about the finer points of university life and just wanted the time to pass. The next few months at Yale went by without major incident, and Ronald made preparations for his final exams.

As was usual, he handed his coursework in early. Once again, when the results came in it was revealed that Ronald was well on course for his degree. All he had to do was keep this up for the duration of his course. This he would manage with little difficulty. The events going on at home took Ronald's mind off politics and also the loneliness of few students talking to him. He was not enjoying life at the university but would reap the rewards of his suffering later.

★ ★ ★

Outside university in the larger political arena events were moving apace, particularly Lyndon Johnson's foreign policy towards Vietnam. President Johnson had made his final decision to increase the number of US troops on the ground, partly due to the failure of the air war to control the North Vietnamese and Viet Cong. This action by the president brought about a sharp increase in the anti-war movement and the numbers involved. At Yale it was students' union policy to oppose the war and leaflets condemning the actions of the United States were distributed. Coupled with the rise in the anti-war feeling the Black Panthers were in their ascendancy. Many students at Yale supported or were clandestine members of this revolutionary organisation committed to civil rights and black liberation. Despite the hype and rantings of the right-wing media, these people were not black thugs but very rational and reasonable people with a just grievance. For the Black Panthers, violence, though accepted as necessary at times, was very much a last resort.

Teddy Crump and Megan had made an appointment at the George Washington Private Hospital. Many 'ordinary' patients had their appointments either postponed or cancelled because the great man needed treatment. The neurologist, Dr Alan Quincy, was a personal friend of the Crumps and had often been a guest at their dinner table.

'Hi Al, how's it going?' said Teddy by way of introduction.

'Great Ted, and how are you, the delectable Megan?'

'I'm fine, Al, how's Veronica?'

'She's fine, probably on the golf course as we speak. Now, what appears to be the problem?' the neurologist asked.

'Well, Al, it's his short-term memory, he keeps forgetting,' Megan informed the physician.

'I can speak for myself, honey,' Crump interjected.

'How long has this been going on, Teddy? Do you have problems recalling long-term occurrences?' Dr Quincy questioned Teddy for about forty minutes then asked if he could recall where his wife was.

'Why, did you not say she was – oh, where did you say? She is I think, she's playing golf,' Teddy finally recalled.

'That's right, Ted, you got it eventually,' Quincy said with a false air of optimism.

'What do you think, Al?' Megan asked.

'Too early to tell. I'll consult my colleague, Dr Franklin Alucard. He's the leading psychiatrist here. If you would both take a seat outside, I'll be back to within the hour,' he told them.

'Thanks,' the Crumps said alternately.

After about forty minutes Dr Quincy returned with his colleague. 'This is the patient, Dr Alucard,' Quincy said, putting his professional hat on.

'I'm going to ask you a series of questions,' the psychiatrist informed Teddy. 'Who is the president of the USA?'

'Uh, John, no, Lyndon Johnson,' was Teddy's belatedly correct answer.

'What rank did you hold in the army?'

'I was a colonel,' Teddy answered without hesitation.

This process continued for about half an hour then the two men retired. Dr Quincy returned a few minutes later and addressed the Crumps. 'It looks like the very early stages of Alzheimer's disease,' he reluctantly informed them. 'I'll know better when we get the results of the blood and urine tests and we would like to do an X-ray on your brain, Ted, with your permission.'

'Yes, by all means,' the arms dealer replied.

When all the tests were completed it was confirmed that the doctor's prognosis was correct.

'Don't worry, Ted, it can take years before deterioration really takes hold, so get on with enjoying life, there's plenty of bounce in you yet,' the physician told him.

'But will my brain deteriorate?'

'Oh yes, eventually, but my guess is not for some time yet,' the doctor said.

'Well, thanks, Al,' said Megan.

'Yes thanks a bunch, Al,' a reluctant Crump added.

Ronald was now ready to sit his final exams at Yale for the first year. Then, as at school, it would be the long summer vacation which for once he was ready for. His results came back before college broke up for the summer and Ronald's marks held up. His course work had improved, and he gained a 2–1 for his dissertation and 2–2 for his exams.

Ronald Crump drove from Yale University to New York in the car his parents had bought him for his eighteenth birthday. On his arrival Megan and Teddy were waiting to break the news of his father's illness.

'It's very early days yet,' Megan informed her son, 'and degeneration will quite possibly take some time, so we still have many happy years ahead of us, God willing.'

'Yes, son,' said Teddy. 'It's just one of those unfortunate things which happen but for the time being it's business as usual. I'll be attending the board meetings when I feel well enough and on those occasional days when I am too tired you can take the meeting on your own. I'll give you full powers. Tell the vultures I'm taking a day off for a round of golf and if they persist with their questions inform them what I do is of no concern of theirs.'

'No problem, Dad, leave it to me,' Ronald reassured his father.

'We must keep this in the family, Ronald,' Teddy emphasised. 'You are already leaps and bounds ahead in the business stakes so when I'm not there things are in safe hands.'

'Thanks, Dad, for the vote of confidence,' Ronald concluded.

The following Wednesday was the day of the board meeting and there was a long agenda. Ronald accompanied his father who made an announcement at the start of the meeting.

'My son will be taking the meeting today. As you all know I will be retiring in a couple of years so this is an opportunity for Ronald to get to know the ropes.'

Teddy had recently appointed a new secretary, Janet Snowden, an attractive woman in her early twenties. She positioned herself adjacent to Ronald for taking the minutes and he gave a cursory look at her stocking tops – later, he thought – before commencing the meeting.

'Now the first item on the agenda I want to deal with is the number of staff we employ. We are carrying too many, especially in our engineering works. The trade is changing, the days of heavy engineering are coming to a close and we must not get left behind. I propose we close our New York works down, or perhaps reduce the output by ninety per cent, concentrating on specialist equipment. For this we will no longer need the huge cooling shops, the moulding plant or half of the tradesmen we presently employ. We shall concentrate on precision equipment such as micro-gyroscopes and high-powered microscopes.'

Of course, this was largely to facilitate Ronald's plans for his venture into real estate, which he chose not to share with the board just yet.

'I propose we close our heavy plants and pay the legal minimum requirement in redundancy payment. I have calculated that it will cost us about the same as one year's rent to pay the staff off, so we will actually lose nothing. If we keep the plants open we will lose on profits and rent; it's a no-brainer.'

'Could we not redeploy?' Bob Tomkinson asked.

'No, Bob, we need to save money to increase profits, not transfer expenditure.'

'Sounds pretty ruthless to me, just throwing people on the scrapheap with no real warning.'

'That's business, Bob, you should know that. What more do the staff want? We have given them plenty of work over the years, protected them from those nasty unions,' – a light laughter rang out at this last remark – 'and now it is time for them to pack their bags and, who knows, enjoy their early retirement.'

This proposal of Ronald's was more of a declaration of intent. There was to be no discussion. Ronald just informed the board as he would inform the workforce, or perhaps more accurately as Janet Snowden would, though she did not yet know this.

'Let's vote on this, a show of hands,' said Ronald. Almost the entire board with one abstainer agreed.

'Carried almost unanimously. Sure you won't change your mind, Bob?'

Ronald then instructed Janet to type up redundancy notices. 'I'll see you in the office shortly we can discuss the wording,' Ronald informed the young secretary.

On hearing this last instruction from Ronald, Sally Seddon muttered, 'Poor girl.'

Ronald and Janet Snowden met in the office as he had instructed.

'You will be working a little late tonight, don't mind, do you?' he said. 'We need to get the wording right on this.'

'Yes, sir, I'll phone my fiancé and tell him I can't make tonight and will see him tomorrow.' Ronald Crump was already removing his jacket and tie!

Ronald arrived back home around eight o'clock.

'How do you think it went, Dad?'

'Great, son, I like the ruthless streak in you, must get it from me. It's the only way in business, son. Remember the staff are working not for themselves but to make a profit for us. When that can no longer be achieved they have to go, where to is not our concern.'

'My sentiments exactly, Dad,' and the two butchers laughed atrociously.

The summer break over, Ronald returned to Yale for the second year of his degree. This would be the 1966–67 year and he intended to keep his head down, work hard and get the fuck away from there, hopefully unharmed. He decided to take the train back as he feared with the increase in student militancy against Lyndon Johnson's foreign policy across campus his car might be vandalised. Better safe than sorry, he thought. This second year would be very uneventful, as far as he was concerned. He just revised in his dormitory and was becoming, purposely, a recluse. He would not bother with the other students, fucking communists, and the girls were all lesbians. They didn't deserve a real man like him, he thought, so let them all rot. Ronald Crump really did have a high opinion of himself. Unfortunately nobody else, outside his family, did! The year dragged on in fits and starts and he finished the term with a respectable 2–2. His coursework was good, but he let himself down a little on the exams; not to worry, as long as he passed. He was now looking forward to his final year, 1967–68. This would be the telling year, so he wished to minimise any possible distractions.

Ronald was fully prepared and studied hard for his final year at university, feeling confident and composed, despite the political situation around him, which was not in line with his views. He felt that in his studies he was fighting with one arm tied behind his back because when preparing his coursework, he could not use his preferred questionable methods in negotiating property contracts he would use in the real world.

It was mid-September and Ronald received a letter from Janet Snowden, now senior secretary since he had taken over much of his father's role. Teddy had instructed her to write directly to his son regarding anything to do with the job losses. The letter read:

Dear Mr Crump

With reference to the job cutbacks we discussed and passed at the board meeting just over one year ago, I am pleased to inform you the last of the workers have now collected their last pay and redundancy money. As you recall, the first batch to lose their employment with the company were put on three months' notice, leaving a scratch team to clear up. These too have now gone, and all the sheds and workshops are vacant and ready for re-leasing to any interested party. We had a little trouble with one employee who tried to stir up trouble with the rest of the workers, agitating for them to occupy the properties. Your father had this man arrested and he has since been sentenced to two years' imprisonment.

I hope this meets with your satisfaction.

Your loyal servant

J. Snowden

Senior Secretary

Ronald was delighted with the outcome and speedy deliverance of disposing of employees that were no longer needed. He had expected the process to take about two years and it had all been done in little over twelve months. It was only right that the man who was causing trouble, trying to save his and other people's jobs, was thrown in prison for a couple of years; it would give him time to cool down. *He was probably a fucking communist anyway*, Crump thought.

It was now break time after the first three-hour lecture and Ronald determined he'd phone Teddy regarding the good news.

'Hi, Dad, it's Ronald.'

'How are you doing, son?' asked Caesar of Tiberius.

'I'm great, Dad. Just to let you know I received a letter from Janet informing me the former employees have all now being disposed of in a very satisfactory and economical manner.'

'Yes, that's right, all gone. Had a little trouble with one fella so I called the commissioner in person who had the lout dealt with.'

'I heard he got two years, serves him right, interfering with the natural order of things like that.'

'That's right, son. I was going to insist on five years but I do have a heart.'

'You're all heart, same as me.' Ronald gave a short laugh. 'Must go now, Dad, another lecture, see you.'

'Bye, son.'

It was now November 1967 and news was filtering through that Che Guevara, the Cuban revolutionary, had been shot and killed. Officially he was executed by the Bolivian Army on 2nd November but in reality, all the evidence pointed in the direction of the CIA. The United States had never forgiven Guevara for the humiliation he heaped on them at the Bay of Pigs. Guevara had commanded the revolutionary forces which defeated the US-backed right-wing attackers. When Teddy Crump heard this news he was ecstatic and almost wept with happiness. This 'terrorist' had been a thorn in the side of the United States bourgeoisie for some time, and now he was no more.

Of course, there was no mention of all the good work Guevara and Fidel Castro had done on the island of Cuba, such as clearing up all the child prostitution centres which former president Batista had turned a blind eye to, and advancements in healthcare on the island. The reasons were twofold. Firstly, the USA wanted the revolution to receive no credit at all, even when it was deserved. Secondly, the clearing of child prostitution in the eyes of many upper-class citizens of the USA was not necessarily a good thing. It was these perverts who used Cuba under Batista as a playground, which was why the USA supported the former right-wing dictator.

Teddy Crump, forgetting his illness, decided to throw a party for all his wealthy neighbours at this great news. But Ronald, at university, though he shared all his father's feelings of delight, was acutely aware that his views would be a tiny minority, possibly of one, at Yale. He also knew it was in his best interests to keep his mouth shut or even, if push came to shove, show an element of sympathy (albeit falsely), and only if he had to.

As the news filtered through, the whole university was in a state of shock. Ronald Crump decided to stay in his dormitory and enjoy the event in private. Suddenly a terrible fear gripped him. What if some of the hotheads wanted a scapegoat? They all knew about him. What if they paid him a visit? He could not go anywhere. He had lectures. No, he would just have to sit it out.

As it happened nobody would have wasted their time on Crump. Even to give him a kicking would have been an insult to Guevara; after all, is that not what fascists did? The following morning at the lecture Ronald kept himself to himself and ignored the looks of hatred aimed in his direction. Even the minority of students who occasionally gave him the time of day were silent. Crump was effectively sent to Coventry. He could live with this, unpleasant as it was.

November passed very quickly and led into December. It would soon be Christmas, New Year and 1968. The murder of Che Guevara passed, though lectures on his life as a physician and revolutionary Marxist continued in the students' union.

9

Ronald Takes the Reins ★ Two Homicides

Ronald was home again for the Christmas and New Year of 1967–68. He had maintained his marks in his coursework and penultimate exams, and his finals would be later in the new year. His actual marks were in the 2–2 or B minus bracket, which was satisfactory. In the imagination of Ronald Crump, his life was under constant threat, with isolationism imposed on him by the intimidating actions of the communists in the students' union. In actual fact there had been no threats to his life. The students' union had much more important things to do than bother about this insignificant, perverse little imp. This was a bad description in terms of Crump's appearance: he was over six feet tall, dark in complexion and slender in build; it was more his perverse attitude which was akin to that of an imp, or a devil. All the students' union said to Crump was that they would not tolerate his sick, racist and fascist rants. If the truth be known, if Ronald had been in less of a hurry to become known by the media at Bishops Court Rise, then nobody would have heard of Ronald Crump. He had in effect created his own cage of solitude!

Ronald was from now on to take a more proactive role in Teddy Crump's empire, soon to be his empire; he was Tiberius, the emperor-in-waiting, in one respect. It was the last board meeting before Christmas and Teddy (Caesar) could not make the venue. He told his son to make his excuse – golfing – that would always cut it. It was a short meeting and Janet was positioned beside the stand-in chief to take minutes.

Ronald opened the meeting. 'Firstly, I would like to thank all of you for the work and dedication you have all put in during the recent closure of our engineering plants which, regrettably, resulted in job losses. The entire closure programme went smoothly, apart from one no-doubt communist-inspired incident, and the buildings are now clear and free for re-letting. I should say a special thank you to Janet here for the diplomacy and skilful wording used when she drafted the redundancy notices.'

'I bet that's not all she drafted,' muttered Sally Seddon.

'Well done all of you,' Ronald concluded. 'Apologies from my father who is indisposed today, he's actually playing golf, and can't make the meeting.'

At this point the board allowed themselves a little appreciative chuckle because if anybody deserved a day off to play golf it was Teddy Crump!

Janet Snowden was an attractive twenty-something-year-old. She was engaged to be married to Richard and they were both living at his parents' house until they got on their feet. Janet had been promoted to senior secretary in recognition of her hard work and dedication by Teddy eighteen months earlier. She was now Ronald's PA, at least for the time being. Janet wore very short skirts and skimpy tops, though she never left Richards parents' home wearing this attire. She left her fiancé's home wearing a respectable knee-length dress and smart blouse, changing into her working clothes when she arrived. Richard Pearson, her husband-to-be, had no idea of this duplicity but this would change, ending in tears.

The board meeting concluded, Ronald instructed Janet to wait for him in the office.

'Yes, sir,' she said.

The work Ronald and Janet had to do was very taxing and exhausting, and therefore the door was locked and a 'Private Do Not Disturb' notice hung on the exterior doorknob. When the chief-in-waiting and his PA had finished their accounting they both sat on the couch. It was very warm, so their clothing was loose for purposes of comfort, of course. It was at this post-work point that she informed her boss of her and Richard's intention to marry.

'We are living at his parents' house,' she told him, 'just until we get a place of our own. That is why the promotion was a great help. I'm very grateful to Mr Crump Senior.'

'Congratulations, Janet,' Ronald said, with the air of a man who was far too important to concern himself with such trivialities. 'Will it make any difference to our little arrangement?'

'Of course not, it will make no difference, business as usual, what I do at work is none of his business,' Janet reassured Ronald.

'That's what I like to hear,' he replied.

'Oh, Mr Crump,' Janet said, 'you will always wear a condom, won't you?'

'Yes, of course I will, unless we do alternative sex,' Ronald answered her, and the pair laughed at this disgusting suggestion, disgusting relative to the times they were living in.

Ronald Crump could not give a shit about Janet. So what if her fiancé found out, what could he do? To this misogynist she was merely a tool to satisfy his urges whenever he felt like it. If it suited him, he would drop her the same as any other woman. Any female who was going to work for Crumps would probably think twice if she were aware of what their duties consisted of! To Ronald these assignations with Janet, or any other female employee, were an expectation; it was part of their job.

★ ★ ★

Despite her husband's diagnosis of Alzheimer's, Megan continued her affair with Derek. Perhaps she and Teddy were created for each other, two from similar eggs! As the reader will recall, Teddy was acutely aware of his wife's little games playing away and was going to put a stop to her assignations. However, now that his mind was in decline he began to think, with an element of bitterness, that he might just say nothing. He no longer had the energy to trail his wife's movements to catch her in the act. With the deteriorating circumstances he knew he was also going to need Megan like he had never needed her before! He concluded, therefore, it might be better to let her have a weekly fling and say nothing. She would never leave him, this he was sure of, because nobody else could keep her in the luxury she had become accustomed to.

★ ★ ★

On 18th January it was reported that over five thousand women had rallied in Washington DC, and among their number was a woman called Colette Hill (née Lugosi) and the actress Jane Fonda. Colette, whom Ronald thought he had heard the last of, had turned up, though he was unaware of her involvement at this moment in time. It would be some time before Colette Hill sprang to prominence as an activist in the anti-war campaign. This was the first all-woman mobilisation against US involvement in Vietnam, and it would not be the last. The rally made the news and Ronald passed a sick comment: 'Fucking lesbians, can't get a fella.' Little did he know a very attractive and married Colette was involved.

On 1st April Ronald Crump was to celebrate his twenty-first birthday. He was taking a few days out from university and a huge celebration was planned for the great man. Unknown to the Crump family and their brigand friends, there would be cause for double celebrations. The event for the other or extended party, macabre as it was, and only the most hate-obsessed of the US bourgeoisie would contemplate celebrating it, was the murder on the 4th April of Martin Luther King. For Teddy Crump and his fascist son, it was not the fact that King was dead, apart from there being one fewer black men, but that the perceived threat he posed to the ruling class of the United States was quashed for the moment. Martin Luther King was a leading activist in the civil rights movement, the anti-Vietnam war campaign, the trade union movement and many egalitarian-seeking causes. Teddy Crump and, therefore, Ronald had King down as a communist. If the Soviet Union was the barometer used to describe communism he was not a general threat, like Guevara was to the USA and all it stood for. King, unlike Che Guevara, was not a revolutionary. He believed in change through peaceful means, not violence.

On 29th March Martin Luther King was in Memphis, Tennessee, to support black sanitary workers who had been on strike since 12th March in pursuit of higher pay. They were withdrawing labour not just in pursuit of a higher basic but also equality with their white colleagues. Earlier in the year the workforce, black and white workers, had been sent home due to inclement weather. The white workers were paid for the whole day, whereas the black employees were only paid for the two hours they were actually present. Obviously, a discrepancy existed which needed addressing. King was there to offer his support, which was everything the Crumps hated about the man. On 4th April at 6.01pm Martin Luther King was shot in the neck, allegedly by a man named James Earl Ray. King died at 7.05pm at Saint Joseph's Hospital. Many believed Ray was used by the secret service agencies in a similar way to how, in their opinion, Lee Harvey Oswald had been used to assassinate President Kennedy. Martin Luther King, despite the crocodile tears wept by sections of US society and the state itself, was perceived as a threat to the established order based on racial disharmony and foreign aggression. As we visited earlier, Kennedy, in the opinion of many, was shot due to his handling of the Cuban Missile Crisis and not going to war with the USSR. This, the hawks in the US establishment saw as a weakness on the part of the United States.

Teddy Crump and again Ronald, whose ideas were beginning to put those of his father into the shade, believed King was a communist and, therefore, perhaps should be eliminated. This assumption was based on a letter King had sent to his future wife, Coretta Scott, regarding his ideological position: 'I imagine you already know that I am much more socialistic in my economic theory than capitalistic...' In one speech he claimed unreservedly that 'something is wrong with capitalism' and continued in his letter, 'There must be a better distribution of wealth, and maybe America must move towards a democratic socialism.' King had read Marx while studying at Morehouse University and while he rejected traditional capitalism he also questioned communism. This was due to the Western media description of Soviet communism, which was not necessarily accurate, and too authoritarian for King. Either way, he rejected capitalism, which to Teddy and Ronald was the only workable system. They, of course, would say that, as they benefitted greatly from the private ownership of the means of production, distribution and exchange and amassed huge profits. The same did not apply to their employees.

King also disagreed with the USA supporting the landed gentry in Central America, claiming the United States should support the shirtless and barefoot people in the Third World rather than suppress their attempts at revolution. The ruling class of the United States, as in any capitalist country, governed the country and looked after their own interests exclusively. Therefore, to expect the capitalist government not to support fellow capitalists in other countries and switch their allegiance to the dispossessed was naïve at best. If the ruling class had supported the 'shirtless and barefoot people' that might encourage their own dispossessed to rise up against themselves!

James Earl Ray was convicted of the murder of Martin Luther King, despite protesting his innocence and that he had been used by persons unknown – possibly state agents – and was sentenced to ninety-nine years. He escaped the death penalty due, on the advice of his attorney, to his guilty plea, which saved the court time and money. He wanted to plea not guilty but the evidence was stacked against him. He received the mandatory sentence and went on to escape from the penetentiary. This gave the conspiracy theorists more proof of skulduggery because to escape he must have been helped at a high level. He was arrested on 8th June 1968 at Heathrow in London, England, trying to get to Canada on a false passport. He died in 1998 aged seventy, protesting his innocence to the end.

When Ronald arrived back at university he was not surprised to find none of his peers had even noticed he had been away. As he walked through the main lobby he looked at the life-sized picture of Martin Luther King and muttered, 'Who's having a dream now?' It was now time to get down to his studies. This was the final lap, and he would be shortly finished with this hell hole, as he perceived it. All he had to do was maintain has grade and he would be happy. After then he would take up his full-time position at the firm. He was already planning a name change to his father's company: Crumps Arms Manufacturer and Real Estate. It had been agreed he would gradually take over from his father, who would retire gracefully on a pension of $100,000 per annum. Unlike the workers, who were thrown out of their jobs without question or recourse with no pension, Teddy Crump would end his days as he had lived, in luxury. The final exams were in late April this year and then Ronald would be on his way. He wouldn't hang around for his results: they could post his on to him, as he knew he would pass, probably in the 2–2 or B bracket.

Having sat his exams, he left his forwarding address with the course administrator. His dissertation had given him a mark of sixty-eight, a 2–1 or B+. Everything ultimately depended on how he did in the written exam. He would wait for this result to be posted on.

★ ★ ★

Ronald sat at his new huge desk in the office giving dictation to Miss Snowden. The letter was to a property developer which Ronald had been referred to by one of his university lecturers. Crump was already scheming how to screw any seller but did not want his PA to be aware of this. He wanted this dictation out of the way so he and she could 'talk things over'.

Janet was enjoying this job, not so much for the satisfaction she got as a glorified secretary but the arcane side of the job, the deviousness behind her fiancé's back. Janet did not get on too well with her future mother-in-law and enjoyed playing behind her future husband's back. Mrs Pearson was a little snobbish and always felt Janet was not good enough for her son. The same would have applied irrespective of who her son's choice may have been; nobody was good enough for her Richard.

With the dictation out of the way he asked her, 'Are you in a hurry, Janet?'

'No, sir, plenty of time, I meet Richard at seven. It's not yet four thirty.' Janet went to her handbag and threw her boss a 'three pack'. 'Put one on and we can get started.'

Crump did this reluctantly as Janet was not yet ready for the alternative sex mentioned earlier. The 'Do Not Disturb' sign was again put on the outer doorknob and activities commenced. Suddenly there was a knock on the door. The couple were naked so there was no time to dress; they would have to hope the intruder would leave. There was another knock.

'Quick, get dressed quietly, they're not going away,' ordered Crump.

The couple made themselves presentable and Janet opened the door. It was Richard, Janet's fiancé.

'Richard, I've told you not to bother me at work. Mr Crump and myself were very busy doing dictation.'

'Oh, that's all right Janet,' Crump condescendingly said.

'Sorry, darling, I tried to phone but it was engaged,' Richard commented.

'Yes, we took it off the hook, now what do you want?' she asked him as one would speak to a child.

'Just to let you know I have to work late tonight so we can't go to the cinema,' the poor wretch told her. If Richard had taken the trouble he would have noticed she was wearing different clothes than what she left home in earlier. 'Well, I'll let you get on with your work, darling,' he said. 'Goodbye.'

'Goodbye, Richard,' Janet said offhandedly.

'Cheerio,' said Crump, with a hint of sarcasm.

If Richard had also been a little more observant not only would he have noticed Janet's clothing change, he would also have noticed a pair of panties just about visible half under the sofa.

'Shall we finish off what we started?' suggested Ronald.

'Why not? He's none the wiser,' the PA answered.

This liaison would not remain secret for much longer: the next time Richard turned up he would be acting on information received but which he had hitherto refused to believe.

Ronald arrived home and Teddy was waiting for a full report on the day's activities. He was not ready to relinquish complete control just yet.

'Everything is fine, Dad,' Ronald assured his father. 'Don't you worry about a thing. I have some interviewees tomorrow and next week for the property branch I was talking to you about.'

'Great, son, I'll be there myself for these interviews, you don't mind, do you?'

'Course not, Dad, I'll benefit from your experience.'

The following morning at breakfast Teddy was reminiscent of his former self, alert and ruthless. 'How many are you interviewing, Ron?'

'Only three, the position is part-time and involves looking at potential property buys and reporting back to me.'

'This is your baby, son, if it goes wrong you bear the brunt. I'll support you as far as I can but if I see a dead duck I will say so.'

'I wouldn't expect anything less, Dad,' Ronald agreed.

They arrived at the office and Janet was already hard at it, preparing the questions. She would be present in her capacity as Ronald's PA. The interview board would consist of Teddy Crump, Ronald and Bob Tomkinson, and there would be one person from personnel to ensure employment law was followed. It was a good job this person was present; the first interviewee was an African American. Employment law in the USA had moved on a little: a person could not be directly discriminated against at an interview on the grounds of skin colour, though this did not offer any protection once the interview was complete. Neither Teddy nor Ronald were aware of this, though Bob had a vague idea about it.

When the young man walked in the interviewers went through the pretence of being nice and polite but that is exactly what it was, a pretence. Once he had left Teddy, Ronald and Bob Tomkinson burst into laughter. Janet was a little uneasy with this overt racism but said nothing. Ronald was indignant that a black man thought he had the right to work in his company, and immediately tore up the man's CV. 'Won't be needing this rubbish, will we?'

'No, son, we certainly will not,' Teddy responded.

The next person to face the Crumps was a white lad about twenty-four years old who was more interested in the secretary than the interview.

'I'm sorry, are we boring you?' Ronald asked the lad, who was staring at Janet up and down. She pretended to be offended by this but in reality she was loving every minute of it.

'What are you looking at?' Teddy asked.

'Oh, nothing sir,' replied the embarrassed interviewee.

'Well, we'll give you a call if we need you, sir,' Ronald informed the stargazer, not even going through the motions of shaking his hand.

The third man to be interviewed answered all the questions perfectly. He knew the property game, price fluctuations, the signs to look for in surveying real estate. Then came the time for him to ask questions of the interviewers. 'Is there a trade union presence here? I'm a card-carrying member of the Surveyor's Association,' he informed them.

This was a red rag to a bull and Teddy almost physically threw the man out. Needless to say, he did not get the job.

'An unsuccessful day, son,' remarked Teddy.

'Not really, Dad, we could not employ the n****r no matter how good he thought he was.'

This man had sailed through the interview but had been rejected before he even sat down.

'The second bloke was more interested in Janet than actually working for a living and the third was obviously a communist.'

'If I have to, I'll advertise again,' said Ronald.

★ ★ ★

While Teddy and Ronald were at the office, Megan took the opportunity to meet up with Derek. They had booked a room for the afternoon at a hotel in the New York suburbs. These occasions would be fewer than before and Megan knew she had to explain the new situation to her lover.

'The doctors have diagnosed Teddy with the early stages of Alzheimer's disease,' Megan told Derek.

'What does that mean for us?'

'We'll be all right, but our meetings may have to be fewer. Some days, like today, he's all right and others he just sits around. Every time he is well I'll call you and even if it's only for an hour we can meet.'

'Yes, let's play it that way,' Derek agreed.

Ronald, now to all intents and purposes at the helm, still needed some part-time staff to help get the real estate side of the business off the ground. He did not wish to pay top wages, and would not employ blacks, Hispanics, Jews, Palestinians, Eastern Europeans, Russians or Chinese. He was running out of options because these were the very groups who, in many cases through desperation, would be more likely to work for peanuts. Nobody who understood real estate would even apply for the posts on the wages Crump was offering.

Then, eureka! The problem was answered before his illustrious eyes: Bob Tomkinson. Although he was on five per cent of post-tax annual profits and as Crump was aiming to buy the properties as cheaply as possible, there would be no extra profits, no extra money for Bob. The five per cent deal had been done between Bob and Ronald's father, but now Ronald was a different proposition. He began scheming how to cut Tomkinson's already miserable five per cent and came up with the 'no extra profit and therefore no extra cash' formula.

The problem was, unlike ordinary employees, he could not tell Bob to take it or leave it. He was, after all, a director. Suddenly Ronald squared the circle in his own characteristic way. As he was aiming to buy the property as cheaply as possible, there would be no profits. Tomkinson's five per cent was on any profits accredited during any deal. What Crump was looking for was buying agents, not sellers. *Problem solved*, he thought. He summoned Tomkinson to kneel before the great man himself in his office.

'Enter,' said Crump in a superior tone, when he heard a knock on his door. Bob came in.

'Hello, Tomkin... uh, Bob, take a seat.'

Crump offered his subordinate a cigar, which Tomkinson gratefully received. 'It's like this, Bob, I need a buying agent and as there will not be enough work to justify employing anybody on the payroll I thought of you. You and my dad go back years, Bob. You're almost part of the family.'

Bob really did feel like a man who had the greatest honour on earth bestowed upon him.

'Would you like to take the challenge on?'

'Will I get extra money, Mr Crump?'

'Ronald please, we can cut the formalities in private, Bob, and unfortunately you will not. You see, we will be buying so there will be no immediate profit, so your five per cent does not kick in. However, we are talking of immediate profit which is what your percentage is linked to. This will be protracted profit which will not be visible for at least two years,' Crump lied. 'When the profits come in, as they will be protracted, and I'll have taken a hell of a hit, I can go to two per cent for you, Bob. After all, I'm only after the property to renovate to give unfortunate homeless people homes. I won't make much out of it. What do you say, Bob? Think about it, this could be the start of bigger things as I've got plans in the future which will involve you, and that you will benefit from.'

The people who would be offered a tenancy by the devious Mr Crump would not be exactly homeless. They were the fortunate few who had been placed on the list of the New York Housing Charity Foundation (NYHCF). The charity provided temporary accommodation in an old renovated warehouse for their listed applicants. This organisation was partly funded by New York State and partly from donations, raffles and collections. The object was that the foundation would pay eighty per cent of the tenant's rent, and the remaining twenty per cent would be paid by New York State for a period of six months. The ultimate aim of this charity was to improve the material conditions of the chosen few, which did not include people with alcohol or drug problems, enabling them to seek and gain employment. With this achieved, the intention was that from then on they could pay their own rent. The NYHCF thought they were dealing with a normal landlord, but Crump was in a league of his own.

'Well, I… I… I'll take it, Mr… Ronald.'

'Great, Bob, can we shake and have a drink on it?'

'Yes, of course we can, sir,' said Tomkinson.

Crump had his eye on some run-down terrace houses which he would renovate and then charge extortionate rents for to 'unfortunate homeless people'. The asking price for the four terraced houses was $80,000. Crump summoned his 'buying agent' to draw up plans.

'Right, Bob, your first little job. There are these run-down old houses. The asking price is $80,000 and I don't want to pay that amount. I'll go to $45,000 maximum.' 'They'll never come down that far,' Tomkinson commented. 'They will after you have done a little damage, Bob,' Crump explained, 'or you can get a couple of unemployed lads, pay them as little as possible out of petty cash, to do the job. Make it plain to them if they get caught they are on their own. Try and find a couple of addicts who need money for a fix. Not too much damage – just enough to give me a bargaining chip to bring the asking price down. Maybe a front door kicked off its hinges, a few broken windows and perhaps a small fire in one of the kitchens. Not an inferno, just a small blaze.

'Then when I go to view the property I can say, there's no way I can give you the asking price, how about $30,000? They will probably haggle, and I'll settle for $45,000 possibly $50,000 absolute maximum. If they say the damage will be fixed in, say three weeks, I'll say too late. Dangle the money in front of them. They are, after all, only small-time. Show them the colour of your money and the property will be ours. When the rents come in so then does your two per cent, Bob. Can you do your part?'

'Yes, Ron, I can. Leave it with me.'

It was Monday morning when the conversation between the two eloquent gentlemen under discussion took place. Crump was to arrange an appointment to view the property and place an offer for purchase. The two bandits arranged their plans with great precision and on Wednesday night 'mindless vandals' would strike, causing damage to the property in question.

However, Tomkinson, after careful thought about using desperate-for-cash drug addicts, decided against this idea. If they were caught, he thought to himself, they would sing like nightingales to the cops and it would be he, not Crump, who would face charges. What Bob Tomkinson did not realise was he had now, albeit unwittingly, made himself Ronald Crump's safety net. He would find out as time went on that this little scheme was the tip of the iceberg regarding hare-brained schemes thought up by Crump and carried out by Tomkinson. He had not realised Ronald was not Teddy; Ronald was less meticulous with his planning and, as long as nobody got near him, could not care a damn for anybody else. Teddy had been ruthless all right but had a certain regard for Bob and his welfare. No such niceties inhibited Ronald.

On Wednesday night, well after dark, Bob Tomkinson made his approach to the terraced houses. He decided he would start a fire in one of the kitchens but would use no paraffin or other flammable agents as it would be a giveaway for a case of arson. He needed to make it look like an accident, an electrical fire, for example. Tomkinson knew where the main electrical box was, and he was more than able to cause a short circuit when needed. The owners had not turned the electricity off, which was foolish, so this to a man of Bob's wartime experience was easy.

He placed old newspapers around the point where the short would occur, the idea being to maximise smoke damage, and he also placed a pile of flammable foam in the same area. This foam would give off toxic fumes, so Tomkinson broke the rear window. He then returned to the first building and caused a short circuit, also setting the paper ablaze. This fire would cause more smoke damage than anything else, which was the idea. Mission accomplished, and Bob Tomkinson made his getaway successfully.

The following morning, Thursday, Ronald Crump set off for his liaison with the agent selling the property. On arriving he and the agent exchanged pleasantries, shook hands, and went to inspect the properties. On arrival both men were shocked to find a fire brigade vehicle at the properties, finishing putting a fire out to the smoking premises.

'Well, what the hell has happened here?' Crump said, putting on a phoney, but impressive, act.

'I really don't know, Mr Crump, I don't know what to say,' panicked the agent.

A fireman told the pair, 'It was a short circuit. Some fool left the electricity on. It happens all the time and no matter how much we warn potential sellers of these dangers they persist in leaving the electricity on. They are so afraid it might cost a couple of dollars to put back on. Well, I can tell them for nothing it will cost them a lot more now. The insurance will not pay out, as it's the present owner's own fault. If the electricity had been switched off the insurance company would have paid for the cleaning up. As it is, no chance.'

Crump pretended to look dejected as the agent struggled for words.

'I can't possibly consider paying the asking price,' said Ronald.

'I wouldn't expect you to, sir,' the agent reluctantly replied. 'If you can hold on a few weeks we can get the property cleaned up with new doors and knock, say, $5,000 off the asking price. What do you think, Mr Crump?'

'No can do, I'm afraid, I need the property now or there can be no deal. What about I offer you $30,000 now, it is, after all, badly fire damaged. I acknowledge it is nobody's fault, but I am in a hurry.'

'I'll phone the owners and ask, I'll put your offer to them. They might accept because they want a quick sale.'

With this news Crump felt a feeling of satisfaction and encouraged the hapless agent to 'do just that'. After about five minutes the agent returned.

'No, not $30,000, sir. Your offer, even allowing for the damage, is too low.'

'What is the asking price now?' enquired Crump.

'He wants $55,000,' was his answer.

'I will go to $45,000 and that's my final offer,' Crump said.

Ronald would go to $50,000 which would have been his top offer, $30,000 cheaper than the original asking price for the sake of a few broken windows and a small fire.

'I'll ask again,' the agent said and a couple of minutes later came back. 'My client will accept, reluctantly, your offer of $45,000, providing it is today.'

Ronald Crump was delighted. His first venture into the property market and he had a result beyond his wildest expectations. 'Here is your cheque,' he said handing the agent the piece of paper and receiving the deeds for the property.

'That concludes our business,' said the agent, shaking hands with Crump as he left.

All Ronald wanted now was some unemployed lads to clean the walls down and put some new windows in. He would then get onto Duke Tillerson about the proper renovation work. A good day's business, he thought. When he arrived back at the office he summoned his new troubleshooter, Tomkinson.

'Well done, Bob, we did it. You will get your two per cent, as we agreed, as soon the rent starts coming in. In the meantime I have a lot of expense clearing up your mess,' he said, almost accusing his new slave of causing the damage of his own accord.

'I won't make much out of this deal,' Crump added, 'so please, Bob, don't be impatient.'

On arriving home feeling very pleased with himself, he asked Teddy if he would speak with Duke Tillerson about the renovation work. He did not want to call or phone himself in case Peter answered either the door or the phone. He could not let Teddy know this, so he said, 'Dad, you have known Duke a lot longer in business than me, so will you speak to him about a special rate for the job? Talk to him as if it was a job for yourself.'

'Leave it with me, son. Remember, it is still, for now, my company so in reality Duke will be doing the work for me.'

Ronald was not entirely happy with this answer; he was getting ideas above his station and his father was reminding him of this. Caesar was not dead yet! In the meantime, Ronald used Jim Kelly, the man who did the advertising leaflets for Tillerson, to supply the labour for the cleaning up. It would provide a couple of days' cheap labour and Kelly was a master of exploitation at that level. When speaking to Kelly over the phone Ronald inadvertently asked, 'Does that woman Karen still supervise for you, Jim?'

'Yes, she does, why Ronnie?' Kelly had a good idea why Crump was asking this question but played ignorant for the laugh.

'Just wondered, Jim. I'll be dealing with her while your lads are doing the cleaning, will I?'

'If you wish me to send her round, Ronnie, I can do that. You do know she is married, don't you?'

'Yes, and I know her husband is a painter and decorator. I might have a couple of days' work for him in the office. I'm thinking of having the boardroom decorated, new wallpaper, top quality, and gloss paintwork. Don't say anything as nothing is yet decided.'

All Ronald had to do was convince his father of the need to spruce up the boardroom which wouldn't be a problem as the cost could be reclaimed on the tax returns. This way he could add Karen to Janet as a 'port in a storm'. After all, if an old fucker like Jim Kelly can have his way, then a handsome godly young man like himself should have no problem. All kinds of thoughts were going through Crump's mind. He could have Karen while her husband worked in the next room! This was the kind of power-crazed individual Ronald Crump was. Ronald put the idea of having the boardroom decorated to his father who agreed, providing it was done to the highest standards.

'I don't want you cutting corners in *my* boardroom,' he reminded his son.

The following morning Jim Kelly phoned Ronald Crump to inform him Karen was on her way to see him. She would look over the job and give him a price.

'It is only washing down and replacing a few windows, not proper tradesmen's work?'

'Yes, that's all, no point paying a qualified glazier. If you have any handymen on your books, which I'm sure you have, they can do it.'

'No problem, Ronnie. Karen should be there shortly, she just has to check another little job first.'

'Thanks, Jim.'

Karen arrived at 11.30am. She looked great. She had that gift women of her age are able to do to men of Ronald's tender years: it's called sex appeal. Ronald at twenty-one was twenty-seven years Karen's junior, but that did not seem to matter.

'Thanks for coming over, Karen. There's something else I want to run by you: I understand your husband is out of a job? I might have a week's work for him if he'd be interested. Let me show you.'

He took the woman to the boardroom and explained what he wanted doing to *his* room.

'Would your other half be able to do it?' asked Ronald.

'Yes, he certainly could.'

'Great. Could he come on Monday morning to price the job?' said Ronald.

'I am sure that will be fine with him, I'll pass that on. Now, I've heard about you. You think of yourself as some kind of stud, don't you? Well, I've eaten bigger than you for breakfast,' Karen told him in a humiliating fashion. Karen was feeling bored. Her husband Tony had been out of work for some time and relations at home were a little strained. This work would put him on his feet. She could now relieve her boredom and have Tony employed all in one swoop. So Karen locked the door and took the phone off the hook.

About an hour later they emerged from the boardroom.

'Can you show me the job we'll be doing then, Ron?' she asked.

'Yes, come on, I'll show you. It's only four terraced houses. Shouldn't take too long.'

'I'll be the judge of that, young man,' she teasingly replied. 'Oh, by the way, what just happened was a one-off. If anybody mentions it, I'll deny it. Then any little treats which may have been in the offing most definitely will not be, and you may well end up with two broken legs. Do you understand me? We can do it when I say so, on my terms and I have insurers who do not recognise the niceties of Lloyds of London!'

'Yes, I get the picture, Karen.'

'It's Mrs Cooper until I say differently.'

They arrived at the houses which needed washing down and windows replaced. This way he could take it off the invoice for Tillerson, and Karen assured him they could do the job in three days.

'Are you sure?'

'I'm certain. Three days, $400 dollars labour and you provide the windows.'

'Sounds good to me, Mrs Cooper,' Ronald said. Ronald knew Kelly would provide the windows for free. All was agreed with Karen and the lads from Kelly's were there the following morning. The work would include bagging up the rubbish and washing down the smoke-damaged walls, replacing the windows and sweeping up ready for the builders to start the renovation work. The work was done, as promised, within the three days and Ronald paid Karen in cash.

Ronald arrived home, with a look of satisfaction written all over his face. Teddy suspected his son had been up to no good and asked no questions.

'I've made arrangements for the boardroom to be decorated, Dad. You know Karen, Jim Kelly's supervisor? Her husband is a professional painter and decorator and is going to do it. He'll be round on Monday to price the job.'

'Perfect, son,' Teddy acknowledged. 'Don't take too long over it, time is money.'

Monday morning came to pass and Tony Cooper arrived at Crumps with his wife. She brought him to the room where the work was to be executed. He measured up, and recommended twelve rolls of velvet paper, the very best for such an illustrious room, and a gallon of brilliant white gloss paint undercoat the same, one gallon.

'I'll have to rub down all the old paintwork, Mr Crump,' he informed the budding tycoon. 'If I do not do that the shine off the gloss will be second-rate and I do not do second-rate work.'

'Glad to hear it, Mr Cooper, your wife was saying you're top of the range. I see now what she meant,' Crump said in a condescending way. 'Get all you need, give me an expenses docket and I'll get you the money to go down to the wholesalers and make the required purchases.'

This done the decorator returned with all he needed. 'I can start first thing in the morning and I reckon ten days will see the job done.'

'Till tomorrow then,' said Ronald, shaking the artisan's hand. Ten days might sound a long time for one room, but it must be remembered this was a large boardroom with bays and crannies to be papered. Karen dropped her husband at the office complex as arranged the following morning and he began the work in earnest. She then was about to depart to supervise some other job for Kelly when Crump called out, 'Karen, wait. What about later?'

'What about later?' she replied. 'I'll tell you when and if there is a later and right now there is not.'

Ronald retreated like a scolded brat, feeling a little peevish. Karen Cooper had certainly got the measure of Ronald, one of the few who would call the shots for the duration of their brief acquaintance.

Ronald then phoned his father. 'Did you speak to Duke Tillerson about the renovation work, Dad?'

'Yes, son, he said he will meet you at the site on Wednesday, tomorrow, and he will give you a price. Don't worry, he's giving "mates rates".'

This is a system where business is done between friends and the builder, who in this case used semi-skilled instead of skilled labour, cuts corners or scamps the work, and charges accordingly. Ronald had stated he did not want to spend much on the renovation; just make the houses habitable for the 'lucky homeless people' for whom Ronald had benevolently bought the property.

Duke Tillerson arrived on site as arranged on Wednesday morning.

'Hi, Duke,' Ronald greeted the contractor with a handshake.

'How's things, Ronald?' Tillerson retorted. 'Right let's see, you will need new drains linking the house's domestic system to the main sewer. We can use sleeving where possible, that'll save you a few dollars. I'll get the CCTV down and we can then ascertain where sleeving can be used. Then the walls need a lick of paint.'

'Don't be too conscientious about the paintwork, Duke,' Ronald interjected.

'No problem, Ron, if we can use sleeving instead of putting in a full drainage system, and with the painting and the sashes that will need replacing and some replacement tiles on the roof, I reckon $2,000. If we do have to put all new drains in then we will be looking at considerably more.'

'How much more?'

'Well, allow another $1,200. That's the best I can do, Ronald.'

'Very well but try to use sleeving if at all possible.'

'I will but it will have to pass the building inspector. Don't panic, I believe Teddy has him wrapped up. Even so, something of a job will have to be made.'

'I get the picture,' Crump said. 'When can you start?'

'Monday sounds all right. I'll have my guys here at seven thirty in the morning. By the way, Ronald, what is going on between you and our Peter? He has not a good word to say about you.'

'Nothing really, Duke, he thinks I'm a racist.'

'Well, you are, aren't you?'

'I believe we as white people are superior, yes.'

'I used to think like that, but a lot of what Peter says makes sense. He also reckons you are opposed to trade unions.'

'I am, vehemently against them,' said Crump. 'Look at the trouble you had a few years ago with the fucking unions at your clothing factory, you can't tell me that was good for business.'

'No, not at first but remember that fire? If a factory inspector who was honest had come like the union threatened, I'd possibly have had to pay a fortune. It was only swept under the carpet in the first place because the inspector was crooked.'

'So, you caved in to the fucking union. Well, I never will.'

'Listen to me, Ron, you are new to this game and in certain circumstances the unionisation of a workforce can have advantages. For example, staff relations at the clothing factory are at an all-time high. We have a pay structure which allows for a pay review every year between management and unions, the staff are happy, and production is up. I have contracts like I've never had before. Think about it… you might reconsider your position, Ronald.'

'I might, but I doubt it,' answered Crump.

'If I were you,' said Tillerson, 'and this is advice: keep away from our Peter. Many of his friends are black and Hispanic and they all hate racism. Everybody down at the gym are anti-racist so mind yourself. See you Monday. I'll do the CCTV tomorrow morning and give you a definite figure.'

Duke came to the terraced houses the following afternoon. He guided the camera down the drainage channel, and as he expected, saw that sleeving would do the job satisfactorily. The figure of $2,000 would be the one submitted to Crump.

The following morning Ronald arrived at the office about nine thirty. He was expecting a special letter that day from Yale University regarding his results. He was not to be disappointed.

'The post came early,' the secretary said, 'and this one is confidential.' She gave it to him and watched as he just looked at the envelope with Yale University emblazoned on it.

'Well, aren't you going to open it?' she inquisitively enquired.

'Yes, pour two stiff drinks, Janet,' a slightly apprehensive Ronald ordered.

The grades were pretty much what he had expected, Bachelor of Arts with Second Class Honours but his marks breakdown on a separate sheet were better than he had anticipated. He was graded in the 2–2 bracket but was only one point off a 2–1. He was pleasantly surprised at this upturn. It meant, in his eyes, he was more competent in the property game than he first thought. Now he could apply his own methods, less than orthodox, in the property market. A form accompanied the letter asking if he was attending the Cap and Gowns ceremony or would he prefer his certificate be sent to him by post? Ronald ticked the latter; he had no intentions of going back among those communists ever again.

Janet poured the drinks and Ronald told her, 'Today we are going to celebrate.'

'What about the workload, Mr Crump?' she asked.

'Don't worry, how much is there? Get the important stuff out of the way and then designate to your juniors. You and me will be out all afternoon. I know a lovely little hotel just outside town where we can book a room for the afternoon!'

Janet left the less important work, that which did not require immediate attention, to her juniors; after all that was what they were there for.

The couple, or at least that is what they were posing as, arrived at the Garden of Eden Hotel about 1.30pm and Crump booked a room under the name of Mr and Mrs Pearson. He did this for devilment and Janet made no serious objection at her boss using her fiancé's name. They departed about 4.30pm and headed back to the office.

'That was great, Janet.'

'You weren't so bad yourself, lover boy,' the slightly tipsy secretary replied.

7.30am Monday morning and Duke Tillerson's men were at the terraced houses which Crump had bought for refurbishing. Duke was present and was awaiting the arrival of Ronald, who was delighted with the way his first property deal had gone so far. Crump arrived around 7.45am and Tillerson explained, 'Sleeving will do the job, Ron. It is a little cheaper so the $2,000 figure is what we are looking at.'

'That's brilliant, Duke, how long do you think the job will take?'

'Let me think, say two weeks for the drains to be completed, that includes linking into the sewer and replacing the old traps and caps, and the roofers can be getting on with their work at the same time. That then leaves the painting which again can be done in the same two weeks, leaving only the landscaping which we cannot do while the drains are up. I'd say about four weeks tops, possibly three.'

'Sounds good to me, Duke, would you like to go for a drink?'

'Don't mind if I do, I'm not our Peter,' he replied, and the brigands laughed in unison.

Tony Cooper was almost finished decorating Crump's boardroom and Karen brought him to the place to finish up. He reckoned by lunchtime he would be finished so his wife said she would go and check up on her own workforce and be back to collect him. She indicated to Ronald she had no need to check on anybody, as she had already done so, meaning she had three spare hours to kill. Ronald got the message and they both went for a drive in the country outside town! This was to be quite an exhausting drive and they got back just in time for Karen to take her husband home. She collected the cheque on her husband's behalf, $250 as arranged and a bonus of $80 as Karen was a friend and he had done a first-rate job. Ronald shook hands with Tony and Karen Cooper. It was unlikely their paths would cross again and, as Ronald pointed out, 'It's been a pleasure!!'

It was now early June and on the sixth of the month news came through of the assassination of Robert Kennedy, the brother of the late President John Kennedy. He was gunned down while campaigning for the Democratic Party nomination as presidential candidate for the next US election. Robert – Bobby as he was affectionately known – was very popular with African American voters as well as Hispanic and younger members of the electorate. He was popular among the poorer sections of society and perhaps epitomised modern US liberalism as opposed to the conservatism of the Republican Party. He was shot in the Good Samaritans Hospital, Los Angeles, California by a Palestinian, Sirhan Sirhan, supposedly because of his recent visit to Israel and complimentary remarks he made about the Jewish people re-emerging after the holocaust.

Teddy Crump, one-time member of the Democratic Party, and disillusioned with that party's swing in support of ethnic minorities, was less than pleased with that organisation's leftwards leaning towards liberalism. He did not agree with their appealing to black voters who, in his and his son's eyes, should not have the vote at all and he did not like Kennedy's pro-Jewish accommodation. This had prompted Teddy and his son to flirt with the Republican Party, who were emerging as the right-wing alternative. Having said that he did not view Kennedy as an enemy of capitalism as was the case with Che Guevara and Martin Luther King, so there were no celebratory parties in the back garden as with the previous two murders. Ronald agreed with his father's political position, partly because he lacked the intelligence to form one of his own, and hated the Kennedys' 'betrayal' of the white race. Like Teddy, he did not see in Robert Kennedy a man who would betray capitalism, accusations he would aim at the eventual presidential winner, Richard Nixon. These future accusations would have no foundations and, like most of Crump's rantings, would be nonsensical, to say the least.

The year 1968 moved on very quickly and by early September the terraced houses which Tillerson had refurbished were ready for rental. The renovation work had been finished for some time and now all the legalities were out of the way. The properties would then be Crump's to rent out to the unfortunate homeless people, as he sarcastically called them. He had it written in the contract that if they missed more than one week in payment of rent they would receive eviction notices. Fortunately for the new tenants the NYHCF would look after the rent, at least initially.

The tenants moved in and Crump was there in person to greet them and welcome them to their new homes. He gave them a rent book and a list of dos and don'ts. If these people had not been desperate they would have told their benevolent landlord where his could stick his less-than-impressive houses. In years to come, due to the sub-standard work which had gone into the renovation of the property, these tenants would have good grounds, had they the means, for litigation and a court case against Crump. Unfortunately, these poor souls, and Ronald Crump knew it, were so desperate for a place to live they would sign any contract placed in front of them. If they had read the small print they would have perceived a clause expunging all blame for any structural defects from their new landlord. They would also have seen that all structural damage, whether old or new repairs, were to be footed by the tenant. Rent was to be paid weekly at an initial rate of $30 to be reviewed every year with a view to increase in line with inflation. Lastly, no businesses were to be run from the properties.

So the new tenants signed the tenancy agreements, in conjunction with the NYHCF, without hesitation or question, agreements which would have given a convict in San Quentin more protection. The landlord from hell, Ronald Crump!

Crump hated the NYCHF or, for that matter, any other charity. However, they did ensure the rent would be paid and this was Crump's priority. This organisation offered the tenants limited protection against the excesses of Crump, something they had never come across before.

10

God's Will

This chapter will give the reader an insight into how Crump's selfish external activities impacted on the lives of others.

The antics going on between Janet and her boss, Ronald Crump, were becoming the talk of the office among the junior members of staff. Crump heard of this gossip and summoned a meeting which he himself conducted.

'I understand much gossip is circulating involving the besmirching of my character and that of Miss Snowden. I must inform all of you, without exception, that any rumours you may have heard regarding Miss Snowden and myself are unfounded. If I hear any more talk on this subject the perpetrators will be subject to immediate dismissal. In fact, I am putting an embargo on any talking about anything unconnected with work during working hours. Any member of staff, junior or otherwise, in breach of this embargo will be sacked out of hand. Do I make myself clear?'

'Yes, sir,' came the reply in unison.

'Right. Back to work, all of you.'

Richard Pearson was twenty-eight years old and lived with his parents. His fiancée, Janet, also lived with them. This arrangement, not really to Janet's liking, was necessary until such time as they could afford a home of their own, and then they could get married. For this reason, it was important for Janet she secured a promotion and a higher salary at work. To ensure this it sometimes meant using unorthodox methods, like sleeping with her boss. So far, Janet had been successful in her quest. She was now senior secretary with three juniors under her, a responsible position. What Janet did not perhaps realise was that this position depended very much on her being available for

Crump, irrespective of her wedding plans. This would have applied to any young secretary in Crump's firm; it was not personal. Ronald perceived women as tools to be used when and if he required. His brief encounter with the streetwise and experienced Karen was a one-off; no other woman would get the upper hand on Crump. Karen was an exception, more than even Crump could handle probably because he had no vantage points on her, she was not his employee and arguably because she had the influence elsewhere to have Crump physically damaged.

Richard had met Janet at her father's funeral. Richard was the presiding vicar of St Giles Church. Unlike the Roman Catholic Church, the Protestant variants did not insist on their priests, vicars and ministers practising celibacy and, again unlike their Catholic brethren, did allow marriage, but they were insistent on no sex out of wedlock. For this reason, Richard had not yet made love with his bride-to-be. 'Wait until we are married, darling,' he would constantly tell the frustrated young woman. Perhaps for this reason, Janet was not wholly to blame for what happened at work; she was, after all, human!

Janet loved Richard but the relations with his parents, particularly his mother, were strained to say the least, and she was the opposite of her fiancé. All the same, they were due to be married and were in the process of discussing a date for the wedding. Before he retired, Teddy Crump had promoted Janet on merit. She was a good secretary, but merit mattered little to Ronald. Availability for 'playing away' was the major criteria, and then came the ability to do the job. Fortunately, Janet possessed both. Like many women in similar situations at the time Janet felt powerless to resist her boss's advances, and therefore pretended to enjoy these liaisons. What made this pretence easier for Janet was the frustration she had regarding her fiancé insisting on no sex before marriage. Janet, again like many women, feared the sack if she resisted her boss, and Crump knew this eternal fear of the slaughter would always carry the day for him. It was an unashamed abuse of power and position by an employer on an employee.

Having just addressed the Women's Institute at St Giles, Richard decided he would walk into town and collect the shoes he'd left for repairs. He collected the footwear and was about to head home when he met an old friend. Richard had not seen Mitch, the friend, for some time and as they said their hellos, Mitch shared the news that he had recently married Sharon, the lady that was accompanying him. An introduction to Sharon and congratulations to both were given, and after a few more words, Mitch suggested they go for a coffee. The trio made for the coffee shop and Mitch ordered three large coffees.

'How's things been, Richard?' enquired Mitch.

'Apologies, Richard, we would have invited you to the wedding but had no idea where to contact you.'

'No worries, Mitch, and nice to meet you, Sharon.'

'Likewise,' the attractive woman replied.

Richard explained he was engaged to be married himself and he and Janet were in the process of fixing a date.

'We are staying at my parents'. Not ideal; far, far from it,' explained Richard, 'but it's only a temporary arrangement.'

'I know,' said Mitch, 'we were in a similar situation but we're on our own now. We've got a place over on the south side of New York.'

'Sounds great,' replied Richard.

'Yes, I like it there,' said Sharon. 'In fact, I've never been so happy,' she smiled.

Richard then began telling of his future wife's employment at Crumps, and how she had recently been promoted to the post of senior secretary. Sharon nearly dropped her coffee, as would have Mitch had he been holding one.

'Did I say something wrong?' enquired the young reverend.

'No, uh, no, not really,' replied Sharon. 'It's just I worked there for a few weeks as a temp and the boss, Teddy Crump, the owner and doesn't everybody know it, could not keep his hands to himself. I reported his behaviour to the agency and they found me another placement. It's all right, you know, but he thinks because he is the employer he can do as he pleases. Maybe he does with his direct employees but not me.'

'Oh, no worries on that score. Mr Crump Senior is hardly ever there these days. In fact, it was he who promoted Janet before his semi-retirement. His son, Ronald, is in charge now and everything appears up and above board,' Richard said, not very convincingly. 'Only the other day I had reason to call in and they seemed to be working as normal, no funny business going on.'

'Is that a fact?' asked Sharon. 'I've heard the son is worse, a right misogynist pervert!'

'Come on, Sharon,' said Mitch, 'you'll be giving Richard nightmares.'

'Sorry, Richard,' Sharon afforded. 'Sometimes I think all bosses are like that, Teddy. The thought of him makes my skin itch. I'm sure your fiancée will be more than a match, if necessary. Don't cause trouble on my paranoid behalf,' she said.

'I'm sure your experiences were a one-off, Sharon,' Richard said. 'Must make tracks now. Great seeing you again, Mitch – and you Sharon. May I wish you all the best for the future, oh, you must give me your address so we can send an invite to our wedding.'

'The very same to you and Janet,' the newly-weds wished, returning the compliment.

While Richard was walking through town his mind wandered back to the day he had reason to visit his future wife's place of work. He was sure, in hindsight, Janet was wearing different clothing when she left his parents' home earlier that day. It was far too late to broach the subject now and maybe he was mistaken. All the same, it was all a bit confusing. *Why am I questioning my future wife's fidelity?* he thought to himself. *I have no reason to. She has never given me any reason for doubting her.*

Richard arrived home and called out, 'Is anybody in yet?'

'Yes,' replied his mother. 'Your father will be late, but I will have your dinner and Janet's ready in about ten minutes.'

'Jan not home yet?'

'No, not yet, son.'

Suddenly the front door opened, and his future wife entered the room.

'Hello, darling,' Richard greeted her. 'A busy day at the office?'

'Yes, I've been rushed off my feet getting these new orders for parts typed up,' Janet informed the company.

Richard's mother took little notice. She did not trust Janet, not wholly, and always suspected she was up to no good. It was nothing personal. No woman, not even Princess Grace of Monaco – better known as the actress Grace Kelly – would have been good enough for her son.

'They work you too hard, darling. Tell them if the work is too much.'

'What do you mean?' Janet snapped at the innocent remark.

'Nothing, I only meant: don't let them walk all over you, you're too good-natured at times.'

'They don't, and I won't. Now can we change the subject?' Janet's response was too aggressive relative to the conversation, something Richard's mother took notice of.

'Why are you so uptight, Janet?' the older woman asked.

'I'm sorry, it has just been one of those days, I didn't mean to snap.'

'That's all right, darling, I understand,' Richard assured her.

His mother didn't respond but was suspicious. However, nothing more would be gained by asking more probing questions. 'Dinner is nearly ready,' she said. 'I am sure you're both hungry after a long day.'

Later, Janet suggested they have an early night.

'Good idea, darling,' said Richard, feeling unaccountably uneasy. He watched her leaving to go to the guest room.

The following morning at the breakfast table an atmosphere appeared to descend on the soon-to-be-weds. Mrs Pearson had gone out early, leaving the couple alone.

'More tea, dear?' Richard asked his fiancée.

'No,' came the blunt reply.

'What's the matter, darling, why are you angry?'

'You don't know, are you just plain thick or just not interested in what to other couples comes naturally, or are you so wrapped up in that damn church that you're incapable of thinking of anything else?' Janet let it all out. 'Oh Richard, I'll be so glad when we are married and we will be free to have sex.'

'That's what it's all about?' he finally realised; a little slow on the uptake was our man of the cloth. 'You know there is more to life than sex.'

'What!' exclaimed Janet. 'I hope you don't mean when we are married you're still not going near me, do you?'

'Of course not, darling, I just meant there is more to married life than just sex.'

'Don't I know it, and we're not even married yet,' the frustrated young woman said. 'I'm off to work now, see you at teatime.' She gave him a peck on the cheek, and stood up.

'Yes, darling, will see you later,' the oblivious Richard replied.

Janet arrived at work in a foul mood. Crump realised all was not well, and he believed he knew why.

'Go and get changed, Jan, I like you in that short skirt, no need for any underwear,' he laughed.

'Mr Crump, I'm not that sort of girl,' Janet pleaded.

Ordinarily this may have been the case but due to the sexless hours at home, coupled with the fact if she refused she felt it would cost her the job, she thought she might as well enjoy it. Perhaps 'enjoy' was stretching it; as she felt she was getting short-changed by Richard, Crump would have to do.

Richard was tidying up the rectory and stacking the prayer books when his mind drifted back to the day he had met Mitch and Sharon. He recalled how she nearly dropped her cup at the mention of Crump and how his fiancée had reacted to an innocent remark the previous evening.

'Was there really something going on?' he murmured.

At that moment the verger walked in.

'Morning, sir,' she said.

The Protestant churches had women vergers and women in other lower religious positions, unlike the Roman Catholic church, which even to this day does not have women priests.

'Anything the matter?' she said.

'No, nothing, nothing at all, but thank you for asking,' Richard replied.

'Mrs Truman, can you hold the fort for me?'

'Yes, of course I can, Reverend. How long will you be?'

'Oh, about two hours I expect, and thank you,' he said.

Richard Pearson went into town, catching the tram to his destination. He was going to allay his suspicions once and for all. His thought turned to a song by Elvis Presley, 'Suspicious Minds'. He was not going to get married while he held these thoughts. What he was about to do would put the matter to bed once and for all! Richard disembarked from the tram at his stop and decided to go for a coffee before attending to the business in hand. With a cup in his hand he sat for what seemed like an eternity, turning things over in his mind. If he was wrong, he thought, how could he forgive himself for suspecting his innocent fiancée? If, on the other hand, he was right, he could not allow the wedding to take place. No, he told himself, I must know one way or the other. After all, if Janet suspected him of infidelity she would, in all probability, do the same.

He finally plucked up the courage to continue on his quest, so he left the coffee shop for the short distance he had to walk. In the window was advertised: 'N. Parker, Private Investigator. Complete privacy and diplomacy shown at all times. Reasonable rates. Call in for a quote.' Richard entered the office and was invited to sit down.

Norman Parker – known as Nosey – was a retired police officer who had set himself up doing private work to supplement his pension. He had a reputation for doing a good, clean and above all, private job on any matter. He specialised in finding out if husbands or wives was cheating on each other. Richard explained his suspicions to the PI who listened and took notes attentively. He said he would take the case on, subject to agreement of a fee. This agreed, Richard gave further details of his questioning thoughts, telling Parker where his fiancée worked. At the mention of Crump, Nosey said nothing, keeping his countenance neutral. He knew the name only too well, having previously had dealings with suspicious husbands involving Teddy Crump. He could not disclose this to Richard, however, so he took the appropriate information down on paper and told the vicar to leave it with him, that he'd be in touch.

Richard returned to his church and thanked Mrs Truman for holding the fort.

'I must get along now, sir, I've Jack's dinner to get ready.'

He felt like a man who had just taken lunch with Old Nick himself! He finished tidying up the place and locked the church doors. No longer could the building be left open for lost souls to come in at their leisure, as these days many of these creatures were more interested in finding themselves via the church silver. Richard returned home and awaited Janet's arrival from work. She arrived shortly after five and was in a far better mood than the previous day.

'Would you like to go out for a drink tonight, darling?' she asked.

'Sure,' Richard agreed as peace on earth descended all around.

A month passed by and Richard was working in the office adjacent to the church sifting through some documents regarding canon law. He was hoping to find a loophole which would allow him to give his bride-to-be the pleasure she obviously craved. Of course, he had his mild suspicions that something was going on between Janet and her boss, but he didn't seriously contemplate she was having sex with him. Anyway, he could not find the required loophole, so it seemed Janet would have to wait. He had hired Nosey Parker just as a precaution, as he did not really expect anything to come out of the investigation. He had arranged with the private investigator that all communications between them should be sent to the church, not Richard's private address. One morning a letter arrived. Richard guessed correctly it was from Parker. The letter read:

Dear Mr Pearson

On foot of the information you furnished me with regarding your suspicions surrounding your wife-to-be, I have to inform you something has surfaced which I believe will be of interest to you. To discuss this matter further, and assuming you wish me to continue with my investigation, might I suggest we meet at my office at a time of our mutual convenience. I shall await your response to this communiqué.

Yours sincerely

Norman Parker, Private Investigator

(Detective Inspector Retired)

Richard immediately telephoned Parker to arrange the suggested meeting. Parker agreed to meet the good Christian the following morning at his premises. Richard was experiencing mixed emotions; he wanted Parker to tell him there was nothing to worry about, but he also wanted the truth. That evening at the parents' family home Richard was calm. His father, who seldom spoke at the best of times, sat reading the newspaper.

'According to this, the economy is expected to shrink this year,' he said to an uninterested audience.

'Will we go for a walk, dear?' he suggested to his fiancée.

'I'm a little tired, darling,' the bored Janet replied. 'I think I'll have an early night.' The truth of the matter was, Janet was having second thoughts about getting married at all. How would she, how could she know if she and her husband-to-be were compatible in bed? She kept thinking it over until she fell asleep.

The next morning Janet set out for the office at the newly renamed Crumps Arms Supplies, Light Engineering and Real Estate Ltd. She was unaware of her fiancé's arcane meeting with the private investigator. Richard also set off but this morning his destination was not St Giles Church but Norman Parker's office. He arrived there at around nine thirty and rang the intercom.

'Come up,' a gruff voice instructed, and the clergyman obliged.

'Come in, Richard, have I got something for you,' the investigator informed him. 'I have been trailing your fiancée for a month now and a pattern appears to be forming. Every Wednesday she accompanies her employer, Mr Crump, to the Garden of Eden Hotel. I have these photographs to confirm this. On the third occasion I followed them, at a distance, and this time I entered the hotel, giving them time to retire to wherever it was they were going. I opened the signing in book. They had signed in as Mr and Mrs Pearson. Using my pocket camera, I took a photo of the page in question. As you can see it says quite clearly 'Mr and Mrs Pearson', your surname! I also made some subtle enquiries about the hotel and it appears to be one of a few in the area which rents rooms out for the afternoon, reportedly on occasions to prostitutes.'

'These on their own prove little if anything conclusively. Even the signing of the book under Pearson is incriminating but not hard proof of any wrongdoings. What do you suggest should be done next?' asked the vicar.

'Well, I think we should follow them this Wednesday. That is tomorrow; are you up for it?'

'Yes,' a reluctant Richard replied.

'Right, tomorrow here at one o'clock sharp, agreed?'

'All right, let's do it.'

The following morning Richard attended to church matters. Fortunately, he had no funerals or other Christian duties to perform, so he was free to go at the appointed time to Parker's. On arrival the private investigator was waiting in his car.

'Over here,' he called.

Richard got into the car and the duo set off for Crump's office. Richard had prayed before he left that nothing untoward was going on between his fiancée and Crump. When the couple approached the main road to the office, they saw Crump's large Mercedes and his chauffeur outside the main entrance, which had not been the case the previous week.

'Unusual,' said Parker, 'this was not here last week.'

Suddenly Ronald Crump appeared alone, and his chauffeur opened the door of the large car for Crump to board. They drove off, followed discreetly by Parker and Richard. They travelled about five miles to a large building where Ronald Crump got out of the car and entered the building, leaving his chauffeur waiting.

'Well,' said Parker, 'he has changed his routine. This is not what has happened the previous weeks. He has a red saloon which he drives himself.'

Richard was naively delighted. This was evidence which proved his fiancée's innocence, he thought.

'Well, Mr Parker, thank you for all you have done but it appears that Janet is innocent, doesn't it?'

'Not according to the previous weeks, I'm afraid.'

'I think you're mistaken. The photo you took, in good faith I'm sure, must have been another couple called Pearson. I'm satisfied of my fiancée's innocence and feel guilty for doubting her in the first place. This must be God's will. Thank you again for all you have done.'

'Very well, Richard, if you're sure, I'll call it case closed. Can I drive you back to your church?'

'Yes please, I would be appreciative,' the clergyman said.

Parker dropped Richard at his church and set off back to his office. Fool, darned fool, Parker thought, this was a once-off and I bet next week they go as a couple to the hotel. Still, he considered, there are none as blind as those who want to be! A true saying as Richard Pearson would soon find out.

Richard arrived home that evening full of the joys of spring. What a wonderful world it was, he thought. He started singing the hymn, 'All Things Bright and Beautiful' to himself.

'You're in a happy mood,' his mother said.

'Yes, Mother,' he replied. 'Have you ever been pleased to be wrong?'

'Never given it a thought,' Mrs Pearson said.

Janet arrived through the front door.

'Good evening, darling, how are you today?'

'Not too bad,' she said, suspicious at her fiancé's cheerful mood. 'Why are you so happy?'

'Oh, no real reason,' was his reply. 'Let's go out tonight. Would you like to go out for a walk? It's a nice evening.'

Janet did not really want to but she did not have the heart to say no when she saw Richard in such high spirits.

'Sure, why not?' Janet was still having serious second thoughts about the wedding, but she did not want to mention anything just yet.

Several weeks passed and Janet kept putting off deciding a date for her wedding. Richard was still convinced all was well, so he didn't notice his fiancée's avoidance strategy. Then one morning he was at St Giles and realised he had forgotten something important which Janet had in her handbag. This left him no option but to call round to the office in her lunch break to retrieve this article.

On arriving around 12.30 he made straight for the office. One of the juniors had an idea what Crump and her immediate manager, the senior secretary, were up to and decided to allow Richard to proceed. He arrived at the office door and heard funny noises, like moanings. The office junior laughed to herself as he knocked on the door. After a few moments the door opened. Crump, his fly still unfastened, stood there glaring at him. Janet was at her desk panting for breath. Then he looked at the sofa, and saw a pair of ladies' panties lying there.

'What have you been doing?' he blurted out.

'What do you think? It gets hot in here, very hot,' Janet said weakly.

Ronald was giggling to himself at the sight of this besotted fool trying to find an explanation other than the obvious for his fiancée's behaviour.

'We'll talk about this when you get home,' Richard said, hurt and angry.

Janet and he exchanged a long look before Richard turned and left.

'Now Janet, get yourself together. Playtime is over. We are very busy so we had better get back to work.'

Ronald Crump cared not one iota for Richard's feelings or, for that matter, Janet's. As far as he was concerned she would do the work and duties of the senior secretary, which included servicing him whenever he wanted.

Despite her public show of confidence over this embarrassing situation, Janet was in reality very upset. Later in the afternoon she began to weep when she thought she was alone. Ronald Crump entered the room.

'What are you crying for, woman?' he arrogantly asked.

'Have you no feelings, Mr Crump?' she sobbed.

'No, not really. Don't start getting all sentimental on me, I've no room here for that sort of thing. It was after all your own fault, you can't blame anybody but yourself. Now I want you to dictate this.'

'Fuck you,' she said in a fit of anger.

Weeks of pent-up emotions spilled over, weeks of barely tolerable sex with her boss.

'What did you say?' Crump asked, with the air of a man who had been greatly offended. 'After all I have done for you, this is how you repay me. It was you who came on to me. In fact I should sack you for bringing the firm into disrepute. So you can cut the waterworks.'

This made the young woman cry even more. 'I resign,' she said. 'I can't work here with you a moment longer.'

In the space of a little over three hours Janet Snowden had lost her fiancé, her job and the roof over her head.

Ronald Crump had taken advantage, as ever, of a situation. He knew his secretary was due to be married but he didn't give a care for either Janet or Richard.

When Janet arrived back at the Pearson's house she was still sobbing.

'You little tart,' Richard's mother said nastily. 'My son is well rid of you.'

'Don't say that, Mother,' Richard pleaded. 'This is hard enough without you spitting venom at her.'

'You've never liked me, have you?' Janet said to Stella.

'I'm sorry it ended like this, Jan,' Richard said with total honesty. He was heartbroken, and Janet was much more upset than she expected. Perhaps if Richard had been more open-minded he could have worked through the mess with Janet, and maybe a happier resolution could have been found for them both. However, both her betrayal and the church's rules led him to believe the only answer was to end the relationship.

Janet Snowden returned to her family home. Her mother was now a widow, and Janet returning home was a great comfort for her. She was a good secretary and soon procured another job. Never again did she let herself be sexually coerced as she was at Crumps, and in time she found love once more. She had learned the hard way, that was for sure, while Richard still believed it was all God's will.

11

Politics and Marriage

The year 1968 saw the beginning of the campaign for the general election in the United States. The incumbent, Lyndon Johnson, had shocked the public when he announced he would not be seeking re-election. The Democratic Party presidential candidate would be Hubert Humphrey, and he would be taking on the Republican nominee, Richard Nixon. A third man in the race was the former Governor of Alabama, the racist George Wallace. Wallace had thrown his hat into the ring after riots among African Americans and the rise of the Black Panther movement whom Wallace implied were terrorists after the murder of Martin Luther King. This may have been an attempt by Wallace to muddy the waters surrounding King's murder. To suggest the Black Panther movement had anything to do with Dr King's murder was the politics of insanity. The riots were worrying many white voters and George Wallace saw a possible fertile hunting ground for his white supremacist policies. Both Teddy and Ronald Crump echoed the views of Wallace.

Teddy Crump had once been a Democratic Party member but had fallen out with them because of what he perceived as moving too far to the left and showing support for ethnic minorities. Teddy and, therefore Ronald – unable to make a political decision of his own based on anything approaching rational – shifted towards the Republican Party until Wallace came on the scene. The racism of Wallace appealed to both Crumps and for this campaign they would promote the outsider, instructing their employees to vote for him. Of course, they could not oversee or supervise this instruction, so they would have no way of finding out if their order had been obeyed. They hoped the fear of the sack alone would be sufficient to frighten their employees into voting the way the Crumps wanted.

They could not openly tell their employees whom to vote for, but they implied very strongly if Wallace did not have a reasonable number of electors' votes, heads might roll. This was, of course, impossible and Ronald along with his ever-sinking father knew it. They just wanted to see how much fear they could inject into their subordinates. Ronald had hitherto been ambivalent towards Lyndon Johnson. He disagreed strongly with his Voting Rights Act but supported increased military action in Vietnam against the communists. When Johnson ordered the blanket-bombing of civilian and military targets in that country to cease both Teddy and Ronald shifted over in the direction of Richard Nixon, later known as 'Tricky Dicky'. However, when Teddy's old hero, Wallace, came back on the scene the support for Nixon was temporarily given to the racist – or perhaps more accurately, the more racist of the two.

The Soviet Union had recently sent the Warsaw Pact troops into Czechoslovakia over that country's moves for more dialogue with the West. The country's leader, Alexander Dubcek, was making sound bites towards Western capitalism which, in the eyes of the Soviet Leader Leonid Brezhnev, was becoming a threat to the region. He therefore ordered the Warsaw Pact forces to move against Dubcek. He was replaced by the pro-Soviet Gustav Husak.

In the eyes of Teddy Crump and therefore his son, the Democrats were appeasing the communists and Nixon appeared, at least in the early days, to take a harder approach. Nixon won the election and in 1969, Teddy and Ronald Crump joined the Republican Party. The Crumps' man in the election, George Wallace, won five states, which was more than expected and showed the level of fear among white voters that the black population might rise up. But there was no uprising. The events were a response, understandably, to the murder of King. The support for the Black Panthers was strong: nobody believed Wallace's silly suggestion that the Black Panthers were terrorists. He did not even believe it himself. Many black communities actually needed defending against such groups as the white supremacist and terrorist group the Ku Klux Klan, whom former Governor Wallace supported. Another worrying sign within the Democratic Party for both Crumps was at their 1968 convention where 212 of 3,099 Democratic Party delegates were African American compared with the Republican Party at the same time where there were only 26 black delegates out of 1,333. Still, 26 too many for Ronald, but an improvement on the Democratic softies! In the following year, Ronald Crump joined the Republican Party.

Ronald Crump's private life was moving in an upward direction. He was going steady with a girl called Tracy Edwards, whom he was thinking of marrying. To his own surprise, for the first time he discovered he had real feelings of affection for a woman. In spite of this he still carried on his activities with the female staff at the office. To Crump, this was an entitlement and none of his girlfriend's business. All the same, the staff involved in this involuntary sexual harassment were sworn to secrecy under fear of the sack.

Tracy Edwards was twenty years old when she first started going out with the businessman and eventual prospective congressman. She was an attractive young woman who, like Crump, pretended to be a Methodist who attended her chapel on a regular basis. Going out with Ronald would seriously make her question her beliefs to the point of eventually dropping them altogether. She had no idea of her boyfriend's infidelity and would remain ignorant of this fact for many years to come.

Ronald Crump, as one would expect from such a figure of popularity, was becoming a striking sight within the Republican Party. He not only looked the part, tall and dark with sharp features, he was making friends among the party's right wing, often referred to as Neo-Conservatives, or neo-cons for short. He also befriended those on the so-called religious right, Christian fundamentalists, all of whom were white. A mouthpiece for this trend was a young religious firebrand called Pat Buchanan. If Christianity was anything the so-called good book professed, then Buchanan was the most unchristian person imaginable, making implied racist remarks suggesting the 'sons of Ham (Negros) were born inferior'. What also appealed to Crump about Buchanan was the man fought in Vietnam and suffered as a POW. God was, after all, a white man and Jesus, his son, a blond-haired, blue-eyed Nordic man as all the pictures depicted. Therefore, it was only right the white race ruled! The right wing of the Republican Party, similar to most of that creed who describe themselves as Christians, blamed a person's poverty on themselves, unemployment on greedy workers and their trade unions asking for too much money. Money the good Christian employers could not afford! Usually, these greedy unchristian souls were only asking for a living wage, a wage to purchase the goods they had collectively produced. Such requests resulted, where the boss could get away with it, in the greedy worker receiving the sack. Where the employers could not get away with this, due to trade union resistance, a pay increase was granted but not until much anti-union propaganda was made by the bosses via the media. The right wing of this political party was a bunch of misfits whom Ronald fitted in with very well. Ronald would often spend time in the bar with his fellow loonies cracking jokes about the Democratic Party.

One such butt for their fun was a very young politician called Bernie Sanders. Sanders was a young twenty-year-old idealist with, by the standards of the USA, socialist views. He believed in health care, free when needed, a small programme of nationalisation in certain industries, and free education for the poor, especially those groups excluded from society such as African Americans, Native Americans and Hispanics.

'Have you ever heard such crap,' roared Crump during a drinking bout with his so-called mates in the congressional bar.

'That's right, Ronnie,' slurred a congressman called Dixie Vileman, sometimes referred to as 'destitute Dixie' because of his constant less-than-humorous jokes about poor people. Of course, this man would never dare crack his form of humour outside the safety of the bar or in the company of anybody possessing a modicum of intelligence.

One day during one of these conversations by the so-called political elite, Crump came up with his solution to the problem caused by 'troublesome' women. Crump's solution to this non-existent problem was a rerun of the Salem witch trials, February 1692 to February 1693. Any woman stepping too far out of line should be, according to Crump, tried as a witch! If a husband thought his wife was acting unreasonably this law could be applied. The rest of his company found this suggestion so funny they almost choked on their drinks.

Ronald Crump knew little if anything about politics, but that didn't matter. It was not a required qualification in the world of US politics. Knowledge of the subject could actually work against a person if they were to be seeking admittance to either the US Senate or the House of Representatives. The last sort of person these bastions needed were people who could spell the words 'political', 'politics' or 'policies', let alone understand anything about the subject. Such people as these would be a hindrance to the progress the US establishment were making on behalf of the bourgeoisie. All Crump was qualified in was exploitation, rape, slave-driving, profiteering and undiluted selfishness. These were perfect qualifications for entry into the political elite and running a large business. Crump was now competent in both these fields.

In the world of politics in the United States – or any so-called liberal democracy – it is the civil servants who do most of the work, thus guarding the politicians' backs. In the arms-dealing world of Crump and his cohorts it was the tradesmen, scientists, machinists and designers who did all the work; Ronald collected the profits. In the world of real estate, which Crump was now established in, it was not he but various secretaries, field officers, chartered accountants and hired estate agents who did the work and who would in turn take the rap if anything went wrong. As a fail-safe safety net Ronald Crump always had good old reliable Bob Tomkinson to sort any problems out. This man was not yet aware what his boss had in mind for him. It would be in a different league.

Ronald Crump was sat at his desk and his thoughts turned briefly to Janet Snowden.

'Silly girl,' he told himself. 'I begged her to stop before we got caught but she would not have it.'

Well, he thought, *she only has herself to blame for her predicament.* Little did Crump know she was now very happily working in a respectable firm. She had a proper job description and was also represented by a trade union. Employer/ employee relations were so much more harmonious where firms employed a pluralist system of industrial relations.

Ronald had a new secretary now, a young girl of eighteen whom he would soon corrupt. All new employees at Crumps Arms and Real Estate, he had dropped the Light Engineering part of the title, were forced to sign a secrecy agreement which stated: 'Any breach of security including duties carried out at work, whether in your job description or not, will be deemed a breach of contract. Such actions will also constitute a civil offence punishable in a court of law.'

One day Crump summoned the new secretary in for some dictation and contract reviews, which involved those who owed him money, and correspondences with governments who were in the market for weapons.

'Mary,' he called on the intercom, 'can you come in here?'

Within seconds the teenager was in his office. Crump eyed her up and down, taking in her short skirt and low-cut top. *She's begging for it,* he thought.

'Mary, come over here. I have some dictation for you. Sit here beside me on the sofa.'

'I'd rather sit at my desk, Mr Crump,' she said.

'You'll sit where I tell you,' he said indignantly, slipping his hand up the girl's skirt.

'Get off me, you pervert, who do you think you are? I have a boyfriend and when I tell him about you, your life will not be worth living,' the girl exclaimed.

She had no boyfriend, but neither was she available for Crump. She ran out of the door in tears.

'I won't be back here,' she shouted.

The fact was, Mary had no intentions of returning to Crumps, but she was also afraid to speak out because of the document she had signed. The document was actually groundless because it had no legal bearing, but she did not know that. If the document had been specific about 'giving away company secrets which may benefit a rival', then a certain amount of legal standing would have been applicable. Mary left Crump's employment but kept her mouth shut about the incident.

Agnes Moorhouse was Ronald Crump's senior personnel officer and she had seen the young woman leaving in tears.

'Mr Crump, sir, why don't you leave it to me for appointments? I could have told you she was not what you were looking for. I know the type, they're just troublemakers. Let me appoint your next secretary.'

'I think you're right, Agnes, I will leave all appointments to you. Don't let me down now. You know the kind of young woman I need,' said Crump, expressing a sly grin.

Agnes Moorhouse was very loyal to he employer, provided he did not break the law, and was honest when it came to legalities. Crump might have been wise to remember this.

That evening Ronald had arranged to take Tracy out for a meal. He had booked a table for two at the New York Caledonian Hotel. Tracy Edwards lived at home with her parents, Stella and Louis Edwards, and Crump arrived at the house as arranged at six o'clock that evening.

'I'll be about half an hour,' he told his chauffeur.

Stella Edwards, Tracy's mother, was not overly struck by Ronald Crump. There was something shifty about his mannerisms which she could not put her finger on. Louis Edwards, on the other hand, thought Crump was a great guy, and a man of the world who had made it in business. His conclusion was the young man must be of sound stock. Louis tended to judge people's credibility by how much money they made; it never entered his head to question *how* they had made that money. Stella reckoned he, Crump, 'had too high opinion of himself, was too cocky by a mile' and she certainly did not trust him. Louis, on the other hand, knew Ronald was worth a fortune and one day, if his daughter played her cards right, they would marry thus entitling her and her family to a sizable amount of Crump's wealth.

The Edwards family considered themselves to be lower middle-class, petit bourgeois, in the great class barometer by which a family's decency is rated in the USA. Louis was a pawnbroker and Stella a part-time secretary for a small firm of solicitors. Tracy herself was a silver service waitress at the New York Hilton.

Ronald rang the doorbell and Stella answered.

'Oh, it's you, is it? You'd better come in, wipe your feet,' she said, vaguely expressing her contempt for her daughter's boyfriend.

Ronald put her attitude down to a mother's concern for her daughter and who she kept company with, especially male company.

'Come in, son,' said Louis, 'would you like a drink?'

'Scotch, please, sir,' replied the tycoon.

'How was the office today, Ron?' enquired Edwards.

'Oh, the usual pressures of business,' replied Crump, omitting being sexually inappropriate with an employee.

'Where are you off to tonight?' asked Mrs Edwards.

'We have a table booked at the Caledonian,' Ronald said.

'Don't you keep her out all night. She has work tomorrow,' interjected Stella.

'Don't worry, Mrs Edwards, 'I'll have Cinderella back by midnight.'

'I shall expect her well before then, young man,' came the abrupt reply.

'I was only joking,' Ronald said in an attempt at appeasement.

'Enjoy yourselves, don't mind Mother,' Louis shouted after them.

Tracy Edwards was a quiet girl who had first met Ronald while she was working at the New York Hilton. He had been on a business lunch with a colleague and she was his table's waitress. He had asked her name and then if she would like to go out for a meal one night with him. She had accepted the offer, spellbound by the request. She remembered the colleague saying, 'You don't let grass grow, Ron', to which Crump made no reply. She was pleased he did not answer his coarse friend. That suggested he was a decent man! They had been on several dates since and romance appeared to have blossomed.

The chauffeur delivered the couple to the Caledonian Hotel where Ronald instructed him to collect them at ten o'clock.

'Very good, sir, enjoy your evening,' to which Crump, forgetting himself temporarily, made no reply. The head waiter showed the couple to their seats.

'Bottle of wine, honey?' Ronald asked.

'Can we have a claret, Ron?' she replied.

'You can have whatever you wish,' Ronald smiled.

'Waiter, we're ready to order,' Ronald indicated. Halfway through their first course Ronald dropped his bombshell.

'Tracy, will you make me the happiest man on God's earth and do me the honour of becoming my wife?'

'Oh my goodness! Oh yes, Ronnie, of course I will,' Tracy said, surprised and overcome with happiness.

Ronald then produced an engagement ring he had bought. The ring had cost $3,000, bearing three diamonds and a ruby in the centre.

'Oh, it's beautiful,' said Tracy, expressing delight beyond belief. 'Ron, when can we set a date?'

'Steady on, honey, we have to tell your parents first. We'll do that tonight after our meal and a celebratory drink. I hope they don't object.'

'I don't care if they do! We can elope if they don't agree,' Tracy said, her eyes flashing with excitement.

'Your mother appears a little frosty, but your dad is great,' Ronald commented.

'Yes, my dad likes you, Ron. But we are getting married with or without their blessing,' Tracy said firmly.

'Right, let's head to your place and give them the good news,' said Ronald.

It beggars the question of how can a man have two such diverse personalities? At work he was a loathsome creature and yet here he was with Tracy, a respectable, kind man. The reader could be forgiven for believing they were reading the book, *Dr Jekyll and Mr Hyde*.

The chauffeur was waiting as instructed for Ronald and his fiancée.

'Everything all right, sir?' he asked.

'Couldn't be better, Creighton,' said Ronald, this time remembering to behave politely. 'Take us to where you collected us, please.'

'Yes, sir.'

On arriving at Tracy's home, Tracy ran in, unable to contain herself.

'Guess what, I'm getting married!'

Ronald entered the room a few feet behind his fiancée.

'You're what!' said Stella.

'You heard me, Mom, I'm getting married! Ronald and I are going to be man and wife.'

Stella looked stony-faced, while Louis was clearly delighted.

'Congratulations, sweetie, and you too, son,' he said, shaking his future son-in-law by the hand.

'Let's have a drink to celebrate. What are you drinking, Mother?' he asked his wife.

'I'll have a sherry,' she reluctantly said.

'I'm pleased for you both,' she said, not wishing to spoil the party.

'I'll have a Scotch, sir,' said Ronald.

'And I'll have a small port,' Tracy said.

'Here's to you both, treat her well, son,' said Louis to Ronald.

'I will, Mr Edwards, don't worry.'

The excitement over his marriage plans to Tracy gave Ronald, for once in his miserable life, something to be genuinely happy about. Now he had to tell his own parents.

'I must be going now, must break the news to my mom and dad,' Ronald informed the company.

'Oh, Ronnie, I would love to go along with you,' Tracy said.

'Of course you can, darling. Come on, I'll get Creighton to bring you home. That's all right, sir, isn't it?' he asked Louis as a matter of politeness.

'Yes indeed, son. Don't be too late though, Tracy.'

'I won't, Dad,' Tracy promised.

Creighton drove them to the Crumps' mansion. 'Wait there, Creighton, and you can drive Miss Edwards home shortly.'

'Very well, sir.'

The happy couple announced their engagement to Ronald's parents.

'Congratulations, son,' said Teddy, who genuinely liked Tracy.

'Yes,' echoed Megan, a little teary-eyed, 'I am so happy for you both.'

'Have you set a date?' asked Teddy.

'Not yet, I only proposed tonight,' Ronald answered. '

'Well, let's have a drink,' said Teddy. 'What are you having, Megs?'

It was only on rare events Teddy used his wife's abbreviated name, and this was certainly one of those.

'A glass of red, thanks. In fact, why don't we bring out the grand reserve wine in celebration?'

After toasting the newly engaged couple, Teddy spoke up.

'We will buy you both a house for your wedding present.'

Tracy looked open-mouthed at Teddy, while Ronald spoke.

'Dad, that is wonderful, many thanks!'

'Yes, thank you so much, Mr Crump,' Tracy just about managed to say.

'Please, from now on it is Ted or Dad.'

Finishing their drinks, Ronald saw his fiancée back to the car, where Creighton dutifully drove the girl home. When Tracy had gone Teddy and Ronald discussed a date for the wedding.

'It must be a date which fits in with business,' Teddy reminded his son that even in these happy times the dollar bill trumped all other considerations, even a wedding.

'I know, Dad, but I can't let Tracy think she's playing second fiddle to the business, can I?'

'No, you can't, but do bear that in mind,' said Teddy, 'I won't mention it again, son.'

The following evening Ronald was at his fiancée's house discussing the plans and date for the wedding.

'I want to get married as soon as possible,' she said enthusiastically.

'Well, today is eighteenth of August. What about a month from today, the eighteenth of September? A short engagement suits me,' said Ronald.

'Yes, oh that's brilliant, just perfect. Only a month to go,' said Tracy, clasping her hands together in delight. 'How about if I go to the church minister and ask if he is free on that date?'

'Meet me tomorrow morning at our offices and we can go together,' suggested Ronald.

'I will, I cannot wait,' said Tracy, 'I'll tell them I need a couple of hours off at work.'

As it turned out, the New York Hilton not only gave Tracy as much time off as she needed, but offered her the banquet suite as a wedding present from them. Tracy and Ronald accepted the gift with gratitude, genuinely on her part, phoney on his; the management at the hotel did this gesture more in the hope of procuring business from Crump than in goodwill for Tracy. The happy couple arrived at the Methodist church office and spoke to the minister. The date they requested was fine and all was set for the eighteenth.

★ ★ ★

Ronald was sitting in his company office when he received a telephone call from Senator Edward Sheath. Sheath informed Crump his presence was required at the White House; the president had summoned him and two other party members. Sheath was to accompany the unsuspecting party activists to the White House for an audience with the president. It would be good news for the trio.

On their arrival President Nixon greeted the four with a firm handshake.

'Mr President, you requested our presence,' Sheath announced, introducing the conversation.

'Yes, gentlemen, I'm looking to the 1971 mid-term congressional elections and possible new candidates to the House of Representatives. Crump, I've heard a lot about you. You will be over twenty-five by the time of the election, won't you?'

'Yes, Mr President, I will,' replied an already scheming Crump. Crump would actually be only twenty-four, but he hoped, and guessed correctly, that this would be overlooked.

'Firstly, Crump, do you want to be nominated to the House?'

'Yes, sir, Mr President, I certainly do,' Crump responded.

'Then I will set the wheels in motion; Sheath, you will second my nomination,' Nixon instructed.

'Yes, sir, thank you. I would be honoured,' Crump responded.

'Good, you will need to complete the appropriate forms and declarations, Sheath will second you. I will then sort out the rest of your nominations required.'

Sheath assured Ronald he would be happy to second Crump's nomination, something he would live to regret as the neo-fascism of Ronald Crump slowly became more apparent.

'Mr President, what about us? What did you need to speak with us about?' the other two party members asked.

'Are you both over thirty years of age?'

'Yes, Mr President,' they replied.

'I would like to offer you positions in the Senate. If you agree, you, Trevor,' referring to one of the men, 'will be nominated for Florida North, and you, Bobby, Georgia.'

The two bewildered men looked at each other and accepted Nixon's offer with open arms.

★ ★ ★

For Tracy Edwards, shortly to become Tracy Crump, her big day could not come quickly enough. Finally, it was 18th September, and all was set for her wedding and future happiness. Ronald Crump had secured the services of his childhood friend, James Rothschild, to be his 'best man'. James had recently married Susie Carter, his childhood sweetheart, and would reflect his feelings in his best man's speech.

Tracy was wearing white for her big day, a lacy confection with a long veil. Louis was a proud father as he accompanied his daughter down the aisle to her Prince Charming, ready to give her away. The reader will recall Tracy's employer, the New York Hilton, had given her the banquet suite as a wedding present free of charge and after the ceremony and marriage vows this would be the rendezvous point for the party.

James Rothschild got on his feet to deliver the best man's speech.

'Ronnie and myself go back many years. We have been friends most of our lives and would, at one point, have been prepared to die for one another,' he told the unsuspecting audience. 'I myself recently married my childhood sweetheart, Susie here, and have never been happier' – this was perhaps the only factual part of the speech – 'and would like now to ask you all to raise a glass to Tracy and Ronald.'

'Tracy and Ronald,' a unified cry rang out.

The afternoon and evening passed pleasantly enough, with all the guests enjoying the celebration. Teddy and Louis made chit-chat about world affairs, with Louis pretending he knew what Teddy was talking about. Megan made small talk with Stella, both pretending they had much in common. The reality was, they were chalk and cheese. Stella still harboured doubts about the suitability of Ronald for her daughter but remained quiet on the subject. As the day drew to a close, Teddy and Louis continued to imbibe the many drinks at hand and engaged in genial drunken banter.

The happy couple took off on their honeymoon to the Greek islands for three weeks. Each week they stayed in a different top-of-the-range hotel owned by associates of Crump's. When they returned they moved immediately into their new house, a five-bedroom mini-mansion. Their benefactors, Teddy and Megan, had also furnished the place so now all the newly-weds had to do was hire servants. Ronald told Tracy they would need a cook and two domestics, and that he would bring Creighton, his present chauffeur, with him. Tracy would cease working, Ronald said without any consultation. Tracy was less than happy about this but said nothing. As long as Ronald was happy then so was she, Tracy tried to reason, not very satisfactorily.

'We must have a housewarming party,' Tracy insisted. 'I'll invite my mom and dad and yours of course, plus all our friends.' This really meant *her* friends. 'It will be a great night,' she enthused. Ronald thought about her friends. They were working-class people from the Hilton, no doubt; still, some of those waitresses were probably up for it, he deviously pondered.

Then reality hit Crump. He'd better keep his hands to himself. He had just married a woman he genuinely loved so he put those thoughts out of his head and let the party go ahead, telling Tracy she could invite whomever she wished. Ronald considered this a great concession to his new wife. For his part he would invite Bob Tomkinson, his new henchman from the office, James and Susie Rothschild and he would send an invitation to Texas for his old school friend, Christopher Johnson. His parents and Ronald's new in-laws would also be asked as they all appeared to get along very well. Yes, it would be a great evening.

'When would you like to hold it?' Ronald asked.

'Let's get the invites out as early as possible,' his excited wife replied. 'Maybe over the next week or so?'

'That's fine, dear. Go right ahead.'

Altogether, twenty-five invitations were circulated and unfortunately for Ronald, due to other commitments, Johnson could not make it. James and Susie were coming as were most of Tracy's friends. Ronald ordered the drinks, and plenty of it: beer, wine, whiskey – Scotch and Irish – plus various cocktails. All tastes were accounted for. The evening of 27th October was the grand housewarming and Ronald gave the newly appointed domestics the day off, on the understanding they would be in early to clear up all the mess the following day. The party went down well, with Teddy and Louis enjoying their now familiar drunken sessions, much to the disgust of Stella and, to a lesser extent, Megan.

Ronald had a word with the police commissioner, explaining the party would go on till the small hours so the normal laws on public nuisance did not need to apply. Passing the chief a parcel of crispy dollar bills, Crump was assured no law enforcement officers would bother them on their grand night.

The housewarming over and the settling-in period coming to a close, Ronald began to reconsider his decision forbidding Tracy to go to work.

'Tracy, come here a minute,' he shouted, which she dutifully did. 'Have you handed your notice in at the Hilton yet?'

'No, Ronnie, not yet. I was going to do so this week. I was hoping you might have had a rethink about me working,' she said.

'Well, I have dear, I've decided as you obviously wish to continue working I must not stop you. Can we come to a compromise? Maybe you could go part-time at the Hilton? That way you would not get bored while I'm at work.'

'Really, Ron, do you mean it? I could ask them tonight if that would be possible.'

There was an ulterior motive in Ronald's change of mind over his wife working. He remembered how bored his own mother had become once he was off her hands. He also recalled those awkward questions his father occasionally embarrassed his mother with, and it was not hard to put two and two together. He was almost sure it was her boredom that led her to being unfaithful to her husband. The control freak Ronald was, he did not want his wife getting so bored she felt she needed to do this. So in truth his decision was little if anything to do with giving his wife a certain say over her own life.

Tracy asked the manager at the Hilton about the possibility of part-time work.

'No problem, Tracy, you can go on twenty hours a week from Monday.'

The manager obliged without hesitation as he correctly assumed this was the idea of her husband, Ronald Crump, whom the hotel wished to court. This was an arrangement that could only benefit all concerned.

12

Prostitution and Arson

It was 1970, and down at the gym where Peter Tillerson trained the mood was buoyant. News had come through that Joe Frazier, Peter's former sparring partner and friend, had become the undisputed world heavyweight champion. Athletes from all disciplines were over the moon for Joe. It was amid all the jubilations with everybody, black, white and Hispanic, that his thoughts drifted to Crump and his bitter little persona. How he hated his former school friend and all he stood for. He knew that one day, if he took over his father's business, dealing with Crump would become a necessity. Peter was not sure he could do this, and decided to talk with his father as soon as possible.

Young Tillerson arrived home.

'Can I have a word, Dad?' he asked.

'Sure, son, what's the problem?'

'When I take over the business from you in a few years' time, I will have to deal with that racist maggot Crump, won't I?

'Probably, Peter, yes you will.'

'Well I'm not sure I can, not without hitting him.'

'I see your problem, Pete,' said Duke. 'You will have managers under you who you could designate all work to do with him to them. Remember, there are many more contracts than just his. In fact, if push came to shove we could drop his contracts. I'd rather not, though.'

'Thanks, Dad, that's a relief. Good to know that can be done.'

Despite being crowned the undisputed heavyweight champion of the world, Joe Frazier had not fought the former champion, Muhammed Ali, and because of this many felt that Frazier's achievement was a little hollow.

Ali had been stripped of his title and had his boxing licence revoked because of his refusal to fight in Vietnam. This was a position supported by Peter's gym and most other sporting institutions across the USA. Peter Tillerson and the other athletes at the gym, and from many other sporting disciplines, decided to launch a campaign to have Ali's boxing licence reinstated, paving the way for a genuine title fight. Frazier would eventually fight Ali and win the first fight later in 1971. Ali would win the rematch, reclaiming his title, though the primary reason for the campaign was to support Ali's anti-war stance.

When Ronald Crump heard of this campaign he was fuming. He contemplated launching a counterclaim, insisting Ali never be allowed to fight again and all those who supported this initiative by the gym have their sporting licences revoked. He then found out Peter Tillerson, himself on course for a crack at the USA light-heavyweight title, was a leading light in this campaign and decided against launching his own counter-initiative. He did not like the thought of having his face rearranged by his former friend.

★ ★ ★

Ronald Crump had purchased two rundown adjacent properties at a knock-down price. He was going to renovate these two flats to the highest standards, perhaps knocking them into one. There was to be no shoddy workmanship here. He intended having new bathroom suites installed, fitted carpets, and the best wallpaper. He wanted new drainage installed and new plasterwork done. He would contact Duke Tillerson about carrying out the work, emphasising quality. Ronald phoned Duke to arrange a meeting to discuss this work, and they met the following morning at the site.

'Hi, Duke, how's it hanging?' said Ronald, welcoming his father's friend.

'Grand, Ron, about yourself?' the builder replied.

He then gave Tillerson a guided tour, explaining what he wanted done as they walked around.

'A bit high-class for you, Ron?' enquired the builder.

'It is a high-class purpose I have in mind,' explained Crump. All discussions complete, Ronald asked Duke for an estimate and time expectancy for completing the work.

'I reckon about, say, one thousand for the drains and plastering.'

'Any chance of "friends' rates", Duke?' asked Ronald.

'Yes, usual rate, Ron, don't worry, I'll sort you out. All the same, it will not be a cheap job even with discounts.'

The builder, along with his head foreman, continued to survey and eventually came up with an estimate.

'About eighteen thousand dollars and the work will be completed in around sixteen weeks. I would prefer cash, Ron, if you get my meaning.'

'Sounds fair to me, Duke,' Crump said, and the two brigands shook on the deal.

The business end out of the way, the two men retired for a well-earned drink.

Of course, Tillerson had already worked out how to cut a few corners and was actually going to charge Ronald the full price. The 'friends' rates' involved Duke manipulating the accounts, that is, those disclosed, so all ultimately appeared above board.

They arrived at the bar and Duke ordered the drinks.

'I hear Peter is launching a campaign to have that traitor Muhammed Ali's boxing licence given back to him. Is that right, Duke?'

'Well, Ron, I keep out of his ideas as far as possible. He feels very strongly about it and so do the rest down at the gym. If I were you I'd keep well out of it.'

'I was thinking of launching a counter campaign based on patriotism and loyalty to the USA, condemning these people for their misguided ideas.'

'I wouldn't do that if I were you; it could result in serious injury to yourself. Peter can't stand you anyway, or more to the point what you stand for, so I wouldn't antagonise him. You would end up in hospital and it would threaten our business arrangements, including your new flats we have just shaken on.'

At the mention of this Ronald Crump, being less than brave when it came to standing up for what he believed in, decided against any countermeasures, especially when profits came under threat!

'Remember, Ron, in a few years our Peter may well be taking over the business, and he will be less likely to do deals with you which are advantageous to your pocket. Even if he does not take over, the company I would sell to might be less inclined to your needs if you are outspoken in these matters.'

The two men finished their drinks and went their separate ways.

'Good luck, Ron.'

'And you, Duke.'

Ronald was planning reductions in staffing levels, and minor reductions in the offices. With the reduction in the size of the engineering works he would no longer need two secretaries. He would leave the announcement of these job losses until after the flats had been renovated for reasons which will become clear later. The staff reductions would only involve the two junior members of staff who would both be offered new employment. This might be more to their liking, who knew? The flats which Duke Tillerson's company were renovating would not be ready until after Christmas.

Crumps Arms Supplies and Real Estate, though one of the largest concerns in the USA, did have a rival, and a rival in New York City at that. Capitalism always preaches to those who would believe it that competition in industry is a good thing. This is a misconception pedalled by those who benefit from this. It is often termed 'perfect competition'. All the bourgeoisie, the private owners of the means of production, claim to adhere to this perfect competition model or industrial organisation because it financially benefits those who win the game. What it actually does in real terms is pitch worker against worker in the brutal game of life. The winners get to keep their employment and the losers are made unemployed, thus providing a reserve army of labour in a particular field of industry. This reserve army, the unemployed former employees, are then used by the bosses to suppress wages of those still in employment.

If, for example, we have four companies employing ten thousand workers, all competing for a specific order which only one company can secure. That means three firms cannot have the order and will therefore, if no other work is in their order books, make staff redundant. Of course, the firm which gets the order will take up some of the surplus workers but certainly not all of them. The majority of the workers who do not get taken on by the company which wins the order are then out of work and are eager to rectify the situation. If, then, those in work demand a pay increase for working productively, they are told the company cannot afford to give them a pay rise. If these workers threaten strike action, thus putting under threat the order which they have won, the employers tell them, 'Strike if you will, we shall bring in the former employees of the other three losing companies.' These former employees become known as scab labour.

This is what the employers call perfect competition and like any competition there is nothing perfect for the losing team. Unfortunately, we are not talking of a game of football or baseball. We are talking about people's livelihoods and the future of their families. The losing employers often sell up for a mint and retire! It was this kind of competition which Crump was often engaged with in the form of T.A. Gunn, another arms dealer, as they constantly tried to undercut each other in this cut-throat world of 'perfect competition'.

★ ★ ★

This would be Tracy and Ronald's first Christmas together in their new home and she was very excited. It was not just the festive season which had brought about this excitement in the young wife – she had just discovered she was expecting a baby. She calculated conception must have occurred while the couple were on their honeymoon and saw this as a positive sign from God for the future. When Christmas Eve arrived, she gave Ronald the news, and he was delighted. Even by Crump's standards, there was genuine happiness at this news. The reader might look on with dread at the thought of another Ronald being set loose on society in the future, but for Tracy, who knew nothing of her husband's split personality, this was the best news she could have received. The baby would be due around June.

Ronald invited some chosen guests round for a Christmas party to celebrate. Both their parents were invited, though Teddy's illness was getting worse. Louis and Stella, Megan and Teddy along with both generations of the Rothschilds and the Carters, were present. James Rothschild proposed a toast similar to the one toasted at the wedding.

'To Tracy, Ronald and their new baby,' he said, and all raised their glasses.

Teddy looked a shadow of his former self with his tie not positioned properly. Louis, a little ignorant of the former businessman's condition, plied him with more drink. Crump Senior began acting similarly to the way young Ronald had behaved at his eleventh birthday party when he sexually assaulted young Lucy Livingwell. Teddy made improper remarks toward Stella and eventually made a grab for her, much to Megan's embarrassment.

'Stop encouraging him, aren't you going to do something?' Stella asked of her husband.

'Come on, buddy, leave my wife be,' he said, at which point Teddy began crying like a baby.

Mortified, Megan apologised on behalf of her husband to Stella, who pretended to accept the situation.

★ ★ ★

With the Christmas and New Year over and 1969 giving way to 1970, it was back to business.

'When are you giving work up, honey?' Ronald enquired of his wife.

'I thought about April time, or when I begin to show,' she replied.

'Yes, that sounds about right, darling, whenever you feel ready,' he said. 'I hope it's a boy, a son and heir, just like I was to my dad!'

'Yes, that would be perfect, then we could try for a little girl,' added Tracy as if the gender of the infant was a decided deal.

Back in the world of business, Ronald Crump had been meeting with the head of personnel, Barbara Simpson, from Gunn's, the rival company. They had struck up a relationship, obviously without the knowledge of Tracy, or Barbara's husband. Barbara had worked for T.A. Gunn approximately ten years and was a trusted member of the management team. Crump was aware of this and for this reason was having an affair with her. Her husband was in the US Navy and was away a lot. This made things easy for Crump who conveniently forgot about his own pregnant wife. Ronald wanted some documents off Barbara, and it was to this aim he had struck up the affair. Barbara was quite besotted by the young tycoon.

At a meeting on the previous Thursday after work he had asked Barbara if she could get him the plans of Gunn's factory plus the estimates submitted for forthcoming orders.

'Why do you need the plans?' she asked.

'Strictly between you and me, Barbara, I intend sabotaging one of his machines, so it will be out of action and the order will not be complete. Nobody will get injured and you, my sweet, will be an industrial espionage agent!'

She was bored with her not-very-eventful existence, so she agreed wholeheartedly to this exciting and secret mission involving industrial espionage. It was early February and he told Tracy he would be away for the weekend. Ronald booked a hotel, reusing the names Mr and Mrs Pearson. Crump, having had a massive impact in splitting up Janet Snowden from Richard Pearson, could not resist using Richard's surname again; it was like a trophy to Crump. Of course, Barbara was unaware of her fellow partner-in-adultery's antics.

He picked her up around the corner from her place of work at Gunn's on Saturday lunchtime. Anxious that nobody would see them, Barbara wore sunglasses and a headscarf, attire she would not usually be seen dead in. They arrived at the hotel and Ronald gave their bogus names and visited the bar for a while. After retiring to their suite, he ordered some bubbly to be sent up to their room and the evening's proceedings began.

Gunn's were on the verge of securing an order from the Iraqi government, whom the USA had supported in getting to power, consisting of over one thousand high-powered assault rifles with a million rounds. They also wanted small arms, revolvers, and a cache of rocket-propelled grenades (RPGs). They also requested four of the Americans' new Patton light tanks. All this merchandise was worth a fortune to Gunn's. However, they would only be paid if the order was completed on time. Ronald planned the order would not be completed at all, meaning the Iraqis would have to shop elsewhere. There was only one other company capable of fulfilling such an order in the USA, and that was his.

Ronald had arranged for Barbara to bring the aforementioned documentation with her to this rendezvous. Barbara was quite taken with the thrilling espionage which she was getting involved in. She was careful to cover her tracks so the theft of the relevant information could not be traced back to her.

In their suite Ronald and Barbara drank champagne and wine after they had sex.

'Did you bring the documents, Babs?' Crump asked her.

'Of course I did,' she said producing the merchandise from her handbag.

'Any problems?'

'None at all, Ron, it was easy. I am completely trusted at work.'

As well as the rampant sex Ronald promised Barbara, at a later assignation she received $15,000. Ronald told her this was because he was so appreciative of her efforts in getting this valuable information for him. The following morning the couple showered, dressed and went for breakfast. As they departed the hotel on Sunday afternoon the concierge asked, 'Did you enjoy your stay, Mr and Mrs Pearson?'

'Very nice, very nice indeed,' came their reply.

On their way back to New York, Ronald suggested they find a quiet spot off the beaten track and take an hour off from their drive for a little more fun and games.

The two adulterers arrived back, and Ronald took Barbara within half a mile of her home. He then headed back across town to his own house and Tracy.

'Hi, honey, I'm home,' Ronald called.

Hi, darling, I've missed you,' Tracy said.

'What's for tea, dear?' he asked.

'Salmon, I think the cook said,' Tracy informed him.

'Great! Let's have a cosy night in.'

He put his hand gently over her stomach. 'I am so looking forward to becoming a father,' he said.

'I can't wait, Ron, I really can't,' she said.

The couple retired to bed around eleven thirty and Ronald brought his wife a cup of Ovaltine to help her sleep.

'Thank you, dear, you do look after me,' she said.

Ronald was up early the following morning and the domestics had the table laid.

'Give me some cereals and fruit juice. I'm taking my wife her breakfast to bed,' he ordered the domestic help.

'He does love her,' the servants said admiringly to each other. 'It's like a fairy tale.'

Ronald's chauffeur, Creighton, was waiting to ferry his master to the office for another hard day's toil. Crump sat in the rear of the vehicle without acknowledging his driver's presence and opened his briefcase, pretending to be reading something of importance. On arriving at the office, he decided that if the flats were finished, today would be the ideal time to inform the two office juniors their services as secretaries would no longer be required. Duke informed him of the completion of the job and Crump decided to postpone his announcement to the women until he had met Tillerson and inspected the job. He phoned the builder and arranged an appointment.

'See you in about an hour, Duke?'

'Yes, that's fine, Ron.'

The two men met at the entrance to the newly furbished flats.

'I'm sure you will be happy with the work, Ron,' the builder said. 'All done to your specifications and the inspectors have checked everything. They also had a look at the drains and brickwork and appear happy. Here's the certificate of completion.'

'Great, Duke, let's have a tour.'

'By all means, buddy,' Tillerson said.

The flats were indeed luxurious, carpets one would sink into and the décor was out of this world. The bathrooms were the size of most people's living rooms with a sauna and showers fit for royalty, coupled with a Jacuzzi and small laundry chute. Whoever lived here was in for a treat, which was exactly what Crump wanted. The lavatories were separate, of course, and both apartments were the same in every way. They were linked by a wide adjoining door making them almost one unit – almost, but not quite. Ronald signed the agreed cheque and the pair retired for a well-earned drink. It was certainly a hard life being an entrepreneur.

Back at the office Crump summoned the two sacrificial lambs. He had a brief word with Agnes Moorhouse, his trusty aide, and dismissed her. This meeting and what would transpire was too secret even for her.

'Now ladies,' Crump said by way of introduction, 'as you will be aware we only now deal in light engineering, and not a great amount of that, it just doesn't pay. We will, therefore, not be needing the number of office staff we now employ, and certainly not two junior secretaries! Therefore—'

'You're telling us we're sacked or redundant,' interjected Linda.

'Not exactly, girls,' Crump continued. 'How would you like redeployment? Two positions where, to a certain extent, you make your own rules. It will be a live-in job. That means you can say goodbye to those crummy little flats where you now reside, if that is the correct description,' he said belittlingly.

'You both like nights out on the town, don't you?' he continued. 'You both like to be wined and dined by rich fellas? I don't blame you, two good-looking young women. If you've got it, flaunt it, eh?'

'Yes, I suppose so. Look, where is this going?' an impatient Carol asked.

'All in good time, ladies, all in good time,' Ronald said, teasing the women as if they were children.

Linda and Carol were both very attractive twenty-five-year-olds with excellent figures, just what Crump was looking for in his new venture.

'How would you both like to live in my luxury apartments?' he enquired.

'What's the catch?' asked Linda.

'No catch, ladies, only what *you* can catch, so to speak. You will be my first hostesses for the foreign dignitaries I'm expecting wishing to purchase arms, contracts worth millions if not more. Part of your job will be to give these gentlemen a good time, good company and above all respect. You will encourage them to purchase off us as opposed to our rivals who will not offer this service.'

'He's putting us on the fucking game, Carol,' Linda exclaimed.

'No, no, no, ladies. You will be hostesses and that's all.'

'What if these posh fellas want sex?'

'That will be up to you, girls. I'll be charging $1,000 per hour for you to wine and dine them. You will receive $200 each of this and me the rest. If you then wish, of your own accord, to engage in further activities, that is your choice. Whatever you do, make your own prices, which I will take fifty per cent of. You will, after all, be living rent-free.'

'Let's at least think it over, Linda,' said Carol.

'Yes let's,' she replied.

The two girls retired to a corner of the room where they engaged in a furtive conversation for a few moments. Then they sat back in front of Crump. He spoke before they had a chance to.

'Now,' Crump added, 'these guests will be few and far between, so if you wish to go freelance then you can. Just be careful of the clientele you engage with. Any trouble from the law when you're freelancing, and you're on your own. I know nothing of it. There is no need for that to arise if you are sensible and you'll make more in one night than in six months as secretaries. When you are freelancing, assuming you decide to, and there is no pressure to do so, you are self-employed and remember, the secrecy document you signed applies to these jobs as it does to your secretarial roles.'

Ronald Crump had updated his secrecy rules, threatening criminal action if they were broken; this had previously not been included.

'Well, ladies, what do you think?'

The ladies looked at each other and nodded.

'Yeah, Mr Crump, let's live a little and get paid for it. We'll give it a try.'

'Great, I knew you would see sense. Just sign here, ladies, and we can all go and have a drink!'

Ronald Crump was aware these wealthy clients from foreign governments he spoke of would indeed be few and far between. In fact, they were only the bait on the hook to entice these two women into prostitution for him. It would become more apparent, after Crump had arranged their first clients, that most of their earnings would come from the freelance work previously discussed. The two women would surrender their present places of abode in return for these perceived luxury apartments. Once they became totally dependent on Crump for their accommodation he would turn the screw tighter and tighter. His percentage of their earnings would increase until eventually these two 'hostesses' would be lying on their backs simply to keep a roof over their heads and bread on the table. In a nutshell, they would in all probability have been better off taking their redundancy, even at legal minimum rates, and seeking employment as secretaries elsewhere. Instead they would, slowly at first, set out on the road to perdition.

Crump, on the other hand would, within two years, have recouped the money he laid out for the renovations and a whole lot more off the immoral earnings of his girls. Of course, should a wealthy representative of a foreign government come along then the facility to entertain would be available. For

Ronald Crump it was a win–win situation. To cover his own backside, he had the job covered by his bogus secrecy document which all employees, legal and otherwise, were illegally obliged to sign. Of course, he had to keep up the pretence that they were bona fide employees of Crump's in case any questions were asked by the law. This was unlikely because the local force, from the Chief of Police down, were all in his pocket. No, the major potential problem for Ronald Crump could be the Mob, who generally ran all prostitution rackets in and around New York. For this reason, he had to keep his two girls looking like employees and would not, at any cost, consider expanding. The Mafia might just swallow this operation, providing it became no threat to them and did not eat into their profits. Crump was aware how far he dared go with this venture. He gave the two women a sizable amount of money and told them to go shopping for clothes, attire which men would be turned on by.

'Sounds good to us,' the two naive ladies agreed.

With the first of Ronald's criminal plans approaching fruition, it was time to move on to his next, even more unlawful, plan. This would involve using the plans of T.A. Gunn which he had gone to such lengths to procure. Barbara had furnished him with all he needed, he now had no further use for her; in fact she was a liability on two fronts. Firstly, should anything go wrong which might involve an inquiry into himself, she would be readily available for questioning. Secondly, she might also, depending on how the situation unfolded, tell Tracy of their sordid little romps.

In the weeks which followed the betrayal of her employer to Crump, Barbara Simpson continued in her job as if nothing had happened. She had a couple of short assignations with Ronald and as far as she was aware, everything in the garden was rosy. Her husband would shortly be home on shore leave and her twice-yearly bonus was due at work. She told Ronald they would have to cool it a little while her husband was home. She had ensured the master copy of the documents, photocopies now in Crump's possession, were back in the safe, so no leak would be suspected. All the same, she did wonder what Ronald Crump *really* wanted with them.

It was now about six weeks since her assignation with Crump had taken place and although they had met in the meantime and sex had taken place, these meetings were nothing compared to that passionate weekend. It was five thirty and Barbara was leaving the office for her bus. She disembarked the vehicle at the same spot where Crump had left her off that Sunday. Suddenly, and without warning, a car sped out of nowhere, hitting Barbara and sending her flying through the air. She was dead on impact with the ground. The driver then sped off into the distance. The offending vehicle was found the next day partially burnt out and devoid of any fingerprints several miles from the scene of the incident.

The next evening, Crump instructed his chauffeur to stop and get him a paper on his way home. He read of the accident and acted shocked and distressed. When he arrived home he was shaking, or he was pretending to be, and explained to Tracy that a senior member of staff from a rival company had been tragically killed.

'How did it happen, darling?' asked his wife. 'Here, I can see you're upset. Let me pour you a brandy.'

'Thank you, darling. I know she was an employee of a competitor, but we are all one of the same club,' he said. 'You know, Tracy, it feels like one of my own family has been killed. We are all working in the same industry and we are all part of the same family.'

'Never mind, darling,' Tracy said. 'At least she had a good friend in you even though you were, in one respect, the enemy. Will you be going to the funeral?'

'That is the least I can do,' he sanctimoniously replied.

'Then I must come with you, dear.'

'Yes, darling, you must indeed,' he agreed. The more people who could see Crump in his grief, the better.

The misguided Barbara's funeral was the following Monday morning at Saint Columba Roman Catholic Church. The previous Friday, Crump had summoned Bob Tomkinson to his office.

'I want you at the funeral of Barbara Simpson with Tracy and me,' he decreed.

'Do you think that is wise?'

'We must show our respects, and our presence will help alleviate any lingering suspicions that intercompany rivalry may have been a factor in her unfortunate passing.'

'Well, if you think it's worth the risk,' said Tomkinson, sounding more than a little doubtful.

'There are no risks Bob, save in your imagination.'

'Well all right, Ron, I see your point,' he conceded.

'Imagine you are behind the enemy lines in Normandy with my dad, Bob. A job had to be done and you did it. Did you panic? No, you didn't. Think of this in the same vein.'

The problem with this analogy was there were no enemy lines. Back in the day Colonel Crump had been a staff officer fifty miles behind the allied lines. The war hero story was made up by Teddy to create an impression of a man who had fought bravely in battle. Crump had pretended he was a war hero, not merely a staff officer. Tomkinson was sworn to secrecy. In fact, Colonel Crump had only taken over the regiment in Hamburg after a brief spell in France, following the Third Reich surrender. It was here he met Sergeant Tomkinson and the 'war hero' illusion was concocted. It was also in Hamburg where Crump Senior had the idea of taking Tomkinson with him as an employee to ensure a potentially dangerous rival was off the stage. Ronald was unaware of this illusion and acted accordingly.

'Very well, Ron. Will I drive you and Tracy to the church?'

'Yes, that's a good man, Bob, I'd appreciate that,' Ronald said. 'I will tell Creighton he won't be needed that day. We will go as representatives of the company and offer our condolences to the family.'

The morning of the funeral arrived, and Crump looked what he was, the height of hypocrisy. Tracy looked very smart in a dark two-piece suit which showed off her blossoming figure. In the case of Tracy, her respects and condolences were genuine, despite not knowing the deceased woman. Bob Tomkinson arrived to drive them to the service and he, like Crump, dressed in black.

After the service in the cemetery graveyard plain-clothed police officers mingled with the crowd. They were seeking a hit-and-run driver, and knew that they sometimes the perpetrator in a tragedy like this would turn up to secretly pay respects. The senior officer, Chief Inspector O'Hanlon, was a friend and golfing partner of Crump's and the pair made small talk. After they'd arranged a round for the coming weekend Crump said, 'Oh Pat, allow me to introduce you to my wife, Tracy.'

'Nice to meet you, Mrs Crump, I see congratulations are in order.'

'Thank you, Pat,' a slightly embarrassed Tracy replied.

'Till the weekend then, Pat,' said Ronald. 'I'll take you on the thirteenth.'

After this sickening sight of Crump and Tomkinson crying crocodile tears over the woman whose demise they were responsible for, it was time to take Tracy home and return to the office.

'Don't forget, Bob, pencil in the next board meeting and let me have the agenda in good time. At least a week before anybody else.'

'Will do, Ron. If there's nothing more I'll head on.'

'Yeah, see you, Bob.'

Crump then hit on the idea, as he had some very rare spare time, to pay Linda and/or Carol a visit at the apartment to see how they were keeping. He telephoned first to ascertain they were not entertaining. Upon discovering they were both free he drove over to them. 'Hi, ladies, I thought maybe you were bored so I'd brighten up your afternoon, call it rent money.'

'He means a freebie, Linda,' said Carol.

'Yeah, I know. Come on, then, let's go to the bedroom.'

The reader must understand that it had been a tiring day for Crump, the funeral, a chat about golf and now two demanding females: little wonder the poor man was exhausted!

The following morning Ronald arrived at the office early. He wanted to examine the plans for Gunn's premises without being discovered or disturbed. He noticed a way in at the rear of the factory, not covered by CCTV. *Yes*, he thought, *this is the best way, I'll speak to Tomkinson when he arrives.*

Bob Tomkinson had yet no idea what his boss had in mind. This would change over the next few days as Crump drip-fed his subordinate little bits here and there. Ronald Crump knew if he disclosed his plans in their entirety to Tomkinson he would run a mile. Tomkinson arrived at Crump's office.

'Bob, I may have a major job for you which, if it comes off, will pay handsomely.'

'What kind of job?' asked the bemused man.

'All in good time, Bob, all in good time,' Crump said. 'If we get this contract, your director's pay will rocket plus the value of your investments with the firm and your two per cent.'

'You mean five per cent, Ron, that two per cent was a one-off, remember?'

'Of course, Bob, five per cent. I don't know what came over me!'

'When do I get the low-down?' Tomkinson asked, the dollar bills revolving around his eyeballs.

'Wait till I have met with my senior scientists, gunsmiths and engineers. I need to know we can do the job. As soon as I've consulted them I'll get back to you. Oh, you used incendiary devices during the Second World War, didn't you?'

'Yes, why?'

'All in good time, Bob, don't be impatient.'

Ronald summoned his technological team of experts to a meeting, and produced the relevant plans furnished him by the late Barbara to show his henchmen.

'Could you, based on these specifications, produce these weapons here at Crumps? Do we have the technology?' he asked.

The men carefully looked at the information before them. Ronald's team were Dr Stephen Hayes, a specialist in specifications, wind, elevation (how climatic conditions and recoil can alter the trajectory of a missile or bullet fired from a firearm) and gas-powered weapons; Colin Jameson, a ballistics expert; Peter Knott, a gunsmith; and Larry Wakefield, an engineer.

Hayes looked at the plans and designs, sharing them with his colleague, Colin Jameson.

'What you think, Colin?' Hayes asked.

'I don't anticipate any real problem constructing these weapons. What do you two think?'

This was reference to Peter Knott and Larry Wakefield.

'Sure, we have done much of this stuff before. Remember the contract for the Saudis some years back? Most of this technology was used in their machines.'

'That's right, lads, I remember now,' Hayes confirmed, so it was decided should Crumps get the contract there were no problems regarding production.

'So, team, between you, me and the garden post we can put this together. Now I must outline the importance of secrecy. I do not want any leaks, which is why only us four and Bob Tomkinson are aware of this project. None of the other directors know about it yet. I trust you all and remember this if it comes off there is work for all our staff in the coming years.'

The meeting thus came to a conclusion and Ronald was left to his own thoughts. He had decided on his next move, and timing would be a major factor.

Suddenly the telephone rang, and his attention was diverted in another direction of major importance. It was mid-June and Tracy was in her ninth month of pregnancy. The message was that his wife was in labour and had been taken to St Mary's hospital.

'I'm on my way,' Ronald informed them, and he summoned Creighton to ferry him to the hospital.

'Take me to St. Mary's Hospital, Creighton, and step on it.'

'Very good, sir,' replied the subordinate. 'May I ask is there a problem?'

'No, on the contrary, I'm going to be a father,' Crump informed his driver.

'Congratulations, sir, I'm delighted for you. If there is anything I can do just say the word,' Creighton said.

'I'll let you know. Now drive,' Crump ordered.

If anybody was unfortunate enough to witness this scene it could be imagined that Creighton would willingly have given birth for the Crumps himself to save Mrs Crump the pain and Crump himself the anguish.

They arrived at the hospital. 'Stay here, Creighton,' said Crump in much the same manner one would speak to a dog.

'Yes, sir.'

Ronald rushed into the reception area.

'You there, yes you,' he shouted to a young nurse.

'Excuse me, are you talking to me?'

'Yes, goddamn it, my wife is giving birth,' he said, his colour rising.

'A lot of women are, sir. Now calm down and tell me her name.'

'Tracy Crump,' Ronald informed the nurse. 'Where is she?'

'Just a moment and I'll find out for you, Mr Crump.' The nurse consulted the receptionist, who was able to inform Ronnie what floor his wife was on.

After rushing up to the relevant area, all Ronald could do then was sit outside the delivery room for what seemed like forever. He simmered in frustration. He could have been present at the birth, but he had turned down the opportunity. This would have involved showing something approaching courage, which Ronald was a little short of. Crump only showed any signs of what he considered courage when it involved bullying women, making racist remarks or abuse, knowing no law in the land would prosecute him, or threatening his workers with imminent dismissal and, therefore, starvation for them and their families.

After about forty minutes a midwife exited the delivery room.

'Congratulations, Mr Crump, you are now the proud father of a baby boy.'

'Thank you, nurse,' acknowledged Crump, hugely relieved. 'May I see my wife?'

'Of course. Come on in,' he was told.

Crump then entered the small delivery room.

'Well done, darling, we have a baby son! I'm so proud of you, Tracy,' he said, reassuring her of his support. He gave his wife a hug and held the infant in his arms. 'He's got my eyes, and my head.'

'I should hope so, there would be something wrong if he had the milkman's eyes and head, now wouldn't there?'

Crump gave an appreciative laugh at his wife's humour.'

'When can my wife come home?' he enquired of the midwife, who was standing nearby.

'She needs a couple of days' rest. Two days and she's all yours, Mr Crump.'

'Have you thought of a name yet?'

'Not yet, we'll have a talk about that when I get home,' Tracy said. 'I'm so excited, Ron, aren't you?'

'Of course, dear,' Crump replied.

'Come along now, Mr Crump, that's quite enough excitement for one day. Your wife needs her rest.'

Ronald did not take kindly to being ordered about by a slip of a woman but he bit his tongue and left as requested. '

'See you tomorrow, darling,' he said.

The following day Ronald arrived at the hospital with flowers he had actually purchased himself.

He entered the ward and saw his wife was sitting up and cradling the baby.

'Hi, darling, I've bought you some flowers.'

'They're lovely, darling,' Tracy enthused. 'Nurse, will you put these in some water, please?'

'Certainly, Mrs Crump.'

'Can we talk about a name for our little boy, Ronnie?'

'Yes of course. What ideas do you have, Tracy?'

'Well, anything you like really, Ron.'

'Very well, you are handing me responsibility to name our son, are you?' Crump joked half mockingly. 'All right then, as he's going to be a man involved at the highest level of business he must have a name to match. He must also have a name befitting his class status. Can I sleep on it?'

'Of course, darling, you can.'

'I'll be back tomorrow with a name,' Crump said. He had already decided in his own mind on Tarquin. All he had to do was sell it to his wife. If Teddy was Caesar and he, Ronald, was Tiberius then his son, Tarquin, would be Caligula in line with the Roman Empire. This is the Crump Empire, he thought.

The following day Crump arrived and much to his delight Tracy was dressed.

'She can go home today, Mr Crump,' the nurse informed him.

'Great news,' said Ronald.

'Have you thought of a name, dear?' said Tracy, getting into the coat Ronald held out for her.

'Yes, I'll tell you when we arrive home. Creighton is outside waiting, and before you suggest it, we are not calling him Creighton,' Ronald joked.

The happy couple arrived home and the immediate topic of conversation was the child's name. The domestics were all making a fuss, with exaggerated congratulations to the master and mistress.

'Yes, thank you all very much. Now back to work,' said Crump, reminding them of their lowly status and not to get too familiar with their betters.

'Now, the name. I thought of a few powerful-sounding titles. Eventually I settled on Tarquin, yes, Tarquin Crump. What do you think, dear?'

'Yes, that sounds very businesslike,' agreed Tracy in a half-hearted fashion.

'That's it then, decided!' cried Crump triumphantly. 'Tarquin it is!'

The following day Ronald sat at his desk in his office. He was pondering his master plan to steal the contract from T.A. Gunn. Yes, he thought, the time was about right. He spoke through the intercom: 'Mrs Moorhouse, will you ask Mr Tomkinson to come and see me?'

'Yes, Mr Crump.'

He was now going to outline his plan to get the Iraqi government contract from Gunn and Co.

'Cometh the hour, cometh the man, Bob, you are that man. We must prevent Gunn's from starting, or certainly completing, that order they have from the Iraqis. If they cannot fulfil the contract, then the Iraqi government will look elsewhere, and we are the natural choice. I know they need that order completed urgently. Perhaps something is brewing in the Middle East. I don't know or care. What I do know is I want that contract!'

'What have you got in mind?' asked Tomkinson.

'We need to sabotage their factory; in fact, we need to decommission it and you are the man for the job, Bob.'

'How do you work that out, boss, I mean, what do you have in mind?' Tomkinson enquired.

'Well Bob, you worked behind enemy lines during the hostilities of 1941–45, didn't you? You were involved in sabotaging the Nazi war machine, I believe?'

'Yes, and therefore?'

'Come here and examine these plans of Gunn's rear exit. I think they have forgotten about it, which would be surprising as they are conducting secret operations in the old part of the plant. You see the back door, here? There are no CCTV covering it, the late Barbara told me, so it is easy access.'

'Where do I come in? You're not expecting me to gain entry and sabotage the place, are you?'

'Yes, why did you think I courted Barbara and asked you to do the wicked deed?'

'I didn't think you had breaking and entering in mind.'

'I think, Bob, after a hit-and-run, this is small beer.'

'Oh, I don't know, Ron, I've done enough.'

'Stop being a Lilliputian. You're up to your neck in shit already so don't even contemplate walking out on me now,' Crump said brusquely. 'Now listen to me, you used incendiary devices in the war, didn't you?'

'Yes, I did but that was on active service. That was wartime, this isn't.'

'It is Bob, it's industrial conflict and like any other conflict, the fittest survive. That's one thing the Third Reich got right: get in our way and we'll crush you.'

'Yes, Ron, but it was they who ended up being crushed by the Soviets, ourselves and the British chiefly, with help from various partisans.'

'Don't you ever speak of the communists in the same breath as us, Bob, ever. Some things are best aired out of history. Anyway, back to our plan.'

'Uh, your plan, Ron.'

'No, goddamn it! We are both in this, you son of a bitch.'

Crump felt he was not getting through to his underling. 'Listen, Bob, your director's salary will rocket, to say nothing of your investments in the company and then there's your two per cent.'

'Five per cent.'

'Yes, OK, OK, five per cent.'

The two men bickered over the plan until Bob finally agreed subject to a full briefing.

'Come here and look at this. As I said, Bob, there are no CCTVs covering this door. All you do is enter the premises at about 8.30pm. Nobody will be there. Then you are going to set these four incendiary devices. I know you have used them before which makes you the ideal man for the job. I'd do it myself,' he said, 'But I haven't your experience. Set them to detonate at 10.30pm. That will give us plenty of time to be out of the way. We will be disguised with wigs and glasses to be on the safe side and—'

'You're coming as well, are you?'

'Of course, I wouldn't leave you to do the job alone, would I? After it's done we drive the old banger I've procured and dump it, wiping the car clean of prints. Earlier in the day you will have left your car in a nearby hidden place, so we can use that to get back to the office. Then we will go to my place to bring Tracy for a surprise drink. That will be our alibi, not that we'll need one.'

'Sounds easy enough, Ronnie, and you say my salary will increase?'

'Yes, Bob, by some distance – as will the other directors, but not by the same amount.'

'There will be no danger to life?' was Bob's last question.

'No,' Crump lied. The truth was, a security guard would be present, a Korean War veteran, and should he be doing his nightly patrols he would be in danger. Still, better not tell Bob; he might get cold feet.

'We go Friday night, Bob. As Eisenhower said, "Let's go!" This, Bob, is our Normandy.'

Friday evening came and the staff at Crumps were finishing up for the weekend. This would leave just Ronald and Bob in the office to finalise plans.

'Have you got the incendiary bombs, Ron?'

'Yes, here they are. Are they all right?'

'Yes, PX fours, perfect. A slight muffled explosion which nobody will hear and then… bingo.'

'You're feeling confident now, Bob?'

'Yes, providing there will be no loss of life.'

'Don't worry about that. Well, are we ready?'

'Yes, Ron.'

'Then let's go.'

The two arsonists arrived incognito behind Gunn's plant and Bob Tomkinson walked slowly to the rear door. From here he made his way unnoticed into the back room, the old part of the complex. He placed the first incendiary bomb adjacent to some gas cylinders, and the second he placed beside a drum of solvent to create maximum fireballs. The remaining two devices he placed in the laboratory, the heart of the operation, which had been converted from an old storeroom. All the devices were timed to explode at 10.30pm that evening.

Tomkinson then headed back to the waiting Crump who then sped off to some waste ground where an old flooded quarry was conveniently awaiting the old banger of a car. The two men then pushed the vehicle into the dark, deep murky waters and watched it disappear and all its secrets with it. That car would never be found; the water was a hundred feet deep.

'A good night's work, Bob,' commented Crump as they made their way back to the office in Tomkinson's car.

From the office at Crumps Arms and Real Estate they drove to Ronald's house to collect an unsuspecting Tracy.

'Come on, darling, we're taking you out for a drink.'

'What about little Tarquin?' she asked.

'Where is the nanny?'

'I sent her home early. She has done a lot today and I thought she deserved some time off to herself.'

'Rubbish, I'll phone and get her back.'

'That doesn't seem fair, Ronnie.'

'Nothing is fair in life, dear. We are celebrating a new deal and a success in the property market,' he partially lied. 'Hello, is that Marigold? It's Mr Crump here. Can you look after Tarquin for a few hours? I want to take my wife out.'

'Your wife gave me the night off, Mr Crump,' the employee complained.

'I will give you generous overtime for this, make it worth your while.'

'All right then, Mr Crump,' the lady replied, irritated she had been discommoded but pleased with this unexpected bonus.

'Be here in half an hour,' said Ronald curtly.

It mattered not to Ronald Crump whether Marigold had arranged a personal night for herself with the unexpected time Tracy had given her, as far as he was concerned the only people who mattered were himself, his wife and, on this occasion through necessity, Bob Tomkinson.

'She'll be here, darling, and then we can go and celebrate. Where would you like to go?'

'Oh, let's go for a meal. Can we go for drinks after?'

'Of course we can. You don't mind old Bob coming along?'

'Less of the old,' Tomkinson interjected.

Ronald chuckled, muttering a faint apology.

'No, of course not,' said Tracy. 'You're more than welcome, Bob.'

They arrived at a restaurant in the New York suburbs, the opposite side of town to Gunn's soon-to-be-crippled factory. Crump ordered for himself and his wife while Tomkinson retained his independence.

'Nice food here, Bob,' Crump said, making small talk. 'You like it, don't you, Tracy?'

'Well, uh, yes,' she replied, unable to recall having ever being there at any time previously.

'Yes, it's very nice, Ron,' Tomkinson commented.

When they had all finished their meal it was time to retire to the bar and the comfort of the luxury sofas the establishment was furnished with.

In the corner was a large television set with hourly news bulletins coming through. Suddenly the main programme was interrupted:

'We interrupt this programme to bring you breaking news of an inferno at Gunn's Arms Manufacturers. A security guard has been killed by one of the explosions that went off at the plant. Thirty firefighters are at present trying to bring the blaze under control. The fire is believed to have started at the rear of the building where an old faulty electrical system may have short-circuited. Police do not suspect foul play. Further updates will be given in the next bulletin.'

On hearing of the security guard, Tomkinson glared at Crump.

'Oh my God, that poor man,' Tracy said.

'Yes, it's a tragedy,' commented Crump.

Tracy was so upset that she had to retire to the bathroom. Tomkinson turned to Crump.

'You said there would be no casualties. You fucking lied.'

'Hang on, Bob, I said I did not expect any casualties. It was just unfortunate. What do you military people call it: collateral damage?'

When Tracy returned from the restroom she was still upset. Ronald tried to act sombre and grave putting his arm comfortingly around her shoulder. If the new mother had not been so emotional she might have noticed her husband was not really bothered at all, it was just a front. She was suffering from post-natal depression, and this tragic news fuelled her condition. Ronald decided to use his wife's emotional state to make his excuses and leave.

'You won't mind if we get a cab? That news has clearly upset my wife and I should get her home.'

'No, that's OK. I'll see you in the morning. Good night, Tracy,' Bob said.

'Good night, Bob.'

The following morning Tomkinson entered Crump's office for a one-on-one.

'You knew that poor fucker would be present, Ron, didn't you?'

'I swear, Bob, I did not. I was clueless, thought the place would be empty,' he lied.

Tomkinson was upset enough about the security guard. What made it more difficult was he was an ex-army man decorated in the Korean War. What bugged him even more was the fact he had allowed himself to be used, first by

Teddy and now by Ronald Crump. All for a meagre, miserable five per cent! But it was too late to turn the clock back now. To make matters worse he was now responsible for two lives being lost at the behest of Ronald. Teddy, for all his faults, had never asked that of him. What could he do? Nothing, was the answer.

'Come on, Bob, looks like we got away with it. All we have to do is wait for the government of Iraq to transfer the contract to us. We're laughing all the way to the bank.'

Tomkinson had no choice but to make the best of it. He would, after all, be somewhat better off and could retire much earlier than anticipated. In fact, if all went to plan, Bob Tomkinson could be out of this malaise within eighteen months. He would sell his stake in the company and retire somewhere nice with his wife and kids, forgetting all about these events. Perhaps things were not that bad after all.

13

Death of Caesar: Tiberius for Congress

The two hostesses, perhaps more appropriately described as high-class hookers, were beginning to realise that Ronald Crump took the lion's share of their earnings. The high-class foreign government representatives were a trickle and certainly not the flood which Crump had suggested. More and more the women had to rely on their freelance work. When the odd occasion did arise when a high-class wealthy client hoping to do business with Crumps Arms took advantage of this service, the money these gentlemen paid, though high, was filtered into Crump's alternative bank account. This was the separate account he had set up to take the women's earnings, or the cream of them, and would pay for Tarquin's education in the future years. Carol and Linda found they were increasingly working for pocket money and rent-free accommodation. The riches which Crump had implied, without promising, were a long time coming; if anything, to say little of the risks involved, their net wages were going down, not increasing.

Ronald Crump, on the other hand, was making a fortune out of these women and already had over fifty thousand dollars in his private account. The scheme had only been up and running for a few months and at this rate, Ronald thought, Tarquin would want for nothing. When the girls got past their sell-by date he would evict them. That would be easy to do as they paid no rent. Then he would find two more attractive young women prepared to work in the good cause of self-sacrifice for Crump.

However, for the time being the girls had no need to worry. Crump would continue for now to 'look after them'. Ronald also took his perks, often in lieu of rent, which involved romps involving himself and the two women.

Of course, Tracy knew nothing of this side of her husband's business. If she had it was unlikely even she, placid as she was, would have put up with her husband essentially being a high-class pimp. She was also unaware of the secret bank account funnelling the women's money for their son's future education, something that was deeply immoral and unconscionable.

The Crump family nanny, Marigold, was a fully qualified childminder who had come to work for the Crumps just prior to Tarquin's birth. She had taken the job because the flexible hours, not part-time, suited her social life. Ronald had hired her himself, as he wanted to make sure she was white, as he did not want his son "contaminated" by non-whites. Of course, he never voiced this to his wife. The position suited Marigold for now. However, she decided if Mr Crump did not improve his bombastic attitude, she would seek employment elsewhere. She liked Tracy; everybody liked Mrs Crump, but him!

The health of Teddy Crump was deteriorating, and Megan was beginning to struggle with her ailing husband. Over a two-week period a marked deterioration had taken place and she was at the end of her tether. For the first time she began to think of having him retired to a care home. She could not, with any confidence, leave him alone for too long in case he had an accident or – worst-case scenario – burnt the place down. She decided to phone their friend and physician, Dr Alan Quincy for guidance.

'Hi Al, it's Megan Crump.'

'Hi Megan, how can I help you?'

'It's Teddy. His health is getting worse. I think I should consider a nursing home as an option.'

'I'll come over in the morning. I'll bring my colleague along as well. You remember him, Dr Alucard? Between us we should be able to make a recommendation.'

'Thanks Al, till the morning then.'

'Yes, bye.'

Megan then phoned Derek. 'We'll have to hold back a little, dear. I'm trying to have Teddy committed to a care home.'

'That'll be great,' he said baldly. 'We can be together more then, can't we?'

'Yes, of course, that's the idea.'

She then phoned Ronald and explained Teddy's situation to him, and about the doctors' imminent visit. She told him of the rapid deterioration in Teddy's health over a ten-day period. One aspect of Alzheimer's disease is the unpredictability of any deterioration. For example, a sufferer could go many months or even years with only minor changes in their behaviour. Then, suddenly, a rapidly deterioration could happen, which was now the case with Teddy Crump. Megan said she needed her son and daughter-in-law with her the next day, and Ronald assured her they would be there. Megan also phoned Hugh Rothschild and explained to him and Mary her husband's predicament.

'Don't worry, Megan, we'll do what we can for you. Unfortunately we are going away for a few weeks but when we get back let us know if you need anything.' The Rothschilds were not, until this point, going anywhere but a sudden crash decision was taken on hearing a 'friend' might need help.

Ronald Crump instructed their nanny that her leave and normal working hours were now changed due to an emergency family crisis. 'You will have to look after Tarquin overnight while my wife and I are away,' he said.

Tracy had to say something about her husband's rudeness. 'Ronald, stop taking Marigold for granted. She might have her own plans. Marigold, would it be too much trouble to look after our son overnight? I shall be back tomorrow to give him his feed so if you can, it will be doing Mr Crump and me a great favour.'

'Of course, Mrs Crump,' Marigold said, ignoring Ronald. 'Leave the little one with me and we can take it from there.'

Ronald was most put out after his wife had publicly humiliated him, as he saw it, but should have been grateful because if Tracy had not intervened with an apology, Marigold was going to tell him to stuff his job.

Ronald and Tracy arrived at Megan's.

'I'm thinking of putting your dad in a nursing home, Ronald,' Megan explained. 'I cannot cope like this much longer. Dr Quincy will be here in the morning and we shall try to sort something out.'

'Whatever you decide, Mom, you'll have our support. Won't she, Tracy?'

'Definitely, Megan, don't worry.'

The following morning Dr Alan Quincy and his colleague arrived.

'Thank you for coming, Al, my son is here,' Megan said.

'Ronald, good to see you. The last time I saw you was after the swimming contest you did well in.'

'Good to see you, Al.'

'Oh, Ronald, this is my colleague, Dr Franklin Alucard.'

'Nice to meet you, sir,' Crump Junior said, offering his hand.

'Right, Megan, where's the patient?' Quigley asked.

'He's through here, Al, I think he's sleeping.'

Megan led them into the lounge, where Teddy was slumped in a comfortable armchair.

'Teddy, Ted, it's me Alan, Dr Quincy, how are you?'

Teddy awoke and looked up at the man.

'Were you in Hamburg after the war?' he said slowly.

'No, Ted, I'm your doctor and this is my associate, Dr Alucard.'

'You were! Both of you were in Hamburg and were SS officers.'

'No, Ted, wrong side, we're friendly,' Quincy said, trying to humour Crump.

'What do you think, Al?' Megan asked quietly.

'Well, it's not good,' Dr Alucard interjected.

Alucard looked at Teddy, who was now staring vacantly into space.

'I think we should take him into hospital immediately,' Alucard said. 'I must advise you, Megan, I doubt he will come home again.' Quincy agreed with his colleague. 'From there we can assess him and arrange for a place in a care home to be found. They are very good, these homes we have now. Only the best for Teddy.'

Tracy Crump arrived back at their house and thanked Marigold for her time and patience. She apologised for her husband's rudeness, explaining the pressure he was under.

'I'm going to be away for a couple of weeks at least, Marigold, so you can take the time off.'

'I can't afford two weeks without pay, Mrs Crump.'

'Who said without pay?' Tracy countered. 'You will be on full pay, at least for two weeks, so don't worry.

'Thank you, Mrs Crump,' Marigold said gratefully.

The nanny packed a few things, thanking her employer once again, and departed.

Tracy arrived back at Megan's house and explained to her husband she had given the nanny two weeks' paid leave.

'You have done what?' Crump complained.

'Look, Ronnie, I need her at least for another two years and she is worth her weight in gold. Stop being so mean with the staff. She is having the time off, end of conversation.'

For once Ronald Crump listened and saw the logic of his wife's argument.

'Very well, darling, I'm sorry. Just a little distraught at the moment.'

'I know, Ron, but I'll be with you all the way.'

The next day Ronald arranged for Creighton to take them all to the hospital to see his father. It never entered Crump's head to invite the old family retainer, the loyal Creighton, if he would like to see his employer of twenty years.

'Creighton,' said Megan, 'would you like to see Mr Crump? You have, after all, been here a long time with us.'

'Thank you, madam, I should like that,' Creighton replied.

Teddy Crump was a sad sight. Even allowing for the rotten, devious things he had done it was pitiful watching another human in this condition.

'Hi, Megan,' said Dr Quincy.

'Hi, Alan. Poor Teddy, he doesn't look good at all. What are your plans?'

'That is very much down to you and your family. All I can tell you with any certainty is he will never come home again.'

Tracy began to cry a little. She liked Teddy. She was unaware of the real Teddy Crump and based her feelings on the man she had got to know since Ronald and she were going steady. 'It's horrible, it does not seem right, a nice man like him lying there like a cabbage.'

'Never mind, darling,' Ronald said, comforting his wife and kissing her on the head. 'He's in the best place now.'

Creighton was visibly upset. 'I'll leave you, Mrs Crump, to be with your family and thank you for the brief visit.'

'That's all right, Creighton, we'll be out in half an hour,' Megan informed the chauffeur.

A week passed, and the telephone rang.

'Megan Crump speaking.'

'Hi Megan, Alan Quincy here. Good news for you.'

For a brief second Megan dreaded they were going to say Teddy had made a surprising recovery and could come home; she did not want that.

'Hi, Al, what's the news?'

'We have found a place for Teddy in a lovely nursing home. Only one problem: it's 350 miles away in north-east New Hampshire.'

That's not a problem, Megan thought, *it's a blessing.*

'Oh I see, Al. Well, I suppose if there's nothing nearer home we will just have to accept that,' she said, hoping above hope nothing nearer could be found.

'Well, there are closer places but they're of poorer quality.'

'We don't want that, Al, only the best for my husband.'

'I knew you would say that. Will I give the go-ahead?'

'Yes, do Al, right away.'

The truth was, Megan could not really care less if it was a nice place or not; the further away her husband was, the more convenient it would be for her and Derek. She informed Ronald and Tracy of the situation.

'It's the best we could do for him, apparently it is a lovely place. We could visit once a month though it is unlikely he will recognise us.'

'Thanks for letting me know, Mom. Tracy and I will return home – oh, and Tarquin,' he joked, pretending he had forgotten about his son.

Marigold was still on leave for a couple more days.

'I'll get in touch and order her back to work,' Ronald told Tracy.

'No, you will not, you'll leave her alone. I gave her two weeks off and two weeks she is having and that's an end to it.'

'Very well, darling, but I think you are too soft with the staff,' Ronald exclaimed.

'No, I'm not, Ronald, I just believe people should be treated as people and not as a commodity in your big business machine. I refuse to adopt any of your managerial techniques when handling any of our domestic staff. This is my department, Ronald Crump, the business is yours.'

Tracy had a nice way of putting Crump in his place when necessary, though how this would hold up if real money, Ronald's god, was at risk and remained open to speculation.

'Very well, darling, have it your way. This is, as you say, your domain.'

Ronald was sitting at the breakfast table when the morning post arrived. It was brought to him on a silver platter by one of the domestics.

'Your mail, Mr Crump,' said the young servant.

He opened the envelope and was pleasantly taken aback at its contents. It was a letter from the Republican Party confirming he had been selected to stand for Congress in the coming midterm elections for Little Neck/Douglaston.

'They want me to enter the House of Representatives, darling,' he conveyed to his wife.

Crump knew he was a year too young, strictly speaking, but he would keep this quiet and see what happened.

'Oh, I'm so pleased for you, Ronnie. You'll make a great congressman, I know you will,' Tracy congratulated him.

'Hold on, darling, I have to get elected first.'

'That will not be a problem. Who would not vote for you? You're made for the job.'

The letter asked for the prospective candidate to complete the acceptance form at the end of the letter and return to the party HQ no later than one month from the above date. Crump immediately detached the form, signed the acceptance and dutifully returned it.

'The constituency they wish me to represent is a good business location, my kind of people whom I can represent with meaning and like-mindedness. If they had chosen me to represent the troublesome residents on the Bronx I would have turned it down. As it is, they have put cream with cream, so to speak. The party machine knows its business.'

★ ★ ★

Megan was out on a date with Derek. Ronald and Tracy were unaware of these assignations, though Ronald had had his suspicions for some time. They booked into a hotel and after a sexual marathon, their pillow talk involved the future, post-Teddy.

'If they had not found him a nursing home, Derek, we would have had to consider moving his demise forward.'

'What do you mean, honey?'

'You know darling, finish him off. It would have been a kindness, but as things are, he will shortly be in a nursing home miles away in New Hampshire.'

'Are you serious?'

Megan sensed disapproval in her lover's tone. 'No, don't be silly,' she lied, 'it was just a fantasy. Just a bit of banter.' This was not strictly the case, she had said it half in jest but with serious undertones. 'I know we are having an affair behind your sick husband's back but making jokes about killing him is macabre, Megan. I don't think we should talk like that. I wish he was out of the way, have done so for years, but not that way.'

'Stop panicking, darling, I was only joking,' Megan reassured him.

'Seriously, Derek: when Ted has been moved and after a few months, you can move in with me if you wish.'

'You mean leave Mavis?'

'Well, I can't have her moving in as well, there won't be room in the bed. Unless she wants a job as my personal maid,' Megan said, trying to keep things upbeat. 'Do you want to move in with me eventually, Derek?'

'I... I... I'm not sure,' he faltered.

Megan's tone changed. 'What do you mean you're not sure, I thought you wanted me for eternity?'

'I do Megan, but leaving the wife—'

'What other way did you think? I haven't minded sharing up to now because there has been no alternative. Now, due to my husband's deterioration in health an opportunity has presented itself which we should grab with both hands. We leave it a few months then I'll introduce you to my son and his wife, easy as that.'

'Well, put like that, darling…'

'You're not getting cold feet, are you?' Megan could sense for the first time a touch of apprehension in her lover. Perhaps he was not the reliable man she had thought.

The reader will recall it was Derek who had once suggested the very same as Megan was suggesting now. She wondered if he had done that because he knew her leaving Crump was an impossibility? Had he been using her over the last few years? *Well, this would be the litmus test* she thought.

'Let's give it six months from when Teddy moves out, darling,' she said awaiting his response. 'Then you can move in.'

'That sounds great darling,' he replied. 'In six months' time, come what may, I shall move into your house, in Teddy's place.'

'No, not in Teddy's place, nobody could ever do that. You haven't got the money,' she laughed.

This last comment said in jest just about sums up the nature of marriage in bourgeois USA, purely and simply a financial matter. Capitalism has reduced marriage to a business transaction performed before a priest or church minister. For those a little less hypocritical a register office ceremony would suffice. Either way it is a business deal, not a mission of love! When a couple come together where there is an element of love and chemistry present it is very much secondary to financial considerations. If a man and a woman genuinely love each other but the financial rewards are minimal or zero, the marriage in all probability will not go ahead. In bourgeois USA the dollar bill trumps all other considerations including a genuine marriage.

Ronald Crump, having accepted his nomination to run as a candidate for Little Neck/Douglaston, was planning his campaign for the 1971 midterm elections. He had the backing of President Nixon and was in favour with the Republican right wing. Back at the office he issued a memo instructing all members of staff to vote for him or risk losing their jobs. To the more politically aware employees he requested their vote, with the threat absent. The religious right had also thrown their weight behind Crump as the door-to-door canvassing began in earnest.

Leaflets proclaiming 'CRUMP IS MADE FOR THE JOB' were distributed in their thousands. Bill posters encouraging people to 'VOTE CRUMP' were also placed strategically around the constituency. Part of Crump's campaign was based on the saying, 'Successful in business equals success in politics' which, of course, is a nonsense. However, a gullible electorate would fall for such folly. Though the majority of the voters in this constituency were not stupid, they would vote for Crump as they had a class interest in doing so. The posters highlighting his business success were aimed at the less well educated members of the electorate whom he considered might need something they could believe in. The hardcore Democrat and Republican voters would remain just that; it was the 'undecideds' the campaign was aimed at.

The day finally came to pass when Teddy was to migrate to New Hampshire and the nursing home. The ambulance arrived with Dr Quincy.

'I'm so grateful to you, Al, for finding my husband a lovely place where he can spend his remaining days in comfort and be well looked after. My son and daughter-in-law and I will visit every month.'

'That was the least I could do for you, Megan,' replied the good doctor, who secretly had ideas of bedding Megan himself.

Alan and Veronica Quincy were having matrimonial problems; in fact, they were on the verge of splitting up, and should this happen Quincy would be a free agent. This would never happen, Megan thought. He was a nice guy and useful in situations like this but a bed partner for Megan, no way.

Dr Quincy and Megan travelled with Teddy to his new home, Ronald being too busy canvassing to be bothered with such trivialities.

On the election trail Ronald was doing door-to-door canvassing in the exclusively white middle-class electorate. The tiny minority of working-class, higher-echelon artisans with skills who lived in the constituency, he left to members of his team. His message was clear and what his audience wished to hear.

'I will stand up for your rights as business people and hard-working folk. I shall defend white rights, I'm sick and tired, as I'm sure you are, of hearing about black power and racial equality. I encourage a hard line against the black terrorist organisation styling itself the Black Panthers. Although I do not agree with the strategy of the Ku Klux Klan, I can understand their point of view.' This was another lie, Crump did agree with the KKK but could not afford to have it known.

This kind of language resonated well with these middle-class white voters who, in many cases, were fascist in all but name. The campaigning continued right up to polling day in November. Ronald Crump and his team had campaigned vigorously, hammering home their racist message to the eager listeners of middle-class Little Neck/Douglaston. He also promoted some economic policies, which he had borrowed off those who knew a little on the subject.

'There are those,' he said, 'who advocate free health care, like they have in communist countries such as Cuba,' – which had the finest health care in the world – 'but I'm here to tell you this folly will not happen on my watch. Has anybody asked these communist fifth-columnists who will pay for this free health care? Well I'll tell you folks, we will, we will pay for the universal health care of those who are too lazy to work and too greedy to pay private health insurance. Why, I have a colleague in business who offers very reasonable health insurance to the less well-off and will they take it? No, they won't, they expect us hard-working, hard-headed business people to pay for it. Well, that is not going to happen.'

For this, Crump received massive support both at his public meetings and door-to-door. His colleague who 'offered very reasonable health insurance' was Hugh Rothschild and his son, James and by 'reasonable' it would cost a poorly paid family a full month's salary before all other outgoings! Of course, the minority bourgeoisie couldn't care less about the majority working class except when they could bluff them into thinking they were all on the same side. Elections were such a time when the ruling class played this bluff.

The night of the election count arrived. Ronald Crump, Republican candidate, was on the stage along with his Democratic Party opponent, Mr Walter, W.A. Walley and a third candidate, Mr N. Hope, whom few had heard of. Essentially it was a two-party, two-horse race. The count was delayed as some ballot papers were late arriving. Walley tried to make small talk with Crump who did not want to know, so the Democrat gave up trying to be nice and just glared at Crump. The adjudicating officer signalled he had received the count: 'The numbers of votes cast in the Little Neck/Douglaston midterm election were distributed as follows: votes cast 31,400; Crump Ronald Republican Party candidate 17,300; Walley Walter Albert, Democratic Party candidate 13,000; Mr Norman Hope, Independent 1,100. I therefore announce Ronald Crump is duly elected to serve in the House of Representatives representing Little Neck/Douglaston.'

A loud cheer went up from the Republican faithful and they all vacated the hall for a prearranged party.

Teddy Crump had settled into his new surroundings, such as he was aware of them, and was receiving the very best attention money could buy. This was the nature of the health system in the USA: the bank balance was checked first, and treatment afforded accordingly, very much based on wealth before health.

★ ★ ★

Teddy had been gone about three months and Megan was sick of being on her own. She decided it was time to bring Derek into the house. She would phone him and tell him he was moving in. Now Megan had the space, she was adopting a similar dictatorial attitude to that practised by her husband on her.

'Derek, it's Megan. Now listen, darling, Ted has been away for some time now,' she began.

'You said six months and it has not been that long,' replied Derek.

'Never mind that,' she said. 'I think three months is long enough, don't you agree? So now it is time for you to move in with me, as we agreed, remember?'

'Well,' Derek stalled. He had hoped this day would never come. He was actually contented enough at the moment with the arrangement they already had. He had every intention of moving in with his lover but at a time of his choosing; it was to be his initiative, not hers. He felt he was no longer in control and besides, there was now another consideration.

'I hope you're not getting cold feet, Derek, I'll be most annoyed if you are.'

'No, not at all, it's just, well, it's Mavis.'

'Fuck Mavis, this is our time.'

'No, Megan, you don't understand.'

'I do, you spineless bastard, it's now or never,' Megan seethed.

'Listen, Megan, Mavis is sick, she has Alzheimer's disease, the same as Teddy,' Derek revealed.

'Then get her to a nursing home as I did with Teddy, that's no excuse.'

'She is not that bad yet, Megan, she is still in the early stages and besides I do not have the money at my disposal which you and Ted have.'

'Well she will get bad, so dispose of her now. Send her to the asylum.'

Megan was showing a side hitherto unknown to Derek and he did not like it.

'I'm sorry, Megan, I will do a lot for you, but I will not have Mavis spend the rest of her life in an asylum when there is no need. When she deteriorates then we'll have another look at the situation.'

Megan was fuming. 'Listen, Derek it's make-your-mind-up time: me or her. It's time for you to grow a pair of balls. You're moving in with me, and that's it.'

'No, not at this moment in time, Megan, I cannot leave Mavis and I won't,' Derek said with conviction.

'Very well, you've made your choice Derek. Now fuck off, you loser, I don't want to hear from you again.'

She slammed the phone down. Derek breathed a sigh of relief. For the first time he had seen the real Megan and he did not like it. Megan Crump had adopted the same attitude and principles her husband had practised on her and thought she could treat Derek the same as she herself had been used, or abused. He had escaped by a narrow margin. Whatever happened now he would not be moving in with that woman.

★ ★ ★

Congressman Crump was due to make his maiden speech in the House of Representatives. His theme would be consistent with his election promises: internal terrorism, namely the Black Panthers. He was supported by the religious right and the neo-cons but very few others. His opening salvo was a tirade of racist filth which he had to be warned about twice.

'I stand against this gang of black, nay, negro terrorists styling themselves the Black Panthers. It is time we, the government, gave our president the power to deal with them accordingly. I propose we move against them, making it a criminal offence to be member of this gang. This crime will carry a prison term of ten years. Making their salute will also carry a jail sentence as will showing any support for such an organisation.'

The Democrats countered with their own proposal that if any action was taken against the Black Panthers then the same rules had to be applied to the white supremacists, the Ku Klux Klan. Crump, Reagan and young Pat Buchanan were outraged by such a suggestion and a huge row broke out in the House. Crump's proposal did not even get to serious discussion stage and was rejected out of hand by the Democrats and majority of the Republicans, the far right exempted. President Nixon himself was not opposed to Crump's ideas but they needed congressional approval, which was not forthcoming. It did not go through as a Bill, not even reaching the Senate.

Ronald Crump called a caucus meeting of the right-wing Republicans to discuss future tactics. The proposal had not been dropped, merely postponed till a later date when they were in a stronger position. They had presidential support, so eventually they would get it through. They decided on a strategic withdrawal for now. Alas for these right-wingers, President Nixon had a massive headache waiting just around the corner, a headache which would cost him his presidency and ultimately the Republicans the government. This nightmare would become known as the Watergate Affair.

Megan Crump had got used to life without Teddy and 'spineless Derek'. She would find another man eventually, someone she could control and manipulate. One man sprang to mind, someone she would not have given a glance to until recently. This was a man who has been secretly besotted with her, the now-separated Alan Quincy. She could control him like a puppet on a string, she thought, reciting the song sung by Sandy Shaw.

Her son, Ronald, would also approve of such a match whereas with Derek she may have had problems in this department. Yes, Dr Alan Quincy, play your cards right and this could be your lucky day!

Megan phoned the hapless doctor. 'Hi Al, it's Megan, how are you?'

'I'm great Megan, lovely to hear from you. How can I help?'

'This is not a professional call, Al. How would you like dinner with me at my place?'

'Sounds swell. When?'

'Tomorrow suit you all right? Would you be free then? I'll tell the cook to prepare something special.'

'Yes, that sounds great, Megan. About eight?'

'OK Al, I'll see you then.'

Dr Alan Quincy was one of the finest neurosurgeons in New York state, if not the United States as a whole. He was now divorced and had had eyes for Megan Crump for some time. Up until now, Teddy was a barrier to any progress in this direction. Megan would not, until recently, have even considered Quincy as a partner; he was a family friend and golfing partner of her husband. He had also been Teddy's private physician for a number of years and medical advisor to the family.

She knew of Alan's feelings for her and was aware she could make him dance the fandango if the mood took her. He might not be the lover that Derek was, and he might not be in Teddy's league financially, but he did have enough money still to spoil her. She could also have flings behind his back, denying anything if she was found out, knowing full well Quincy would be gullible enough to believe her. In a nutshell Megan had, in Alan Quincy, someone she could manipulate like putty in her hands. She liked him but did not in any way love him. *Still, what did that matter?* she thought. She only had to pretend she had feelings for him and he would give her anything she desired.

It was eight o'clock and the doorbell rang. The butler answered the door.

'Come in, sir, and I'll tell Mrs Crump you're here.'

'Al, do come in,' she welcomed the physician.

'Good to see you, Megan,' Quincy said, giving her a warm smile. 'You're looking well.'

'Oh thank you! Dinner will be served shortly. Would you like a drink?'

'Scotch on the rocks if you have it,' he replied.

'Of course, Al. I'll pour you one.'

With that the maid served up the meal, roast pork with apple sauce, vegetables and potatoes. After the meal the pair relaxed on the huge sofa and discussed Teddy. Megan did not really want this to be the topic under discussion but also realised it would have to be, save Quincy finding out what a cold, calculated person she had become.

'Yes, Al, I go once or sometimes twice a month to visit him. It really is a lovely home. You did him proud. Ronald and Tracy come with me most times but, what with his business and now he's a congressman, time is a little limited for Ronald.'

'Of course, that's understandable, Megan.'

'Another drink, Doctor?' she said with an element of teasing in her voice.

'I'll have same again, Megan, thank you.'

The evening drew on and eventually Dr Quincy had to leave but not before making another date for the weekend, when the pair would spend the day together. Everything was going to plan for Megan; all she wanted now was for her husband to die. Of course, she could not allow this private consideration to be known. When her husband did pass away, she would pretend to be the heartbroken widow. Then she would spring her trap which the good doctor would be defenceless against!

★ ★ ★

Ronald Crump was on his way home from the office when he received a call on his car phone. He answered the phone and it was bad news. Teddy Crump had passed away that afternoon, 16th November 1971.

'Bad news, sir?' Creighton enquired, sensing something was wrong.

'Yes, Creighton, and sad news for you too,' said Crump, acknowledging Creighton's long service for his father. 'My dad passed away this afternoon.'

'May I pull over, sir?' a clearly distressed Creighton asked.

'Yes, Creighton, if you feel the need to do so, feel free,' Crump advised.

The news had obviously hit Ronald hard as he never spoke to Creighton in any way approaching civil, but on this occasion he did. 'Take your time to absorb the bad news and then we'll go to see my mother together after we collect Tracy.'

Creighton was close to tears and one could be forgiven thinking he had lost a lifelong friend, not somebody who had bullied him for the best part of his adult life. Many times Teddy Crump had spoken to Creighton as one would speak to a stray dog in the street and yet, despite all the humiliations, Creighton appeared heartbroken.

They collected Tracy Crump, Ronald breaking the news which greatly upset the compassionate young woman. Ronald telephoned his mother to inform her they were on their way. 'Oh do hurry, Ronald,' she said, playing the grief-stricken newly widowed woman.

On arrival Ronald gave his mother a hug as did Tracy, while Creighton was compelled to stay in the car. Ronald was anxious the sad occasion was not allowed to become a pretext for too much familiarity with any staff members. They could show their sorrow without being over-familiar with the family. It was important they did not forget their place!

'We'll stay the night, Mom,' Ronald told her.

'We've brought your grandson with us,' Tracy said. 'Here he is. As one door closes another one opens,' she said philosophically.

'Alan Quincy is on his way. He had been a great friend to me over the last few weeks, Ronald,' Megan explained as a kind of introduction to the new scheme of things.

'That's great, Mom,' said Ronald, appreciative of Quincy being on hand, which would save him bothering. 'When will he arrive, or when is he expected?'

'Any time now, son,' Megan acknowledged her son's interest.

Quincy arrived and hugged Megan.

'Not too close, Al,' she advised him. 'Not yet.'

The body was to be taken from the nursing home in New Hampshire and returned to New York for burial in the Gate of Heaven Cemetery after a short service. Ronald visited the Methodist minister who agreed to conduct the funeral. The burial was also arranged and would be in the cemetery of the family's choosing. Megan said Teddy wanted to be buried in Arlington Military Cemetery, but it was pointed out that as her husband was not killed in action this would not be possible. The family therefore settled on the Gate of Heaven, which was local and would allow easy access for the family to visit his grave. The funeral would take place on 22nd November at the Methodist chapel which Teddy had attended.

The day arrived and Megan, acting out the part worthy of an Oscar, dressed in black and led the mourners. At the graveside Ronald said a few words to complement those he had already uttered in the chapel.

'Today we lay to rest an honest, good man, a philanthropist and genuine Christian who was always on hand to help the poor.'

Truth be told, any good person would feel nauseous listening to this diatribe of lies. It was also noticeable how many so-called friends of Teddy's were absent. Most of those who attended did so merely out of duty.

When the funeral was over and Teddy laid to rest in peace, the brigands retired back to Megan's for drinks and sandwiches prepared by the servants who were not allowed to attend the funeral. They were told firmly that this would not be possible due to their workload. The domestics were grateful they received an answer at all and had to make do with expressing their sympathy with tears.

The convoy of cars drove up the drive and Betty, now ageing in years, was waiting to open the door for the 'grieving' widow and the family.

'I'm so very sorry, Mrs Crump, and on behalf of all the staff may we express our sympathies and condolences.'

'Thank you, Betty,' Megan acknowledged, 'and do thank the staff for their kindness.'

This was much more than Teddy himself would have afforded them had he been burying his wife. Betty would have had to settle for a grunt from him and count herself honoured at that. Drinks were being served and all the staff were standing around with trays of wine, port and whiskey. Dr Quincy was partial to a drop of whisky and consequently had a little more than was good for him.

Fortunately, he was not working for three days so the excess alcohol would not impair his ability to perform his duties. The mourners made pleasantries for a few hours, and one by one they began to leave. Ronald and Tracy were among the last to depart, and only Dr Quincy outstayed them. Creighton, despite being Teddy's chauffeur of long standing, was not invited in and was forced to await Ronald and his wife in the car. Eventually Megan was left alone with Quincy, something she had half planned

She refilled his glass.

'Why don't you stay the night, Alan?' she suggested. 'I could make the sofa up and you can sleep down here.'

This was not really what she had in mind, but it was her starting point. Quincy was feeling a little worse for wear at this stage.

'I think you're probably right, honey. I'm feeling a little drunk and perhaps would not make it home safely.'

'That's it decided, then, Al,' Megan confirmed.

They both had another drink and sat close to each other on the sofa.

'Forget the sofa, Al, come upstairs with me,' she invited him, guiding him to her bedroom. Megan's latest fling had begun.

14

Crump's Learning Curve in Politics and Business

Dr Alan Quincy had spent the night with his late friend and patient's wife and was beginning to reproach himself. Had he acted unethically? He grappled with the question and concluded that he had done nothing wrong. Teddy was, after all, now deceased and Megan was a free agent, as now was he. Perhaps the only point which might have raised a few eyebrows was that it happened so soon after the man's funeral. He decided to speak with Megan about his fears and see what she felt about it.

The new couple sat having breakfast which the maid brought to them.

'Megan, do you think we were a little early sleeping together?'

'Nonsense, Al, we're both mature adults with no ties, so what is the problem?'

'I just thought with Teddy barely cold, us jumping into bed with each other may be seen by some as a little off.'

'Don't mind what other self-righteous people may think, Al. Do we interfere with them? No, we don't, so what right have they got to stick their noses into our affairs? None, that's what, none at all.'

'Well, put like that, dear, we are in the clear.'

Megan was trying to decide when to tell the physician he would be moving in with her. She had now become a female variant of her deceased husband, making decisions for other people without asking them what their views were.

'Ronald will be here shortly, Al. We can tell him you stayed the night. He'll have to find out at some point, so why not now? Get in while the iron is hot, that's what I say.'

'Wait a minute, Megan, he may not see things our way. Remember, we only buried his father yesterday and, the way he may perceive it, I slept with his grieving mother.'

'Well, Al, if it bothers you, we can tell him you slept on the sofa this time, but I expect you will be staying a lot more. We will be seeing much more of one another, won't we?'

'Of course we will, darling.' Quincy had started calling her more affectionate names like 'darling' and 'sweetheart' after their previous night's romp.

After about an hour Ronald and Tracy arrived. Quincy was glad she had accompanied Crump in case he disapproved of his overnight stay. He had no need to worry; Crump had already reckoned on the doctor staying over, as that was exactly what Teddy would have done and what he himself would also have embarked upon.

'No problem, Al. You say you slept on the sofa? I thought you might have... never mind, that's your own affair, life has to go on.' Privately, Tracy was a little less cavalier about what was happening but kept her opinion to herself.

Tarquin sat on his mother's lap and the foursome made a fuss of the baby until Tracy indicated she had to go into the next room, as it was time for his feed. Ronald and Tracy left with Tarquin after a few hours, with Tracy going home and Creighton taking Crump to the party offices. Ronald had much to do in pursuit of his political career which would run parallel to his business enterprises. The two would complement each other. Business and politics to Crump were one of the same.

★ ★ ★

Something was in the air. President Nixon, who did not usually come to the HQ without good reason, was speaking to the right wing of the party.

'Come in, congressman, and take a seat,' he instructed Crump. There were five people present: Ronald, Pat Buchanan, Senator Cecil Harding and the State Chairperson Douglas Fairchild.

'Listen to what I have to tell you,' Nixon began. 'There has been a burglary at the headquarters of the Democratic Party and I am eager to distance the Oval Office from any blame. Ronald, will you come and see me when we've finished?' the president asked Crump.

Crump nodded. Nixon continued. 'This break-in was nothing to do with the Republican Party, myself or any of my staff. However, there are those in opposition who may wish to sling mud in our direction, particularly those on the left wing, our natural political enemies. I'm just telling you to be on your guard against any slanderous comments and/or accusations.'

Ronald Crump then followed the president to his chauffeur-driven car and the chief beckoned him to get in. They were going to the White House and even Crump was a little humbled at this gesture so early in his career as a politician. They arrived at the hallowed building and entered the great hall.

'Sit down, young man,' Nixon said, when they entered the Oval Office.

'Thank you, Mr President.'

'I've brought you here, Crump, because you remind me very much of myself as a younger man. I am going to fill you in on something that may have sparked outrageous lies. I was talking about the dirty tricks the Soviet Union get up to, spying on political opponents and said, in jest, wouldn't it be great if the president had the power which the Kremlin has? We could tap phones and listen in to our opponents. Now five of those present at my off-the-cuff remark have been captured breaking into the headquarters of the Democratic Party. I don't want anyone to think for one moment that I sanctioned these misguided fools to carry out this burglary.'

Of course, Nixon was guilty as hell, as time would tell and as the plot unfurled.

'I see, Mr President. What do you want me to do, or can I do anything?'

'Yes, Ron, you can. You can be my eyes and ears on this matter. You can report back to me anything you hear either within the ranks of our own party or from the opposition.'

'Yes, Mr President it will be a privilege and an honour. Leave it to me, sir.'

At that point the two men shook hands and Crump left to walk back down Pennsylvania Avenue. Ronald was thinking: he could tell Nixon was not revealing everything to him – he would be a fool to do so – and he also knew his own long-term plans were to sit where President Nixon was sitting right now. He had learnt one lesson today: always keep your cards close to your chest, and do not tell people like himself too much confidential information.

Ronald ended up in a bar that was popular with politicians. He engaged in conversation with Edward Sheath, the man who had introduced him to the president well before the election in midterm. Sheath was what may be called a 'soft marshmallow', meaning he was a little too concerned about the effects of government actions on the poorer people. He was not a fan of Nixon and was unaware Crump was working hand in glove with him.

'Drink, Ronald?' he asked.

'Whisky, Scotch please, Eddie,' Crump replied.

'Let's sit over there, Ron.'

Crump was aware of Sheath's soft policies, but he was a senior congressman and could be useful to Ronald in climbing the greasy pole. Once he had outlived his uses Crump would drop Sheath like a hot potato.

'Did you hear about the break-in at the Democrats' offices?' he asked Crump.

'No, not a word, Ted, can you enlighten me?' Ronald lied.

He sensed there may be something in this for him. Sheath could become useful much earlier than anticipated.

'I think Nixon is up to his neck in it. Between you and me, I think he planned the whole rotten job,' the foolish Sheath revealed.

'No, I couldn't imagine that Edward, not Mr Nixon.'

'Yes, Mr bloody Nixon, they don't call him "Tricky Dicky" for nothing, you know.'

This was referring to the President's first name, Richard.

'"Tricky Dicky". I didn't know he was called that behind his back.'

'Not just behind his back: some of his closest confidants call him that to his face; he quite enjoys the title.'

The Watergate plan was to essentially wiretap the telephones of the Democratic Party and photograph secret election strategy documents. This political espionage was done clandestinely under the Committee for the Re-election of the President (CRP). The problem arose when illegal means were adopted to this aim, as was the case with Watergate. On 27th January 1972, G. Gordon Liddy, Finance Council for the CRP, presented the illegal plan to the committee's Acting Chairman, Jeb Stewart Margruder, the Attorney General John Mitchell and Presidential Council John Dean. The Watergate conspiracy was underway and Nixon, despite his ducking and diving, was up to his neck in it. Ronald was to watch points which led to the demise of Nixon and would learn from them. Whether he learned enough, time would tell!

Throughout 1972 the President's story about being misunderstood regarding a conversation surrounding the power held by Leonid Brezhnev, leader of the Soviet Union, began to hold less and less water. Watergate was an appropriate name, as Nixon's tale was full of leaks. Later in 1972 President Nixon was on record saying, 'I can say categorically that… nobody in the White House staff, no one in this administration, or presently employed was involved in this very bizarre incident.'

These were all lies, and as time went on the lies and contradictions got bigger. Ronald Crump was watching every point of what not to do or say in the political amphitheatre of the USA.

He decided it would soon be time to drop Sheath in at the deep end by revealing to the president the contents of their conversation regarding this issue and Sheath's claim that 'Nixon was up to his neck in it.' He would be failing in his duty to the president of the United States not to inform Nixon of Sheath's mistrust of him. Of course, the president would be appreciative of the information that one of his own was a backstabber and might give him, Crump, promotion. Who knew? Perhaps he might get a junior government position. He phoned Nixon up on the number the president had given him.

'Mr President sir, I think we should meet. I have some news for you.'

It was arranged for Crump to meet Nixon in the Oval Office the following Thursday, when he would reveal all he had on Sheath, and a bit extra he had made up. Ronald Crump had also heard that Sheath was a homosexual which, he was sure, would not go down well with the president. He would dress this up for all it was worth and by the time he had finished he, Sheath, would be lucky to remain in the Republican Party, let alone be a junior government official. He might even be stripped of his position as a congressman, Crump thought.

Among all the other groups Ronald Crump hated, he was also homophobic. Edward Sheath, despite being a great help to Crump, was a legitimate target.

Ronald arrived at the appointed time for his chat with President Nixon. He told the president what Sheath had said about 'him being up to his neck in it'. He then started making things up to tell on top of the facts which took place during the conversation with Sheath.

'Mr President, Sheath also said he would do all he could to bring an end to your presidency, up to and including – if he could get the evidence – going to the Attorney General.'

Ronald Crump was unaware that the Attorney General was also involved in the malaise.

'Well, thank you very much, Ronald, for the information, particularly about Sheath and his underhandedness and treachery. I shall not forget this.'

'Oh, Mr President, before I forget: I have heard through the grapevine that Edward Sheath is a practising homosexual. Should such people be in government?'

'Thank you, Ronald, you have done well,' Nixon said non-committally. They then shook hands and Ronald left.

Nixon did not wholly trust Crump. He had only been in Congress a few months and already he was dropping his friends in the shit. Was it not Sheath who had introduced him to the political elite, including himself, the president? If Crump would do this sort of damage to somebody who had helped him, imagine what he would do to somebody with real power if he thought he could gain something out of it? Keep Crump at a distance and do not trust him, he decided. Use him by all means and drop him as soon as possible. Fortunately for Ronald, Nixon would not be around long enough to do him any real harm.

All this hard work and pressure was taking its toll on Ronald and when he arrived home he was bone-weary, or that was the impression he wished to portray.

'Fancy a night out, Tracy?' he asked.

'I thought you were all-in, Ron?' she replied.

'I'm never too tired to take you out if you want to go, or would you prefer a trip with Tarquin over to Mother's?'

'Yes, that sounds a better idea, I haven't seen Megan for some time. I wonder how she and Alan are getting on. I'm glad she has found a nice partner after the sad loss of your dad.'

'Yes, so am I, darling,' Crump agreed. So it was decided they would go and see Megan and Alan for a change.

The following morning Ronald set off for the office, courtesy of Creighton, and on his arrival, he opened a letter. It was from the representative of the Iraqi government:

Dear Mr Crump

In view of the tragic circumstances which led to the terrible fire at T.A. Gunn and Co, we have found ourselves in an impossible position, with which you may be able to assist. Gunn's and we had signed a contract for some weapons which the aforementioned will be unable to fulfil. We would be eternally grateful if you could consider completing this very lucrative order for us. We are available to meet at a time of your convenience. Please contact us on…'

'Bob, Bob, come in here at once and read this, we've got the contract if we want it. Read it, Bob, what you think?'

Crump's assumption the Iraqis had only consulted his company was premature, as we shall see.

'Dammit, Ronnie, we did it, your plan worked.'

'Quiet, Bob, walls have ears. I must phone their embassy immediately and let them know we are interested in taking over the contract subject, of course, to satisfactory negotiations. Call an emergency board meeting for tomorrow morning. We will not need an agenda; there is only one item for discussion. I'll need to pick a high-powered team beginning with you.'

Ronald knew he could not trust the Seddons on this one. Sally might put the spanner in the works, ruin the deal for badness, he thought, but he could not let Bob Tomkinson know his reasons. He would tell Bob, who was bound to suggest the Seddons, that they lacked the necessary experience at this level to be of any use. *Besides*, he considered, *we only need three negotiators and he and Bob would be two of them.*

'Who do you think, Bob, for the third position? And please don't say Sally Seddon just because you are attracted to her.'

'Well, what about Charlie Kearns? He has a wealth of knowledge going right back to your dad's early days. Charlie would be a good asset.'

'You reckon? Then Charlie it is. I'll tell him at the board meeting he will be our third man.'

Tomkinson then sent a memo out to every board member informing them of the emergency meeting the following morning. The memo advised them of the importance in this meeting and that only one item would be on the agenda: the contract passed over from Gunn's. That evening Crump instructed Creighton to drive him over to the apartments. He said he wished to inspect something.

'No need for you to wait, Creighton,' he said. Ronald decided after all this stress he needed a bit of Linda, whether she was busy or not!

Tomkinson summoned the local brigands to the board meeting. Crump sat at the head of the table and opened the meeting.

'Today, as we only have one point for discussion, I shall chair the meeting myself. We are here to discuss our good fortune, due to Mr Gunn's misfortune. We have been asked to take over the contract previously assigned to Gunn's,' he outlined, presenting the ill-gotten figures. 'The question is, how much do we charge? I happen to have the figures which they were paying Gunn's.' What Crump did not realise, and perhaps should have, was that they were not the only firm to be asked to 'take over the contract.'

At this point Sally Seddon raised her head. She was asking herself, *How did that devious bastard get those figures?*

'Now, I thought we should take the figure they were paying Mr Gunn and, due to short notice and having to cancel other smaller contracts—'

'What smaller contracts?' interjected Matthew Seddon.

'The ones we tell them we had, you cretin,' Crump abruptly answered. 'Now, Gunn's were looking at $7,500,000 gross, which would yield after tax and expenditure, wages, depreciation of machinery around the $4,000,000 figure. As we pay lower wages than they did and our machinery mysteriously does not depreciate to the same extent and given the short notice, we should charge for the rest of the contract, given it is half complete, the sum of $7,000,000,' said Crump sporting a sly grin.

'That is almost the full price for the whole contract,' Matthew Seddon noted.

'That's right, Matthew,' said Tomkinson. 'We can always come down a little and I know the Iraqi government are desperate to have this order completed. It is very short notice! Do I have the board's permission to tender this figure of $7,000,000 to complete the contract, with a guarantee we can and will complete on time?'

Tomkinson was thinking of his five per cent, and increase on his director's salary.

Matthew Seddon voted in favour, with reservations, Sally abstained, and Charlie Kearns voted in favour. Kearns had seen this done before masterfully by Teddy Crump and if Ronald was half as cunning he would get the contract.

'Now', continued Ronald, 'the team will consist of myself and Bob, so we need one other. I thought of you, Charlie. You've got the experience in this field and if Bob and myself miss anything you will be there as a safety net. How about it?'

'Well, Ronnie, as you said I have the experience. I was taught by the master of cunning and deviousness, your dad, so yes, if there are no objections, I will be the third man.'

'Any objections to Charlie being our "goalkeeper"? We do need a safety net and I can think of none better,' said Crump.

'You mean, Ron, that even you can make mistakes? I thought the great man was infallible,' Sally sarcastically remarked.

'I don't, as you know only too well, Sally, don't you?' Ronald replied cuttingly.

Sally said nothing.

With the negotiating team decided upon, Crump then arranged a meeting with the Iraqi government officials. The 17th of March was the date arranged for the crucial meeting. Crump, Bob Tomkinson and Charlie Kearns would have a preliminary meeting beforehand to decide on their bottom line. It was agreed that the figure of $7,000,000 would be negotiated down, and it was concluded by the three wise men that their bottom line would be $6,200,000; they could afford to come down by $800,000, which was a sizable concession.

Unknown to Crump and his negotiating team, they were not the only arms manufacturing company in the running for the unfinished contract. The Iraqi government had made representations to other companies in different countries, and the two who had stood out were an Italian firm and another company registered in West Germany. The figure of $6,200,000 bottom line which Crumps Arms had in mind was far higher than the purchaser was prepared to pay. In the eyes of the Iraqis, the contract was already half complete if not more so and Crumps were trying to charge the full price, as if the contract was being started all over from scratch. The Italian firm could do the work for $5,700,000, which was half a million dollars less than Crumps' bottom line. The West German company were in or around the same figure, so Crumps were out of their depth.

Ronald might have thought he was very clever procuring the figures out of the hapless Barbara Simpson which, if he had been dealing with a smaller concern and not a government, may have been the case. Unfortunately for him, he was now dealing with a foreign government which had more cards to play with, something had his father been around he would have had pointed out to him. Foreign governments are not restricted by the same rules of commerce as are domestic organisations. Had Teddy been around and was of sound mind, and should Ronald have asked him, the flaws in his strategies would have been pointed out. Ronald had brought in Charlie Kearns too late in the day. Had he involved him earlier these pitfalls would have been brought to Crump's attention, and a woman would still be alive. This was all unknown to Crump, who attended the meeting full of optimism.

The two sides turned up for the allotted meeting to discuss a price for the unfinished contract. This was the world of dog eat dog which Ronald Crump championed from the rooftops as the finest system available to mankind. Crump was unaware of the Italian offer to the Iraqis who were already working on their own figure of $5,200,000, a million less than Ronald Crump's 'bottom line'. The representatives of Iraq were still below by $500,000 the Italians' quote but felt they could go up a little if the company came down a touch. This was skilful negotiating which, had Ronald sought advice, he would have known. Like the world of politics this was a learning curve for Crump.

When the Crump team tabled their offer, the Iraqis glanced at each other and laughed.

'You cannot be serious, Mr Crump. You expect us to pay that amount for a job which is already half finished. Come, come, make a realistic offer. You are far too expensive.'

The purchaser could, if they were forced, be prepared to pay $5,700,000 but the contract had to be completed on time. They did not disclose this to the Crump negotiators, and insisted Crumps come down to $5,200,000.

'Impossible,' said Ronald. 'It can't be done, no way.'

'Can I suggest a short adjournment?' Charlie Kearns requested.

'Twenty minutes, Mr Kearns,' the Iraqis said.

Crump's team convened in a small room adjacent to the meeting room.

'Ronnie, we could come down and still be in pocket considerably. We could do the job for $6,000,000. I recommend we do that.'

Crump pondered, his greedy eyes darting around the room.

'I wanted maximum break out of this,' he said.

'Very well, let's dangle the carrot and see what they say.'

All the bodies were back at the table and Charlie made the company's final offer. 'We can do the job for $6,000,000.'

'Mr Kearns, you are still too expensive,' the chief Iraqi negotiator explained.

'Right,' said Charlie, throwing caution to the wind, 'what other quotes have you had?'

'We have had several, all lower than yours,' he was told. 'And the contract would be completed on time and clauses would be inserted that we pay less for every delay.'

'Can we have a figure?'

'Yes, $5,000,000,' the Iraqi lied. This was powerful negotiating and Ronald was out of his depth. He could not bully his way out of this one.

'Another adjournment, Mr Kearns?'

'If we may.'

The Crump team went back into the smaller room.

'Look, Ron, even if we could do the job for the price mentioned we could not finish it on time. Our machinery, as you pointed out at the board meeting, does not depreciate as much as other firms'. That is correct because our machinery could not depreciate any more. In a nutshell, it's antiquated. We need new modern machinery and a staffing reduction of around fifty per cent. Then and only then will we compete in the modern world.'

'So, we will have to leave empty-handed?'

'Yes, that's about the strength of it, Ron. We must modernise. Your dad was talking about this before he took ill, and we must now complete his wishes. Call this a lesson learned, a kick up the ass.'

They re-entered the room and explained to their opposite numbers they were withdrawing from the negotiations.

'Mr Crump, maybe you should take a lesson out of your late father's book. He was greedy, like you, but also, what is it you Westerners say? Artful. He knew when a tactical retreat was of benefit. Can we conclude negotiations are at an end?'

'Yes, we concede,' a dejected Ronald admitted.

He then instructed Tomkinson to call a board meeting for the following day. This would be hard to swallow.

The next day Crump delivered the news.

'You mean we didn't get the contract after all that,' Sally Seddon shouted.

'After all what?' Ronald asked her to clarify; he was suspicious she had found something out.

'After the meeting and secrecy, you, the great man, come back empty-handed,' Sally said heatedly.

'Hold on, Sally,' Kearns interjected, unaware why the woman was hammering Crump, 'we tried our best. The fact is our machinery is old, it needs updating and we need to cut staff. With the new machinery we can do away with many manual tasks. I would say we need at least fifty per cent staff reduction and that would pay for our new technology. The money we save on wages will pay towards the upgrading.'

As can be gleaned from these last statements, it was the workers who suffered in the end for management's errors. It is true to say Crumps missed out on the contract, but it would be half the firm's workforce who would lose their livelihoods. This will continue to be the case for as long as the means of production are in private hands, and profit is the only word in town. The same machinery under public ownership would mean a shorter working week for all with the means of production working for the benefit of humanity and not the greedy profits of the minority. Now, and because of this private ownership, working people, families, would suffer, not the likes of the Crumps who own the means of production for their benefit and their profits! Of course, all the board were 'sorry' about men losing their jobs, over a thousand of them, but there was nothing they could do. They, the former employees, would of course receive the legal minimum redundancy payments and a thank you for all they had done.

Perhaps working-class people should start questioning what, in generations to come, will happen to them if and when all the means of production become automated? Presently the bourgeoisie require workers, which is becoming less and less the case, and soldiers to go and fight their wars for them. As we know automation of the means of production, distribution and exchange is already happening with increasing rapidity. What happens next? What happens when workers are no longer required to make profits? Are the ruling-classes going to give everybody money for doing nothing? They will not be needed for work machines will be doing that! Karl Marx once said, 'Capitalism would be its own gravedigger.' He never said when. And Crump epitomised the private ownership of the means of production.

As the year progressed it was mid-June and Tarquin's second birthday. Tracy did not want a fuss, so the couple decided on a low-key affair. They decided they would invite Megan and Alan as well as Tracy's parents and they could all make a fuss of the toddler. Ronald's mind was half on his son's birthday and the rest of his concentration was on the political situation surrounding President Nixon. Crump was watching these events closely and only drip-feeding the president some of the information which was coming his way. Ronald kept his side of the bargain in giving Nixon information but only scraps of information he felt would not get him into trouble at any stage down the line. The position of president of the US was the long-term post Ronald had earmarked for himself, and he wanted to keep himself squeaky clean. He would give the president information on other members of the party who might be plotting against him; that way if any suspicions were aimed at Crump there would be enough clear blue water separating fact from fiction to put Ronald well in the clear.

The date for Tarquin's birthday arrived, and Tracy had arranged with Cook a special meal for their guests. Ronald wanted to invite the Rothschilds, including James and Susie. The day went very well and young Tarquin, oblivious to what all these daft grown-ups were doing dancing around like idiots, fell asleep.

'Oh, look, Ronnie, he's tired already,' Tracy commented.

All the guests had bought the child presents, but Tracy was determined her son would not be ruined. If she had been around for some of Crump's childhood birthday parties it was unlikely they would be together now. Tracy eventually put the child to bed, and the grown-ups then had a few drinks. Alan Quincy, who could not take a great deal of alcohol, began showing himself and Megan up, so she had to chastise him in public. She made him look an even bigger fool than he did himself through the drink.

At the White House the pressure over the Watergate break-in was mounting on President Nixon. He was determined to stand by his story, which he was beginning to believe himself: of passing a harmless comment over a desire to hold the same power over his political opponents as did the leader of the Soviet Union. Ronald thought that if Nixon had any sense he would put the entire blame for this debacle on the USSR, something he would later come to learn would perhaps not be the wisest move. An afterthought of Ronald's was that it might be better for the president to go public, thus admitting to a silly little joke which had unfortunately led to this very serious matter. It would be better being fingered for culpability on making crass comments than the possible alternative, impeachment!

If Nixon was impeached then the vice-president would assume the office, as had Johnson after the assassination of Kennedy, and Crump could watch from a distance the whole affair unravel. This might serve him in future years.

What with the business deals, or lack of, with the Iraqis and the political turmoil unravelling at the White House, Ronald Crump gained invaluable experience in both politics and business. The whole chapter had been one big learning curve.

15

The Mass Slaughter

After the severe body blow suffered by the inexperienced Ronald Crump at the hands of the Iraqis, despite his father's teaching and theory work, a board meeting was called. Ronald had learned a valuable lesson which only experience could deliver. If he had brought in veteran Charlie Kearns earlier a more positive result may have been the outcome. Now he would have to make his own mark and with the help of Kearns and the ever-loyal, though misguided, Bob Tomkinson to take the blame for every mishap, there was no reason why he could not become a name as big as the late Teddy.

He was certainly more ruthless than his father, who was bad enough, but Ronald had no respect for anybody, especially women and ethnic minorities. Ronald was determined to make it big and whoever got in his way would be sacrificed. He would use his hostess service to lure contracts and take every penny those women made for his son's education. If they complained, he would have them prosecuted for practising prostitution from his property. The defeat at the hands of the Iraqis would be avenged ten times over and the innocent would pay.

Crump summoned all directors to attend the meeting and to have some figures and ideas for huge-scale redundancies. The company was going to modernise, as Charlie Kearns had pinpointed that as the fault line which needed fixing. Kearns had noted the antiquated machinery needed replacing but until now had little leverage with which to apply pressure. After the Iraqi debacle he now had the ear of Crump himself and could ignore all opposition. Kearns was right, Ronald was not interested in the cautious strategies of the 'wets' on the Board, he wanted action, and now.

It was 11am on a Thursday morning and the brigands of Crumps Arms and Real Estate, now the official title of the company, gathered for their council of war in the boardroom. Crump sat at the head of the table, ready to take some flak – he may even have to bite his tongue if that slut, Sally Seddon, had a dig, he muttered to himself – but this was the price of temporary failure.

'We need to make redundancies and a lot of them,' Crump opened up the meeting with this less-than-encouraging cry. 'I shall pass you over to Mr Charlie Kearns, whom we should listen to and who will outline where we went wrong and are continuing to go wrong.'

'Why, did those Iraqi men tie you up inside out?' Sally Seddon interrupted. Then she started making gestures, using her pointing finger of her right hand inserting in and out of a loop made by the thumb and index finger of her left. 'You may not have done enough of this, Ron, we may need soft toilet paper.'

Crump knew what she meant as did she, but few others had an inkling. Sally had waited some time to get one back after Crump's crude remark to her some years past about needing 'soft toilet paper' after he had forced her into having anal sex with him.

Thankfully for Ronald nobody, bar those two, had a clue about Sally's little joke, or were aware of the significance of her indications and comments. Ronald glared at Sally.

'I'll now hand you over to Charlie,' he said to the board.

'Listen up, everybody, this is paramount to my case. All our machinery is, and has been for some time, out of date, antiquated. In today's world of business, we cannot be left behind, which was one reason we lost out to an Italian company on the Iraqi contract. The late Teddy Crump was concerned with this area and I believe we should carry out his plans. We are also overstaffed for today's world, we don't owe the workers a thing. They have had plenty of work and steady wages, now they must go. There is no room for sentimentality in modern business. Now I recommend you all go and speak to your line managers and so-called workers' representatives and ask them to draw up a list for the chop.'

'I thought the reps were supposed to defend the staff and their jobs?' said Matthew Seddon.

'Don't be ridiculous. Why do you think we select the candidates for election onto these bodies? So, we can control them. They are not like a proper trade union, thank God,' said Kearns. 'Why do you think we only allow lower-grade workers to be representatives? Sweepers and cleaners, labourers at best. The answer is simple, like them: the only jobs they will be defending are their own!'

'How many jobs have to go, Charlie?' asked Bob Tomkinson.

'About 1,500 from New York and Detroit.'

All the directors agreed to instruct their line managers to draw up lists for redundancies, including their own jobs; these were no times for 'people being selfish'.

Ronald now had a new secretary, a Mrs Alexander, who had been chosen by Agnes Moorhouse. She had interviewed the woman herself as she did not want any young strumpets who led Mr Crump on, and Mrs Alexander fitted the bill. Previously, young women had tried to imply Mr Crump was after sexual favours; nothing could be further from the truth as far as Agnes was concerned. This time she would pick the candidate, a good, honest, loyal secretary with impeccable credentials.

Beth Alexander fitted the criteria like a glove. She had been a secretary for a number of large companies, and her CV was exceptional, as were her references. A happily married woman of strong morals and principles, even Ronald Crump would have been unwise to make any sexual advances in her direction.

He asked her, 'Can you type up the redundancy notices, Mrs Alexander?'

'Yes, Mr Crump. What's the deadline?'

'Beginning of next week if you can.'

'Leave it with me.'

Bob Tomkinson, Charlie Kearns and a handful of leading scientists and engineers were searching for the aforementioned new machinery, state-of-the-art equipment which could carry out the tasks of half a dozen manual workers. The machines were designed to bring Crumps up to date, so they would be able to compete with other companies in the cut-throat game of dog-eat-dog. This upgrading would be expensive but much of the cost could be offset against money which would be saved in payment of former staff wages. With the fortune Crump had amassed over the few short years he had been in charge, coupled with the billions left by his late father, the tycoon could have easily paid for all the new equipment out of his own pocket.

It was estimated Ronald Crump was one of the richest men in the USA, worth at least $1.5 billion in 1972, a phenomenal amount of money, perhaps worth three times that amount today. Of course, this was not his personal wealth; much of it was tied up in the business and investments abroad, and in Swiss bank accounts, hidden from prying eyes, which were tax-free but undeclared. Either way, he could have upgraded the factory and kept staff employed if he had a mind to do so. The same applied to most large employers but because the capitalist system does not work like this, men and women had to be let go. Of course, Crump, being a good Christian and dedicated disciple of the lowly carpenter of Nazareth, said he was very sorry people had to lose their livelihoods but that was the way of the world. The men could always come back and see him in a month or year when he might have an opening but until then it was thanks and good luck.

The final figure for redundancy was 1,500, though some men were kept on a little longer for salvage work. Of course, this kind of work did not pay the same as they would have been getting as tradesmen and laboratory technicians, but it was better than nothing. It was surprising how many men volunteered for this work, even offering to undercut each other in how little they would work for. One man, Tommy Crassly, offered to work for nothing on the understanding Crump put him at the top of the list if any more work came in. Ronald gave this careful consideration but unfortunately 'after much deliberation', he declined this man's offer. The way Crump viewed it was, he didn't mind a man working for nothing, but the 'on the understanding' bit appeared the man was placing conditions on Crump, so he had to decline.

'You can take your place in the queue like the rest of them,' he told Crassly.

'Fucking creep,' Ronald later commented to Matthew Seddon.

The new technology arrived on a daily basis and was soon installed, performing tasks which were once done by men.

'We'll soon be back at the top, eh, Charlie, what you say?' Crump asked of Kearns.

'At this rate, give it six months and we will be competing with the rest. Shame a war doesn't break out somewhere like the Middle East,' Kearns commented.

'Actually, lads,' Bob Tomkinson interjected, 'those Iraqis were in a hurry for that super gun and the parts as well as the smaller weapons. I wonder if they're planning a run-in with one of their neighbours. There is political unrest in that part of the world. I noted on a CBS news bulletin the Soviet Union were talking to the Egyptians. I wonder if they and the Israelis are going at it again?'

This last statement was not far from the truth, just a year or so out.

'Well,' said Crump, 'if it does kick off we will be tendering for every contract irrespective of which side the weapons will go to. With these new machines, and more to come, we'll triple or even quadruple our output in half the time.'

To these men, arms-dealing was all about money. How many people lost their lives, providing of course it wasn't them or their children, was irrelevant. All they cared about was how many dollars would keep coming in.

The day finally came when the men received their redundancy both in New York and Detroit. They lined up like sacrificial lambs to the slaughter to collect their meagre cheque for a lifetime's work in the good service of furnishing the Crump family with all the luxuries they themselves would never be able to afford. Some of these men believed that Crump, like his father before him, had done his best by them and they were actually grateful of the years of employment they had had in the company. One man actually suggested buying Mr Crump a present for the service which they had provided. But then he realised with only three years' employment with the firm he would not have enough to pay back his debts, let alone buy his god a present!

★ ★ ★

Bradley Morgan was working with the diplomatic corps in the United Arab Emirates as part of a team promoting US business in that part of the world. Ronald had asked Morgan to keep his ear to the ground regarding any defence or related contracts in the UAE. As it happened, Bradley was in communication with the personal bodyguard to the sultan. This was a stroke of luck because this man was responsible for the sultan's security. The conversation was guided, by Morgan, in the direction of small arms. The bodyguard expressed an interest in the purchase, for the sultan's personal police, of two hundred sub-machine pistols. Bradley was aware Crumps Arms were now fully automated and suggested the firm to the security chief. It was not a huge contract, but the object was, similar to Duke Tillerson in Kuwait, to get known in the region. If Crump could land something like this, even running at a slight loss, then the world could be his oyster. Morgan telephoned Crump explaining the situation.

'Great, Brad, can you get the contract?'

'Yes, I'm sure I can, Ronnie,' Morgan said.

He suggested this to the security chief, who was most interested. He had a brochure of all the small arms Crumps could produce and he showed this to the sultan's man. A contract was quickly drawn up and signed by the security chief of the UAE and a representative of Crumps was flown out rapidly on hearing of the possibilities. The deal would only be worth a few hundred thousand dollars but that was not the point. Crumps would have a foothold in the UAE, and Ronald was already planning to invite the security chief over for a week of meetings and make the deal more attractive by offering him the use of his hostesses and extra services.

This small contract which had been signed, albeit in haste, also offered a short reprieve for some of the redundant workers. Crump reckoned he would need around twenty staff to remain for a month to complete the order. The wages would not be as high as before because the machines did most of the work now. All the same, there was no shortage of applicants for the jobs.

Crump received a telephone call. It was the sultan's chief of security. Then and there, Ronald invited the sultan's right-hand man over for a week of discussion and possible contracts. This was the perfect opportunity, and the great man graciously accepted. March 1973 was the month both men pencilled in for the summit, which gave Crump time to make the appropriate arrangements.

Although the contract for the machine pistols was a small concern, Ronald knew he could make up some of the shortfalls by evading income tax. Crump would use his own mathematical abilities and also fall back on the advice and lectures given him by his late father. He would, by using his skills with figures, only pay a quarter of the tax officially owed. Ronald intended submitting half the order, and the rest would go into his Swiss bank account. If he disclosed the fifty per cent, then he could also claim tax relief, meaning he would be out of pocket due to paying tax by just five per cent of the total figure.

The contract signed and sealed, Ronald Crump retained twenty men especially for this job and had them working at the reduced rate at breakneck pace. He wanted the client to be ecstatic about the efficiency and quality of the order as a whole. He was aiming for much larger orders from the tiny UAE armed forces. The small medium-range armoured personnel carrier was well within Crumps' operational capacity and the firm's designers had updated their original design to outrange their competitors. Crump hoped to use the coming visit, with the help of his hostesses, to convince the Arab that these vehicles were ideal for his purpose. They could outpace any other vehicle of their class on earth; in a nutshell they were the very best within their class. Of course, Ronald had to sort Bradley out with a sweetener, but it could not be huge. This Morgan understood and, like Crump, he would wait for bigger and better things in the future. He would receive a sizable lump sum if Crumps landed bigger contracts, which looked likely.

27th March 1973 was the date pencilled in for the UAE security chief's visit to Ronald Crump's factory. Crump would give the man a guided tour of the works so he could see at first hand the efficiency which the company worked at. The date came around quickly and Crump had informed Linda and Carol their 'professional' services would be required. The two women knew the score; it was too late to get out of this malaise now, as they had nowhere to go. This had always been Ronald's intention, to have them as slaves for eternity or until he decided to offload them.

'Listen, you two,' Crump instructed, 'It is vital you persuade this gentleman to place a huge order with the firm. It is your job, using your charms, to ensure he signs. Whatever this man wants, and I mean whatever, you will provide everything. Do you understand?'

'Yes, Mr Crump, crystal clear.'

The day arrived, and the sultan's security chief and entourage arrived in the USA. Crump was at the airport to greet the man in person, going through the Arab greeting ritual of kissing on both cheeks.

'Good to see you, my friend,' Crump grovelled.

'Likewise, Mr Crump. We have heard a lot about you and the deals you may offer for our armed forces. May we take a look around the factory, Mr Crump?'

'Of course, sir, all in due course. Let me introduce you to Mr Tomkinson and Mr Kearns, two of our senior directors.'

The three shook hands and all made their way to the arms-producing complex where a guided tour had been arranged for the emissary. All Crump's staff were working like their lives depended on it.

'This is where we will produce the Tiger Armoured Personnel Carriers, which I'm sure will suit your needs, sir.'

'Yes, I'll be interested to have a look at where our future backbone of the army will be produced.'

Encouraged by this affirmative statement Crump proceeded. 'We have just had the factory completely refitted. These are our new computerised digital turners which do the work of ten men and twice as quickly.'

'I'm impressed, Mr Crump, very impressed. Tell me, I understand you recently lost out on an order to the Iraqi government?' the Arab police chief said.

'Yes, that was why we completely modernised the works. This is all new machinery,' said Crump, anxious to know how the UAE man knew of the Iraqi contract.

He decided against asking, it might be seen as rude and that would never do. On this occasion he would have crawled under a rattlesnake if it served his purpose.

'You acted very quickly. A model response to a perceived weakness, Mr Crump. I like that.'

'Thank you.'

With the tour of the factory complete and the potential customer more than satisfied, the summit had so far gone well. They then retired to the office for further discussion. At the end of the day Crump suggested some company for the security chief and his entourage.

'No, they will stay in the hotel,' said the main man, and, clapping his hands, dismissed all of them. There was a valid reason for this dismissal of his staff. Under Arab law alcohol is forbidden, as is sex out of marriage. The sultan's man expected both and did not wish his subordinates to know. He wanted nobody having any kind of hold over him, least of all those who would stab him in the back if the occasion suited. The sultan and government of the UAE were unaware of these 'perks' involving sex and alcohol their emissary was receiving. Had they been informed the security chief would almost certainly have faced punishment.

Ronald then arranged for Creighton to take them to the apartments.

'I think you will enjoy the social evening and company, sir,' Crump advised his honoured guest.

Both of them then travelled to Crump's apartment where he introduced the Arab emissary to Linda and Carol, his hostesses for the evening. The UAE man had been on many similar missions to this one and took sexual favours, with payment of course, as read. The champagne and company would be on Crump, a small price to pay for a lucrative contract. Anything over and above this would be charged by the women. Ronald would then call the following morning to take the lion's share of what the women had charged, leaving them with a roof over their heads and a little money.

After Crump departed, the threesome sat comfortably on the sofa talking and getting closer.

'More champagne, sir?' asked Linda, wearing a provocative low-cut top and short skirt.

'Are you staying long?' asked Carol.

The small talk out of the way, the girls moved the conversation towards the arms trade, telling their guest how they worked in the administration side of the industry before Mr Crump 'promoted' them. They showed their guest some samples of weaponry which Crump had left for them and began moving closer to him on the sofa.

'Would you like to come with us to our room?' Linda suggestively asked.

'Yes, indeed,' replied the security chief.

'Then come right this way,' Carol informed him.

The following morning the three campers rose at 7am and dressed.

'Did you enjoy the night, sir?' Linda asked their guest.

'Yes, very much so,' came the reply. 'I have here a little gift for you both, a solid gold necklace with diamonds,' said the sultan's man. He had brought these gifts with him expecting the services provided by the women. He had anticipated correctly that sex would be forthcoming.

'One each?' asked Carol.

'Yes, indeed,' the man laughed. 'One each. You were both well worth it.'

The girls were delighted; these necklaces had to be worth at least $5,000 each. The bulk of the money the girls received went to Crump but, as a perk, he allowed them to retain any gifts they were presented with. At nine o'clock Crump arrived, driven by Creighton, to collect their honoured guest. They retired back to the office for a short time before the UAE security chief left on his private flight.

'Did you enjoy your evening, sir?' Crump enquired.

'Very much, Mr Crump, we Arabs are men of Allah, but we are still men, ha, ha,' he joked.

'The next time you come I'll book you in with the girls for the week,' offered Crump.

'That would be very satisfactory,' he said. 'Now Mr Crump, let me see those carriers again, I think we can do business. Your female sales staff are very persuasive.'

With the contracts signed, business for Crumps looked good. A much smaller workforce and new machinery gave the works a new modern look and feel. Once the sub-machine pistol order was completed, the twenty men were laid off. Crump now felt, in order to complete this new large order, his existing workforce may need some extra hands, even with the robotic factory. He would take back ten of the twenty at an even lower rate of pay than they were previously on while engaged on the machine pistol order. Crump rationalised this further reduction in wages.

'As you will be employed on this job for a longer period,' he told the men, 'the machines will be doing more work, therefore your tasks will be shorter and easier. As not as much labour-intensity will be involved, your rate of pay must reflect that fact. You can take it or leave it.'

As Crump expected, all the men chose to take it.

Many of the men formerly employed by Crump were walking the streets now looking for employment. Occasionally they would stray into one of their former workmates and ask if there were any vacancies at Crumps. The answer would usually be, 'There is nothing. Sorry, wish I could help.' But they did not mean a word of it. Most of the men in employment despised those unfortunates who had been made redundant. It was, they believed, all their own fault. If they had worked harder for Mr Crump instead of idling, then he, Mr Crump, might have given more consideration to their plight. That Mr Crump was a firm but fair man, was the consensus of opinion among those still working for the firm.

Ronald had decided, despite the good work they had done in helping secure the UAE order, it was time to offload the women, Carol and Linda. One major reason for this was the pressure coming down from the Mob. The Arab visitor, the highest ranked guest Crump had yet entertained, had not gone unnoticed by the Mafia. They ran all the prostitution rackets and if Crump thought he was having some of it he was mistaken. Hitherto the Mob had taken a blind eye approach to Crump's apartments but with the arrival of such a wealthy guest there was obviously money to be made.

They paid Ronald a visit. Leaving him under no illusions, they told him that if his activities continued they wanted their cut! But if he just let the girls go then they would probably end up working for the Mob who would in all probability confiscate his apartments which had cost him enough to refurbish and redecorate. However, if the women were out of the way, say in prison for some years, they could not work for the gangsters and he would also be free to sell his apartments. So then there would be no bait to attract the Mob.

Ronald immediately began scheming what to do. He did, after all, have the chief of police in his pocket so any trumped-up charges would stick as Crump also had the judges where he wanted them, and one senior judge in particular, Early Greasley. As things stood so did the Mafia, but take away their interest, the women, and Crump had a free hand.

Crump decided he would arrange for a rich punter, somebody he knew well, to have some entertainment with the girls, a threesome. Ronald knew just the man, a politician named Eugene Mathis, a centre-right man who trusted Crump for some reason. Crump knew Mathis was single and desperate for company of the female nature, so he would be ideal.

Ronald worked things out meticulously. Crump would turn up early at McGrath's Bar in New York City with the unsuspecting punter and when the time was right, would administer a slow-acting non-fatal poison in the man's drink. A feeling of drowsiness and nausea would kick in after about fifty minutes. The punter would never suspect Crump and the girls would be blamed, especially when the man's wallet would go missing. This Crump would do by sneaking into the apartment while the threesome were otherwise engaged in the bedroom, and before the punter began feeling sleepy and ill. He would take the man's wallet and put it in one of the women's wardrobes. He would position the wallet in such a place where it would not be easily seen. Then when the police arrived, bingo! Attempted poisoning and robbery, bound to carry ten years at least. The women would be out of Crump's way, the mob off his back and the apartments would go up for sale, bringing in a tidy profit!

Dwight Connman was the Chief of Police in New York and was a personal friend as well as golfing partner of Ronald Crump's. Judge Early Greasley was also a member of the golfing fraternity and, like Connman, was a friend of Ronald's. Both these men were also in the pay of Crump. Brown envelopes were regularly passed to them in return for certain favours and the stitching up and subsequent 'slaughter' of these two women would be no exception.

The plan was well laid, and Crump arranged to meet the unsuspecting Mathis at McGrath's Bar. He had also arranged for Linda and Carol to arrive soon after the two men's arrival. Crump had told them that he would reward them well if they entertained a lovelorn friend of his. In his pocket Crump had the tiny sachet of odourless and colourless powder which was the pivot of the plot.

'Take a seat, Eugene,' Crump said pointing to two vacant chairs. 'What are you having?'

'Let me get the first one, Ron,' said Eugene.

'Fair enough,' Ronald ordered. 'I'll have a beer then.'

'Two beers, please, bartender,' Mathis ordered.

As they both sipped their drinks, the two vixens entered the premises.

'Let me introduce you, Eugene, to two friends of mine: Carol Hawkins and Linda Lowry.'

'Nice to meet you.' Both parties exchanged pleasantries.

They all engaged in an enjoyable conversation. The girls gave a lot of attention to Eugene, who was surprised and completely taken in. After about an hour, Eugene asked: 'Would everyone like another drink?'

'I'll get this one,' said Ronald. 'More beer for you?'

'More beer!' said Eugene jovially.

'And more vodka for the ladies,' Ronald said, smiling a fake smile.

He got up and ordered for himself and the others. But this time, before he went back to his seat, he furtively looked around and then when he saw no one was looking, poured the powder into Mathis's drink. Then he joined the others, being very careful not to mix the beers up. Mathis took a long slurp of his drink, oblivious anything was wrong, as then did Ronald.

After another fifteen minutes or so Crump told them that he had to go home.

'What a shame,' said Carol. 'Eugene, would you like to join us for a few more drinkies over at our place.'

'You wouldn't mind, yes – yes, that sounds great,' replied the slightly merry Eugene, hardly believing his luck.

'I will leave you all, then,' said Ronald. 'Enjoy yourself, Eugene! Bye now, ladies. We must catch up again soon.'

Crump gave the girls a smirk before he turned and left.

Eugene, Carol and Linda then retired to the apartment. The girls were oblivious of Crump's devious plan, that they were being used far beyond what they knew. Crump waited at a safe distance outside the apartment for about forty-five minutes. When he noted the the bedroom light was on, he knew the trio were engaged in that particular room. He entered the apartment using his key and stealthily moved around. He could hear the three enjoying themselves as he found Mathis's jacket. Fumbling in the pockets, he found the man's wallet and placed it in the wardrobe; whose it was mattered not to him. He then left the property and headed homeward.

He arrived home and called Tracy. 'Are you in, honey?'

'Yes, darling,' came the reply.

They had just sat down to eat when the telephone rang.

'Hello, Mr Crump, it's Linda. Your friend took ill and has been taken to hospital, I knew you would want to know.'

'God! I hope he's all right,' said Crump. 'Thank you, Linda, I must check on him as soon as I can.'

'Anything wrong, dear?' asked his wife.

'A friend of mine suddenly became ill and was has been taken to hospital.'

'Oh my goodness. Anybody I know?'

'No, he's a party member. If you don't mind I'll go look up the hospital number and make the call in the other room.' Ronald left the room but did not make the call. He gave it a few minutes and told Tracy that he found out the friend was stable and he would visit him the next morning.

The plan so far had gone perfectly. Now for the second phase. By the morning Mathis would have realised his wallet would be missing and the blood tests would confirm the presence of a mild non-lethal stomach poison. Ronald called at the hospital the next morning as he had planned.

'A patient was brought in last night, a Mr Eugene Mathis?'

'Oh, yes. Mr Mathis. He's in the Liberty Ward just along the corridor,' a young orderly said, and directed him to the room.

'Eugene, what happened?' Crump innocently enquired.

'I don't know, Ronald. It's all a bit of a blur now. I was so sick... but thankfully I feel much better now. There's one thing I do know – my wallet is missing, along with my credit cards and $500.'

'Have you reported it to the police?'

'No, not yet.'

'Bother yourself not, Eugene. I'll look after this,' Crump assured him.

Ronald Crump reported the incident to his friend and conspirator Commissioner Dwight Connman. Connman ordered a search of the flats and, lo and behold, the wallet was discovered hidden in one of the women's wardrobes.

'Anything to say?' the leading officer asked them both.

'No, officer, we've never seen that wallet,' both women pleaded. 'It has nothing to do with us and we don't know how the hell it got into the wardrobe.'

'Right, I'm arresting you on suspicion of poisoning with the intent to steal, prostitution and illicit behaviour,' the policeman said.

A junior officer present felt not enough questioning had been carried out. *For a start, if these two were indeed prostitutes what then were they doing in the property of one of America's richest men?* he thought. He began to question his sergeant and was told to 'leave well alone'. The young rookie was less than satisfied.

'Shouldn't you question Mr Crump?' he asked his superior.

'No, Mr Crump is one of the wealthiest men in the land and an upright citizen. His record is beyond reproach and he is a congressman. These are just common whores. How dare you speak of a man like Mr Crump in the same sentence! If you are going to get on in this job you'd better learn fast,' the Sergeant concluded.

The charges were read out to the women who offered, apart from some perceived lies about being stitched up by Crump, no real credible defence.

'We were stitched up, fucking stitched up by them, Mathis and Crump. We don't know why, but we were.'

'Do you want slander added to your charge sheet of poisoning, theft, prostitution and illicit behaviour?'

The two women were remanded in custody and the duty solicitor was informed. The police might just as well have informed Hanging Judge Jefferies for all the use the duty man was. He considered the two women guilty before he heard a word they had to say. Linda and Carol were remanded in custody until a trial date could be set. Crump had a word with Connman and Greasley, urging them to move it up the list. They agreed to pull some strings.

Ronald Crump arrived home and sat down with Tracy. On the wall of the living room was a picture of dead people rising from their graves and Jesus saying to them the words, 'Cometh to me, sinners. Repent and be saved.' Underneath were the words, 'God is the master of this house.' As we know Ronald Crump was a dedicated Christian, as was Tracy. The difference was that she was genuine in her faith. When Crump told her of these two terrible women, she was aghast.

'I didn't think such evil people existed, Ron. They should throw the key away and keep the sinners locked up,' Tracy said, never for a moment suspecting her husband's involvement.

This was perhaps the first flaw in Tracy's religious conviction. There was a time she would have pleaded for mercy for unfortunates. Had Ronald begun to have a negative effect on the previously innocent girl? If only she had known the truth! One day she would.

The trial date was set to take place in three weeks' time, remarkably quick under the circumstances. The verdict was pre-set by Connman and Greasley who had 'by coincidence' landed the trial. The young officer who had been asking awkward questions insisted on giving evidence for the defence. Connman suspended and then sacked him for telling the judge that in his opinion a proper investigation had not been carried out. Judge Greasley ignored this evidence, which he deemed as inadmissible. He informed the court, 'A junior officer's opinion of an investigation is of no relevance.' The defence lawyer, Mr Joe Weedy, presented many irregularities surrounding the investigation, information which in any other court might have led to an acquittal. This did not apply in Judge Greasley's court. Almost all the defence evidence was deemed inadmissible by the so-called trial judge whose authority was never questioned.

The trial lasted two days, and despite overwhelming discrepancies, Carol and Linda were sentenced to ten years each. What a price they paid for Crump's unorthodox form of employment. These two women had, albeit foolishly, trusted Ronald Crump who had used and abused them. When in court, they tried to plead with the judge that they had been abused sexually and had their employment rights violated. Greasley just ignored their pleas.

These two women suffered the most unjust fate: imprisonment for something they had not done. This was a miscarriage of justice at the highest level and one which eventually would be part of the overall evidence which would bring about the ultimate demise of Ronald Crump. The final outcome is for the future; there are still a few miles to travel before justice is finally achieved.

These women, who had made so much money for the good Mr Crump, were now out of the way for the foreseeable future. Crump had no regrets about the tactics of corruption he used which led to denying two innocent women their freedom. He felt he had to take this avenue to preserve his own interests, otherwise he may have lost the all-important contract with the UAE if it ever leaked that hostesses were used by high-ranking UAE officials. With the two women out of the way Crump could sell his property at a huge profit, given what he had paid for the run-down buildings, with no chance of leakage about the UAE official. The only two who could say a word would be in prison.

Crump was also well aware of the Mob's interest. He also knew that the NYPD's high-ranking officers were also in the pocket of the Mafia. Ronald Crump's reckoning was, if he had dismissed the girls, they could have gone to work for the Mob and also told them about some of Ronald's underhand dealings.

In the eyes of Ronald Crump, prison was the safest place for them.

16

Tracy

Tracy Crump was a mildly religious kind of woman, well bred with impeccable manners. How she and a misogynist beast like Ronald Crump became one is anybody's guess. Her family, particularly her father, Louis, liked Crump and now her mother, Stella, was beginning to take a shine to him, despite earlier misgivings. Tarquin, their little boy, would be three years old in June, which was only a couple of days away.

Ronald Crump was two, even three, different people, similar to the characters in the novel, *Dr Jekyll and Mr Hyde*. Contrary to the story of the good doctor taking a wicked potion and changing into the evil Mr Hyde, Crump needed no such potion to complete his metamorphosis. One character was charming and homely, like the one Tracy had fallen for, the other a ruthless monster capable of anything up to and including the taking of life if it suited his ends. Would Tracy ever find out what her husband was really like? Time would tell!

Tracy was beginning to show signs of her husband's personality rubbing off on her. This was not the ruthless Crump who would trample on anybody to get what he wanted but some of his milder traits. All that said, Ronald was to Tarquin what Teddy had been to him, a good father in most respects. Like Teddy, Ronald believed the dollar bill could sort out any problems, something Tracy did not agree with. She would also apply a calming lotion on Ronald, something Megan failed to do with Teddy. Tracy was one, if not the only, person who could influence Crump in any way.

Ronald Crump now had ideas of bringing Tracy into the business. He might need somebody, family, to take the reins in years to come if his long-term plans came to fruition. This would be where his wife came in. She could not, however, do that without the appropriate training and manipulation, which only he could give her. He was aware of the importance of knocking aside the innocent streak which threaded through Tracy's personality. There was no room for decency in the murky world of business. The main question for Crump was, where to begin?

★ ★ ★

At the large complex which constituted the main Republican offices and social club, Congressman Crump was mixing with the party's right wing. The group with which Crump found common grazing ground almost amounted to a faction within the party, a kind of elite was how they viewed themselves. This wing was made up of two groups, each sharing certain political ideologies. The Christian Right had people like the very young Pat Buchanan, along with people like Alfie Slyme, Robert Crass, Norman Hunter, Garfield Sprake, Jean Dibley and Margaret Prosser. The other group comprising this motley little circle were the larger Neo-Conservatives (neo-cons) and consisted of congressmen and women like Theresa March, Mable Allen, Leon England, Francis Pym, Stuart Perverse, Tony Acomb and Meghan Windsor-McAndrew.

Overarching both these groups was the governor of California, Ronald Reagan, who, although agreeing with them also realised they could be a liability as far as elections were concerned. For this reason, Reagan kept the 'loony right', as some moderates referred to them, at arm's length. He would socialise with them occasionally and even vote their way in the House of Representatives but that was as far, for now, as he would go. When these two groups had a get-together over a few drinks, to the casual observer it could be questioned if these people should be allowed out on their own, unsupervised. The truth was these people stuck together not only because they shared similar views but because no sane person would have anything to do with them. How ideas changed within the Republican Party over the next few years. Ironically, it would be the aloof Reagan whom Crump would defeat in the 1980 primaries to be the Republican candidate for the election of the same year. For this reason, Ronald needed Tracy on board, even though no concrete plans had been formulated. The basis for such a move on the presidency was still in the embryonic stage.

Ronald Crump was working on a hate-filled, racist Bill he wished to present to the House. It would be imagined the author of such an obviously ethnically biased piece of work would be a person with a very disturbed mind. Like most of the content which was passed off as serious political debate, the Bill which Crump hoped to present was a diatribe of right-wing rhetoric which nobody of average intelligence would insult themselves by reading. However, when we are talking about the likes of Ronald Crump the words 'average intelligence', certainly politically speaking, are non-applicable. Only his cronies on the religious right and neo-cons would give such literature the time of day.

Crump was proposing forced conscription for all African Americans into the armed forces of the USA. This, Crump argued, was the opportunity for the black population to show their appreciation to their white superiors, though he stopped short of using this wording for introducing the various acts granting them selected rights. These dated back to the Civil Rights Act 1866 following up on the abolition of slavery, the Voting Rights Act 1965, the Civil Rights Act 1966, and many others. These acts, according to Crump and other like-minded racists, were bestowed upon these people as a favour allowing African Americans some of the rights enjoyed by white people. Basically, being allowed to breathe was a great favour handed down to the black population by the whites. For this reason, they could show their eternal gratitude by joining the armed forces or be conscripted into doing so. Crump also wished this Act to be extended to Native Americans who for too long had moaned about it being their land. Well, now was their chance to fight for 'their land'. Crump had support among his usual cabal, but Ronald Reagan stayed clear. He perceived pitfalls in this proposed Bill and, though he agreed with some of it, knew it was detrimental in electoral terms. Most of the House of Representatives also saw in this as certain suicide and it never even reached its first reading. Not a great start for Crump in the political arena!

Ronald Crump had long-term plans for himself which would involve eventually getting himself nominated as a candidate to stand in the presidential elections. He had his eyes fixed on the 1980 election and would need the support of his friends on the far right of the party for nomination to stand in the primaries of that year. He also knew that should he win that nomination and then the primaries his next stop could be the White House. Should this occur he would have to surrender all his business interests as they would be incompatible with the top job. His son, Tarquin, would not be old enough so that left Tracy, whom he would have to get trained up.

He had plenty of time to educate her in the ways of business and would eventually introduce her to the board and board membership. She would then become the senior board member, standing in for Crump himself. He had one potential major problem: Sally Seddon. Would she keep quiet about the incident in Crump's dormitory all those years ago? He concluded she possibly would not, so what could be done? Maybe he could seek the advice of Agnes Moorhouse, his new female troubleshooter. But that might mean needing to inform her of what had taken place that night on his sixteenth birthday, and that would never do. He would have to make Sally out to be a compulsive liar to Moorhouse, and that should not be too difficult. She did, after all, believe the young secretaries were to blame for leading him on and causing most of the trouble in the office. In the office, Agnes outranked virtually all other staff so making things up about young 'tarts' was no problem. But Sally was a director and in Crump's absence she could fire Moorhouse. Perhaps he could find another way of silencing Sally, perhaps by using Matthew. Blackmail sprang to mind. Her antics essentially as a high-class hooker might have to become public! Yes, this could be the answer.

In the meantime it was more pressing to get Tracy interested in the business. The question here was where to start? This would not be easy. Tracy had always directed the conversation down another avenue every time he mentioned her becoming involved. What if all failed and she was just not interested? All these thoughts were passing through Ronald's head when, eureka, he hit on another idea. He would try to get Tracy interested but if that failed, as the majority shareholder in his business, he could transfer his sixty per cent to her in trust – that way he could still, in real terms, own them. Tracy would never go behind his back, she was too naive, he thought. That would leave the rest of them in a position where they either sold their collective forty per cent or bought his shares. Either way, he would be in pocket and if this doomsday scenario came to pass and he was successful in his bid to become president he would be free to run the country as he pleased, or so he thought. If this was Ronald's understanding of being president of the USA he had learned nothing. Perhaps instead of working out how to screw the incumbent, President Nixon, he should have concentrated more on the constitutional issues. *Well*, thought Crump, *for now I have two options, both of them healthy*.

Tarquin's third birthday had been and gone, a quiet family affair, and Ronald was pondering, early days as they were, whether to test the water with his wife. After the couple had sat down and eaten and the domestics had cleared all the plates away, Ronald and his wife were at last alone.

'Tracy, I've been thinking, dear, and I was wondering if you would like to get involved a little in the running of the company?'

'Me, Ronnie? Why, I've no head for that kind of work. How could I run the business? Besides, that's your department. You have always said my domain is the house and Tarquin, and dealing with the staff, and you would concentrate on the business. I like things that way.'

'I was just thinking though, darling, Tarquin will be at school shortly and that will leave you free all day, so maybe a couple of hours at the office?'

'Well, I don't know, Ron, let me think about it.'

Ronald was satisfied with this answer. He had not been given a cold and definite no; at least she was considering the proposal. He would now leave it a few days before mentioning the subject again. The following morning Ronald mentioned in passing to Bob Tomkinson his idea of bringing Tracy on board.

'What do you say, Bob?'

'Oh, Ronnie, I don't know, that is something between you and Tracy. How would she handle the dodgy dealings we occasionally are involved with? I'd be very careful if I were you, but it will be your decision.'

Ronald could not help but agree with Bob's caution. It would be a risk, not only with the less-than-honest deals, but there was the threat of Sally Seddon, and keeping police and judges sweet. Could Tracy do a full conversion from honest Jane to crooked Laura? Crump continued to ponder his options. It would be a huge risk even with full training and manipulation, and was it really worth the risk? No it wasn't, he finally concluded. He kept his doomsday option about selling up to himself. Best not let Bob know too much. He was an ally but if he felt his position was under threat that could change. He definitely would not mention anything to Charlie Kearns; he was an old campaigner from Teddy's day and would smell a rat immediately.

That evening Ronald was playing with his son on the carpet, pretending to be interested, but really waiting to get the child off to bed so he could have another question-and-answer session with his wife.

'Have you given any more thought to what we were discussing last night, dear?' he casually asked, after Tracy put Tarquin to bed.

'What about, Ronnie?'

'About getting involved with the business. Did you consider the possibility further?'

'Well, yes I did for a little while and I decided I'm happy as I am. If I got involved and you, for whatever reason, were not there, I would have to make huge decisions, wouldn't I?'

'Yes, you would,' said Ronald, now happy enough that it would not be a good idea for Tracy to be involved.

'Do you think you could handle it, with training from me of course?'

'I don't think so Ronald, I mean, how much training? You were taught by your father over how many years? And how long would I have to learn the basics, let alone the intricate side of business dealings?'

'Not very long. It is a ruthless game… Maybe it was unfair to ask you, darling, I just thought for the coming years of a husband and wife team, but if you think it is a little much for you perhaps we'll leave things as they are.'

Ronald was pleased with the outcome, or the way it appeared to be heading. He had given his wife the opportunity to become involved and, if he was reading the situation correctly, she had thought it over and decided against.

'So, you're not really interested, dear?'

'Oh, I wouldn't say that, Ronnie, I just think I'd be out of my depth.'

'I'll tell you what, darling, we'll leave it for now, shall we?' Ronnie suggested, having no intentions of ever bringing the subject up again.

'Yes, for now, Ron, I think that will be for the best, but thank you for having confidence in me, believing in my ability to emulate you and your father.'

The next day at the office Ronald informed Tomkinson, his partner in murder, that he had spoken at length with his wife and they both thought it for the best if she did not take an active role in the running of the business.

'I agree, Ron. Imagine if she found out about – you know? She is such an honest woman and the thought of being, or her husband being, involved with anything like that could lead to all kinds of problems. Remember, Ron, you can't buy every official off or rely on Teddy's reputation forever.'

'That's true, Bob. Don't know what I was thinking,' Crump lied, 'but it is probably for the best if Tracy leaves this side of things to me and I leave the house, Tarquin and the staff to her.'

Tarquin was almost ready for prep school, just as Ronald had been at the outset of our story. Tracy was secretly delighted Ron had dropped that silly idea about involving her in the business. What was he thinking of? She was happier than she had ever been with Tarquin, the apple of her eye, with running the house and the domestics, who were like sisters to her. This was a view, of course, not shared by Ronald but he kept his counsel in Tracy's domain.

'No,' she said to herself. 'I don't want to have to deal with those kind of high-powered decisions. Leave them to him.'

As we come to the end of 1973 and begin 1974 it was going to be a year of huge political turmoil in the USA. This was a year which would see a president resign his office under the threat of impeachment and a vice-president take over. Ronald Crump would be watching these events unfold with great interest for his own future. The events about to unfold would be another educational for Crump, one which he failed to grasp sufficiently. These events would become known as 'Watergate'.

17

Impeachment or Resignation

This year, 1974, would be when Tarquin began prep school. For Tracy it was the end of a maternal era never to return, just as happened many years previously when Megan had suffered the same turmoil. This is the kind of change in routine which perhaps only mothers can experience and appreciate. Both Ronald and Tracy had Tarquin's name down for some time at the school of their choice. They had decided to send him to Wetherspoons, the same school Ronald had attended.

It would be a few months before Tarquin would begin his new experience, after his fourth birthday in June 1974. Prep school began a little earlier than compulsory education, starting in August as an introduction before classes proper began in September. Tracy was looking forward to taking Tarquin there on his first day. However, she was feeling a little out of sorts about the inevitable steps that were soon to take place. For these reasons Tracy decided to phone Megan for a little mother-in-law advice on the subject.

'Hi Megan, it's Tracy. It's Tarquin's first day at prep school tomorrow and I'm feeling really anxious. Can you give me any advice?'

'Tell you what, Tracy, why don't I come along with you?' Megan suggested.

'That would be great, Megan, thank you.'

The two women took little Tarquin along to Wetherspoons and the grandmother took the initial lead. She introduced herself and Tracy to the young teacher, Miss Cherney.

'I remember bringing my son, Ronald, to this very school many years ago,' she commented with a smile.

Miss Cherney introduced the women to the other mothers and conversations were soon struck up. With the ice broken, Tracy felt much more at ease and looked on as young Tarquin began playing with the other children. It was time for the parents to leave, and on their way home Tracy took Megan for a coffee and thanked her for the intervention.

It so happened that at this same time the biggest political turmoil to hit the USA and principally the Republican Party was to blow up. Rumours were rife throughout Congress in both the House of Representatives and the Senate regarding the future of President Nixon. The reader will recall how Nixon had asked Ronald to be his eyes and ears, something Crump had enthusiastically accepted but with far more sinister ulterior motives. Ronald Crump never did anything for anybody, outside his home, unless there was an advantage in it for him. This included the President of the United States.

Ronald had seen several congressmen speaking with the Attorney General, and he thought they were talking about the president. However, what was being discussed was just general conversation about nothing in particular.

Ronald Crump wished to examine and digest Nixon's body language in this tricky situation regarding Watergate. How would he get out of it and what could he, Crump, learn from the exercise? Once the Attorney General knew that the president was not only aware of the Watergate break-in but had all but sanctioned it, there could only be one outcome. Ronald was determined, for possible future reference, to gain as much knowledge on how to escape the inevitable as he could. Which way would Nixon turn? Who would he turn to? What if he survived and found out Crump had withheld valuable facts which could have saved him? Crump began making contingency plans in case the president did a Harry Houdini and escaped. Who could Ronald blame to save his own skin?

The vultures were now flying lower and lower over the White House as a special team was deployed to investigate Watergate. The president continued his denials of any break-in or equally any attempted cover-up. He was also denying the team access to some perceived tapes, recordings of conversations involving the president which could throw light on the whole affair. But the team could prove Nixon was lying through his teeth, if these tapes became public. President Nixon claimed that to 'release the tapes would undermine the position of the office of president and would give cause not to trust the office again in the future.' This claim perhaps was credible but Nixon, many felt, was using this wall of presidential security and credibility to hide behind.

Ronald Crump perceived a president in deep trouble. He might now start drip-feeding his boss with snippets of information. Whatever he gave the president had to hold an element of truth with heaps of lies and innuendoes piled on. *Yes*, thought Crump, *the time was right*.

This drip-feeding would begin with a fact, not a very important truth, but nevertheless an actuality. He would inform the president he had seen Senator Harry Kirkpatrick speaking in private to the Attorney General. Crump could only guess at the contents of the conversation, but was it not a coincidence that shortly after this conversation the investigation at official level into Watergate began? This was the kind of stuff he, Crump, would fill the president's head with.

The fact was, many senators on a daily basis spoke in passing to the Attorney General; in fact there was a rule that in the social club legal matters were taboo when speaking with the USA's top lawyer. However, to circumvent this unwritten rule Crump would tell Nixon the conversation took place not inside the social club, but in the lobby outside. Inside the warped world of Congress a seemingly innocuous event like this might be deemed anything but.

Ronald Crump phoned Nixon suggesting an urgent meeting. This way if, by some quirk of nature, the president survived, Crump would be perceived as a reliable, dependable troubleshooter, not the troublemaking spineless jellyfish he really was. Crump would also suggest Soviet involvement with the break-in and that Kirkpatrick might be having dealings with the Kremlin. He would imply this without actually accusing; that would be going too far even for him.

'Mr President, it's Congressman Crump. I think we should meet. Remember you asked me to inform you of anything relevant I overheard or witnessed? Well, that time is now.'

'Very well, Ronnie, well done. I need some help at the moment.'

Ronald and President Nixon met in a sub-office without the knowledge of anybody else. This was top-secret stuff.

'My advice, Mr President, is stick to the story, sorry, fact, about your little jest being overheard and taken seriously. Somehow this reached the Kremlin, possibly via Senator Kirkpatrick – and it may have been the Soviets who orchestrated the break-in at the Watergate complex. Now, Mr President, I saw Senator Kirkpatrick talking secretively to the Attorney General outside the social club. May I suggest the reason they were colluding, or possibly colluding, outside the club was because of the unwritten rule about discussing points of law or breaches in the legal system while inside the club?'

Crump knew these allegations, untrue as they were, could mean the end of the senator's career, but so what! He was one of the centre-lefts, the type, who, in Crump's opinion, should be ousted anyway. All he was doing was helping him on his way. President Nixon listened to what the young congressman had to say.

'Why did you not come to me earlier, Crump?' Nixon enquired.

'I only saw the pair meet last night, sir, and called you first thing,' Ronald said.

It should be remembered President Nixon was up to his neck in the Watergate scandal and would listen to anything, no matter how far-fetched, which might be constructive in saving his skin.

'Well, thank you, Crump, you have been a great help here. I'll remember this in the future, assuming I survive.'

'Oh, I'm sure you will, sir, in fact I'm positive,' Crump said reassuringly. 'If I were you, sir, I would concentrate on possible Soviet involvement; that would at least muddy the waters. Anything to do with the USSR causes a stir, sir, and it is perfectly feasible they *could* be involved.'

'Yes, good point, Crump. I'll put the wheels in motion,' Nixon said, indicating it was the end of the audience.

President Nixon, on Ronald's departure, contacted his Chief of Staff and legal advisor. The two high-ranking officials reported to Nixon who then held a council of war. Sandy Gall was the legal advisor and John McQuillan the White House Chief of Staff.

'I've heard some nasty things today about Senator Kirkpatrick stirring the shit,' Nixon opened the conversation with this information.

'How do you know this, Mr President?' enquired McQuillan.

'I will not disclose my source, not yet,' Nixon replied.

'You may have to, sir, and it would not do for you to withhold information at this point. Such an assumption would cast further doubt on your sincerity Mr President,' Gall advised. 'From a legal point of view, they will force you to reveal your source.'

'Well,' said Nixon, 'let's get Kirkpatrick here and see what he has to say. If it is relevant I'll reveal my source, how's that?' said the President.

'That'll do for now, sir,' Sandy Gall informed him.

'Get me Senator Kirkpatrick here now. No excuses, I want him now,' said Nixon on the intercom.

'Very good, sir,' his secretary replied. Half an hour later Kirkpatrick arrived.

'Sit down, Harry,' Nixon invited him.

'Thank you, Mr President.'

'Now, Harry, you were talking to the Attorney General outside the social club, is that right?'

'The Congressional grapevine moves fast these days!' exclaimed Kirkpatrick.

'Yes or no, Harry?'

'Well, yes, I was.'

'What were you talking about, Senator? This is important.'

'Well, if you really must know sir, and you'll feel foolish as it was nothing, I was discussing Saturday's baseball game at the New York Oval. I have a ticket and he is a baseball fan.'

'And that's it?'

'Yes, sir, that is it. May I ask why?'

'No.' It was plain to see that Kirkpatrick was telling the truth. 'Sorry to have dragged you in here, Harry, you can leave. Oh Goddammit, have a drink, it's this Watergate nonsense getting to me, I'm seeing conspiracy everywhere. Again, Harry, I'm sorry.'

'Not to worry, sir, I think you are innocent,' the naive senator said. He actually did believe in Nixon's innocence. In fact, Harry Kirkpatrick, unlike Crump, was one of the most loyal people Nixon had around him. If the president wanted eyes and ears he should have actually employed Kirkpatrick, not the rattlesnake Crump who would stab his own mother if it suited him.

The meeting dissolved, and the President now had some serious questions for Crump. What was he up to? Or was he up to anything at all, or were his albeit misguided concerns genuine? President Nixon sat in the Oval Office as the evidence mounted up against him. He pondered the situation, worried about the tapes the investigation team wished to see. Nixon was hiding behind presidential privilege, credibility and security which, if an outside body such as the National Security Agency had been involved, may have been a valid reason for denying access. However, the truth was, the break-in was carried out by persons who were members of the Republican Party and he, Nixon, was not only aware of the operation, he had sanctioned it. The tapes would be incriminating, yet denying access was equally so. He felt like Nero watching Rome burn except he was not playing the fiddle. In fact, arguably, it was his *fiddling* which had placed him in this untenable situation.

President Nixon felt it was perhaps a matter of time before the cries for his impeachment came from all corners, not just the Democrats. Only two nights ago he had gone on national television and claimed 'there would be no cover-up'. On the contrary, he was conducting the cover-up of all cover-ups and the ground beneath his feet was becoming softer and softer by the day.

President Nixon called Crump to his office. He wished to know more about what he had been up to. For the first time he was beginning to look at the young congressman through questioning eyes. Nixon had enough problems. Had he known or even suspected Crump's deceitfulness, he would not have had him around the place. As it was, Nixon was not aware of Crump's willingness to sacrifice anybody or anything in pursuit of his own aims.

Ronald arrived at the office.

'You wished to see me, Mr President?'

'Yes, Ronald, take a seat. Why have you been pedalling false information, Crump? Why did you tell me, or lead me to believe, that Kirkpatrick was passing dubious information to the Attorney General?'

'With all due respect, Mr President, I did not pass on false information. I never once said I knew what their conferring was about. I never suggested that, I just thought you should know.'

Ronald knew the president was on the defensive despite his aggressive front. He estimated, correctly, he only had to stand his ground and maybe engage in a little grovelling when and if necessary.

'You asked me to keep my eyes and ears open, sir, and report back to you. This I have done to the letter of your instruction,' he lied. 'I'm sorry there was nothing tangible in Kirkpatrick's conversation with the Attorney General.'

'How do you know there was nothing tangible, Crump?' Nixon countered. 'I never told you that.'

'Well, sir, I thought that was why you had summoned me? I just assumed you had gained nothing from the information I passed to you.' Crump was going on the mini-offensive. 'Mr President, I don't know what they were talking about, only that they were talking. Given the rules about discussing law or points of law relevant to the times inside the club, I was a little suspicious as to why the conversation was taking place outside. Mr President, I do not like spying on people, but my president asked me for help and help I gave.'

'All right, congressman, calm down. You did as you were asked. I shouldn't have a go at you for doing as you were told.'

'Do you wish me to continue keeping you informed, sir?'

'Yes, carry on, Crump, you may go.'

'Thank you, sir.'

'Oh, Crump, the next time you believe to be witnessing an important conversation, try to ascertain the content of the discussion.'

'Very well, sir, I will do my best.'

Ronald Crump had succeeded in manoeuvring his way out of a potentially damaging situation. He thought at first Nixon suspected him but in the end any doubts he had were dispelled. He was as safe now as he had been before the grilling. He convinced himself President Nixon was no match for himself, which, given the pressure the chief was under, may have been the case. *No need to worry, I'll just watch the events unfold and draw up mental plans should I find myself in a similar situation in the coming years*, Ronald thought. Ronald definitely had eyes on the top job now.

He acknowledged in grim irony how Nixon couldn't have employed a worse man to be his unofficial advisor.

Ronald now had Creighton collect him from the party offices.

'Home, Creighton, home. It has been one of those days. Thankfully tomorrow I'll be at my day job,' he joked.

Creighton, not known for his sense of humour at the best of times, either did not see the little joke or chose to ignore it.

'I'm home, honey,' Ronald called. 'Did you have a busy day? Did you take Tarquin to school or have the nanny do it?'

'No, darling, I took him. I'm making friends with the other mothers. Your mom told me that is what she did when you were little.'

Crump was privately seething that his mother should discuss his formative years with his wife, but he didn't let on. To do so might suggest there were things he wished his wife not to know about. The particular incident he was thinking of was the occurrence at his eleventh birthday. He did not let Tracy see his apprehension.

'Glad you're making some nice friends, dear,' he remarked.

'Yes, I am. Megan was telling me they were some of her happiest years, taking you to prep school while your dad was at work, just like I am now.'

'How is Tarquin doing at school?' Ronald asked pretending to show an interest. This stage of the child's education was of little concern to him; the youngster was not yet ready to be corrupted. That would come later when he separated Tracy from their son for a few hours per day, like Teddy had done with him.

'His class teacher, Miss Pratt, says he is showing great early promise, especially in the measuring of liquids department.'

At this Ronald coloured up. It brought back memories of having water thrown all over him by those he would eventually become friends with.

'Yes, I was good in that department, I'm told,' he said, allowing a slight grin.

Ronald began playing with Tarquin with a ball, which involved passing the object to each other across the lounge floor. Tracy sat drinking her cup of tea. *What a perfect life I have*, she thought – *a caring husband and my beautiful son.* If only this lovely, though perhaps naïve, person knew. She was too good for Ronald Crump, as one day she would find out.

The following day at the company office, Crump was dictating to Mrs Moorhouse. 'Take this down, Agnes,' he said. '"To the United Arab Emirates Department of Defense— "'

Ronald had a radio in his office which relayed world news. Just then an emergency news bulletin came on, which only happened in the event of war or national emergency.

The newscaster said: 'Information is coming in of calls to impeach President Nixon over the situation surrounding the 1972 break-in at the Watergate office complex. First reports suggest the calls are coming primarily, though not exclusively, from the Democratic Party, but sections within the Republican ranks are also calling for impeachment. That is the end of this emergency bulletin.'

'We'll leave the dictation for now, Mrs Moorhouse,' said Ronald. 'Get Creighton to collect me at the front. We are going to the party offices.'

On arriving at the party offices Crump noted a large crowd had gathered.

'Drive me to the rear, Creighton,' he instructed his chauffeur.

It was August 1974 and the place was awash with rumours. Nixon had been impeached, then he had been arrested. It appeared not to enter the heads of the proponents of the latter untruth that a sitting president cannot be arrested. Crump sought out the Governor of California, Ronald Reagan, his future nemesis, though this was unknown to either man at this point.

'What's happened, Governor?' asked Ronald.

'Everything is a blur at the moment, Congressman, we'll have to wait and see. Rumour has it an announcement of the most sensitive nature will be announced some time. It appears the main concern of the security officials is keeping any announcement away from the media.'

Then a man appeared. 'Can all senators and congressmen please make their way to the main hall? Priority will be given to sitting members of the Senate and the House.'

Crump and Reagan – the two Ronnies – made their way to the one-thousand-seater hall, complete with huge screen at the front, and awaited the next turn of events. The hall soon filled up and everyone was informed that a broadcast from the Oval Office would be given in the next few moments. This would be shown live on the big screen at the front of the hall. The date was 8th August 1974, a date which would go down in the political history of the USA. The senators and members of the House waited patiently and equally anxiously for the president's face to appear on the screen in front of them. Then with no further ado, the image of President Richard Milhous Nixon was on the screen, ready to make his announcement.

He began: 'This is the thirty-seventh time I have spoken to you from this office, where so many decisions have been made which shaped the history of this nation. Each time I have done so to discuss with you some matter which I believe affected the national interest.'

The speech was very long and the full content is unnecessary for our purpose. After outlining his position and that of the events which led to this announcement, Nixon added: 'Therefore, I shall resign the presidency affective from noon tomorrow. Vice-President Ford will be sworn in as president at that hour in this office.'

He finished with: 'To have served in this office is to have felt a very personal service of kinship with each and every American. In leaving it, I do so with this prayer. May God's grace be with you in all the days ahead.'

Ronald Crump retired to the bar with his fellow right-wing and religious hypocrite, Alf Slyme.

'Nice speech, but he had no choice,' voiced Slyme.

'I wouldn't have,' said Crump. 'If he hadn't been in such a hurry to make friends with the commies of the Soviet Union he could have heaped the blame for the break-in on Moscow. That way he would still be the man in charge instead of that clown Ford.'

'I hadn't thought of that, yes you're right, Ronald. Pass the blame onto others, even if it is another superpower. Lie through your teeth, that's the way to survive,' Slyme agreed.

Like most of those who lay claim to be the modern disciples of the lowly carpenter, this man forgot all about paying special attention to the commandments, especially the one about 'bearing false witness'.

'The Soviet Union will run rings around this fella, Ford. He is too soft,' Crump commented.

This opinion was based on Ronald having no knowledge of the man under discussion.

President Nixon was unlucky in the game of capitalist dishonesty and fraud. He got caught and subsequently paid the ultimate sacrifice demanded by the bent system he served. Nixon was not the first, or indeed the only, dishonest president of the USA, or world leader. The problem is not isolated to the USA, although due to the power that country's bourgeoisie wield, it is the most noticeable. Other countries' leaders are all part of the same club, a club which has evolved over the centuries via revolutions, as in England in 1641–49, France 1789–93 and 1848, and the Soviet Union, which was perhaps of them all the one which showed early promise. This club consists at our time of international bankers, which the USSR were not part of; huge conglomerate capitalist companies, again non-applicable to the USSR, the only counterbalance on the planet; and legalised corruption and robbery. From the early days of mercantile capitalism, evolution of the process coupled with manipulation by the benefactors has done the rest.

Ronald Crump would, from now on, keep his plans for his push for the future presidency to himself. The next election, due in 1976, was too early for Crump but the one after that, 1980, might well be his time. What he had to do, he perceived to himself, was to get nominated under protest; make out he did not wish to be nominated and having everybody on the right wing pleading with him. Eventually Crump would, apparently very much against his will, succumb to this peer pressure, making out it to be his 'moral duty' to do so.

★ ★ ★

The rest of the seventies offered little to our character that we do not already know. Gerald Ford replaced Richard Nixon in the Oval Office and he was defeated by the Democrat, Jimmy Carter, in the 1976 election. Carter's claim to fame was the Camp David Accord in 1978, bringing the Egyptians and Israelis to the table together for the first time. This was an historic achievement by President Carter, one for which he would be remembered. Egypt became the first Arab state to recognise the Israeli state's right to exist.

Ronald Crump was secretly seething at this agreement towards peace. His company made billions of dollars selling arms to both sides. Of course, he could not publicly voice opposition to the accord, one which even the USSR,

Egypt's one-time backer, applauded. Indirectly this agreement, though not satisfactory to many Arab nations like Syria and Jordan, made the world a safer place. The two superpowers, the USA and the USSR, had been fighting a proxy war in the Middle East. The Americans backed the Israelis and the Soviets backed Egypt, until recently. This game was greatly reduced and along with it the risk. Only somebody like Ronald Crump could have reservations, based on profit, about such an accord. He would in the future scupper many similar agreements which were aimed towards peace, or at least relative stability in the capitalist world.

18

The Call Girls

1980 was an election year in the USA and Ronald Crump, by use of stealth and his double-bluff strategy, intended being the presidential candidate nominee for the Republican Party. The favourite to take this mantle was Ronald Reagan, the incumbent Governor of California, so it could well be a battle of the Republican right wing. There were of course other contenders, but none of these were expected to fare too well against the heavyweights of Reagan and Crump. The Republican Party right wing was split as both these potential presidents were from the right. Crump, not surprisingly, took the religious right and many of the neo-cons who had been expected to back Reagan. Ronald Reagan took the rest of the neo-cons and the centre right and moderate lefts. The battle lines were drawn.

Other candidates to enter the race for the Primaries were George H. W. Bush, the former head of the CIA, John B. Anderson, Phil Crane and Bob Dole. All these hopefuls were to concede at varying points when it became apparent they would not receive the numbers in terms of votes. This left the way clear for a two-horse race between the two darlings of the right. When all the debating and discussions were over it was down to who would have the numbers. The results came in and a few eyebrows were raised: Ronald Crump received 7,709,793, amounting to 53%, and Ronald Reagan obtained 3,500,700, which gave him 25% of the vote. The remaining 22% was shared among those who had withdrawn earlier.

Ronald Crump was to be the 1980 presidential candidate for the Republican Party. His opponent was the incumbent Jimmy Carter. Crump had not forgiven Carter for costing his firm money with his Middle East peace deal at Camp David. Crumps Arms were supplying primarily the Israelis, but the Egyptians placed smaller orders if the USSR refused to supply them. Either way, Crump had lost a lot of money thanks to this imbecile, as he saw Carter. Revenge would be sweet. Ronald Crump could not allow this personal bitterness to become apparent, so he bit his tongue and kept his feelings under wraps. That said, in all the debates all Crump could see were missing dollar signs going round and round.

Creighton collected Crump to take him home to Tracy, the all-innocent Tracy, to whom he shouted his usual announcement informing her of his arrival. But this day was different.

'I'm home, honey, and guess what?'

'What, darling, do tell me?' Tracy asked.

Ronald then informed his wife. 'You may well become the First Lady of the United States. I'm to be the party candidate for president.'

'Oh, Ronald, I'm so happy for you! Imagine me, a waitress from the New York Hilton becoming the First Lady, imagine it, Ronnie! Imagine it!'

Tracy was on cloud nine with this news and began dancing around the room.

'Hold on, honey, I have to beat Carter first. He might have ideas on spoiling the party,' Ronald informed his ecstatic wife, sobering her up a little.

'You'll beat him, I know you will,' she enthused.

Tarquin looked up at his parents with an air of superiority regarding their behaviour in much the same way a sensible person would regard the antics of a circus clown.

'Tell Nanny – sorry, ask Nanny if she will work tonight as I'm taking you out for a celebratory meal. We will go to the New York Hilton. I've told Creighton he's needed so if you sort it with the staff we'll be on our way.'

'Oh. Marigold won't mind, especially when she knows the reason why we are celebrating.'

'No, Tracy, please don't tell anybody just yet. We must wait for the party to issue a statement. Tell her we are celebrating but do not breathe a word as to why.'

'Oh, very well, dear, if those are the rules, I suppose you don't write them.'

'Now for the bad news, honey. I have to be away next week at an arms dealers' convention in Michigan. I'll be gone a week. You don't mind, do you?'

The way Ronald asked this question might give the impression the outcome of this discussion depended very much on his wife's answer to this question. In reality it didn't matter he was going anyway. He asked the question merely out of politeness, something which was an improvement for Crump, as at one point he would not have even gone through the motions of asking.

'No, not really, you must do what you must do, and business is business. You see now why I didn't want to get involved? All this running about and inconveniencing is not for me, darling. You go and good luck.'

Ronald Crump had already arranged for private entertainment while he was at the convention, in the form of two high-class call girls. Of course, there was no need to tell his wife this; she would be miles away bringing up their child while he was philandering.

Creighton collected the Crumps and drove them to their destination. The reader will recall the New York Hilton was Tracy's former employer and she was looking forward to seeing old friends. Ronald reminded her again about the need for secrecy.

'Talk about anything but that,' he reminded her.

The Hilton had been good to Tracy at her wedding, giving her the banquet suite free as a wedding present, and she wished to thank them properly. The couple sat down at their table and it turned out that the waitress who served them was a former friend of Tracy's. They were both delighted to exchange a few pleasantries with each other. When Ronald and Tracy finished their meal, Tracy decided to go and see Mr Jackson, who was the manager who had facilitated her wedding. Tracy, by marrying one of the richest men in the country, helped him come to this compassionate decision.

'I'll just be a few moments, Ron,' said Tracy, as she stood up.

'Take your time, darling,' he replied.

Tracy went to Jackson's office.

'Tracy, what a nice surprise! How are you, my dear,' Jackson said. 'And how is your husband?'

Jackson had never met Crump and even if he had, Ronald could have been on his worst behaviour, his rudest, and Jackson would still make out he was a nice man.

'I'm very well, Mr Jackson. I just want to thank you in person for the room at my wedding.'

'Think no more about it, and if there is anything else we can help you with in the future let me know,' Jackson said obsequiously.

'Of course I will, sir.'

'Oh, drop the sir, Tracy. It's Jeff.' He believed in treating Tracy as an equal these days.

To listen to Jackson grovelling one could be forgiven for believing him to be a nice man who treated all the staff like this. Nothing could be further from the truth: he docked girls' pay for the slightest offence and would not tolerate lateness. Tracy remembered this but was too polite to remind her former boss of his demonic arrogance. All things considered, Jackson, like most agents of capitalism, made the life of the staff a living hell.

★ ★ ★

Ronald Crump and Charlie Kearns, the veteran arms dealer and Ronald's right-hand man who was the seasoned dealer of many a campaign with the late Teddy, arrived for the convention. There were representatives from many firms including T.A. Gunn and Co., the company Ronald and Bob Tomkinson tried to put out of circulation.

'I'll just go and offer my condolences to Tommy Gunn's representative for the tragic deaths of their secretary, the hapless Barbara, and security guard,' Ronald said.

Crump walked across to shake the hand of their representative, wishing him congratulations from Crumps on their return to the big league and sorrow for the firm's loss. The reader will recall the plot concocted against Gunn's by Crump and executed by Tomkinson which resulted in the deaths of two people for a contract Crumps still did not win. Of course, the representative from Gunn's had no idea about Ronald's involvement in the inferno which engulfed the company factory he represented, but Charlie Kearns had a feeling Ronald had more involvement in the matter than he was letting on. Charlie had been around for many years, and had seen Teddy pull some strokes, but never involving murder.

The convention was a huge international affair with representatives from all over the world. The French firm G. Renade were showing off their new high-tech cluster grenade, while Crumps had on show a new upgraded variant of their long-range sniper rifle, accurate for up to three miles. Gunn's, as part of their comeback, had designed a new chemical weapon dispenser capable of knocking out the population of a large city with the smashing of a test-tube. These weapons were supposedly banned under international treaty, but like most aspects of this business these treaties were always trumped by those who had the most dollar bills. One thing all these rival companies had in common was that they all were in the business of making money out of mass extermination.

The convention was to go on all week and the first day was very much about introductions and formalities. Crump and Kearns mixed with the other mass murderers, all of whom were worth billions, or perhaps more accurately, the companies they represented were. Only Crump and Kearns were the owner and senior director of the company they were representing. The other reps were from the various firms' marketing departments. After the day's work all the delegates retired to the bar for a few drinks. It was traditional at such gatherings to get drunk on the first evening before the real work began.

As the evening gathered pace some of the delegates began acting in a fashion one would expect from a poor unfortunate in the county asylum as opposed to so-called captains of industry. These normally devious souls were, in many cases, reduced to the level of semi-imbeciles as one by one they sloped off to bed. Of course, the following morning they would pray to God they would never act in such foolish manner again. But all the hypocritical praying in the world would not prevent such events occurring again and again. The truth of the matter was, none of these people were capable of carrying out any meaningful work or useful tasks. Going to conventions such as this one, which produced nothing of any practical use, was about the limit of their capabilities. In an ideal world these people would serve no purpose whatsoever.

Next morning started off with a film demonstrating the new cluster grenade, designed by the French company G. Renade, blowing up a village in what was at the time of filming French Algiers. Renades had upgraded the weapon and the second part of the film showed a mock village ten times the size of the previous one with cardboard cutouts as opposed to living people. The result was devastating; the area representing an entire village was blown to bits. All the dealers in death agreed this really was a wonderful weapon.

Following this remarkable piece of 'entertainment' it was a bus ride out of town to witness a marksman demonstrate Crump's sniper rifle. A target was erected three miles away and due to the distance involved, the delegates watched the result of the marksman's shooting on film. The target in question was a pile of bricks about four feet high, held together by cement and erected the previous evening. The marksman took aim three miles from the target, his weapon fitted with ultra-telescopic sights, and the rifle fired an explosive bullet. The four-foot-high target of solid brick and cement was obliterated, and a round of applause followed from the delegates.

'Imagine if that were a tower block, bingo,' said one of the bloodthirsty delegates. 'There would be bodies everywhere,' he continued, and all the brigands agreed.

At this point it was decided they would all retire for a well-earned four-course lunch after which, due to the morning's exertions, they would bring proceedings to an end for the day. It had been a long hard morning for the dealers, watching a film about murdering Algerian civilians and a sniper blowing up a pile of bricks from three miles away.

Ronald Crump suggested a pay freeze or even wage reduction for their employees to pay for all this extravaganza and all the delegates agree to suggest it to their relevant companies. The truth was that this convention, four-course meals included, would be reclaimed in part from income tax returns. In short all of them were having a free week away from the day-to-day 'hard toil' at the office. For the coming evening Ronald Crump had arranged some light entertainment for himself. He decided not to tell Charlie Kearns, who might not approve. This consideration would not normally bother Crump but the last person he wished to alienate was Charlie. What Charlie didn't know, he could not worry about. But Charlie Kearns was a wily old fox and unknown to Ronald had a fair idea what Crump was up to.

Crump lay on his bed, satisfied the day had gone well, when a knock came to his door. Crump answered to the beholding sight of 'Sharon Storm' and 'Stephanie Lust', two call girls he had hired.

'Come in, ladies. Drinks?'

'Yes, after we have discussed business,' Sharon said.

At this point Crump handed them both $500, instructing them both to undress for a threesome and more.

Charlie Kearns was down in the bar having a few drinks. He too could have had call girls but firstly he could see the possible pitfalls and secondly, he was a little old for the casual sex scene. He preferred the loving caring build-up, but had he been Ronald's age he may well have joined in. Kearns was a little concerned about Ronald's flippant attitude towards Tracy being left at home carrying out her maternal duties. He was worried that if she ever was to find out about her husband's antics it would cause no end of problems for the company. She would not take it lying down, that was for sure. Best she never found out; therefore it was essential nobody else here knew about his chief's exploits.

Kearns was making his way back to his room when he heard a terrible commotion coming from Crump's suite. He heard raised male and female voices and ushered closer to improve his eavesdropping position.

'You fucking pervert,' was among the milder accusations coming from one of the women.

'Fuck off, my ass is my own,' was another female exclamation.

'I've paid good money for you two tarts and you'll provide a service or I'll—''You'll what?'

Charlie approached the door and knocked hard.

After a moment Ronald opened the door. By the looks of things he had hurriedly pulled his pants on. In the background stood two naked ladies. 'Oh, it's you, Charlie.'

'Yes, and lucky for you it is, Ron.'

'These two tarts are prostitutes and I want them prosecuted,' said Crump. What he didn't realise was that the women, as was the practice for insurance purposes, were recording the whole conversation.

'Ronald, did you call these girls to your room?' asked Charlie.

'No, they just showed up.'

'You're a liar and we can prove it,' said Sharon.

'Who do you think the authorities will believe?' sneered Crump. 'You two, a couple of call girls, or me, one of the wealthiest and respected business men in the USA?'

'They'll believe us, Mr Crump. Just check the hotel communication lines and your call to us will be recorded. The hotel will not hang us out to dry, there are too many other equally wealthy Johns who come here and request our services. And, don't you forget this: in Michigan the John as well as the escort are prosecuted. If you are stupid enough to go down that avenue it is your own throat you'll be cutting.'

'They're right, Ron, better off cutting your losses and calling it a draw. Anyway what is the argument over? You called these to your room, they are not refusing what you paid them for – just the extra you're demanding is how I see it,' said Charlie.

Ronald had not been content with the basic threesome and vaginal and oral sex; he had wanted something extra which the girls did not wish to give. This was the same act of sodomy he had forced on Sally Seddon that night on his sixteenth birthday, but these two escorts were refusing to do it. Both women had bruising down their arms where Crump had tried to coerce them against their will.

'Ronnie, the girls are here to provide a service. They are not here to be physically, verbally or psychologically abused in any way. You've pushed them outside the area of services they provide, now cut your losses.'

'That's good advice,' Stephanie said.

'Yes, it is,' echoed Sharon. 'We'll be on our way for now!'

They grabbed their clothes and left the room in great haste.

Just as the Watergate tapes had come back to haunt President Nixon, so too would these for the future President Crump.

'Fortunately the other delegates are all out probably doing the same as you, Ron,' said Kearns, 'but a long way from the hotel. With luck, nobody will get to know about these fun and games as there were no witnesses apart from me. Therefore, the chances of Tracy getting to know are slim, but for Christ's sake be careful. Let's just get on with the rest of the week and no more games, eh?'

'Yes, you're right, Charlie, it was my fault. I pushed them too far.'

'Well, Ronnie, let's call it a lesson learned and if you see those two again, ignore them.'

The rest of the week went down with no major incident. Ronald did engage in paid sex behind his wife's back but this time he went far away from the hotel, and did not breathe a word to Charlie though it was likely he suspected. The last day, Friday, eventually came and the overworked arms dealers had an even shorter day as they were all to finish off for opening time at the bar. As on the first evening of the convention, most of them got drunk again.

However, Ronald stayed reasonably sober; after his escapade this was just as well. The two prostitutes he had engaged were in the bar on that last day and they both disappeared with one of the delegates.

'Leave it, Ron,' the ever-watchful Charlie warned. 'Only a couple more hours and we're away back to New York.'

When the time came for them all to go their separate ways they all pretended to be best buddies. Nothing could be further from the truth. They all represented different companies and despite the public showing of camaraderie they all knew not one of them could be described as a friend of the other. In a nutshell these captains of industry hated each other's guts.

19

The Race to the White House

Ronald Crump arrived back home on the Friday evening. Creighton had been on hand all week but fortunately had been given the night off when the incident with the call girls occurred. Not that Crump had any need to worry; Creighton was as loyal to the Crump family as any Labrador dog, which was about the same level of respect his master, Crump, afforded him.

'I'm home, honey,' called Crump, as Tracy and Tarquin ran to welcome the great man's safe return, and Ronald felt like a great white hunter having just returned from a safari having bagged the heads of several defenceless animals.

'Did you have a good week, darling?' asked Tracy.

'Yes, I met some great guys there. The arms business is certainly on the up and up,' he boasted.

These 'great guys' could not stand the sight of each other, but lying was never a problem to Crump.

'Any problems? Did you keep away from any loose women?' Tracy enquired in jest. If only she knew.

Ronald laughed, and gave his wife a gentle kiss. 'The only woman I want is you,' he murmured smoothly.

Ronald knew that an announcement was due from the party announcing him as their presidential candidate for the up-and-coming election. He informed his wife of the imminence of this great presentation by the Republican Party, and she could hardly contain her excitement. Time to put the events of the previous week behind him, especially the unpleasantness of those couple of tarts, and concentrate on his campaign. He was prepared for the televised head-to-heads with his opponent, President Jimmy Carter, and had no qualms about any subjects that would be discussed. He felt certain he could handle Carter, if only through verbal bullying, confident that most of the people who voted had not a clue what they were voting for. In fact, a chimpanzee would have more of an idea than the average voter, was Crump's analysis. Therefore, it was only necessary to shout louder than your opponent. The debates where just a little knowledge was necessary – foreign policy and defence – he would copy the manifesto of his primary opponent, Ronald Reagan. Crump would just alter the wording a little to mean the same. It didn't matter so long as the next president was a Republican named Ronald Crump.

It was Monday morning when an announcement came on the television and radio channels from the Republican Party headquarters.

'For the forthcoming presidential campaign, we in the Republican Party will nominate Congressman Ronald Crump as our candidate for the White House.'

'Did you hear that, darling?' said Tracy, jumping for joy, with Tarquin looking on with that now-familiar expression of superiority.

'Yes, dear, it's official now. The race for the White House is on. We are under starters' orders,' Ronald enthused.

'Can I tell all my friends now?' asked Tracy.

'Yes, of course, dear, you tell the whole world if you wish and tell them we are going to win. I mean, how can I lose with you by my side? We make a formidable team, you and me!'

The first televised debate between the two hopefuls for the White House, the incumbent Jimmy Carter and challenger Ronald Crump, would be on defence. Both camps were geared up for the debate, which would be viewed by millions. The Crump camp had laid out their strategy and their man would go on the offensive.

Crump immediately attacked the Carter administration's defence policy, accusing Jimmy Carter's government of weakening the United States in the face of Soviet aggression. He went on the attack over the Strategic Arms Limitation Talks (SALT) II which were aimed at limiting the number of warheads a missile could carry. These talks differed from SALT I, which merely dealt with the actual missiles, the delivery system, not the number of warheads each missile could carry. Nothing was actually signed after these talks due to the alleged Soviet invasion of Afghanistan. The Western governments, including the United States, claimed the USSR had invaded, a position supported by the ever-dependable capitalist media. However, given a more objective examination, the invitation theory is the more realistic of the two. The socialist government of Afghanistan had asked the Soviet Union for help against Muslim fundamentalist rebels, the Mujaheddin guerrilla forces who wished to put the country back centuries, denying women any of the rights they had gained – and although nothing was signed, both sides abided by the terms of the SALT II talks.

Crump argued these favoured the USSR and criticised Carter for not taking a more proactive role in backing the forces of the Mujaheddin against communism. Carter countered this with the accusation that Crump, with his hawkish policies, would plunge the country into an unwinnable war with another superpower.

'Afghanistan is within the Soviet orbit of influence, as Nicaragua is within ours, so the best way of registering our disapproval at Soviet actions was to pull out of the talks.'

The reality was, Crumps Arms and Real Estate were supplying the rebels and making money hand over fist in the process. Ronald kept this under wraps, hoping Carter would not raise the issue. Unlike Crump, Jimmy Carter played a straight game and bringing in Crump's business interests was, to him, below the bar. If the situation was reversed Ronald Crump would have had no such scruples. Crump acknowledged the talks were never signed by the United States, but Carter still abided by the terms of them, 'as did the USSR', Carter countered.

Crump then accused Carter of being willing to sign up to the talks, but that Congress had refused Carter permission. 'A good thing they did,' said Crump.

'A man like you, Congressman,' Carter responded, 'cannot be trusted with our nuclear arsenal.'

Crump counter-attacked: 'A man such as yourself will weaken the USA and turn us into a second-rate power.'

The debate lasted about two hours after which both men shook hands. Public opinion as to who won was split, as were the media. The result was a draw.

The following day Tracy took Tarquin to prep school and the topic of conversation was the presidential debate. Tracy was still getting to know the other mothers, all of whom took to the likeable young woman.

'You don't remember me, do you?' a voice asked. 'I was at your wedding. I'm the wife of your husband's best man, James Rothschild,' Susie informed Tracy.

'Of course, how blind of me not to recognise you! Would you like to go for a coffee?'

'Love one,' said Susie, and the pair formed an easy friendship almost straight away. Susie told Tracy how their husbands, James and Ronald, had met at Wetherspoons many years previously. She regaled Tracy with some of the antics, as children, they and the rest of the gang, herself included, got up to! After they had finished their coffee and discussion about the past they found out they both lived quite near each other, so they walked home together. The discussion moved in the direction of the presidential debate the previous evening, and both women agreed Ronald had the edge over Carter. They arranged to meet later on and collect their children together. Tracy and Susie would become good friends, as had Megan and Mary Rothschild all those years ago.

Tracy and Susie arrived to collect their children, Tarquin Crump and Quentin Rothschild, and the topic of conversation was still the presidential debate. It was at this point the other mothers realised Tracy was the wife of one of the candidates. With this knowledge they all suddenly wanted to be her friend, or at least on first-name terms with the possible next First Lady. The only genuine one among them was Susie Rothschild. Tracy was aware what these women were doing but being the placid person, she was polite with each of them engaging in discussion about their children. But for the most part, she stuck to Susie.

The next televised debate between the two contestants was again surrounding Carter's foreign and domestic policies. Crump attacked Carter over his decision to pardon all 'draft dodgers' during the Vietnam War.

'You took it upon yourself to grant pardons to all these traitors, cowards who refused to answer their country's call to arms. Unforgivable! Heroes are regarded like unwanted trash and these cowards receive a presidential pardon. It beggars belief and is beyond contempt,' Crump argued.

Carter countered, 'The war was unpopular, even unconstitutional, as no state of war was declared. There was never Congressional approval which, if you had taken the trouble, Congressman, to read back papers of Congress you would be aware. Therefore, I decided to pardon people who had technically broken no law, as no war had been declared. Perhaps you, Congressman, would prefer the rule of law to be changed to "guilty till proved innocent" instead of the present, "innocent till proved guilty"? What kind of dictatorial president will you be, Congressman?'

386 ★ THE MISOGYNOUS PRESIDENT

'I will be a president who will always put America first. The interests of the USA and its people, not a few cowards, will always take preference on my watch. The watchwords will be "America first" and always,' the Republican candidate ranted.

On this patriotic note Crump scored some points, questioning Carter's patriotism. Crump then attacked the Carter administration's decision to give back the Panama Canal to the Panamanians. 'This,' he argued, 'once again weakens the US position on the world stage. That canal is vital to our interests. Even Teddy Roosevelt recognised its strategic importance.' Crump was referring to the incumbent President at the time, the early twentieth-century, when the canal was dug. Teddy Roosevelt called the Panama Canal, the 'Big Ditch,' vital to US interests at the time, linking the Atlantic and Pacific oceans. The situation on the American continent at the time of this debate was somewhat different to that of the time when the canal was constructed.

'We can still use the canal. Panama is not a hostile country. We cannot continue holding parts of other people's lands just because one day, as you would appear to want, a hostile government might emerge,' Carter stated. On this point Carter regained some of the ground lost over the draft dodgers' pardons. Many people over the age of forty-five supported Crump's views on draft dodging; equally, many between eighteen and forty were less sympathetic towards Crump and favoured Carter's pardoning approach. The consensus in the various media was this debate was a score draw.

Ronald Crump was in his Crumps Arms and Real Estate office when a letter arrived, causing the presidential hopeful concern. The letter was from the attorney of Sharon Storm and Stephanie Lust (real names Sharon McKinley and Stephanie O'Donnell), the two call girls Crump had had an altercation with at the hotel during the arms convention. He had thought all that was water under the bridge but it appeared not. Crump immediately contacted his own attorney, Marcus Bendall, in a state of near panic. The last thing he wanted with the presidential race gathering pace was these two raising their ugly heads and telling the world all about him.

'Don't panic, Ron,' the attorney told him, 'or try not to. I'll contact their man and arrange a meeting; that way we can find out what these two ladies want. It appears on the surface they are after compensation for an assault causing actual bodily harm. Would there be any truth in that?'

Crump hesitated.

'The truth now. Did you or did you not cause one, or both, of them grief?'

'Yes, Marcus, but it was their fault, they started shouting and screaming and swearing. I had to shut them up.'

'You did that all right by the sound of this. It will be their word against yours.'

Ronald assumed, wrongly, that this would not be a contest: two hookers against one of the most highly respected businessmen in the United States. Surely the jury, any jury, would believe him.

'Not necessarily, Ron, not in 1980; twenty, even ten years ago, no problem, but today it is not as clear-cut as back then.'

'I see,' said Ronald, a little downbeat. 'Well, you arrange the meeting with their attorney. Who is he, by the way?'

'Augustus Cleveland, he's good. Always plays a straight bat, no messing. I'll arrange a meeting with him and see if we can keep this away from the courts and the media.'

Ronald then hit on an idea, or he thought he had. 'What about a few dollars, a few thousand dollars, to the jurors?'

'Are you stark raving mad? As you know I tend from time to time to twist things a little but tampering with a jury these days? You'd get time, Ron, wealth or no wealth, and the White House would be a distant memory. No leave it to me, I'll sort something out.'

Bendall contacted Cleveland and arranged a meeting between the two attorneys at Cleveland's office. Marcus Bendall would need all his cunning in this one and would have to concede quite a lot to keep his client out of the public eye. Apart from his presidential campaign, which would be derailed beyond repair, there was also Tracy to consider. How would she take such a shock? It would almost certainly signal the end of their marriage. No, he must keep proceedings local and out of court. Bendall knew Cleveland reasonably well. They were not drinking buddies, but nevertheless they were on first-name terms.

On arriving at the office Cleveland greeted Bendall. 'Marcus, do come in and take a pew.'

The two men shook hands and had an introductory drink to break the ice.

'Now, Marcus, you wish to discuss your client's problem with the pending damages claim by Sharon and Stephanie?'

'Yes, that's right, Augustus. Come on, we can sort something out. They are, after all, only a couple of hookers.'

'Careful, Marcus, they are my clients and I will defend them as I would anyone else. They have a case and you know it, otherwise you would not be here.'

The two men pondered over the case and swapped points of law for two hours and eventually came to an agreement which they would put to their clients. If the women agreed to drop their claim in court, then Ronald Crump would afford them $200,000 each, providing they were sworn to secrecy. They would also hand over the tapes of the events that occurred that evening which Sharon had in her possession. The two women and Crump would sign an affidavit in the presence of both attorneys.

'I think I'll be able to sell this to Ronald, Augustus.'

'You'd better be able to, otherwise it's goodnight White House, Marcus.'

Bendall was all too aware of the consequences for his client should Ronald, for whatever reason, refuse the offer, or, for that matter, if the women did!

Crump agreed to this deal under duress, until the alternatives were pointed out to him. He had already worked out a scheme where, if he kept everything quiet, he could cream most of the compensation payout from his election campaign budget. This would be wholly illegal but only if he got found out. He would have a story made up as to where the missing money had gone should any campaign accountant get a little nosey.

Crump accompanied Bendall to the meeting with the two women and Cleveland.

'Listen Ronnie don't refer to them as "hookers", "prostitutes", "escorts" or any other name pertaining to their employment. We are not holding a trial here, merely going through the formalities of signing a legally binding document incumbent on both parties.'

Sharon McKinley and Stephanie O'Donnell were with Augustus Cleveland, who approached Bendall with a handshake.

'Got the cheques, Ronnie?'

'Yes, here they are, two hundred thousand dollars each.'

Here was where the problem arose. The time was five o'clock and Crump had a live election debate with Carter at six thirty, so time was short. In his haste Crump forgot to sign the affidavit, which was also missed by both attorneys. Sharon and Stephanie, however, did not miss this detail but kept their mouths shut. They took their copy of the document which had been signed by them and bade the lawyers a grand farewell. To all intents and purposes, the document was null and void! They had Crump in their pocket should they wish to run the risk of a blackmail trial if Crump decided to play awkward. They knew he had influence and was well capable of hiring thugs to get his money back, so they decided to keep quiet for the foreseeable future. They had surrendered the incriminating tapes to Crump's attorney, which were now of less relevance than the unsigned affidavit. They had also copied the tapes as a backstop just in case, but the unsigned document was far more important.

Ronald Crump set off for the television studios in the assumption that this matter was over. For the time being it was, but eventually it would come back to haunt him.

Both men arrived at the television studio for the live debate. Tonight's subject was to be the economy and unemployment. Jimmy Carter was concerned with keeping inflation low even with the risk of creating unemployment. Crump too was eager to tackle inflation and had his own plan to deal with unemployment and tackle the problem of inflation. Both these diseases are symptoms of capitalist economics and could be sorted easily by abandoning capitalism. Neither of these political warriors would even contemplate such a move: what, communism? Never. At any rate, it would be unemployment where Crump would attack Carter, whose record was not great in this area.

The Carter administration had advocated and enacted an extension of the Employment and Training Act, first introduced by the Nixon administration. This act aimed to provide training for the unemployed, granting them jobs in the public service. Of course, this would not provide work for all, but it would begin to address the problem. The truth was, neither man had much idea how to solve this problem within the realms of capitalism.

With the means of production in private hands, no employer can be compelled to employ labour. To the employers, labour is a commodity to make profits. If a profit cannot be made then there is no use for the commodity. This is Marxism working in reverse to suit the bosses: all agree the only commodity the working class has to sell, as a commodity, is their 'labour power'. If this labour power is not profitable then what is the purpose of purchasing it? From the employer's viewpoint, there is no purpose.

Crump then came in with his solution for unemployment and tackling inflation. To spur economic growth, he advocated huge tax cuts for the wealthiest and modest cuts for the workers; the lower down the scale, the less the cut. He wanted a huge reduction in government spending, thus reducing the size of the public sector, which was the opposite of what Carter wanted. Carter wanted to increase the public sector to provide work under the Employment and Training Act, but if Crump had his way the public sector would be shrunk to about half its size with private companies taking over many of the tasks or, as Crump called it, the 'slack'.

'Tax cuts,' argued Crump (or perhaps somebody who had an idea on the subject had told Crump), 'will spur economic growth.'

If anybody had asked Crump what he meant by 'economic growth' he would have struggled to give a digestible, literate answer. It was on the unemployment front where Ronald Crump showed his true colours. Crump claimed many if not all the unemployed were just too lazy to work and would not take work even if it were offered. This was highly offensive and completely untrue, but it suited the US bourgeoisie to think it, or pretend to.

'Therefore,' continued Crump, 'I propose to launch a scheme which would conscript the unemployed onto a labour plan which would be run and organised by the private sector. The scheme would be similar to conscription to the armed forces and would be compulsory. It would provide private employers with a labour force, which could also be used by the public sector if needed. Failure for any unemployed person to register for this scheme would give the impression they did not want to work and could result in a custodial sentence for repeat offenders.'

Jimmy Carter countered this ridiculous scheme which in any free country must be condemned as fascism, citing Hitler's remedy for curing unemployment in Nazi Germany – which was Crump's blueprint. He accused Crump of steamrolling unemployed people into slave labour, and what would happen if no employer needed them?

Carter was very careful how far down this road he ventured, fully aware he was approaching a communist answer which neither man wanted. Jimmy Carter then accused Congressman Crump of scapegoating the unemployed for the country's economic woes.

'No, Mr President, I'm not scapegoating or blaming the unemployed in any way for the country's economic problems. That honour goes to you and your administration, sir.'

Ronald Crump then went on to explain what would happen if placements could not be found for the unemployed, or those for whom placements could not be located.

'I propose we build huge camps where they would reside collectively until an employer needs them. That way we will pay no unemployment benefit as they will not need it; they will work in the camp. If a placement comes up they will be released from the camp and return home with a job.'

'You mean, Congressman, put the unemployed into a form of prison, don't you?'

'Not at all, it would be a social answer to a social problem, firm but fair, and society will thank us for it one day. The problem with you on that side of the House,' said Crump, his voice now raised, 'you oppose anything which is beneficial to society. You would end up giving these people easy lives for ever,' he continued. Crump went off on a political rant, implying people once in employment purposely put themselves out of work to claim state benefits.

At this point the time for the debate was over and again the customary handshake, now a little weaker than after the first debate, took place like the pointless ceremony it was.

The following day a huge protest march was organised by the unemployed against Ronald Crump. Many banners bore pictures of Crump surrounded by a swastika, the sign of the German NSDAP or Nazi party. The march was intended to collect more people on the way and culminate at the Republican Party headquarters. Organisers estimated around 80,000 to have been on the demonstration, though police estimated, as was usual on such occasions, that there was actually less than half that number. Such marches by the unemployed, trade unions, women's groups, black equality organisations and black liberation groups along with lesbian and gay rights organisations would increase in number over the coming years.

★ ★ ★

Tracy was taking Tarquin to school and called for her new friend Susie on the way.

'Did you see the debate last night?' asked Susie. 'I thought your husband was correct, there are those who do not want to work. He may have overgeneralised but in essence he was right. Good luck, Ronnie, is what I say.'

Tracy was a little taken aback because she thought her husband's argument about the unemployed was wrong in its entirety. For the very first time she was a little embarrassed that he was her husband. She knew she should keep out of Ronald's political world, but she had not expected a sensible woman like Susie to agree with him. Tracy decided the best way out of this was to say nothing. She had few enough proper friends, excluding the gold-diggers, and she did not want to lose Susie. If Susie persisted, then she would pass on her opinion in a tactful way.

On arriving at school all the mothers, eager to ingratiate themselves with Tracy, all rushed towards her, frightening the petite woman half to death.

'Great speech, Tracy. We all think your husband will make a great president,' was one of the less grovelling orations.

If Mrs Carter had been there instead of Tracy, these women would have made exactly the same overtures to her. The problem Tracy had was she agreed with neither her husband nor these women. She would have to say something if this diatribe of rubbish which insulted her intelligence continued. Fortunately, things quietened down as all the children headed for their appropriate classes and their mothers went their own way. Tracy then walked back with Susie, grateful she did not bring the subject up again.

The final live televised debate was due out in three days' time and one of the subjects was one Ronald had been waiting for: the Iranian hostage crisis. The main theme of the debate was the subject and question of immigration. Crump had very strong anti-immigrant views which he intended transmitting to the nation. He would tie this in with the Iranian crisis, rounding off the campaign in true right-wing fashion. He was certain that middle America, whose votes he particularly counted on, would come around to his way of thinking.

At the gymnasium where Peter Tillerson trained, political opinion was the opposite of what Crump stood for. The athletes decided to oppose Crump with a view to launching an anti-Crump campaign. As we know, the athletes at the gym consisted of black people, particularly in the discipline of boxing, as well as Eastern Europeans, and white Americans. The athletes committed themselves to countering Crump's vile policies and spreading the word to other gymnasiums. They would call themselves American Athletes Against Crump (AAAC) and hoped to enrol every gym in the country in their campaign. This was a tall order as there were thousands of gymnasiums in the USA. For now, they decided to concentrate on the larger and better-known ones, such as their own.

They highlighted their own Joe Frazier, the black boxer from the gym who had once been world heavyweight champion, as their standard bearer. Joe accepted this position without reservation. Peter was elected publicity officer with responsibility for transmitting information to other gymnasiums and sporting venues. In the southern states where the far right of the Ku Klux Klan had a strong presence, part of the job for the black athletes was to counter their extremist white supremacist positions. Up till then, this racist body prevented black athletes getting a foothold in sport. The campaign received great support from across the northern states where support was almost unanimous. The southern states were a little more mixed with the Klan gaining support in a minority of venues where an unofficial and illegal 'white only' policy was applied. The AAAC decided that one of the first things they would do was boycott the southern state gyms where this unofficial apartheid was practised. It was also arranged to hold a national convention of the AAAC should Crump be elected. In the meantime, their job was to campaign against such an eventuality.

The evening of the final televised debate came around and Crump was in bullish form. He took the initiative against the wimpish Carter, attacking from the word go. Crump was aware that Middle America was concerned with the levels of immigration into the country, so this would be his starting point.

'We have a problem, a big, big problem in the United States, that being the number of non-Americans walking our streets.' This was Crump's opening salvo. 'I intend to reduce immigration with a view to stopping all non-European people coming in. We have a skills problem, not a labour problem. What is the point of me initiating my plan for eliminating unemployment if we import the problem from Sub-Saharan Africa? No point whatsoever. We must stop this mongrelisation of our white race, allowing in only the skills we require from Europe, Western Europe primarily. After Sub-Saharan Africa I notice we have a large number of Muslims entering our country from lands which may be considered hostile to the US. This influx I propose to stop. Finally, we are playing host to a number of Southern and Central Americans, Nicaraguans, Bolivians and Mexicans. This too will cease.'

Jimmy Carter countered this clearly racist policy. 'What you really mean, Congressman, is all non-white immigration will stop. You will only allow White Europeans into our country. Why don't you just say what you really mean? You, Congressman, are a racist which this country does not need, least of all inhabiting the White House.'

Crump came back. 'Not true, sir, not true at all. You, as usual, are ignoring what every sane American can see: we have too many immigrants. You are trying to twist what I'm saying in order to further your multicultural campaign with no consideration for the consequences. I, sir, am not a racist. I am looking after the interests of the USA. I am also looking after the interests of Sub-Saharan Africa. If all their people with intelligence are over here, who then will those countries rely on to solve their own economic, medical and social problems?'

The fact that many problems faced by Sub-Saharan African countries are the symptoms of United States and other so-called developed world countries foreign policies appeared not to enter Crump's head.

Crump then moved on to the Iranian hostage crisis and the Carter administration's handling of it. Crump claimed Carter was too soft, misusing the military option by giving the army half instructions, tying one hand behind their back, and refusing those hawkish generals permission to take military action, thus tying their hands. The military assault to save the US hostages resulted in the deaths of eight US servicemen, one Iranian and the destruction of two helicopters. Crump argued a full-scale military intervention was needed, not a half-hearted military assault. He never once considered what the response of the Soviet Union would be to such folly, let alone the United Nations.

'You called this "Operation Eagle Claw", which turned out to be more like "Operation Blunt Claw". You humiliated the USA in the eyes of the world when you ordered this assault on the 24th April 1980, humiliating Irish America on their national day.'

Crump had no love of the Irish; he was using them for opportunist reasons. This was the anniversary of the Easter Rising in Ireland 1916, not officially a national day but very important in Irish eyes. He continued. 'A direct military no-kid-gloves invasion of Iran would have sorted the problem, released the hostages and regained our primacy as the world power.'

'Your strategy, if that is what you have just proposed is,' said Carter, 'would have possibly led to a third world war with the USSR. They would not have stood by and watched their interests in the Middle East compromised.'

Carter's counter-attack was perfectly true. The Soviet Union would not, as we shall see later, stand by and watch the USA take over the Middle East, which was what Crump was indirectly suggesting.

Opinions on this debate fluctuated within the media, some outlets claiming victory to Crump, other more liberal news channels and newspapers claiming Carter came back to place some great counter-punches. Carter, according to one paper, exposed Crump for the racist he was. Opinion was split. This was the final debate and the handshakes were becoming increasingly feeble. The first debate ended with a firm and sincere handshake, the second a little less so and after this final confrontation between the two men the hands barely made contact.

The athletes' anti-Crump campaign was gathering momentum. Peter and the other sportsmen and women had listened with horror to Crump's political position, and all agreed their campaign must be intensified. Peter had now leafleted and faxed every gym in the country and was embarking on universities which had sporting faculties. This would prove a relatively successful campaign. Interestingly, it was Yale University, Crump's former establishment, which contacted Peter first. Perhaps more specifically, it was Yale students' union which contacted him, sending him a faxed letter with the following content:

Dear Mr Tillerson

It was with great interest and support that we received your fax outlining your concerns and fears in the event of a presidential victory for the Republican, Ronald Crump. We here at Yale students' union share your worries as we did when the same Ronald Crump studied real estate here. We made it plain to him that the union would not tolerate the kind of racist and sexist, to say nothing of misogynist, comments he was renowned for making while at private high school. We monitored Crump and kept him quiet from the day he darkened this university's doors.

We welcome and support your campaign to counter the racism as epitomised by this vile politician and our athletes fully endorse your anti-Crump campaign. Not only our athletes but the student union in general at Yale are fully behind you and wish the campaign well.

We would appreciate any updates you may have on coming events and venues. We would very much like to help and become involved in any way we can.

Yours sincerely

Larry Johnson (Students' Union, Yale)

Peter Tillerson was very encouraged by this and many other positive replies to the campaign against Ronald Crump and all he stood for. Not only were responses coming from universities with sporting facilities, but also from many bodies, societies and organisations not involved in sport. The campaign base was expanding.

The gymnasium set up a committee and after the final televised presidential debate it was decided to call a national demonstration opposing the Republican candidate. It was decided to make the campaign an anti-Crump initiative to be held in October, opposing racism, misogyny, xenophobia, homophobia and all the negatives espoused by Ronald Crump. It was not intended to be a rallying call or election support campaign for Jimmy Carter.

Other organisations of the left wing and socialist leanings ranging from hard-line Marxist revolutionaries to moderate left-wing organisations were beginning to stir. One such group was the New York Women's Solidarity Group fronted by Colette Hill, nee Lugosi, who had known Crump as a young girl. Colette was now married to a radical trade unionist, Joe Hill. She had been involved in radical feminist groups since her mid-teens and had met her husband on a left-wing rally. She wrote a letter to Peter reminding him of their childhood friendship when she hung out with Ronald Crump and the rest of the gang. She also reminded Peter, who was delighted to hear from her after all these years, of the incident at Crump's eleventh birthday party. She pointed out in her letter, as well as well as voicing support for the campaign, the analysis she reached regarding that incident:

I thought his assault on my friend Lucy was perhaps a sign of his immaturity. I realise now how wrong this analysis was and what we witnessed that day was a microcosm of what we have today. This man has every chance of becoming president of the United States and must be stopped by all reasonable means.

Our group will be attending the national demonstration in October. I personally look forward to renewing our old acquaintance.

In Solidarity
Colette Hill

Peter was delighted with this 'blast from the past' and shared her enthusiasm. They agreed to meet for a coffee in the city, where Peter was also introduced to Colette's husband. They agreed to expand the campaign once the initial aims had been realised into a mass movement against racism and fascism and the growing problem of misogyny. Joe committed himself to promote the campaign through the American Federation of Labour, a large confederation of trade unions in the United States. Colette told her husband she was in great admiration of Peter having started the campaign. Tillerson corrected her.

'The gym at which I train collectively began the idea, and it has spread. The former heavyweight champion, Joe Frazier, trained there and has lent his weight and support to the campaign. The present champion, Michael Spinks, has also given his support as has perhaps the greatest of them all, Muhammad Ali.'

'It is a great initiative, Peter,' expressed Joe Hill, 'and I believe we can get the whole trade union movement behind it. I shall speak in favour and support of the whole operation.'

Joe agreed to fax various trade unions and Colette backed this by saying she would liaise with groups such as Lesbians for Freedom, black liberation groups and of course her own organisation, New York Women's Solidarity

Group (NYWSG). Colette assured Peter she would fax all these groups as she had built up many contacts over the years.

Soon after this meeting, Colette went to a feminist meeting which was attended by the Hollywood superstar Jane Fonda, the veteran anti-Vietnam War campaigner and supporter of civil rights. Colette never took much notice of a person's fame or reputation – to her all were equal – so she approached the actress with a view to securing her support for the October demonstration.

'I'd be delighted to not only give my support, Colette, but if you wish I could speak,' the superstar said. 'I don't want to steal the limelight from anybody else, so do check with your committee first.'

'Thanks, Jane, I will and either way I'll look forward to seeing you there. I shall inform you of the exact date and venue as soon as I know. I strongly expect New York will be the place.'

The date was set for 8th October 1980 in New York City centre as the venue, subject to police approval. It was hard to see how the authorities could refuse such a large demonstration though Dwight Connman, the NYPD Commissioner, tried. He reasoned a demonstration of this size and nature could represent a threat to the peace. However, he was also aware a downright refusal could result in trouble and he could not afford to allow his friendship with Ronald Crump to be seen as clouding or influencing his decision. Connman therefore passed the book to the Assistant Commissioner who carried less baggage. After consultation and in the perceived spirit of free speech, it was decided to give the demonstration the go-ahead.

The police gave permission for the demonstration to begin in New York's Manhattan area and agreed to keep a relatively low profile. The organisers expected a huge turnout and were not to be disappointed. Banners from many organisations were present, from the Black Panthers movement to various women's organisations. The trade unions were also well represented with hundreds of banners visible from those affiliated to the American Federation of Labour (AFL), as promised by Joe Hill. At the time of high political tension in Northern Ireland, banners expressing support for Irish Republicanism were also present. But the most numerous banners being held aloft were those depicting Crump as a fascist.

The organisers claimed there was in excess of 100,000 on the march, a figure which over the next year or so would be dwarfed. The main speakers were Jane Fonda, the Reverend Jesse Jackson, a leading civil-rights activist, and Joe Hill from the AFL. The message was loud and clear: Ronald Crump and his vile policies were not welcome here. As large as the demonstration was, it would be the election result, to be announced early in December, which would be the final arbiter. The demonstration went off peacefully with few incidents of concern. The organisers and speakers had all appealed for calm in the face of what many claimed were deliberate police provocations. This was despite the low profile the forces of law and order adopted. Not low enough, it would appear, for some.

As previously described, Ronald Crump was a tall slender man of an almost Mediterranean complexion. With the televised election campaigning over he had taken to sporting a short moustache about two inches in width just below his straight nose, adding to his already dark appearance. This gave Crump a kind of triple hybrid appearance between a very young Oswald Mosley, the founder of the British Union of Fascists; Adolf Hitler, who needs no introduction; and the actor Tyrone Power. Crump liked to slick his dark brown hair back, giving him a stylish and polished demeanour.

Early polls had Crump and Carter neck and neck, and right up to polling day it was anybody's guess as to who would be the next occupant of the White House. With election campaigns finished and demonstrations finally over, it was eyes down for the result. December came in what appeared the blink of an eye. The problem with the US presidential electoral system is it can be and is often misleading. Contradictions and ambiguities are frequent as the winner is not necessarily the one who receives the most popular votes. The voting system is known as the 'Electoral College' and it is the result of this voting which decides the outcome irrespective of the number of votes cast for an individual. It is necessary for the winner to secure at least 270 Electoral College seats to claim victory.

To the surprise of many, it was looking like Crump would edge it. The 1980 election result was as follows: Carter, Jimmy, Democrat: 277 electors, Crump, Ronald, Republican: 304 electors. This meant Crump had secured above the required number of Electoral College votes as had Carter, but it was Crump who had the larger number. However, if the result had been based on the popular vote, then Carter would have carried the day. Carter received 65,900,212 compared with Crump's 62,784,628 votes, meaning Carter had secured over 3,000,000 more votes than Crump. The Electoral College system of voting has frequently raised concerns regarding its questionable democratic nature.

Ronald Crump was the new president of the United States of America.

20

President Crump

It was not until 20th January 1981 that Ronald, Tracy and Tarquin Crump would take up residence at the White House. Ironically, on that date the Iranian hostages were released, due to former President Carter's efforts. However, Crump was determined to take the credit for his predecessor's achievement. Crump claimed it was the fear of him which forced the Iranians' hand, but this was just wishful thinking by the new incumbent.

Tracy Crump, the former waitress and generally downtrodden former employee of the New York Hilton, was shortly to become the First Lady of the United States. Tracy was worthy of that title, unlike her husband. For Tracy, still oblivious of any wrongdoings by the monster she had married, it was the ultimate dream come true. Her beloved little boy, Tarquin, would spend at least the next four years in the White House. When the presidential results were announced, Tracy Crump was bombarded with telephone calls from her former workmates, offering genuine messages of congratulations. The management of the New York Hilton, those who had once bullied and ruled over her with a tyrannical grip, were now grovelling for her friendship. These former slave-drivers of Tracy and her colleagues were now bending over backwards to enrol her as their number-one friend.

Tracy still did not have a cruel or bad word to say of them. She also still thought her employers had given her the wonderful wedding present of a free reception and suite at the Hilton because she was a popular employee. The principle reason was actually because she was marrying one of the richest men in the United States. How would this gift promote the local management of the New York Hilton in the eyes of Ronald Crump? This was their principle consideration. Such a cynical thought never entered the head of Tracy Crump. This was the kind of person she was: nothing bad to say of anybody, not even the tyrants who had worked her half to death. The poor woman would eventually come down with a bang. Fortunately, her former workmates would always be there for her along with, perhaps more relevant, a new set of friends from a very different circle.

Young Tarquin was to be taught by private tutors within the confines of the White House. He would enjoy a lofty position even by the standards of the US bourgeoisie as the son of the president of the USA. When the time finally came for the family to leave the White House he, Tarquin, would attend the finest educational establishments in the land, that was, providing Dad did not make a mess of the job!

Before the family moved into the presidential residence, Crump was to have his swearing-in ceremony on 10th January. Here he would take the oath of allegiance and loyalty which for him, Crump, would be the most fantastical work of fiction since the Bible. Ronald Crump was already scheming to undermine the US Constitution and the checks and balances enshrined within it. These political checks and balances were primarily inserted to check the rise of the far left and defend the interests of the ruling classes of the USA. These checks enshrined the right of private property and the private ownership of the means of production, distribution and exchange as well as defending all the points and amendments of the US constitution. Much of the constitution Crump agreed with, particularly the 'right of citizens to bear firearms', which had over the years reaped great profits for his former company.

There were, however, certain checks and balances which were not to Crump's liking and it was these which he was scheming to dispose of. The checks and balances designed to defend the interests of the US bourgeoisie against the hard left could also, if necessary, be used to stave off fascism and the far right. Ronald Crump, president-elect, decided he wanted rid of the barriers which would prevent him imposing his form of far-right politics on the country. He dreamed of passing a United States version of Hitler's Enabling Act of 1933, which gave the Fuhrer all the powers he needed to make decisions without recourse to the Reichstag. Crump wanted to be able to unilaterally make decisions, and it was this aim he was privately, very privately, scheming to bring about.

The Christmas of 1980 was to be the last Christmas the Crumps would spend in their mansion for, at least in principle, four years. Ronald and Tracy, at her insistence, invited all the domestic helps to spend Christmas Day with the family. Ronald hated this idea of familiarity but went along with it to keep up the appearance of being a decent human being. Tarquin had all the trappings which had helped create the ogre he would be unfortunate enough to call his father, as the staff all bought the little boy gifts, similar to the three wise men in the story of Christmas. Fortunately for Tarquin, Tracy was nothing like Ronald's mother, Megan. Protective, yes, but contributing towards her son's ruination, a resounding no. The Crumps intended renting their home out to a well-to-do family, Mr and Mrs Gifford, for the duration of their stay in the White House. This way the building would be protected for the time they would be away, and an income would be coming in every month. Tracy wanted a clause put into the rental agreement safeguarding their employees' jobs, but Ronald prevented this.

'We cannot force our tenants to employ our staff,' he argued with certain justification; this was part of the nature the capitalist beast dictated.

Tracy then held a meeting behind her husband's back with all the staff. 'I would like to keep your employment open while we are away. My husband's job is not for life, after all. I would like to give all of you a verbal assurance that when we return I shall endeavour to find a place here again for all of you.'

The staff were doubtful this commitment could be kept but all agreed Tracy was genuine and sincere in her oration. She certainly meant every word of what she said, and they believed she would try.

With the Christmas and New Year period over it was now approaching the time for Ronald's inauguration ceremony. The 10th of January was the date set and many anti-Crump demonstrations were planned before and during the event. At this moment in time Tracy could not understand the animosity from sections of the people towards her husband. This would, of course, change within the first year. Crump had chosen Alf Slyme, who had been his running mate, as his vice-president. Slyme was one of those Bible-bashing, psalm-singing right-wing hypocrites whom Crump could control and manipulate simply by quoting some fictitious passage from the so-called 'Good Book'. If Slyme disagreed with anything Crump said, he would just find a quote, and this would keep his vice-president in check. Slyme would be the voice of the religious right in the White House and would represent this group well.

President Crump's inauguration was attended by an estimated 100,000 people. Due perhaps to the divisions in society over Crump and his extreme right-wing policies, the turnout was much lower than previous presidential inaugurations.

Now he was president, Ronald Crump was forced by US constitutional law to relinquish his interests, financial and managerial, in Crumps Arms and Real Estate. He handed over the reins of power in the company to Charlie Kearns and Bob Tomkinson respectively, or at least this was the official position. Privately, Crump ordered his leading henchmen not to do anything requiring executive consultation without consulting himself first.

He was planning to ostensibly support Saddam Hussein in his war with Iran and their leader, the religious maniac, Ayatollah Khomeini. Saddam had come to power, covertly backed by the CIA, in 1979 though he held unofficial power long before then. President Crump intended the Iraqis, and if possible the Iranians, to buy arms from his company, now under the control of Kearns and Tomkinson. The CIA were providing the Iraqis with information via their satellite network, which Crump was aware of, and Crumps Arms stood to make a fortune. As president he intended politically ruling the entire Middle East by proxy. His plan was well in place, and there was no way any arms deals could be traced back to him. At the same time, as president he would exert political influence in the entire area. If the Iraqis were to be victorious thus winning the war, President Crump would then remove Saddam from power and put in his place a more subordinate puppet. These were to be some of Crump's early initiatives once he was installed. These actions were wholly illegal, like much of US foreign policy, but international law does not appear to apply to that country. This situation was bad enough with a relatively sane man at the helm but with somebody as unstable as Ronald Crump, the dangers were infinitely more severe.

One of the first tasks for the new president was to choose his political team for the White House. He wanted young women in positions close to himself and picked Carol Barnes, a young undergraduate, as the White House press officer. Crump already had eyes on this young woman for extended breaks away. He would, however, find it significantly more difficult to have affairs behind his wife's back as president than he did as head of the Crump Corporation. As president, all eyes were on his every move and any assignations he might plan would be very risky indeed. Besides, if the young woman turned out to be an unwilling conspirator, Crump would find his presidency seriously under threat.

He decided to give the post of White House Chief of Staff to Clodagh O'Neill, a thirty-year-old former chemist whom Crump also had an eye for. He decided to allow vice-president Slyme to pick a small group to manage domestic policies, giving himself some freedom to deal with the more pleasurable aspects of the job. Crump was contemplating offering his old troubleshooter, Agnes Moorhouse, a position in the Oval Office. He would sleep on this one because he was aware he needed reliable people back at the ranch at Crumps Arms and Real Estate.

The Department of Defense he gave to Mr Vernon Greengrass, a retired army officer and a former mayor of New York. In the Department of State, Edward Crawford was the president's choice. He was a man of vast experience in many fields, but primarily in business. There would be no change in the Head of the CIA with Anthony James remaining in his position as Director General. Regarding the FBI, John Rowlands would remain at the helm, a decision which would one day come back to haunt Ronald. The Department of Transportation – under Crump, 'Deportation' may have been a more appropriate title – would go to Mr William Needy, while that of Immigration would be held by Mr Mitchel Bernstein. These two departments would be of special need and interest to Crump once his policies were in full swing.

President Crump would now begin his pursuit of sole presidential power with dictatorial authority without recourse to Congress. The Senate and House of Representatives would become symbols with neither meaning nor relevance, a bluff for the citizens of the US. He could not propose an Enabling Act as Hitler had on the back of the Reichstag fire – he could not burn down the White House and blame the communists – neither could he propose to Congress to transfer such powers to himself thus, effectively, dissolving itself. He would never get that through. The economy was doing reasonably well when he became president, therefore there was little if any appetite among the bourgeoisie for a fascist dictatorship. He did not have the economic, social and political advantages which Hitler had during the early thirties. There was no communist threat within the shores of the USA, only the threat of the other superpower, the Soviet Union, which was ever-present. People had become used to the so-called Cold War and no longer became afraid at its mention.

Despite all these perceived negatives (from Crump's point of view), he was still determined to become the sole dictator of the United States. The reader might conclude this man had lost the use of his mental faculties, and they would not be wrong. The president would consider his options for an Enabling Act and would discuss it with Vice-President Slyme, a man who was interested in his own self-advancement to anybody else's detriment.

The president summoned Vice-President Slyme to his private quarters for an informal chat. Here the two began formulating plans for total power for the president, and that he would be president for life. Elections, even those governed by the questionable Electoral College rules, would soon be an inconvenience of the past. President Crump was acutely aware he could not trust Slyme, and that he was a devious, cheating, lying hypocrite. Ronald's upbringing with Teddy had taught him all about this subject. However, Slyme would serve his purpose for what he had in mind.

'Come in, Alf, take a seat,' the president invited his deputy.

'Thank you, Mr President,' the good Christian replied.

'Alf, I need to pick your brilliant mind for a while with no distractions,' Crump said. When the vice-president heard his boss's plans he suggested deceit and gradualism as the best modus operandi. Slyme then proposed the Middle East as a starting point: intervention by stealth in Saddam Hussein's war with Ayatollah Khomeini and Iran. The United States' involvement in the already bloody conflict would inevitably lead to more deaths but this consideration meant little to Slyme. Vice-President Alf Slyme simply placed a different interpretation on any annoyances which interfered with his own self-gratification.

'Firstly, Mr President, put the United States forces' advisors at the disposal of Saddam. Do not inform Congress and see if we get away with it! If Congress kick up about it, we can claim to be politically naive as newcomers to our posts. If, as I expect, they do not catch on we have got away with it and can move to stage two of this plan.'

'What is the next part of our plan, Alf?' the President asked.

'We make US armed forces available to Saddam Hussein, as observers initially then, again if we get away with it, as combatants with the Iraqis. Remember, Mr President, you always have the sixty-day rule to fall back on.'

'Sixty-day rule?'

'Yes, it means in certain circumstances you can declare war in the national interest, without Congressional approval for sixty days. Remember the war in Vietnam was never declared by any president from Eisenhower to Nixon.'

'That's great, Alf, I picked the right man for the job in you.'

'If we tread carefully, I doubt we will get much opposition from our own side. It is those soft puddings in the Democratic Party who may present problems. The longer we go undetected the more difficult it will be for them to reverse any of our decisions.'

Crump was delighted his vice-president was prepared to be a willing accomplice. President Crump liked the way Slyme used terms like 'our plan' and 'we will get away with it'; this suited him down to the ground. If Congress found out what was going on, Crump would heap all the blame on his vice-president. President Crump decided the deceitful, gradual approach suggested by Slyme would give his plan for absolute power the best chance. He would adopt this approach and bit by bit, piece by piece, things would fall into place.

He decided to arrange a meeting with two of his most trusted generals, without informing Congress or Vice-President Slyme. Slyme had served his purpose for now so he had no need to know of this meeting. Crump knew these two generals, Batten and Howitt, both favoured a military dictatorship minus Congress. This was not exactly the same as what he had in mind, a fascist corporate dictatorship with him as supreme commander and dictator. They, the generals, would be subordinate to him, not the other way around. However, these two power-hungry military brass hats would serve his purpose for now, and should they inform Congress of Crump's plans he would deny everything and claim to have uncovered a military plot to subvert democracy.

At this meeting the purpose was to discuss the sending of six military advisors to Iraq to be at the disposal of Saddam Hussein. There would then be an offer of napalm explosives to the Iraqi leader, which he could use against Khomeini.

The two generals arrived. 'Come in gentlemen and take a seat. Would you like a drink?'

'Not on duty, Mr President,' the pair replied.

'I want to pick your brains in strict confidence, gentlemen,' Crump opened with. 'I want to send military advisors for Saddam against Ayatollah Khomeini, with a view to sending "boots on the ground" at a later date. What are your views on this, gentlemen?'

'Well, Mr President, we have a list of six perfect candidates for your initial plan, all good loyal men of the highest calibre. Can we assume that if we can do this without Congress finding out, and that it would serve as a precursor for a larger military venture?' Batten enquired.

'Of course, gentlemen, I have eyes on the whole Middle Eastern region. I've calculated the longer we keep it from Congress the longer we keep it from the Soviets. By the time they catch on it will be too late: the Middle East will be ours. When we send ground forces, supposedly to support Saddam, they will in reality be the first stage of an army of occupation,' the president finished up.

'Sounds great, Mr President,' Howitt said, 'but remember, sir, confidentiality is the key word.'

They were all in agreement, and the meeting came to a close.

Inside the Democratic Party there were some young guns who were permanently suspicious of President Crump. One such young Congressman was Bernie Sanders, a young progressive politician with, by the standards of the USA, left-wing views. He advocated a free-at-the-point-of-need health service funded by taxation, among other progressive ideas. The other was another young man called William Clinton, more of a liberal than Saunders' socialism, but equally suspicious of President Crump and his intentions. It would be these two men who would first voice concern at the President's behaviour on foreign policy and lack of communication with Congress.

Outside the world of US party politics the FBI chief, John Rowlands, was beginning to have doubts about the integrity of the New York Police Department and its chief, Dwight Connman. These factors, along with many other external issues, past and present, would eventually conspire against Crump and lead to his downfall. For now, though, everything in the garden appeared rosy for the president.

President Crump, now in his first month of the job, was sitting in the Oval Office when his thoughts drifted towards Carol Barnes, his press officer. His wife, Tracy, was in the other side of the White House in their private quarters so he decided it was a good time to call in Miss Barnes to give her instructions for her first press statement. He would send her to answer questions and when she returned he would try his hand with her. If she objected, which he felt she had no right to do, he would blame her poor performance at the press conference and sack her. He called her in.

'Miss Barnes, Carol, at today's conference they will ask about the poor turnout at my inauguration and you will tell them they are mistaken. The turnout was as good as any previous president's.'

This was not true: the popular vote figures in the election were reflected by the relatively low turnout for the inauguration of Crump and Slyme.

'They may also ask what my intentions are towards the USSR, which are of course perfectly honourable. I, like any other President, will defend US interests, preferably through co-operation with the Soviet Union,' he said, adopting a conciliatory tone.

'Very good, Mr President, leave things to me,' Carol said, eager to make her mark. President Crump had already had an introductory chat with Soviet leader, Leonid Brezhnev, on his first day in office. This was protocol dialogue between the two most powerful leaders on the planet. Good communications since the Cuban Missile Crisis had been an important feature of United States and Soviet relations. The hotline which was set up by President Kennedy and Soviet supremo of the day, Nikita Khrushchev, after the crisis over Cuba had thankfully never had to be used in anger. It was put in place to avoid any further misunderstandings occurring. Everybody, including the Soviets, hoped this president would be sensible irrespective of what his election campaign speeches had contained.

The media had gathered in strength for this first news conference. Young Carol Barnes had taken her seat at the head of the stage for her first event. She was a little nervous but confident of her own ability. President Crump watched with a certain envy at the young woman's performance, which was almost perfect. The first question was from CBS News, Daryl Morgan.

'What was the White House view of the relatively low turnout for the inauguration of President Crump and Vice-President Slyme?' he asked.

Carol remained seated and composed. 'The attendance at the inauguration was the same as that of former President Carter and allowing for the terrible weather conditions that day it could be argued the turnout was actually better. You were perhaps only looking at the front of the podium when, in fact, there were many present at the rear,' she said.

The next question came from Mark Austin of the *Chicago News*. 'Has the new president any plans to deal with the problem of unemployment out west?' he asked.

'To my knowledge, the president, along with the Department of Labour, have plans to encourage employers to invest "out west", which will include curbing trade union power to call lightning strikes, which have affected your part of the country for some years.'

Then came Tony Fools of the *New York Journal*. 'What about the slowly rising rate of inflation? Has the president any plans to stem this before it gets out of hand?'

'Yes, the president plans to impose a wage freeze to counter the inflation threat. He is working with the Department of Finance,' was the press officer's reply.

The reader may have noted the president's answers to all social laws were aimed at the working class and their trade unions. It is not the working class or the unions who increase prices; it is the bosses (in the private sector), yet this president was hell-bent on union-bashing, which would solve nothing.

'Allan Downey, ABC News,' came the cry from the floor.

Carol pointed him out and invited his question. 'How does the president aim to counter the Soviet threat in the Middle East?'

Carol was on the ball. 'Do you know of some threat which the president is unaware of, Allan?' was her answer.

President Crump was watching this with grudging admiration. He wanted to find an error which he could fire her for failing to satisfy his urges. However, he might have to wait for a while as the country would also be watching this maiden performance by her. Carol had, frankly, handled the news conference with the expertise of a veteran. If he fired her for a non-existent error many questions would be asked. All he wanted to do was treat the young woman as a sex slave, where was the harm in that? The problem here was that he, Crump, actually believed his analysis of his predicament. It would be all Carol's fault if she refused!

Another hard day over and the president retired to his private quarters for some quality time with Tracy. This was a man who, only a couple of hours earlier, had planned to rape his press officer. Now he was sitting down with his wife and child as if he was a faithful husband and true pillar of society. After tea he chatted with his wife.

'How was your day, darling?' he asked.

'Great, Tarquin's tutors are very professional. I think he will learn much more and much faster here than even at the best private school,' Tracy voiced.

'Yes, well, I am the president of the United States, you know, dear,' said Crump with a mega dollop of egocentrism about the comment.

'Yes, I do know, it must count for something, and I'm the First Lady,' explained Tracy uncharacteristically, as she never had hitherto boasted. Tracy was not the kind of person to allow the euphoria experienced with her new position to go unchecked. At root she was a homely person and very maternal and when the newness of being First Lady wore off, which would not take very long, she would revert back to her natural role: bringing up Tarquin, despite the presence of her servants. This was the real Tracy Crump, not the pretentious bourgeois which her new position tended to demand.

Tracy decided to broach the subject of what appeared to be her husband's unpopularity. 'Why do you think there's so much hostility towards you, Ron?' she asked.

'Godammit, Tracy, not you as well! It's the commies and people like that Colettte Hill on television trying to set me up. I vaguely knew her as a kid,' Crump let slip.

'What, you knew her?' Tracy interjected.

'Only through somebody else, a kid named Peter. I didn't know her well,' Crump lied. 'Don't you believe me?' 'Of course I do, darling, I just thought, oh, I'm not sure what I thought,' Tracy conceded.

★ ★ ★

With the basics of an aggressive and illegal foreign policy laid and his intentions of domination in the Middle East clear to his leading generals, the way was clear for the president to put into place his equally aggressive domestic policies. Immigration would be the cornerstone from which he would move towards a permanent right-wing direction. He intended stopping the immigration into the USA of all non-whites from outside the American continent and all Hispanics from Southern and Central America. His confidence was growing day by day and after he had his telephone conversation, as protocol demanded, with Soviet leader Leonid Brezhnev, he felt the world was his oyster. Crump had deployed six advisors to Iraq and the Soviets had no idea about this, as neither did Congress, and there had been no phone calls from Moscow enquiring as to the purpose of this action. This could only mean they were unaware of the US military presence. He felt he could now proceed with his next step. Before this, though, he felt it important to introduce domestic policies to Congress, or part of these policies, retaining the rest as a presidential secret!

President Crump had now been in office for six months and so far, he had had little difficulty keeping Congress at bay. With his domestic policies due for a reading, he anticipated this situation would change. His initial proposal would be outspoken; he knew that and was prepared for it, believing a large proportion of the United States electorate would agree with him. Immigration had been a pivotal point of his election campaign, but nobody was prepared for what he had in mind. He proposed to erect an electric fence, ten feet high, running the full length of the US border with Mexico. This was the major crossing point for people outside the USA to gain access and this fence would certainly stop that. The fence would carry 10,000 volts through it for the entire length of the border. Anybody touching this death trap would be immediately incinerated. Even his own allies in the religious right and neo-cons would be somewhat wary of such a move, which would amount to cold-blooded murder. This proposal could well be defeated because although he outnumbered the Democrats he would need the support of every Republican, not just those on the far right. For this reason, he needed a distraction, something which would draw attention away from this loony idea.

He would need to work closely with the departments of labour and transportation and both heads of these were his allies. The two men, Mitchel Bernstein and William Needy, were of the same fascist mindset as himself. Bernstein was in charge at the department of immigration and Needy held a similar position in the transportation (deportation) department. To this aim he summoned the two men, in much the same way he had his trusted generals, for a private chat at the White House. He arranged for Clodagh O'Neill to summon the pair to his office for the following morning.

The two men arrived wondering what this private meeting was about. They would not be disappointed when they heard the plan.

'Gentlemen, come in and take a seat,' was the now customary greeting offered by Crump when he wanted something.

They both sat down.

'What I'm about to say,' Crump said, 'is for now strictly confidential. I want you both to work together on a deportation strategy. You, Mitch, at immigration, will list all those of a coloured complexion for deportation. You, Bill, will look after the transportation of these people back to Africa.''But Mr President, some of these people have been in the US for generations,' exclaimed Bernstein.

'Doesn't matter, if their papers are even slightly inaccurate, they are here illegally. Therefore, I'm entitled to deport them. Some of the electorate will demand it, and I gave them a promise. After that I want you to look at those whose papers are in order. Find some discrepancies and act accordingly. In both cases make sure their papers are false! Those who are serving in the US armed forces can stay for as long as they remain combatants. Should they leave the armed services then they come under the same scrutiny as any other black person.'

President Crump then poured three brandies to seal the deal.

'What about those non-black immigrants whose papers are not in order?' Needy enquired.

'Well, Bill, we will have to make an example of some white illegals, the Irish, for example. They are known as "undocumented", so we begin with the blacks and then deport some, though not all, Irish. While you are doing this list, Mitch, I will try and get my plan for an electric fence on Mexico's border through Congress. I do not expect to be successful in this venture –

yet – but while we are arguing through both Houses, nobody will notice the deportations!'

At this point the president concluded and invited comments from his two allies.

'Why that's brilliant, Mr President,' said Mitch Bernstein, whose praise for the great man knew no bounds.

'Yes, poetry in motion, sir,' Needy complimented Crump.

Either these men were devoid of intelligence or they thought Congress believing such a scheme would work. Did they really imagine that convoys of black US citizens being deported would go unnoticed? If they did then the already bizarre world of US politics had really gone off the edge of a cliff. Nevertheless, President Crump was deadly serious, as were Bernstein and Needy.

Away from the White House and Congress, FBI chief John Rowlands was leading an enquiry into the NYPD commissioner Dwight Connman. Connman, as the reader will recall, was a friend of the president's. Rowlands had taken an interest in allegations of corruption at the top of the NYPD and during the course of his preliminary investigations one of his agents came across a case involving two women. These women had been jailed but allegations of an unfair trail from a junior officer in the force had come to light. The young policeman had been dismissed by Connman who refused to even contemplate examining some of the evidence, which suggested the innocence of the two women, Carol Hawkins and Linda Lowry. The case had involved Eugene Mathis, a friend of the current president's. The women were accused of administering a mild drug to this man, causing drowsiness and stomach cramps. Added to this, they also allegedly engaged in prostitution and stole his wallet.

The young officer had CCTV footage which showed a figure strongly resembling President Crump entering the apartment where the three were engaging in sexual activity. Footage also showed incriminating evidence in the pub where Ronald, Mathis and the girls had met on the evening in question. A camera showed Crump pouring something into Mathis's drink. All this had been deemed inadmissible by the trial judge and shortly after the case, with the women in prison, the young policeman was fired by Connman.

John Rowlands ordered the case to be re-examined, sending agents into the women's correction centre where the two were being held. What emerged prompted the FBI chief to order a full investigation into the case.

In Congress, President Crump was having a hard time selling his bizarre idea about building an electric fence. The Democrats were outraged and voiced their opposition accordingly. Bernie Saunders spoke up.

'Mr President, have you taken leave of your senses? If you press on with this murderous plan and, if we are all stupid enough to allow it, you could well be prosecuted for crimes against humanity. You, as the representative of the United States, will have heaped irreversible shame on this country and will go down, rightly, as a mass murderer. I call on you, Mr President, while the White House still holds respect and credibility, to withdraw this ridiculous proposal.'

These condemnations were becoming common as senators and congressmen alike, apart from the religious right and a few neo-cons, lined up to oppose the president. When the vote on the fence was put to Congress it was defeated out of hand. President Crump was not too bothered; when he finally had ultimate power the fence would go up anyway and besides, he had now bought time for his mass deportations, or so he thought. However, news spreads fast and on learning about the deportation strategy, many members of the public across the entire USA wrote letters of concern to their elected representatives. This was not regular, normal behaviour by the authorities and people wished to know what was going on.

Congressman William Clinton was the first to raise the issue as a matter of urgency in the House of Representatives. He demanded an explanation as to why US citizens were being transferred to holding camps for suspected deportation.

'On whose authority are these outrages being carried out?' the young politician asked.

Clinton demanded the heads of the departments of immigration and transportation be brought before the House to explain who gave them the authority and, indeed, orders to carry out these illegal acts. Neither Bernstein nor Needy, when they saw their president was going to hang them both out to dry, were eager to be the sacrificial lambs. They did not wish to lynch their chief but he, it appeared, was more than happy to hang them.

President Crump urged calm and denied having given orders for any deportations to either men. He did, however, concede: 'Gentlemen, there appears to have been some misunderstanding. I asked the Department of Immigration to compile a report of all foreign aliens, including those who had resided here for some years with questionable papers, who had criminal records. I had a view to bringing to Congress proposals, as I said in my election campaign, a Bill to deport or consider deportation of such individuals. It seems the entire request I made has been taken as a literal done deal by these two departmental heads.'

Congress were not entirely happy with this explanation but short of accusing their President of lying had to accept, reluctantly, his interpretation of events. President Crump, the man who had given the orders to his underlings, sacked both men out of hand. He accused them of acting far and above any request or instruction he had given them and told them they were therefore unfit to hold their positions. For the moment the two men, who were out of their depth, left quietly – but they would not forget what Crump did to them.

Carol Barnes was due her second news conference and the president once again briefed her on what to say and what not to reveal.

'Have you got a boyfriend?' he asked.

'No, Mr President, not at the moment.'

'Must get lonely at night on your own,' he continued.

'Mr President, with all due respect, is that the sort of question you should be asking?' the young woman remarked.

Crump thought hard: was this a come-on? 'I was only having a bit of fun, my dear,' he said. 'Go on then, Carol, don't let me down, which I know you won't. You're one of the few I can trust.' He heaped exaggerated credit on the young press officer to cover up his belittling remarks.

This press conference was going to be difficult as it concerned the suspected deportations and electric fence. The next day Carol took up her position on the stage.

'Is there any truth, or indeed is it an exaggeration, that the president was planning mass deportations similar to those Hitler carried out in his early years?' a reporter from ABC News asked.

'No, sir, there were no plans for any such deportations, but there were dangerous crossed wires, not of the president's doing, which may have led to giving that impression,' Carol replied. This answer appeared to satisfy the questioner but not everybody was convinced.

'Alan Galvin, *New York Times*. Is it true the president wished, or wishes to build an electric fence across the Mexican border, which could potentially kill hundreds if not thousands of people?'

'This was something which the president suggested hypothetically during his election campaign. He never intended for one minute building the thing,' she said. 'Yes, if such an abomination was erected it would kill hundreds of people, but it will not be built.'

Once again, the young graduate performed like a veteran and President Crump knew it would be a bad idea to upset this priceless ally.

President Crump had now been in office for ten months and was contemplating putting the second part of his aggressive foreign policy into action. He consulted his generals, not just Batten and Howitt, but the entire general staff of his armed forces. He wished to know their opinions on moving United States ground troops into Iraq, ostensibly to assist Saddam Hussein in his struggle against Ayatollah Khomeini. The six military advisors had been there four months now and the feedback was encouraging. What nobody suspected was that one of these military elites was working for the Soviet intelligence agency, the KGB.

'Gentlemen, what is the state of play in Iraq? Can I move ground troops in?'

Batten informed the president, 'Mr President, the Iraqi government have been told of our willingness to give them support troops, and a figure of twenty thousand foot soldiers to fight alongside the Iraqi army has been provisionally agreed.'

'Very well, gentlemen. Will we set a date for our invasion… whoops… invitation,' – rapturous laughter broke out – 'will we say December, a year to the month since my election victory announcement?'

Howitt agreed wholeheartedly with this date. 'Will I inform our men on the ground in Iraq to tell the Iraqi government we shall be sending two divisions early in December?'

'Yes, go ahead,' the president instructed.

Once this information reached the military advisors in Iraq the mole immediately informed the Kremlin. This had the potential to equal the threat to world peace posed by the Cuban Missile Crisis to world peace. A telegram arrived on the desk of Soviet leader, Leonid Brezhnev reading:

United States military involvement on the side of Iraq imminent stop – twenty thousand ground troops expected December stop – military advisors being present for some time aiding the Iraqi side. End

Obviously, the USSR could not stand idly by and allow these activities to go ahead unchecked. Brezhnev could not use the hotline set up after Cuba, as he would risk giving away his top agent. The mole had to be one of only six and the odds of blowing his cover were too great. Brezhnev summoned his commanders and between them it was decided to place ten divisions in Iran. It would be necessary to arrest the so-called religious leaders of that country, including Khomeini. The Soviets had bases in Egypt and Soviet Central Asia, which were well within reach of Iraq, in the time span permitted. Two divisions of paratroopers would be sent in advance, and would wait for the United States to move from their territories, which were further away. The Red Army would be in Iran and in control of the area awaiting the arrival of the US forces. During the Iranian religious revolution Khomeini had locked away some of the former Shah's finest airmen in prison. These fighter pilots were equal in ability to anything the USA or USSR had at their collective disposal. One of the first jobs of the Red Army would be to release these men for combat. The Soviet High Command formulated a plan to counter and if necessary repel the forces of the United States.

With the foundations laid for an aggressive, albeit illegal, foreign policy which bypassed the Department of Defence and the Secretary for Defence, Vernon Greengrass, President Crump now felt confident enough to formulate an equally aggressive domestic policy based on immigration. He believed Soviet leader Brezhnev had been bluffed by his articulate conversation with him months earlier so with the Middle East open to him, he believed attention on domestic affairs was now in order. During his election campaign, Crump had made much of immigration into the United States. His comments during this campaign were blatantly racist and were aimed at non-white immigration including Hispanics from Central and South America.

Fortunately, neither Congress nor the US population were as stupid as Crump had believed and the ridiculous fence plan had been defeated. The President's proposal for the fence was, as far as Congress were concerned, dead in the water. The genuine concerns of the US citizens regarding convoys of trucks carrying helpless black people to camps had, at least for the time being, stopped this act, which aped Nazi Germany. Crump had not allowed for this public backlash when news eventually leaked out. He thought that some people's misguided concerns over immigration meant he could just start deporting at will. There were, it was true, a tiny minority who shared this fascist opinion, but by no means a sizeable number. The United States, even those on the right of politics, were not yet ready, and did not need, fascism of any sort. Crump was going to find his pursuit of dictatorial power less than easy. Even the bourgeoisie, who, given the right economic conditions, would not shrink from fascism, did not agree with Crump's proposals.

The Soviet Union held the advantage, unknown to Crump or the minority of hawks in the US military, whom he had taken into his confidence. The USSR intended occupying Iran the moment they received news of the US troop movements towards the region. It was early December and now two divisions of US ground troops were heading for the Middle East where they would link up with Iraqi forces, ready for a full-scale invasion of Iran. The majority of US troops would come from their bases in Europe with others coming from special units in the USA under radio silence. On receiving this news the Soviet Union made their move. Ten divisions moved from Soviet Central Asia with two divisions of paratroopers going in advance. President Crump had kept the Department of Defence and Congress in the dark while he moved troops to the edge of war. It would take the US Army longer than their Soviet counterparts to reach their destination and Crump might have got away with this devious move had the USSR not been forewarned. He and his generals were in for a huge surprise, which would cause eruptions both inside Congress and on the streets of the USA.

On entering Iran, the Soviet Army had the advantage of complete surprise. The Revolutionary Guard of Iran, fanatical as they were, proved no match for the Soviet paratroopers. The Soviets arrested the Iranian government, including Ayatollah Khomeini, and placed them under 'protective custody'. They then gave the Iranian Armed Forces an ultimatum: surrender or face annihilation. They chose the latter option. The next task for the Soviets was to release the imprisoned former fighter pilots from the deposed Shah's air force. They told the men their former leader, the Shah, would not be returning but they would be fighting for the future of Iran against a combined Iraqi/US invasion attempt. The importance of these fighter pilots could not be overestimated should hostilities break out. They were as good as any on the planet. They would fly their own aircraft flying Iranian colours and these men were ready to go. They were delighted to be doing what they were good at and fighting their nemesis from the Iraqi fighter squadrons. The United States air force posed no fears at all for these pilots. This was of course music to the ears of the Kremlin: it would save their own pilots for later engagements.

'The enemy presents us with no fears or problems,' the pilot's commander assured the Soviet marshal in charge of operations.

Soviet Red Army troops were positioned right up to the Iranian/Iraqi border and were ready to cross into Eastern Iraq if the order came from Moscow. The United States troops, far fewer than the Soviets had, were at least one day away from their destination in Iraq. Then the order came from the Kremlin: 'Cross the border and occupy Eastern Iraq.' This was an order which was carried out with maximum efficiency. By now the CIA had become aware of Soviet military activity in the Middle East and of their own forces heading in the same direction. Congress was oblivious to anything untoward going on. This situation would now change rapidly as the news spread like wildfire. Their president had taken unilateral action with no consultation, neither with Congress nor his entire High Command. Furthermore, only a minority of Crump's trusted hawks, headed by Batten and Howitt, were aware of what was happening.

It was unlike the CIA to be so far behind with events, but their intelligence had been frustrated by the presence of the Soviet mole inside the six military advisors to Iraq. The CIA Director General, Anthony James, immediately contacted the White House to update the president. He needn't have bothered. Crump was more than aware and understood it would be a good idea to act surprised and shocked for now. What President Crump, clever as he thought he was, did not know was that the Soviets were waiting for the US troops, and in greater numbers. The man deserved an Oscar for his performance as he was told of the events unfurling in the Middle East, pretending to have no knowledge regarding the deployment of US troops into the area. Did he really expect people to believe that these divisions of the United States Army could be deployed without presidential knowledge?

Initially this tactic of blind oblivion to the situation appeared to at least buy him time. He then took the path of blaming his generals for acting unilaterally without his knowledge. He even hinted they could be involved in a military coup against him. At this point both generals, George Batten and Howitt, decided it was time to drop the president before he dropped them. For them to take the blame for this mess could result in their dismissal from the army and loss of very lucrative pensions. This would not be allowed to happen.

The CIA advised the president to order an immediate return to base to the troops still on their way to the Middle East. President Crump decided under the circumstances this was his best option. His plan for domination, he thought, could be put on hold for reconsideration at a later date. Crump, after he had hinted his two top generals were involved in a coup against him, expected these men to support another hare-brained scheme. Was he totally mad? The US Congress were now fully briefed of the situation and Batten with Howitt had decided to issue Congress with a full report which would, as he had tried with them, point accusing fingers at the president. They were not going to take the rap for this essentially unilateral decision by Crump to seize power. There were for the first time demands in Congress for the president's resignation which, for now, would not gain sufficient traction. The generals began to close ranks and distance themselves from their Commander in Chief. Remember, Crump, no matter his high opinion of himself, was very much a novice.

This state of affairs would not last as more and more allegations both inside and outside Congress built up against Crump. Ronald Crump was thirty-three years of age when he was elected to the office of president. He was beginning to look a very shrivelled imitation of his former self. On the streets mass demonstrations were being organised; the anti-war movement, which had been mothballed after the Vietnam War came to an end, was now reactivated. As if this was not enough, the news of the attempted deportations had reached the streets and black liberation and equality groups were once again mobilised. Women's groups and women against war were once again part of this anti-Crump movement which now, unlike during the election campaign, could call two to three hundred thousand people out.

One demonstration against the president, accusing him of fascist subversion, was stopped only after the National Guard opened fire on the crowd. The time would come when the National Guard and police would not be sufficient to prevent the rising anti-Crump feeling. Central American governments had also voiced their concerns at the policies of the US president, especially Mexico, along whose border his electric fence would have run. The US public were outraged that their president had almost caused a war with the Soviet Union, possibly the only country which could match the USA militarily. This was not some Central American republic where the USA could march in and 'kick ass'; this was the USSR, and Crump was prepared to risk world destruction in pursuit of his own power-hungry ego. This was the same US public which detested the USSR and all it stood for, actually blaming their own president before pointing the finger at the Soviets.

On hearing the news that US troops were being recalled to base, Soviet leader Leonid Brezhnev issued a statement:

'The Soviet High Command had received reliable information from our agents of a huge US military build-up in the Middle East. The Soviet Union was left with no alternative but to send troops, including airborne soldiers, into the Iran/Iraq area to protect our interests. We shall now begin a gradual withdrawal over a number of months of our forces back to bases in Egypt, Syria and Soviet Central Asia.'

With great reluctance the US Congress accepted the word and interpretation of events issued by the USSR and all breathed a sigh of relief. President Crump's selfish actions had brought the world nearer to nuclear war than had the events of Cuba in 1962. Congress were also worried about the accusations of Generals Batten and Howitt, who pointed the finger of blame in the direction of the president. It was a silly move by him of trying to shift the entire blame for his wild scheme onto his generals. Once again, Crump bought time through bluff.

'It had all been a misunderstanding between Generals Batten, Howitt and me,' he claimed. 'National security' – always a good catchall excuse – 'prohibits me from going into detail.'

The generals played along with this, remembering their own hands were not exactly clean.

21

The Downfall

The pressure of what was going on was taking its toll on Tracy Crump. If any person did not deserve this it was she; she was not equipped to deal with pressures of this magnitude. Her first priority, as with any good mother, was her son, Tarquin. She had hitherto always supported her husband but as evidence mounted up against him, she began to doubt him for the first time. It was not so much about what was happening regarding his misuse of power, but what was beginning to emerge from the FBI enquiry. The talk of two women put in prison after being forced into escort work by her husband was concerning. Had she ever really known the man who gave her Tarquin? For the time being she would continue to give him a begrudging benefit of the doubt, as nothing yet was proved against him. This situation and attitude would change dramatically. John Rowlands, head of the FBI, was currently investigating the NYPD Commissioner, Dwight Connman.

This investigation was intensifying. The terms of reference were widening, and the cases of Carol Hawkins and Linda Lowry were to be looked at again. Commissioner Dwight Connman was coming under more scrutiny by the day as was his relationship with Ronald Crump before he became president. As the case for Carol and Linda gathered momentum, with the evidence of the fired young policeman now considered relevant, talk of a retrial abounded. The relationship between Crump, Connman and the trial judge, Greasley, was coming under the microscope. John Rowlands assembled a six-person team, three male and three female agents, to conduct the inquiry into the case.

John Rowlands decided to re-interview the two women and he despatched agents Hillary Starling and Natasha Gordon to the prison where Carol and Linda were being held. The agents' terms of reference would be wide and far-reaching as Rowlands set about cleaning up the entire system of justice in New York.

Starling and Gordon arrived at the Women's Correction Penitentiary and met the women.

'Tell us in your own words what happened on the night in question, from meeting Mr Mathis to his drowsiness, sickness and wallet going missing. You should include everything, including any sexual activity which took place. Also, we would be interested in the part played by Mr Crump in the events of that evening,' Agent Starling pressed.

'Well,' said Carol, 'Mr Crump said he had a special job for us both, worth a good packet to us two "lovely ladies" with an associate of his. He arranged to meet us at a beer bar in downtown New York for an introduction, at which point Mr Mathis would be made known to us.'

'Were you aware Mr Crump was using you essentially as prostitutes?' asked Natasha Gordon.

'We thought, as he said, we were employees of Crumps Arms and Real Estate and were covered by the same rules as the other employees.'

'Mr Crump led you to believe this, did he?' the agent continued.

'Yes, he did,' Linda interjected.

'Were you at any time alone with Mr Mathis's drink that evening? Could you at any time have administered a mild toxin causing him vomiting and drowsiness?'

'We were alone with him, but neither of us fixed his drink.'

'What happened at the apartment?' asked Starling.

'Well, when we arrived there,' said Carol, 'Mr Mathis had a bit of a stagger on, so we propped him up a little. We then retired to the bedroom and all three of us undressed. Mathis was a little drowsy, but we thought it was the effects of the alcohol. Sexual intercourse took place.'

'Did Mr Mathis fall asleep then?'

'Yes, he was a bit worse for wear,' said Linda. 'He complained of nausea and then started vomiting. We got really concerned because he seemed so sick, and so we called an ambulance for him.'

'We heard he was OK, thank God. Poor fool,' added Carol.

'Did either of you go to his jacket and remove a wallet?'

'No! At no time did we do anything like that,' Carol attested.

'Very well, ladies, will you give us written statements outlining what you have just told us?' Natasha Gordon asked.

Carol and Linda agreed.

'Good. Here are some sheets of paper for you, and pens,' Starling said, offering them the materials.

The two agents returned to the FBI chief, armed with the women's statements.

'Let's have a look,' Rowlands said, 'and we'll have another look at the CCTV footage from the bar that evening.'

The footage showed Crump and Mathis arriving followed, shortly after, by the two women. Mathis sat down for what looked like an introductory conversation while Crump ordered the drinks. The CCTV showed Ronald Crump putting his hand in his pocket and producing a packet, from which he poured something into a drink. Sitting in on this viewing was another FBI Agent, Ray Franks, and he came to the same conclusion.

'This certainly casts doubt on the entire case,' said Rowlands. 'If it was Crump who administered the dose then what else were the women innocent of? The only crime they may have committed, and even this had mitigation, was that of prostitution. We must continue. I want to interview the trial judge. Deal with that, Franks.'

'Yes, sir.'

John Rowlands acquired the correct documentation to interview the trial judge, Greasley, and showed him the CCTV footage.

'Why was this evidence deemed inadmissible at the trial, Judge?' he asked the eminent man.

'Well, I thought it unclear and not sufficient quality to offer any credible evidence to the trial,' the judge said.

'It looks clear enough to me, Judge. What do you think, Ray?' he asked Franks.

'Looks very clear to me too,' the agent agreed.

'So, Judge, if this had been admitted as evidence you may have come to a different verdict, wouldn't you agree?

'Well, it's possible,' said Greasley, 'but at the time the quality did not look as good as it does now.'

John Rowlands was not altogether happy with the judge's response to his questions.

'I want to access his bank statements for that period,' said Rowlands. 'I also want to view those of Connman, the New York police commissioner, for the same time.'

The bank, reluctantly and under threat of a court order, gave the FBI access to Greasley's account. For the period under review a transfer from the account of Crumps Arms for the amount of thirty thousand dollars had been transferred to the judge's account. On the examination of Dwight Connman's account an amount of ten thousand dollars had been transferred from Crumps Arms' account in the same period. On this evidence Rowlands was considering arresting the judge and commissioner, but he really wanted Crump, the paymaster. The problem he had was: arresting an incumbent president without absolute proof was almost impossible. Within the US constitution were 'structural principles' which made it difficult, though not impossible, to arrest a United States president while still holding office. Rowlands did not have enough yet for these principles to be broken.

Rowlands calculated it might only be a matter of time before Congress impeached the president. The way would then be open as Crump would probably resign, as had Nixon before impeachment. The retrial of Carol and Linda would be major news, especially with the perceived involvement of the president. If it became proven that Crump had arranged for these women to be imprisoned to suit his purpose the scandal would rate alongside Watergate and in Britain the Profumo affair of the early sixties. This was an incident which shook British parliamentary politics to their foundations in 1961. The Minister for War, John Dennis Profumo, was having an affair with a nineteen-year-old prostitute, Christine Keeler. She was also sleeping with agents of the Soviet Union, so the problems were obvious. In 1963 then British Prime Minister, Harold Macmillan, was forced to resign over the affair, which became known as the Profumo Affair and shook not only Britain but the whole Atlantic alliance (NATO).

★ ★ ★

On hearing the news on the radio, television and reading about it in the newspapers, the two call girls whom Crump had hired while at the arms dealers' conference decided to act. Sharon Storm and Stephanie Lust, real names Sharon McKinley and Stephanie O'Donnell, had in their possession the unsigned agreement which Crump hoped would keep the incident at the hotel quiet. They would now make a fortune selling their stories to the newspapers starting by touting around for the highest bidder. With all the issues surrounding the president, the papers would pay handsomely for these women's tale.

They ended up in the *New York Times*. The editor, Dicky Hitchcock, told the women, 'Spice it up, ladies, our readers like sex and scandal. Don't hold back, it will be a seller.'

'All very well,' Sharon said, 'but let's see the colour of your money. You're not having a scoop like this for nothing.'

'But hold on, ladies, have you not already received money from Crump?'

'Mind your own business, that is our affair. All you need to know is our deal is perfectly legal.'

She was telling the truth, the lack of Crump's signature on the document about not going to the press made it just a piece of paper with no legal clout whatsoever. They did not need the incriminating tapes; publication of the unsigned document would be sufficient. The two former prostitutes walked out of the newspaper's offices $300,000 richer. They decided to retire from the high-risk occupation of prostitution. They already had the $200,000 each Crump had paid them, and now with this bonus, they were made. Now it was time to turn their backs on this profession, which had been good, though risky, while it lasted.

★ ★ ★

As damaging as the call girls' story would be, what would happen next to President Crump would lead to his eternal destruction. The reader will recall Crump spending an evening with Barbara Simpson, the Secretary at T.A. Gunn's, in order for her to deliver him the plans and contracts of the rival arms dealer. It will be remembered she ended up dead after a hit-and-run accident about which, after much investigation, the New York Police Department came up with nothing.

The receptionist from the hotel where Ronald and Barbara spent the night recalled the incident when all the news about Carol and Linda hit the streets. She approached the FBI Chief, John Rowlands, informing him that the woman who was killed in the hit-and-run accident had been a guest at her hotel with Ronald Crump. She was dead a few weeks later, and the receptionist wondered if there was anything sinister about it all. She said she would have come forward earlier but thought the investigation was closed. She was really after self-gratification and publicity under the guise of helping the police and also hoping for a financial reward for her efforts. Rowlands thanked her for her vigilance and promised to investigate. He had seen through the lady's ulterior intentions straight away but did not wish the gold-digger to think her evidence was of more value than it actually was.

Rowlands called Ray Franks to his office and shared the information with him.

'Get me the CCTV footage for that day, you know the day Barbara Simpson was killed. Who investigated the case, Ray?' he asked.

'NYPD I think, boss,' the agent replied.

The two men viewed the CCTV of the Barbara Simpson incident.

'Zoom in on that car speeding off after it hit her, Ray. Who is driving?'

A clear image of Bob Tomkinson appeared.

'How the fuck did the NYPD and that Commissioner miss something as plain as this? Unless they had been bribed,' Rowlands concluded.

This evidence was clear enough to order the arrest of Bob Tomkinson, and Ray Franks ordered a convoy of police cars to head to Crumps Arms and Real Estate. As luck would have it, Tomkinson was in his office when the police arrived with the warrant for his arrest. After a short chat the arresting officer read Tomkinson his rights before uttering the words: 'Robert Tomkinson, I am arresting you on suspicion for the murder of Barbara Simpson. You have the right to remain silent...' Tomkinson was in shock; he felt like he had just stared Medusa in the face and had been turned to stone.

'Take him down, officer,' Ray Franks ordered.

★ ★ ★

With all the ado over Crump now involving more acts of misogyny, women's groups, along with anti-war, black liberation movements and the trade unions, were on the streets. Colette Hill, along with Jane Fonda and other leading celebrities, were among the brethren. Joe Hill, Colette's husband, was pushing anti-Crump motions through the American Federation of Labour and the affiliated unions were demanding action from Congress against a man who was clearly unfit to govern. He was a risk to the stability of the USA and working-class people in particular. He had been blaming union power, as reflected by Carol Barnes in a news conference, for the state of the economy out west. The man was at very best corrupt and at worst a fascist, misogynist, racist and xenophobic, who might now also be complicit in murder.

The deceased woman, Barbara Simpson, had been a member of the white-collar secretarial union, the Union of Office Secretaries and Clerks. Her union was now pushing for an enquiry on foot of what the receptionist from the hotel had told the FBI and anybody else who cared to listen.

The anti-Crump lobby had organised a huge demonstration in Washington DC and New York to coincide with Crump's first year in office. An estimated half a million were expected on this monster rally and it was decided that they would march on the White House. The state organised a reluctant National Guard for the day, giving them orders to shoot if things got out of hand. What they had not anticipated was that this time the demonstrators were prepared for martyrdom if necessary. In other words, they would accept some losses with a view to disarming the National Guard. This was entering socialist revolutionary territory.

The Soviet Union was watching events in the USA closely. They still had a policy of assisting workers in struggle though whether this would include going to war with the USA was highly doubtful. They could, if events went far enough, offer advice and assistance short of troops. The day arrived and upwards of three-quarters of a million people were on the anti-Crump, anti-corruption demonstration. Regular troops tried to block their path, but sheer weight of numbers pushed them aside. Unlike the novices in the National Guard, these regular troops were not trigger-happy and would only fire as an absolute last resort. Many were in favour and in sympathy with the demonstrators; after all, this president had almost got them into an unnecessary war with the USSR.

The marchers kept walking, despite appeals from the authorities to stop where they were. Eventually a senior army officer holding the rank of colonel asked to meet a delegation from the protesters. Joe Hill and Jane Fonda were chosen to negotiate with the army.

'What are your demands?' the officer asked.

'We want that animal in there who is masquerading as our president placing under arrest with a view to Congress impeaching him. He has had two women falsely imprisoned and according to two call girls, wished to engage in acts of gross indecency with them. They refused, and he became very aggressive and nasty. We also want to talk to Tracy Crump. She is a victim in all of this. Either you grant us our demands, or we come in and get Crump and save Tracy ourselves. You know there are not enough troops on US soil to stop us. Please, Colonel, use your discretion. If we go back to the demonstration with nothing we will not accept responsibility for what happens next.'

The officer agreed to their request providing his men accompanied the delegation. It was agreed and the small party of six of the campaign leadership, including Colette and Joe Hill, with two soldiers, moved towards the White House.

★ ★ ★

Ronald Crump, perhaps for the first time, was thinking of the reality the situation presented. He was in a bad place. *This was not in the script!* he thought. He was possibly on the verge of losing his wife, his son and possibly his presidency. He felt a very lonely man.

As for Tracy, she knew she had to face the inevitable, that the evidence against her husband was overwhelming and undeniable. 'Oh Ronnie, we were so happy. But now it's all fallen apart. I can't stand beside you any more, I'm so sorry.'

'No, Tracy, no, you must believe me,' Crump said, grasping at straws. 'The commies are trying to set me up.'

Tracy gave him a long look. 'I'm sorry, Ron. It's no use. You can't keep saying that. I know you are lying to me. I was trying to convince myself over and over that none of this was true, but I must accept the facts now.'

The telephone rang, and as Tracy was nearest, she lifted it up. It was the colonel, who filled her in on the demonstrators' requests. What he said confirmed her decision. Then she offered the phone to her husband.

'Do you want to talk to the colonel? He says Colette and Joe Hill can bring me and Tarquin away to safety for a few days. I must go down to talk to them.'

Ronald just shook his head. 'No. Just go,' he said sadly. 'And tell my son I love him.'

★ ★ ★

The small delegation of demonstrators met Tracy in the reception room.

'Tracy, you have nothing to worry about, we are not here to harm you,' Colette assured her. 'Please come with us. We feel you are in danger here, and bring your little boy with you.'

Tracy nodded. 'You are right. Tarquin and I can't stay here any more. Wait here for a few moments so I can pack some things in a bag.'

Twenty minutes later Tracy took her son by the hand and left the White House. Accompanied by Colette and her group, they walked back to the main event.

'Take Tracy home, back to New York, Colette,' her husband said. 'We'll get on with what we need to do: report back to the march and the organisers giving them an account of the events which have just taken place.'

The army Colonel then assured the crowd that Congress would be discussing the president's future the following day and it was likely he would be given the option of resignation or impeachment.

'Please let due process deal with this,' the colonel pleaded.

This satisfied the campaign leadership for now, but they had to sell it to the rest, the larger body of almost a million people. A huge screen was erected with several smaller ones along the march route at Washington and New York, with Washington DC being the main focus. Joe appealed for calm, telling the crowd what the army had told him. This appeared for now to be sufficient for most of the organisations which constituted the campaign. It must be pointed out that the army would not usually have taken such a softly-softly approach; it was the sheer weight of numbers which forced their hand. This campaign had not yet reached the high-water mark and the colonel hoped the establishment would see sense before it became all-out revolution.

Colette Hill and three other women took Tracy back to New York and the Hills' apartment.

'Come in, Tracy, and bring Tarquin with you. Would you like a tea or coffee, perhaps something a little stronger?' Colette asked.

'I'll have a cup of tea please if that's no trouble,' said Tracy, 'and a glass of milk for Tarquin, thanks.'

'No problem. Make yourself at home.'

One of the accompanying ladies kept the little boy occupied while Tracy and Colette talked.

'Are you ready for the truth, Tracy?' Colette gently asked.

'Yes I am,' Tracy said. 'Tell me everything.'

Colette began with Ronald Crump's infidelity behind Tracy's back and the assignation he had with Barbara Simpson who, a few weeks later, was killed in a hit-and-run case. Colette went on. 'He also hired the services of two prostitutes while at an arms dealers' conference. When he demanded more than the two women were offering and was refused, he turned very nasty and aggressive. He also planned, behind the back of the US Congress, the illegal deportation of black citizens and Hispanic people and was arranging for the erection of an electric fence along our border with Mexico. The fence would carry ten thousand volts and would fry anything which came into contact with it. I understand you probably did not involve yourself with the political side of your husband's life, and perhaps find what I'm saying difficult to believe, but I do think you should know the kind of man he is.'

'I had no idea, Colette,' Tracy said, which was perfectly true. 'He was always so gentle at home, a bit of a bully towards the staff which I corrected him on numerous occasions but apart from that he was a perfect husband. Are you sure he is all the things you say he is? There have been no charges brought against him.'

'Trust me, Tracy, you and Tarquin would eventually be in danger. You are victims. I don't expect you to believe all I say but please stay here tonight and watch events unfold this week. Your husband as we speak is under house arrest and will be called to Congress tomorrow. Tonight, you and your little boy can have the spare room. Try to get some rest – it must be a lot to take in.'

Joe Hill and the other members of the United Against Crump campaign leadership were waiting in Washington to ensure the army colonel was not simply playing for time. If no action was taken against the president, the next march would be even bigger and more aggressive. The target would be the White House itself, of which the colonel was acutely aware. Over five hundred coaches had travelled from New York to Washington DC and along with the local population they made up a huge crowd. Another equally large demonstration was taking place in New York City and collectively around a million plus people were involved. In the mid-west of the country demonstrations against the Crump administration were taking place, the largest being in Chicago. Here around three hundred thousand people took part and the police struggled to maintain order.

Watching these events with great hope that it would signal the end of Crump, for different reasons, was the good Christian, Vice-President Alf Slyme. If the President was impeached or resigned then he would become the top man. Oh, how he prayed to God for such an outcome. Slyme obviously did not know Crump as well as he thought he did. He, Slyme, was part of the administration and if he thought Crump would go under alone he was even more unrealistic than the religion he pretended to worship. That evening the vice-president attended chapel praying for the downfall of his colleague.

All the negative publicity surrounding President Crump was taking its toll on his mother, Megan, now installed with her new lover, Dr Alan Quincy. This was the woman who had given birth to Ronald, defended him against the indefensible, made sure he would never have to face up to his responsibilities and frankly ruined him from birth. Megan was greatly responsible for the person her son had become; she even defended him against a sexual assault claim when he was merely eleven years of age. His late father, Teddy, was one of the most dishonest, lying, cheating and vilest people imaginable. He had taught his son every devious trick in the book, which shaped the future Ronald Crump. Now that the media was exposing shocking revelations about Ronald, Megan and Alan decided it was time to move. Alan Quincy secured a position as a senior neurologist at Montreal Hospital, Canada, and they had a buyer for the huge mansion which had been Megan's home since Ronald was a baby.

★ ★ ★

The police station where Bob Tomkinson was being held in downtown New York appeared a million miles away from the events on the streets of Washington DC and New York City. John Rowlands had seconded the station for the purpose of extracting as much as possible from Tomkinson. The FBI wanted Crump and were prepared to do a deal with Tomkinson in order to get him. If Crump resigned, as expected, it would be straightforward. First the Bureau needed Bob to talk.

Tomkinson and Rowlands sat in the interview room. 'Come on, Bob, you would not have driven that vehicle unless acting under instructions from somebody else,' Rowlands said. 'You are not a killer so why go away for life, or risk the remote possibility of the death penalty?'

New York in 1982 still retained the death penalty for a minority of cases, after a decision was taken back in 1967 allowing for this. Bob Tomkinson's case was unlikely to fall into this category, but a life sentence was a real possibility, unless he talked.

'If you give us what we want it may be possible, with a word in the right ears, to get you off with a ten-year sentence as an accomplice to the hit-and-run. If you give us information leading to uncovering an even greater crime, we may get this down to five years. Think about it, Bob. Do you really want to do time for somebody else who may not give you a second fucking thought?'

John Rowlands for once was offering Bob Tomkinson a way out. The man considered. If the boot was on the other foot would Ronald Crump have thought twice about dropping him, Bob, in the mire? No, he would not, nor would he care a shit about Tomkinson's family.

'Come on, Bob, think about it. Was he or she worth it? Who gave the order? Who was the paymaster? Are you really going down for the rest of your natural to shield them?'

The FBI decided to let Bob sleep on the day's events. They would recommence interviewing first thing in the morning. If the crimes were not exactly covered over then vital evidence may well have gone conveniently missing, on Connman's watch! As yet, John Rowlands knew nothing about the fire at Gunn's, executed by Crump and Tomkinson, and resulting in the death of a security guard. He just suspected strongly more corporate crimes had taken place which may have included further loss of life. The key to these suspicions lay with Bob Tomkinson, and Rowlands with his team would make an early start on him.

The following morning Bob Tomkinson, after a sleepless night and with the damning CCTV evidence against him, decided to cooperate with the FBI. He began singing like a canary. The information he gave was far over and above John Rowland's wildest dreams and expectations. Tomkinson concluded he was not going down for Crump. That family had had more than their pound of flesh out of him and they would have no more. He told the FBI of how Ronald Crump had secured the plans from Barbara Simpson of Gunn's arms factory, including the rear buildings where the fire started. He also told of the contract for the arms deal which Gunn's, due to the fire, would be unable to complete and therefore the logical answer to the client's dilemma would be to allow Crumps to finish the job.

This all began to add up in the calculative mind of John Rowlands: kill the secretary who knew too much. Arrange for the crime to be covered up by Connman and then, on foot of the plans given to Crump by the unfortunate lovesick woman, arrange a fire at the plant. Timing devices were used giving both Crump and Tomkinson, if ever suspected at all, the perfect alibi. This information, Rowlands felt, was perhaps not all Tomkinson knew.

'Go on, Bob, keep going. Remember, five years as opposed to life.'

Tomkinson had told just about all he could and Rowlands, an experienced officer, sensed this. Tomkinson agreed to give Rowlands a word-for-word account of his involvement, on Crump's orders, in the death of Barbara Simpson.

'That's great, Bob. Now what I need from you is an account of your knowledge regarding the fire at Gunn's. If I get this I can speak to the right people about getting you a light sentence.' There was no copper-plated guarantee about this, but Rowlands would do his very best to deliver what he was promising Tomkinson.

John Rowlands went right to the top and did eventually manage to secure leniency for Tomkinson, if he came up with the right information.

★ ★ ★

The demonstrators in New York had made their way home but many of those in Washington, most of them in fact, remained surrounding the White House. They were waiting for Congress to decide whether Crump would be impeached or whether he would resign. They wanted to keep their forces large, thus restricting the actions the army could take. The plan to sacrifice martyrs was still there should a fudge by Congress occur. They were still prepared to fight and disarm the army if necessary and occupy the White House and other government buildings. Some of the people in the demonstration were firearms-trained, the Black Panthers, for example. In the southern states fights between anti-Crump demonstrators and the Ku Klux Klan had erupted, with the Klansmen taking a hiding. They were not too good when the numbers of combatants were anything approaching equal in numbers. They preferred odds of five or six to one in their favour but considering a large proportion of their make-up were businessmen not used to street fighting, the result was perhaps not surprising.

The United States Congress met on Monday 21st January 1982 to discuss the president's future. Many Republicans were lining up with the Democrats to order their president's impeachment, with only the religious right and neo-cons in the president's corner. He had effectively been under house arrest since the huge demonstrations demanded action and today was the day of reckoning.

The president had the charges read out and asked to give his account. The two generals, Batten and Howitt, were also to give evidence regarding the illegal move towards war with the USSR; and they had decided they were not going to be hung out to dry.

President Crump claimed he firmly believed an imminent Soviet threat was waiting to happen in the Middle East. 'I must admit to this Congress, I got that totally wrong,' he said. 'Myself and Vice-President Slyme discussed the situation around the Iran/Iraq region and we both agreed there was a threat to the United States, or at least potential threat. I acted accordingly as we saw fit.'

Notice how Crump had immediately brought Slyme into the theatre! All the vice-president's praying for Crump to be impeached, thus allowing himself to take the top job, had proved fruitless. If Slyme thought Crump would go down alone, he was sadly mistaken.

The congressional chairman then asked: 'Was Vice-President Slyme involved with the whole unfortunate incident?'

'Yes, sir, he was, right from our first meeting,' replied the president.

'Liar, liar, may God forgive you, Crump. I knew nothing about any of this,' the good Christian shouted.

More people were questioned, including the two generals, who did just enough to save themselves without hanging the president. Eventually Congress retired to decide Crump's fate on this charge of war-mongering and threatening the integrity of the USA. They returned with a verdict that the president would be severely sanctioned due to political immaturity. This was better than the president had expected, but his troubles had only just begun. The charges of forced deportation, involving the secretaries of two departments, Deportation and Transportation, would have more far-reaching affects.

'First you, Mr President, wanted us to erect a twelve-foot-high electric fence, in breach of international law, across our border with Mexico. While you kept this ridiculous proposal under discussion in Congress, your henchmen, Mitchel Bernstein and William Needy, were illegally deporting young black citizens and Hispanics. You also contacted Vernon Greengrass in the Defence Department asking for military help for the police in carrying out this act. Are these allegations true, Mr President?'

'No, they are not, it was Bernstein and Needy that did all this. I tried to stop these actions.'

'Tried to stop these actions? You're the president, you do not try to stop illegal acts. You just order them stopped. You are lying, aren't you? You got away with passing the buck over the Middle-East situation and you are trying it again, aren't you, Mr President?'

The Chair was not letting the president get away with any more buck-passing. 'Are you going to blame all your heads of departments for every wrongdoing?'

Congress then retired again to discuss the president's future, based on these hearings. After about an hour the Congressional Committee returned.

'President Ronald Crump we, the Congressional Committee and on behalf of the entire US Congress, have decided you are to be impeached, subject to you not submitting your resignation from the high office of President.'

At this point Crump was unaware of the evidence held by the FBI in the civil courts. If he had he would perhaps have been better off fronting out the impeachment. He did not know about the information Bob Tomkinson had given the FBI or that the former police commissioner, Dwight Connman, was under investigation. When Rowlands received access to Ronald's bank account and if the figures tallied with the payments to Connman and Greasley, he would face charges of bribery and corruption in the civil courts. This would be coupled with charges of double homicide and arson.

When news of the Congressional Committee reached the crowds surrounding the White House, pandemonium erupted. All the demonstrations had been worth it. President Crump was to be impeached or resign. The FBI were as anxious as the demonstrators for this decision. Crump would in all likelihood resign, as had Nixon. The difference was Richard Nixon did not have other serious charges awaiting him. For Nixon it was resignation full stop. For Ronald Crump his resignation allowed him off with the impeachment, but then left the gate wide open for charges of bribery and corruption, murder, arson and on top of all these, charges of blackmail and rape that had yet to surface.

When Tracy Crump heard the verdict of Congress she was could hardly believe it. But her main concern now was her child, Tarquin, who had to be protected from the fallout. She burst into tears at the thought of the future. Fortunately, she had a good friend in Colette who, ironically, might have been the only person who could have saved young Ronald Crump from himself all those years ago.

During one of their increasingly regular discussions, Colette asked Tracy what her plans for the future were. 'You're welcome to stay with Joe and me as long as you need to,' she said.

She also invited the former First Lady to join one of the women's equality movements.

'You would be welcomed with open arms to any of the groups,' she reassured Tracy. 'My husband, Joe, may also be able to find you a job in one of them but only when you are ready.'

'It's all been a lot to take in,' said Tracy. 'Firstly, these accusations against my husband which, I must admit, I refused to believe until so much evidence stacked up. Then I found out he was unfaithful and if all this talk is correct a lot more, even murder! But we're done, Ronald and myself. It's over. I don't want to call him my husband any more, and I don't want to see him again,' she added, with a new firmness in her tone. 'And when I'm ready, I'd like to start over, start afresh.'

'Of course, Tracy, I understand,' the feminist assured her. 'There's no hurry, no rush at all, just take your time readjusting to life. Have you given any thought about visiting your parents, even to reassure them their grandchild is well? If you wish, I'll go with you. Joe will drive us there in the Land Rover.'

'Will you, oh please! That would make it much easier. I'd like them to see I'm not on my own, Colette.'

'No problem, we can go in the morning. Joe will be back from Washington shortly… surely a decision will have been taken in Congress by now.'

At seven o'clock that night Joe Hill arrived back from Washington.

'The president has resigned rather than be impeached,' he informed the two women. 'It will be on the news tomorrow, Monday, so keep it under your hat for now.'

'That's good news, Joe. Tracy was saying she wants to start afresh, and I told her we'd help her. Will you drive us to her parents' tomorrow?'

'Of course, what time do you want to leave? I would suggest early because when the announcement becomes public tomorrow, we must protect Tracy.'

'That's perfect,' said Tracy. 'I'll tell Tarquin we are going on an adventure to Grandma's and Grandpa's.'

It was arranged they would leave at 7am for the forty-minute journey to Tracy's parents.

The following morning the group set off for Tracy's parents. Setting off early would avoid any chance of the former First Lady being spotted. When the demonstrators told the army if they did not hand Tracy over they would come in and get her, it was agreed to keep her destination secret. They arrived at the Edwards' house around eight o'clock and Stella, Tracy's mother, was there to greet them at the door.

'Tracy, darling, do come in,' an enthusiastic Stella said. 'Louis, guess who's here, your daughter and grandson. Come down! Get out of that bed and see your family.'

She turned to her visitors with a cheeky grin. 'He's as lazy as ever. Bed, bed, and more bed if I'd let him,' Stella said.

'This is my friend, Colette, and her husband, Joe,' Tracy said. 'They have been so good to me. I would not have got through this without them. Colette and Joe, this is Stella, my mom.'

'Nice to meet you, Mrs Edwards,' they both said.

'Call me Stella, cut the Mrs Edwards. I never let that Crump fella call me that. I never trusted him. I know genuine people when I see them, and you both fit the bill.'

At that point Louis Edwards came downstairs to greet his daughter and grandchild.

'Tracy, how are you? And how's my little soldier, Tarquin?' Louis said warmly.

Louis was then introduced to Colette and Joe.

'Nice to meet you, Colette. Hello, Joe,' said Louis, greeting Colette's husband. 'I recognise you from the television, you're the trade union man, aren't you? I think you are doing a great job, keep up the good work.'

Whether Louis was such a big fan of the unions was debatable. Maybe he was, in so many words, responding to everything Crump stood for. Joe was aware his host's enthusiasm may have been a little exaggerated but did not make an issue of it.

'Good to meet you, sir,' Joe said courteously.

The scene inside the Edwards' house was one of a long-lost daughter coming home. She had only been gone a year but to her parents it seemed like a lifetime.

'The last time you were here with the little fella was when he was just six months old. Where have you been since?'

During her time with Crump both before and while she was First Lady, Ronald had implied visiting her parents was an unneccessary distraction. Tracy was not convinced of this argument but lacked the courage to stand up to her husband. She didn't dare tell her parents this, so she said the workload had a huge effect on the time available to her. Stella and Louis appeared to accept this, though Colette guessed there was more to all this than was apparent on the surface. However, she said nothing. Tact was the order of the day.

'Tracy, where are you going to live?' asked Stella. 'You're welcome here if you wish, no problem.'

'I may get a flat. Colette and Joe are helping me with all that, but first I must sort out Tarquin's education.

Stella and Louis accepted their daughter's plan and agreed with it.

It was now time to leave the Edwards. Just as they were about to leave an announcement came on the radio: 'PRESIDENT CRUMP RESIGNS.' Of course, Colette, Joe and Tracy knew this was imminent though they said nothing. By now Tracy was secretly delighted; the initial shock had now turned to anger against her husband.

★ ★ ★

Tracy had been staying at the Hills' a little over a week when Joe came in very pleased with himself. He had a job for Tracy, if she wanted it. The post had been advertised for some time in the union journal, but there had been no applicants. The job came with accommodation and, if she accepted, it would be ideal. The position was in the AFL library as assistant librarian. She would be working with Elizabeth – Lizzie – Flynn, the union librarian there. This was the same Elizabeth Flynn who had been a negotiator with the United Textile Workers Union for employees at Tillerson's years earlier. The salary was not great, but the accommodation was very reasonable and subsidised by the union congress.

'I've found you a job, Tracy,' he said to her. 'Only if you think it might suit you, of course! The AFL congress has a large library of socialist and trade union literature, and they are looking for an assistant librarian. The post has been advertised but there have been no applicants, so we are in a position, without breaking policy, to offer you the post. There is also accommodation with the job, which is subsidised, making the rent very reasonable indeed. Have you ever worked in a library before, Tracy?'

'No, I haven't, but I'm keen to learn, very eager. When can I start?'

'I'll take you in tomorrow and introduce you to Lizzie Flynn, our head librarian, and we can sort everything out from there. Then we can take a look at the flat. I think it will be ideal for you and Tarquin. While we are at the union offices we can begin to sort Tarquin out for a school place. He is still at prep school, isn't he?'

'Yes, he's in his final year at prep level, and then he'll be starting junior school.'

'No problem, just as the rich and powerful have schools we have ours, fully accredited with a junior school and senior level. We can, if you wish, get him in at our school.'

Tracy accompanied Joe to meet Elizabeth Flynn, who would give her a description of her duties and what the library was all about. Joe said he would leave them both to talk and would call back later to pick Tracy up again.

'Nice to meet you, Tracy. I understand you've been through the mill in the last few weeks. Not to worry, you'll be all right with us. Now, let me explain the layout of the library. These shelves contain Marxist and internationalist literature. Over here we have general and socialist books, while the shelves along the rear contain industrial relations and law, state by state. This huge almanac is all about Federal Law, which includes industrial relations and guidelines for resolving conflict. Your job, to start with, will be ensuring all returns go back on the appropriate shelf and under the correct category.'

It was agreed Tracy would begin her duties in the AFL Library the following Monday, thus allowing her time to move into the flat. She could also sort out Tarquin's education, having decided he would go to the union school, the Bill Haywood Preparatory and Junior Education Centre. Lizzie Flynn, a seasoned trade union militant, assured Tracy if she needed a little time off to settle her son it would not present any problems.

'We are not like those bastard employers,' she said.

Perhaps for the first time in many years Tracy Crump, soon to revert back to Edwards, felt safe and secure. For her, clouds certainly did have a silver lining and her life would now flourish in this new and alternative society.

22

The Arrest and Trial of Ronald Crump

The FBI had a warrant for the arrest of Ronald Crump after he resigned the presidency. They already had enough evidence of bribery and corruption against former police commissioner Dwight Connman, and former judge Early Greasley. Now the jewel in Rowland's crown, former President Ronald Crump, was for the taking. His political misadventures were a matter for the US Congress but the other charges outstanding were a case for the courts.

Reading what had been going on with great interest was Madeline Atkinson, née Copley, the teacher Crump had blackmailed and raped while at Bishops Court Rise school. She had waited a long time for this day and was determined to have her day in court. Who could blame her? When Crump had committed this despicable act against the young teacher he was nearly fifteen years of age, old enough to accept criminal responsibility.

When Ronald Crump left the Congressional Chamber, having submitted his resignation to avoid imminent impeachment, he was under the impression this would be the end of the matter. Unfortunately for Crump his troubles were only just beginning. He probably would come to wish he had stayed on as president and faced the impeachment, which may not have got past the Senate. As Crump emerged from the building, John Rowlands, in the absence of a police commissioner for the state of New York, was waiting.

'Ronald Edward Crump, I have a warrant for your arrest regarding events surrounding the mysterious death of Barbara Simpson. We also wish to question you about a blackmail and rape allegation made against you which occurred some years ago. Time does not diminish the severity of the allegation which it is claimed you committed while still at boarding school. We also have information linking you to the fire at T.A. Gunn's Arms Manufacturers which led to the death of a security guard and caused extensive damage to the plant. I must ask you to accompany us, sir.'

Madeline Atkinson and her husband, the former games teacher Bob, had gone to the police, having first sought legal advice. The desk sergeant listened to what happened while they were both teaching at Bishops Court Rise involving Ronald Crump and the then Miss Copley. The desk sergeant then directed the Atkinsons to the incident room set up by the FBI. Madeline Atkinson recounted what had happened at the school in detail, telling how the adolescent Crump had taken a photograph of her and her then future husband in a compromising position. Due to the nature and sensitivity of the case, agents Starling and Gordon were put on the case.

'Ronald Crump had taken these photographs of myself and Bob, who is my husband now. He then arrived at my classroom while I was alone and instructed me to be at his dormitory later that afternoon or he would make the photographs public. He knew that should these photos be made available both of us would be out of a job. When I arrived at his dormitory, he told me to undress and lay on the bed. He said he was "going to have me". I felt I had no choice and did as he said, feeling dirty and ashamed. I still do.'

'Don't worry, Madeline,' said Starling, 'you did nothing wrong. It was certainly nothing many others haven't done in similar situations.'

Madeline voiced the opinion, with a tremble in her voice: 'This surely must be rape through blackmail, as I was unwilling to participate in this act.'

'It certainly is, Madeline. You did the right thing reporting the incident. Can you give us a written statement outlining in detail what you have just told us?'

'Yes, I can, just give me a pen and paper.'

'Excellent,' said Gordon. 'Just one more question. Is there any way these photographs are, to your knowledge, still in existence? If we can find them it would be a huge help in securing a prosecution.'

'I would doubt it, why would he keep them? He got what he wanted so why keep incriminating evidence?'

'People like Crump are power freaks. Keeping the instrument which gave him the power over you probably gives him some kind of turn-on. You would be surprised how these people think.'

The agents then left the room for a few minutes as Madeline wrote down her statement. As they eventually wrapped up the interview, the agents thanked Madeline and her husband for coming to the police station.

'That will be all for now, Mrs Atkinson. We will keep in touch with you and inform you of every positive development,' said Natasha Gordon.

The two agents pondered their next move to find these photographs; both were convinced they were still in existence. It was decided a search warrant be obtained for the Crump's former home. They arrived at the library where Tracy was working to ask her if she had any knowledge of the pictures.

When they arrived at the union building Lizzie Flynn asked abruptly, 'Have you a warrant?'

'Calm down, Miss Flynn, we only wish to ask Tracy some questions and you may sit in as a witness if you wish or contact your union legal team.'

'I will do just that, sit in as a witness,' the union militant accepted.

'Did your husband ever talk about events he was involved with at high school, Tracy?'

'No, not once, in fact his schooldays are as much of a mystery as is the man I married.'

'Did he ever mention a French teacher named Miss Copley?'

'No, I've never heard that name until now,' Tracy answered.

When they had finished, satisfied Tracy had no idea about the photographs, they asked if they could search the house where they had lived. Tracy gave them her permission to conduct a search but in case the tenants created a problem, they secured a warrant.

'That will do, Tracy, we'll say goodbye for now and will keep you up to date. Good day, Miss Flynn,' they also bade the librarian as they left.

Armed with the warrant, FBI agents Starling and Gordon arrived at the huge dwelling which had once been home to the Crumps.

Mrs Gifford answered the door. 'Tracy told me you would be coming and to cooperate all I can. You don't need a warrant, but I understand why you thought it safer to have one. Come in and search away. Try not to leave too much of a mess.'

'We'll be as thorough and tidy as possible,' Gordon assured her.

They searched high and low to no avail and were about to leave when Starling came across some beading at the side of some shelves which was loose.

'Natasha, look here. Did you see this?'

Gordon came over. 'Well spotted. That is worth looking at all right.'

They gently removed the strips and to their delight, bingo, they found a series of photographs showing a young woman naked, kneeling in front of a half-dressed man in a very compromising position. These were the photos, the Holy Grail. On their arrival back at the station they contacted Madeline Atkinson and asked her if she would come in and confirm these were indeed the offending photographs. Madeline agreed and was on the next bus to comply with the agents' request.

It was true; Tracy Crump had little knowledge of her husband outside the man she knew in the home. He had a Jekyll and Hyde personality, both of which were incompatible with each other. Tracy had fallen for the side which appeared nice, never witnessing the demon which epitomised the real Ronald Crump. She really did have a narrow escape because it would only be a matter of time before Crump would be unable to mask the true self.

Ronald Crump was now in FBI custody, in downtown New York. Ordinarily the case would by now have been passed on to the State police but because there was no police commissioner in place the investigation, for the time being, was led by the FBI. John Rowlands, assisted by Agent Ray Franks, began questioning Crump about an evening in a hotel where he and Barbara Simpson spent the night together.

'We have witnesses, Ronald, eyewitnesses, so there is no point denying you were present. The receptionist remembers you and Barbara very well; in fact it was she who presented herself to us having heard the woman died shortly after.'

Crump responded quickly. 'Come to think of it, you're right. I met Barbara at her request because she was a little worried about the legalities involved with something she was involved with at Gunn's. I was giving her advice on this matter.'

'What was your advice?' asked Franks.

'I told her she must speak to the police.'

'About what?' interjected Rowlands.

'About what she had told me.'

'Which was?'

'She told me in confidence, I never break a trust,' said Crump.

'Put it this way then, Ron, either you tell us, or we will assume you are hiding something in what is now a murder case.'

'I can't quite remember,' said Crump.

'Well, Ron, let me tell you what I think happened, will I? Then you can let me know if I've got it right. Then again, Ron, you always play for high stakes, don't you?

'I think you met Barbara Simpson whom you knew was having a tough time of things. Her husband was always away, and you promised her sex and money in return for the plans of Gunn's and you wanted a copy of the huge contract they had secured. You were aware, as was the rest in the arms dealing game, that Gunn's had secured a lucrative contract supplying state-of-the-art weapons to a Middle-Eastern government or agents thereof. You then planned to ensure the company would be in no position to fulfil this contract because their premises would, most mysteriously, catch fire. You then planned, being the benevolent man which you undoubtedly were, to come riding on a white charger to the rescue, helping the stranded client out by offering to complete the contract yourselves. Am I right so far, Ron? You would be well versed with the terms of the contract because you had a copy, courtesy of the hapless Barbara, so you would have ironed out any pitfalls before your offer was pitched. Then you executed the final part of your plan, which was getting rid of the only witness and, therefore liability, who had made the whole thing possible.'

Crump remained stony-faced but visibly paled.

'Now, Ron, you wouldn't have the balls to carry out a murder yourself, so you had to find somebody greedy, stupid, and frightened enough, or a combination of all three, to do your dirty work. You would have told this person, whoever they may have been, that due to your connections in the police there was virtually no chance of being caught. Evidence would either be ignored or destroyed, and this person would be financially rewarded by you for doing what you asked,' Rowlands probed. 'How am I doing so far, Ron? What you neglected to take into account was that the CCTV footage might be destroyed, but there are always backup copies which your mate Dwight Connman would not have accessed. It was this backup which placed Bob Tomkinson behind the wheel of the vehicle which mowed down Barbara Simpson. How did I do, Ron?' Rowlands concluded.

'I want my attorney present before I say any more,' Crump demanded.

The attorney, Percy Sugden, was an Englishman who had emigrated to the USA a decade previously. He was competent in UK and US law. Upon hearing his services were required, Sugden advised Crump to say nothing for the moment. The attorney was as yet unaware of Bob Tomkinson's incriminating statement, as well as the statement from the hotel receptionist.

In reality the FBI had more than enough, even at this early stage, to charge the former president with murder one and arson. John Rowlands wanted to add rape and blackmail to the list along with bribery and corruption, and he would not have to wait long for enough evidence to add the former. The

Crump case was a prime example of the US bourgeoisie being prepared to sacrifice one of their own who, even by their standards, had become too greedy. He had become a liability to the entire deceitful gravy train, and had to go in order for their system to survive. By now the compromising photos of the Atkinsons had been shown to Madeline and Bob, who confirmed their authenticity and, along with Crump's former employee Janet Snowdon's character witness statement, blackmail and rape were added to Crump's charge sheet.

Ronald Crump's legal team were flabbergasted, especially Percy Sugden, when FBI Chief Rowlands, agents Franks, Starling and Gordon presented all the witness statements, including that of Bob Tomkinson along with the CCTV footage. Bribery and corruption were also added to the ever-lengthening charge sheet, bribing a senior police officer and a judge. Crump's legal team were at a loss as to what to advise. Remaining silent or suggesting saying 'no comment' would not be of any help for Ronald now that the evidence was too great and incriminating!

Former Commissioner Connman and one-time judge Early Greasley agreed to give evidence and statements providing they were not incriminated in any other crimes other than the wrongful imprisonment of Carol and Linda. Greasley had no problem with this as he had not been involved in any of Crump's other felonies. Dwight Connman, on the other hand, had much to concern himself with, like destroying or losing evidence to a murder case. John Rowlands agreed in principle to the two men's requests, though in truth he could not guarantee with any certainty he could deliver to Connman. That didn't matter to the FBI: he could honour his word to Greasley, but Connman? He would word it in a noncommittal way. As a former police commissioner, Connman should have been aware of the way these things worked and usually panned out. He was in such a state of panic he was incapable of thinking anything. When agreeing to these terms Rowlands made sure no legal representatives were present.

'Come on, Dwight, policeman to policeman,' was the line FBI chief took. 'There's no need for anybody else to be involved. Legal people, you know what they are like. Just you and me, Dwight, you do trust me, don't you?'

Connman took the 'old pals' act hook, line and sinker.

The problem Connman had, but was unaware of, was that Rowlands was only running this case until a new commissioner could be appointed to the NYPD. Then the FBI would hand over all evidence to the new person in charge. The only deal which was safe, come what may, was Bob Tomkinson's, as authority for his lighter sentence came from well up above. The bribery and corruption charges would stand against Connman, but Greasley would escape prison with a lifetime ban from the legal profession plus a hefty fine. He would, courtesy of bourgeois America, keep his pension. This was considered for services rendered. Greasley had been a very accommodating judge for the ruling class in his time!

Jenny Bradley had been a police officer for over twenty years and was about to be appointed to the position of New York's Police Department Commissioner. She would become the first woman to hold such a high position in any police force in the USA. This could be seen as an indication of how far middle-class America had come regarding the appointment of women to top jobs. The middle class were equally determined this kind of equality would not spread down to the working class; it was to be the preserve of middle-class women. The orthodox feminists, mainly bourgeois, were delighted, but Marxist feminists like Colette Hill were not impressed at all. John Rowlands handed all the evidence from the Crump case over to the new commissioner, explaining the case of former commissioner Dwight Connman and that of Bob Tomkinson.

'Sorry, John, no can do,' Bradley said. 'Tomkinson I have no say in, as the order came from above, but as for giving my predecessor an easy time, no way. He brought the force into disrepute, which I have to sort out, and he is going where he belongs, the state pen. As for Greasley, he had no other involvement other than the Carol Hawkins and Linda Lowry case, so I can keep your deal with him.'

'See your point, Jenny, I never promised Connman anyway. I said I'd see what I could do, which I have,' said the FBI boss.

★ ★ ★

Monitoring events in the daily newspapers and on the various TV channels was Janet Snowdon. She had never forgiven Ronald Crump for the treatment he afforded her having destroyed her wedding plans then dismissing her out of hand. She had heard about the allegations Mrs Atkinson was making and decided to make contact with the former teacher. She found her telephone number and arranged to meet her and Bob, Madeline's husband. Janet told the Atkinsons of her ordeal while working at Crumps Arms and Real Estates and offered to give the police a statement, giving Madeline's allegations more weight, while outlining her experiences with Crump and the kind of person he really was.

'That would be great, Janet, would you do that?'

'Of course, I'll go to the police today and offer my account. Who do I ask for?'

'Hillary Starling and/or Natasha Gordon of the FBI,' Madeline informed her.

★ ★ ★

Armed with all the evidence furnished to her by the FBI, new commissioner Jenny Bradley approached the Crump legal team.

'My name is Mrs Bradley and I'm now in charge of this case. I shall be charging your client with the following: murder first degree, murder second degree, rape, blackmail, bribery and corruption. I should start preparing your case, gentlemen, if I were you.'

Percy Sugden asked the new chief if a deal was possible. 'What about he pleads guilty to manslaughter along with the bribery and corruption and we forget or drop the murder and rape/blackmail charges?'

'I have been in this job a little over a week and already you are asking me to turn a blind eye? No, Mr Sugden, all the charges will be brought, I shall forget the implication of your request.'

Sugden advised his client to plead guilty to the lesser charges and not guilty to murder. He suggested blame be shifted to Bob Tomkinson for the killing of Barbara Simpson and the fire which cost the security guard his life. What Percy Sugden did not realise was Bob Tomkinson was protected, and that he would go to prison but for a much shorter period than would Crump. Ronald Crump had upset the very system which afforded him and parasites like him a life of luxury based on the principle of exploitation of the working class. He had roused the wrath on the streets of the working-class who had forced their army – the army of the ruling class – to back down. Crump was a liability to the bourgeoisie and would have to pay for that. He had become a danger to the idyllic life of luxury that middle-class America had become used to. If the proletariat – working class – ever rose up in unison, which they had very nearly done thanks to Crump, then bourgeois power was finished. For this Crump had to be punished to ensure his selfishness could never again endanger the US ruling class. An example had to be seen to be made!

Percy Sugden now realised, perhaps for the first time, the magnitude of the task which lay ahead. The police appeared to have irrefutable evidence against his client who, in turn, had nothing or very little in his defence to offer as a counterbalance. Sugden asked to see his client in his cell with a view to formulating a plan of defence.

'Ronald, you'll have to hang Tomkinson to stand any chance. We must discredit his evidence. The problem is, his evidence is complemented by statements. Can we call anybody from your company, someone who owes you, who may counter Tomkinson?'

Percy Sugden was grabbing at thin air, and he knew it, even if somebody came forward to slate Tomkinson, the prosecution still had the CCTV footage. The chances of anybody coming to Crump's defence were slim; in the world of people like Ronald Crump, it is survival of the fittest. If the boot had been on the other foot Crump would not have put himself forward to help anybody else unless there was something in it for him.

'Hang on, Ron, the CCTV shows a vehicle being driven by Tomkinson. We can claim your involvement in the entire scene was made up by him, diverting attention away from himself. This claim must cast reasonable doubt on his evidence.'

'That's great, Percy, will it work?'

'It's a long shot but if you stick to the story,' – which was all it would be – 'this man, the man you helped and cultured, repays you by casting blame in your direction for a murder he committed. You must act emotional, hurt and disgusted at this man, after all you had done for him,' – the truth was Tomkinson had been in place since Crump was a little boy, in fact just after World War Two when Teddy had started out – 'you must act the injured party, and the jury might just buy it.'

'What about the receptionist from the hotel where I and that Simpson woman stayed? I signed us both in as Mr and Mrs Richard Pearson. What happens when she tells them I gave a false name?'

Even now Crump could not show the deceased woman any respect, let alone her grieving widower. Crump was also aware Navy personnel stuck together; even if he got away with the crime he would still have to meet her husband. The thought of this terrified Crump. Who could he get to protect him? There was nobody, everybody hated him, never mind, he had to beat the rap first!

'Don't mind her, so she saw you together, so what does that prove? Nothing, it proves nothing and giving an assumed name is not an offence,' Sugden assured his client. 'We will make out Tomkinson was having an affair with Mrs Barbara Simpson, found out about you and her then decided, in a fit of rage, to kill her.'

The way these two were talking of the dead woman was as if she was a loose and available slut who could be had by any male. This was not the case; she had been foolish to entertain Crump, but he had shown her what she considered compassion while her husband was at sea. She did not make a habit of these things as Sugden was proposing to imply as part of Crump's defence.

'So, Tomkinson got jealous when he found out I was banging her.'

'Yes, Ron, but let's be a little selective with the language. That kind of talk will alienate the jury.'

Crump then gave what was once a regular ghastly grin at the besmirching of Barbara Simpson's memory. 'OK, OK, that is the line we will take on Mrs Simpson's death. Now what about the fire?'

Percy Sugden began to quiz Ronald about the fire at Gunn's. 'Have they any evidence to link the fire to you? If they haven't, we can again cast doubt on Tomkinson's evidence. What was the contract you were allegedly trying to finish? Who was the contract with and did you win the tender to finish the job?'

'No, we didn't. The contract was with the Iraqi government and we did not win the tender to finish it.'

'Right. In order to maximise revenge on you for taking his "bit on the side", Tomkinson was not satisfied with setting you up for her death. He decided a perfect opportunity existed to blame you for the fire at Gunn's. We can say Tomkinson got the plans and contract from Barbara. She is not here to contradict, is she? And place the entire blame for each event on him.'

Of course, not a word of this was true and the court case would soon unravel this, but from Sugden's point of view it was probably the most practical believable defence attainable. Neither Percy Sugden nor Ronald Crump was aware of CCTV footage showing Crump on the night of the fire, in the vicinity of Gunn's. This was while he was awaiting Tomkinson's return, not very convincingly disguised. There was no footage of Bob Tomkinson.

'What about the bribery and corruption charges, Percy?'

'Well, Ron, you may have to swallow those charges, but they are small fry compared with murder. I'll put it to the prosecution team you are prepared to plead guilty to bribery and corruption in return for them dropping the murder rap.'

Sugden then took a long pause, looked at Crump and said, 'That leaves the blackmail and rape charge. We can say you had an adolescent crush on your teacher, and as it happened so long ago it is impossible for Mrs Atkinson to remember with any clarity or certainty what happened.'

'The fucking slut deserved it, she was begging me for it,' spat Crump.

For the first time Sugden had serious doubts about his client; he even began to question Crump's sanity. 'Ron, you must keep thoughts like that to yourself – the jury will hold such comments against you. We may beat the rape charge on the grounds it was a schoolboy crush, but you may have to accept the blackmail charge, as they have the photographs.'

'That's great, Percy, I have a great feeling about this. We'll win, won't we?'

Percy Sugden had his work cut out here and he knew it, not least because he did not fully believe his client himself. All the same he was being paid a fortune to get Crump off, and he would do his best. Sugden approached the prosecution team with his offer of Crump pleading guilty to bribery and corruption plus blackmail, in return for them dropping the murder and rape charges.

'Can't do that, Percy. If it were down to us lawyers alone then maybe, just maybe, we could concoct some deal. Unfortunately, the new police commissioner is not one for deals, especially when the evidence against your client is so compelling. We could not even argue insufficient evidence because there is so much of it we will have no problem, Mrs Bradley believes, in getting it over the line. She has only been in the job a short time and she feels this will be her big case. She will not allow us lawyers to take it away from her. Sorry Percy, no deal.'

The date for the trial was set for 12th July 1982 and the jurors would be sworn in accordingly. Judge Caoimhin O'Muraile – a third-generation Irishman, a distant relative of the Kennedy clan, who had kept his Gaelicised name – was nominated and accepted as the trial judge. He was known for his objective outlook and fair play, which suited the defence and prosecution alike. Ronald Crump was now thirty-five years old and the visible affects of recent events were taking their toll, he already looked much older. The jet-black hair, thinning on top, was showing signs of grey and his face looked withered. Crump had genuinely believed his wealth and reputation, or perhaps more accurately his late father's reputation, would let him get away with anything, and he still did believe he would walk away from this 'little mess'.

For once, putting his wife and child's needs above himself, Crump, in a brief memo, agreed to give Tracy a free rein with the family house. *It was only a house,* he reasoned. *I have plenty of money to set myself up somewhere else when this is all over, and start afresh.* If only he knew.

★ ★ ★

Tracy wanted to visit the house, which had been rented out while she and Ronald were in the White House. She was keen to get matters sorted out there. She decided to sell it, offering those who were renting it first refusal. Joe advised her not to go to the house.

'Some reporters are bound to try their hand there, I recommend going to the house later in the week when the press will be either at the White House or the courts. The media will be stalking the entire eastern United States like wolves in search of anybody who may give them a story. You, Tracy, would be a prize catch.'

Three days later, with the press still no wiser to Tracy's whereabouts, she telephoned her former home to ascertain how the ground lay. She was reassured by Mrs Gifford there were no reporters around, so she was safe to visit the house.

The Giffords were the couple who had rented the property with the expectation of staying there for four years. This arrangement would now have to be reviewed, though if they wished, the couple could continue renting for the four agreed years and then Tracy would sell. To tempt them into accepting a review of this agreement she would use the first refusal as bait. If they decided to stay for their full four years, renting, then at the end of that period Tracy could not guarantee giving the Giffords first refusal. Such tactics were uncharacteristic of Tracy; perhaps the recent events had given her a more aggressive approach to life.

Joe agreed to drive her across town at the arranged time, again early before any press activity got seriously underway, to negotiate with Mr and Mrs Gifford.

'Come in, Tracy, sit down,' invited Mrs Gifford. 'My husband will be with us shortly. By the way, this letter arrived for you. I thought it strange coming here and not the White House but with all the news perhaps it is understandable.'

Tracy opened the letter. If she had any doubts about discontinuing Tarquin's education at Wetherspoons this letter would put the problem to bed:

Dear Mrs Crump,

In view of recent reports and events which have overtaken all of us we feel it prudent to contact you regarding your son Tarquin's educational future at this establishment. Unfortunately, all the places here at Wetherspoons are taken, as we expected Tarquin to be absent for four years minimum before starting here. We therefore are not in a position to offer your son, should you wish him to return to Wetherspoons, a place here. Might we suggest you seek a place elsewhere for him in order he does not miss out on any of his education.

Yours sincerely

Mrs M. Langshaw

Headmistress

That didn't take long, Tracy thought. She recalled how the same headmistress had grovelled before her and her husband once she found out how much money they had at their disposal. What vile people this class really were. Slowly but surely, she began to understand why genuine people, such as Colette and Joe Hill, detested these creatures and all they stood for. *Thank God for that,* she mused. *At least I can start from scratch with Tarquin's education.*

She put the letter away and resumed her discussion with her tenant.

'Now Mrs Gifford, I am thinking of selling this house. I am aware you have a four-year rental lease and I will honour that, but first I would like to make you an offer. If you are prepared to forget the lease, release me from my obligations, so to speak, I will give you first refusal on the property. I will let you have it at a reasonable price.' This she could afford to do as Crump had paid for the property outright with cash.

'Why, Tracy, that's very good of you. My husband will be down in a moment. Can you wait?'

'Yes, of course, Mrs Gifford,' and at that point Mr Gifford entered the scene.

'Hello, Tracy,' he said, sitting down beside his wife. 'Sorry for everything you are going through.'

Tracy gave a small smile in acknowledgement.

'Listen, dear, Tracy wants to offer us the house at a reasonable price. I think we should accept.'

'What price, Tracy?' asked Mr Gifford.

'Well, let's say for a quick sale $350,000, which is about $75,000 less than my husband paid.'

The reader will recall the house was a wedding gift to her and Ronald from Teddy and Megan meaning Crump had paid nothing for the house. Tracy really was hardening up to the stark, less-than-pleasant realities of life.

This was a very reasonable price for a property of the size of Crump's former residence. Mr Gifford gave a quick and unambiguous answer: a resounding yes.

'Very well, the union solicitors will draw up the legalities,' Tracy said. She now used the AFL legal team, which Colette had recommended. 'They will then be in contact with your legal team. Can we shake on it, Mr Gifford?'

Tracy and the Giffords shook on the deal and agreed all communications would now be done through the solicitors. The Giffords thanked Tracy and reiterated their disappointment that things had not worked out for her. The reader should remember at this point Ronald Crump had been found guilty of nothing, but all the signs were that that things were, in all probability, soon to change.

★ ★ ★

The scene was now set for what many were calling the trial of the century. The defence had put together a reasonably good case, that is with the cards they were dealt, given the overwhelming evidence in the possession of the prosecution. The prosecution had one more weapon in their armoury which would sink Crump once and for all, assuming the case got that far.

The trials of former Commissioner Connman and ex-judge Early Greasley had taken place in early June. They were both charged with accepting bribes and, in the case of Connman, illegally disposing of vital evidence which might aid a suspect relating to murder. They were both charged with manipulating the verdict which resulted in two innocent women being sent to prison for crimes they did not commit and bringing their respective professions into disrepute. Greasley was fined $10,000 and banned from practising law for life. Connman, whose part was the more serious of the two, was sentenced to four years' imprisonment, dismissal from the force and loss of pension. Thirty years' service lost through his own greed. Commissioner Bradley had wanted a longer sentence for her predecessor but settled for the four-year sentence laid down.

Tracy Crump was already suing for divorce and decided not to attend her husband's trial. She wanted, if possible, to forget the entire chapter of her life with Crump – apart from her son, Tarquin, who was now her priority. She had now and perhaps for the first time some genuine friends, not rich, not powerful, but genuine and principled. She did not wish to hear the name Ronald Crump ever again and certainly had no desire for her son to bear it. She set about using her maiden name, Edwards, and changing Tarquin's to the same.

Percy Sugden now had to break the news to his client that the prosecution was unwilling to play ball and cut a deal. 'Due to the overwhelming weight of evidence, as they see it, the police department see no reason to do a deal with us. They feel enough evidence is in their possession to get all the charges over the line. We'll have to really go to town on that former director of yours, Bob Tomkinson; we must at all costs discredit him and his evidence. At least this way you may beat the murder rap.'

Sugden thought for a moment. 'Then there's that former teacher, Mrs Atkinson or Copley, which was her name at the time. We'll concentrate on you having a schoolboy crush on her. That's perfectly normal among adolescents. The photographs were, we can claim, a bit of stupid fun. There was no blackmail and certainly no rape – this was a figment of her own fantasy. As for bribery and corruption, I'm afraid we'll have to swallow that as they have already found Connman and Greasley guilty. I have received information that the FBI checked your account and found that the day you paid out those exact sums they received them on the same date. They are unlikely now to find you not guilty. No, Ron, we must take that one on the chin,' the Englishman said.

'Well, Percy, we can only do our best. I am not guilty, and their evidence is either prefabricated or circumstantial, I should know!'

This Percy Sugden was beginning to doubt, not the bit about Crump knowing about prefabricated evidence, but the presumption of innocence.

'Less of that kind of talk, Ronald, you are a squeaky-clean businessman, you know nothing about fabricating evidence or committing perjury, you were unwittingly dragged into Connman and Greasley's scheme designed to promote their images. You will be found guilty of those charges, but the judge may go easy on you if he sees before him a victim as well as a participant.'

The problem was, the jurors were not silly: they had wives, daughters and nieces, the kind of people who could fall victim to a demagogue like Crump. The jurors were not like some of the people Crump employed at the lower end of the production line, folk who would believe anything provided the boss said it. The jurors had been vetted and were of reasonable intelligence. Sugden's analysis of the jurors was the realistic one, unlike Crump who thought they, the jurors, were of the same imbecile level as some of his employees. Former employees of Crump's scaled from highly skilled and intelligent to, through no fault of their own, not very bright. It was this perceived lower stratum which Crump cajoled, bullied and exploited to the hilt. Even now the topic on the shop floor at Crumps Arms and Real Estate was that Mr Crump had been treated very harshly. These were the very people Crump had exploited, sacked, kicked around all their working lives, feeling sorry for the tyrant they should have been wishing dead! There were those, usually in the offices, who did not share this semi-imbecile viewpoint. One of these would be the prosecution's secret weapon, not yet revealed.

The day of Crump's trial came around and Judge O'Muraile met with both counsels in his rooms to remind them of the intricate finer details of US law. Under the rules all witnesses had to be disclosed to the judge and each counsel by the other. It was at this point the prosecution revealed their hitherto mystery witness who worked in the admin office at Crumps. Rachel Warren, the prosecution attorney, revealed they intended to call Agnes Moorhouse, who had a great deal to add to their case.

Percy Sugden was totally wrong-footed by this and it was too late now for him or his team to counter this move. He would have very little time with his client before the trial began, so he decided to withhold this information so as not to panic an already vulnerable Crump. As we know, Ronald Crump had aged somewhat during these weeks and his stress was compounded when he found out Tracy had left him, and that she was seeking a divorce. *How dare she*, he thought, feeling indignation mixed with self pity.

The counsels left the judge's rooms and returned to the theatre of engagement. The court usher called out, 'The case of the State of New York against Ronald Edward Crump, all stand for Judge O'Muraile.'

Sugden began outlining the case for the defence. 'Members of the jury, my client is pleading guilty to the charges of bribery and corruption with mitigation. He is pleading not guilty to both charges of murder. The prosecution evidence is in many cases circumstantial and questionable. I will show their chief witness was out for revenge on my client which included framing him for murder. The devious and vindictive Bob Tomkinson was having an affair with Barbara Simpson. He found out my client was also seeing her and decided to dispose of Mrs Simpson and set up my client for her murder. There is no evidence linking my client to the unfortunate fire at T.A. Gunn's factory resulting in the tragic death of the security guard. As for the allegations of rape and blackmail, they happened so long ago I'm surprised anybody, including the woman making the claims, can remember with any clarity what exactly happened. My client may well have had a schoolboy crush on his teacher but that was where it ended. There was no rape and no blackmail, this I shall prove.'

Rachel Warren for the prosecution set out the case for the State of New York. 'Members of the jury, I intend to prove beyond all reasonable doubt the accused, Mr Ronald Crump, conspired with Robert Tomkinson, his junior director, bullying him into executing the murder of Mrs Barbara Simpson, after he, Crump, had done all the planning. I also intend to prove this murder was part of a grand plan to put a rival company, T.A. Gunn's, out of business, thus procuring a lucrative contract from the Iraqi government. For this, he, the accused, needed the plans for the factory layout and a copy of the contract which, when the time was right, he would tender to finish the necessary work as Gunn's would be in no position to complete. These plans and contract could only be procured from Barbara Simpson, apart from Gunn himself, so the accused promised her money and sex, while her husband was at sea, in return for these plans and contract. Her decision to play this game of industrial espionage with Crump would cost her dearly. Resulting from the procurement of these plans and contract a fire was started at the Gunn's complex, planned, on foot of the plans, and executed by the accused.

'The incident involving blackmail and rape back in the sixties while the accused was at high school was not a schoolboy crush at all. It was a well-thought-out plan aiming to force a young attractive teacher through blackmail into having sexual intercourse, and other forms of sex, with the accused.

'The ridiculous claim by the defence that the bribery and corruption involving two senior public servants made him, the accused, a victim is laughable. Mr Crump wanted both Carol Hawkins and Linda Lowry out of his apartments and would go to any lengths to achieve this. Not happy forcing them into what was essentially prostitution he wanted them now homeless. He approached his old friend Mr Connman, who introduced him to then Judge Greasley who would ensure they went to prison for a long time and he could sell the properties for a huge profit. To this end a fantastic illusion was created, suggesting the two women administered a mild toxin to Mr Eugene Mathis while inviting him back to the flat for sex with a view to stealing his wallet. Mr Crump wanted the two women found guilty of these charges and sent to prison. Vital evidence was ruled inadmissible by Greasley and evidence was tampered with and destroyed by Connman to ensure a guilty verdict would be arrived at. A young police officer was fired by Connman for asking awkward questions and suggesting evidence existed which might prove the women's innocence. I will prove beyond all reasonable doubt Mr Crump's guilt on all counts. He abused his position to further his own ends.'

Judge O'Muraile then thanked counsels for their presentations and briefed the jury on the finer points of US law. Crump sat upright in the dock dressed in a light tan jacket with matching trousers, a white shirt and blue tie. In his jacket lapel he wore a badge depicting the flag of the United States, as if to prove his undying loyalty to his country. In the case of people like Crump, in any land, it is their country. They own the means of production, distribution and exchange. Everything belongs to them, the ruling class.

Mrs Warren then called the prosecution's first witness, a Miss Nugent, the receptionist from the hotel where Crump and Mrs Simpson spent the night. Miss Gina Nugent had worked at the hotel for seven years and was on duty the night Crump and Barbara had their assignation.

'Miss Nugent, can you tell the court what you witnessed on the night in question?'

'I saw the accused with a woman, who I later recognised as the person who was run down and died. They retired to the bar where she handed him a buff folder after he ordered drinks. Then they retired to their double room.'

'Miss Nugent, do you have any idea what was in the folder?' Rachel Warren asked.

'Well, when I was collecting glasses, to help out, you see, I noticed some papers with Gunn's letterhead on it. As I looked, he passed the papers back to her very quickly and she put them back in the folder. Then they left.'

'They definitely had Gunn's letterhead on them?'

'Yes, in bold, I only caught a glance, I was not being nosey, you understand.'

'I put it to the court that the papers Miss Nugent caught sight of were the plans and contract which the accused was seeking,' Mrs Warren said.

Percy Sugden for the defence was now on his feet for cross-examination of the witness.

'Miss Nugent, do you drink?'

'Objection, what has the witness's social habits got to do with the case?' Rachel Warren interjected.

'I was trying to ascertain if her judgement might have been impaired,' Sugden countered.

'I'll allow it, but do not dwell on it too long, Mr Sugden,' the judge instructed.

'No, I do not drink,' the witness said.

'No further questions,' Sugden conceded.

'Thank you, Miss Nugent, you may stand down. You may be required at a later time, and you will still be under oath,' the judge informed her.

The next witness for the prosecution was Bob Tomkinson who would repeat the statement he had given to the FBI, now in the possession of the NYPD. Tomkinson repeated how one thing led to another resulting in Crump ordering him, under threat of financial ruin or worse, to dispose of Barbara Simpson.

'I refused at first, but he said, if we did not get that contract, I'd lose all my investments with Crumps Arms. He also reminded me of my time working for his father, Teddy, and how he knew on Teddy's orders I had double-crossed the Mob! I knew this could not be true because Teddy Crump was shrewd enough to stay clear of the Mafia, but Crump Junior could make things up and pass them off as true. I was very worried that Ronald would do this to me, and the Mob would accept Crump's version of events.

'I then asked Crump why Barbara had to be got rid of. He said it was because she was a material witness. She was no longer any use to Crump and as she was a liability she had to be disposed of. "You are going to dispose of the problem, Bob, aren't you?" he said to me. "I would hate the Mob to get your name, after all my dad is dead now therefore they'll take it out on you." I was terrified.'

'Did you know what he had done with Barbara Simpson?'

'Not at this stage, he said she was a witness to what he had done.'

'What *he* had done?'

'Yes, that's what he said,' Tomkinson concluded.

'You were afraid for your life?'

'Yes, and he said he would ruin me financially, so even if I lived I would be in poverty.'

'Tell us about the fire at Gunn's, what happened there?'

'Mr Crump had the layout of the buildings and he wanted Gunn's out of action and not able to complete the contract for the Iraqis. He decided on a plan involving a fire using incendiary devices. I had used such equipment during the war, so he used more threats to secure my compliance.'

'Thank you, Mr Tomkinson, no further questions.'

It was now Percy Sugden's turn to cross-examine.

'Do you expect the court to believe that tissue of lies, Mr Tomkinson? You were having a sordid affair with Barbara Simpson behind her husband's back. When you found out my client was also meeting her for sex you got jealous, didn't you?'

'No, I don't know what you are talking about. I wasn't having an affair with the deceased woman, no way, that is very insulting. I never knew the woman existed until Mr Crump mentioned her. As for this affair, I don't know where you get that from.'

'I put it to you your affair had been going on some time and when Mr Crump came on the scene you decided if you couldn't have Barbara then neither could he. You then set about planning her murder and blaming it on your former boss. Is this not the case, Mr Tomkinson?'

'No, it is not, have you gone mad?'

'You then make up this fanciful tale about a fire at Gunn's,' Sugden continued, 'again trying to blame my client. Is it not nearer the case that you, Mr Tomkinson, started the fire, using your expertise as you said, and once again tried to blame Mr Crump. Is that not nearer the truth, Mr Tomkinson?'

'No, it is not.'

At this point Judge Caoimhin O'Muraile interjected. 'Have you any evidence or witnesses to substantiate these claims, Mr Sugden?'

'No, sir, only circumstantial evidence,' Sugden conceded.

The prosecution now felt it time to up the stakes a little as Rachel Warren called her next witness.

'Call Agnes Moorhouse.'

Crump's mouth dropped open as Agnes Moorhouse, his one-time troubleshooter, took the stand. Though Agnes was Crump's right arm at one point, she was also incredibly honest.

'Ms Moorhouse, you overheard a conversation involving the accused and Mr Robert Tomkinson, is this correct?'

'I overheard many, but they were not my business,' the one-time old faithful replied. 'Can you tell the court the contents of one particular conversation involving the accused threatening his junior, Mr Tomkinson?' Rachel Warren pressed.

'Yes, I can, I overheard Mr Crump tell Mr Tomkinson that he had information about some deal his father had going which involved double-crossing a leading Mob member. He told Mr Tomkinson he was aware he,

Mr Tomkinson, was the man to execute the plan and how he would hate the Mob to discover, even at this late date, that it was he who had cost them so much money. However, Mr Crump could make this disappear if Bob – Mr Tomkinson – did as he was told and got rid of that woman. He also assured him there was no chance of being caught because he could "square" it with the commissioner. He also threatened Mr Tomkinson with financial ruin if he did not comply with these instructions.'

'Thank you, Ms Moorhouse, no further questions.'

The judge then asked Percy Sugden if he wished to cross-examine.

'Yes,' the defence lawyer replied.

'Could you have been mistaken about what you heard? Were you listening through a closed or open door?'

'The door was closed,' Agnes replied.

'So you could not be certain.'

'No, sir, the intercom had been foolishly left switched on. You see, I was not eavesdropping at the door, being nosey as you are implying, I heard every word on the intercom.'

Sugden then switched to the theme of Tomkinson's affair with Barbara Simpson.

'Ms Moorhouse, were you aware that Mr Tomkinson was having an affair with the dead woman?'

'Inadmissible, Mr Sugden, you have no evidence to substantiate your claim,' the judge ordered.

'No further questions,' Sugden once again conceded.

Crump had laid his own death trap. Leaving that intercom on was very, very foolish.

The prosecution now called Colette Hill, who had fulfilled all her early promise of attractiveness. She could have entered and won any beauty contest on earth but, as a Marxist and a feminist, saw such shows as exploitation of women. She was very principled, as the reader may recall, and saw no reason why she should put herself on show.

'Mrs Hill, do you know the accused?'

'I did at one time, many years ago when we were children.'

'In what capacity were you acquainted with the accused?'

'He was my first boyfriend; my father and his then occasionally played golf together. They got to know each other through our friendship.'

'What happened to your friendship, Mrs Hill?'

'I had to dump him. He assaulted my best friend at his eleventh birthday party, sexually, so he had to go.'

'But your father was an acquaintance of the accused?'

'Yes, they were both businessmen.'

'Thank you, Mrs Hill, no further questions.'

Once again Judge O'Muraile asked the defence to cross-examine. Sugden got to his feet. 'Mrs Hill, what was your maiden name?'

'Lugosi, Colette Lugosi.'

'You are the daughter of Benito Lugosi, a leading gangster.'

Sugden had taken the bait carefully laid by the prosecution; they had not mentioned Benito Lugosi or his alleged involvement in organised crime.

'How dare you, how dare you make allegations against my father, you straight-faced old streak of gnats' urine!' Colette let loose, her family loyalty veil coming down. 'Can I remind you my father was acquitted of any offence in Chicago?'

'Mrs Hill, I must remind you this is a court of law,' O'Muraile said, struggling not to laugh. 'And Mr Sugden, I must remind *you*, Mrs Hill is not on trial, neither is her father. I rather think you have done the prosecution's job for them by introducing this theme!'

Sugden had indirectly confirmed the suggestion that Colette's father may have been the Mob leader in question, the one Agnes Moorhouse alluded to. This was evidence that perhaps the threatening conversation involving Ronald Crump and Bob Tomkinson regarding Tomkinson doing the late Teddy Crump's dirty work taking money from the Mafia might well have been true. Therefore, the claim of Bob Tomkinson being afraid of Crump due to knowledge the accused claimed to have in his possession also held more than a drop of water.

'The prosecution calls Madeline Atkinson.'

The former French teacher took the stand.

'Can you tell the court, Mrs Atkinson, your recollection of the events under discussion which occurred at the school where you were employed on the afternoon in question.'

'Yes, he, the accused, came to my classroom having in his possession some photographs of my then future husband and myself in a sexually compromising position,' the former French teacher explained. 'If the photographs had been made public then we, Bob and I, would have lost our jobs and at that stage we were planning our wedding. We could not afford that to happen; if we had lost our employment, we would have been unable to afford our wedding. I felt and still do feel dirty.'

'Then what happened?'

'He told me if I came to his dormitory that evening and had sex with him that he would keep the photographs private.'

Nobody was prepared for what happened next. Ronald broke.

'You fucking slut, you were begging for it. You prick-teaser! You couldn't get enough, you bitch, fucking whore,' Crump bellowed across the court, standing, leaning as far over the podium as the height would allow. He was slavering from the mouth and his eyes were wide and revolving. He was banging the front of the podium with both clenched fists like a man possessed!

Chaos erupted in the court.

Ronald, clearly out of control, spat out more obscenities. His reddening face contorted to an evil grimace as he pointed his finger over and over at Madeline.

'Silence, silence!' The judge pounded the gavel.

Finally the people quietened down, but Ronald continued to rage incoherently. The judge shouted over his voice, 'I'm calling an adjournment for psychiatric reports on the accused after this outburst. I must apologise to Mrs Atkinson for the verbal abuse she has been subjected to. I need to know if the defendant is of sound mind, if he is mentally fit to stand trial. This trial is adjourned for two weeks,' the judge ordered.

Madeline Atkinson was in tears. Colette and Janet Snowden, another character witness due to be called, comforted her. Crump was taken down. Outside, Bob Atkinson threatened to kill Crump if he ever laid eyes on him again. The former president was dragged kicking and screaming by three burly court policemen off to the cells. He was literally foaming at the mouth and it was clear to all that the man had gone berserk.

Judge O'Muraile then summoned both counsels to his quarters. 'Now, as we witnessed, it appears the accused has taken leave of his senses. What we need to know is: is this condition likely to be permanent? What is your early view, Mr Sugden? He is, after all, your client.'

'Well, not being a medically qualified man I'm pretty much in the same position as you, sir. What does Mrs Warren think?'

'If he was putting on an act he deserves an Oscar, I'm not qualified in the field of psychiatric disorders and am prepared to leave it to those who are,' the prosecutor conceded.

'I think we should leave it to those who know what they are doing, the experts,' the judge said. 'If his condition is permanent or will last longer than what could be considered temporary then obviously a trial is out of the question. He will be sectioned and placed in a secure unit for as long as is deemed necessary. My view is: leave it to the psychiatrists.'

Crump was taken from the cells to the New York Mental Facility for the Criminally Insane, until such time as it could be ascertained whether he was mentally fit to stand trial. Even though he had not been found guilty of anything yet, there was no other safe place to keep him. He was, after all, expressing violent intent towards a witness, so for now that would be where he would stay.

A team of top psychiatrists from across the USA was appointed to take over Crump's case. Professor Richard Head hailed from Chicago in the west of the country, Dr Brian Stephen Hitter came from New Jersey, Dr Philip Looney was stationed at the state mental institution for the state of Texas and Dr Randolph Trevor Bend was from South Carolina. The last man was a replacement for Dr Peter Quincy, the brother of Dr Alan Quincy, Megan Crump's live-in lover in Canada. Quincy pointed out that, through his brother, he had connections to the Crump family and declined to be on the team. It would be the job of these eloquent men to decide, over the coming weeks, the state of Crump's mental health and its likely duration. Judge O'Muraile, as the trial judge, was furnished with the list of psychiatrists. The judge voiced no objections to this list and the team began their analysis of Ronald Crump.

Judge O'Muraile concluded that although the sanity of Ronald Crump was now under serious question, at the time of the rape involving Mrs Atkinson he was of sound mind. Crump's outburst, sound mind or not, suggested the former teacher was telling the truth. It appeared it was this truth which triggered Crump's outburst of madness. The judge awarded Mrs Atkinson, on the limited evidence he had heard, $500,000. As for Carol and Linda, the two wrongly convicted women, he awarded $275,000, each again on the available evidence. He would have preferred to give them more, but he couldn't because they had been conducting acts of prostitution and the evidence was incomplete.

Had the full case against Crump been heard it was likely Madeline Atkinson would have received three times the amount awarded by Judge O'Muraile. As it stood he could only give what the limited evidence allowed by law on the evidence available. Fortunately, he had seen in private the incriminating photographs located by the FBI at Crump's former home.

Elsewhere, the trial of Bob Tomkinson had taken place. As he had pleaded guilty, arranged as part of the deal he did with the FBI, Judge Peter Sankey gave him a ten-year sentence. Ten years was twice what the FBI chief, John Rowlands had agreed but far shorter than would have been the case with no deal in place. Bob Tomkinson was almost relieved it was all over, and he was sent to a relatively lenient prison, not a penitentiary where psychopathic killers resided. Tomkinson was viewed as a soft consequence of Crump's actions and although he had to be punished, a grade A prison would not serve anybody's purpose. Judge Sankey also stated Tomkinson could qualify for parole after five years. He inserted this clause mindful of what had been agreed behind the scenes but also aware of the court of public opinion. Five years was too lenient, and ten years would be more acceptable. With the parole clause inserted Sankey considered he had satisfied both sets of opinion.

★ ★ ★

Ronald Crump, now considered a patient, was given a padded cell for his own protection as he had continued to throw violent tantrums. He sat in this small compartment sucking his thumb for most of the day. It was unquestionable the man had suffered a mental breakdown. The question was, for how long? The psychiatric team worked all day every day, all being given leave of absence from their usual duties to work on this case for a number of months. At the end of their analytical investigation it was decided, unanimously, that Crump had to be sectioned under the National Mental Health Act. He was unfit to stand trial and was likely to remain so for an indefinite period.

As he had not been found guilty of any offence he could not, by law, be kept in any institution for the criminally insane, as he officially was not in this category. The question was, where should he be placed? He had plenty of money; he had amassed a fortune through the exploitation of others, so the cost of his care was not a problem. If he had been an ordinary working-class person who had unfortunately suffered a breakdown, the county asylum would have done. Crump was not. He would receive, despite all he had done, the very best treatment even if it was for the rest of his life, which it might well be! One thing was for certain: Ronald Crump, whether he remained in a psychiatric care home or if he recovered and was able to stand trial, would be unlikely to smell freedom again for the rest of his life.

Back at Crumps Arms and Real Estates the talk of the workforce was about 'poor Mr Crump' and how he had been hard done by. 'After all he has built up here, all the hard work he and his father before him put in, this terrible thing happened.'

Nobody, particularly the lower paid workers, thought Crump capable of doing such evil deeds as people were accusing him of.

'That rotten French teacher, telling lies about poor Mr Crump,' was a regular line heard among the disciples. It never once entered their vacant heads that it was they who had put all the work in. It was they who had created the goods which Crump sold, amassing a fortune, and it was they who had created all the wealth which Crump had hitherto enjoyed. This sensible argument was far over the heads of these empty-headed unfortunates. But the higher up the pay scale the less sympathy there was for Crump. The skilled workers were saying, 'It's our labour that created all this. Crump and that gang of brigands on the board are nothing more than robber barons.' The problem was, under the present idiotic system, these people's employment depended on this gang of thieves.

Tracy Crump, now settled in her job with the American Federation of Labour and with Tarquin doing well at school, secured her divorce. If ever there was a mismatch of a marriage it was surely that of Tracy Edwards to Ronald Crump. From now onwards she would be called Tracy Edwards and her son would adopt her maiden name.

When she found out about what her husband had done to his teacher at Bishops Court Rise she made an effort to visit Madeline Atkinson. Madeline and Bob made Tracy very welcome and made a fuss over young Tarquin. A friendship grew between them and visits to and fro were regular. She continued to be active, along with Colette and Joe Hill and with other socialists like Lizzie Flynn, syndicalists, communists and feminists of various degrees in the trade union and socialist movement.

Epilogue

The characters portrayed in the previous pages are of course fictitious, as are the events involving them. Some incidents mentioned above, like the Watergate scandal, did happen and it was used as a background for our main character, Ronald Crump. The question may be asked: do such people really exist? And do events, extreme as these appear, happen in real life? If they do, then reports of such people and events are quickly quashed. Back in the 1980s in Britain, former members of Margaret Thatcher's cabinet were reportedly involved in cases of child abuse. These reports were in various newspapers and then disappeared from view as quickly as they came. The story was replaced by cases of lower-ranked persons being involved in similar atrocities. Was this one of those cover-ups?

The United States Presidential Election of 1980 was won by Ronald Reagan – as Ronald Crump was fictional – and as right-wing and divisive as Reagan's policies may have been, it is difficult to imagine him being involved with anything outlined above. Ronald Crump was not supposed to represent Ronald Reagan; just the election date was used to fit with the story. There have only been two cases of impeachment in US political history: in 1868 Andrew Johnson was impeached by the House of Representatives, as was Bill Clinton in 1998. Both men were acquitted by the Senate who were, in both cases, unable to reach a two-thirds majority. Both men sat out their full presidential terms. Richard Nixon, mentioned in the story, resigned rather than face impeachment over the Watergate scandal. In our story President Crump did the same, though as events conspired, would it have been better for him to hang on in there and face impeachment? Who knows, like in real life with Johnson and Clinton, the Senate may have acquitted him!

We are constantly told we live in a democracy, but do we? The system which brought down our character, Ronald Crump, capitalism, will occasionally sacrifice one of its own in order to maintain its grip. Capitalism as an economic system is based on greed, profits and private ownership of the means of production, distribution and exchange and is the system which allows the few to rule the many. The electorate, in any capitalist country, never get a vote on whether we like the system, merely who we wish to govern it. This is not for one second to suggest people abstain from voting; on the contrary it is the only democratic right we have.

Could anybody imagine if an election question was put, before voting for any candidate, to the electorate:

Would you like to live in a society where every able-bodied person is employed, where all the modern technology is working to make life easier for everybody, not merely those who can afford the benefits? A society where health care is free at the point of need and not being run down as it appears the American health system is? Would you like to live in a society where the means of production are under common ownership and we produce for the benefit of all, not the profit of a few? Would you desire to see a world free of wars, usually caused by capitalism or capitalist greed, be it in pursuit of another country's natural resources or to stop another gang of thieves getting their capitalist hands on them? A society where homelessness is vanquished? Private ownership of properties is the cause of homelessness. By private ownership I'm not referring to somebody who has bought their own house, I mean big properties which cannot be touched because of the rights of private property. The retirement age should not be going up, it should be coming down. We are told technology can do much of the work once carried out by humans; true enough, so why are we expected to work longer? The answer to this is similar to so many others: all this technology is owned for, and for the benefit of, a few private individuals to make profits. The rest of us must, if we are lucky, work until we drop. We are never asked if we agree with this system, are we?

If such a question were to be asked on a ballot paper the answer would undoubtedly be a resounding YES: we would like to live in such a system free of poverty and unemployment, wars and homelessness. Then should such a socialist party stand for election on this ticket, and win, the state run by the ruling class – the clue's in the name – would send the army out, declare the election null and void and probably arrest the newly elected government. We elect governments not to run the affairs of the majority, but to look after the interests of the rich and powerful.

In most countries, the only democracy that exists in almost all privately owned industries is where firms, usually those state- or semi-state run, recognise trade unions. Here we see democracy in the workplace in action, the shop steward being elected usually on a yearly basis. We do not elect our bosses – they own the firm, the means of production, distribution and exchange. They own us, they rule by fear, fear of the sack and the poverty trap. Ronald Crump was such a person, with his wealth based on the exploitation of the many by the few. Liberal democracy is a smokescreen to present an illusion that because we get a vote we have a real say in how things are done. Admittedly, it is better than some totalitarian regimes, such as Pinochet's Chile, Mussolini's Italy and certainly Hitler's Germany, but in crisis, would capitalism resort to these measures? History suggests it would if we elected the wrong party to government, as happened in Chile 1973. It masks the reality which is the dictatorship of the bourgeoisie – and the aristocracy – in the case of Britain and other monarchies.

History teaches us real change comes about through revolutionary struggle. The English Civil War 1641–49, won by Cromwell and the Parliamentarians, put an end to the divine rights of monarchy. It was finally finished by the misleadingly termed 'Glorious Revolution' of 1688. The French revolution of 1789 gave rise to the Parisian bourgeoisie and, as in England one hundred and forty years earlier, resulted in a king losing his head. These violent acts resulted in real change. Modern socialism certainly does not advocate depriving a monarch of their head, but we should be prepared for a bourgeois backlash should a genuinely socialist party be elected into the British, or any other country's, government, for example. Perhaps in Britain Jeremy Corbyn's Labour Party is the nearest thing, and in Ireland perhaps Sinn Fein and social democratic parties, advocating change to the system within the status quo. Unfortunately, across Europe, we are presently witnessing various electorates, having been fed poison by the middle-class media, voting for parties which are likely to contain people like our Ronald Crump, far-right-wing neo-fascist organisations. In the United States, 2016, socialist policies were perhaps epitomised by the democrat, Bernie Sanders. The Democratic Party, equally opposed to any form of socialism, chose as their candidate Hillary Clinton, not Sanders.

In reality, could it ever become possible that the USA becomes a fascist dictatorship? Within US liberal democracy there exist checks and balances primarily to prevent the rise of any form of socialism and all the benefits to the working class such ideology offers. These same checks and balances can be used to prevent the rise of the far right unless the ruling class demand drastic measures. In the past the United States, again to suit their ruling-classes needs, have a record of protecting war criminals. While some of the former German Nazi regime were being tried at Nuremburg the USA was protecting others who were of use to them. An example of this protection was the use of the Nazi and SS rocket scientist Wernher Von Braun, the man ultimately responsible for the United States Apollo moon landings, assuming this was not another US hoax! Von Braun and other leading Nazis were afforded protection by the USA because they were anti-communist. Admittedly Von Braun was a brilliant scientist but should this have been his get-out-of-jail card? This stance would fit in with parts of our story. The United States and her allies, including Britain, have a history of protecting fascists who were of use. Just as the system protected Crump, until he got too greedy, the USA protected Nazis until they were no longer of any use, like Klaus Barbie, the butcher of Lyon. The reason this man was protected was because, like our character, he was anti-communist and would be of use to US Intelligence against the Soviet Union.

The feminist movement is very broad-based and there is no single homogeneous strand. Orthodox feminism demands equal rights for women within the present system. An example in our story was the appointment of the police commissioner for the State of New York, Jenny Bradley. This was an example of middle-class feminism, which, as the story suggests, must not extend to the majority of working-class women. Marxist feminists, epitomised by the character Colette Hill, generally tend to see women's liberation as being tied in with the working-class revolution. Class emancipation will automatically include women's liberation. This does not mean Marxist feminists reject all gains won outside the class struggle; they do not advocate waiting for the masses until their advancement can be achieved. By the same token they see these gains, within capitalism, as progressive but not the end of the war. Then we have radical feminists, some of whom envisage a world without men or the involvement of men. This includes, in a minority of cases, becoming pregnant without the use of male impregnation: parthenogenesis.

Misogyny and racism, along with other antisocial and reactionary behaviour, appear to be on the rise. Right-wing politics would seem to be rising around the globe. Our character, Ronald Crump, epitomises the very worst of these ideologies. In the real world much is made by those who claim to be anti-racist and opposing misogyny by highlighting minor, though politically incorrect, behaviour. An example is that the use of the word 'blackboard' in UK schools is no longer acceptable. This is fair enough, but are there not far more important and vicious attacks on ethnic minorities in society to be addressing? Misogynist attitudes in the workplace need combatting as does domestic violence against women in the home – of course it must also be mentioned that there are a small number of cases involving violence by women against men.

Our character, Ronald Crump, summed up the worst forms of all discrimination. The story also showed how people power, including Marxists, all strands of feminism, anti-racist groups, gay and lesbian organisations, liberals and trade unions, played a major role in his ultimate downfall.